HIGH FLIER

HIGH FLIER

A romance about horseracing
set in the early 1980s

Jane McKerron

MICHAEL JOSEPH
LONDON

MICHAEL JOSEPH
Published by the Penguin Group
27 Wrights Lane, London W8 5TZ
Viking Penguin Inc., 375 Hudson Street, New York, New York 10014, USA
Penguin Books Australia Ltd, Ringwood, Victoria, Australia
Penguin Books Canada Ltd, 10 Alcorn Avenue, Toronto, Ontario, Canada M4V 3B2
Penguin Books (NZ) Ltd, 182–190 Wairau Road, Auckland 10, New Zealand

Penguin Books Ltd, Registered Offices: Harmondsworth, Middlesex, England

First published in Great Britain 1993

Copyright © Jane McKerron 1993

Typeset in 11/13 pt Sabon
Printed in England by Clays Ltd, St Ives plc

A CIP catalogue record for this book is available from the British Library

ISBN hardback 0 7181 2952 0
ISBN paperback 0 7181 3728 0

The moral right of the author has been asserted

To my Ws, who knew I'd stay the distance

Acknowledgements

I should like to thank the following for their help with this book:

My publishers, Michael Joseph – in particular Susan Watt for her support and invaluable suggestions for improvements throughout and Anne Askwith for her calm and constructive assistance with the final draft.

Racing friends such as Jonathan Irwin and Graham Rock who nobly ploughed through the manuscript, Mary Bromiley for her advice on equine ailments and their cures, Robert Armstrong, Sir Mark Prescott, Clive Brittain, John Biggs, Bob McCreery, and Sally Sands of the Grovewood Stud for their patience in answering all my queries.

Non-racing friends Paula Leigh and Georgina Howell for their informed advice on fashion.

All those who had to put up with me when I was actually writing the book, in particular my brother Colin McKerron and my neighbour in Suffolk, Elizabeth Grant.

My friend and fellow racing enthusiast, John Barnard, for taking such good care of my whippet Woody for me during some seemingly endless spells at the typewriter.

PROLOGUE

Leaning against the paddock gate, Lady Kitty Leverton gazed reflectively at the dapple-grey mare cropping the grass in the autumn sunshine.

'Kate, I've had an idea. It's time I told you about it,' she announced, turning to the dark-haired girl at her side.

Kate glanced at her sharply. She knew that purposeful look on her mother's face only too well. It usually heralded some surprising new plan to which she, being of a more cautious disposition, would take some time to adjust.

'Well, go on then. Let's have it,' she replied as Lute, one of her mother's blue whippets, nudged her leg with his long nose.

'I think we should try to get Misty in foal again, before it's too late,' her mother said, narrowing her large china-blue eyes. As she gazed into the distance, the mare lifted up her head slowly and started to amble towards them. 'I love her to death, of course, but I can't hack her around any more, now that this wretched hip has got so bad, and I really can't afford to keep her in idleness indefinitely.' She sighed. 'I'd like to give her one last chance to get in foal again, to earn her keep. Otherwise I honestly think we'll have to sell her. What do you think?' She turned to Kate with raised eyebrows.

'Well, it's worth a try, I suppose,' Kate replied thoughtfully. 'I'd hate to lose Misty – she's a real family pet, but getting her in foal would be quite an expense, wouldn't it? Would it be worth it? I seem to remember Uncle Harry telling us before he died and left her to us that those two foals she produced in Ireland were not much good.'

Lady Kitty snorted. 'They were useless,' she replied. 'I don't think either of them ever saw a racecourse at all, but that could have been Harry's fault. I don't suppose he could afford to send any of his mares to anything decent, poor lamb. I don't think he really gave Misty a chance.' She turned to Kate, her eyes shining. 'But this time

ix

we should send her to something with real class – like that Northern Dancer colt which Lyle Saunders is going to stand at his stud in Newmarket, Three Swallows. Greek Dancer, I think his name is. I was just reading about him in *Pacemaker* magazine the other day.'

Kate felt a surge of alarm. This sounded like one of her mother's more fanciful and extravagant ideas. 'Hang on a minute! Isn't Northern Dancer just about the most fashionable stallion in the world? The one that Sangster and O'Brien and now the Arabs are so keen on?' she asked with consternation. 'We can't possibly afford to send Misty to one of his sons, surely?'

'Not one of the proven stallions, no, of course,' Lady Kitty agreed calmly. 'But the point about this Greek Dancer is that he's such an unknown quantity. He ran only once, as a two-year-old in Ireland, I gather. After that he broke a sesamoid bone and never set foot on the track again. Next year will be the first season at stud.' She gave Kate a quick sidelong glance. 'As a result they are charging only £2,500 as a stud fee – on a "no foal no fee" basis. I think that's remarkably cheap,' she added casually.

'What! You must be joking!' Kate spluttered. 'I know £2,500 may be cheap for some people – chicken feed to the likes of Robert Sangster or the Aga Khan – but it's a great deal of spare money for *us* to find, particularly just at the moment, isn't it? Only the other day you told me that your builder bloke in Bury says we'll have to find over £20,000 over the next few years in roof repairs to the Old Rectory alone.' She cast a despairing glance over her shoulder at the tall Georgian house behind her, its pink-washed façade glowing rose in the late afternoon light.

Her mother did not reply. With her little head on one side like a bird, she was watching Misty with affection as the mare plodded up to the gate and stretched out her nose, whinnying softly.

'There, there, girl. You'd enjoy a bit of romance again, wouldn't you? A bit of a fling?' she said softly, scratching her under her chin.

'Well?' Kate asked impatiently.

Lady Kitty fished in her pocket for a packet of Polo mints and fed the mare a handful, waiting for them all to vanish between her long yellowing teeth. 'There,' she said, 'that'll do. Davy will be coming to get you in for your tea in a minute.' She turned back to her daughter. 'You've missed the point,' she said briskly. 'If we send Misty to Northern Dancer we could make a *real* profit at the yearling sales, particularly if she produces a colt. Also Greek Dancer has got Hyperion blood, you know – his dam's Astral Girl, was by Aureole and Misty's pretty well bred herself too. Roan Rocket was a top-class miler. If the foal's conformation is good it could fetch anything from 20,000 to 200,000 guineas at the sales. The market's pretty buoyant at the moment.' Her eyes lit up with enthusiasm.

'That would give us enough for all the roof repairs, with a little bit left over, *and* mean that we could enjoy having a foal about the place for a year as well. We'd have to send it off to be properly prepared for the yearling sales, of course. But just think how proud we'd be if it actually got to the racecourse. We might even go and see it run. Think about that!'

Kate leant against the gatepost looking at her mother with resigned amusement. 'You're such an optimist,' she complained. 'Trouble is, I can see you have quite made up your mind!' She shook her head. 'Look, even if you are right and we could make a profit out of this foal idea, it wouldn't be for two years, would it? How are you going to afford the stud fee and Misty's and the foal's upkeep for a year in the meantime? Have you thought about that?' She shivered as she spoke, suddenly aware that the sun had finally dropped behind the chestnut trees. There was a definite chill in the air now, along with the scent of wood smoke drifting over from the row of cottages that fringed the village green. Pulling her jacket more tightly around her, she went over to her mother and put an arm around her shoulders. 'Come on now, you reckless old thing! It's getting cold. Let's go back inside and I'll light the fire. I think we need to discuss this further over a cup of tea.'

Ten minutes later, with a feeling of satisfaction, Kate sat back on her heels in front of the fire. Despite the absence of any firelighters (which her mother had forgotten to buy), she had at last managed to get the logs burning properly. Pushing her dark hair out of her eyes with a grimy hand, she glanced around the darkening room, its familiar objects illuminated in the fire's flickering light.

Above the Adam fireplace hung the famous Herring portrait of one of her ancestors, the second Earl of Rathglin, with his thoroughbred colt, Gadfly. On the far side of the fireplace were the two delicate Ingrès drawings that her father had acquired just after the war and a John Nash watercolour of the Stour Valley, given to him as a wedding present, of which he'd been particularly fond.

The Old Rectory had been his family home, of course. He had inherited it after his parents' death and had used it as an English base in between foreign postings with his regiment, the Irish Guards, until he had been killed in a freak helicopter accident in the Middle East fifteen years ago. After that, there had been no question of her and her mother going to live anywhere else – even Ireland: the Old Rectory would always be their home from now on, they had decided.

Kate was devoted to the shabby old Georgian house, with its light, beautifully porportioned rooms and long windows looking out over the garden and parkland beyond. It was full of memories of a happy childhood, apart from the horror of her father's death. It also had a tranquillity and reassurance about it that never failed to comfort and sustain her, particularly when, as at the moment, she felt buffeted by events in the world outside, for she had recently separated from her husband Hugo, and she suspected that the temporary rift would become a permanent one. So, in the last few months she had decided to come home.

Now she was living at the Old Rectory, she realized that there were other pressing, even if less emotionally disturbing, decisions to be made. First of all, there was the problem of her mother's increasingly painful and debilitating hip: should she or should she not have a replacement operation? Then there was the rapidly deteriorating state of the house itself. Quite apart from the structural repairs needed to the roof, the whole building needed painting both inside and out: no small undertaking for a house of that size. Helping her mother and Davy, their old Irish groom-cum-gardener, prune the wisteria the other day, she had noticed another large crack in the plasterwork spreading ominously across the pink-washed wall under her bedroom window. Surely, therefore, every extra penny they had in the next year or so, either as income from her mother's small number of shares or any increase in her own earnings as a freelance photographer, should go into keeping the Old Rectory going, not into some madcap scheme to breed an expensive foal? As her mother came limping back into the room with the tea trolley, she was determined to be as firm with her as possible.

'Now, I've made some Earl Grey. And we've got some of your favourite seedcake. At least I remembered to get that this morning,' Lady Kitty said cheerfully as she manoeuvred herself down into her usual armchair, careful not to disturb Lute's mother Liffey, who was already draped over the cushion, her long blue nose dangling.

Kate sighed. 'You are deliberately trying to butter me up, Kitty! It won't do any good.' For some reason, she couldn't recall why, ever since her father's death, she had called her mother by her Christian name. Her forehead creased into a frown. 'Look, how on earth are we going to afford the nomination *and* the horses' keep for the next two years? Come on, out with it. You've had at least twenty minutes to come up with a convincing reply!'

Lady Kitty leant forward to pour the tea. 'Don't worry,' she replied soothingly. 'I know exactly what I'm going to do. I have the perfect solution.' She paused, her hand on the tall silver teapot. 'I'm going to sell that Munnings sketch of me and Skittles.'

Kate shot forward in her chair. 'What? I don't believe it! You can't do that,' she replied indignantly. 'I love that sketch. Daddy did, too; he would never have wanted you to sell it – I know he wouldn't.'

She was aghast. Her mother had been a brilliant rider to hounds in Ireland in her youth. The toast of Tipperary, Limerick and half Galway too: 'always up there with the thrusters', Uncle Harry used to say with pride. Staying briefly one winter at Rathglin, Alfred Munnings had sketched her setting off for a meet on her hunter, Skittles. It had been an impromptu sketch, done on a piece of loose paper, but Lord Rathglin had been impressed and had immediately had it framed. Her father had always liked it, too, and ever since Kate could remember it had hung in his old study at the Old Rectory which Lady Kitty now used as a dining-room. She could not bear the thought of it being sold.

'David would have wanted me to do what I want to do. He would have understood,' her mother replied firmly. 'I never liked that sketch much anyway. It makes me look like a doll.'

Her daughter still looked so thin, she thought. Her usually alert, snub-nosed face was pale and peaky and her large grey eyes unusually wary. Since Hugo had got involved with this American woman, Amy, Kate seemed to have withdrawn into herself somehow, her confidence and even her work obviously affected. Lady Kitty hated to see her suffering like this and hoped, privately, that when Hugo did return from his next visit to California, he would request a divorce and set Kate free. He had never really made her happy. He had waltzed her into marriage with great determination, seeing in her, perhaps, qualities that he did not possess himself but which might well be useful to him. On the surface it had seemed a suitable match: Hugo was not only good-looking, energetic and ambitious but had clearly valued Kate too; but he was too shallow and self-seeking to love anyone whole-heartedly, Lady Kitty had always suspected.

'I really don't want you to sell that sketch, even if you don't like it,' her daughter was saying, her grey eyes pleading. 'If you are so set on this idea of trying to breed from Misty again, I am sure we can find the money from elsewhere. I could take on more commissions, for a start.' She stirred her tea purposefully.

Lady Kitty glanced at her fondly. 'Oh, no, you won't,' she insisted. 'You've got enough on your plate as it is. This is my folly and I'll pay for it.' She leant over and put her hand on Kate's arm. 'Look, dearie, this is no time to be sentimental about possessions. Other things are more important. Indulge me, please, just this once.' She patted Kate's hand. 'You're having a bumpy ride at the moment and it's not over yet. And, if I do decide to have this hip operation, it'll hardly be a picnic, will it? So, we both need something to take us out of ourselves at the moment, don't we? I'd say that what we both needed is an adventure.'

PART ONE

CHAPTER ONE

The Sunday Chronicle *Magazine, Fleet Street*

'Princess Michael! Don't make me laugh! I know the ed. says the magazine needs more glamour, but this is a series about *professionals*, sweetheart. Not raunchy members of the Royal Family who hunt occasionally – that's amateur stuff.' Reg Gunn, the picture editor, was scornful. 'What we're looking for is a bird who actually makes a living working with horses. She'll have to be a looker too, though, of course.'

He picked up the phone at his elbow. 'How about some coffee then,' he barked at his secretary in the next-door office. 'We could do with a bit of stimulation this morning. Some people's imagination seems to have packed up completely!' he added, glancing across at Kate Leverton. 'You're not with us at all, are you, sweetheart?' he inquired, not unkindly. 'Not still brooding about that wanker of a husband of yours, I hope? How many times do I have to tell you that getting shot of him is the best thing you've ever done?'

Kate gazed at the notepad in front of her. She *had* been thinking about Hugo, of course. Reg might be vulgar but he was also shrewd. He had met Hugo only a few times but had immediately taken against him, describing him as 'that pretentious pup'. The day Kate had finally confessed that the marriage was over and she'd agreed to a quick divorce, citing Amy as the cause of breakdown, Reg had been so delighted that he'd marched her down to El Vino's for some champagne in the middle of the afternoon. What Kate had never even attempted to explain to him, then or since, was that rather than seeing the divorce as a cause for celebration, she saw the whole débâcle as a miserable failure on her part. Being a Taurean, she tended to be obstinate, proud and a great self-blamer. Maybe her attitude to the marriage had been wrong from the start, maybe she should have subjugated herself more, tried harder, she still rebuked herself.

3

'Sorry! My mind *had* rather wandered on to the subject – you're right, Reg,' she admitted with a rueful grin. 'I've just come from my lawyer, you see, and everything seems to be going through so quickly and tidily, mainly because we didn't have any children, I suppose.' She sighed. 'It all seems so clinical and final somehow, like having your wisdom teeth removed. I find it all rather depressing.'

'Hmm . . . Well, you know my views,' Reg said. 'When the bloody Absolute comes through I might even take you out to dinner – and you know what a rare occurrence that is!' He stubbed out his cigarette. 'Now, look. Let's get back to the business in hand, for Christ's sake. You must know *someone* in the horse world who'd fit in with the bloody series – some bird who trains or breeds horses or even a "lady jockey",' he added disparagingly. 'Though they're not much cop, I'm told.'

Kate's face cleared suddenly. 'I know! Of course, Diana Saunders!' she announced excitedly.

'Never heard of her,' Reg frowned.

'She manages the Three Swallows stud near Newmarket,' Kate explained. 'I know her quite well, actually. I took some pictures for the stud's brochure in the spring. Also, Achilles, the colt my mother and I bred, is by one of Diana's stallions, Greek Dancer. Achilles is back at Three Swallows at the moment, as a matter of fact, being prepared for the yearling sales,' she added proudly.

'Never mind about all that. What does this Saunders bird look like? Is she sexy?' Reg asked impatiently.

Kate grinned. 'Very. In an open-air, Lauren Hutton sort of way. Probably a bit thin for your taste, but certainly glamorous enough for the editor. She's a millionaire's daughter, of course. The stud belongs to her father, Lyle Saunders – you know, the Australian media tycoon.'

'Lyle Saunders's daughter! Christ, the ed.'ll have an orgasm. He's convinced that our lords and masters here are selling out to him right now and he's shit-scared about losing his job.' Reg rubbed the side of his nose gleefully. 'He even put up the idea of a piece on Saunders himself a few months ago but we talked him out of it, saying that it was too arse-licking, but the daughter'd be different, of course. If we do a legitimate feature on her, in her own right as it were, we might all get a pay rise!'

He got up and pulled on his jacket. 'Well done, girl. You seem to have cracked it. Ring her up today, will you, and book her in. Insist. Exaggerate our circulation figures a bit but don't take no for an answer. Come on! They're open. We'll forget about the bloody coffee. I'll buy you a drink.'

Tattersalls Sales Paddocks, Newmarket

The mid-afternoon sun streamed down through the glass dome and high windows of the elegant, mock-classical sales pavilion on to row upon row of intent spectators. Some of the world's richest racehorse owners and breeders were there, packed unceremoniously on to the seats and into the gangways. Flanked by their bloodstock agents and trainers like an army of casually dressed predators, they were waiting, with a mere flick of a catalogue, to pounce on the yearlings of their choice.

'One hundred and ninety-five thousand, ninety-six, ninety-seven, ninety-eight, ninety-nine,' the auctioneer prattled on, his head flicking from side to side like an agitated bird as he scoured the packed arena for bidders. 'Two hundred thousand, ladies and gentlemen, two hundred thousand I am bid for this exceptional colt, a son of Mill Reef, out of a Stakes winning mare. A lot of potential – he could be a classic winner,' he pleaded.

Kate, perched high on one of the gangways, watched fascinated as the electronic scoreboard above the auctioneer's head flashed the six-figure bid simultaneously into four different currencies. So many millions of francs seemed an awful lot for a horse, she thought. She glanced down at the huddle of backs in front of her to where the object of the bidding, a neat bay colt by the Derby winner, Mill Reef, was being led round in a circular ring, seemingly undismayed by all the attention.

As the bidding, slower now, headed towards the half-million guineas, Kate sensed a tightening of tension around the ring. With the best European and American blood in his pedigree, the Mill Reef colt had been billed as one of the sales' biggest attractions. The television crew in front of her swung their lenses in the direction of a billionaire Kuwaiti prince as he sat by the ringside, trying to look inconspicuous in a regulation flat cap perched incongruously above his dark glasses and beard.

Suddenly, for no apparent reason, the composure of the colt in the ring snapped. He flung up his head, eyes glassy in the electric light, and skittered sideways, whinnying with dismay.

He may be worth over half a million, Kate thought, but he's only a baby. Just like Achilles. Her heart thumped suddenly at the thought of how she would feel when the colt she and her mother had bred, the colt they had known since birth, was up for grabs in front of this ultra-critical audience, all his shortcomings revealed in the glare of the lights. She was dreading the moment, yet it was only two weeks away now.

There was a chestnut filly in the ring now, looking considerably less happy than the Mill Reef colt. She waltzed sideways, staring at the crowd, her tail swishing and ears back.

'Don't like the look of that temperament. Course, she's out of a Red God mare. They can be dodgy,' commented a man with a moustache sitting just below Kate.

'She looks cow-hocked to me. And she's too straight in front. I wouldn't touch her with a barge pole,' replied his companion, a heavily made-up woman with a streaked blonde pony tail and Hermès scarf.

Some of the people she'd observed at Newmarket sounded so bossy and opinionated, Kate thought, quite unlike the horse people she had met in Ireland. Their Irish voices were softer, somehow, and they gazed at horses with a mixture of wistful shrewdness and affection that she had always found attractive. They seemed to regard the owning of horses as such a privilege too, Kate reflected, as she watched the chestnut filly tittup on round the ring. She was reminded, once again, of how her mother had insisted that getting Mystical in foal again would be such a positive thing to do: such an advantage, she insisted. In retrospect, Kate had to admit, Achilles had certainly been that.

Diana Saunders had suggested that the foaling should take place at Three Swallows where Misty had already been booked in for a date with their other resident stallion, Grand Hotel, but Lady Kitty was insistent that it should be at the Old Rectory. Davy was the best stud groom they had ever had at Rathglin, she said, and it would be an insult to his competence not to let him foal his own mare.

Kate was in Brighton in the middle of photographing some exhibits from a collection of Victorian toys that day, a pernickety job requiring all the patience she possessed. She finished as quickly as she could, though, and drove furiously northwards to Hazeley to see the foal before it got dark. She found her mother and Davy brewing up a final cup of tea in the tack room before they settled the mare and foal down for the night. She would never forget her first sight of the spindly-legged colt, rolling his eyes warily as he leant against his mother's flank.

6

'There's not much of him, but he's sure got the bone all right,' Davy said proudly.

The colt was black all over with lop ears and only one distinguishing mark, a long white sock or stocking stretching up to his hock on his near hind leg.

'It looks as though he's been dipped in pitch, except for that one leg,' Kate observed with amusement.

Lady Kitty looked up sharply from beside the manger where she had been checking Misty's feed. 'That's it!' she said, delighted. 'We'll call him Achilles. After all, he's by Greek Dancer out of Mystical. It's perfect!'

Watched over with loving care and nurtured on good grass, Achilles had prospered as a foal, with only an occasional run-of-the-mill problem with worms or a runny nose to contend with. He stayed at the Old Rectory until he became a yearling, when they reluctantly decided that they must send him to Three Swallows to run with the other colts, as an essential part of what Lady Kitty described as his 'social education'.

Although he showed no sign of viciousness, he sometimes seemed to resent being treated as a family pet, standing aloof in the paddock when his mother was being fed titbits, staring out over the neighbouring parkland as though he glimpsed something particularly fascinating in the distance.

'Perhaps it's his Hyperion blood,' Lady Kitty mused. 'He used to do the same thing, you know: stand stock still on the gallops suddenly and refuse to move. That could be the explanation.'

Achilles also disliked being groomed, and would shift his feet, snorting with irritation, and even give Davy the occasional nip as he went painstakingly over his baby coat.

He had been greatly missed when he departed for Three Swallows, particularly as by then his mother, Misty, was back there too. The Munnings sketch had fetched a mere £2,800, less than Lady Kitty had hoped for, and the moment the mare had been confirmed as being in foal again to Grand Hotel, she reluctantly decided to sell a half share in her to Diana and to board her permanently at the stud.

'It's for the best,' she told Kate. 'Horses are herd animals, remember. She'll be happier along with the other mares and it means that we can well afford to pay Achilles's board and lodging too, until he comes up at the sales.'

Lady Kitty also finally decided to go ahead with her hip replacement operation, so Kate stayed on at the Old Rectory to keep an eye on her.

Now that she and Hugo had agreed on a divorce, she also wanted to stay out of his way while he was in London finishing his book on Napa Valley wines before returning to California.

Glancing now at her watch, Kate realized with horror that it was past four o'clock, the time she had agreed to meet Diana Saunders for another picture session. Picking up her camera bag, she hopped around the clumps of people sitting on the stairway and hurried out through the doors of the sales pavilion on to the well-kept gravel outside.

It was her first visit to the Tattersalls sales paddocks and she found it all rather bewildering. From the central sales pavilion and office and restaurant complex, a maze of neat yards, made up of dark wooden boxes, spread out over the lawns in complicated geometrical patterns. Casually dressed, the hordes of buyers, bloodstock agents, trainers and breeders stalked around the boxes, greeting each other cheerily enough, as though in a holiday mood, yet also obviously driven by a sense of serious purpose. Yearlings of various shapes and colours, lurking behind closed doors, suddenly bounced out into the sunlight as Kate passed by. As they were led up and down they were regarded by the *cognoscenti*, unsmiling, with all the intensity of art critics at some prestigious private view.

Kate finally found Diana, in the middle of a row of boxes marked 'O'. She was standing, hands on hips, looking like a cowgirl in a film, in tight black jeans, black silk shirt and silver low-heeled boots, as she watched one of her yearlings being put back into its box. She also looked like a rich man's daughter, Kate reflected, as she started organizing her cameras. The Alice band that held back her sun-streaked blonde hair was no doubt from Gucci; and heavy gold glinted around her wrists and throat. She also looked remarkably healthy, as usual, with her apricot-coloured silky skin, clear blue eyes and dazzling, rather sexy buck teeth.

'This is a Run the Gauntlet colt, out of that mare of mine, Dreamer,' she informed Kate in her strong Australian accent. She led out a leggy bay colt with a crooked white blaze and stood by his head, scratching him affectionately under the chin. 'I thought we'd use him in the pictures as he's usually quite a good boy and he hasn't been out of his box much today, have you, sport?' she added.

Ten minutes later, concerned that the colt, rather than Diana, was beginning to dominate the pictures, Kate requested a halt while she explained the sort of pose she wanted. Diana, obliging as ever, was just passing the lead rope back to the groom when a low-flying jet suddenly screeched overhead, a violent roar of sound rippling in its

8

wake. The bay colt, startled, reared up without warning and spun round, pulling the rope from the man's hand. Giving a buck and a kick, it then cantered off purposefully along the row of boxes.

'Shit!' Diana helped the groom back on to his feet. 'Run round the back and try to head the little bugger off, will you?' she instructed him urgently.

She gazed anxiously after the colt who jinxed as someone made an attempt to catch him and increased his speed still further.

'Christ! I hope he doesn't try to jump the paddock railings at the end. He could go arse over tip and really hurt himself,' she muttered, setting off in pursuit.

Minutes later, however, Diana re-emerged through a gap in the boxes looking considerably less worried, to Kate's relief.

'It's OK. We've got him. Charlie Kyle managed to catch him,' Diana called out as she got nearer. 'In the nick of time, though. He could have caused mayhem with some of the fillies.' She pushed her hair back with a tanned hand and fell back against a box door. 'Whew! Thank Christ that's all over,' she said breathlessly and with feeling.

'I'm really sorry. Perhaps it was my fault,' Kate apologized quickly.

'Nonsense! You weren't flying that flipping plane, were you?' Diana retorted firmly. 'I've a bloody good mind to complain to the base.'

She turned, her expression softening, as she watched her errant colt being led round the corner towards them. He was obviously still very much on his toes, jig-jogging along, his coat dripping with sweat.

At his head was a lean, good-looking young man with ash-blond hair cut unfashionably short at the back. Wearing a blue and red plaid shirt and faded jeans, he walked quietly along beside the horse, one hand on its neck to soothe it.

'Thanks, Charlie. You really are a pal,' Diana said, smiling, as she took the lead rope. 'Come on, you scamp. Let's get you back in your box.'

She indicated Kate with her free hand. 'Charlie, this is Kate. Kate Leverton. She was just taking some pictures of me when that frigging plane came over.'

Charlie Kyle stared at Kate, unsmiling. With his bony face and high-bridged nose, he had the keen, aggressive look of a bird of prey and although his green eyes were fringed with unusually long lashes, they held a definite expression of contempt.

'Photographers should be banned from these sales in my view,' he remarked coldly. 'There's enough pressure on the yearlings as it is.' He had an odd accent, Kate noticed: a blend of public school and somewhere colonial that she could not place. 'You've got a nice colt here, Diana,' he remarked. 'Better take better care of him. See you.' He raised his hand and strode away.

'Who's *he*?' Kate asked indignantly.

Diana seemed unperturbed. 'Charlie Kyle.' She grinned. 'Bit of a dingo, isn't he? But his bark's worse than his bite.' She kicked the bottom of the box door shut with the toe of her silver boot.

'He could do with some manners, if you ask me,' Kate complained. 'Who is he, anyway? I mean, what does he do?'

'He's an assistant trainer, works for Tod Beckhampton at Barons Lodge. He's a weird sort of mixture. Chippy as a load of timber. His father used to train, too, years ago, I gather, but he went to prison and lost his licence. Burnt down his own yard or something dippy like that.' She walked slowly along the row of boxes, checking that all the bolts were in place. 'Anyway, Charlie's devoted to him. He followed him out to a sort of exile in Zimbabwe some years ago. He's only recently come back.'

Zimbabwe! So that was what the odd inflection in Charlie's voice was, Kate thought.

'Is he always that uncouth?' she asked, picking up her camera bag.

Diana shrugged. 'No. Not always. But he doesn't suffer fools, particularly the female version. I rather fancy him, as a matter of fact. He's quite a challenge,' she grinned. 'Come on. Let's go and get a drink. You look like you need one.'

The sales bar was doing its usual hectic trade; the babble of conversation and clinking glasses was almost deafening as Kate followed Diana through the restaurant, its white-clothed tables, bright with posies of flowers, already laid for that evening's dinner.

As Diana elbowed her way through the throng, people turned to greet her enthusiastically, some of the men planting a kiss on her cheek, others flinging an arm around her slim shoulders. The horse world was a hard one to break into, Kate suspected, but Diana's direct Australian charm was clearly effective. She had been living in Newmarket for only three years, yet was obviously popular.

She stopped now to talk to two middle-aged men leaning over the bar. One of them was a big man with an indolent patrician air about him and silvery sleeked-back hair that reminded her of an actor she'd always admired, Charles Gray; the other was leaner and more casually dressed, with dark hair and horn-rimmed glasses. She paused, a sudden blast of cigar smoke making her eyes water.

'What'll you have?' Diana called out. 'Glass of white wine?'

The man with the glasses shook his head. 'I honestly wouldn't advise it by the glass, Diana – it's pretty undrinkable. We've just ordered a bottle of quite decent Meursault. Why don't you have a glass of that instead?' He held out his hand to Kate. 'No one introduces anyone round here. My name's Tod Beckhampton.' He had a firm grip and an attractive lop-sided smile, Kate noticed, and behind the glasses his brown eyes were friendly.

'Oh, sorry,' Diana said good-humouredly. 'This is Kate. Kate Leverton. She's a terrific photographer. She's been taking pictures of me today for the *Sunday Chronicle* magazine. This is Tod, my favourite trainer, by far.' She tapped the silver-haired man on the shoulder. 'And *this* is the famous Basil Hunter, lord of the press room, oh, and Tod's brother-in-law too. Perhaps you two have met already? In Fleet Street or somewhere,' she added rather vaguely.

Basil Hunter turned to Kate with an unctuous smile. 'Unfortunately not, I'd most certainly have remembered.' He eyed her up and down appreciatively.

Basil was the racing correspondent of the *Daily Post*, Kate knew. Lady Kitty read him regularly and occasionally followed his tips. 'Racing's eyes and ears,' they call him. 'Must have been playing blindman's bluff yesterday,' she recalled her mother snorting recently when two of his selections had trailed in last.

'Kate and her mother are selling a colt here in a fortnight's time,' Diana was telling Tod. 'He's from the first crop of our lad, Greek Dancer out of a Roan Rocket mare. Very exciting. He's small. Got a lot of growing to do but you might like him. He's a well-made little sod. Will you take a look at him?'

Tod nodded. 'Sure. Ring me with all the details. I'll be busier that week than I am this, that's for sure. With the exception of Stelios, perhaps, and my new Arab, this week's prices are way beyond my owners' reach. Doesn't stop some of them looking though, I'm afraid, and endlessly complaining, of course!'

He took a crumpled packet of Gitanes cigarettes out of his pocket and offered one to Kate. 'No? – Come to think of it, you don't look like a smoker,' he remarked, giving her an appraising look. 'How many broodmares have you and your mother actually got?' he asked politely.

'Only one. Mystical,' Kate replied. She went on to explain about Misty and about how they had called the foal Achilles. 'I know we shouldn't have actually given him a name ourselves but we just couldn't resist it. It seemed so suitable. We're dreading selling him, of course, but needs must.' She gazed wistfully into her wine glass. 'I know it sounds pathetic but I'll never be able to watch him actually being sold in the ring. It was pretty nerve-wracking just now, when I hadn't even got an interest in any of the horses.'

Tod smiled sympathetically. 'It's not pathetic at all. Most small breeders feel like that. But why isn't your colt in this sale, by the way, rather than the October? His pedigree's good enough, I'd have thought.'

Kate frowned. 'He was turned down for the Highflyer,' she explained. 'I think it had something to do with him being so small. He's barely fifteen hands. That and the fact that he's black are definite minus points, Diana says.'

'Ah, yes, I see,' Tod replied thoughtfully. 'Black is a pretty unfashionable colour, I'm afraid. It's supposed to indicate a dodgy temperament.' He grinned. 'Black horses are usually listed in sales catalogues and racecards as being dark brown, you know. I never really see the point in that myself: people have got eyes, after all.'

'Well, he may be the wrong colour, but he's a real character and we think he's got class,' Kate replied loyally.

'All right, all right. I believe you! I'll certainly take a look at him myself and tell you what I think,' Tod replied with amusement.

The girl was very pretty, he thought, with her snub nose, wide grey eyes and tousled dark hair – very Irish somehow. Her name, too, was familiar. He frowned as he struggled to remember why.

'Leverton? Mmm . . . Your mother isn't Lady Kitty Leverton, by any chance, is she?' he inquired.

Kate nodded.

'Oh, well then! We've already met, years ago. I hunted alongside her in Ireland once. Or perhaps I should say in her wake! I seem to remember that she and the hounds were in the next county by the time I caught up with them. I felt most inadequate.' He smiled at the memory. 'Where is she living now?' he asked.

'Quite near here: the Old Rectory at Hazeley. It was my father's old home,' Kate replied.

Tod raised his glass. 'Well, I must invite her over to Barons Lodge for a drink some time. You must come too, of course. In the meantime, here's to your little colt. May he do his breeders proud.'

Glancing at his watch, he turned to Basil Hunter. 'I've got to run. Got to take a look at that Sir Ivor colt and those two fillies before I go home.' He sighed. 'Hassim's coming up again tomorrow, cheque book at the ready, and Myra insists I check all the horses on his shortlist thoroughly by then. She's right, of course.' He adjusted his glasses and levered himself away from the bar. 'Look. If you get back to Barons Lodge before me, tell Myra where I am, will you? Engaged on legitimate business and all that – OK?'

Basil, who was deep in a flirtatious-looking conversation with Diana, looked round. 'Try not to be late for dinner though, won't you?' he insisted in a pained voice. 'I don't think the old girl's in the best of moods.'

Before Tod could reply, a tall girl with long dazzling chestnut-coloured hair, dramatically dressed in a black leather jacket and trousers, wove her way deftly through the throng beside the bar and flung her arms around his neck.

'Daddy! At last I've found you. You haven't seen Alain, have you?'

Tod, who seemed delighted to see her, kissed her warmly on both cheeks. 'Lucy! We were expecting you for lunch. Myra must have got it wrong. Does she know you're here?'

Disentangling herself, the girl flung back her hair and looked round the bar with huge amber eyes.

'Sure. Don't panic. I rang her from London this afternoon. Actually, I suspect I'm in her good books for once. Only because of Hassim. She was incredibly polite on the phone – I couldn't believe it.'

Tod put his hand on her shoulder. 'Well, so she should be. It's only thanks to you, sweetheart, that we've actually got an Arab in our sights at last. It's what she's always wanted.' He made a face. 'Look, I've got to dash now.'

Kate had been listening to this exchange with interest. She had never met Lucy Beckhampton before but of course she knew her face well. It was difficult not to: Lucy was a very successful and highly paid model both in Europe and America and over the past few years her waif-like face had adorned the front cover of numerous magazines. She also featured regularly in gossip column items, along with her lovers who included the French jockey Alain du Roc. Kate remembered colleagues in Fleet Street returning from picture sessions with Lucy complaining of her capricious behaviour but usually captivated by her charm.

Tod turned back to Kate. 'I'm so sorry. How rude of me. Kate, this is my daughter, Lucy. Kate's a photographer, I gather,' he explained.

'Probably the only one around who hasn't photographed you,' Kate joked, holding out her hand. 'Hello.'

Lucy shook it firmly. 'Hi,' she said, with a friendly smile, remarkably like her father's.

Tod put his arm around her waist. 'Come on, Lucy. I really must be off.' He held out his hand to Kate. 'Goodbye, then. Glad to have met you. I won't forget to look at your colt, I promise.'

He turned with a smile and headed off through the crowd.

'Kate, Kate. Come here a sec.' Glancing towards the bar, Kate saw that Diana was beckoning her over. 'Listen, Basil's just invited us both up to Barons Lodge for a drink.' She grabbed Kate's arm enthusiastically. 'I think we should go. Give us an opportunity to rustle up some interest in your colt – there are bound to be various odds and sods of owners and bloodstock agents up there. OK?'

Kate frowned. 'Well, yes, I suppose so. But I'm really not the best person to promote Achilles, you know. I'm so ignorant.'

'Oh, you can leave all the hard sell to me, don't worry. I'm good at that sort of thing,' Diana replied cheerfully.

CHAPTER TWO

Barons Lodge

Barons Lodge was a large, forbidding-looking Victorian house fringed by laurel bushes and a high brick wall, on the north-eastern side of the town. As they drove there Diana gave Kate a quick rundown of the yard's recent history.

'This place was famous in old Sir Digby Hunter's day. He was the father of Myra Beckhampton, Tod's wife. He trained for a lot of nobs including the Queen and was champion trainer several times. Bit before your time, of course!'

'So Tod inherited the yard from his father-in-law, then?' Kate asked, gazing to her left at the great sweep of ghostly-looking gallops, stretching up to the brow of Warren Hill.

Diana swore as the car hit a rut in the road. 'Shit! Yep, that's right. He did pretty well right from the start, too. He was champion trainer twice, I seem to remember. Certainly the year he won both the Guineas and the Derby with Mafioso.' She slowed down to turn through an imposing tall brick archway, flanked by two weatherbeaten bronze eagles. 'He's had a lousy run recently though, I'm afraid. He inherited a lot of Sir Digby's posh owners but most of them have dropped off their perches or left racing in the past few years. Also his horses have been running so badly. He seems to have had the virus on and off for the past three years. Quite a few owners have taken their animals away.' She peered ahead at the curve of cars lining the drive, looking for somewhere to park.

'I think Barons Lodge have only had about twenty winners this season and none of them anything to write home about. God knows when they last had a Group winner. Tod's pretty dispirited about it all, I think. He's certainly drinking a lot more than he used to.'

She turned round to back the car expertly into a small space. 'Right, let's go and see who's here, then. Barons Lodge may be on the skids but that won't stop people turning up for a free drink.'

Clutching her glass of white wine, Kate leant against the window ledge, breathing in the sharp evening air. The twenty or so people in the room in front of her were still all discussing horses: their shapes, sizes, pedigrees and the amounts they had managed to fetch at that day's sales. All this concentrated horse talk was giving her a headache.

'That filly of Timmy's fetched 200,000 guineas, you know. Hell of a lot for a Lord Gayle, isn't it? Particularly one with a parrot mouth,' a young man had commented indignantly as she brushed past him, heading for the window.

Although she was learning fast, she was still so ignorant about thoroughbreds. She dreaded having to answer any more serious queries about Achilles. She wished her mother was present: she knew so much more about it all.

Myra Beckhampton, in particular, had given her a particularly withering look, when Diana had introduced them earlier.

Myra was a rather imposing-looking woman. Tall and broad-shouldered, with metallic blonde hair swept up into a French plait, she had the same wide forehead and slanting eyes as her brother, Basil, but her chin was more determined. She was immaculately if rather heavily made up, particularly around the eyes, and her high heels and dark pencil-slim skirt revealed excellent legs. The high-necked lace blouse and Victorian pearl choker she was wearing gave her a somewhat regal air, but the face above them was discontented, as though life was not going exactly the way she wanted.

'Diana tells me you are a photographer,' she had said briskly, holding out her hand. 'Should I know your work?'

'Maybe,' Kate replied evenly, determined to be polite. 'I don't work for any racing magazines, though. Mainly general features for *Harpers* and some of the colour magazines at the moment.'

'Well, I see *Harpers* every month, of course,' Myra replied. 'I'll look out for your name.' She turned to a thin, faded-looking woman with wavy brown hair hovering at her side. 'Organize some more glasses, will you, Pam,' she ordered. 'Get Charlie to do it.' She indicated a plate of canapés. 'And circulate with these. We don't want people getting too drunk,' she added.

What a bossy woman, Kate thought, as Diana waved her over to be introduced to one of the Barons Lodge owners, a squat, florid-faced middle-aged man called Joe Weston who was, he soon told her, a bathroom-fittings manufacturer from Bradford.

Kate then talked to a butch-looking woman in tweeds who turned out to be a bloodstock agent.

'This colt Diana has been telling us about, your Greek Dancer. Isn't the dam a half-sister to that Irish-trained animal that won the Cork and Orrery last year?' she asked eagerly.

Kate made a face. 'I'm awfully sorry, I've no idea. You had better ask Diana,' she replied apologetically.

To bloodstock *aficionados* the names of races were like signposts in a familiar landscape, she was beginning to realize. The Cork and Orrery, the Gimcrack, the Cesarewitch, the Ebor. She had heard them all referred to in the past half-hour, with little idea of what they signified. Yet to most of the other people in the room, a horse's performance in any one of such contests seemed to give an exact clue as to its ability and class. When Basil Hunter had introduced her to the dark-haired woman whom Myra had been ordering around and who turned out to be his wife, Kate plucked up the courage to ask him to explain what a Group race was. They were the top races, Basil told her: particularly prestigious contests, graded Group One (like the Classics and the Prix de l'Arc de Triomphe), Two, or Three under the Jockey Club's Pattern System, but she had still not really grasped how exactly that worked. It was a good thing in a way, she reflected, that Achilles *did* have to go to the sales and she was not going to become a serious owner. That would mean doing a lot more homework.

Through a half-open doorway, on the far side of the room, she glimpsed a dining-room with a massive mahogany sideboard festooned with silver trophies. Barons Lodge did not look like the home of an out-of-form trainer to her, but Diana had been adamant that things had been slipping badly in the past few years. Maybe the house had become a sort of museum and the trophies were all relics of previous triumphs, she mused. On a quick visit to the downstairs cloakroom on the way in she had found herself in another shrine to the past. Row upon row of faded photographs of winners decorated the dark-green striped walls interspersed with a few *Spy* cartoons of owners, trainers and jockeys. Sir Digby had certainly given Tod a lot to live up to.

Kate realized with a start that a tall figure was standing in front of her carrying two bottles of wine. It was Tod's assistant trainer, Charlie Kyle, the short-tempered young man she had encountered earlier at the sales. She felt immediately wary.

'More wine?' he asked abruptly, proffering one of the bottles.

'No, thanks,' she replied equally curtly, thrown by his presence and aware how ungracious she sounded.

Charlie shrugged his shoulders. 'You seem a little left out,' he observed. 'If you're looking for Diana, she's just been out in the yard looking at one of our horses, but she's back now – over there, talking to Lucy Beckhampton.' He indicated with his head before moving on.

It was time she got back to the Old Rectory, Kate thought. It was getting late: she'd had quite enough to drink, and she certainly did not want any more patronizing remarks from Charlie Kyle. She would walk back to the sales paddocks to collect her car. A bit of fresh air was just what she needed.

As she made her way to the door, Lucy Beckhampton caught sight of her as she gazed languidly around the room and waved a hand in greeting.

'Hi! Kate, I hope you're having an amusing time.'

She was looking very striking in what looked like a pair of jade-green silk pyjamas. On one of her slender fingers she was sporting a large emerald and diamond ring.

'You haven't seen Daddy, have you?' Lucy inquired.

'I'm afraid not,' Kate replied, with genuine regret. She had been wondering where Tod had got to and hoping she might see him before she left. Their meeting had been brief but she had found him attractive, particularly his lop-sided smile and low soothing voice. Also he had not bombarded her with a lot of jargon, like some of the horse people she had met today.

'Oh, well!' Lucy shrugged her elegant shoulders. 'He's probably dropped in for a drink with someone somewhere and is busy getting pissed.' She turned to Alain du Roc at her side. 'Alain, come and meet a new face. Always welcome in stuffy old Newmarket. This is Kate: she's a photographer.' As Kate shook the jockey's hand, she continued, 'Well, I'll leave you two together.'

Kate had never met Alain du Roc in the flesh before. Although he was a top jockey in France, he also rode frequently in England and she had seen him in the distance both at Newmarket racecourse and on the television. He was shorter yet more substantial than she had imagined, with broad shoulders bulging under his white polo-necked sweater and a powerful handshake. He was older and more simian-looking too, but with his dark hair and rather leathery skin reminded her of her first real lover, a half-French photographer called Georges who had taught her a great deal about photographing landscapes as well as about sex and who had had similar amused, berry-black eyes.

Du Roc's English was fluent, she discovered, although he spoke it with a strong French accent. He would be riding again in England next season; the international art dealer, Maurice Weinburger, for whom he rode in France, was switching a small string of horses to Newmarket over the winter. He might well be riding occasionally for Tod Beckhampton, too.

'Tod and I go back a long time,' du Roc explained. 'His first wife Monique and her parents, Guy and Jeanne de Bernay, were old friends of my father's. They owned neighbouring stud farms in Normandy. My parents were devastated when Monique was killed. Such a terrible thing to happen.' He shook his head sadly. 'Particularly as Lucy was so young.'

So Lucy was not Myra's daughter, then; Kate was not surprised. They certainly did not look at all alike. 'What happened to Monique?' she asked tentatively, aware of du Roc's melancholy expression. 'I'm afraid I don't know anything about it.'

'She was killed in a car crash when Lucy was only two.' He sighed. 'She was very beautiful, Monique. Just like Lucy, although perhaps a little softer, *plus douce*.'

'How awful!' How awful for Tod, Kate realized she meant. She knew what it was like to lose someone you loved suddenly and unexpectedly. It had happened to her, after all, when her father was killed in the helicopter crash when she was only fourteen. She knew how long it took to recover from a shock like that and what scars it could leave.

'Yes, indeed, it was,' du Roc nodded solemnly. 'The whole village went into mourning, I recall. Jeanne de Bernay hoped that Tod would stay in France and take over the running of the stud; she was always fond of him. But he came back to England instead and took the job as assistant to old Sir Digby. And then, soon after, he married his daughter. *Voilà!*'

Kate listened to all this with interest. 'So Tod took over the yard when Sir Digby retired, then,' she said. 'It must have been quite a challenge.'

Du Roc smiled. '*Bien sûr*. But Tod is a very good trainer, you know. He had many great triumphs in the seventies with horses like Mafioso and the filly, Prism. Unfortunately, I never rode her myself' – he made a face – 'but I got very tired of the view of her backside. She was a real flier!' He took a sip of champagne. 'But things have not gone so well recently, I am afraid,' he went on. 'So many of the original owners have gone and Tod has had such bad luck with the wretched virus.'

He shrugged his shoulders. 'However, as we say in France *"il n'y a chance qui ne rechange"*.'

He swung round as Joe Weston, who had been waiting impatiently for him to stop speaking, tapped him on the shoulder. 'Mr du Roc, we are just leaving, but my wife is longing to meet you. She's a real fan of yours.'

The jockey smiled and held out his hand to the plump, homely-looking woman in a plaid dress who was gazing at him with obvious admiration. '*Enchanté, madame,*' he said with unselfconscious charm.

Kate watched his profile as he bent over Mrs Weston's hand. His was a very interesting face, she reflected, sensitive yet scarred by experience; the result of years of wasting and struggling to keep in peak fitness clearly etched in those lines on the forehead and around the dark eyes. She would definitely like to photograph him some time, she decided. She must talk to Reg Gunn, her picture editor, to see if she could persuade him to commission a feature.

Glaring at her reflection in the dressing-table mirror, Myra Beckhampton shook her powder puff angrily, dabbed it across her face with a shaking hand and banged it back in its bowl. It had been a present from her father: part of a whole silver and enamelled dressing-table set which he had given her for her twenty-first birthday. She dreaded what her father would have said about the way things were going at Barons Lodge at the moment. The yard might well be down to less than forty full boxes next season. In Sir Digby's day they had sometimes had over a hundred horses, owned by respected members of the Jockey Club and some of the other grandest and most sporting owners in the country. Many of them used to come and stay for the big race weeks and the sales, of course, and Myra would never forget accompanying her father when he took them on his evening stable rounds, particularly during July week when the horses were always at their gleaming best and the lads, standing quietly at their heads, specially dressed in smart white drill jackets for the occasion. Nowadays, with the exception of Stelios Alexandros, what owners they had left either seemed to be syndicate members, car dealers, or bathroom manufacturers from north of the Trent, she reflected bitterly.

As she selected a hairpin from the little tray in front of her, there was a knock on the bedroom door.

'Myra? Are you there? Can I have a word?' Pam asked plaintively.

She opened the door and peered into the room. 'Ah, here you are! We didn't know where you'd got to. Everyone's starving and Dorcas is agitating about dinner. She insists that unless we eat soon her duck will be ruined.' She hovered anxiously in the doorway.

'Well, that's not my fault, is it?' Myra replied crossly, smoothing back her hair and fastening it more tightly at the back. 'It's Tod who's holding us up. God knows where he's got to.'

Pam's face cleared. 'Oh, it's all right. He's just rung up. Said to start without him if we're in a hurry. He spoke to Basil. He's just popped into Gerry Carnegie's for a drink. That Sir Ivor colt he's been looking at for Prince Hassim is quite something, he told Basil. Anyway, he'll be back soon.'

'Mmm, well, he'd be in even less of a hurry if he knew what I've got to report,' Myra replied, picking up her lipstick.

'Why? What's happened?' Pam asked, concerned.

'I've just had a phone call from that dreary little man Simons. He's taking his horses away at the end of the season, he told me, which means we won't be getting any of his yearlings either.'

Pam sank down on one of the beds. 'Oh dear,' she said, sympathetically, smoothing the pink satin bedspread beside her. 'That is bad news.'

Myra swung round on her stool to face her, her eyes narrowed. 'Yes, it is, isn't it! It's bloody disastrous, in fact. Stelios is the only decent owner we've got left and it's only a question of time before he sends all his horses over to Ireland,' she added despairingly. 'Prince Hassim is our last chance, Pam. We simply have to get him to send us some yearlings. If Tod blows this one, I'll never forgive him!' She turned back to her dressing table and seizing her bottle of Mitsouku sprayed it vehemently on one side of her neck and then the other.

'I'm sure Tod won't blow it – why should he? He wants Hassim's horses as much as you do, surely?' Pam insisted.

Myra picked up her lipstick and painted her mouth with care. 'I'm not so sure,' she said slowly. 'I know we've had a lot of bad luck with the virus and everything but I really do think it's more complex than that. I think Tod's lost his ambition too – resigned himself to being a failure from now on. I really can't handle that.' She grabbed a tissue from the box in front of her and clamped her lips down on it. 'But Hassim is loaded with money and wants to buy horses that win races, and we need him.'

As she got up slowly, smoothing her skirt over her hips, a door banged downstairs in the hall and there was some excited yapping followed by the sound of claws skittering across a wooden floor.

'Cool it, girls! Gert, Daisy. Come here. Calm down.' Tod's voice in the distance sounded relaxed and slightly slurred.

Myra headed briskly towards the door. 'Hmm, well, he's back all right but he sounds tight to me,' she said disapprovingly. 'I'd better go and break the news to him. If he's capable of taking it in, that is.'

CHAPTER THREE

Fleet Street – the **Sunday Chronicle**

Kate stood by the window of the sixth-floor office watching the rain sluice down the long plate-glass windows. The open-plan room behind her, partitioned off from the main section of the magazine, with its journalists' clutter of desks, phones, typewriters and computers, was the domain of the art department and although it was early evening, several members of the staff were still bent quietly over their layout pages. Some of their work areas were incredibly untidy, with a jumble of proof pages, packs of transparencies, books and rulers as well as numerous dirty coffee mugs and used ashtrays. It was amazing, Kate often thought, that the magazine's pages came out looking as clean and professional as they did.

She had been called in for a discussion of the pictures they were going to use for the Diana Saunders piece, and had brought in the final batch she had taken at Three Swallows over the weekend of Diana with her two resident stallions, Grand Hotel and Greek Dancer. The picture editor, Reg Gunn, was a newspaper photographer by training, who some years ago had chosen to abandon the pursuit of news stories, war and natural disasters in favour of a desk job in the more tranquil pastures of magazine journalism. As a result he often complained that magazine work was boring. Some photographers found him impossible to work with, as he was so passionately opposed to any attempt at lyrical, 'arty-farty' pictures as he called them. But Kate found his sharp newshound's eye educational and she knew that her work had improved under his tuition.

Today, however, he was beginning to irritate her. The pictures were 'OK', but they weren't sexy enough, he complained. He was also taking even longer than usual to choose the ones he wanted to use, poring over the light box with his habitually critical expression, a cigarette drooping from the corner of his mouth. Perhaps she was being unduly impatient, Kate told herself – after all, it was important to get the feature right; but it was a dark, dismal afternoon and she was longing to get the whole matter settled and be heading back up the M11 to Hazeley. That was the only drawback to living at the Old Rectory really, having to drive all the way back there when she was tired, as she was today. The moment the sale of the Battersea house where she had lived with Hugo went through, she really must find herself another *pied-à-terre* in London.

'Ah ha!' Reg suddenly exclaimed with relish. 'These ones are more like it.'

Kate swung round with relief. She had a good idea which pictures he was referring to.

'This one here – *la* Saunders rubbing noses with one of the beasts. Or this one, with her gazing into its eyes. That's more like it, sweetheart – just the ticket.'

'If we use either of those, I'd prefer it to be this one,' Kate replied, pointing to one of the transparencies.

'Why's that?' Reg pulled at his cigarette.

'Because that's Greek Dancer. The sire of our colt – the one that's going to the sales tomorrow. The year before last was Greek Dancer's first ever year at stud, you see. So he needs all the publicity he can get.'

Reg gave her a withering look. 'Come off it, girl. Since when have we been in the free advertising business? What a cheek!'

Kate shrugged. 'Maybe,' she replied equably. 'But I think you'll find it's the better picture. I made sure of that!'

Tattersalls Sales Paddocks, Newmarket

Less than twenty-four hours later, Kate and Diana, sheltering from the slanting rain under a large golf umbrella, were standing by the paddock rail, watching Achilles being led round before he went into the ring, his lot number 506 prominently displayed on his quarters. Lady Kitty had declined to be present. She had become so fond of the colt, she confessed, that she really could not bear to witness him being sold. The Levertons' groom, Davy, though, had insisted on being present and was standing beside Kate now, his craggy face anxious as he watched Achilles and his tall gangling Three Swallows groom.

'They might have given him to a smaller lad, to be sure,' he muttered unhappily. 'Back home we always had a rule, never be giving an undersized yearling to a tallish groom. This one makes our fella look like a Shetland pony.'

Achilles was an impressive walker, though. Even Kate could see that. He strode out in a bold fluid manner, his hind feet overstepping his front hoofprints; but he was clearly not in a very good mood, constantly shaking his head in an irritated way at the wet and laying back his long lop ears.

'Tod Beckhampton liked him, you know. Said he reminded him of a tricky colt he trained years back who'd also got Hyperion blood,' Diana informed Kate cheerily. 'But I have to admit that the other buggers that have had a look at him – and there have been about twenty of them – have been pretty bloody critical. They obviously think he's too small, and a lot of them don't like his being black. Trouble is, he's in such a lousy mood too. He hates being pulled in and out of his box so often.'

When the colt was finally led into the ring it was obvious that his spirits had not improved. He looked tiny, bedraggled and thoroughly put out, Kate observed with a sinking heart. Halfway round the ring he halted, refusing to move at all, and just stared suspiciously about him at the lights and tiers of people, swishing his wispy tail.

'Strewth! He's not the best advertisement for the stud as a yearling's finishing school, is he?' Diana joked. 'He looks like Muffin the Mule.'

By the time Achilles agreed to stride on, the auctioneer was already in full flood, intoning the colt's pedigree and running through all his illustrious antecedents with as much enthusiasm as he could muster.

'A grandson of the great Northern Dancer, ladies and gentlemen, out of a Roan Rocket mare. He may be small but he's a May foal and has got plenty of time to grow. He could have it all. Speed and stamina, and as you can see, he's as sound as a bell. Five thousand – he's worth ten times more than that, but we'll start at five, ladies and gentlemen.'

He looked searchingly around the half-empty auditorium, finding little response. There was a bid of ten thousand guineas, then ten and a half, then eleven, but as Kate watched the colt reluctantly following his handler round the ring like a recalcitrant dog, her embarrassment mounted. Why was he making himself look so unappealing? she wondered in despair.

'Christ, he's not even going to make his reserve,' Diana whispered, as the bidding faltered yet again at thirteen and a half thousand guineas and the auctioneer, however valiantly he tried, seemed unable to revive any more interest.

Yet when, seconds later, his hammer fell and he announced that Lot

506 was being led out unsold, Kate experienced an overwhelming sense of relief. They would have to try to sell him privately now, she supposed, but at least he was still theirs, for a short while.

Diana led the way out, maintaining her usual good humour despite the battery of sympathetic looks and commiserations.

'Oh, well, you can't win them all,' she remarked philosophically. 'I sold a Habitat filly for precisely double the amount I expected yesterday. It's all swings and roundabouts as usual! I'll try to rustle up some interest in a private sale, of course, but it might be wise to wait a bit, until he's grown some more, I mean.' She turned to have a word with James Delahooke, a bloodstock agent Kate knew she particularly admired, and was soon deep in discussion about another of her yearlings, her disappointment over Achilles temporarily forgotten.

Kate, followed by Davy, hurried on, anxious to catch up with the colt before he was led back to his box. They found him, standing disconsolately on the raked gravel, still quivering with nerves.

Davy ran his hand gently down his neck. 'There, there, fella. You can relax now. There, there,' he reassured him. 'He'll not be easy to train, this one,' he went on gloomily, turning to Kate. 'Need all the patience in the world, I'm thinking. He's terrible highly strung.'

Lady Kitty's reaction to the news that, for the moment at least, they still owned the colt was predictable. Levering herself up abruptly from her chair, dislodging an indignant whippet in the process, she hopped round the floor, clapping her hands with delight, her enthusiasm in no way diminished by the fact that despite the operation she was still in considerable pain from her hip.

'There you are, it's fate: that's what it is. We're not meant to lose him yet,' she exclaimed. She caught sight of the look on Kate's face and sat down again more slowly. 'It's all right, dearie. I know: I'm a sentimental old fool. We can't afford to keep him and that's that. I just wish we could, that's all!' She looked unusually wistful. 'Diana will find a buyer for him sooner or later, I'm sure. She's a very resourceful girl. You'd better pour us a stiff sherry, or a whisky, if you'd rather. I can't say I've done a thing today but I feel completely worn out! Oh, by the way,' she added, settling herself back in her chair, 'there's a letter for you in the hall. From Hugo by the look of it.'

As Kate sat down with her drink and tentatively opened the envelope plastered with unfamiliar American stamps, Lute leapt gracefully on to her lap and curled up, settling his long blue nose in her crotch.

26

Dear Kate,

There's been a major change of plan. Amy's father has, at last, offered me a job. Am also about to land a weekly slot on local TV. What looks like being a pretty tasteless (sic) food and wine show but who cares – the money is fantastic. So there's no question of us living in London now. Amy thinks she's already found us a house, in St Helena. Also, Christmas in London is off too although I shall have to come back to sort things out finally in the New Year. Suggest you put No. 12 on the market as soon as possible.

As we agreed, half the money from the sale therefore is yours. I hear prices in Battersea have rocketed, so get cracking.

All the best to Kitty,

Love,

Hugo

Kate put the letter back in its envelope, gulping down some sherry as she pondered its implications. It was good news indeed. She wouldn't now have to face Hugo and the toothsome Amy at Christmas, which she had been dreading, and she'd been longing to get rid of the Battersea house anyway. Also, it meant that she would have quite a bit more money. Her mind started sprinting along several different tracks.

'Well?' her mother asked cautiously.

Kate looked up with a smile. 'Sorry, I was just trying to take it all in. It's good news, you'll be happy to hear.' She explained the contents of the letter.

Lady Kitty looked relieved. 'Well, that's grand then. How much do you think the house'll fetch?'

Kate shrugged her shoulders. 'I'm not sure. The last valuation I got was £100,000 but that could be a bit high.' She paused reflectively as an idea began to crystallize in her mind. 'Kitty, I've had a brilliant wheeze. My turn for once!' she announced, her eyes bright with excitement. Scooping up Lute she carried him over to her mother's chair and flopped down cross-legged at her feet.

Lady Kitty looked down at her, her face concerned in the lamplight. 'Have you, now? Well, we'd better hear it,' she replied gently.

She knew her daughter well. Normally Kate was far more cautious than she was herself. But she was also very determined and occasionally would decide to do something unexpected and out of character, like when she decided at the last minute not to go to art school but to become a photographer instead, insisting that she did not have enough

27

talent to make it as an artist, although that was not the general view. She wondered, with a certain apprehension, what was coming now.

Kate settled Lute on her lap again, tucking in his dangling paws.

'You don't mind if I stay on here for a while, do you? I'll put No. 12 on the market next week, of course, but I don't think I feel ready to go back to London just yet.'

'This is your home as long as you want it to be. You know that,' her mother replied patiently.

'Well, look: my share of the house sale could be around £50,000, couldn't it?' Kate continued. 'Even including all the expenses of selling and everything I should have at least £40,000 left. Well, we could use it to keep Achilles in training for a year, couldn't we, and just see what happens. What do you think?' She searched her mother's face eagerly for her response.

Lady Kitty eased herself up in her chair, grappling with several different emotions. 'You're a grand girl, Kate. I love the idea. But I can't let you do it. It's out of the question,' she replied as firmly as she could manage.

'Why? It's my money. Or rather it will be. I can do what I like with it.' Kate was indignant.

Lady Kitty shook her head. 'I can't let you squander your money on a horse, dearie. He may be useless and then it's all been wasted. Not what your Hugo would call a very shrewd investment now, is it?'

'He's not "my Hugo" any more, Kitty, he's Amy's. And it's exactly what you would do if you had the money, isn't it? Go on, admit it!' Kate replied heatedly. 'And you most certainly don't think Achilles will be useless. You've always had faith in him.'

'I've often been wrong about horses. Who hasn't?' Lady Kitty said firmly. 'Look, Kate. You'll need that money for your future. You won't want to be staying on here for ever. You'll need every penny you've got to get yourself a nice place in London. I may be old enough and stupid enough to go wasting my money on horses but you are most certainly not!'

'I'm not planning to "waste" very much,' Kate insisted. 'Only £10,000. That's about what it takes to keep a horse in training for a year, isn't it? I'll put the rest down on a flat and take out a mortgage and all that sensible stuff in my own good time.' Her face assumed an innocent expression. 'Perhaps you'd rather I gave you £10,000 towards the roof? After all, as you say, this is my home too. I ought to share the responsibility of making sure it doesn't fall down, shouldn't I?'

'Oh, to hell with the roof!' her mother retorted. 'It doesn't seem to be getting any worse. The major repairs will just have to wait.' She got up and, limping over to the fireplace, lit one of her cheroots.

'It's no good your trying to put me off. You know how obstinate I can be,' Kate went on. 'The more I think about the idea, the more I like it. Look – just think of it as a thank-you from me, for all the worry I've put you through recently.' Her cheeks flushed, she gazed at her mother imploringly. 'You started all this, Kitty, you got us going on this particular rollercoaster. We can hardly jump off now, can we? We can't just abandon Achilles, when no one else wants him.'

Lady Kitty regarded her affectionately through a haze of smoke. It was uncanny, she reflected: Kate argued just like her father, instinctively knowing how best to appeal.

'You remind me so much of David sometimes. It quite takes my breath away,' she observed.

'Well, there you are then,' Kate replied triumphantly. 'Daddy would have wanted us to have an adventure, I know. You said so yourself at the start. Well, now it's my turn to make a contribution. That's fair, isn't it?' She looked at her mother defiantly, her head on one side. 'You of all people wouldn't want to spoil my fun now, would you?'

Lady Kitty put down her cheroot, her face breaking into a delighted smile. 'That I would not,' she agreed. 'All right, Kate, you win. You little witch!' She held open her arms. 'Well, go on! What are we waiting for? There's a bottle of Krug at the back of the fridge. Let's drink to the rebirth of the Rathglin colours.'

An hour later, the two women were up in the attic, rummaging through a collection of dusty boxes, suitcases and trunks, watched with some curiosity by the two whippets curled up on a pile of old brocade curtains. Lady Kitty, looking girlish and dishevelled, had dived into the contents of a particularly ancient trunk with all the keenness of a terrier digging out a fox.

'They must be in here somewhere. I packed them myself. I even remembered the mothballs,' she muttered.

Reaching down she seized upon a mound a tissue paper and, unwrapping it, handed Kate a tiny pink and white smocked dress, delicately embroidered with rosebuds.

'Heavens! I'd forgotten all about this,' she exclaimed.

'What on earth is it?' Kate asked in surprise.

29

'Your first party dress. I had it made for you in Hong Kong. You never liked it,' her mother replied smiling.

'But it's beautiful. Look at the sewing. It ought to be in a museum,' Kate replied. She couldn't imagine any daughter of hers ever wearing it. Of course, she might never have any children herself at all. She had never wanted them with Hugo because she'd not felt ready to embark on such an enormous responsibility and had then realized she didn't love him enough to want his child anyway. Hugo himself had never been keen on the idea. Babies were a bore, he said, an impediment to all the good things in life like travel, entertaining and sleeping in late.

'Here we are. Now then, Kate, just take a look at these!' Lady Kitty laid a long cardboard box on the floor in front of her and reverently lifted up the racing silks for Kate to see. 'There you are: the Rathglin colours. They haven't been seen on the racecourse for twenty years – not since that day Father's Mr Mullingar pulled up lame at Fairyhouse. He'd been hoping to run him in the National later in the season but he'd broken down. We were all devastated. That was it, Father said. He'd been looking for an excuse to pull out of racing and just concentrate on the breeding side.' She lifted the silks and held them up to the light. 'So our colours, dark green, old gold epaulets and cap, went into mothballs. But your uncle kept them registered over the years. It was one of his little extravagances. And, as you know, he left them to me in his will, the sweetheart.'

Kate lifted her glass of champagne. 'Here's to Achilles,' she said. 'It's all up to him now – and whoever we can get to train him, of course.' She gazed lovingly at the silks before dropping them back into the box.

When, the following morning, they rang Diana Saunders to tell her of their decision she was delighted. 'Good for you – very sporting. Let's hope he turns out to be a champ. He'll be a late developer, though; there'll be no point in hurrying him. He's an awkward little sod.'

'Who do you think we should ask to train him?' Kate asked. 'Kitty thinks it should be someone in Newmarket so that we won't have far to go if we want to go to see him or watch him on the gallops.'

'Hmm . . . I'd go for a small to middle-sized yard, if I were you,' Diana suggested. 'He might get lost in one of the one-hundred-plus jobs. You could send him to Tod Beckhampton, of course. He seemed to like the colt, after all, and whatever problems he is having, he's still a good trainer. He's not greedy either, like some of them. Shall I give him a ring?'

Kate hesitated. 'Well, I thought I'd go racing tomorrow and maybe put it to him myself.'

'Good idea. If you look for me outside the weighing room after the first race, we'll go and find him together. He's got a couple of runners, I think – quite a fancied one in the Cesarewitch. You'd better allow plenty of time to get to the course, though: there's always a whopping big crowd on Champion Stakes Day.'

Rowley Mile Racecourse, Newmarket

Diana was dead right, Kate realized the following morning as she joined the slow-moving queue of traffic from London and Cambridge at the July course roundabout and began to crawl bumper to bumper over the heath. She had had a sudden desire to see Achilles before she went to the racecourse and had called in at Three Swallows on her way. The colt seemed much happier now that he was back in his old box and Kate stroked his nose for a minute, trying to convey to him that all was well and that they had not deserted him. Diana and her house guests had clearly already left for the races so Kate followed them on alone.

She was having trouble with the slow running of her MGB which Hugo had given her as a present to assuage some of his guilt, she presumed, just before he had left for California the second time with the seduction of Amy obviously on his mind. She had got very fond of the car, though she did not usually get attached to inanimate objects. 'It's a bit flashy for you. More Kitty's style really,' Hugo had joked. 'Still, you can always sell it.' He'd been wrong, as he often was about her. The only reason he regarded her as a cautious driver was that she hardly ever drove when they were together. He had criticized her driving so frequently that it had affected her confidence and she'd given up, except when he had had too much to drink. The moment she got the little car to herself, though, she soon got her nerve back and revelled in its compact power and speed.

Stalling again by a gap in the hedge, Kate caught sight of the racecourse and the Rowley Mile stands away to her left, looking like a great beached liner stranded on the wide sweep of the heath. A Mercedes behind her hooted impatiently and alongside her a chauffeur-driven Rolls, crammed with people in hats all perusing *The Sporting Life*, seemed intent on forcing her off the road. There was obviously a shortage of patience, if not of money, among some racegoers, she reflected, as the gleaming line of cars crawled, as though magnetized, towards the Members' Enclosure.

Later, as she queued for her Daily Members' Badge, she was almost swamped by a line of men hurrying on to the course as though late for a train, and dressed in what seemed like a regulation uniform of trilbies, dark blue and camel hair or 'covert' overcoats.

'Hello, Caroline. Your mare should run well today. Looks a snip at the weights,' one of them called cheerily over his shoulder.

'The trip'll suit her but she'll hate the going,' the girl stalking behind him replied, as she bent to adjust the metal badge on her lapel. A lot of racing women looked a bit like horses themselves, with their long limbs, long necks and glossy hair, Kate reflected, except that their eyes were closer together.

By the time she'd got her bearings, the runners for the first race were already leaving the paddock. She squeezed into a gap on the wooden rail to watch them being led out on to the course. It was not just the sight of racehorses that was exciting, but also the sound and the smell of them as they came bouncing past, half a ton of bursting pent-up energy about to explode down the track. Alain du Roc, in the Weinburgers' well-known lime-green and white silks, was the last to leave the paddock and was having some trouble with his mount, a big-framed bay. He bent low over the horse's head, easing himself effort-lessly up in the stirrups as the horse gave another cheeky buck. '*Tiens, tiens, calme-toi*,' said softly, placing a soothing hand on the horse's shoulder. He looked unconcerned and totally in control. Mmm, she must pursue that idea of photographing him, Kate thought, as she turned away.

Du Roc won the race, a mile and a quarter handicap, skilfully settling his horse at the back of the field before unleashing a run in the middle of the course in the last half-furlong to win cosily by a length.

Kate tried to watch the race from in front of the stands but she found that she could see nothing but the backs and heads of the people in front; also, the horses seemed to be running straight towards her. Presumably, to see anything at all at Newmarket it was advisable to climb to the top of the stands. She was gazing upwards, wondering how to get there, when she bumped into a smallish man in a camel-haired coat smoking a cigar who immediately raised his trilby. It was Joe Weston.

'Hello there,' he said. 'So you didn't manage to sell that colt of yours after all. Can't say I'm surprised. Not enough of him, for my taste. Didn't like the look of his temperament, either.'

'We're keeping him, as a matter of fact. Putting him into training ourselves,' Kate replied coldly, annoyed by this disparaging comment.

Weston raised his eyebrows. 'Are you, now? Well, the best of luck to you,' he replied cheerily. 'Don't forget to back our Southwold Jack in the Cesarewitch. He's got an each-way chance, especially now that the ground's come up soft and the frog's riding him! The wife's over the moon!'

An intimidating man in a dark suit and bowler hat was blocking the way to the weighing room, scrutinizing everyone's badges. Not certain whether her badge guaranteed entry to this holy of holies or not, Kate waited outside, peering over the shoulders of the *cognoscenti* milling around on the weighing-room steps. Diana was easy to pick out in a red and white checked suit with a scarlet trilby and matching boots. She was leaning on the rail gazing knowledgeably at the winner as he was led round and round by his delighted lad, steam still rising from his back. Kate recognized a few other people in the mêlée: the tall figure of Henry Cecil, a cheerful-looking Michael Stoute, talking to fellow trainer, Peter Walwyn and the dapper Barry Hills – but there was no sign of Tod. Everyone seemed to be involved in animated discussion with much gesticulation and laughter, as though they were guests at some private reunion. Racing people certainly squeezed every drop of enjoyment they could out of their sport, Kate reflected.

As the horses were led away, Diana detached herself from the group she was with and came over to join Kate. 'Hi! Seen Tod yet?' she asked.

Kate shook her head. 'No, but I haven't really been looking,' she confessed.

'Well, no doubt he'll show up. He's got a couple of runners later. Come on, if we want a decent view of the Champion Stakes field, we might as well head straight for the paddock right now.' Diana took her arm briskly.

Kate noticed with surprise that clumps of people had already drifted over from the weighing room to the pre-parade ring and were milling around the entrance to the stable block and saddling boxes. Diana stopped every few paces to greet someone she knew, including a burly man in a flashy light-grey suit with a great head of matching oiled back hair and dark heavy-lidded eyes.

'Diana, hello. How are you?' he asked solicitously, holding out a tanned hand.

'Fine, thanks,' Diana replied, introducing Kate.

'How do you do?' the man said, shaking Kate's hand energetically. 'Do you have an interest in a runner here today?' he inquired. He had a gravelly voice and an unusual accent, a mixture of American and Mediterranean, presumably Greek.

'I'm afraid not,' she smiled. 'I'm just an observer,'

'Well, I envy you,' Stelios told her, solemnly. 'I get more nervous when my son's horses run than I do when my own are out on the track. Perhaps it's because they often have more of a chance!' He gave her a ponderous smile, revealing several gold-capped teeth, and his head tipped in the direction of the saddling boxes. 'I must go and join Nik now. He thinks Devilry will win today.' He looked from Kate to Diana with obvious appreciation. 'Well, goodbye then, ladies. Enjoy the race.' He raised his hand and set off purposefully in the direction of the stables.

'Who's he?' Kate was curious to know. 'He seemed rather sweet.'

'Don't know about that!' Diana made a face. 'He's a hell of a tough businessman, according to Daddy. They've done some deals together in the Far East. Stelios made his money in shipping – he's the boss of Alexandros Maritime, but the company have diversified into real estate and hotels too. He's got a few horses with Tod. He's probably his best owner, but that could all change when his son Nik takes over the licence at Kilmarron.' Turning her shoulder, she eased her way effectively around a group of people standing at the paddock's edge.

'Nik is assistant trainer to Hugh O'Donnell at Kilmarron in Tipperary,' Diana explained. 'O'Donnell's really past it now – getting very shaky, I hear. Nik really does all the training, and the moment O'Donnell snuffs it he'll be taking over the licence properly. Stelios is bound to send his horses to him then. You know what the Greeks are like about family.' She pulled out her racecard and started to study it. 'Nik's good, too, and very ambitious,' she said approvingly. 'I'd say he may *well* win this with Devilry. The colt's certainly got the form and he could even be improving.'

Watching the ten runners for the Dubai Champion Stakes tread delicately around the paddock, immaculately groomed, oiled and polished and clinking their bits, Kate noticed how mature they looked compared with yearlings like Achilles, although they were only two or three years older. She commented on this to Diana, who seemed amused.

'Sure, they are a completely different ball game,' she grinned. 'Horses have a very rapid adolescence, you know. Unlike humans, they grow up really fast, particularly once they're in training. Ah, here comes Devilry. Looks great, doesn't he?'

34

As the bell rang for the jockeys to mount, Devilry halted right in front of them. He was a powerful, deep-girthed bay, with a small white blaze on his forehead. His black mane and tail were neatly plaited and there were diamond patterns meticulously groomed on the top of his quarters.

'Wow! Nik certainly believes in having them well turned out,' Diana commented, obviously impressed.

As the horse's girth was adjusted, he danced sideways, revealing Stelios Alexandros standing behind with a tall young man who stepped forwards to leg Pat Eddery into the saddle. Hatless and wearing a navy-blue overcoat, he was very pale and slim, with jet black hair and brilliant blue eyes. Frowning intently, he watched his charge bounce off, before turning to the girl at his side, who looked uncannily like him.

'That's Stella,' Diana said. 'She and Nik are twins. Spooky, isn't it? People say they can always tell what the other one's thinking. I'm not sure I'd like that myself! Come on, let's get back to the stands.'

'What does Stella do? Is she in the horse business too?' Kate asked as she hurried after Diana.

Diana nodded. 'Sure. She runs the Alexandros's Mountclare stud. It's close to Kilmarron. Devilry was bred there, of course.'

The twins were certainly a striking-looking couple, Kate thought as she stepped on to the escalator carrying racegoers to the top of the stands. 'They don't look very like their father, do they?' she commented, turning to Diana on the step above.

The Australian shook her head. 'Nope. They look just like their mother – Stelios's first wife, Tessa, apparently. She was Irish, of course – the daughter of some dotty old aristocrat called Lord Henry Fitzgerald. He died only the other day. Anyway, Tessa drowned, so they say, when the twins were kids. Tragic really.' She broke off to wave at someone higher up the escalator. 'They're not popular, though, I'm afraid. Respected, but not liked. They're too bloody arrogant for a start.' She seized Kate's arm as they got to the top of the escalator and propelled her through the crowd swarming out to the front of the stand.

From the top of the packed stands, Newmarket Heath, shimmering below, looked like a lake of gold. Its surface was broken only by the undulating line of Devil's Dyke in the distance and the curve of the plough beyond. As the runners for the Champion Stakes peeled away from the parade and cantered down to the start hundreds of pairs of binoculars swung right to watch them blurring into the haze.

Five minutes later, as the commentator announced that they were about to go into the stalls, Kate sensed a tangible tightening of tension all round. Although there were television cameras suspended at various intervals from the roof of the stand, from where she was standing she couldn't see the runners clearly on the screen. As a result, when the off was announced and the distant clump of horses began to speed towards the stands, she had to rely on the commentator and additional information from Diana pressed against her in the crush, her binoculars glued to her eyes.

'*As they come to the end of the first furlong, it's Abbeville, followed by Morne Mountain, Weatherman tucked in on the rails. Screen Dancer going well on the stands side. Angelica's Pride leads on the far side with Devilry on a back markers.*'

'Eddery's really dropped him out,' Diana muttered. 'Du Roc's well placed on Weatherman though – they are going at a hell of a pace.'

By the time Kate, standing on tiptoe, could really see the horses, they were passing the famous Bushes and meeting the rising ground, and there was such a crescendo of noise all around that she had a sudden fear that the roof of the stands might be blasted off by the volume. Trapped in this wall of noise, she watched du Roc's lime-green colours surging ahead on the far side of the course.

'Christ, he's hit the front too soon,' Diana said beside her.

Suddenly, in the centre of the track, Devilry shot out of a pack of horses and began eating up the ground with long, seemingly effortless strides. As the two horses passed the winning post in a blast of cheering it was impossible to know which one of them had won.

Diana clapped Kate on the shoulder, her face glowing. 'Wasn't that terrific? Weatherman really ran for du Roc. I don't think he hung on, though; a mile is his best trip. I think Devilry just got up on the line. Anyway, I'm off to find out. See you.' She darted off, pushing her way through the crowd.

There was such a crush of people shuffling towards the exits now that Kate decided to stay up in the stands for a while. Jumping down the emptying tiers she leant on the parapet and gazed down at the crowd below, swirling impatiently round the bookmakers as they waited for the result of the photograph to be announced. She could see why her mother loved this course and said it reminded her of the Curragh: there was the same great sweep of uncluttered grassland and sky. She envisaged Kitty, watching the racing at home with the whippets beside her, and wondered whether she had been on the winner of the last race. One of her mother's most cherished extravagances was

36

her credit account with William Hill. If Achilles ever gets to the racecourse, Kate mused, God knows what Kitty will risk on him. But Achilles might never race at all. There was a high percentage of yearlings who never did, due to some mishap, injury or ailment, she'd gathered from Diana. She was beginning to realize the extent of their financial gamble.

Turning back to the stands, she suddenly noticed Tod Beckhampton, hatless in a brown tweed suit, standing on the steps above her, polishing his glasses on a silk handkerchief, his eyebrows slightly raised.

'Ah, it *is* you!' he said, stepping down to her side. 'I'm getting blinder by the hour. You were looking very pensive.'

Kate smiled. She was pleased to see him, she realized. 'Hello. I was about to come looking for you, as a matter of fact. There's something I want to ask you.'

'Really? I hope to God it's something I can answer! I'm not feeling exceptionally bright today.' He gave her a lop-sided grin.

He did indeed look strained, Kate thought. There was plenty of colour in his face, due to riding out in all weathers, no doubt, but his eyes behind the glasses looked bloodshot and tired.

'It's about our Greek Dancer colt – Achilles. Diana Saunders says you had a look at him at the sales and quite liked him.'

Tod looked at her thoughtfully. 'Yes. I did like him. He's got a hell of a lot of growing to do and his temperament could be tricky. But he's definitely got something and I think he's an athlete. Reminds me of another little horse I had once when I'd just taken over from Digby. He had Hyperion blood too. He was difficult to train and we never got him right at two but his three-year-old career went exceptionally well until he broke down. He was beaten by only a head in the St James's Palace on ground that didn't suit him, but he went on to win the Prix Jacques le Marois at Deauville. Anyway, that was years ago. How can I help you? Didn't you sell him yesterday, then? I never got up to the sales myself, I'm afraid!'

'He didn't make his reserve,' Kate told him. 'I can't say I'm surprised. He is such a titch and he put on a miserable display in the ring, which put people off too. He was obviously in a foul mood.' She paused. 'So we've decided to keep him ourselves and run him in my mother's old family colours. We are ridiculously excited about it. We wondered whether you would like to train him for us?' she asked as casually as she could manage.

The public-address system crackled overhead. 'The result of the photograph is first No. 3 Devilry, second No. 11 Weatherman. The third horse was No. 6 Morne Mountain. The distance was a neck and three lengths. A neck and three lengths.'

She was very appealing, Tod thought, as she stood there expectantly in front of him in the sunlight in her becoming russet outfit. Even if the yard had been full, he wouldn't have been able to turn her down.

'Of course I'll train him for you,' he said, smiling. 'It would be an honour.' God knows we've got the room, he thought to himself. Myra would be delighted, too, of course. She was a raging snob and Lady Kitty was an Earl's daughter, after all; it would cheer her up considerably to add the Levertons to Barons Lodge's dwindling list of owners.

'He'll be a bit of a challenge, I suspect, your little colt,' he added thoughtfully. 'Where is he at the moment – back at Three Swallows?'

Kate nodded, still smiling broadly with delight.

'Right, I'll give Diana a ring, then, and arrange for him to be brought over. Perhaps your mother would like to give me a ring over the weekend – to find out the worst about the training fees, etc.' He made a face. 'I'm not the most expensive in Newmarket by any means, but we have just had to put them up, I'm afraid. You might change your minds!' He glanced at his watch. 'Christ, it's time I went and saddled up old Southwold Jack.'

On a sudden impulse, Kate stood on tiptoe and kissed him on the cheek. He smelt pleasantly of Eau Sauvage, French tobacco and also, faintly, of alcohol.

'Thanks so much, Tod,' she said gratefully. 'Kitty will be thrilled. I can't wait to get home to tell her. We'll call you tomorrow.'

As the escalator bore him down to ground level, Tod realized that his flagging spirits had lifted noticeably. Kate's kiss had completely taken him by surprise. He would not have expected her to be so demonstrative. He wondered if she was married, or seriously attached to anyone. If so, it was obviously not anyone in the racing world. There was an honesty and softness about those grey eyes which he found particularly appealing. But he really must not allow himself to fantasize about her further, he was in no position to get involved with anyone, particularly someone so young and vulnerable as Kate. And, after all, if life got too bleak, he could always seek out his old friend and mistress, Marie Claire – although she was so seldom in London nowadays that he hadn't seen her for over a year.

He was glad that the little Greek Dancer colt was coming to Barons Lodge. He was very small and had an awkward temperament, obviously, but he liked him for some reason; he couldn't put his finger on why. But what with him and Prince Hassim's three yearlings now installed in the yard, and the possibility that Southwold Jack could run quite well today, there might even be a few smiles around the dinner table this evening, just for a change.

CHAPTER FOUR

Barons Lodge

Prince Hassim's bay colt, Bahir, threw up his head, his eyes glassy in the electric light, as Tod, followed by his head lad, Sam Shaw, strode in to his box. Tod was at the end of his usual evening stables routine, checking the well-being of each horse after it had been fed and dressed over for the night, with all the care of a Harley Street physician visiting patients in an expensive private clinic.

He glanced in the manger. 'How's he been doing today, then, Angie? Settling in all right at last? He certainly seems to be eating up better.'

The stable girl, holding the colt's head collar, reached over and gently stroked his nose. 'He's been heaps better this week, Mr Beckhampton. Seems to have got the hang of the lungeing at last, haven't you, sweetheart?'

Angie, Sam Shaw's nineteen-year-old daughter, was a stocky girl, with curly blonde hair, friendly brown eyes and a cheerful expression.

'Good. He's a nervous colt, though, so we'd better go slowly.' Tod turned to his head lad. 'We'll try a saddle on him tomorrow and aim to back him by the end of the week.' He looked at the colt with his head on one side. 'He'd better be good. He cost nearly half a million. Right, Sam, I think that's it, isn't it? Check Southwold Jack again later, will you? Let me know if there's any more heat in that leg. He had a hell of a hard race.'

'He could have won, sir, if he had been ridden differently,' Sam commented dourly, picking up a broom that had been left outside the box door.

Alain du Roc had ridden a brilliant tactical race on Southwold Jack, an inveterate front runner with bottomless stamina and not much speed. He had set up such a lead in the first half-mile that he had only just been caught on the run in by one of the bottom weights. Most of the staff at Barons Lodge had had the sense to back him each way, so

40

they were reasonably satisfied with the result, but Sam had been more than usually critical of the French jockey. He had come south to work for Tod when he had first taken over from his father-in-law Sir Digby Hunter and he had old-fashioned views about what he called 'flashy riding'. He was also a loyal supporter of Barons Lodge's retained stable jockey, a fellow Yorkshireman called Jack Massam, and always disapproved when Tod or one of his owners wanted him jocked off.

Tod put his hand on his shoulder. 'Come on now, Sam! Alain rode a cracking race. Anyway, it was my idea to try to set up a lead like that, so don't blame him. Right, see you in the morning, then.' He closed the box door carefully and switched off the light. 'Oh, by the way, I think Angie's doing a great job with Bahir,' he added. 'I thought they'd get on. He's a nervous character and she handles him with a lot of confidence.' He grinned. 'I thought it was time I gave her a challenge.'

'That's right, sir,' Shaw replied proudly. He pursed his mouth. 'I doubt if she's up to riding the colt, though.'

Tod laughed. 'We'll see, we'll see. One step at a time.'

Bolts were being kicked and scraped home and lights switched off all round the yard's maze of boxes now, as the lads shut down their charges for the night and headed for the pub or back home to their digs or hostel in the town. When he had first come to Newmarket, Sir Digby had acquired a dilapidated house in the Hamilton Road which he had had done up as a hostel and which many of the lads still used. Passing the little office next to the tack room, Tod saw Charlie Kyle still poring over the *Racing Calendar*, working on some of the entries for the following month. Tod tapped on the window and went in.

'God, Charlie! You're a real glutton for work. Why don't you come up to the house for a drink when you're through?'

Charlie shook his head. 'No, thanks. I'd better get on home. I was checking the runners for Castaway's race at Leicester next week. I reckon he's got a chance at the weights.'

'He might have if we can keep him sound. That's the problem,' Tod replied, glancing at his watch. 'Christ! Look at the time. I'd better get a move on before all Myra's good mood vanishes. Oh, by the way, we have got an interesting new yearling arriving next week. Belongs to Lady Kitty Leverton. He's by that new Three Swallows stallion, Greek Dancer, very small and very black, I'm afraid, so he didn't fetch his reserve at the sales. Amazingly enough, the Levertons have asked us to train him.'

Leverton, Charlie thought to himself. That rang a bell. Wasn't that the name of that girl photographer who had upset one of Diana's yearlings at the sales and who had come up for drinks the other day? Oh, well. It was none of his business. Barons Lodge needed all the owners it could get. 'Good. Who do you think should "do" him then? Any preferences,' he asked Tod.

Tod looked thoughtful for a moment. 'Why not Liam Byrne? He's a bit of a loner – doesn't seem to have any friends in the yard but he's very good with tricky animals. He's an excellent work rider, too.'

'Hmm ... He's not the most relaxed of people, though, is he?' Charlie commented. 'He looks as if the furies are after him sometimes. But I agree, he's a good worker.'

Tod hid his amusement. Charlie was hardly regarded as a bundle of laughs in the yard himself; although generally respected, even by Myra, he was too strict and insistent on discipline to be really liked by most of the staff.

'Well, he's never been away from home before. No doubt he's missing Ireland,' Tod replied. 'If, as I anticipate, this Leverton colt proves to be a handful, it'll take Liam out of himself perhaps.' He moved towards the door. 'The colt is still at Three Swallows. Perhaps you'd like to give your girlfriend a ring and see when she can send him over.'

Charlie looked up, frowning, the colour flooding over his high cheekbones. 'Diana's hardly my girlfriend,' he replied sharply. 'I like her, though, I admit,' he added, pushing his chair backwards. 'There's no bullshit about her. Probably because she's an Aussie.'

'She's also jolly sexy,' Tod replied, grinning. 'Anyway, you colonials should stick together.' He dodged sideways to avoid the rubber Charlie sent flying in his direction.

'OK, OK, have a good weekend. See you on Monday,' he said, pushing open the office door and heading back across the yard to the house.

Keepers Cottage

Swinging his Rover round the July course roundabout, Charlie Kyle felt suddenly weary. He was longing to get back to Keepers Cottage for a hot bath and a meal. It had been a busy week. Quite apart from the racing in Newmarket and the sales, he had had to take a runner up north to Catterick and had only returned that morning. As he was a bachelor, he had had several invitations to dinner that evening, in and around Newmarket, but he had turned them all down. When he was tired, he always preferred his own company. And besides, he wanted to ponder the next move in his quest to clear his father's name.

Tod reminded him of his father, he thought, half an hour later as he lay soaking in the bathtub. Tod was more sophisticated and tougher, perhaps, but he shared Johnnie Kyle's casual, laid-back approach to training horses. They also both had considerable charm – although Charlie did not have much respect for charm alone. After all, it had not helped his father very much. In the six months since he had been at Barons Lodge, Charlie had come to like Tod and admire his quiet, instinctive skills, but he was also occasionally irritated by his lack of ambition and fatalistic attitude to the yard's decline. If it wasn't for Myra, Charlie suspected, Tod might well have decided to pack up training altogether. He did not particularly like Myra; he found her bossy and snobbish but he respected her efficiency and devotion to her father's old yard. The two of them also shared similar views of discipline. Tod was far too slack, in Charlie's view, inclined to spend too much time wandering around the yard gazing at the horses and chatting to the lads, not even insisting that they call him 'sir'.

Charlie knew that his devotion to his father always took people by surprise. 'Oh, Johnnie Kyle's a nice enough chap,' they used to say in Zimbabwe, 'but nothing special. He's had a rough time, of course. There was that dreadful business in England.' What they could never understand was how Charlie had idolized his father as a small boy and how his realization, later, that his father was not perhaps of heroic material had not changed the way he felt.

After the evening of the fire, which had altered all their lives, Charlie's love for his father had grown even more, swelling inside him like a growth, painful, inconvenient and inescapable. Johnnie Kyle had been accused of starting a fire in his own small jumping yard, Coombe Place, near Yeovil in Somerset, with a view to defrauding his insurance company; but Charlie, only twelve years old at the time, had never for one moment, then or since, doubted his father's innocence. He just knew that his father was incapable of doing anything like that and couldn't understand why everyone else didn't feel the same. Johnnie Kyle had been convicted largely on the evidence of his head lad, a Londoner called Keith Warrender. When he'd been sent to prison for two years the whole structure and security of Charlie's life had collapsed like a house of cards.

Just the memory of that time, all these years later, made him shiver. His father had not wanted him to go to court for the verdict, he remembered; he had come into his bedroom early that morning in his favourite lovat green suit and reassured him that it was, of course, all a terrible misunderstanding and he would be acquitted but, if by any chance he did have to go away for a while, Charlie must be brave and courageous and look after his mother. At this point, much to his embarrassment, as he was trying to be as grown up as possible, Charlie had burst into tears and clung to his father, telling him how much he loved him and believed in his innocence.

That was the last time they saw each other for months. Charlie had wanted to go to visit his father in prison as soon as possible but his mother had insisted that this would be too upsetting for both of them and she had made him wait until Johnnie was transferred to another more open establishment. In the meantime, Charlie had been sent off to Marlborough, as planned, his grandfather agreeing to pay the fees.

He had absolutely hated his first term there but on the eve of the Christmas holidays he had had to endure another even greater trauma. His mother had turned up to drive him home, looking particularly dazzling, he remembered, in a new mink coat. She immediately told him that she and his father were going to separate and that Johnnie would be going out to farm in Zimbabwe the moment he came out of prison.

'I know it's upsetting. Particularly for you, darling, as you're so fond of Daddy. But I promise you it's for the best. You see, Daddy and I really haven't been getting on for ages and after the terrible business of the fire, we both feel we ought to make a new start.' She smiled one of her brilliant, tragic smiles. 'Of course, it will mean selling Coombe Place. But don't worry about that. You and I will move to London, darling. That will be more fun, you'll see.'

Charlie had been aghast. His mother had always loved London; she had had a short career as a fashion model there before her marriage and was always complaining that life in the country was dull. But to Charlie the country had always seemed the only place to be. The idea of moving away from his beloved Coombe Place with all the horses and other animals, and local friends like Pete the Poacher who used to take him up to the High Wood to watch badgers, was unthinkable. How could his mother just let Coombe Place go? Why wasn't she making more of an effort to save it? His grandfather had some money, after all. He didn't understand. It was at that moment, he realized later, that he had really become wary and mistrustful of his mother: feelings that had later hardened to dislike.

The very next holidays, which they spent in a rented mansion flat in

Kensington where Charlie was left most of the time with an elderly housekeeper, his mother announced that when her divorce came through she was going to marry one of her current escorts, a stockbroker called Neville who lived just up the road. Charlie disliked Neville and his house on sight. With its polished parquet floors, expensive rugs and prized collection of porcelain and glass, it seemed to him more like a museum than a home; and there was, of course, a ban on all animals. When his father came out of prison, Charlie vowed to himself, he would follow him out to Zimbabwe.

After he came out of prison Johnnie Kyle came down to see him at school before he left and Charlie would never forget that wet, squally day and how his initial delight at seeing his father again evaporated at the thought of their future separation. They had driven miserably around Wiltshire in the rain, not knowing how to comfort one another.

'I have to go, Charlie,' his father explained. 'Farming's the only thing I know about, other than training horses, and there's no life for me now in England. Old man Strutt has offered me this bit of land, twenty miles south of Salisbury. I've no option,' he added sadly, looking out at the desolate garden of the little hotel where they were having lunch. 'Anyway, it's probably less embarrassing for you too, if I'm out of the way.'

Several years at boarding school had taught Charlie a lot about how to bottle up emotion, but he broke down at that point, unable to bear the sight of his father's gaunt face forcing a smile.

'Don't worry, Dad. I'll come out to join you as soon as I can,' he said, leaning across the table and grabbing his father's hand. His voice broke into a sob. 'I hate England now, anyway. It's horrid and unjust. You're completely innocent, Dad, I know you are, yet you have to be punished for the rest of your life.' By this time the tears were streaming down his face. 'It's so unfair. But if you have to go because of it all, I promise you I'll go too.'

There was a furious scene with his mother, of course, when he announced his intention of leaving school after he'd taken his O-levels. In the end, she had to give in, knowing how determined he was and that she couldn't legally keep him there once he was sixteen.

'It's a frightful waste, of course. Neville thinks you're quite bright enough to go to university,' she said. 'I must say Johnnie's bloody lucky to have such a devoted son. I can't think what he's done to deserve it. You've never shown me such consideration. I sometimes think you don't care for me at all.'

Charlie looked at her coldly. 'I blame you for the break-up of the family and for us losing Coombe Place. It may be unfair but I do. I can't forgive you.'

He left for Salisbury with eight O-levels under his belt and never saw his mother again. She wrote occasionally at first: long rambling letters in her childish hand all about friends and first nights and people that Charlie either disliked or didn't know. He threw the letters away. And then, when she got ill with cancer, she wrote, asking him to come home. Neville wrote too. 'Come on, Charlie. She really does need to see you, you know. It's been a long time and you *are* her son. I'll wire you the fare, if that's a problem.'

Charlie refused to go. He knew it was harsh and he suffered the occasional pang of guilt about it, but he felt he would be dishonest to pretend to care.

The more he talked to his father about the past, the less convinced he was that his mother had told the complete truth at the trial. It was possible, he suspected, that she had known more about the origins of the fire than she had been prepared to admit.

'She was having an affair with Neville even then, you know,' Johnnie Kyle told him one evening on the verandah. 'That's what our row was about that night. She wanted a divorce, you see. I was desperate. I loved her so much. Despite her faults. Yet I sensed I'd already lost her.' He sighed. 'She behaved very oddly when I was charged, I remember. Furious, shocked, self-pitying – all in turn. It seemed a bit of an act to me. I couldn't make out what she really felt at all. She broke down hysterically the first time she came to see me in prison, though, which, I suppose, did indicate that she cared.'

Six months later, when Charlie had left the farm and was working for a trainer in South Africa, he heard from Neville that his mother had died. Much to his surprise, he felt devastated. He lay on his bunk and wept for hours, only thankful that most of the other lads were away that day. It was not his mother's death he was grieving about, he realized, but the fact that he had had a mother whom he had been unable to love.

The memory of that day now was painful and, wanting to banish it, he hopped swiftly out of the bath and, folding a towel round his lean body, padded through to the sitting-room. Keepers Cottage was an old brick and flint gatehouse, a bungalow, with all its rooms leading off a central living-room. Charlie appreciated its compactness; it was, he felt, his own little corral against the outside world and tonight it seemed particularly cosy.

Sumi, his large black cat, was stretched out in front of the wood-burning stove and a delicious smell of braising pigeons was wafting in from the tiny kitchen. Charlie had learnt to cook in Zimbabwe, tutored by Benji, his father's Mashona cook. In Mashona, both cooking and cleaning were traditionally men's work. Johnnie Kyle had not really approved; in his view, cooking was a sissy occupation, suitable only for women or African servants. But Charlie disagreed. He enjoyed it and he wanted to be able to look after himself and be self-sufficient in the future.

He had just poured himself a stiff whisky and soda when the phone rang. It was Tod, sounding slightly slurred.

'Charlie, hello. Hope I'm not disturbing you. Look, I've just had an idea which might help you to track down that Warrender man you're looking for. I've just been going through some old copies of *The Sporting Life* – looking up something for Myra – and I noticed an advertisement put in by some bloke who's writing a book about old racing yards. He asks anyone who's any memories of places like Druids Lodge or Danebury to get in touch. Well, what occurred to me was that you could put in a similar sort of ad – you know, say you are researching into West Country jumping yards in the fifties and sixties and would like to hear from anyone who has worked at Coombe Place. What do you think?'

Charlie leant back, cradling the receiver against his ear. 'I think it's a very good idea,' he replied thoughtfully. 'Well, worth a try. I'll concoct something over the weekend and maybe you could glance at it on Monday. Thanks, Tod. Thanks a lot.'

Charlie had become more and more convinced that it was the head lad, Warrender, whose evidence had been so detrimental at the trial, that he needed to talk to him to find out what had really happened the night of the fire.

When last August he had confided in Tod about his determination to find him Tod had, in his usual amiable way, offered to help in any way he could. Why didn't he go down to Somerset? he suggested, and see if anyone in Yelperton, the nearest village to Coombe Place, knew of his whereabouts.

At the end of August Tod had given Charlie an extra-long weekend off to go down to Somerset to see if he could find any trace of Warrender in the area. Charlie had dreaded revisiting his old home. He had such a clear and loving picture of it in his memory that the possibility of defacing this with reality after all these years was painful but still, he felt, it had to be done. Parking his car in the lane by the entrance to the drive he could see that the place was mainly just a dairy farm now. The farmer who lived there kept a few horses but hadn't actually ploughed up all the gallops. There were two quite decent-looking part-thoroughbreds grazing in the paddock on one side of the drive and in the other were a couple of ponies and a collection of ramshackle show jumps. The 'Horses Crossing' sign, very rusty now, was still up in the lane leading to the old gallops but otherwise there was no sign that the place had once been a racing yard.

Charlie turned up the track that wound past the house and the walled garden, to the high paddocks and the wooded ridge beyond where he and Pete used to wait by the badger setts at dawn. He sat on a gate and looked down on the back of the familiar mellow brick Queen Anne house with its long windows, and the little conservatory that his grandparents had built, leading out to what the family had always called the croquet lawn. He felt racked with nostalgia, remembering those summer evenings when he had lain in his bedroom as a small boy, cocooned in happiness, listening to the click of the mallets on the ball and the sound of amiable rivalry and laughter.

All this had been destroyed on the night of the fire. Blinking angrily to stop the tears, Charlie got back in his car and revved back along the muddy track. He had to find Warrender somehow, if he was still alive and try to clear his father's name before he died. His other ambition was to make it as a trainer himself and redeem the family name that way; but that could wait.

According to his father, the head lad had bought a saddlery business in Yelperton when Coombe Place had been sold, but Charlie soon found out that that had closed several years ago. The landlord of the local pub, though, remembered Warrender well and had clearly not liked him.

'We was glad to see the back of him, I can tell you. He wasn't popular in the village. Not at all. Had a pleasant enough wife, though – or fancy bit, more likely, name of Beth. Always called her his wife but you couldn't be sure with him.' He sniffed disapprovingly. 'But they split up and I think she went up north somewhere, but where he went I couldn't say. Couldn't care less either.'

The landlord had, however, given him the address of another of his father's old employees, a man called Bill Plant who still lived on the outskirts of the village. Bill had been one of Coombe Place's older, more reliable lads, Charlie remembered. He would be getting on a bit now and probably would not recognize him, but Charlie put on a pair of sunglasses just in case and introduced himself under a false name, saying that he was an acquaintance of Warrender's from way back, a customer of his who wanted to track him down because of a long-standing debt. For some reason, he was not sure why, he had been reluctant to explain what he was really up to.

'I'm not surprised. Keith could never be trusted with money,' the old man commented, as he hobbled over to switch on the kettle to make some tea. 'Tell you the truth, I often wondered how he got the cash to buy up that saddlery business in the first place,' he said, shaking his head. 'Maybe he'd been lucky with his bets or something – though the guv'nor never approved of any of us betting that big. Dead straight, that Mr Kyle was, you know. That's why most of us were so sure he couldn't have started that fire in his own yard, deliberate like. He wasn't that sort of a bloke.' He limped over to the fridge and got out the milk. 'But I'm going on a bit, I'm afraid. Mr Kyle's nothing to you. Probably never even heard of the bloke. It's Keith you want to know about.'

'Have you any idea where he went when he sold up the saddlery business, then?' Charlie inquired quickly.

Bill Plant shook his head. 'Not a clue. I met up with a lad who used to work at Coombe Place last time I went to Wincanton about a year or so back now. He said he'd heard a rumour that Keith had gone to prison in Australia.' He shrugged his shoulders. 'Wouldn't surprise me! He was as crooked as a corkscrew. Tried to get a jockey to pull one of Mr Kyle's horses once, I remember. The guv'nor found out and threatened to sack him. He should have done! Too soft-hearted for his own good, Mr Kyle was, if you ask me.'

Too true, Charlie thought again now, as he lay stretched out on the sofa, waiting for the pigeons to finish cooking. He also remembered, with a pang of longing, how beautiful Coombe Place had looked the afternoon of his visit and how many happy memories it had brought back. He could not imagine that any house, anywhere, would ever be so dear to him ever again. Even though his mother was dead, he would never forgive her for letting it go.

As he swung his long legs off the sofa and got up slowly to go and check on his dinner, the phone beside him rang again.

'Hello. Charlie Kyle,' he barked into the receiver.

'Charlie! Hi! It's Diana. What's the matter? You sound in a bitch of a mood!'

'Sorry,' Charlie apologized. 'I didn't mean to be so abrupt. How are you?'

'Hunky-dory,' Diana replied cheerfully. 'You spend too much time on your own, you know. It's high time we remedied that.' She paused.

'Look, I know it's short notice but can you come over to lunch tomorrow? Dad's just arrived: he flew into London unexpectedly yesterday and came straight up here. I think he wants to check up on some of the changes I'm making to the stud. I've rounded up a few people already but I'd love you to meet him too.'

'Thanks. I'd love to come,' Charlie replied with genuine enthusiasm. He would like to meet Lyle Saunders. The man was so successful internationally now, with newspapers, television and radio stations all over the world, that he very seldom had the time to come to Newmarket. He would be interesting to talk to – a change from the usual Newmarket brigade, some of whom Charlie found rather snobbish and limited in their interests.

'Good-oh,' Diana said enthusiastically. 'Look, the temperature in the pool is just great at the minute. So, why don't you come really early, around eleven, and bring your swimming trunks? Or better still, don't bother,' she chuckled. 'Dad'll be playing golf. There'll only be me here. See you tomorrow.' She rang off.

Charlie sat quietly on the sofa, his mouth relaxing into a grin. That sounded remarkably like a proposition, he thought, and he was definitely interested. He had been wondering about making an approach to Diana for some weeks now. He both liked and fancied her. She was professional, ambitious and direct, all of which he appreciated. She would also, he suspected, be a good lover. He knew that she was running several boyfriends at the moment, but that didn't worry him at all. The last thing he wanted was some sort of commitment or deep relationship. Padding into the kitchen to take the pigeons out of the oven he decided that the following day was definitely going to be fun.

CHAPTER FIVE

Elsinore Court, St John's Wood
Wrapped in her black silk Sulka dressing-gown, Lucy Beckhampton lay stretched out on the sofa in the living-room of her London flat, the telephone cradled against her shoulder.

'It's definitely *on* with Helmut Newton? Wow! When did you hear?' she asked, her amber eyes widening with excitement. 'Well, sure, of course I'm available. *Make me* available, for Christ's sake. Cancel something. You're supposed to be my agent!' Yawning, she shook the receiver before pressing it back to her ear.

'What? The *Vogue* shoot? Oh, it went OK, I suppose,' she said wearily. 'The guy's a good photographer, very "Bruce Weber" though. He had us all hanging around in this wood in the middle of Oxfordshire in Vivienne Westwood clothes, half naked with twigs and things in our hair. We must have looked like we were doing some weird performance of *A Midsummer Night's Dream*. Except that it's midwinter – well, late October,' she shrugged her shoulders. 'Anyway, it was *freezing*. I'll want more money if I have to work with him again. Two grand's not enough.'

She sneezed once, then a couple of times more. 'Shit! Did you hear that? I've definitely got pneumonia!' she said crossly, fumbling in the pocket of her dressing-gown for a handkerchief. 'Another thing. The guy's an eyebrow freak. Made me make up mine so that they met in the middle, *à la* Margot Hemingway. Crazy!' She blew her nose loudly.

'Who wants my number? Kate Leverton? Who's she?' she frowned. 'Oh yes. Sure. I met her the other day in Newmarket, with Daddy. She wants to ask me something about Alain? What cheek!' she grinned. 'OK, tell her to call me on Sunday then, but not too early, for Christ's sake. Is that it? OK, see you on Monday, then.'

Replacing the receiver, Lucy sank back against the cushions again.

51

She couldn't think why she was feeling so tired. It had been a long month, of course. The Paris collections were always exhausting and then she had had to go on that trip to Bali for *Elle*. Or perhaps she really was sickening for something; her sinuses were certainly playing up again, which was a real bore. She was due to fly back to New York with her flatmate Celeste, also a model, on Monday to do a studio shoot for *American Vogue* with Irving Penn and she couldn't possibly cancel that. She must go and roust Celeste out of her bathroom, she thought, sitting up slowly. If her date with Hassim was still on she'd need a hot bath to liven her up a bit.

She must also reorganize and redecorate the flat when she got back from New York. She had bought it a few years ago, from a doctor acquaintance who had offered to drop the price if she agreed to store some of his belongings whilst he went off to do some research work in Baltimore. Apart from the price, she'd liked the flat because of its position on the sixth floor of a red and white brick Edwardian block at the bottom end of St John's Wood High Street with a view over Regent's Park, and because of its address, No. 60 Elsinore Court, which had appealed to her sense of humour.

She had never really seen it as home though, she reflected: more as a comfortable lair where she could rest up between modelling jobs, with all the travelling they entailed and her various sexual adventures. She had had her bedroom and bathroom redecorated in what Alain du Roc called her *'poule de luxe'* taste but the sitting-room was badly in need of attention. She had never bothered to replace the doctor's faded grey Wilton carpet, shabby Hessian wallpaper and sixties Heals' furniture, and the room was an incongruous mixture of his belongings and hers. Massive glass-fronted bookcases packed with medical tomes mingled with her own odd assortment of pictures and other objects given to her by admirers or picked up on magpie shopping trips around the world. Above the fireplace hung her favourite piece of furniture, the ornate Directoire mirror, given to her by her French grandmother, Jeanne de Bernay, on her twenty-first birthday. In a weak moment, she had promised to leave it to her half-brother Toby, who adored it, rather than to any children she might one day have herself. Remembering this as she paused to gaze critically at her reflection, Lucy made a face and extracted the note she had received earlier from Toby from her dressing-gown pocket. He had apparently been up from his boarding-school for the day to visit the dentist and had called by earlier in the hope of seeing her.

Where are you? Waited as long as I could but have to catch the train back to Hadleigh. Ugh! School is an even worse nightmare than usual this term. Escaped for the day for a boring visit to dentist and very boring lunch with Aunt Pam. Please try to be home weekend of 10 November when I'm allowed out of prison. Lots of love

Toby

Frowning, Lucy stuffed the note back in her pocket. She hoped Toby was all right. He had been so clammed up and moody last holidays, shutting himself up in his room for hours, listening to pop music and watching TV, that even Tod had got irritated.

Tod had complained about what a business it was getting him up in time to ride out any more, let alone help about the place: he was becoming an idle little bugger, he'd said. It was probably just his age and the pressure of his O-level year, Lucy thought. She remembered how difficult she'd been as an adolescent; he'd grow out of it, she reassured her father. Still, if she wasn't abroad, she would try to get back to Barons Lodge on that weekend. Maybe it was time she and Toby had a talk.

'Helmut Newton wants to photograph you?' Celeste queried some minutes later as she lounged in a wicker chair in the black-tiled bathroom, smoking a joint. 'Rather you than me, sweetheart. No, honest, I mean it. Helmut's too decadent for me.' She looked pretty raffish herself, Lucy thought. The effect of the drug was making her pupils enormous and the thick white towel she had wrapped around her like a sarong emphasized her luminous dark skin. Celeste was American, the daughter of a jazz musician from Chicago (black) and a dancer from New Jersey (white), and with her doe eyes and cropped black hair she made an interesting contrast to Lucy's tawniness. As a result, photographers often liked to work with them together; and as they shared an agent in London and New York and had the same insouciant attitude to life, particularly sex, they had become friends.

'Nonsense! You're much more his type. Much more corrupt-looking than me,' Lucy replied, grinning. Pinning up her hair more securely, she slid down into the fragrant steam.

Celeste raised one of her delicate eyebrows. 'Oh, really,' she drawled. 'What about you and your Arab, then?'

'Oh, that's just a game. Nothing serious,' Lucy replied lightly, sinking further.

'Anyway, Newton uses such weird locations,' Celeste went on. 'Where did you say he wanted you to go – Prague? In January! No thanks,' she shivered. 'He'll probably keep you hanging around in some icebox of a disused church or something for hours on end. I intend to spend January in the Bahamas myself,' she added smugly, picking up the glossy magazine at her feet and starting to flip through the pages.

As Lucy lay there soaking, her nose just above the water, she pondered on her liaison with Prince Hassim. She was actually looking forward to seeing him again. She had not made love to anyone for over a week and despite her fatigue was feeling decidedly randy. She liked a lot of sex; it calmed her down and also gave her the satisfying feeling of power over men. But Hassim's intense, almost brutal love-making seemed to fulfil some other inner desire of hers to be used, even punished, for some unknown sin. Her instinct from the start had told her that their sexual liaison might well lead her in a direction she did not sensibly want to go without being able to stop, which gave the whole affair an added frisson.

She had met the Saudi prince at the Deauville sales last August. Hearing from a bloodstock agent friend that he was looking for another trainer in England and, glimpsing him on the racecourse, she had decided that it might be fun to try to seduce him and persuade him to send some horses to her father. She knew that Tod was becoming increasingly despondent about the situation at Barons Lodge and she was in the mood for a challenge.

The plan had been an instant success. When she was introduced to Hassim at the yearling sales that evening, he had looked her up and down, gimlet-eyed, as though she was one of the fillies on offer. He listened impassively while she prattled on about Tod and his former triumphs, interrupting her only to inquire which hotel she was staying at. Later that evening, after a visit to the casino, he telephoned her to ask if she would like to join him for a nightcap in his suite. She accepted with alacrity. She was, she knew, looking particularly good that evening in a white, almost backless Bruce Oldfield dress. She was not surprised when, after asking her some polite questions about Barons Lodge, Hassim announced that he would indeed consider sending a few horses to her father. He then got up suddenly and stalked over to her chair, his black eyes gleaming.

'I want you,' he said urgently, grasping her wrist. 'You are beautiful, I want to possess you. But there must be no publicity, no scandal: nothing to upset my people back home. Do you understand?'

Lucy was amused. Such immediacy turned her on. There was obviously going to be no sophisticated courtship. Like two dogs who had met in the street and circled round sniffing appreciatively at each other, no time was going to be wasted here. 'All right,' she promised with a demure smile. 'If that's the way you want it.'

Since that night in Deauville, she had seen Hassim only a handful of times, always in London, at his suite at the St James's Plaza, the hotel he owned overlooking Green Park. In September, he had returned to Saudi Arabia, telling her that he would be back in a month's time. 'I shall expect to see you if you are in town,' he added. 'In the meantime, I shall send you something to make sure you do not forget me.'

The next day, just before she left for Paris, a small parcel was delivered to her flat. It contained a large emerald and diamond ring, set in eighteen-carat gold from Van Cleep and Arpels; and a note ordering her not to wear the ring in anyone else's company but his and certainly not to tell anyone who had given it to her. With the exception of close friends, Lucy decided to comply with the second request but to take no notice whatsoever of the first. Emeralds were her favourite stones, after all, and the ring was exquisite. 'What's the point if I can't flash it around a bit?' she complained to Celeste. 'I might as well do the full bourgeois bit and keep it in the bank and I've never understood the point of that!'

As she looked forward now to seeing Hassim again, the phone rang at the far end of the room.

'I reckon it's your beau, Miss Lucy,' Celeste said in a parody of a Southern accent. She picked it up. 'Glory be! Looks like you're in for some fun tonight.'

St James's Plaza Hotel

While Prince Hassim's trusted bodyguard and chauffeur gossiped and played cards in the anteroom next door, Lucy lay spread-eagled on his huge bed at the St James's Plaza, quivering with anticipation.

After wolfing down a large quantity of caviare and toast, a roasted quail and several glasses of vintage Krug, her fatigue had vanished completely. Giggling slightly, she had allowed Hassim to tie her hands behind her back with a black silk scarf and to knot another one around her face, placing it like a bit between her teeth as she lay face downwards on the satin sheets, her long body gleaming in the dimmed lights, her magnificent hair spread out on the pillow.

'Now, I will do with you what I wish,' Hassim said, his normally impassive eyes gleaming. 'You cannot stop me. You cannot speak or stop me now.'

Crouching between her legs, he ran his muscular hands repeatedly down her slender back and over her thighs, as though soothing a fractious horse. Then, parting the taut cheeks of her bottom, he explored urgently between them, first with his fingers and then with his tongue, his coarse beard rasping against her delicate skin.

Tingling between her legs, Lucy swung her pelvis up off the sheets and clenched her bound hands in anticipation of the initial searing pain of being penetrated from behind. Instead, Hassim hooked his arm, silky with black hair, around her waist and lifting her up still further, insinuated two then three fingers into her vagina. 'Ah . . .' he exclaimed, delighted by her wetness. 'You are ready for me now, my beauty.'

Flipping her over on to her back, he plunged into her with the certainty of a skilled diver entering a pool and started to thrust upwards with long rhythmic strokes. Twisting from side to side as he speared through her, Lucy felt her excitement mounting. Because of her looks and deceptively fragile appearance men were so often in awe of her physically, tending to treat her like porcelain. She found being plundered like this, in silence, unable to initiate or explain, even if she had wanted to, far more satisfying. Hassim's penis was not particularly large, but it seemed to be unusually long and mobile as it slid over her clitoris and mercilessly probed all her inner crevices as well. She flicked her head from side to side and began to moan softly through the silk.

This seemed to arouse Hassim still further and, thrusting into her more powerfully, he began to mutter to her in Arabic, exhorting her to a climax. As her tremor started, he froze for a moment, then exploded into her with a great groan of pleasure, the weight of his body crushing her back against the pillows. When he finally withdrew and their combined juices spilled over the sheets, he ripped the scarf off her mouth and kissed her fiercely, something he only ever did after she had come. As she finally opened her eyes and gazed at him lazily, he cupped a muscular hand around her neck.

'Never forget,' he said, his jet eyes narrowing. 'I am your master.'

CHAPTER SIX

Barons Lodge

Tod Beckhampton stood in the kitchen, looking at his wife with dismay. 'What!' he asked in astonishment. 'Prince Hassim wants to come and look at his yearlings later this *morning*! Well, that is a surprise we can do without. Why on earth didn't he give us more warning?'

Myra shrugged her shoulders, her back to him as she hovered over the Aga. 'God knows!' she replied, prodding the frying bacon with a fish slice. 'But we were warned that this might happen, remember? Penny Carnegie says their Kuwaiti owners often drop in with no warning at all.'

'Well, what the hell are we going to do about it?' Tod inquired, frowning, as he padded across the floor in his stockinged feet. He sat down at the kitchen table, littered with breakfast things, and opened copies of the racing papers. 'If he's coming at about eleven thirty, there'll be no one here to show him round.' He glanced up at the kitchen clock. 'Charlie's halfway to Redcar by now, you're going to London and I have to leave for Leicester straight after second lot. Jam Jar runs in the First, remember?' He fumbled in the pocket of his worn jodhpurs for his packet of Gitanes. 'Oh, well, Sam will just have to cope somehow, I suppose. He can show him how Bahir and the fillies are getting on, if we pull him off everything else.'

'Of course Sam can't show Hassim round on his own. That would be giving completely the wrong impression,' Myra replied impatiently. 'He is, after all, our most valuable owner, wouldn't you say?' She pushed the frying pan to the side of the Aga before turning back to Tod. 'It's perfectly simple, I'm afraid. I'll just have to reorganize my day completely. If I go to Leicester and cope with Jam Jar you can stay here and put on a show for Hassim. That's by far the best solution.'

57

Tod shook his head uneasily. 'But that means you've got to cancel your lunch. Weren't you going to give Toby a bit of a treat? I don't want you to cancel that.'

Myra's mouth snapped down at the corners. 'Well, we haven't got much option, have we?' she replied tartly. 'One of us has to be here and in this instance it had better be you. You know what Arabs are like about women working! They think we should all be shuffling from the kitchen to the bedroom in yashmaks or whatever they're called. Hassim'll have a fit if he thinks I'm in charge here!'

Tod reached over to pour himself some coffee. He definitely had a slight hangover this morning, he realized. He must have overdone the brandies at Gerry Carnegie's last night. He really couldn't remember what he had said or done in the latter part of the evening at all. 'We may have some trouble with Toby,' he warned Myra. 'He wasn't in the best of moods earlier, when we were out on the Heath. I put it down to the fact that Lucy's not coming this weekend. He was so looking forward to seeing her. This latest change of plan will really piss him off.'

'Well, it can't be helped, can it?' Myra retorted. 'After all, it's hardly the end of the world. I can always take him to that restaurant tomorrow instead. We've got plenty of time before the dentist. Anyway, if he's going to be a trainer himself, the sooner he learns about the ups and downs the better. Rule number one: owners come first. After all, *they* pay the bills – or at least some of them do. Hassim certainly does, thank God.' She jammed two pieces of bread into the toaster.

Tod took a pull at his cigarette. She was right, of course. Toby had always said he wanted to be a trainer, even take over Barons Lodge himself one day – something Myra in particular very much hoped would happen. It had also been his idea that first of all he should try to qualify as a vet. But Tod had sensed recently that his son might be having doubts. He had certainly seemed more and more reluctant to ride out these days, which was worrying. He had had a fall in the Easter holidays when one of the older horses, usually traffic-proof, had bolted with him along the Bury road, and Toby could well have lost his nerve although he had denied this. Tod had not mentioned his fears to Myra as yet. She would be horrified. She still rode out frequently herself and was absolutely fearless in the saddle. It would be inconceivable to her that anyone with her Hunter blood would be nervous of horses.

Watching Myra lounge impatiently against the dresser as she waited for the toast Tod remembered the first day he had seen her out with the Quorn and how impressed he'd been by her competence and dash as a horsewoman. He'd found her attractive too, in a hard-bitten sort of way. Considering that she was nearly fifty, she was still a handsome woman, of course, he reflected, although the green cords she was wearing today bulged uncomfortably round her thighs and there was a distinct droop about the curve of her breasts under her tight black sweater. He wished sometimes that he fancied his wife more. Not that she would have appreciated it if he did, he suspected. The main emotions he seemed to engender in her these days were irritation and impatience and it was years now since she had shown much interest in sex. It had never been very important to her, even when they were first married, and Tod had always sensed that she valued him more as a partner and companion than as a lover. As a result he had sought sexual and emotional release elsewhere, mainly with an old school friend of Monique's, Marie Claire. They had become lovers the year after Monique's death, when Tod had first come back to England, and had continued the affair on and off ever since. 'It's what Monique would have wanted – us to love each other,' Marie Claire had always insisted. She had been the perfect mistress: highly sexed, sophisticated yet affectionate and undemanding. She too had got married shortly after Monique's death to a wealthy French industrialist with whom she enjoyed a discreetly open marriage. In the past few years Marie Claire had spent more and more time in Paris – her husband's health was poor – and Tod had hardly seen her at all, though they had kept in touch by phone. He had made a point of telling Myra about her existence and insisting that, as an old friend of Monique's, he would be lunching with her in London from time to time, but he had taken great care never to let Myra suspect that there was anything more serious going on.

Plonking the toast rack down on the table, Myra pulled back a chair. 'What exactly do you plan to do with the yearlings this morning, then?' she asked briskly.

Tod took another pull at his cigarette, breathing the smoke out sideways. Myra did not approve of him smoking in the kitchen.

'Well, now, let's see,' he said thoughtfully. 'Bahir will be trotting in the paddock with some of the other colts. You know, figure-of-eight stuff and all that. Hassim can take a look at that. Then I had intended to give the fillies another look at the starting stalls.' He grinned. 'That should be fun. Be My Guest behaved like a right cow when we introduced her to them last week – lashed out all over the place. Let's just hope she behaves herself today.' He scratched his head. 'That's about it, I suppose. Oh, and we are lungeing some of the other colts, including the little Greek Dancer, Achilles, in the far paddock. Hassim can take a look at that too if he wants.' He glanced across at Myra. 'By the way, what about lunch? Can Dorcas put something together?'

Myra shook her head, her mouth full of toast. 'Not necessary. Hassim's not staying for lunch. He made that quite clear. He's lunching elsewhere – with one of his more successful trainers, no doubt.'

Tod grinned. 'Actually, I meant *my* lunch,' he explained.

Myra stared at him impatiently. 'Oh, that! Yes, well I should think Dorcas could cope with that. I'll get her to organize some cold meat or something and some shepherd's pie for tonight.' Glancing at the clock, she got up, brushing some crumbs off her trousers.

'What the hell's happened to Toby? He went up to change half an hour ago,' she frowned. 'His breakfast will be inedible at this rate. I'd better go and chivvy him out of his room and break the news of the change of plan.'

Tod picked up *The Sporting Life*. Barons Lodge had three runners at the Doncaster meeting on the last two days of the flat-racing season. One of them, a five-year-old handicapper, Castaway, actually had a chance, if they could just keep him sound for another few days. The gelding had worked surprisingly well on the gallops this morning out on the heath. With a fresh easterly wind scattering the coloured leaves like confetti, it was very much the sort of late autumn day Tod usually found so invigorating, but he had felt distinctly jaded and lethargic today; it wasn't just a hangover or the usual, post-sales fatigue but more a deep weariness that seemed to penetrate his very soul. He had always found the continuity of the racing year very comforting and appreciated the way the education of the yearlings came straight after the rather dreary end to the flat-racing season. Then there was always some excellent shooting in the Christmas holidays to look forward to, followed by several weeks' holiday in Barbados, perhaps, or on the ski slopes before the new season loomed. In the old days, he had always liked to take one or two of the horses down to Cagnes-sur-Mer in the south of France in February and March to pick up some nice prize money and get them one hundred per cent fit for the start of the English season; and of course one could always enjoy a few good meals down there too. But for the past few years he had not bothered. He was beginning to feel he was on some tedious treadmill with one increasingly unsuccessful year merging into another, with little point in any of it any more. Maybe one of Hassim's yearlings would turn out to be a world-beater, but he doubted it somehow. However expensive, well bred and good-looking they were did not in any way guarantee that they had any real guts or speed.

He really must try to get out of this defeatist frame of mind, he told himself, as the phone rang behind him. He reached over wearily and picked it up. It was Bill Sink, one of the sharpest, most persistent and generally accurate members of the popular racing press.

'Hello. Tod Beckhampton. Yep. Castaway runs on Saturday if the ground doesn't get any firmer,' he said; 'you know how dodgy his old legs are. What? Oh, you can forget my other runners. The filly's only running for her education – that's not for publication, of course. And the other one, Green Jet, is over the top but you try telling that to the owner. He's a big cheese in South Yorkshire and no doubt he's invited all his mates racing. I won't be very popular when the horse finishes out with the washing but he won't listen so what can I do?' He spread his hands. 'Not at all. See you around.'

As he was pushing back his chair there was a sudden clatter on the steep back stairs leading down to the kitchen, and Toby stumbled through the door and made his way without speaking over to the Aga. He looked remarkably spruce, in a pair of grey flannels and a new tweed jacket and his curly fair hair slicked back tidily – a remarkable transformation from the windswept figure out on the gallops – but the boy's pale face was preoccupied, truculent almost, as he bent down to get his breakfast out of the oven.

'From the look on your face, you've obviously heard the news that you and Myra have been rerouted to Leicester,' Tod said cheerily, as he got up. 'Sorry, old chap! But that's one of the drawbacks of being a trainer.' He put his hand on Toby's shoulder. 'Somewhat at the mercy of your owners' whims – I'm afraid that's the way it is.'

Toby carried his plate over to the table. 'It's OK, Dad. I've already had a lecture on the ups and downs of a trainer's life. Mother waxed very lyrical.' He flopped down into a chair. 'I'm sorry, Dad,' he said apologetically. 'I know it's not your fault. It's just that this three-quarter term is turning out to be such a wash-out. Lucy's had to go back to New York' – he made a face – 'and now our lunch at Joe Allen's, the only other thing I was looking forward to, has had to be cancelled. Mother says we can go tomorrow instead but I doubt if they'll have a table. They get fearfully booked up, I know, and anyway, we've got to be at the dentist at three, so there won't be time.' He turned his attention, moodily, to his bacon and eggs.

'Never mind,' Tod reassured him. 'Perhaps we can all go there in the Christmas holidays. Lucy too. She has absolutely promised to come to Barons Lodge for Christmas, by the way. So that's good news, isn't it?' He looked around for his jodhpur boots. 'And, by the way, I've just been checking out the Leicester card. Jam Jar's race has cut up nicely, I'm glad to say. Who knows? You may even be saddling a winner!'

Glancing out of the window, Tod noticed that some of the horses for second lot had already been led out of their boxes and were standing impatiently looking about them as their lads waited for a leg-up. Christ! He was going to be late, he thought, hurriedly pulling on his boots. He was just reaching for his quilted jacket when the phone rang again.

Irritated, he strode over to the dresser. 'Yep. Tod Beckhampton,' he said briskly. 'Yes, this is Tod,' he repeated impatiently. 'Who am I talking to? Oh, Kate.' His voice relaxed. 'Sorry. You've rather caught me on the hop, I'm afraid. I'm running a bit late with second lot. No, it's OK. What can I do for you? Your colt's fine, by the way: he's coming along very nicely. I was going to ring your mother on Sunday.' Cradling the receiver to one ear he struggled into his jacket. 'This evening!' His eyebrows shot up in surprise. 'No, no, that's fine,' he grinned. 'We're having rather a social day, actually. I can't remember when we've been so popular! Prince Hassim's dropping in before lunch as well. No, really. That's fine. Come just before six. Then you can catch the end of evening stables and see some of the other horses as well. OK? Sorry I've got to dash. See you then.

'I'm not sure that I'd have taken on all these new owners if I'd known they were going to keep popping in like this,' he commented jokingly to Toby as he headed for the door.

As he stepped out into the cold air and hurried along the laurel-fringed path leading down the side of the house towards the yard, he realized that he was feeling distinctly more cheerful. It must be the thought of seeing Kate Leverton again; he could not think of any other explanation.

'Good fella. Good lad. You're sure getting the hang of it all now,' Liam murmured encouragingly as he leant forward to pat Achilles's dark neck. The colt was slowing down his walk in response to Sam Shaw's pressure on the lunge reins and swung left obediently as they neared the paddock fence. He seemed to turn more easily and naturally to the left than to the right, Liam had noticed. They would have to do

62

some more work on that when Achilles started trotting out with the other yearlings; it was so important to get young horses evenly balanced. Apart from that, though, Achilles was proving to be an excellent pupil. He had shown the usual initial panic, of course, when they first backed him: Liam had laid the full weight of his body across his back in the box, but after five minutes of playing up, rearing and plunging all over the place, he had calmed down and just stood there, still quivering but quiet, whilst Liam went on talking to him gently and Sam Shaw gave him a carrot. The next day they had been able to lead him round the yard with Liam balanced over his back and now he seemed to be rapidly getting the hang of being ridden properly and how to respond to the vital signals from rein and leg.

As Sam Shaw stomped over, his flat cap jammed tight down on his grizzled head, his shoulders under the dark blue Husky hunched against the wind, his expression was less dour than usual and Liam sensed that the head lad was pleased with Achilles's performance this morning, particularly as the colt had been on show. Tod, flanked by Prince Hassim and another dark-bearded Arab companion, was still leaning on the paddock gate talking. 'Walk him round for a minute or two and then give him a pick of grass,' Sam ordered as Liam slipped lightly from Achilles's back.

'We won't be needing these any longer, any road,' the Yorkshireman added as he unbuckled one of the lunge reins. 'The guv'nor wants him out trotting with Bahir and the others tomorrow.'

With his hands in the pockets of his plain navy overcoat, Prince Hassim did not look like one of the richest owners in racing, Liam thought, though Angie Shaw had insisted to him earlier that he was. 'Perhaps he's a billionaire, or even a trillionaire,' she'd said excitedly, as she'd put the finishing touches to Bahir's appearance and tucked up his rug more securely under the saddle before leading him out of his box.

Angie was completely devoted to Prince Hassim's bay colt, Liam knew, but good-looking and precocious though he undoubtedly was, Liam would not have swapped Achilles for him for the world. Bahir had a daintiness and fragility about him which made Liam wonder whether he would stand up to really tough competition on the track. Achilles, on the other hand, although still small and very immature, with a lot of physical developing to do, seemed both physically and mentally tough and had a presence about him which Liam found impressive.

Liam had learnt to break in horses at an early age, mainly through helping his father and elder brother at home in Kildare. His father had been a horse dealer, just outside Newbridge, and Liam could not remember any time in his eighteen years when he had not been surrounded by horses and ponies of all shapes and sizes. Although there had never been much money about, it was a carefree, relaxed place on which to grow up – that is, until his father fell in love with a girl groom from Limerick who was fifteen years younger than himself and decamped with her to Canada. Liam was only thirteen then but when his mother decided to return to her family in Dublin he insisted on staying on in Kildare, living with one of his father's relations. He started riding out for a short-staffed trainer up on the Curragh, lying about his age and frequently bunking off from school.

The moment he was sixteen, with his elder brother Rory's help he got a proper job with Tom McGuire, a more successful local trainer, who actually gave him some race-riding experience on some of the smaller tracks. He was doing remarkably well – five winners and a couple of places from twenty-five rides – when he had the accident to his foot. That was the beginning of the black time: months of pain and despair which he tried not to think about now, particularly when he was lying in his narrow bunk in the lads' hostel late at night. His bitterness about the ruin of his riding career was still intense. He knew he could have been a good jockey: not as brilliant as his idol, Pat Eddery, perhaps, but good enough to be retained by a decent stable. McGuire had always told him that he had unusually good hands and 'a particular understanding of what goes on in those creatures' heads' and would undoubtedly have taken him on himself in a year or so had his foot not been permanently injured. He was strong for a lightweight and McGuire specialized in running horses off a low handicap mark. The only positive thing that had happened since was that he had got away from Ireland, got away from Rory and his friends, and managed to find a decent job in Newmarket. Mr Beckhampton was hardly a very successful trainer these days but he was a good guv'nor, all the lads thought so, and obviously appreciated Liam's riding skills. He had been giving him more of the trickier horses to ride recently and, after initially restricting him to the older handicappers, had now given him an interesting yearling to 'do'. Liam had already christened the colt 'Jacko'. The animal reminded him of a particularly temperamental part-Arab his father used to let him hunt called Black Jack, who had also been spirited and difficult to handle.

As a couple of the other Barons Lodge lads came jogging past the

64

paddock fence, one of them snorted with laughter, startling Achilles, who stopped cropping the grass and threw up his head in alarm. Both the lads were smoking, Liam observed – something they would not have dared to do if Charlie Kyle had been around. Mr Beckhampton was more lenient, of course – maybe because he was a heavy smoker himself – but Mr Kyle never allowed it and anyone caught with a cigarette anywhere in the yard always received an explosive ticking-off. The assistant trainer was respected by all the stable staff at Barons Lodge but was too strict and aloof to be popular. This gave Liam a fellow feeling for the man; he knew that he too was generally regarded with suspicion. Shy and homesick for Ireland and still in a state of trauma about his accident and what had happened afterwards, he had buried himself in his work from the moment he arrived at Barons Lodge, often offering to do other lads' horses when they were away or off sick. This had given him a reputation as a 'keenie' and, together with his mysterious limp and what some saw as favouritism from Tod, had not endeared him to any of the other lads.

Only Angie Shaw had been consistently friendly, often trying to include him in conversations and jokes around the yard. Recently she asked him to supper at the cottage attached to the main yard where she lived with her parents, but Liam had refused the invitation; he was nervous of sitting through a meal with Sam Shaw, who he sensed did not like him. The head lad had given him no encouragement what-soever, despite the hard work he had put in during the months he had been at Barons Lodge.

'Don't worry about Dad,' Angie had reassured him cheerily. 'He just can't stand the Irish! Thinks you should all stay at home. Don't worry – it's nothing personal. He'll come round to you in the end!'

Liam was not just grateful to her for her friendliness: he was spellbound by her prettiness and sunny charm, and was thinking about her yet again now, as he led Achilles quietly back towards the main yard, under the old Victorian archway with its original weather vane and clock. He recalled the smile she flashed him earlier in the week when they were cantering upsides on the gallops and she was struggling to keep her horse balanced. He felt flooded with happiness and hope for the first time in months.

When Angie's head popped out suddenly from over one of the box doors, he was as startled as Achilles, who spooked and cavorted backwards.

'Oh, Lord! I didn't mean to give you such a fright. Sorry.' Angie smiled apologetically as she emerged from the box, carrying her grooming kit. 'I just wanted to ask you something. Tried to catch you in the tack room earlier but you slipped away. We were all in a bit of a panic about Prince Hassim. Anyway' – she turned and bolted the door carefully behind her – 'how did he do in front of an audience, your little black titch?' she inquired, smiling. 'Did he behave himself?'

'Sure,' Liam nodded proudly, his heart thumping. 'The guv'nor wants us out trotting with you and Bahir and the others tomorrow.' He looked down at his boots, sensing an embarrassed flush to his cheeks.

'Great!' Angie replied cheerfully. 'Look, Liam, I want to ask you to supper again tonight.' She raised a hand. 'Don't look so worried: I know you're a bit wary of Dad but he won't be there.' She stood in front of him, hands in pockets, her brown eyes beseeching. 'Oh, come on, say yes,' she pleaded. 'It'll be steak and kidney, Mum's speciality, and you could do with a good meal in my opinion – you're skinny as a bird.'

Liam nodded, realizing that this time he was incapable of refusing her. 'Thanks, that would be grand,' he mumbled. 'What time shall I be coming over, then?'

'Oh, about seven,' Angie told him. 'Mum will be popping out after the meal, too. It's her evening-class night. She's brushing up her shorthand so she can be of more help to Mr Beckhampton in the office. She's on her own there now, you know.'

Hearing a whinny behind her, she swung round, zipping up her quilted jacket.

'OK, baby, I'm coming. Keep your hair on,' she called out as Bahir's handsome head appeared over the top of his box door.

'Best get back to work,' she added to Liam. 'That Music Boy colt trod on Dad's foot earlier so he's in a right old mood. We'd best not be seen slacking. See you this evening, then. Don't forget now.'

He would be very unlikely to do that, Liam reflected as he led Achilles off. The prospect of spending an entire evening with Angie, particularly away from her father's eagle eye, was so exciting that his hand shook as he slid open the bolt on the box door and he narrowly avoided an indignant nip as he fumbled uncharacteristically with the girths. 'Hey! That's enough of that, yer little devil,' he told Achilles happily. 'You keep yer teeth to yourself. I'll not be wanting more bumps and bruises before this evening now, will I?'

*

'Hope you don't mind the back door,' Tod said. 'It's just so much easier than going all the way round by the front.'

'Of course not,' Kate replied as she followed him eagerly up the path.

'Good. Come along in, then. Hey, girls, steady now!' Smiling, he held open the door as the two Jack Russells bounded over his feet and into the warm.

'We'll have a drink in my study, commonly known as "the Den",' Tod said, kicking off his boots. 'It's cosier in there. Myra's probably turned the heating off in the drawing-room, and anyway, that's forbidden territory for the dogs,' he grinned.

As Kate followed him through the tidy kitchen, she couldn't help comparing it with the kitchen at the Old Rectory, where bunches of herbs, drying onions and garlic, mingled with dried flowers, festooned the low ceiling above the Welsh dresser and a jumble of copper pans gleamed on the wall. Myra's kitchen was far too impersonal and institutional-looking for her taste.

'Sorry about the gloom,' Tod said, switching on the lights at the end of the passage leading to the hall.

He led the way down the corridor lined with photographs of racehorses in action and opened a door into a small square room with shabby, comfortable-looking chairs, a long sofa covered with an oatmeal-coloured rug and an antique paper-strewn desk. Two tall alabaster lamps with honey-coloured shades threw pools of light on to the dark wall hung with pictures and framed photographs, not all of them of horses. There was a particularly striking black-and-white photograph of Lucy, leaning forward out of the shadows, her hair streaming behind, her eyes dreamy, and another portrait of her in oils above the tiled Victorian fireplace.

Tod indicated the little fridge beside his desk. 'White wine? I seem to remember you like that. I've got a few bottles of Frascati here.' He swung round in mild irritation. 'What we don't seem to have, though, is any glasses. Never mind, I'll fetch some from the dining-room. I'll be right back; make yourself at home.'

Kate sat down on the sofa, carefully moving one of the dogs, and watched Tod as he went out of the door. She liked the back of his neck, she thought. There was something appealing yet vulnerable about the way his springy, dark hair, speckled with grey, curled over the back of his collar, and something reassuring, too, about the shape of his head; she had noticed it earlier when he was showing her the horses. She had also realized what a pleasant voice he had: low-pitched and gentle, yet capable of considerable authority. As he had traipsed from box to box, reciting the pedigrees, track records and assorted ailments of the horses, he had, at times, she thought, seemed almost bored with the plethora of information. There had been nothing phoney, though, about his obvious concern as he bent down to feel the heat in a leg or listen to one of the lads reporting a new, worrying symptom.

'Wonderful, isn't it? Lame, coughing and in season,' he had commented with a wry smile at one point as Sam Shaw buckled the rugs back on a little chestnut filly. 'Thank God she's due to go to the sales any minute! One of the most notable things about thoroughbreds is the number of things that can go wrong with them,' he remarked, turning to Kate. 'I'm frequently amazed that any of them ever get to the racecourse at all!'

He insisted that they go and look at Achilles first of all. 'Well, that's what you came for, isn't it, and I doubt if you'll be interested in the others until you've had a good look at him.'

The colt looked happy enough as they leant over his box door but the moment Tod approached him his ears went back and he began to shift uneasily on his feet.

'Not got the most gracious of stable manners, has he?' Tod commented cheerfully. 'Doesn't seem to bother Liam here, though, and that's what counts.'

Liam stood solemnly by Achilles's head, talking to him softly and scratching him under the chin until he resumed a more amiable expression. The boy was so skinny and slight himself that he made the colt look taller than usual, Kate noticed, but his dark winter coat was sprouting through in patches now, making him look slightly scruffy and pony-like.

'Don't worry,' Tod said, following her gaze. 'We'll be trace-clipping him in a day or so – giving him a bit of a shave. He'll hate that! I'd advise protective clothing that day, Liam.'

Liam's peaky face relaxed into a smile as Tod explained how well the colt was coming along and how he would be out trotting, off the lunge rein, the following day.

'He won't be cantering for a while, though, so we won't really be able to tell much until then. Liam thinks he's something special, I suspect, but even sensible lads are prone to optimism, I'm afraid.' Grinning, he closed the door kicking the bottom bolt shut with the toe of his boot.

'How do you like my den?' Tod asked now as he came back

through the door carrying a tray of glasses. 'I spend a lot of time here.'

Kate smiled up at him. 'Very cosy. There's a marvellous photograph of Lucy over there, I notice. It's by Snowdon, isn't it?'

Tod nodded. 'Yes, I'm very fond of it myself. Lucy at her most beguiling. She's got reservations about it though – says it makes her look like a witch.' He opened the wine with a final jerk of the corkscrew and poured Kate out a glass.

'Thanks. I rang Lucy the other day,' Kate said. 'I hope she didn't mind. I wanted to find out where I could contact Alain du Roc. I've persuaded the *Sunday Chronicle* magazine to commission a profile on him. I've wanted to photograph him ever since we met here; he's got such an interesting face.'

Tod nodded as he squirted some soda into his whisky. 'Yep. All human life is there, as they say. Or all his life anyway. He's had a hell of a struggle with his weight over the years, you know, and it shows. He's a good friend of mine, actually, apart from being a brilliant jockey – I've known him for years. His parents were neighbours of the de Bernays, my first wife Monique's parents, in Normandy.' He paused for a moment then, as though on some sudden impulse, strode over to the fireplace and switched on the light above the oil portrait that Kate had noticed earlier.

'That's Monique,' he said softly. 'Painted at our home, Le Bourg Fleuri. It had only just been finished when she was killed. She's lovely, isn't she?' he added tenderly.

Kate gazed at the picture with fascination. Monique's face was remarkably similar to Lucy's, she thought; it had the same delicate bone structure and remarkable eyes, but it was also somehow more innocent, more ethereal and serene. She was seated by a vase of bright daffodils, iris and narcissi, against a background of dark oak furniture and dim ornate mirrors, and the impression of spring beginning and bright hope that shone out of the picture was, in the light of what had happened, very poignant.

'She's so beautiful,' Kate commented, unexpectedly moved. 'You must have been devastated when you lost her. You must have missed her so.'

Tod went on staring at the picture. 'I still do,' he said quietly. It was true. Even after twenty-five years there was hardly a day when he did not think about Monique or was reminded of something about her. Usually he would try to obliterate the image as quickly as possible, concentrating on some immediate practical problem so as to avoid

69

rekindling the pain, but occasionally he knew it helped to let the memories flow.

It had been a particularly warm scented May evening at Le Bourg Fleuri, he remembered. The smell of the lilac hedge behind the old dovecote was especially sweet and the orchards fringing the paddocks frothy with blossom. Monique had been up to Paris to see her father, Guy de Bernay, off on a business trip to South America and was expected back later for dinner. Tod had already tucked up Lucy for the night in her little attic nursery and he could still remember the scent of the fresh linen, mingled with baby powder and lavender, that filled the room as he bent to kiss his daughter goodnight. The sight of her lying there, cocooned by care and love, long chestnut lashes curling on her pale cheek, moved him once again to feel a fierce sense of happiness. He had had some good friends at Eton, but all in all he had had a lonely boyhood since his mother died, with only his unbending father for company in the school holidays and no one to love or feel close to except animals.

At Le Bourg Fleuri he felt he had at last come home, to a place where he was loved and needed and where affection and laughter flourished. Ever since his first visit there to learn both French and the stud business when he was still up at Cambridge, the de Bernays had treated him like their own son and their daughter, Monique, had, from the start, seemed delighted to have him there.

Since their marriage she had become so completely a part of him that, although she had only been away for a day, he was longing for her to come home so that he could hold her and tell her how much she had been missed. He had also insisted that they had one of her favourite dishes, *lapin au gratin*, for dinner.

He was out in the paddocks, bringing in one of the mares who was obviously about to foal, when Marie, the stud groom's daughter who helped in the kitchen, came running to the gate, her floury apron flapping.

'Monsieur Tod! Monsieur, venez vite! C'est la police à l'appareil. Il y a quelque chose qui se passe.'

A sliver of panic had pierced his stomach as he vaulted over the gate and ran towards the house. Something, he knew, had happened to Monique. He could never bear to remember the rest of that evening in too clear detail, although some images would be etched on his memory for ever: the fearful look on his mother-in-law's sweet, normally tranquil face, as she handed him the phone; the calm with which he had listened to the details of the accident, unable to absorb that they related to the person he loved; then the great blast of rage and despair that had engulfed him later as he sat gripping his mother-in-law's hands in the darkening salon, tears coursing down his face, when he realized that Monique had been taken away from him for ever.

A tanker had been leaking oil badly on to the road between the nearby villages of Alouis and Le Bec Frenet, the police told him. It should not have been travelling on such a narrow byroad, of course, and the police had been on their way to put up warning signs before a particularly sharp bend, but they had been too late. Skid marks showed that Monique, obviously in a hurry to get home, had braked hard on seeing the oil, slid into it and crashed straight into a stone wall. She had been killed on impact, the police said, recommending that neither Monsieur Beckhampton nor Madame de Bernay should see the body for the moment.

'I'm a religious woman, Tod. *Comme tu sais*,' Jeanne de Bernay said as they had sat in the semi-darkness. 'But when God takes away someone so young and so beautiful, he demands too much of us.' She slammed her small fists into the cushions beside her. 'There are times when I have no faith. To take Monique away like this was not fair – *une erreur. Elle était une source de lumière*, a life-giver. They are so rare.' She wept silently in the gloom, curled up like a wounded animal.

The only things that had kept Tod sane during the dreadful days that followed were his duties with the mares, several of whom chose to foal that week, and being with Lucy. Any spare moments were spent just watching her playing with her toys or toddling through the house, tugging her favourite teddy bear by the hand. He watched her with an intensity that had alarmed him even at the time. She was so like her mother that he felt that if he took his eyes off her for a moment another vital emotional link with Monique might be lost. He had also insisted on bathing Lucy himself every night, soaping her so gently as she splashed around that he'd sometimes tickle her, causing her to chortle and roll her shining brown eyes. This had so reminded him of Monique that he would lift her out of the bath and crush her to him, his eyes filled with tears.

Glancing away from the portrait, Tod pulled himself back to the present, aware that, all these years later, his eyes were embarrassingly damp.

'I'm so sorry,' he said. 'Memories! What a mistake it is to indulge in them.' He flopped down in his usual armchair and took a gulp of his whisky. 'I don't know what came over me. I'm sorry. It must be your sympathetic presence.'

Kate stared at him with a strange intensity. 'You mustn't apologize,' she said, almost angrily. 'It's essential to remember people you have loved, even if the memories are painful. The worst thing that can happen is to forget how much you loved them and how much they meant to you.' She leant forward, clenching and unclenching her hands, her face flushed with emotion. 'After all, if it was I who was dead, I'd hate people to keep grieving over me in a morbid sort of way, but I know I'd hate it even more if they tried to forget me altogether – wouldn't you?'

She must have had a similar experience herself, Tod realized, feeling suddenly concerned. 'It has happened to you, then – losing someone you love, suddenly?' he asked gently.

Kate nodded, her eyes huge with sadness. 'My father. He was killed in a helicopter crash in the Lebanon when he was just about to leave the army and come home. He wasn't shot down or anything: it was just some sort of mechanical failure. A freak accident, they said at the inquiry. I was fourteen when it happened; I'd just gone to a new boarding school.' She took a gulp of wine, her face abstracted. 'I can still remember every detail of the night I heard,' she went on. 'I had gone to bed, ridiculously early – you know how you do at boarding school. Matron came to the dormitory, looking very peculiar, and said that the headmistress wanted to see me downstairs. They were all terribly embarrassed. The English so often are by death, aren't they? I couldn't think what was wrong except that it must be something bad. The headmistress was so nervous that she had to smoke a cigarette while she told me. A Craven-A it was – I can still see that black cat on the packet. I remember staring at it, concentrating very hard, to stop myself from crying.'

She shivered at the memory and looked across at Tod, her grey eyes shining.

'I loved Daddy so much. He was such an honourable man and wise too, but never pompous or boring. He adored Kitty too; she was lucky.'

She sighed, thinking of the contrast with herself and Hugo. She had tried so hard to love him and had indeed convinced herself for a while that she did; she would not have married him otherwise. He had been so insistent that they were right for each other, and had announced with great certainty that marriage was the stage they were at and what they both needed. He had been wrong, of course. That was exactly the stage she was *not* at with him, but she had allowed herself to be persuaded. And now she did not even like him any more. It had all been so draining, she reflected; such a waste of emotions. She wondered whether she would ever have the energy to fall in love again and whether it would be wise to do so. Her judgement, after all, seemed so suspect.

Tod leant forward to pour some more wine into her glass. 'It's odd, you know. I feel as if I have known you for a long time and yet we've hardly met,' he remarked. 'I actually know very little about you. I don't even know if you are married or not, for example.' He leant back and took a pull on his cigarette, watching her with interest.

Kate frowned. She too was finding it remarkably easy to talk to Tod and had in fact already told him far more than she had intended; she might as well explain about Hugo, too. 'I'm married, yes, technically speaking,' she replied, 'but not for much longer. The divorce should be through pretty soon. It was a short marriage, I'm afraid, and never really a love match, like yours obviously was with Monique.' She made a face. 'Hugo's a wine writer, very ambitious, and a lot more worldly than I was when we met,' she went on. 'I think I was rather overawed by him then. He had so much energy and confidence. Anyhow, he's found someone far more suitable now, called Amy. They met when he was writing his book on Californian wine; her father's a big wine grower in the Napa Valley. They're getting married as soon as our divorce comes through, I gather.' She shrugged her shoulders. 'I wish them luck.'

Tod gazed at her thoughtfully. She was, he suspected, more upset by the failure of her marriage than she was letting on, but he didn't want to press her further. 'God knows what the best prescription is for marriage,' he said eventually, taking a long sip of his whisky. 'Love, obviously, but I am not sure about "being in love" myself. That means starting off on such a high and rarefied plain that you can really only go down.' He blew some smoke out through his nostrils. 'Perhaps I was lucky to lose Monique when we were both so tremendously happy. That way neither of us ever let the other down.' He paused. 'People say that friendship is the best basis, shared interests, a lot in common and all that. That's fine as long as things go well but when they don't, it doesn't leave much in the emotional locker, does it? Oh, well, marriage is probably best avoided altogether!' He grinned, stubbing out his cigarette. He couldn't believe, though, that Kate would not marry again. Quite apart from her prettiness and intelligence, there was a vulnerability about her which would be an added attraction to a certain type of man. He was pondering on this when the telephone rang on the desk behind him, immediately disrupting the intimate atmosphere.

'Here we go again. Another anxious owner, no doubt,' he groaned, swinging round and putting his hand over the receiver. 'They tend to start ringing about now. Myra usually copes with them, actually – it's one of her specialities. Hello. Tod Beckhampton speaking. Stelios! . . . How are you? Yes, yes, I know.' He made a face at Kate. 'I was going to ring you. The little filly's still not sound, I'm afraid. I'll get the vet to look at her again tomorrow. It's nothing serious, I'm sure, but we can't be too careful. Sure. No, I'm afraid you can't have a word with Myra, as a matter of fact. She's in London. She'll be back tomorrow night, though. Why don't you give her a ring after nine o'clock? OK. Talk to you soon. Cheerio.'

He turned back to Kate. 'That was Stelios Alexandros. You've probably seen him around: he's a large bloke, Greek, wears rather flashy clothes.' He smiled. 'I rather like him, actually. I inherited him from my father-in-law, Digby Hunter. He's got a very soft spot for Myra. He's known her since she was a child, of course. She gives him advice about his psychopathic twins from time to time. Not that it does any good, in my view – those two are a law unto themselves.'

'Diana Saunders introduced me to Stelios at Newmarket the other day,' Kate told him. 'He seemed quite pleasant to me. I also caught a glimpse of the twins in the paddock. They are quite extraordinarily alike, aren't they? Very handsome, like a pair of well-matched carriage horses.'

'More like well-designed robots,' Tod retorted. 'They're both very talented, of course – Nik's an exceptionally good trainer.'

That seemed to be the general opinion, Kate mused, glancing at her watch. She was amazed to see it was well past eight o'clock, high time she headed back home.

She drained her glass and got up slowly, brushing the dog hairs off her skirt. 'I'm afraid I really must be off, Tod. It's getting late and Kitty will be waiting for supper. Anyway, I'm keeping you from yours.'

Tod snorted. 'Hardly! It's only cold shepherd's pie. Can't you stay for just one more drink? Please?' His brown eyes were entreating. Kate shook her head, smiling. She really liked Tod, though, she decided, as she followed him down the corridor and out through the back door. Despite the cold, she found herself lingering by her car, reluctant to say goodbye.

'Well, thanks so much, Tod,' she said eventually, holding out her hand. 'I loved seeing all the horses and Achilles in particular, of course. Kitty'll be thrilled that he's settled in so well. Can I bring her over to see you some time soon?'

Tod nodded. 'Of course. Any time. Just give me a ring.' He took her hand and gripped it tightly, before pulling her gently towards him and kissing her full on the mouth. As their lips met a tremor of excitement shot through her and she responded immediately, pressing her body against his. Folding his arms around her, Tod held her there, trembling for a minute.

'Hmm,' he murmured appreciatively, blinking behind his glasses. 'That was delicious. Sorry! I couldn't stop myself.' He stepped backwards, a dazed look on his face, as Kate fumbled with the car door. 'Anyway, drive carefully. The roads may be a bit icy. Take care.'

Kate slid into the driving seat, her emotions spinning. 'I will,' she said, winding down the window. 'See you soon, then, and thanks again.' Her voice was steady enough but as she started up the engine she realized that she was shivering all over. It was partly the cold, of course, but it was also, she knew, the effect of Tod's kiss. It seemed to have awakened desires she had kept dormant for a long time and her reaction to it was alarming. She had wanted to burrow beneath his coat and cling to him for comfort. Pull yourself together, she told herself. It would be idiotic for her to get emotionally involved with Tod; he was married, although clearly not all that happily, and she had always had a practical as well as a moral aversion to married men. She knew from her experiences with numerous tearful girlfriends that after the first initial excitement was over, it was always a case of diminishing returns. She must put the idea completely out of her head, she decided, as she turned out of the drive and headed towards the Clock Tower roundabout. But she suspected, instinctively, that it was too late. She had left Tod only minutes ago, but already she was longing to see him again.

CHAPTER SEVEN

Eaton Square, SW1

'Myra! How glad I am to see you,' Stelios exclaimed in his gravelly voice. He looked up from his desk with genuine pleasure as she came through the double doors separating his study from the drawing-room and stood there, pulling off her gloves.

Pushing back his chair, he got up to greet her, his bulk silhouetted against the long window behind him, further obscuring the murky daylight filtering in from the foggy square outside.

'You look splendid,' Stelios said appreciatively, eyeing her up and down as he might do a horse. He laid a gold-ringed hand on her shoulder. 'Just excuse me for a moment, my dear. There's a call I have to make before lunch. Carlo will get you a glass of champagne – or something else, if you prefer. I'll be with you in a minute.' With an avuncular smile, he retreated back into his study and closed the doors behind him.

Myra looked around the drawing-room with its thick white carpet and primrose silk walls, festooned with some of Stelios's valuable collection of Post-Impressionist pictures, and sank down thankfully into one of the more comfortable chairs.

She was was still feeling surprisingly apprehensive about why Stelios had summoned her to lunch at all. 'There is something I want to talk to you about,' he had said portentously on the telephone. What on earth could it be? she wondered. Obviously something important; he occasionally took her and Tod out to lunch in Newmarket but she had not been invited to his London home for years. The worst thing, she thought, would be that he had decided to take his horses away from Barons Lodge. Myra did not think she could stand that at the moment: it would be the last straw. It would happen one day, of course, no doubt when Nik took over the licence from Hugh O'Donnell at Kilmarron, but there was no sign of that happening yet. But she must not be so neurotic. It was probably just a perfectly innocent invitation to lunch: a treat from an old friend who knew she was having a bad time. She must try to relax, Myra told herself; she had had so little opportunity to do that recently. As she sank back into her chair, she could hear Stelios booming away on the telephone next door, to his secretary who worked on the floor below.

'No, no, my dear! You don't understand. I have to talk to Marcos in Monte Carlo *first* – before we even approach the Californian people about buying their refinery. I need to know whether that deal with the Filipinos for their dry cargo ships is going through before I get back to Constantine in New York. Understood? Oh, I see. You already have Marcos on the line now. Good. Good. Put him through.'

After some rapid discussion in Greek, Myra heard Stelios give a great bellow of laughter. 'Yes. Yes. Not bad, eh? Four million dollars. And remember, it was *you* who wanted to sell the ships as scrap! And so . . . what about the Manila deal, then? It's going through as planned, I hope? OK. We'll talk tomorrow.'

Myra had never been sure exactly how much tonnage, oil tankers and other cargo ships – as well as his yacht – Stelios actually owned. 'Oh, they never know themselves, those Greek shipping wallahs. They are always wheeling and dealing,' her father had once informed her. She had always known, of course, that Stelios was extremely rich and presumed that in the past ten years he had become even richer. He had bought and sold an airline in that time, she knew, and launched numerous subsidiary companies to Alexandros Maritime, most of them involved with real estate in New York or the Far East. Pondering on what he was actually worth these days, she experienced a wave of envy. If only she had some money, real money, she thought; all the problems with Barons Lodge would be over. It wouldn't matter that they had so many empty boxes and owners were so slow to pay their bills. She wouldn't want Stelios's life, though – all that travelling around the world. Myra did not like 'abroad' much: she hated not being able to understand what the people around her were saying, and unfamiliar food invariably made her ill. Her father had been the same; he even used to take his own hamper when he took a horse over to the races in France or Germany, something the other trainers always used to rib him about.

Myra got up and wandered towards the window. If only her father were still alive, she thought. With his determination and bluff certainty, *he* would have found a way to galvanize Tod and somehow restore the fortunes of the yard. She still missed him so much. She was wearing one of his gifts today, as a sort of talisman to give her support: a handsome Victorian ruby and pearl brooch which he had bought at an auction at Sotheby's in the fifties. It looked particularly good, she thought, on the lapel of the charcoal Chanel dress she was wearing – this autumn's only extravagance. To boost her confidence further, she had taken considerable trouble with her make-up and hair. It had paid off, she hoped, as she studied her reflection in one of the long Louis XV mirrors. Her hair, swept up into an immaculate pleat, shone like gunmetal in the chandelier's electric light, and the length of the dress, with its well-cut skirt just above the knee, showed off her still shapely legs to some advantage. 'Hmm. Not bad for nearly fifty?' she thought to herself with some satisfaction.

Stelios certainly seemed to appreciate the effort she had made with her appearance, she reflected some minutes later when they finally sat down to lunch. She had caught him looking at her several times over his pre-lunch Martini with a sort of peculiar satisfaction, as though she had just passed some sort of secret test. He certainly did not give the impression of being about to present her with bad news. It was all very peculiar.

'It's just a simple menu,' Stelios said as he reached for his napkin. 'Just a little caviare, followed by *sole véronique* and a lemon soufflé. Caviare, I know is one of your favourites,' he smiled at her benignly. 'And the other dishes too, if I remember rightly. I have not forgotten that birthday dinner your father gave for you at Pruniers, when you were working in London. I was so honoured to be invited. You chose *sole véronique* then, if I am not mistaken.' He tapped his forehead. 'You see! The old elephant does not forget,' he said proudly.

Myra was genuinely touched. She was indeed partial to sole cooked this way but she had completely forgotten that she had ordered it at the birthday party. She had been working as a secretary to a bloodstock agent in Knightsbridge at the time, and was desperately missing the horses and Barons Lodge and riding out every morning. But her father had insisted she did a stint in London, so there was no escape. To cheer her up though, he gave her a birthday dinner at Pruniers, inviting a few of her friends from Newmarket and a handful of his owners. Myra had been rather surprised to find Stelios amongst them. He had only recently started sending horses to Barons Lodge, after all, and she had not realized that Sir Digby particularly liked him. He had been on his best behaviour, although he was gauche in company and his table manners were even worse than they were now. He had been married to

Tessa then but she had not been present; she disliked London and preferred to stay at home in Ireland with the young twins, Stelios had told Myra. He phoned her several times a day of course, no matter where he might be in the world, to see if they were all right. Myra had been impressed by that. When she had a husband, she had thought, she would expect him to be similarly attentive.

It was only when Carlo emerged through the dining-room door, carrying the large crystal bowl of caviare surrounded by crushed ice, that Myra experienced another wave of panic. Why was Stelios spoiling her so? she wondered. What blow was he aiming to soften? Fortified now, by several glasses of Dom Perignon, she determined to find out as soon as she possibly could.

Stelios launched into a complicated story about a Modigliani picture that he had seen in New York and was trying to acquire. It belonged to Nik's godfather, apparently, another Greek, who had fallen on hard times and was down to his last million.

Finding the story tedious, Myra decided it was time to interrupt.

'By the way, how *is* Nik?' she asked brusquely, spooning some more caviare on to her toast and sprinkling it with lemon. 'I don't think I've seen him since the Champion Stakes. That was an impressive win with Devilry, I thought. I imagine Nik would like to keep him in training as a four-year-old.'

Stelios glanced up from his plate. 'That is the plan, I believe, though the owners are reluctant, it seems. They want to syndicate him as soon as possible. I'm considering making them an offer for the horse, as a matter of fact. Nik thinks he will need at least a mile and a half next year, and he deserves a go at the King George and maybe the Arc. I'm going to sound out his owners as soon as I can to see if they'll sell. I'm also going over to Ireland next week to look at a stud farm, Ballinvale Stud near Lucan, with a possible view to standing him there eventually.' He gave Myra a crafty smile. 'Neither the horse nor the farm are officially for sale yet, of course, but I have a hunch they may be. And I am usually right about such things.'

'A stud farm! What on earth are you considering that for?' Myra asked in surprise. 'You've already got Mountclare. Surely if you do acquire Devilry or another stallion, you could stand them there?' She flicked a crumb from the side of her mouth with a well-manicured finger.

'Mmm ... I'm not happy about pouring any more money into Mountclare, if you really want to know, Myra,' Stelios replied, his expression clouding over. 'Stella has made a very good job of things there, I know, but I am finding it increasingly difficult to deal with her these days.' He sighed. 'She is so unco-operative: very obstinate and strong-willed, I'm afraid.' He wiped his mouth noisily with his napkin.

'But if you bought the stud, who would you get to run it for you?' Myra inquired. 'Stud managers like Stella don't grow on trees, you know.'

Stelios's heavy features creased into a smile as he signalled for Carlo to remove the plates. 'That is perfectly true, my dear, but I can think of someone else who could handle it perfectly well if she were interested.'

'Oh, really! Who?' Myra asked with curiosity.

'You,' Stelios informed her.

Myra's carefully plucked eyebrows shot up in surprise. 'Me? What on earth are you talking about?' she asked indignantly. 'How could I possibly run a stud farm in Ireland? I've got enough to do trying to hold Barons Lodge together, I can tell you.' What on earth was the man talking about?

'Well, you have at the moment, I agree,' Stelios agreed calmly, 'but that could all change, you know.' He sat back, staring at Myra, his eyes hooded. 'You would be able to run Ballinvale very well, my dear. But it would mean leaving Barons Lodge and your life there altogether and coming to live with me in Ireland.' He paused. 'As my wife, of course,' he added in a matter-of-fact tone.

Myra shot back in her chair in astonishment, unable to believe her ears. 'Stelios! Have you gone completely mad? What on earth are you talking about?' Her voice was shrill with indignation. 'How could I possibly become your wife? As you well know, I've already got a husband.'

Stelios leant forward with a concerned expression. 'Of course you have, Myra: I am very well aware of that,' he replied soothingly. 'I am very fond of Tod. That is not the point.' He paused, obviously choosing his words with care. 'You have never said anything to me, my dear. You have been very loyal but I have watched you over the past few years and I am not stupid, you know. I know how unhappy and worried you have been. You have had a great deal to put up with. So many problems and disappointments; so much bad luck.' He shook his head sadly. 'And Tod has been little help to you, I'm afraid. In fact, it seems to me that Tod has become one of your problems. Perhaps your most serious one! Not only is he drinking too much but he has, I fear, lost all his drive. That is very serious indeed, in my view.' His broad forehead furrowed into a frown. 'And I'm afraid I do not see things improving, my dear. I know Tod was a brilliant trainer once, but that was a while ago. I have been very worried about you, Myra, and what will happen to you in the future. That's why I am offering you a way out.' He sat back, waiting for her reaction, aware that it might not be immediately favourable. He'd given her something of a shock – he realized that.

Myra gripped the side of her chair, struggling to retain some composure. 'Are you seriously suggesting that just because you think Tod has lost his touch that I should leave him and marry you?' she asked in disbelief. 'What unbelievable cheek!'

Stelios turned to Carlo, hovering in the doorway.

'Just pour the wine, will you?' he barked. 'Then give us five minutes before you bring in the sole. I want to talk to Mrs Beckhampton alone.' He turned back to Myra, his face grave.

'Yes, I am indeed,' he said seriously. 'I know it must seem an extraordinary idea but I have given it a great deal of thought, I assure you. I will explain.' He ran his massive hands back over his oiled grey hair, a preoccupied look on his face, reminding Myra suddenly of a physician about to launch into a lengthy explanation of some unusual disease. She took a gulp of her wine. My God, he was serious, she thought.

'I have known you a very long time, Myra, have I not?' he continued. 'Ever since you were a little girl in pigtails. I will always remember the first time you and Sir Digby took me round the horses. You recited all their pedigrees for me. Your father was very proud of you, I recall.' He paused, his expression softening. 'I was impressed with that little girl, you know, Myra, and now, so many years later, that has not changed.' He leant forward, his eyes pleading. 'I only want to help you, my dear. To ensure that your future is financially secure. It's what your father would have wanted for you, too: of that I am sure.'

This unexpected mention of her father had an instant effect. 'Well, I very much doubt if he would have wanted me to abandon Tod and Toby and Barons Lodge just like that,' Myra replied indignantly. 'It's the most extraordinary suggestion I have ever heard.' She sat back in her chair, her heart pounding.

'There would be absolutely no question of your abandoning Toby,' Stelios replied, obviously pained. 'Greeks never abandon their children – you should know that. Toby would have a home with us as long as he wanted one. And I would treat him as I would treat a son of my own, of course. I like the boy.'

Myra regarded him with suspicion. 'I don't understand,' she said, puzzled. However high your regard for me, it doesn't quite make sense. What's in the whole thing for you? Tell me that.'

Stelios held up his hand, an indulgent smile on his face. 'If you will do me the courtesy of listening carefully, I will explain,' he said patiently. 'As you know, I shall be retiring soon. My brother-in-law, Constantine, is keen to take over the various companies. He is already practically running Alexandros Maritime. And he is hungry for more responsibility, as I once was. But I am an old man, sixty-four next year, and I am tired.' He sighed. 'Tired of running round the world, always being one leap ahead of the competition. The time has come for me to step down, my dear. Relax a bit. Why not? I have earned it and I am, after all, a wealthy man. Right now I am probably worth about eighty million – pounds that is, not dollars,' he glanced at Myra to ensure that she had taken this in.

'Not bad, eh? I see that you are impressed,' he said with satisfaction. 'And the old man has not quite finished yet,' he went on before she could reply. 'He has one or two ambitions left.' He leant forward, his dark eyes gleaming.

'I would like to build up my bloodstock interests, Myra. Try to breed one or two really decent horses before I die. That is one of the reasons I want to acquire Ballinvale; but, more important, I would also like to have some real respect from those people I have always so much admired: the English Establishment, if you like. Respect which up until now, I can tell you, has not seemed possible.' His voice was laden with resentment. 'However much I have put into racing, however much money I have invested here, I have been deliberately kept an outsider. The Inner Circle, the people who make the rules, have seen to that. They do not rate me very highly – I know that. Oh, old Stelios is all right, they say, not a bad chap, I suppose, but he is not, of course, one of us.' His expression darkened. 'You do not know, Myra, how much I have wanted to become a member of the Jockey Club. You cannot imagine what that would mean to me. And I have deserved it, in my opinion. I have been an owner for many years. I have put a lot of money into racing charities and my company sponsors several races. But I have not even had an approach. Never. Not from anyone.' He lifted his fist and banged the table. 'Not many arrows get through this old hide any more, but that one has hurt, Myra, believe me.'

Myra stared at him in amazement, so distracted by this unexpected outburst that she almost forgot her own emotions. She had never seen

Stelios so worked up before or had any idea that he felt so passionately about being excluded from the Jockey Club. What an extraordinary lunch this was turning out to be!

'But now I hope all that is going to change,' Stelios continued firmly. 'I will let you into a little secret now, Myra. I know I can trust you and anyhow, what I'm going to tell you concerns you too: it could well affect your decision.' He sat back, folding his hands, a self-satisfied look on his face. 'The Greek Ambassador to Ireland retires in two years' time and my government have asked me to be his successor,' he announced with quiet triumph. 'I'm well known in Dublin, of course, because of the Fitzgerald connection, and also because both my children are doing so well over there.' He sat back, looking as though he had just pulled a particularly spectacular rabbit out of a hat. 'So, you see. You are lunching with a future ambassador today, Myra. What do you think about that?' He paused. 'And one who is asking you to become his wife,' he added, beaming broadly.

'You are a very competent woman, my dear. You would be a real asset to me in Dublin and at Ballinvale. You also have certain social graces that I lack – I am well aware of that.' He spread his hands in a gesture of submission. 'That is why I need you, in answer to the question you have just put to me so bluntly. But you must believe me when I tell you that I am as concerned about your future as I am about mine,' he said, his face serious. 'If things go on deteriorating as they have been at Barons Lodge, have you thought what would happen? You would have to sell the yard, the yard that your father made into one of the finest in England, the place that has always been your home. How would you feel about that?'

'Wait a minute! You're jumping the gun a bit. It really hasn't come to that yet, you know,' Myra replied. 'Barons Lodge may be going through a bad patch but it's still very much in business. After all, what about those yearlings we've just got from Hassim? He would hardly have sent us those if he thought the yard was finished, would he?' She glared at Stelios defiantly before turning to help herself from the dish Carlo was proffering.

'Mmm. You can't rely on those babies to put things right, as you well know,' Stelios replied. 'They may turn out to be useless. And what happens if any more owners take their horses away? I myself will be transferring mine to Ireland, of course, when Nik takes over the licence at Kilmarron – I'm sure you realize that.' He held up his hand, his face contrite at the sight of Myra's expression.

'Please don't be angry with me, my dear. I am not deliberately trying to wound you by saying all these things. I am your friend, I am trying to help you. I am offering you an alternative to any more years of disappointment and struggle; a comfortable future where you will be taken care of in the way you deserve. Surely that is not so terrible, is it?' He turned to help himself to the fish.

'If you agree to my proposition, my dear – and when it is made public – I would settle some money on you straight away – £500,000, perhaps. But that is something we can discuss later.' He turned his attention, enthusiastically, to the fish on his plate.

Myra stared at him, mesmerized, her emotions in turmoil. She had entirely lost her appetite, she realized, glancing down at the sole in front of her. The pale grapes seemed to be winking at her from their bed of sizzling sauce and she felt decidedly dizzy. It must be the amount she was drinking, she presumed, added to the shock of Stelios's extraordinary proposal which, it seemed, she was being bribed to accept. Right now, £500,000 seemed like a fortune.

She suddenly felt near to tears; it was all too much to cope with. How could she possibly even consider leaving her family and Barons Lodge, with all the disruption that would cause, particularly to Toby, who was already going through a difficult phase? It was unthinkable. Yet Stelios was only voicing some of the fears which she herself had lain awake night after night in the past year trying not to think about. It *was* possible that if Barons Lodge did not have any success in the next two years, the yard would be running at such a loss that they would have to consider selling it. That would break her heart. Glancing down at her brooch, she thought again of her father. He had liked Tod a lot but he had always warned her that he was not as determined as the Hunters were themselves and that the future of Barons Lodge would always rest equally on her shoulders. Surely he wouldn't have wanted her to give up now, without more of a struggle?

'I wouldn't be so quick to write off Tod, if I were you,' she said defensively. 'He may have lost some of his fighting spirit, but with one or two decent two-year-olds in the yard next year, our luck could well change.' She took a gulp of her wine. 'Anyway, even supposing your depressing scenario comes about, it's not my character to quit, is it? Surely you realize that?'

'There would be no question of your losing Barons Lodge if you accepted my proposal,' Stelios retorted.

Myra put down her knife and fork. 'What do you mean?' she asked, puzzled.

84

'Because I would provide the money to keep it going. Barons Lodge would come in very useful for Nik. I can hardly believe he will want to stay on at Kilmarron for long. Or we could continue to lease it to Tod, or some other trainer if Tod decides to pack up, until Toby is ready to take over.' Stelios looked across at Myra, his eyes gleaming with triumph. 'That is what you would like to happen, one day, is it not? Well, if you accepted my offer there would be no problem, would there?'

Myra was speechless. Stelios had an answer to everything, it seemed. He had obviously thought the whole thing out very carefully. She suddenly remembered her manners: preposterous though his plan was, he obviously did have her interests at heart, she thought – more than anyone else seemed to at the moment. It would be churlish, therefore, for her not to show some sort of appreciation.

'I don't know what to say, Stelios,' she said eventually, shaking her head. 'I'm dumbfounded. In a way, I should say thank you. I know you mean well but you are asking me to leave Tod, you know. That is pretty damn drastic.'

Stelios nodded. 'I know it is, my dear,' he said soothingly. 'And you must know how sorry I am that things have got to the state they have. I am very fond of Tod, you know. I have nothing against him personally – nothing. It's just your future I am concerned about. You and Tod had much success together in the past but those days are over. I'm a realist, my dear. I'm sorry if I have offended you by my bluntness but I had to speak out.'

Myra felt near to tears again. 'Tod and I made a very good team once, you know,' she insisted. 'One of the reasons he infuriates me so much at the moment is that he doesn't seem to care any more that it's all gone wrong.' She sighed. 'But I am still fond of him, you know. We've been married for a long time.'

'I know, I know,' Stelios said sympathetically. 'But that does not mean you should stay together in the future.' He sat back and began picking his teeth with a gold toothpick. 'I know what I am suggesting is not, as they say, "love's young dream",' he continued. 'I am an old man now and even you too have reached your middle years – though you are still, if I may say so, a very attractive woman. What we would have would be a partnership. An affectionate partnership, I would dare to hope.' He leant forward confidentially. 'There need be no sex between us, if that's what you wished. That would not distress me too much. I've had problems with my health recently as you may know,

85

my diabetes in particular. My powers in that direction have faded fast, I'm afraid.'

He smiled sadly, then glanced at Myra's plate with concern. 'You have eaten so little, Myra! What a pity!' He turned to Carlo. 'Clear this away, will you. I'm afraid Mrs Beckhampton is not very hungry.'

He swung back to Myra, his face concerned. 'My suggestions have clearly come as something of a shock for you. I understand that. That's why I want to give you plenty of time to consider them, quietly, and in your own time. I will be travelling a lot in the next six months, so I do not need your answer until the spring or even the early summer. I think that is fair.'

As Carlo left the room, Stelios leant forward again, his expression solemn. 'It will be our little secret, of course. Until we next meet. I shall tell no one what we have discussed and I expect you to do the same.'

Reaching across the table he laid his great hand over hers. 'Don't forget, Myra, I am offering you comfort and security for the rest of your life,' he insisted. 'I am giving you the chance to escape from an unhappy situation which will only get worse and which is already making your life a misery.' He paused meaningfully. 'I want you to consider it very carefully indeed, my dear,' he said with emphasis, fixing her in his hooded gaze. 'Before it is too late.'

Myra shivered as he pressed her hand. That sounded remarkably like a threat, she thought.

Three Swallows Stud, near Newmarket

Halting at the T-junction to let a horsebox lumber past, Charlie Kyle wound down his window and gazed across the expanse of plough tinged now with a faint green down of winter wheat.

Despite a certain end-of-season fatigue, he was, he realized, feeling more cheerful than he had been for some time. It was partly because he was going to lunch with Diana, of course. Charlie had enjoyed meeting Lyle Saunders on his previous visit to Three Swallows – he had been impressed by the man's approachability and surprisingly liberal views on apartheid – but he had had no time alone with Diana, as promised, as some of her other friends had turned up early for a swim before lunch as sell. Today, however, she had insisted that they really would be à deux.

The other reason Charlie was feeling optimistic was that, at last, he had had a response to his advertisement in *The Sporting Life* asking anyone who had any memories or photographs of Coombe Place to get in touch. The previous day, when he returned from evening stables, he had found a letter on the mat at Keepers Cottage from a man called Wally Pines, who he vaguely remembered his father putting up occasionally as a lightweight jockey. Pines lived just outside London now, apparently, somewhere near Harlow in Essex, and his story was a sad one: he had broken his back in a fall at Taunton racecourse some eight years ago and had been in a wheelchair ever since. But he still kept in touch with the racing scene, he told Charlie, and always read *The Sporting Life*. He'd seen Charlie's advertisement and realized he still had some pictures taken twenty years ago of himself on some of the Coombe Place horses, including a couple of photographs in the Winners' Enclosure at Newton Abbot, his favourite course. He would be very happy to send them to Charlie if that would be of any help.

Charlie had decided to get in touch with Pines as soon as possible. The ex-jockey would be bound to have known Warrender and might even have a clue as to his whereabouts, but when he'd rung earlier this morning he realized he'd been over-optimistic. 'Keith Warrender? No. Sorry. I've no idea where *he*'s got to,' Pines had told him. 'I did hear a rumour that he'd ended up in prison, though. Can't say I was surprised. I never had much time for the bloke myself.' He paused. 'But I tell you who might be able to help you, come to think of it: Beth. Beth Arnott, her name is now. She worked for your Dad, too, and was thick as thieves with Warrender. They ran a saddlery business together, down in Yelperton, I seem to remember. Anyway, she's up in Yorkshire now, got married to some bloke called Arnott who was a travelling head lad for one of the Middleham trainers. Or was a few years ago. I only know because she wrote to me after my accident, saying she'd read about it and was sorry. Mind you, that was a few years back, now – she may well have moved on since then. I haven't kept her letter, I'm afraid, but if Arnott still works up there, she shouldn't be too hard to find.'

Charlie had liked the sound of Wally Pines and was sorry things hadn't worked out better for him. His voice still had that West Country burr that always reminded him of home. He promised to visit him some time soon to take a look at the pictures. In the meantime he would get in touch with his friends in Middleham, the trainer Jack Crow and his wife with whom he often stayed when he had to take any of the Barons Lodge horses up to Yorkshire.

Middleham was a very close community and if this man Arnott was still working up there Jack would be bound to have come across him. Beth might well know what had happened to Warrender; she had lived with the man for several years, after all. At last he had a proper lead, Charlie thought with excitement, as he slowed down to turn into the Three Swallows drive.

Five minutes later he had run Diana to earth down by the stallion boxes. Wearing dark-blue jodhpurs and a matching Husky, her blonde hair tucked up under a flat cap, she was talking to Derek, her stallion man, as he led the young horse Greek Dancer back into his box after his morning exercise.

'Hi there!' she called out as she caught sight of Charlie. 'Come and say hello to my pride and joy.' She slapped the horse affectionately on his bay rump. 'He's been in terrific form this morning, haven't you, sport? Tearing round his paddock like a lunatic. Christ knows what Derek's been feeding him on.' She grinned. 'We were just discussing cutting down a bit on his oats − to conserve his energies for the start of the covering season!'

Charlie approached the box quietly as Greek Dancer clopped inside and, leaning on the half door, gazed into the interior. With its thatched roof, dark wood beams, panelling, brass fittings and high leaded windows it was like a little mock-Tudor cottage, he reflected, only the deep straw piled up around the sides of the box indicating that it was for an equine occupant. Greek Dancer, though, his head already stuck into his manger, seemed oblivious to the luxury of his surroundings.

'Wow! You certainly do your stallions proud. This box is palatial,' Charlie observed, impressed.

'Sure. We like to make our boys comfortable!' Diana replied cheerfully. 'You never know, they might pass the word around to some of the young stock. Try your guts out on the track, kid, and you too could end up in a place like this.' She gazed fondly towards the main yard as a couple of leggy foals came into view, skittering in from one of the paddocks led by a groom. 'If only we could get that message across. Think what a difference it might make,' she added, jokingly.

It was amazing how healthy she always looked, Charlie thought. At the end of the season, when most flat-racing people tended to look grey and fatigued and in need of their annual January blast of sun, Diana still looked remarkably perky and glowing. Presumably some of it was make-up, but her eyes, too, were clear and sparkling as they squinted into the late-morning sun.

She gazed over the box door at Greek Dancer's quarters. 'This one could be anything at stud, of course. We simply won't know until next year!' she said thoughtfully. 'His fertility's fine – 98 per cent – and we had a great-looking crop of foals this year – not too many fillies either, thank goodness. But we've no idea whether they can really go or not until we see them out on the track.' She made a face. 'That's when we'll know whether Daddy's bought a dud or not.' She glanced at her watch. 'Christ, is that the time? We'd better get a move on. I thought we'd have a swim before lunch – OK?'

They could have a 'session' in the sauna first, she told Charlie as she took his arm and started back towards the house. Her touch excited him and he began to feel randy. He decided to relax into his seduction and let Diana make the pace.

As he stepped through the side door into the pool room, its glinting blue water fringed by hanging baskets of tropical plants and exotic-looking ferns, Diana was already peeling off her clothes and throwing them casually into one of the changing-rooms.

'It's OK. There's no one around,' she reassured him, pointing to a large basket. 'You'll find clean towels in there. Just in case you are feeling shy.' Pulling her shirt over her head she stood there unselfconsciously in her bra and knickers and began to twist her hair back into a ponytail.

She had neat, sharply pointed breasts and long firm thighs like a boy, Charlie noticed, as he slipped into the nearest cubicle and started to strip off hurriedly himself. By the time he had emerged, a towel round his waist, Diana was completely naked.

'Come on, then,' she said to him, grinning. She held out her hand. 'Let's go and sweat a bit.' Charlie felt his erection stirring as he followed her into the sauna and watched her fling a bucket of cold water on to the coals, causing a great gush of steam to envelop them both. When it had cleared Diana was already lying on a pile of towels on one of the lower benches, an inviting grin on her face.

Wrenching his towel off with one hand, Charlie knelt over her and kissed her fiercely on the mouth, his erection hardening.

Diana lifted her head and gazed down at his penis with interest. 'Hey! that's some fella you've got there. Mmm ... I can't wait,' she said appreciatively, as she sank back again and let her legs fall open. As Charlie bent down to lick her nipples, firming them into points with his tongue, her breathing quickened. 'For Christ's sake, just fuck me,' she murmured urgently. 'I'm in no mood for messing about. Just get in there quick. I'm dying for it.'

Charlie rammed into her instantly, not needing any encouragement. As he thrust up and down, revelling in all the sensations it was giving him, Diana started to squirm beneath him, her lips parted with pleasure. 'Terrific. Great. Harder, Charlie. Harder. That's it. I'm going to come quickly. Then we can do it again.' Leaning back on her elbows, she tilted her body upwards, grinding her pelvis against his. 'Hmm . . . That's it. That's bliss,' she breathed.

As Charlie drove into her again with renewed vigour, he felt her vagina suddenly go into spasm and she began to shudder violently, her nails biting into his shoulders.

'Oh, wow, yes, oh yes, Charlie,' she yelled out ecstatically as her orgasm reached its peak and she flopped back on the pile of towels. 'Sorry,' she murmured finally, her eyes still closed. 'Couldn't control myself.' She grinned lazily. 'Don't worry. I'll see to you in a minute, I promise.' She patted the towel next to her. 'Come and lie down here. On your back,' she ordered. 'I'm going to mount you this time.'

Charlie was longing to get inside her again, to ease himself into that hot, inviting tunnel. As she rolled over, he stretched out beside her, his heart thumping. The next minute she was on top of him, guiding him inside her deftly with one hand and wriggling about sensuously before sinking down on her elbows.

'Now relax,' she whispered. 'Just leave it all to me. I'll do all the work this time.'

She started rotating her body gently but firmly in small circles, pleasuring herself slowly and leaning down to brush her swollen nipples against his chest. 'It's OK. We're nearly there,' she murmured, shifting her weight to one elbow and beginning to caress his balls expertly with one hand. Charlie, who had been drifting along on a swelling tide of pleasure, could hold back no longer and as she pushed herself up and down more fiercely again, he started to come. 'For Christ's sake, Diana. You're too much,' he moaned as he bucked into her, throwing her upwards, his fingers digging into her back.

After she had come again, almost instantaneously, and they lay there panting in the steam, limp with satisfaction, Charlie reflected on his luck. He had always enjoyed Diana's company, of course, and suspected that she would be an excellent lover, but she had surpassed even his expectations. Very few women, in his experience, were able to come so quickly and enjoy sex so blatantly, in such an uncomplicated way. It was exactly what he had been looking for.

As the confirmation that Alain du Roc had just got up to win the fifth race by half a length came crackling over the public-address system, Kate was already sprinting through the crowd towards the Winners' Enclosure. She must try to get a few more shots of the jockey being led in on the winner, Mois d'Avril, before the light finally went. The racegoers had just witnessed a classic example of du Roc's determination and skill, which some of them did not seem to appreciate too much as he had managed to defeat a well-backed favourite. As she dodged round a couple of disgruntled-looking punters in expensive raincoats, they were already tearing up their tickets in disgust before heading for the car park. There was only one race left on the card now and many of the Parisian punters, not noted for their hardiness, had already left, but a few stalwarts were still assembled around the Winners' Enclosure, waiting to applaud one of their heroes as he was led in.

'Quel audace! Ça fait cent vingt-neuf, n'est-ce pas?' inquired a tiny grizzled old man who must be a retired jockey or stable lad, Kate thought, as she adjusted the focus on her camera.

She shook her head. 'Pas encore. Vingt-huit, je crois. Il a perdu la première course, rappelez-vous,' she replied in what she felt was embarrassingly rusty French. She realized that she had become far more knowledgeable about racing in the past year, which would be useful, of course, when Achilles finally got on the track.

The man shrugged his shoulders in typically Gallic fashion. 'Cela m'est égal,' he said. 'Il va gagner la Cravache d'Or quand même.'

I hope to goodness that he's right, Kate thought to herself, hastily wiping her lenses. Having sold the idea of an immediate du Roc profile to both Reg Gunn and the editor of the magazine, who had suggested that his old friend, Frank McLachlan, sportswriter of the year, should write it, she had been alarmed when Reg had started to waver about the timing. They should run it at the beginning of the next flat-racing season, he suggested, rather than at the end of this one.

'I've just been talking to the sports editor,' he explained over a drink at his favourite local, the Bunch of Grapes. 'He insists it's not odds on that du Roc *will* win the championship this year. He's only fifteen winners ahead, apparently, with quite a few weeks to go. Supposing he gets injured or something? That Yank who rides over there, Del Mar, could still catch him up if something like that happened.

We'd look right Charlies then, wouldn't we?' He shook his head. 'I
don't like it, girl. I think we should wait until the spring.'

Kate looked at him in disbelief. 'But we went into all this,' she
complained. 'We agreed that we should take the risk, as this is such
an important year for du Roc. He could land the championship *and*
beat his own best ever total of winners. But all this will be really
old hat in March.' She poured herself some more Frascati. 'Anyway,
he's riding like a dervish at the moment. He had four winners at
Longchamp on Sunday, including the Prix Royal Oak.' She frowned.
'What's the matter with you all of a sudden, Reg? I thought you
liked a challenge?'

But Reg had been persuaded to go ahead only when, in the course
of another drinking session with the sports editor and his friends,
he had heard the rumour that Dale Del Mar, the American jockey
who was running second to du Roc in the French jockey table, had
reactivated an old neck injury in a fall on the gallops and was thinking of packing it in for the season and returning home to Florida
for the winter.

In the past few days, however, Kate had begun to question her
own judgement. Du Roc had not had a winner for several days and
Del Mar, who showed no sign of returning to the States, had closed
his lead to eleven. It was quite possible that if anything should
happen to du Roc and the American decided to really go for the
title he could win it. Du Roc, however, remained confident. She had
been out photographing him on the gallops at Chantilly early that
morning and had had a chance of a quick chat with him in his car
after he had ridden work on a couple of horses. Despite looking
drawn and suffering from the tail end of a cold, he insisted that he
had an excellent chance of riding the winner of the first race that
afternoon, on a colt of Weinburger's who always came right in the
late autumn when the ground was really soft.

The colt had indeed started the firm favourite and had looked all
over an easy winner at the furlong pole, but he had stumbled in the
last hundred yards, been overtaken by his nearest rival and pulled
up lame. Then, in the third race of the afternoon, du Roc's fortunes
had taken another, more drastic, downturn. His mount, a leggy
chesnut colt who had been particularly edgy in the paddock and
taken a very strong hold on the way down to the start, had reared
up backwards as the handlers were trying to put him into the stalls.
Du Roc had no option but to slip off his back, but unfortunately
his toe had caught in the stirrup and he had fallen heavily on to his

left shoulder, which he had already injured earlier in the year. A sleet shower had been threatening at the time, and the sky grew so dark that Kate abandoned all attempts to take pictures until the light improved again and watched the incident on closed-circuit television in one of the bars. Seeing du Roc get up slowly, clutching his shoulder, she felt a wave of panic. Suppose he were badly hurt and had to pack up riding for the rest of the season? There was no chance that the magazine would run the feature then. She admired and liked what she knew of du Roc and felt immediately guilty that she should be worrying so much about her feature rather than feeling concern for him. But it was vital, if she wanted to build up any sort of reputation as a photographer in the racing world – which she definitely did now that she and her mother had decided to keep Achilles in training – that the du Roc pictures should be memorable and out of the ordinary. Much against his will, in one of his more hungover moments, Reg had agreed to let her shoot them in black and white. They would be more dramatic, she insisted, and more truthful, and would better capture the essence of the relationship between rider and horse.

As du Roc and the winning filly trod towards her now, it was hard to say which of them looked the most exhausted. Mois d'Avril's white face was spattered with mud and she was still blowing hard, her flanks heaving. Her jockey, staring impassively between her ears, managed to crack a smile when a ripple of applause broke out; Kate guessed that this was more through relief that he had no more rides today than anything else. As she ran alongside him, taking a few more shots, he turned to her, raising one hand wearily in protest. 'Alors, ça suffit. Have mercy, Kate, please,' he said good-humouredly. 'Give me un quart d'heure. Then we'll leave. I need to get cleaned up a bit.' He flicked some mud disdainfully from his arm before slipping his feet out of the stirrups.

Kate was delighted when he'd offered her a lift back to Chantilly after the racing. She was staying on there at her hotel for one extra night in the hope of having lunch with Frank McLachlan at some restaurant off the Champs Elysées tomorrow; but ten minutes drive away from the racecourse she was starting to regret that she had not booked a taxi, however expensive. Du Roc had already cut up several people on the way out of the car park and once on the main road weaved in and out of the traffic at terrifying speed, seemingly impatient to overtake anything that got in his way.

'I'm afraid I'm making you nervous,' he observed as she gripped the side of her seat. 'Jockeys are terrible drivers, I know – so competitive. They can't help it, I'm sorry. They like to test their cars to the maximum.'

Not liking to admit how nervous she actually was, Kate did not reply. She noticed, however, that du Roc winced visibly as he settled back more firmly in his seat.

'Does your shoulder hurt a lot?' she asked him, with genuine concern.

'*Bien sûr*,' he replied casually. 'But I have an appointment with my physio this evening and again tomorrow morning. No doubt he can patch me up for the time being.' He made a face. 'That idiotic colt. *Il est complètement fou.*' He gripped the wheel more tightly as he accelerated past another Porsche. 'I gave the little filly too hard a race, I fear,' he went on reflectively. 'I had intended to look after her better. It's not really her ground – she has such small feet.' He shrugged his shoulders, wincing again. 'But I had so little luck earlier and I knew she had the ability to win today if I really pushed her. She's very genuine.'

'Your determination certainly communicated itself to her,' Kate remarked. 'You seemed almost to carry her over the line.'

Du Roc smiled. 'That's why the will to win is so important. Most animals would pack it in under pressure, left to themselves, and who can blame them?'

'Well, you were equally hard on yourself. Don't you sometimes wonder whether it's worth it? I mean, you could be out in California or Florida or somewhere, enjoying a bit of sunshine with some of the other European jockeys.'

Du Roc turned to her, his dark eyes suddenly hard. 'You don't understand,' he snapped. 'I want to be the best, here in France on my own home ground. I have won a lot already, *bien sûr*: certainly all the major races in France and the Arc de Triomphe four times. But it's not enough. I want to win them again, and the championship, of course. It's what motivates me at all times, even now at the back end of the season in this terrible weather, when I'm taking rides that in other circumstances I wouldn't touch. But when I lose this will to win, I shall pack it up, *tout de suite*. It would be dangerous to ride after that.'

'What will you do when you do retire? Train perhaps?' Kate asked, taken aback by his vehemence.

Du Roc shook his head emphatically. '*Non, jamais ça.* I lack the necessary patience, I'm afraid. Tod and I have often talked about it.'

94

Just hearing Tod's name mentioned so unexpectedly gave Kate's nerves a jolt. She had been thinking about him again on this trip to France and of how she had felt that evening when he had kissed her. Clutching her seat as du Roc revved up the engine again and prepared to swoop around the car in front, she realized another reason why the pictures of him had to be good: she wanted them to impress Tod. Somehow now, that seemed very important.

CHAPTER EIGHT

The Old Rectory

Lady Kitty raised her glass. 'Well! Happy Christmas again, everyone. It's grand to have you here.' She rolled the ruby-coloured wine around her glass slowly, holding it up to the candlelight, her neat little head, with its cap of snowy hair, tilted to one side like a bird. 'Now, this is an excellent drop of claret you've brought us, Professor,' she commented, her blue eyes wide with pleasure. 'Pichon Longueville 1978, did you say? Well, you always were the connoisseur. It's as smooth as satin.' She looked round the table appreciatively at her two male guests and at Kate sitting opposite, looking so pretty and glowing in cherry-coloured velvet, and put down her glass. 'Now! Not too much talking until we've tasted Kate's goose,' she ordered.

Although it was barely three o'clock in the afternoon and not yet dark, the Christmas weather was so damp and dismal that the Levertons had decided to shut out the day completely, pulling the curtains and lighting the candles. They were eating their lunch in the little panelled room that had been David Leverton's study, its dark oak walls bright with cards and holly, rather than in the large dining-room which was never used in the winter, being far too draughty, with leaking radiators and a chimney that smoked. The small walnut dining-table sat four people easily and the old gold curtains, relics from Rathglin, could be relied on to keep out the cold with the help of a wood-burning stove in the fireplace.

Lady Kitty had insisted on using the best of her Waterford crystal and the remains of her beloved white and gold Crown Derby dinner service. In the centre of the table was a simple Wedgwood bowl of white anemones flanked by two Georgian silver candlesticks and assorted dishes of nuts, raisins, quince jellies, fudge and chocolates.

Kate had enjoyed cooking the goose, stuffing it with mashed potato and onion rather than with the traditional sage mixture in order to absorb more of the fat. Taking a mouthful, together with a sliver of spiced parsnips, she looked across at her mother and smiled. They both always enjoyed Christmas, keeping the jangling commercialism at bay as much as possible, decorating the house with holly and the sweet-scented hyacinths Lady Kitty nursed in her greenhouse sheds and spending leisurely hours in the kitchen making the cake, mince pies and puddings. Last year, however, had been a sadly low-key occasion with Kitty still in pain with her hip and Kate suffering from flu and brooding over the break with Hugo. They had not felt much like entertaining anyone, so had spent a quiet few days being visited by local friends, watching old films on television and trying to bolster each other's flagging spirits.

This year, however, Lady Kitty had been determined to be more festive and had invited an old friend from Dublin to stay. Desmond Kiely, always known as 'the Professor', was a contemporary of her older brother's at Trinity College; they had first met at a party during the Horse Show week just before the war when Lady Kitty was just nineteen and, remarkably, had remained friends ever since, corresponding when Lady Kitty was abroad as an Army wife, and the Professor was climbing steadily up the academic ladder to become a respected expert on medieval history. He had had various adventures with women in his youth, enjoyed their company and was certainly not homosexual, but he had never married and lived in a solid stone villa at Blackrock with a succession of devoted housekeepers, the most recent of which had recently died. When Lady Kitty had heard the news she immediately wrote to him ordering him over to the Old Rectory for Christmas.

Watching them now across the table, reminiscing happily about some Christmas they had both spent at Rathglin when the old Earl was still alive, Kate could see that her mother's invitation had been an excellent idea. The Professor always reminded her of Mr Pickwick, with his bald dome of a head fringed with white hair and twinkling brown eyes behind little gold-rimmed glasses, and this afternoon he looked even more Dickensian than usual. She caught his eye as he sat back, surreptitiously undoing another button on his cardigan, and he raised his glass and smiled.

'To the cook,' he said. 'The goose is perfection, as indeed the company, too.' He reached for the decanter beside him to pour Lady Kitty some more claret.

Judging by the way their other guest was attacking his plate and spooning sauce enthusiastically over his remaining slice of goose, Geoffrey Barlow was also enjoying himself, Kate observed.

'It's all so delicious. Much more interesting than turkey. I'm afraid I'm making a pig of myself,' he announced cheerfully through a mouthful of mashed potato.

Kate had invited Geoffrey on a whim two weeks ago when she had been sitting in his Bloomsbury office, still stunned by the offer he had just made her. The director of a small publishing company taken over a few years ago by a large international conglomerate, he was now responsible for the art book list, or, as Hugo always put it, 'the coffee-table crap'. Geoffrey had published Hugo's first book, *Wines of the Iberian Peninsula*, which had been quite successful, and they subsequently became friends. Kate always welcomed the visits of Geoffrey and his pretty but scatty actress girlfriend, Bettina, to the house in Battersea; she found them agreeable company and considerably less pushy and pretentious than a lot of Hugo's friends. She always found Geoffrey rather too earnest and pedantic, though, with his devotion to the Labour Party and a penchant for Victorian Gothic architecture and corduroy jackets, but he had always been easy enough to entertain. He was always so appreciative, perhaps because Bettina, Kate knew, was an absolutely hopeless cook.

Geoffrey had always shown enthusiasm for her work, often going on at embarrassing length over the dinner-table about some spread or series of pictures of hers that he had seen in one of the magazines. She had not heard from him at all, however, since Hugo's last departure for California so had been genuinely surprised when he had rung her up one morning to tell her he had an interesting proposition to put to her.

One of their New York directors, he told her at their meeting, had landed rather a coup. He had persuaded the American Sandy Diss, previously the TV actress Sandy Dacre, who had recently become a decorative addition to the English aristocracy through her marriage to the Marquis of Diss, to do a coffee-table book on the British and their horses.

'Of course, she's not actually going to write very much,' Geoffrey explained. 'Just a series of long captions and comments. I shouldn't think she can write for toffee, but she does know about horses. Her father is a big breeder in Kentucky, apparently, so she grew up on a stud farm. Anyway, she's very well known in the States from that soap she was in, the one about an expensive clinic. She played Nurse Julie, I seem to remember. The one that was always getting shagged by the doctors. Anyway, that should really boost the US sales and now she's got a title too – you know how they love that over there,' he rolled his eyes.

'I'll be honest with you, Kate,' he went on earnestly. 'Sandy initially asked for a real "name" photographer to do the pictures. You know, Snowdon or Lichfield – I think she even suggested Prince Andrew! She wanted to make up what she described as a "real aristo package".' He made another disapproving face. 'Well, of course, we can't possibly afford someone like that, particularly after the advance her agent is asking, and it turns out that none of them are interested in horses anyway, so that's that.' He leant across the table, blinking enthusiastically behind his glasses.

'So then I thought of you, Kate, and how well you could do it. I thought those pictures you took the other day of that French jockey were absolutely brilliant: he looked so brooding and world-weary in some of them, yet so completely relaxed on his horse.' He beamed at her. 'They really were awfully good and Jacky, the commissioning editor in New York, thought so too. I sent them over to her straight away, together with some of the features you've done recently.' He pushed back a strand of lank brown hair. 'Anyway, I've managed to sell you to them, I think,' he said triumphantly. 'They're in a real hurry to get cracking, too – want to start as soon as possible. So, what do you say? I ought to add that there won't be much of an advance, I'm afraid – £3,500 – but you could make quite a bit on royalties. I could speak to your agent about the details.'

Kate was overjoyed. The book was exactly the sort of commission she had been looking for. She *knew* it had been important that those du Roc pictures were good. Thank God, too, that he had won the Jockey's Title – it was by less than ten winners at the end, but still he had won it and exceeded his previous totals. The book would give her a real opportunity to improve and experiment with her techniques of photographing horses, too, and as, according to Geoffrey, it would entail covering most of the major horse events, like Badminton and the Windsor Horse Show, as well as such highlights of the racing calendar as Royal Ascot, Derby Day, Cheltenham and Liverpool, she would be able to sell plenty of extra pictures to newspapers and magazines.

This additional money would be vital. Although she had found a cash buyer for the Battersea house, £10,000 from the proceeds of her share of the sale would have to be immediately put aside to cover Achilles's training expenses and it would be sensible to invest the rest immediately until she decided to buy herself somewhere else to live in

London some time next year. An increase in her freelance income was therefore essential.

'Geoffrey, you're an angel! Of course I'll do the book,' she replied, jumping up from her chair and impetuously giving him a kiss. He insisted on opening some champagne to celebrate and while they were drinking it she asked him about Bettina. Things weren't going so well, Geoffrey informed her morosely. Bettina was away filming in Brazil and he suspected that she'd got involved with some unsuitable man out there. Anyway, she wasn't coming back for Christmas. Kate, still feeling euphoric, immediately invited him to the Old Rectory.

'Oh, do come,' she insisted. 'Kitty will have an old flame from Dublin and I hate playing gooseberry!'

Geoffrey seemed delighted at the idea and arrived on Christmas Eve, laden with presents. He was a model guest, being both appreciative and accommodating. What a pity she didn't fancy him in the slightest, Kate reflected, as she got up to go into the kitchen and cope with the Christmas pudding.

As she waited for it to cool slightly before unwrapping it from its swaddling clothes, she switched on the ancient radio to catch the end of a carol service she'd noticed in the *Radio Times*. Geoffrey was certainly a welcome change from Hugo too, she reflected. *He* would have just sat around, pontificating about some obscure wine he was forcing them all to try and complaining of indigestion.

'He's an amiable fellow, all right, your Geoffrey,' Lady Kitty had commented when they were laying the table. 'Very keen on you too, I'd say.'

Kate had grinned. 'Maybe. He's a good friend. But don't go getting any ideas in that direction, will you? He's definitely not my type!'

Her mother would not be overjoyed if she knew who was obviously very much her type, Kate thought, turning up the radio. The choir had started singing 'In the Deep Mid Winter', one of her favourite carols. She had not, after all, seen Tod since that evening in early November. She and her mother had gone over to see Achilles one day but both Tod and Myra had had to go to a funeral up north that day and it had been left to Sam Shaw to look after them. Achilles was making good progress, though he was still overkeen and moody in his box, the head lad had informed them. 'Liam Byrne's got his measure though, I reckon,' he added. 'He's not doing badly with him at all, specially for an Irish lad.' Kate had been delighted to hear all this but also desperately disappointed not to see Tod. When he had folded her briefly in his arms that evening she felt as if she had come home.

There was no other way to describe it: it had seemed so right. Despite all her reservations about getting involved with a married man, she so wanted to see him again. But Tod was probably not really attracted to her at all, she kept telling herself. Talking about Monique and her death had perhaps released painful memories which in turn had induced an emotional reaction which had really had nothing to do with her. She had just happened to be there; Tod had probably got carried away on a wave of nostalgia.

She could understand that: it happened to her sometimes. There had been moments today when she had felt a wrenching sadness just remembering Christmases past, spent with her father when he was home on leave, in this very house.

'Snow had fallen, snow on snow, / In the deep mid winter, long ago.' As the last bars of the carol faded away Kate bent down and gently moved Liffey, curled up on a beanbag in front of the Aga, so that she could get at the pudding more easily.

'Whatever are you listening to this dirge for?' Lady Kitty asked briskly as she came bustling in from the larder with a large bottle marked 'Medicinal'. 'Right, let's get the show on the road,' she said, rolling up her sleeves. 'I've found that old brandy we keep to pour over the pudding.'

Minutes later as Kate bore the pudding, blue flames rippling down its sides and topped with holly, into the darkened dining-room she felt a surge of excitement. For the first time since things had started to go seriously wrong with Hugo, the future seemed full of promise. There was the book to do now, and there was Achilles too, and the chance that they might actually see him on a racecourse, carrying the Rathglin colours, some time next summer; and then, of course, there were her feelings for Tod and the growing suspicion that, whatever the risks, she would follow wherever they led her.

The Professor observed her, eyebrows raised, as she placed the pudding down in front of him. 'A penny for them, Kate. You're miles away.' He smiled. 'And your eyes look like stars.'

Lady Kitty, sitting next to him, glanced sharply at her daughter. When Kate looked dreamy like that, she knew of old it meant she was up to something.

Barons Lodge

'Right, now. Let the festivities continue,' Tod said, a touch wearily, pushing back his chair.

'It's open house in the Den for anyone who wants to watch *Some*

Like It Hot on the video. At least we should end the day with a laugh, I thought,' he raised his eyebrows.

'Oh, great!' Toby leapt from the table with enthusiasm. 'I'll go and tell Lucy. I think she's still on the phone.'

'You do that,' Tod replied, getting up slowly. 'And tell her to make the next call to New York collect, will you? Otherwise we'll be bankrupt.' He leant on the back of his chair and peered across at Myra, blinking behind his glasses. 'You'll join us, I hope,' he said politely. 'You've done quite enough work for today. Why don't you leave all this' – he indicated the clutter on the table – 'and come and relax for a change?' He stood there, swaying slightly, his expression concerned.

'No, thanks,' Myra replied abruptly. 'You know I always like to clear everything away ready for Dorcas to deal with in the morning. I'll get Pam to help me.'

Tod really must be drunk, she thought. He knew perfectly well that she did not like Marilyn Monroe. All that wriggling about like a performing seal. She could never see what all the fuss was about.

Tod shrugged his shoulders. 'All right, please yourself,' he replied amiably, heading unsteadily for the door. 'I think I'll just go and get some more glasses from the drawing-room. I want Basil to try that Armagnac.'

Relieved at last to be alone, Myra poured herself a small glass of port and surveyed the debris of the Christmas dinner. Despite her protests that they were vulgar and a waste of money, Tod and Toby had insisted on buying a large box of crackers. As a result, multi-coloured shreds of paper and crumpled mottoes now littered the table, along with the remains of the Christmas pudding, mince pies and bowls of fruit and nuts. Toby had also bullied everyone into wearing those ridiculous paper hats. On leaving the table Lucy had hastily flung hers over the centrepiece, a Skeaping bronze of a galloping horse that had been one of Sir Digby's favourite trophies; it was typical of Lucy to treat it with such irreverence, Myra thought. The girl had been even more than usually maddening today. After offering to lay the table for dinner, she had then got bored and gone upstairs to change, leaving it only half done. Then, when she had finally re-appeared she had been absolutely no help at all, just lolling about in a silver boilersuit which, as Basil had commented, made her look like some sort of pre-Raphaelite space woman.

Although Myra, with Dorcas's help, had put a great deal of trouble into preparing the dinner, as usual no one had seemed particularly appreciative. Tod had remarked on how tasty the apricot stuffing was, but had hardly actually eaten anything at all, presiding over the other end of the table in a sort of benign stupor. She presumed he had been drinking quietly ever since he had come in from checking the horses at midday. He had certainly seemed quite unable or unwilling to control either Lucy or Toby, who had sat on either side of him arguing, particularly about the merits of some pop group called the Clash and giggling over the cracker jokes, all of which, in Myra's view, had been extremely unfunny. It was good, of course, to see Toby more animated and cheerful than he had been lately, but his improved spirits had had a hectic quality about them and his pale cheeks had been abnormally flushed. Probably he, too, had been getting drunk; Tod had certainly not bothered to control what went into his glass. Basil and Pam had made various attempts at general civilized discussion at the start of the meal but then they, too, had got involved in a tedious argument about what money and clothes they should take on their planned holiday to Barbados next week.

All in all, Myra decided, it had been one of the worst Christmas Days she could ever remember. She was utterly fed up with all her family. It would serve them right if she did take up Stelios's offer and just clear off.

When she had recovered from the sheer shock of his extraordinary proposition, she had decided not to brood about it too much but just put it on 'the back burner', as her father would have said – at least until the New Year when she would have more time to think. But despite all the hectic Christmas preparations, it had kept popping into her mind, no doubt because it presented such a very real dilemma.

On the one hand, the whole idea was quite unthinkable, of course. Barons Lodge was her home. She could not even envisage living anywhere else. She could not possibly abandon it, and Toby and Tod, however irritating the latter was being, to run off with a man she didn't love. On the other hand, she had always quite liked Stelios and, as she had begun to realize, she was rather flattered by the offer: after all, not many women coming up to fifty actually received proposals of marriage from serious millionaires. Also, now that the flat season was over and she and Betty were going over the accounts for the past year, it had become even more obvious what a dire financial position Barons Lodge was in. She wouldn't be at all surprised if their accountant suggested that they take out a mortgage on the whole property this year, just to ensure that they could keep the yard going.

If she accepted Stelios's offer, of course, that would never become necessary. Even if she did not actually live there, Barons Lodge's future would be secured for the rest of her lifetime. That, in itself, would be a terrific weight off her mind.

Draining her glass of port, she got up slowly. She couldn't help thinking that Christmas with Stelios might be rather more pleasant than the last few days had been. There would be proper staff, of course: a cook, maids and a butler that she could just give orders to. There would certainly be no more slaving over the stove, let alone coping with such a disgruntled family. There would also be plenty of money to ensure that she had the clothes and the jewellery to look her best, something that would matter to her more and more as she got older.

It was a real dilemma, she brooded, as she started to clear the table. What she needed to do was to talk it all over with someone she could trust. Ironically, the person she trusted most in her family was Tod but she could hardly discuss it with him. It would have to be Basil; he was her brother, after all, and presumably had her best interests at heart. As she collected the dirty glasses on to a tray, an idea occurred to her. She would go with Basil and Pam to Barbados and they could talk there; and the more she thought about it, the more it appealed. Feeling suddenly more energetic, she headed towards the kitchen.

Clutching her black Sulka dressing-gown around her, Lucy bounded up the stairs leading to Toby's attic bedroom. He had headed up there, she knew, the moment *Some Like It Hot* had finished and although it was nearly midnight she was certain he would still be awake, either watching television or listening to music. Whether he liked it or not, she would try to have a little chat with him before saying goodnight. She herself did not feel in the slightest bit tired – probably because the whole day had been so boring and dreary. She also found it upsetting that the two people she loved most, Tod and Toby, were clearly not happy at the moment, though Tod did make a considerable effort to conceal it. She had decided that this was the last Christmas she would ever spend at Barons Lodge. There was no point in pretending: she didn't belong here any more. If only Tod had not been so insistent, she would have stayed with Celeste in New York as originally planned. Judging by what she had already said on the phone, Celeste was having a very jolly day, starting with lunch with her father and a couple of his old musician friends at a restaurant in Little Italy, and ending with a party given by an extremely camp English art dealer and his Russian boyfriend in a penthouse overlooking the East River.

All in all, it sounded a lot more fun than Newmarket, Lucy thought enviously, as she padded along the passage towards Toby's room and knocked on the door.

'Yeah? Who is it?' he called out suspiciously.

'It's only me. Don't panic,' Lucy reassured him. 'Myra went to bed hours ago and Daddy would be quite incapable of climbing these stairs in the state he's in. I suspect he'll spend the night in the Den, cuddled up with the dogs. Oh, well, *chacun à son goût*.' She stood surveying the untidy clutter of Toby's room before closing the door behind her and sinking down on to the nearest chair.

'You've got some new posters in here, haven't you?' she commented. 'I don't remember seeing that one of Al Pacino in *Scarface* before.'

Toby lay stretched out on his bed, its old patchwork quilt strewn with magazines, papers and record covers. A cigarette smouldered between his fingers and Ginger, an ancient marmalade cat, lay across his stomach like a large fur hot-water bottle. Myra would not have approved of that, Lucy thought: she got furious if people encouraged any of the stable cats to come into the house. But her stepmother would have been far more incensed had she known what sort of cigarettes Toby was smoking, Lucy thought with amusement: there was no mistaking what Toby was up to. It also explained why he had looked so guilty when she'd barged into his room.

'Toby, you little devil! You've got some dope,' she exclaimed. 'I didn't know you were into that these days. You naughty old thing!' She made a face. 'You might have told me. I left all my stuff in London. Never think there's much point in carting it around if you have to smoke alone in your room. Very antisocial! Where did you get it from, anyway?' she asked with curiosity.

'A mate of mine at school gave it to me. A guy called Giles,' Toby replied casually. 'Or rather he swapped two joints for all my David Bowie albums. I decided that I didn't like them any longer.' He gave Lucy a sheepish grin. 'I was going to say they were herbal cigarettes if Mother should suspect anything,' he confessed. He proffered the smouldering joint to Lucy. 'Here, try some. It's pretty ace stuff.'

Lucy sauntered over and whisked the cigarette from his fingers. 'Myra would probably believe you – she's pretty naive about dope and things,' she remarked. 'But for heaven's sake, be careful at school, Tobes, won't you? They'll expel you if you get caught smoking there.' She took a long pull at the cigarette before pushing some of the magazines on to the floor and draping herself gracefully across the end of the bed.

'Look, Tobes, there's nothing else bothering you at the moment, is there? Apart from the dreaded work, I mean. You did say a month or so ago – the day we missed each other in London – that there was something you wanted to talk to me about. You're not in any sort of trouble or anything, are you?'

Toby sat up abruptly, disturbing Ginger, who opened one eye and gave him a baleful look. 'Of course not,' he said vehemently. 'Everything else is fine. Look, I really don't want to talk about school any more, Luce. I'd just like to forget about it for a few days, OK?'

'Oh! Keep your hair on. I only asked,' Lucy replied, surprised by his tone. She pushed up the sleeve of her dressing-gown and glanced at her watch. It was nearly 12.30 a.m. – high time she made that final call to New York. She uncoiled herself from the end of the bed and put her hand on Toby's shoulder. 'Right, I'm off then. Got to make one last call to Celeste.'

She looked down at her half-brother with affection. 'Look, Tobes, I know you're getting very grown up and everything, but don't forget: if there is ever anything bothering you, you can always talk it over with me. I know I'm not always around, but you can always call or write, *wherever* I am. You know that, don't you?' She bent down and kissed him lightly on the top of his head. 'See you tomorrow, then. Sleep well.'

After she'd gone, Toby lay motionless on the bed, staring into space until the cigarette began to burn his fingers. As he stubbed it out with great care, he felt a powerful regret that he had not been able to confide in Lucy. The trouble was, he suspected, that despite her desire to help, she still saw him as her baby brother. He was terrified that if he told her the truth about his relationship with Giles, she might be shocked.

Liam Byrne looked around Angie Shaw's cosy little bedroom, unable to believe his luck. She was being so friendly to him, he thought, and the prospect of being alone with her here, for the next hour, filled him with joy. The room was like a little pink box, with its pale walls festooned with photographs of ponies and horses and pop posters of the Sting and Wham, rose chintz curtains and fluffy pink bedspread piled high with cuddly toys. Angie had insisted they come up here to listen to her Christmas present to him, a Chieftains tape, before they had to go back out to the yard to feed the horses and settle them for the night. Lunch had been a very friendly occasion: there had been much talking, laughing and pulling of crackers, in between large helpings of turkey and pudding. He had sat next to Angie, as promised, and had her young cousin Tracy on the other side, who asked him lots of questions about the ponies he had had in Ireland which had soon put him at his ease. Jack Massam, Barons Lodge stable jockey, who he knew fancied Angie, had been up at the other end of the table next to Betty Shaw, he'd been glad to say, so he had hardly had to talk to him at all; and apart from the occasional curt glance from Sam Shaw, the meal had passed off very pleasantly. The nearness of Angie, with her faint flowery scent and the sight of her breasts pushing through her new tight scarlet sweater, had excited him so much that by the time the meal was over and the Queen's broadcast had been switched on, he had drunk far more beer than he intended and was feeling unusually relaxed.

Sitting in her room now, alone with her at last, he had not, therefore, been particularly alarmed when she confessed that there was a question she was longing to ask him.

'I don't want to be nosy or anything, but I'd really like to know why you left Ireland at all, really, and came over here. I don't want to be rude, but you seem such a fish out of water sometimes.' She grinned at him amicably.

Liam jerked back in his chair, feeling instantly tense. 'Now why would you be wanting to ask me about that, all of a sudden?' he asked suspiciously. 'I suppose one of the other lads put you up to it? Well, it's none of their business, I'd say.'

'Don't be daft. I wouldn't dream of talking to any of the others about you,' Angie replied indignantly. 'It's just that if you and I are going to be friends, I'd really like to know.' She popped another of the chocolates Liam had given her into her mouth. 'Look, I know about your accident, of course,' she continued sympathetically. 'Dad says Mr McGuire explained all about it in your reference – how a lorry went out of control, hitting one of the horses in the string and forcing your filly up against the wall, crushing your foot so badly. He also said that although you'd had an operation, your foot would never mend properly, which is why you couldn't go on as a jockey.'

She gazed across at Liam, her brown eyes brimming with concern. 'I'm really sorry. It's a real shame. You're *such* a brilliant rider. We can all see that.' She sighed. 'It's why some of the other lads have got it in for you a bit, I think: they're jealous – the stupid sods!'

She paused, a puzzled look coming over her face. 'But why didn't you stay in Ireland, when you were able to work again? With your family and mates, I mean. Surely that would have been easier for you?

I can't understand why you wanted to come over here, so far away, where you don't seem to have *anyone* close. Anyway, that's why I want to be your friend. I reckon you could do with one!' She grinned at him shyly.

Liam felt torn by conflicting emotions. Angie's interest in him seemed so obviously genuine and she was being so sympathetic and sweet that the desire to confide in her was overwhelming. Yet another part of him was still trying to resist it. He was grown up now: a man on his own, which meant he shouldn't trust anyone, he told himself. Or, at least that's what Rory always used to say. Then he remembered what his older brother had tried to involve him in and all the bitterness against him returned. Feeling suddenly miserable again, he dropped his head in his hands.

'Oh, forget it!' Angie said abruptly. 'It's none of my business, I know. Don't tell me if you don't want to. Let's listen to your new tape, shall we?' She eased herself along the bed towards her radio cassette player.

Liam looked up at her, his mind suddenly clear. 'No, no, it's OK, I'll tell you – if you really want to know,' he said urgently. 'But you'll not be talking to anyone else about it, will you? You must promise me that.'

Angie's face relaxed into a smile. 'Don't worry, it will be our secret, I promise,' she reassured him, patting the bedspread beside her. 'Come and sit here and tell me all about it.'

Haltingly, Liam began to describe how he had felt when he had come out of hospital and was recuperating at his mother's tiny tenement flat in Dublin. At first he couldn't even bear to watch the racing on the TV, he confessed. Seeing the other jockeys out there doing what he was born to do just reinforced all his bitterness about what had happened and the collapse of his dreams. It had been a lonely time, too: although his mother's friends and relations were constantly coming and going, none of them were connected with racing in any way, so they couldn't really understand what he was going through. He'd therefore been greatly cheered when he'd had a letter from his elder brother, Rory, who was working at Mountclare, the Alexandros's stud down in Tipperary, saying that he'd be coming up to see him shortly.

That had all changed, though, when Rory had finally appeared and it became clear what he was up to. He was sympathetic about the accident, of course – ''Tis a terrible shame, Liam. Just when we'd got you off and running' – but he had not wasted much time in explaining the real point of his visit. He'd been doing a few favours for some 'friends' recently, he told Liam meaningfully. As a result he was under surveillance from the Garda, and wanted Liam to do him a favour. When he was mobile again, he wanted him to go down to Wexford and hand over some money, £500, to a fisherman who lived down there. He had the name and address and everything. The man had no bank account apparently and, as Rory was being watched, it was not wise for him to go himself.

'It's not *that* urgent. Within the month will do,' he said. 'But I need to take care of this soon. He'd not be trusted not to do a bit of talking otherwise,' he added darkly.

'They picked Rory up the following week,' Liam told Angie bleakly. They charged him with illegal arms smuggling. They'd found an arms cache down the way and had been keeping tabs on him ever since his car had been spotted in the area. Two and a half years he got in Mountjoy. But he'll be getting out a while before then, if I know him at all,' he added sarcastically.

Angie looked at him in bewilderment. 'But I don't understand. Why should he be involved with arms smuggling? Whatever for?'

Liam snorted. It was amazing how ignorant most English people were about Irish politics, he reflected. 'For the IRA, of course,' he told her wearily. 'Rory was always a sympathizer. I knew that all right, though I'd never let on to anyone, of course, but I hadn't realized he was actually working for the bastards. And he'd certainly never tried involving me before,' he added angrily.

Sitting bolt upright on the bed, Angie struggled to absorb all this information. 'I see ... So you did as he asked and then decided it would be best to get away,' she said eventually. 'Well, I can understand that. I can see why you wouldn't want to get mixed up with horrible people like the IRA.'

'Indeed I would not,' Liam replied vehemently. 'That's the whole point, don't you see? Once you get in with those people you're with them for life, unless they decide to get rid of you, that is. They're none too keen on deserters!' He paused, summoning up the courage to tell Angie the worst bit. 'So I never went down to Wexford at all, you see. Made no attempt to see that bloke and give him the money. I kept it myself and used it to get myself over here. I stole it.' He gazed miserably down at the floor, not wanting to observe Angie's reaction.

'There was no other way to get away quickly,' he went on defensively. 'After all, I had no money at all of my own. I'd been out of work for months, remember?' He turned his back on Angie, clutching his arms round his bony frame for comfort.

'You shouldn't have done that. I wish you hadn't; it was wrong,' Angie said quietly, taking hold of his hand. 'But I'm glad you told me about it. You must pay the money back, of course – get it back to Rory somehow, whatever he's been up to. Two wrongs don't make a right.' She squeezed his hand more tightly. 'I'll help you, in any way I can. Get Dad to give you extra work, maybe, so that you can get more overtime,' she went on more cheerfully. 'Never fear, Angie's here.' She kissed him lightly on the cheek.

CHAPTER NINE

Three Swallows Stud

Kate had turned up late at Diana Saunders' New Year's Eve party, on Diana's own advice, leaving the Old Rectory, with some reluctance, at around ten. It was a freezing, moonlit night and the back roads were treacherous with ice. After a tricky drive from Hazeley through fields stiff with frost she had found chaos at Three Swallows: the drive was packed with cars all attempting to decant their occupants in some confusion. The whole place had looked very welcoming, though, with pink lanterns swinging from the gateposts and pink and white fairy lights looped along the great avenue of beeches. On either side of the front door, two life-sized model jockeys, wearing the Saunders' pink and blue silks, held flaming torches that flared dramatically into the frosty air. Inside, the hall, with its thick white carpet, fetlock deep, and pale yellow panelling, was bright with flickering candles, wreaths of holly and an enormous bunch of pink and blue balloons suspended under the dome at the top of the stairs.

Diana had decreed that dress should be formal. 'We Aussies like an excuse to tart ourselves up,' she informed Kate. She herself was looking spectacular in a strapless flame-coloured chiffon dress with a diamond and ruby choker glittering at her throat and her hair swept up into a chignon, fixed in place with diamond-tipped pins. As Kate joined the queue of muffled-up women heading upstairs in their furs, wraps and clouds of scent, she hoped she was not too soberly dressed in her Irish grandmother's high-necked lace blouse, and Edwardian cameo brooch and a long moss-green Jean Muir velvet skirt.

'Hi, Kate! Glad you could make it. You're looking ever so demure and "olde worlde",' Diana commented, giving her a toothy grin.

'There's a right old hotchpotch here tonight,' she announced cheerfully. 'We've even managed to get an Arab or two, which is rather surprising as they are usually back home racing camels or running their governments, or whatever they do at this time of year. Prince Hassim is in Dad's study right now discussing a stallion deal with one of the Maktoum's stud managers. I left them together with a bottle of champagne but they said they'd prefer coffee.'

Kate had always heard that the Newmarket fraternity suddenly took off like a flock of migrating birds to such favourite haunts as Barbados, Aspen, Mexico or Mustique straight after Boxing Day, but a fair number seemed to have delayed their departures to attend Diana's party. As she threaded her way through the guests towards the drawing-room, where a small band was playing a medley of songs by Andrew Lloyd Webber, she recognized some familiar faces. Jockeys Walter Swinburn and Greville Starkey, Newmarket trainers Michael Stoute and Clive Brittain. Over in a corner she also glimpsed the lined, yet oddly innocent face of Lester Piggott listening intently to his friend Charles St George.

In the room beyond the drawing-room, which Diana usually used as a bar, a massive glass panel had been pushed back to reveal the swimming pool, glinting under hoops of coloured lights reaching over hanging baskets of tropical plants and ferns. Pink and blue tables, gleaming with silverware, packed the covered patio beyond. 'Poolside breakfast for those who stay the course, so bring your bikini,' Diana had scribbled on Kate's invitation. The atmosphere Diana had created, Kate reflected, was an odd mixture of informal barbecue and traditional hunt ball.

She had already bumped into Joe Weston, the Yorkshire owner she had first met at Barons Lodge who had been so disparaging about Achilles. Slightly the worse for wear, he had insisted on asking her to dance, prattling on about a couple of yearlings he had just bought, and his plans for his gelding Southwold Jack in the New Year, as they shuffled uncomfortably around the floor. He was on his own tonight, he made a point of telling her. 'The wife's back home in Bradford, looking after her mother who's poorly, but I wasn't going to miss this do just because of that, I told her. So, here I am, footloose and fancy free.' He leered down at Kate, clasping her more tightly in his sweaty grip.

Escaping with relief when the band broke off to make an announcement about someone's Mercedes blocking the drive, Kate came face to face with Charlie Kyle, looking so spruce and formal in a dinner jacket that she hardly recognized him. Determined to be friendly, she re-introduced herself firmly as the part-owner of Achilles in the hope that that unfortunate incident at the sales might be forgotten. It was ridiculous anyway, she felt, to go on being intimidated by Tod's assistant now that she had become one of the Barons Lodge patrons. Emboldened by the champagne, she asked if Tod were present; she had to admit to herself that it was mainly in the hope of seeing him again that she had decided to come to the party at all.

Charlie glanced at her sharply. 'I've no idea. I certainly haven't seen him,' he replied. 'I know he was invited but that doesn't mean he'll be here. I expect it depends on how he's feeling.'

Or how much he had been drinking, Kate thought to herself as Charlie turned away.

At that moment the band struck up 'These Foolish Things', a song that always reminded Kate of Hugo, who had been particularly keen on the Brian Ferry version when they were first going out together. Fighting off an unexpected pang of nostalgia, she had just decided to escape upstairs to the landing when Diana spun down the stairs in a flurry of red and grabbed her arm.

'Kate! I've been looking for you all over. I've just been talking to someone you ought to meet, Sandy Diss. Didn't you tell me you were going to do a horsey book with her or something? Well – she and Bertie are here, but they won't be staying late as he's stewarding at Leicester. Why don't I introduce you before they bugger off? Come on.'

She propelled Kate back across the hall towards the library, where a middle-aged man with dark thinning hair and an erect military bearing was talking to a couple of young Newmarket trainers and the TV commentator and ex-jockey Jimmy Lindley. Standing beside him, her arm looped through his, was a Jerry Hall look-alike: a tall, striking-looking girl in a shimmering silver sheath of a dress and long white-blonde hair that looked as though it had just been ironed.

As Diana tapped her on the shoulder, she detached herself from her husband and swung round with an instant photographic smile. All her features – mouth, chin, eyes and nose – seemed over-large, Kate thought, although the overall impression they created, if not one of beauty, was certainly striking.

Sandy Diss's well-plucked eyebrows shot up in surprise as Kate was introduced and she immediately held out a dazzling hand. Not only was she wearing an enormous diamond ring, Kate noticed, but her long silver-frosted nails glinted like knives.

'Kate! My, this is a surprise,' she drawled in a honeyed, Southern accent, stretching out her hand and shaking Kate's firmly.

'Yes, indeed,' Kate replied, smiling. 'It's good to meet you at last. I've been asking Geoffrey to arrange it for ages but he seemed rather evasive – said you were going away on holiday, he thought.'

Sandy's lips spread into another winsome smile. 'Sure, that's correct. We leave the day after tomorrow to visit my folks in Kentucky. Then we move on to Florida, down to the Keys. Bertie's keen to go shark fishing.' She indicated her husband still deep in conversation behind her. 'I guess that's what he's talking to Jimmy Lindley about. Jimmy knows those parts well.'

In her glittering silver dress, Sandy looked rather like a mermaid, Kate decided – a remarkably healthy one, too. Why was it, she wondered, that so many American women, despite the sort of junk food they were reared on, always looked so glossy and had so much hair?

'Then we go on to LA to see some friends of mine and my agent, of course,' Sandy was drawling on. 'So, let me see: we won't be back in England until the end of February.' She spread her hands in a gesture of helplessness. 'Crazy, isn't it, but I guess we won't be able to meet to talk about the book until then.'

'I see,' Kate said, thoughtfully. 'Well, I know Geoffrey wants us to get our act together as soon as possible, but it looks like he'll just have to wait, doesn't it?'

'Sure. Don't worry, there's plenty of time,' Sandy reassured her firmly. 'Why don't you both come over to Rockington the moment I get back? Come to lunch so that we can talk at our leisure, in comfort.'

'Fine,' Kate nodded. She certainly was not going to turn down a chance to see Rockington, which was supposed to be one of the finest Tudor houses in England. She could not quite imagine how Sandy fitted in to such a setting but she was certainly looking forward to finding out.

'Great. Well, that's settled then. Give my secretary a ring next week and fix a date, can you? Bye,' Sandy said, with a wave of her hand and another radiant smile, and swivelled round on her high heels.

Kate regarded her back with a mixture of amusement and annoyance. She had been definitely dismissed, she felt, with no chance of any further discussion about the book. She hoped she was going to be able to work with such a bossy person as Sandy. Under that sugar-sweet exterior, she suspected, lurked pure Bessemer steel. She must be quite a handful, she mused, particularly for such a conventional member of the English upper classes as Bertie Diss. Still, her money must come in handy – Rockington was reputed to cost hundreds of thousands of pounds a year in upkeep alone; or perhaps she was remarkably good in bed, whatever that meant. Pondering on all this, she was startled by a sudden roll of drums.

Diana, standing at the top of the stairs, leaning over the banisters like a ship's figurehead, was making an announcement: 'Right everyone,' she said. 'Midnight's coming up. So hold everything for "Auld Lang Syne". And grab a balloon – they're all numbered for a prize in the breakfast draw. Right then, here goes.'

As the chimes of midnight died away and the band struck up, Kate was swept up in the general mêlée; her arms were seized on either side by complete strangers and pumped vigorously as she haltingly joined in the singing. She had always disliked the ritual of 'Auld Lang Syne' and was already wondering whether the New Year boded as well as she had hoped when she felt a light tap on her shoulder. Turning round she came face to face with Tod, standing there quietly in a dark-green smoking jacket, regarding her with his lop-sided smile.

'At last!' he said. 'I've been looking for you everywhere.' He drew her towards him. 'Happy New Year,' he said softly. As her lips touched his, Kate felt her mood instantly change to a state of joyous expectation. As though an emotional switch had been flicked on, happiness sizzled through her and she longed to fling her arms around him. Remembering where she was and the public nature of the embrace, however, she wrenched herself away with an immense effort and looked around, slightly dazed, for any sign of Myra.

'It's all right. She's not here: she's on holiday in Barbados with Basil and Pam,' Tod said, laughing, obviously reading her thoughts. Still keeping hold of her hand he too peered around. 'Hmm, we're surrounded by gossips, though, I'm afraid. Come on. Let's go and get a drink.

'By the way,' he added quickly, 'I must congratulate you on those extraordinary pictures you took of Alain. They were quite brilliant, I thought. Captured absolutely his mixture of sensitivity and steel.' He gazed at her with obvious admiration. 'I really was very impressed. I should have rung you up to congratulate you but I was hoping I'd see you here tonight.'

Kate felt flooded with delight. It mattered so much that Tod had liked the pictures. He knew du Roc well and she trusted him, somehow, to give her an honest verdict.

'Thank you,' she said, her face beaming. 'I did my best.'

Reluctantly letting go of his hand, she followed him towards the bar, stopping to shake hands with the various people he introduced her to but feeling too happily preoccupied to take in most of their names or make much conversation. Greeted affectionately all round, Tod seemed to know everyone and she was beginning to feel impatient, longing to be able to talk to him on his own, when he turned to her suddenly and touched her arm. 'I know,' he said gently. 'Social obligations are a dreadful bore but this town is like a goldfish bowl. But I think that'll do. Look, grab two glasses from that waiter over there, can you, and we'll go upstairs and try to find somewhere quieter to talk.'

As they headed eagerly up the stairs, their way was barred by a phalanx of swarthy-looking men, led by a stocky, bearded figure with a certain air of superiority about him and imperious black eyes. He raised his eyebrows as he caught sight of Tod.

'Ah. Good evening, or perhaps I should say good morning. I was hoping indeed that you might be here,' he said in a husky, perceptibly foreign accent.

'Prince Hassim, how are you? Happy New Year,' replied Tod with a smile, holding out his hand. 'I tried to call you in London yesterday but one of your staff said you were in Newmarket.' He indicated Kate, standing on the step beside him. 'I don't think you have met Kate. Kate Leverton, another one of my owners. Kate, His Highness, Prince Hassim.'

Prince Hassim shook her hand firmly, eyeing her up and down with a solemn black stare. 'How do you do?' he said politely. 'Do you have many horses at Barons Lodge?'

'Just one,' Kate replied cheerfully. 'In partnership with my mother. A yearling by Greek Dancer.' She glanced at her watch. 'Oh, sorry, correction: he's just turned two.'

'I, too, have two-year-olds with Mr Beckhampton,' Hassim said, continuing to stare. 'So, we shall perhaps meet again.' He turned to Tod. 'I should like to come and see my horses around midday, if that is convenient,' he said.

Tod nodded. 'Of course, whenever you like. I think you'll find that they're coming on quite well, though the filly in particular has a lot of growing to do.' He was speaking more slowly than he had been earlier and with extra care, Kate thought. His breath had smelt only faintly and certainly not unpleasantly of alcohol but she suspected that he was slightly drunk.

'His horses really are coming on well; I wasn't bullshitting for once,' Tod confided as the Arab group proceeded down the stairs. 'Let's hope one of them is some good. I don't think he's the sort of chap to tolerate failure for too long.' He sighed. 'Though if he knows half as much about horses as he says he does, he should know that it's all a bloody lottery.'

Pausing in the doorway of Lyle Saunders' study, he indicated an empty sofa in the far corner. 'Why don't you go and grab those seats for us? I'll join you in a minute – I'm dying for a pee.'

Glimpsing her reflection in a heavy Victorian mirror hanging above Lyle Saunders' desk, Kate realized that although her dark hair was looking unusually tidy, her nose was shining and her grey eyes were huge with excitement. Pulling out her compact, she chided herself for being so emotionally transparent; it must have been so obvious to Tod that she was overjoyed to see him. Why was she never able to conceal her feelings and play it cool?

'How was your Christmas, then?' Tod asked when he reappeared, slumping down on to the sofa beside her and stretching out his long legs. 'Jollier than mine, I trust?'

'It was fine. Kitty had an old friend from Dublin staying and a publisher bloke I know came up from London for the day. We had rather a prolonged celebration, I'm afraid, as he's actually commissioned me to do a book – my first, on the British and their horses.' She went on to outline Geoffrey's proposition and to recount her unexpected encounter with Sandy Diss.

Tod looked amused. 'Oh, the Sugar Plum Fairy! That's what some people in racing call her. No one can quite understand why Bertie Diss married her, except that he's broke and Rockington's always about to fall down. She's a rather bizarre choice for your book, I'd have thought. Shouldn't think she's exactly a literary type, though I can see the advantages of her title for the American market. Also, she's quite a celebrity over there, I believe.'

'Do you think she knows anything about horses, though?' Kate asked. 'My publisher certainly thinks so.'

'Well, she should do. Her father is one of the most respected stud owners in Kentucky,' Tod replied. 'What did you make of her, anyway?'

'I'm not sure.' Kate wrinkled her nose. 'She seemed rather forbidding to me. Still, she may turn out to be more accommodating than I think!'

'Mmm ... and I'm a blue-arsed baboon,' Tod replied, grinning. 'Mind you, given my training record of late, that's entirely possible.'

Kate burst out laughing, relieving some of the tension she was feeling. It was hard, she found, to be sitting so close to Tod yet unable to touch him.

He sank back against the cushions, his hands behind his head, regarding her with obvious admiration. 'You look incredibly pretty tonight, you know,' he commented, 'so glowing and young – you could be sixteen.'

Kate felt herself blush. 'You look in pretty good shape too,' she replied, trying to keep her tone light. 'I love the smoking jacket. It's almost the same green as my skirt. Isn't that extraordinary?'

Tod pulled out a silver cigarette case from his pocket and took out a Gitane. 'Is it?' he asked, raising his eyebrows. 'I think we match very well together. Too well, maybe.' He lit the cigarette carefully, giving her a sidelong glance.

'I'm going to level with you, Kate,' he said softly. 'I've thought about you ever since we last met. Just haven't been able to get you out of my mind. I so enjoyed talking to you that evening and then, when I kissed you – well, that was pure magic.' He gave her a hesitant smile. 'There, I've confessed it: I've been bewitched. It's as simple as that.' He took a gulp of his champagne. 'You can tell me to piss off if I've offended you,' he went on. 'I won't refer to how I feel again. It certainly won't get in the way of any professional relationship or, I hope, of our being friends. I shall just admire you from afar.'

Kate reached for his hand. 'You know I feel exactly the same,' she said urgently. 'You must do, otherwise you wouldn't have said anything, and anyway I'm hopeless at concealing what I feel.' She gripped his hand tighter. 'I thought about you all over Christmas, too. I was longing to see you again; it was really the only reason I came here tonight.' Her eyes clouded over. 'It has been bothering me a lot. I don't like the idea of getting involved with someone who's married; I'm not a disrupter. But I think it's too late.' Her voice sounded shaky. 'I felt so close to you that evening, too. So totally in tune and then, when you kissed me goodbye, I felt as though I had come home. I don't know how else to describe it.'

Tod was staring at her, a delighted grin spreading across his face as though he couldn't believe his luck. 'How amazing! I really wasn't sure.' He shook his head in disbelief. 'I couldn't imagine you really being interested in someone like me.' He squeezed her hand. 'I'm so glad.'

He looked at her thoughtfully for a moment. 'Look, about being married. I just want to say . . .' He broke off as a tall, suave man in a midnight-blue dinner jacket came bursting through the doorway with a red-haired girl in tow and waved to him merrily.

'Tod, hello! I wondered where you were hiding,' he called out, glancing with curiosity at Kate. Dropping down into the chair behind Lyle Saunders' desk, he picked up the phone in front of him. 'Now, hush everyone,' he ordered. 'Let's have a bit of decorum. I'm going to phone the wife: wish her a Happy New Year and all that. If anyone else wishes to have a word with her, now's your chance.' He pushed the red-haired girl down on to the arm of his chair. 'And that doesn't include you, sweetheart,' he said firmly.

'That's Gerry Carnegie,' Tod explained. 'He's incorrigible, I'm afraid. His wife, Penny, is on holiday in Switzerland somewhere with the kids. He's very fond of her really – would fall to pieces without her – but he likes to pretend he's a bit of a rake.' He glanced at Kate quizzically. 'You probably think we're all the same,' he added wryly. 'Well, not quite, I hope. But we'll talk about that later.' He took her hand again. 'Look, I've got to get you out of here,' he said with quiet intensity. 'Quite apart from wanting to talk to you, I desperately want to kiss you again – properly, I mean. Look, why don't we go back to Barons Lodge? There's no one there tonight. Myra's in Barbados, as I said, and Toby's gone to some party in London. What do you say?' He leant forward to stub out his cigarette.

Kate could feel her heart pounding. Whatever her reservations about Tod's circumstances, she knew she could not pull back now; she was longing to be alone with him again.

'I'd love that,' she said simply, without hesitation.

'Right then,' Tod said purposefully, getting to his feet. 'We'd best say our goodbyes separately, I'm afraid. Let me go first so that I've got time to get home before you. Give me five minutes, OK?' Keeping his back to the rest of the room where Gerry Carnegie and the others were still clustered around the phone, he leant forward and kissed her lightly on the nose.

'See you shortly, then,' he said tenderly. 'For God's sake, drive carefully, won't you? I couldn't bear anything to happen to you now.'

An hour later, they were lying together on the rug in front of the fire in the Den, an open bottle of champagne on the table beside them.

When he had met her at the front door, Tod just took her hand and led her urgently across the hall and down the passage, not saying a word until he had closed the door of the Den behind him. Then he took her in his arms and kissed her long and lovingly.

'There. That's better, isn't it?' he said after several minutes. 'We are, as they say, alone at last. Even the dogs have been banished – they're sulking in the kitchen.'

Flinging his jacket over the chair, kicking off his shoes and removing his glasses he had pulled her down on the sofa beside him, gently kissing her face and hair. 'God, you're so lovely,' he said at last, stroking the outline of her cheek with a finger before burying his face in her hair. 'Hmm . . . and you smell delicious too.'

Kate cradled his head in her hands, unable to remember when she had felt so happy. She felt Tod's hand slide gently up her thigh. 'Gosh, stockings and suspenders. What a treat!' He grinned before straightening up, his face suddenly serious. 'Look, I'm not going to let you go tonight. You know that, don't you? It's making me so happy being here with you, and anyway the roads are far too icy. But we don't have to go any further than this, if you don't want to. You'd better decide now or I won't be able to vouch for my self-control.' He made a rueful face. 'We can just talk for a while, if you'd rather, and I promise you can sleep in one of the spare rooms completely unmolested. You just have to say.' He grinned. 'But I shall insist on giving you some breakfast and taking you to see Achilles before you go home,' he added.

Gazing at him longingly, Kate reached over and gave him a kiss. The very fact that he was being so considerate made her want him even more. 'Don't be silly.' She smiled. 'I want to get as close to you as I possibly can. We'll take the rest of my clothes off in a minute, if you like, and then we can make love properly.'

She was surprised at her own temerity. She seldom liked to make the running. But it was clearly what she wanted and somehow, when she was with Tod, emotions seemed to come spilling out, unchecked by her usual reserve.

Tod pulled a couple of cushions on to the floor and knelt in front of her. 'I'd adore to make love to you properly,' he said tenderly, taking her hands. 'If I'm capable, that is. I may well not be, what with the amount of booze I've put away this evening and the fact that I am, believe it or not, rather out of practice.' He grinned. 'I don't make a habit of doing this with my owners, you know. Or anyone else for that matter.' He stroked her fingers. 'Anyway, let's just see what happens, shall we? If I don't get it right tonight, don't worry. We've got plenty of time.'

Kate slid down the rug, her whole body feeling limp with longing.

'I want so much to give you pleasure,' Tod whispered, starting to unbutton her blouse. 'And I won't always disappoint you. I promise you that.'

PART TWO

CHAPTER TEN

Mountclare, Co. Tipperary

Stella Alexandros, accompanied as usual by her Irish wolfhound, Tara, was doing her afternoon round of the boxes at her Mountclare stud. It had been one of the mildest January days she could ever remember, even for Tipperary, and the mares and yearlings had been able to spend longer than usual out in the paddocks. The water meadows beyond, though, were becoming unpleasantly muddy with all the rain; and the little river, a tributary of the Suir, which flowed close by the house, was unusually swollen.

Stella paused for a moment and leant against the corner of the stable block, letting the fine drizzle drift down on to her face. Darkness was descending now, faint slivers of yellow-grey light streaked the horizon and the last of the roosting rooks wheeled noisily round the gaunt branches of the elms. In front of her, the pale shape of the old house reared up, reassuring and familiar, from the jumble of slate stable roofs. Stella loved Mountclare more than anywhere else on earth. As a child she had always resented time spent away from it in fashionable places such as Gstaad, Beaulieu, Martha's Vineyard and even Athosini, her father's island. She had also particularly loathed holidays on his yachts, the *Tessa*s *I*, *II* and *III* where she had invariably felt claustrophobic and seasick. Growing up, she had found that wherever she went in the world Mountclare would always be tugging her back like a magnet. Its setting, in the soft Tipperary plain with Slievenamon and the mountains in the background, never failed to enchant her. The place also restored her, in a way that no drug or chemical potion could ever do. Tonight, however, as she breathed in the damp evening air, she was feeling abnormally tense. When she had finished her work in the yard, she had a very special task to attend to.

Today was the second anniversary of the death of her grandfather,

Lord Henry Fitzgerald, and early that morning she had driven up to the family vault in County Kildare to put a sheaf of white lilies, his favourite flowers, on his tomb. Her twin brother, Nik, had made the pilgrimage with her last year but he was away skiing in Aspen, Colorado, this week, so she had resigned herself to going alone. She had been rather irritated, therefore, when old Horace Prendergast, her grandfather's solicitor, had insisted on meeting her there and taking her to lunch at a nearby hotel. There was a letter that he had to hand over to her in person today, from Lord Henry, he told her solemnly: he had left specific instructions in his will that Stella should receive it on the second anniversary of his death, when he supposed the worst of her grieving would be over and she would be better able to absorb its contents. Prendergast himself had absolutely no idea of what these might be.

Stella had immediately decided not to open the letter there and then, in public, but to wait until she got back to Mountclare. That would be difficult, but she had the discipline and she was convinced it would be better to wait until the evening, when she would have done her rounds of the horses and be able to give it her undivided attention. Some of the mares were heavily pregnant by now and would be foaling in the next month, so it was essential to see them personally each night to check on their well-being.

Moving on, she let herself quietly into the box of one of her favourite yearlings, a burly roan colt by Rusticaro. Preoccupied as she was this afternoon, she immediately noticed that his salt lick needed replacing and that his wispy tail and woolly belly were streaked with mud. As Tara sat down on her haunches in the straw, her yellow eyes glowing, Stella examined the colt's mane and tail more closely, talking to him softly all the while, before picking up one of his hind feet. Her look of displeasure deepened as she dislodged a clod of dirt from his hoof with her fingers. The wet weather meant that all the horses were picking up a great deal of mud, and although Stella liked to leave their coats rough to protect them against the damp and the cold, it was vital that their manes and tails were brushed thoroughly and their feet properly picked out every day. 'None of the young'uns will ever trouble the judge if they've got bad feet,' the head groom at the Irish National Stud used to say, and Stella always lectured her staff on the importance of foot care from the moment a foal was born. Annoyed at what she had seen, she placed the colt's hoof gently back on the straw and stuck her head out over the box door.

'Sean, come here, will you?' she called out after a fair-haired boy scurrying past with a bulging hay-net. The very tone of her voice made him halt abruptly in his tracks. 'This colt is an absolute disgrace,' Stella told him icily. 'Drop that hay-net – I'll deal with it. Come and clean him up properly and any of the others that you've been skimping on and report back to me when you've finished. You're not going home until I've checked them all.'

The boy's expression was stricken under his thatch of pale hair. 'I'm sorry, miss, but I did this fella over extra special yesterday and you said I could get off early today seeing as it's my sister's wedding over Limerick Junction way,' he replied nervously, his eyes pleading.

Stella was unmoved. 'Yes, well, I've changed my mind,' she replied coldly. 'I'm not letting you go until I'm satisfied all your horses are all right. No one slacks around here – surely you've grasped that by now? If you haven't, you'll soon have all the time in the world to enjoy parties at Limerick Junction or anywhere else!' She gave him a withering look before bending down to pick up the hay-net. 'Well, get on with it, then. Who's this for?'

'That little chestnut filly, the little Grundy. I've done *her* over all right, that's for sure,' Sean mumbled nervously.

Stella swung the hay-net over her shoulder and strode across the darkening yard, Tara loping behind. Although unobtrusively dressed in black riding-out boots, dark jodhpurs and quilted jacket, Stella's very presence in the yard made most of her staff apprehensive. There was not an employee at Mountclare who did not respect her or dread the dressing-down they got if their work failed to come up to scratch.

'It's quite the martinet with you, you know,' Rory observed once, overhearing her lay into a couple of grooms. 'Can't say I've known a woman like you! You've a soft enough voice all right, but a tongue like a viper.'

Stella had missed Rory since he had been away in Mountjoy prison. In his few years at Mountclare he had learnt fast, becoming an invaluable ally against the old stud groom, Dermot, whose views Stella found irritatingly old-fashioned; and Rory's standards matched her own. She'd noticed that discipline around the place had got slacker since his departure. She was also, she had to admit, missing him for more personal reasons. When she had taken the unprecedented step of taking him as her lover she had known exactly what she was doing. Dalliance with an employee was usually out of the question, but apart from needing a loyal lieutenant in the yard, she had sensed that Rory was as unlikely to get emotionally involved as she was herself. They both had strong sexual appetites which could be satisfied with the minimum of sentimentality and fuss. She was also sympathetic to Rory's fanaticism for the Republican cause. Although she had never had any dealings with the IRA herself, an extreme Irish patriotism had been instilled in her at an early age by her grandfather, who at the age of seventeen had taken part in the Dublin Easter Rising. She had therefore written to Rory in prison, promising him that when he was eventually freed he could come back to Mountclare as her head groom. She had ambitious plans for the expansion of the stud and Rory would be the ideal man to run it for her, she decided.

She was determined to make Mountclare the most successful private and public stud in Ireland; but to achieve that the stud needed a large injection of capital in the near future, and the only person who could provide that was Stelios. It was all very annoying. Stella had never had much respect for her father but there was no other obvious alternative than to persuade him to finance her. She had always found him coarse and primitive compared with her more fastidious Fitzgerald grandparents and she had always felt Irish rather than Greek. She was also convinced that Stelios was in some way responsible for her mother's death. If only he had been there on holiday that summer with the rest of the family at Fairlight, her grandmother's house in Kerry, instead of empire-building abroad, her mother would not have got into that restless state and taken the little boat out that day on her own. Maybe that was unfair – she knew that Nik thought so – but she did not care: in her view, her father had been negligent and that was that. She would never forgive him.

She waited until the Grundy filly was pulling appreciatively at her hay before stepping quickly out of the box and turning off the light, feeling increasingly impatient to finish her work for the day and get back to the house. She wanted to open Lord Henry's communication in his old study: it was the only appropriate place. Although she had brooded about it all day, she still had absolutely no idea what the letter might contain; she just knew it must be very important. Her grandfather would never have arranged for her to receive it so mysteriously and so long after his death unless that were so.

An hour later, after a quick bath, she was finally seated at Lord Henry's great oak desk. Despite the tranquillity and familiarity of the room, with its soft lamplight and tomes of Irish history, poetry and Gaelic legends that lined the wall, as well as the comforting presence of Tara stretched out in front of the fireplace, Stella felt an increasing trepidation and inner excitement. She glanced at the oil portrait of her grandfather by Sir John Lavery that dominated the room from over the fireplace. Lord Henry's pale eyes glittered down at her, his cheeks hollow, his thin lips curled as though in private amusement; it was a cruel face – that of an alert, imperious bird of prey – but Stella had always found her grandfather's arrogance a source of comfort. She and Nik had felt completely secure in his affections, and having faith in his judgement made them unusually confident of their own worth and immune to other people's opinions: if their grandfather, with his exacting standards, believed in them, what did they matter? Lord Henry had also convinced them that they could achieve anything if they wanted it badly enough, and he had always encouraged them to accept a challenge. Stella stared down at the envelope in front of her. It was, she thought, the last challenge he would ever present her with and, whatever it might be, she would not let him down. Seizing an ivory paperknife, she deftly slit it open and spread the contents, several pages of vellum covered in her grandfather's neat writing, on to the desk. Smoothing them down impatiently, she began to read.

He had not intended to tell her what he was about to impart, Lord Henry wrote. She had been too young to understand at the time of her mother's death; then later he decided he had no right to cause her and Nik any more pain. It was not until he was dying, in what he described as 'this confounded hospice', that he had become obsessed with the desire to tell her what he knew. 'The last act of a selfish old man, maybe, but I have become convinced that you yourself would want to know the truth.' He wanted her to receive the letter now, some time after his death, so as not to add to her emotional burden at the time. And he wanted to tell her, rather than Nik, as 'it was you, you alone, who saw your mother out there on the beach that afternoon when they brought the darling girl back from the sea. Also, you are stronger than Nik: resilient as the finest steel.'

A sudden feeling of nausea came over Stella at this point. She tried never to think about that dreadful day when her mother drowned, but the letter made this unavoidable. It had been late August and unpleasantly sultry and airless all day, with those gun-metal clouds piling up over the sea, that usually heralded a storm. Everyone had been on edge all morning, but it was her mother who had been restless for days, she recalled, who had seemed to find the weather most oppressive and who had announced after lunch that she was going for a walk and a swim, alone, to try to clear her headache. What none of them realized at the time was that instead of swimming at her usual place down by the jetty, she had taken the little dinghy out past the point where the currents that year were abnormally fierce.

Later in the afternoon, when Tessa had still not returned, Stella, desperate for air, ran out of the schoolroom where she was supposed to be reading and made her way across the fields to the beach, with the vague idea of going to look for her mother. As she rounded the final bend on the cliff path, she saw two of the local fishermen beaching their boat a few hundred yards down the shore and tenderly lifting out a long bundle on to the sand. As she ran closer, Eamon, the elder of the two men who often took the twins out with him when he was laying his lobster pots, looked up in horror and came stumbling towards her in his great seaboots, his arms held wide, in an obvious attempt to stop her from getting any closer. 'Now, you just stop right there, Miss Stella. 'Tis a terrible thing that's happened,' he called out. 'You'll not be wanting to take any sort of a look.' Dodging past him, Stella ran on, propelled by panic. She was sure now that something dreadful had occurred. As she drew closer, she could barely recognize the form on the sand as her mother. Her face, with its perfect skin and brilliant eyes, had always seemed so vibrantly alive; now, after several hours in the sea, it had a greenish pallor and a dark purple bruise spreading across one temple. Her long black hair, usually so shining and sleek, lay streaked across her cheek, matted with seaweed.

Stella turned away, falling to her knees and heaving rapidly like a sick dog until she vomited on to the sand. As Eamon lifted her up and started to carry her back to the house, the first few drops of rain splattered down and a sudden flash of lightning crackled over the bay.

She locked herself in her room as the storm raged, refusing to open it to anyone and hugging herself silently until Lord Henry had the door broken down. That night the twins slept in the same bed, clinging to each other under the bedclothes in stunned misery and reciting 'The Ballad of Brian Boru' to each other over and over again in mechanical fashion until they fell asleep. Much later, after the funeral, when they were back home in Mountclare, they mingled their blood and swore a pact never again to let anything hurt each other as much as their mother's death. By sheer willpower Stella then forced the painful memories away. The one thing that could instantly revive them was the sight of anything resembling a mermaid. Once, in a fish restaurant in Acapulco, just seeing a crude sketch of a mermaid on the menu reduced her to a nauseous wreck.

Everyone assumed that Tessa's death was a tragic accident. She was not the strongest of swimmers and had been warned that the currents beyond the point that month were particularly dangerous. It was presumed that she had just ignored this warning, swum out too far and got into difficulties. But now, as Stella read on, she experienced a mounting sense of shock. What Lord Henry was telling her was that the drowning might not have been an accident at all: Tessa had been wrestling alone with a dreadful dilemma and might well have wanted to end her life herself.

The day after her death, when he had been prowling around her room, stunned by grief, Lord Henry had picked up the morocco-bound diary that she kept beside her bed. He didn't know why he'd done that, he told Stella; he normally had a horror about prying into private possessions. It was perhaps an unconscious desire to share his daughter's last thoughts, he explained. Starting to read the final pages, his eyesight blurred by tears, he found himself plunged into an even deeper despair as he discovered her shocking secret.

All summer, a young Englishman, Ashley Spence, had been staying on a neighbouring estate belonging to his uncle, a relative of the Duke of Connaught. Spence had been over to Fairlight, the Fitzgeralds' house, on several occasions for lunch, dinner or croquet parties in the afternoons. What was immediately clear from Tessa's diary, though, was that she had been seeing a lot more of him than that. There had been secret meetings down by the jetty or at the old Doric folly in the woods and the two of them had eventually become lovers. Beautiful, restless and insecure without her husband, Tessa had obviously drifted into the liaison lightly, seeing it as some sort of amusing summer game or distraction. But that had all changed dramatically a week or so before her death when she realized she was pregnant.

'She was clearly distraught,' Lord Henry wrote. 'She felt there was no one in the family she could turn to: she felt too dishonoured. She did not think that Cecily or I would understand. She had not even told Spence himself. He had already gone back to England and she knew he was aiming at a political career; any sort of scandal, particularly the fathering of a child with another man's wife, would have put an end to that. She did not even go to old Father Clancy, though it was clear from her diary that she had thought of it. Abortion, of course, was out of the question: she was too strong a Catholic even to consider that. But she felt there was no way she could go ahead and have the child either. It could not have been your father's: he had been away too long, and she knew that her having a child by another man would have ruined their marriage – your father is Greek, after all, and it would have been a catastrophic blow to his pride. No, it was obvious from reading her diary that even if she did not take the boat out that day with the express purpose of ending her own life, she was in a state of mind to do so. The poor darling girl was in complete despair.'

He had no doubt whatsoever where the real blame lay, he added. 'I regard Spence as being responsible for your mother's death, albeit indirectly. I have never been able to forgive him, or hear his name mentioned without hatred rising in my heart. And now that I am dying, selfish though it may seem, I had to share my bitterness with you, the only person in the world I can really trust.'

Stella turned away and gazed into the fire, profoundly shaken. She simply could not believe that her mother had been so involved with Spence. She remembered him vaguely from that holiday at Fairlight: she had immediately taken a dislike to him, with his patronizing English manners and pink and white good looks – he reminded her of an albino stoat one of the dogs had once caught in the woods.

She understood her grandfather's feelings absolutely. Of course he could never forgive Spence. Now that she, too, knew the truth, neither could she. That day in Kerry had been the most dreadful and traumatic of her life: suddenly, without warning, both she and Nik had been deprived of a beautiful loving mother. Lord Henry had made no suggestions in his letter about how such an injustice could be remedied, but gradually, as she brooded on the whole thing, late into the night staring into the fire's dying embers, an idea formed in her mind. It was up to her, some time, somehow, she resolved, to avenge her mother's death.

Middleham, North Yorkshire

Crouched low over the withers of one of Jack Crow's three-year-olds, Charlie Kyle could not remember when he had ever been so cold. It could be bitter out on the Newmarket gallops when the vicious easterly winds were blowing, and he had had some difficulty in adjusting to the climate in general after so many years in Africa; but here, on Middleham Low Moor, high on the backbone of England, the wind seemed to come straight from the Arctic. Julie Crow ranged alongside him on the grey filly, fighting for her head.

'Kick on a bit, Charlie, can you?' she shouted. 'We're rather full of ourselves today.' As Charlie changed his hands on the reins and let his colt stride on, she yelled at him again, against the wind, 'Thanks. Cold enough for you, is it?'

She always insisted that the scenery around Middleham made up for the cold. It was certainly spectacular. Ahead of them, the Low Moor rolled on up to the neat stone-walled sheep pastures that rose gently and symmetrically up to the High Moor, with its springy turf gallops lying like a green sickle against the heathery slopes of Penhill. On the right, far below, lay Wensleydale with its fields, farms and villages illuminated by patches of sunlight as the wind drove the clouds eastwards. On the left, the long line of hills above Coverdale, stretching purply-brown to the horizon, were still tipped with snow.

Charlie eased his colt up again as they reached the brow of the hill. The horse was blowing a lot and was, Charlie assumed, only half fit, so he had probably had enough. Standing high in his stirrups as the canter became a jog, Charlie swung in a wide circle back towards the town and the rest of Jack's second lot strung out ahead of him, their manes and tails streaming in the wind, their lads hunched into waterproof jackets.

He liked to ride out first and second lots when he was staying with the Crows, as they were usually short-staffed and Jack seemed to value his opinion as to the horses' abilities; it was also some repayment for the Crows' generous hospitality. Jack had a small dual-purpose yard of around forty boxes which usually housed only moderate horses, although his patient handling brought him a fair number of winners throughout the year.

Glancing at his watch, with some difficulty as his colt was passaging sideways, buffeted by the wind, Charlie realized that he should be getting back to Jack's yard as soon as possible if he was going to be on time for his appointment with Beth Arnott in Leyburn just across the valley. She had sounded friendly enough on the phone. 'See you at eleven, then, on Saturday,' she'd said. 'We're the third bungalow on the left past the garage, as you come out of Leyburn on the Bedale road.' She retained a faint West Country accent, Charlie noticed, which had pleased and rather surprised him.

An hour later, as he walked up her garden path, neatly paved and flanked by clumps of snowdrops and early crocuses, he felt surprisingly nervous. He'd met Beth before, of course, all those years ago at Coombe Place, but she would have changed a lot since then and he only had the vaguest memories of a shy girl with dark hair. Also, after months of waiting he was actually just about to meet the person most likely to be able to give him a lead on Warrender. As he pressed the front-door bell and heard it chime inside, he realized that his hand was trembling.

The door was opened almost immediately by a short plumpish woman of about thirty, with a weatherbeaten complexion, kindly brown eyes and dark hair scraped back into a bun.

'Well, well, Charlie Kyle! You've grown up a bit since I last clapped eyes on you. I don't think I'd have recognized you.' She smiled. 'Come along in.'

The house smelt pleasantly of lavender polish and baking; and the little sitting-room into which she led him was bright and cheery with hyacinths, early primulas in pots, horse brasses, a long picture window looking out over Wensleydale, and a coal fire burning in the grate.

'Sit yourself down, then. I'll go and see to the coffee,' Beth said. 'Just make yourself at home.'

As Charlie settled in the nearest armchair, a sleek black cat leapt down from the windowsill and sprang on to his knee, purring. The cat's warmth, together with the simple comfort of the room with its gleaming surfaces, animal ornaments, knick-knacks and familiar racing photographs, made Charlie feel instantly at ease. The photographs, he noticed, were mainly of the same dark wiry-looking man with a number of horses in various Winners' Enclosures. He presumed they were of Beth's husband who, Jack Crow had confirmed, was a well-respected travelling head lad for one of the local trainers.

'What a pleasant room,' Charlie said, as Beth came back through the door carrying a tray with the coffee on it and a plate piled high with biscuits. 'Is that your husband in most of the pictures?'

Beth nodded. 'That's right. That's Bob,' she said affectionately. She plonked the tray down and sat in a chair opposite Charlie. 'He's a good man – I'm very lucky. He's gone to Newcastle today with a couple of runners. One of them has quite a chance, they reckon.' She smiled across at Charlie as she poured the coffee. 'I don't often bet these days but old habits die hard. I popped up the road to the betting shop and put two quid each way on it earlier, I'm afraid.' She handed Charlie the plate of biscuits. 'Please try one of these. They're still warm from the oven and nice and crisp.' She sat back in her chair, looking at him reflectively, her face glowing with colour against the snowy white of the antimacassar.

'I suppose you do look a bit like your father. You're both tall chaps, although you look a bit thinner than I remember him being. I did hear, though, that he got ever so thin when he was in prison.' She shook her head. 'That was a terrible business. But you've got your mother's eyes, that's for sure,' she went on, taking a sip of her coffee. 'Of course we didn't see much of your mother around the yard. She wasn't one for horses, was she, but she was a looker all right, I do remember that.' She paused, before continuing in a matter-of-fact tone. 'Well, now, tell me why you want to find Keith and how you think I can help you?'

Feeling surprisingly relaxed about confiding in such a stranger, Charlie began telling Beth how he had always been convinced of his father's innocence and how they had gone over the whole awful business so many times on those long evenings spent together on the farm in Zimbabwe. 'I came to the conclusion that so few real *facts* had come out of the trial,' he said. 'If Dad didn't do it, who did – and what motivation could they possibly have had? Or maybe the fire *had* started by accident but, if so, surely someone was to blame? I became more and more determined that when I eventually came back to England – as Dad and I had agreed I should after he sold the farm – I must try to find out what really happened so that I could clear his name. It was so incredibly unfair that people should go on thinking he was some sort of criminal.' He looked across at Beth, his expression grimly determined. 'The whole business ruined his life and broke his heart, you know. I have to try to put it right for him before he dies.'

When he did get back to England it had not taken him long to realize how much prejudice he was up against, Charlie continued, with feeling. 'Most people in racing who remembered him seemed to accept completely that he must have been guilty! Some of them were quite sympathetic, actually, obviously thinking that he'd just had some sort of brainstorm, but others just looked at me pityingly, which I couldn't bear.' He made a face. 'Then there were others, like that old sod Ditcher, who trains near Chepstow now, who were downright unpleasant. As he'd been a neighbour of ours in Somerset, I wrote to him for a job. He wrote back saying that although I had excellent references he wouldn't dream of taking me on. "You've got a bit of a nerve, putting yourself about after what happened, haven't you?" he wrote. "There's no escaping bad blood, you know. You learn that in this business!"' Charlie's eyes glittered with anger. 'That made me see red, of course. I'll show the old bastard, I thought. I'll prove to him and all the others that Dad was innocent.' He banged his coffee cup down on the table.

'Dad does admit that he was drunk that evening, of course,' Charlie went on more calmly. 'He and Mother had had a terrible row – about Neville, the bloke she eventually married. They had a shout-up in the yard before she drove off to London. Dad just went back to his study and went on drinking, he remembers; he must have fallen into a stupor. Then your pal Warrender burst in to say that he'd called the fire brigade as the stables were on fire. That was the first Dad knew about it.'

Beth stared at him, her face concerned. 'I see,' she said quietly. 'Very few of us believed at the time that your father had had any hand in it. We knew how devoted he was to the place and to his horses. He'd never have put any of them at risk.' She shook her head. 'Keith, my pal as you called him, was convinced that your father was responsible, though – I remember that. I wasn't living with him at the time, of course: I had digs in the village. The first I knew about the fire was when one of the other lads picked me up on his motorbike to give me a lift to work the following morning.' She shivered at the memory. 'I couldn't believe it when I saw the yard, all blackened and smouldering and smelling of fire, with everything spoiled. I cried my eyes out, to tell you the truth, and just thanked God that none of the horses had been seriously hurt.'

'What did Warrender tell you when you saw him that morning?' Charlie asked intently.

Beth put down her cup of coffee. 'Oh, he was in a right old state, I remember. He'd heard your parents quarrelling in the yard, he said – he was sleeping in the little flat above the tack room at the time. But he'd gone back to sleep thinking no more about it; he knew they weren't getting on at all at the time. The next thing he knew, someone was shouting outside his window and the whole yard was on fire. It was really frightening, he said.' She paused and glanced across to Charlie, her face perturbed. 'You've really got it in for Keith, haven't you?' she observed. 'I can understand: it was really his evidence that did for your father, I suppose. I'm afraid he's not the most likeable bloke in the world anyway,' she sighed.

'I expect you're wondering what it was that I ever saw in him, aren't you? I do too, now: now that I'm so happy with Bob. You have to remember that I was only a kid then. It was my first job away from my family in Devon and Keith seemed to take such a fancy to me, believe it or not!' She smiled. 'Love, or sex, or whatever you like to call it, can make fools of us all at times!'

Charlie's face relaxed into a grin. 'You can say that again,' he admitted ruefully. 'Do you think Warrender really believed that Dad had started the fire, though, or do you think he was just determined to nail him, out of sour grapes?' he went on persistently. 'I mean, they didn't get on, did they? I gather Dad almost sacked him on a couple of occasions. If only he had! But he has always been useless at that sort of thing, I'm afraid.'

Beth looked thoughtful. 'Well, there was no love lost between them, that's for sure. Though he did say something rather odd, much later, about your mother not being all that sorry about the fire.'

'Really? What was that?' Charlie stiffened.

'It was when we had the saddlery business in Yelperton. People who came in and remembered Keith from Coombe Place would occasionally refer to the fire, of course, though Keith was always reluctant to talk about it. One day, when one of the local farmers came in and started on about it, saying how sorry he was for your father and everything, Keith got really angry. "I don't want to hear any more about that bloody fire," he said to me when the man had gone. "What none of the stupid sods around here seems to realize is that Kyle was a bloody useless businessman. He'd have gone bust completely the way he was going, fire or no fire – at least that's what Suzie Kyle told me, and she should bloody well know, shouldn't she? Coombe Place had become a right liability, she said. She was glad to see the back of it as well as the back of him, I can tell you."'

Charlie sat very still, clutching the arm of his chair. His mother had obviously regarded Warrender as some sort of confidant. It was unbelievable! It was also possible that if she had known more about the fire than she had let on, she might well have said something to the head lad about it. That made it even more vital to try to track him down.

'There was something else I thought rather peculiar at the time,' Beth continued. 'It was to do with the money: the way Keith was suddenly able to lay his hands on it, just when he needed it. He'd had his eye on the saddlery shop for some while. Went on and on about how glad he would be to get out of racing and how he wanted me to help him with it, but, of course, he couldn't afford it, he grumbled.' She looked puzzled. 'Then, all of a sudden he got this windfall: this uncle of his in Australia had died and left him £10,000, he told me. I didn't believe him at first. It seemed so unlikely that he'd have relatives in Australia or anywhere else who'd leave him money like that!' She smoothed back her dark hair with a plump hand. 'He got ever so annoyed then and showed me a letter from some lawyer out there which did indeed mention a legacy, though it didn't say how much it was.' She shrugged her shoulders. 'But he had relatives in Australia all right. It was some cousin he went to stay with out there when we finally packed in the saddlery business and went our own ways.'

She got up and went over to the mantelpiece where she carefully removed a folded piece of paper from behind the clock. 'Here: this is the address he gave me at the time. It's somewhere just outside Melbourne, I think. I thought I'd lost it but I found it again just the other day, when I was looking through some of my old stuff – you know, photos and things.'

Charlie slipped the piece of paper into his wallet. 'It's a bit of a long shot, I agree, but it's the only lead I've got. Thanks,' he said, glancing up at the clock. It was time he got going, he thought. He'd made an arrangement with Jack Crow to go and look at a hunter chaser for one of his owners over towards Thirsk and he'd be late if he didn't get a move on. He uncoiled himself reluctantly from the chair. 'Thanks, Beth,' he said again, holding out his hand, 'for the coffee and the talk and everything. I know I'm obsessional about the whole business, but it's so important to me to try to find out what really happened. Anyway, sorry I went on a bit. I've enjoyed meeting you again.'

He meant it, he thought, as he climbed into his car. He liked Beth: she was friendly and direct. He was glad she had got away from Warrender and married someone nicer. She seemed genuinely happy with her Bob.

'Let me know if you have any luck,' she said, smiling as she stood in the porch. 'But if you do track Keith down, please don't tell him where I am, will you? You never know, he might feel like getting in touch with me again and Bob wouldn't like that! Goodbye, anyway, and good luck!' She gave him a cheerful wave.

She had given him a lot to think about, Charlie reflected as he accelerated down the road towards the Coverbridge Inn. It was his mother's chumminess with Warrender which really baffled him. What on earth was that all about? He would not rest easy until he had found out.

Cheltenham Racecourse

Cursing the weather, Kate fumbled in the pocket of her Barbour jacket for a cloth to wipe her camera lens. The rain, beginning to turn to sleet again, was being whipped horizontally over the rim of the Cotswold hills by the freshening wind.

She was on Cheltenham racecourse for the highlight of the National Hunt season, the Tote Cheltenham Gold Cup, huddled along with other racing photographers and hardy observers by the last fence into the straight. Below them, the track, an undulating green ribbon curving under the slopes of Cleeve Hill, was barely visible through the driving sleet. Up the hill, a crowd of fifty thousand or so were crammed into the warren of bars, terraces and private boxes that made up the great concrete stands. Beyond, rows of cars and coaches spread like a glittering metal tarpaulin over the hillside towards the town.

Her collaborator on the book, Sandy Diss, was up there somewhere in the warm and being lavishly fed and watered, Kate thought enviously. To be fair, Sandy had invited her up for a drink, but when she had refused, explaining that she would be in her working clothes, Sandy had not repeated the offer. 'OK, we'll take a raincheck then. Some other time,' she'd replied. Much to Kate's frustration, the long-awaited planning lunch at Rockington had not yet taken place, as Sandy had been delayed in New York and had to cancel it. Instead, they had all had a hastily arranged and very brief meeting in Geoffrey's office a few days ago. Sandy, delayed at the hairdresser and apparently late for another appointment with her dressmaker, had swept in, in a flurry of mink, and handed out copies of the itinerary she had drawn up for the horsey events she intended to visit throughout the year.

'I'll be taking in most of these, so you'd best come along too,' she'd ordered Kate, with a dazzling smile. When Kate attempted to discuss possible more low-key events like gymkhanas, ploughing contests and horse fairs that she wanted to photograph, Sandy was already collecting her various packages and preparing to leave.

'Oh, sure! You just go ahead and snap those little Olde England things, honey. I can always think up something to say about them later – no problem,' she said dismissively before sweeping out in search of her chauffeur.

After exploding to Geoffrey, Kate decided that she would just go her own way for the moment and try to tackle Sandy more seriously when their Rockington lunch eventually took place. 'God knows what made you think we could ever work together, though,' she told Geoffrey crossly. 'Arguing with that woman is like trying to halt the progress of a Panzer division!' Turning up the collar of her jacket, she moved closer to her companion, a burly photographer from *The Sporting Life*.

'Christ! I can't see a bloody thing,' he complained. Raising his binoculars to study the Gold Cup runners circling around at the start, he stepped backwards without warning, treading on Kate's toe. She didn't know the man well but he seemed determined to take her under his wing today. After photographing the favourite and some of the other fancied runners earlier in the paddock, he had propelled her urgently back across the course. The runners would be jumping this particular fence twice, he explained, which would give her a good chance of getting some decent shots.

'They're off!' he announced suddenly with obvious relief. 'Poor buggers. If there's one thing worse than shivering out here by the fence, it's having to actually ride round Cheltenham in this weather. The jumping boys sure earn their money!'

Standing on tiptoe to peer over his shoulder, Kate got an eyeful of stinging sleet. She dropped back again, pulling her coat more tightly around her. Uncomfortable though she was, she was enjoying herself. The past two days had given her a definite taste for steeplechasing, she realized. She had always enjoyed watching it on television, which was certainly far more comfortable, but you missed out on the real thrill of it all: the sound of the horses thundering up to a fence and the crash of the birch twigs as they hurled themselves over, and the smell of the flying mud, mixed with leather and sweating horseflesh. As the runners neared the fence now, her whole body began to tingle with excitement. One minute they were thudding close, out of sight, the next they had burst into view, in a commotion of noise, colour and straining limbs. In the middle of the field, one of the horses hit the fence hard and stumbled down on his knees, but miraculously, by letting the reins shoot through his fingers and sitting right back, his jockey kept him on his feet.

'Christ! I thought we'd lost one there,' commented a wiry little woman in a headscarf at Kate's elbow, glued to her binoculars. 'The Irish mare's going well, isn't she?' Her neat head swung left as the field thundered on up the hill.

Kate checked her film quickly, before leaning back against the rail and relaxing for a moment. She immediately forgot the cold and discomfort as her thoughts turned to Tod, as they inevitably did at the moment. She was possibly already in love with him, she realized, and he with her. Or that's what he had told her the last time they met, and she believed him. Despite all her initial reservations, it made her incredibly happy. They had managed to meet alone several times since their momentous New Year's Eve encounter when, as Tod had predicted, their love-making had not been altogether successful. He had had real difficulty sustaining an erection, so they spent much of the night talking, caressing, or just lying in each other's arms; but a bond had been created between them which Kate knew would grow stronger and more special. Apart from Tod's married state, the only other shadow over her joy was the certainty of her mother's disapproval. It wasn't that Lady Kitty disliked Tod – the reverse was true – but Kate knew her mother's views about getting involved with married men. She always tried to be honest with her, yet found herself already lying, telling Lady Kitty that she had not gone to bed at all after Diana's party but stayed on at Three Swallows for breakfast and a swim before calling in at Barons Lodge to see Achilles. Her return to the Old Rectory in mid-morning, still clad in her party clothes, had therefore not caused any comment, although Lady Kitty had inquired if Myra had been at the party too.

'Barbados indeed! Lucky woman!' her mother had commented. 'I wonder why Tod didn't go too. I thought he looked in need of a holiday the last time I saw him.' She looked across at Kate, her blue eyes innocent. 'He's an attractive fellow, Tod, don't you think?'

'Hmm . . . I suppose so,' Kate replied, as casually as she could manage, avoiding her mother's gaze.

She would have to level with her soon, though, she thought, as a growing tension all around indicated the approach of the Gold Cup runners. Clicking furiously, Kate concentrated on the two leaders as, streaked with mud, rain and sweat, they crashed over the fence, neck and neck, heads outstretched, nostrils distended, and heaved on up the hill to a crescendo of cheering. The roar seemed almost to pull them along like a magnet; Kate had never heard anything like it – she half expected to see the blast of noise lift the roof clear off the top of the stands. As the leaders passed the post, the rest of the field straggling in their wake, the peculiarity of it all struck her. How extraordinary it was that a mere horse-race in the middle of Gloucestershire in such foul weather could attract so many people and generate such amazing excitement.

Fifteen minutes later, exhausted by her efforts in pushing through the crowds to photograph the winner on his long triumphal walk back to the paddock, she sat slumped on the weighing-room steps, packing away her camera. She had photographed Queen Elizabeth the Queen Mother, too, as she made the presentations to the winning connections – the horse's owners, trainer and jockey – and had feared at one point that the small, brightly clad figure would be completely swallowed up by a section of the crowd, mainly Irish, as they thronged and jostled around her. Although the Royal party had departed now, back to the stands, the tiers around the paddock were still buzzing with enthusiastic punters. Kate suddenly felt enormously weary, as well as damp. Now that the action was over, she thought, she would go and get herself a cup of tea. She was just getting slowly to her feet again when a familiar figure emerged from under a large yellow umbrella in the centre of the paddock and came striding towards her.

It was Diana Saunders, clad in a startling canary-coloured suit and black fedora hat. She did a double-take as she caught sight of Kate. 'Strewth, Kate – I hardly recognized you! You look like the original drowned rat!' she joked. 'Great race, wasn't it? I hope you got some good pics. Do you fancy a drink?' she asked before Kate could reply. 'Charlie and I are on our way up to a friend's box right now, but I've got to collect something for them from the weighing room first. You look like a whisky mac might do you the world of good.'

'It probably would,' Kate replied, 'but I don't feel really dressed for box company, thanks. I've already turned down an invitation to join Sandy Diss.'

'Oh, well, please yourself,' Diana replied amiably. 'But look, call me soon and come over to Three Swallows for a meal or something. You'd better make it early next week. We're going to have another go at getting Misty in foal again. How's that little sod Achilles coming along?'

'He's fine. Tod seems pleased, anyway. He's taking him along very slowly still, though. He's hardly grown at all since you last saw him,' Kate replied, hoping she was not blushing.

If she was, Diana did not appear to notice. 'Never mind, he will. Call me soon, then. See you – bye.' With a cheery wave, Diana dodged in front of one of the runners for the next race who was slouching around, heavily rugged up and wearing a waterproof hood. Gazing across the paddock, Kate could just make out Charlie Kyle sheltering under Diana's vast yellow umbrella. She presumed the two of them were still lovers. They had got involved before Christmas, she gathered from Tod, and the liaison seemed to be doing Charlie good: he was more relaxed than he had been before.

If only Tod were here right now, Kate thought wistfully as she went off in search of a cup of tea. How lovely it would be to have his company on the long drive back to London! But she must not start thinking like that, she told herself. Even if they were ever able to go racing together, they would never be alone; Tod would inevitably be accompanied by his usual retinue of stable staff and family. There could be few people more difficult to have a secret affair with than a married trainer, she reflected ruefully. Why was it that, once again, she was making things so difficult for herself?

Barons Lodge

'Rather a sub-standard Gold Cup, wouldn't you say?' Myra observed. She and Tod had been watching the television coverage of the race from either end of the sofa in the drawing-room at Barons Lodge over a cup of tea.

'Actually, I don't agree,' Tod replied quietly. 'The going looks atrocious and the winner is pretty inexperienced, you know – scarcely out of novice company. I thought it was an impressive performance.'

'Mmm . . .' Myra snorted, obviously unconvinced. She leant forward suddenly, pointing at the set. 'Good God! There's Diana Saunders, and Charlie too,' she said excitedly. 'Look, under that ridiculous umbrella. She looks like an overgrown canary.' She shook her head. 'She's got no taste at all, of course. All those bright colours – typically Australian. Still, she seems to be keeping our assistant trainer happy, which is all that matters!' As she spoke, the telephone rang on the table beside her. Indicating to Tod to turn the sound down, she picked up the receiver.

'Hello, Myra Beckhampton,' she said rather crossly. 'Who? Oh, Gordon! How are you?' She made a face to Tod. 'Glad it's the end of term, no doubt.' She listened for a few minutes, a look of growing annoyance on her face. 'I see. Well, we'd better have a talk about it all on Tuesday, hadn't we? We obviously can't go into the whole thing now. No, I'll be collecting Toby on my own. Tod's got to go up to London that day, apparently.' She glanced at him irritably. 'Right. See you then. Goodbye.'

She put back the receiver, her expression concerned. 'That was Gordon, as you probably gathered,' she said. 'He's worried about Toby, apparently. His work, his attitude – everything, by the sound of it!' She sighed. 'He says he's getting into bad company. But there isn't supposed to *be* any bad company at Hadleigh! That's why we send him there at such vast expense, isn't it? God knows what's going on,' she added in a tone of despair.

'Perhaps I'd better come with you on Tuesday, then,' Tod offered tentatively, putting down his cup of tea. 'I can always cancel my appointment with this new eye man.' That was the last thing he wanted to do, of course. He had arranged to see Kate for a late lunch afterwards and it might be their only chance to be alone together for a while. He could see, however, that Myra was genuinely worried by what Toby's housemaster had said.

'No, no, it's taken you months to get that wretched appointment. There's no point in cancelling it now,' Myra snapped.

He would have to have a long talk with Toby this holidays, Tod decided. The boy was obviously finding coping with adolescence and his O-levels very hard going. Perhaps both he and Myra had not been sympathetic enough. Well, that could easily be remedied.

'I shouldn't worry too much, if I were you,' he said, getting to his feet. 'Gordon's probably exaggerating – you know what an old woman he is. I'll try to have a heart-to-heart with Tobes as soon as he gets home. I'm sure we can find out what's going on. Anyway, I must get back to the yard. I'll see you later.'

When he had gone, Myra poured herself another cup of tea and sank back against the cushions. It was worrying that Gordon was so concerned about Toby. She was, too, of course; she didn't know what was eating him these days. She had tried to talk to him in the Christmas holidays, about being more co-operative and helping out more in the yard like he used to, but she had just met with sullen resistance. He couldn't at the moment, he told her: he had too much work to do. He was still obviously attached to his pony, Watson, but other than that he didn't seem to care too much about what went on at Barons Lodge. All in all, he wasn't the same person at all as that cheerful, affectionate boy they had sent off to Hadleigh a few years ago. In view of all that, she dreaded to think how he might react if she did decide to leave Tod. If she did, eventually, decide to accept Stelios's offer, she certainly wouldn't be able to break the news to Toby until after his exams.

Basil's reaction to the whole idea had been fairly predictable. At first, he had seemed not only astonished but also rather shocked. It was only when she explained how serious the financial situation at Barons Lodge actually was, and how desperately worried she was about the future, that he had become more sympathetic. 'The whole thing is becoming a nightmare,' she said vehemently. 'I think Stelios might be right: we may well have to sell the yard in a year or so, at this rate, and that would break my heart. The shame of it – just think what Daddy would say!' She fixed her brother with a fierce look. 'And Stelios's proposal was a complete bombshell: I'd no idea he was planning anything like that. But now I've got over the shock, I have to admit that I am tempted. It would secure Barons Lodge's future as well as mine. Surely that's what Daddy would have wanted?'

Basil's gradual appreciation of this point was not only due to concern for her welfare, she suspected: her brother was strongly motivated by self-interest and, when he had had a chance to mull the whole thing over, the idea of having a millionaire for a brother-in-law had become more and more appealing.

No, if she did accept Stelios's offer, neither Basil nor Pam would represent a real problem in the long run, Myra reflected. Nor quite possibly would Tod. In his present mood, he might well accept her departure with the same philosophical shrug of the shoulders with which he seemed to greet most setbacks these days. It was Toby she really had to worry about. She could not risk upsetting him further: he seemed so vulnerable at the moment. She would have to proceed with considerable care.

CHAPTER ELEVEN

Mountclare

Stella leant on the paddock gate, tears streaming down her face. In front of her a handful of her pregnant mares ambled slowly towards her against the soft blue backdrop of Slievenamon, the leader whinnying softly. In the field beyond, clumps of black-faced sheep were grazing and lambs were skittering about in the sunshine, their bleating mingling with the song of the larks.

It was an idyllic scene but, for once, Stella could not appreciate it. She was exhausted and grieving. Dermot, the old stud groom, had been ill with pleurisy and she had had little rest for several days and nights, supervising and assisting with the foaling. The mild weather seemed to have brought some of the mares on quicker than expected and the last few days had been unusually hectic. She had wished, not for the first time, that Rory had been there to give her his moral and practical support.

And now, less than half an hour ago, she had lost one of her favourite mares, Petra, who haemorrhaged in the course of a difficult foaling and had to be put down. Petra was fourteen and had produced a foal every year of the eight she had been at Mountclare, but this delivery had been difficult from the start, the mare sweating profusely and straining hard the moment her water bag had slipped out. When she started, most uncharacteristically, to panic, Stella realized that something was seriously wrong and sent one of the grooms to fetch the vet. At one point Petra had been thrashing around in the straw so fiercely, with the foal's head and forelegs sticking out of her vagina, that Stella had been seriously worried that they might lose the foal as well. But it had survived, a shivering, trembling little creature with a chestnut coat and a white blaze down its face, just like its father, Be My Guest. The foal was now being fed from a bottle with some of its mother's milk heated up on Dermot's kitchen stove. Petra had been put down with a humane killer the moment the foaling was over. Now came the vital and time-consuming business of finding a foster mother as soon as possible.

Stella had been on her way back to the house to make some phone calls to another stud who had helped her out in the past when she had been overwhelmed with grief and, not wanting any of her staff to see her in a moment of weakness, had walked down to the far paddock gate to try to pull herself together. Tara, who was standing beside her gazing mournfully into the middle distance, nudged her hand gently with her cold nose. Stella looked down. 'OK, you're right,' she said, pulling her handkerchief out of her jeans pocket, 'I must get on.' Blowing her nose briskly, she turned on her heel on the crunchy gravel and began to walk slowly back towards the house.

A scarlet Mercedes parked alongside her black BMW indicated, to her irritation, that her father had returned. He had been staying for a few days, though she hardly had time to see him, and had insisted on going over all the stud accounts – which she thought rather curious as he'd seen them all before: copies were always sent to his various offices in Athens, New York and London. Then, yesterday, he had vanished up to Dublin for twenty-four hours on what he described as 'personal business'. Stella could not envisage what that was, and did not particularly care. She did not imagine that her father was pursuing women any longer, although he still squired various actresses and wealthy widows to the opera or fund-raising dinners and balls in New York; and she could not think what else of a 'personal' nature in Dublin's little socio-cultural pond could possibly be of interest to him. Perhaps he was after a picture. She had never been able to share his passion for modern or even Impressionist art. She liked the work of the best horse painters, Stubbs and the Herrings, and the primitive animal pictures of Roelandt Savery and Henri Rousseau she had first seen as a schoolgirl when her stepmother took her to Paris.

Pulling off her boots outside the scullery door, she padded through the kitchen in her socks and poured herself some coffee.

'It's really sad about the mare, Miss Stella,' Brigid, the housekeeper, said sympathetically as she slapped another lump of dough expertly on the table and sprinkled it with flour.

'Yes, well, I've got to find a foster mother as quickly as I can,' Stella said brusquely. 'The little foal's very weak.' Her mistress looked tired out, Brigid thought, shivering with fatigue and even paler than usual under her black bobbed hair, but she knew that she was a lot tougher than she looked and disliked anyone's attempts to mollycoddle or over-sympathize with her, however well intended.

As Stella approached her study door, walking silently on the stone-flagged floor, Tara at her heel, she could hear her father's voice booming away on the telephone. Instinctively, she halted, instead of going straight in, and leant against the wall.

'I've told you, Stavros,' she heard him saying, 'I want the contract drawn up precisely as I suggested when we last talked in Athens. No, I don't think it's too generous: the woman deserves it, and I can afford it, for heaven's sake. No . . . there's no immediate hurry. I have not asked for her final answer yet; I want to give her plenty of time. Yes, yes . . . What *about* the Thai hotel chain? I told you, we are not interested in that.'

Stavros was Stelios's old friend and trusted lawyer, Stella knew; but what on earth were they talking about? Some sort of business contract with a woman apparently, she thought wearily, reaching for the doorknob. She must get her father off the phone and get on with the business of ringing round for a foster mother for her foal, which seemed rather more pressing.

At Stelios's next words, she stiffened with surprise, her hand frozen in mid-air.

'Ballinvale? Yes, I took another look at the place yesterday,' he was saying. 'It would be ideal, of course, but they can't make up their minds whether to sell or not. They're asking too much anyway. I won't go beyond two million. Yes, yes, I should get first refusal, so we shall see. Regards to Melina and the family. Goodbye.' He put down the phone.

Stella could not believe what she was hearing. Revitalized by a mixture of curiosity and indignation, she strode into the room, her eyes glittering.

'Father, what on earth are you up to? I overheard part of your conversation – I couldn't help it. What's this about Ballinvale? You're not seriously thinking of buying that place, are you?' she asked incredulously. 'Whatever for?'

Stelios looked up from Lord Henry's old desk, a look of consternation on his heavy features. 'Ah, my dear, I had no idea you were outside the door,' he said uneasily. 'So you overheard what I said to Stavros then, did you? Mmm, that is unfortunate.' He tilted his head back against the chair and stared at the ceiling for a moment. 'Well, never mind,' he said eventually, turning back to Stella. 'I was intending to tell you about the whole thing, of course,' he said placatingly,

146

'but not just yet, not until I have had a decision. However –' he shrugged his massive shoulders.

Stella had dropped into an armchair and was staring at him coldly, one hand on Tara's collar. 'What decision? What are you talking about?' she asked crossly. 'And what on earth are you interested in Ballinvale for? I don't understand.'

Stelios did not answer for a moment. Then he swung forward, bracing his fingers against the edge of the desk, his expression solemn. 'You know, my dear, that I am retiring next year, do you not? Handing the burden of running Alexandros Maritime and the other companies over to your cousin Constantine.' He raised his heavy eyebrows.

Stella nodded with impatience. 'Yes, yes, of course,' she replied curtly.

'Well, what you do not know, however, because I have not chosen to discuss it with you, is what I shall be doing in my retirement,' Stelios went on. 'The Greek Government has done the honour of asking me to represent them here in Ireland, to become their ambassador in Dublin.' He paused, glancing slyly at Stella to let the significance of this sink in. 'This is, of course, a very great honour,' he continued, 'and it will mean a few changes, naturally. To carry out my duties properly I shall need to make some acquisitions.' He paused, rubbing the side of his nose with his index finger, something he tended to do when stirred up. 'One of these is a home near Dublin where I can relax away from my official duties. Would you agree?'

Stella looked at him in amazement. This really was the most extraordinary news she had heard for a long time. Her father an ambassador? It was a joke. 'Well, maybe,' she replied cautiously. 'But you don't need a stud farm, somewhere like Ballinvale, surely? It doesn't make sense.'

Stelios smiled at her patiently. 'On the contrary, it makes very good sense, my dear. I have decided that I wish to build up my breeding interests here in Ireland in the next few years. My official duties will not be very onerous, you know.'

'Yes, but you don't need to buy Ballinvale to do that,' Stella said impatiently. 'You've got Mountclare. I know that legally it belongs to me but you have a share in it too.' She frowned. 'After all, it's your money that has enabled me to build up such a strong band of broodmares and to renovate the whole place. And that was just the beginning. As you know, I've got great plans for expansion here – plans for which, of course, I was hoping to get your financial backing.' She leant forward, her eyes narrowed.

Stelios stared at her thoughtfully. 'Mmm,' he said slowly. 'It did not occur to you that I might have other plans, I guess,' he sighed. 'Ah, well, that does not altogether surprise me. There has been a growing lack of communication between us recently.' He leant forward, his elbows on the desk. 'You have done very well, my dear. I have just been going through all the accounts again, as you know. You seem to be managing Mountclare with great dedication and efficiency and you will, I am sure, continue to do so.' He flashed her a patronizing smile. 'I have been happy to finance you up to now,' he continued. 'I am proud of what you have achieved here. But now, as I see it, you really do not need any more help from me. You are able, as they say, to stand on your own two feet.' He spread his hands in a gesture of resignation. 'So, the time has come for me to find a place of my own. A place where I could stand at least a couple of stallions, starting perhaps with Devilry. Ballinvale would be ideal: the facilities there are excellent.'

Stella leant forward, her face pale. This was really too much, she thought. Both she and Nik had been pressing their father to buy Devilry, but only with a view to managing him themselves one day as a stallion – she herself had bred the colt, after all. It was quite intolerable that Stelios was now thinking of standing him somewhere else.

'But all that is perfectly possible *here*, Father,' she insisted. 'You know it has always been my ambition to turn Mountclare into a public as well as a private stud, and Devilry would obviously be my first choice as a stallion. You must realize that!' Her blue eyes blazed.

Stelios sighed. 'You may have been thinking along those lines, my dear,' he replied soothingly. 'But I personally do not believe that Mountclare would be suitable for that type of expansion. I really do not believe that the right additional land will become available, either in quality or quantity.'

'That *was* so, maybe,' Stella replied, 'but things are changing. It really does look now as though the McCarron land this side of the river may be sold off in the next year or so, and that would be ideal: that would change everything.' She frowned. 'Anyway, it's not just my plans here that we are talking about. They are linked, as you well know, with Nik's ideas for Kilmarron. When O'Donnell dies Nik would like to transform the place – build it up into one of the best training centres in Europe. Together we could have the most successful breeding/training operation in Ireland. Surely, Father, you don't want to stand in our way?' Her voice was incredulous.

Stelios got up slowly and moved around the desk towards the fire. 'Hmm . . . that is pie in the sky, in my opinion,' he replied. He ran his fingers slowly along the top of the spines of the books on the shelf as he passed, dislodging a thick plume of dust. 'Nik may very well be able to lease Kilmarron from the O'Donnell family when the old man dies but, without my financial assistance, I do not see how he could afford to buy it and make all these changes,' he went on. 'Nor do I think it would be wise to try.'

He sank down on the sofa opposite Stella and reached into the pocket of his corduroy jacket for a small leather case of cigars.

'Nik will inherit a great deal of money when I die. He can do what he likes then. In the meantime I feel it is my duty to try to guide him in the right direction.' He smiled benignly. 'After all, surely that is what fathers are for?' He extracted one of his Davidoff cigars and started to cut the end. 'I don't think Nik should make his career in Ireland at all,' he continued. 'It has many advantages in the stud business, the VAT in particular, but as far as training is concerned, I think it is too parochial.' He reached over to the desk for his gold lighter. 'I think Nik should move to Newmarket and be a big fish in a bigger pond.' He paused, nodding to himself. 'I might well be prepared to help him then, buy him a yard. In fact, I have even got one in mind,' he added casually, flicking his lighter open and starting to puff energetically away at his cigar.

'Really! May I ask which one?' Stella's tone was glacial. She could not believe what she was hearing. She was furious with her father's sudden ridiculous whim that he must acquire a stud of his own. Her father was pulling the rug out from under all the plans that she and Nik had been plotting. This ambassadorial appointment had really gone to his head – softened his brain, even. It was intolerable.

'Barons Lodge,' Stelios replied with quiet triumph. 'Tod Beckhampton may well want to sell soon, the way things are going.'

'I can't see why,' Stella retorted. 'He may be having a bad run but I'd be amazed if he wanted to sell up. His wife's particularly devoted to the place, I gather. Old Sir Digby probably left it to her anyway.'

'You have neglected to ask me what is the other possession I need to acquire before taking up my Dublin post,' Stelios replied silkily. 'It is, of course, a wife.' He sneaked a quick look at his daughter through the cloud of smoke. 'Myra Beckhampton would, I believe, be more than willing to sell me Barons Lodge. For, you see, my dear, she is the one I plan to marry.'

*

Screeching into the yard at Kilmarron, Stella parked her BMW next to her brother's black Mercedes and jumped out on to the gravel. With all the horses back in their boxes after their morning exercise, there were only a couple of lads in sight, sweeping up the cobbles in a dilatory way. Turning up her coat collar, Stella called over to the one nearest her, asking him where she would be likely to find Nik.

'It's urgent,' she added tersely.

'He'll be over in the office. Or maybe in Devilry's box, Miss Stella,' the lad told her respectfully. 'The big fella slipped up on the road this morning and banged his knee. Gave us a terrible fright, to be sure.'

Striding under the archway into the main yard, a square of mellow-brick boxes with faded yellow doors backing on to the side of the rambling old house itself, Stella caught sight of her brother emerging from Devilry's box, accompanied by his head lad, Tim. He was looking as immaculate as usual in his well-cut jacket, breeches and long boots, but his expression, she thought, was distinctly vexed.

'Stella!' he exclaimed in surprise. 'Whatever brings you here? I'll be with you in a minute.' He turned to the small gnarled figure at his side.

'Don't mention this incident to Mr O'Donnell, Tim,' he ordered. 'We don't want to upset him, do we?' Lifting off his cap, he ran a hand over his shiny black hair. 'Just tell him that Seamus gave in his notice, will you? But make sure all the lads know what really happened. Make sure they understand that if any essential tack is left off their horses, they'll be dismissed too. Understood?'

Tim nodded. 'Right you are, sir,' he replied, without expression.

'Devilry went down on the road this morning and he wasn't wearing his knee boots,' Nik explained to Stella. 'He only grazed himself, thank God – we were lucky. I've sacked the lad responsible, of course. A pity, as he's a good work rider, but I will not have that kind of sloppiness in the yard.' He glanced at his sister with concern. 'What's up?' he asked. He raised his eyebrows. 'We're dining together, with Father, remember, this evening? Couldn't it wait until then?'

'No, it could not,' Stella replied firmly. 'I need to talk to you right now, in private. Can we drive up to the top of the gallops?'

'But it's practically lunchtime,' Nik protested. 'You know how the old man likes me to be punctual for meals.' His tone was ironic.

'To hell with the old man,' Stella snapped. 'He can wait. This is important, I promise.'

Nik listened to his sister in silence as he accelerated along the long avenue of chestnuts that divided the home paddocks and flung the car expertly round the bends in the road as they climbed slowly up to the old Norman watchtower that marked the top of the gallops.

'Father, an ambassador! Good God! How droll! No wonder he's been a bit above himself recently!'

'It's not funny,' Stella rebuked him. 'Wait until you hear the rest.'

By the time Nik had eased the car to a halt at the top of the hill, close by the little cairn of stones where one of Kilmarron's most famous horses, a dual English and Irish Derby winner, lay buried, his expression too was perturbed.

'It may never happen, of course,' he said reflectively. 'This plan of father's, I mean. Ballinvale is not even on the market at the moment, and there's no guarantee it will be – not in the near future, at least.' He turned to Stella. 'Also, more important, how do we know that Myra Beckhampton will accept his offer? Barons Lodge may be in trouble, but women don't leave their husbands just like that, even for money, surely? She's always looked a rather conservative, tight-lipped bitch to me. Hardly the sort to create a scandal, I'd have thought.'

'I can't imagine anyone in their right minds wanting to marry Father,' Stella remarked despairingly. 'The woman must be off her head. Still, he seems to think she'll accept him!'

'*He*'s off his head if he thinks he can bribe me to move to Newmarket,' Nik remarked grimly. 'I have absolutely no intention of doing that. Training cheek by jowl with all the others, everyone knowing what I'm up to – no way!' He lowered the car's electric windows and gazed out at the familiar landscape spread out before him. 'That's not what I have in mind at all, oh no!' he added firmly.

In front of him, basking in the thin spring sunshine, lay his territory, his kingdom. Or it would be one day soon, when he could get his hands on it. On the downland to his left he planned to extend the old gallop to form a perfect replica of the Epsom Derby course, with all its extraordinary twists and gradients. No colt of his would ever take his place in the Derby line-up if it couldn't, to use the trainers' perennial excuse, 'act on the course', he thought scornfully. Down in the valley below, beyond the old yearling yard, he planned to put in a seven-furlong, American-type dirt circuit alongside the existing oval-shaped turf gallop. Such projects and many others were part of the plans he and Stella were formulating to breed and train horses specifically to go on and race in America. That way, they calculated, they would attract more support from owners who wanted to race horses in the States as well as in Europe. This was what they wanted their father's financial backing for and no half-baked plan of his to set up his own breeding operation and run off with someone else's wife must be allowed to get in the way.

'Well, what are we going to do?' Stella asked impatiently. She was shivering, Nik noticed – probably due to a mixture of rage and shock, as much as cold, he reflected. He pressed the button to wind up the windows and sat quite still, staring into the middle distance.

'I think we should sit tight – certainly not panic,' he said eventually. 'We mustn't let Father see how put out we are by his idea. We mustn't quarrel with him. That would be foolish, and would only stiffen his resolve to go through with it – you know how perverse he is. So, I think we should just try to humour him for the moment.' He frowned. 'We must persuade him to go ahead with his offer for Devilry, though. I'm convinced that the owners are in financial trouble and want to sell, and it's essential that, for the moment, we keep the colt in the family. I'm more and more convinced that he needs a mile and a half now, and that gives him a real chance of winning the King George and the Arc. That would make him a very exciting prospect at stud.'

He looked across at his sister. 'But we must, of course, do everything we can to stop this ridiculous marriage,' he insisted. 'That's more important than Ballinvale, in my view. We could still persuade the old fool to come in with us if it weren't for this Myra Beckhampton. The stud is obviously a toy, or a bribe you could say, specifically for her, don't you think?'

He narrowed his blue eyes. 'How well do you know the woman?' he asked.

Stella shrugged her shoulders. 'Hardly at all. I've bumped into her here and there, of course.'

'Well, I suggest you get to know her better,' Nik's smile was sardonic. 'Become her friend. It shouldn't be too difficult. She should need a confidante if she is as unhappy as Father seems to think she is. Anyway, you've got considerable charm, when you choose to exert it! Then, when you have become her friend, you can tell her a few home truths about Father, even invent some dreadful skeleton in the cupboard if you like. It doesn't matter what you tell her as long as you don't let on that you know he's asked her to marry him.'

Still smiling, he flicked the car's engine into life again.

'You know how inventive you are. You might even enjoy it. If you can't put Myra Beckhampton off marrying Father, I don't know who can! Right, let's get back to the house for lunch. I'm starving.'

Dropping the body brush on to the straw, Toby leant his cheek against Watson's warm neck. The pony's calm presence as he contentedly snatched at his hay was reassuring: balm to Toby's feelings of guilt and unhappiness. If only he could go back a few years in time, he thought, back to the days when he had no fear of riding any horse, even a thoroughbred, and everything seemed so simple and secure.

It was only the second week of the Easter holidays, but already both his parents had insisted on a 'talk' with him about his work and general attitude. His mock O-level results had been even worse than he had expected. He'd failed Maths completely and only scraped a C in everything else, except Art where he had managed a B.

Toby put his arms around Watson's neck and buried his face in his mane. He knew why the results were so bad, of course: it was his obsession with Giles Anstey. It haunted him day and night and made it so difficult to concentrate on anything else. He supposed he was in love. He had certainly never felt anything like this before, but whatever it was, it was a torment.

He had always been attracted to Giles, of course; everyone was. Tall and athletic, with his mischievous brown eyes and dark curly hair, he had an aura of power and assurance about him that none of the other boys had. Even Matron seemed to eat out of his hand. But it was only when they had been cast as lovers in the house play, *The Servant of Two Masters*, at the end of the Christmas term that Toby had had any real contact with him. There was a volley of whistles and cat calls from the other members of the cast the first time they'd actually had to kiss at rehearsals, Toby recalled, but Giles, of course, made a joke of it.

'God, Beckhampton. You're a lousy kisser! I must introduce you to one of my girlfriends some time,' he commented, his dark eyes amused.

A few nights later, when the two of them had been tidying up the gym after rehearsals, Giles came over to him and, turning off the lights, pushed him gently back against the wall.

'Right, now, let's see what sort of kisser you *really* are,' he whispered. 'I suspect you could be pretty hot.' When his mouth, smelling faintly of peppermint, sought his in the darkness, Toby's first instinct was to duck away in horror, but far from feeling any revulsion, he found himself gripped by a delicious excitement. When Giles started to explore his mouth with his tongue, he felt an erection stirring.

Hearing footsteps in the corridor outside, Giles hastily switched on the lights again and moved away. He had not touched him again, except during the performances of the play itself, which had been an agony of embarrassment for Toby as he struggled to conceal his degree of arousal. One afternoon last term though, when most of the rest of the house were out watching an important game of rugby, he bumped into Giles by chance in the empty cloakroom and was again grabbed in a lustful embrace, Giles kissing him full on the mouth then reaching down and pressing his crotch. 'Sorry we can't do this more often, but things are a bit risky at the moment,' he murmured. 'Old Gordon's definitely got it in for me. He's a poofter himself, if you ask me!'

Toby, in a state of fevered excitement, kissed Giles passionately back, confessing, impetuously, that he loved him.

The older boy stepped back in alarm. 'Here! Steady on!' he remarked, his eyes suddenly serious. 'You're not supposed to get *involved* or anything, you know. It's only a bit of fun,' he added, pushing Toby away from him.

This incident completed Toby's misery. Giles clearly did not reciprocate his feelings, he realized; it was all just a game to him. He was also seriously concerned that not only was he in love with Giles but he was also possibly irredeemably homosexual. He couldn't imagine how he was going to cope with that or be able to conceal it from his parents.

He wouldn't be able to keep his other problems from them for much longer, he realized, as he clutched Watson for comfort. Tod, he knew, suspected that he had lost his nerve and would know it the moment he saw him out again on the gallops. God knows what his mother would say; she would be absolutely horrified. It was all so shamemaking; he felt such a wimp. He sank down in the straw at his pony's feet and buried his face in his hands.

Whistling softly under his breath, Liam sauntered across the main yard. Despite the bitterly cold wind, he was feeling unusually cheerful and he would soon warm up, he knew, when he got into his usual evening stables routine. He had decided to start early this evening, so that he could get back to the hostel for a shower before he took Angie out to the cinema. Luckily he had only three horses to 'do' today, as none of the other lads was away and the guv'nor was making Master Toby look after Watson during his holidays. He'd just drop in to Watson's box himself too, though, before he started work, he thought, just to check that everything was OK.

Thanks to Angie's friendship he was feeling a lot more confident these days. He was still worried about what Rory would do when he found out about the money, but he agreed with Angie that he should try to save up so that he could pay it back when his brother finally came out of prison. He'd been working as much overtime as he possibly could and had also taken an occasional evening job in a pub, which was tiring, but Angie's support made any amount of hard work bearable. He longed to tell her that he loved her but the time, he felt, was not right. He wanted to earn her respect as well as her friendship before he declared his feelings.

Another problem was that Jack Massam seemed to be taking her out a lot, too, at the moment, to proper restaurants and country pubs – but then he had a car and a lot more money. Liam's growing jealousy of the jockey was also inflamed by the knowledge that it would be Massam who would be riding Achilles in his first piece of serious work in a few weeks' time; and Liam was not convinced that the Yorkshireman had the ability or sensitivity to get the best out of the colt.

Achilles was a difficult ride. He tended to whip round on the gallops and was generally over-keen. When they started cantering Liam had to use all his skill to keep him settled in behind the others. One day recently, when the colt cocked his jaw and managed to get away from him for a moment, Liam felt such an exciting burst of power beneath him that it almost made up for the bollocking he received from Mr Kyle as a result.

As Liam limped on, through the fillies' yard and on to the last row of boxes down by the paddock, old Silverlight, Tod's dapple-grey hack, poked his nose over his half-door and whinnied softly in welcome. There was no sound, however, from Watson's box. That was odd, Liam thought. Toby's pitchfork and muck sack were clearly visible as usual. Approaching the box cautiously and peering inside he was astonished to see the boy crouched down in the straw, his head in his hands.

'Hello there! Is anything wrong?' he inquired hesitantly.

Toby looked up, startled, the colour flooding into his face. 'Er, no, no. I was just having a bit of a think, actually,' he replied, scrambling to his feet, obviously embarrassed.

'Is everything OK with Watson, then? I just thought I'd check. I've got so used to doing him myself, you see,' Liam explained shyly.

Toby nodded. 'He's fine. Thanks very much for looking after him so well, by the way. He seems in great shape. No sign of that laminitis he had before, is there?'

'No, no, none at all,' Liam reassured him, looking at the pony affectionately. 'He's a grand old thing, isn't he? Gets on a treat with my little two-year-old colt, too, you know. I tied Watson up next door when he was being shod the other day and he became as quiet as a lamb. The farrier couldn't believe it!'

'Oh, which colt is that, then?' Toby asked with interest, his embarrassment forgotten.

'The little Greek Dancer. Jacko we call him,' Liam glanced at his watch. 'I must be away to see to him right now. Why don't you come up and take a look at him when you're through down here? We'll be in the third box from the left, just past the clock.'

He liked Toby, he thought, as he headed back to the main yard. He was shy and obviously wary of people, as Liam was himself, and he certainly didn't throw his weight around as he could have done, being the boss's son. But there was clearly something bothering the boy. Perhaps he was ill, or even in love, maybe. Liam knew only too well how unsettling that could be.

He was pleased, when Toby appeared in Achilles's box a quarter of an hour later, to see that he seemed a lot more cheerful.

'He's a bit small, isn't he?' Toby observed thoughtfully. 'And not very friendly either,' he added as Achilles's black head snaked round and tried to take a nip out of Liam's jacket.

'Oh, being so disagreeable is only a game for him,' Liam replied affectionately as he unbuckled the colt's rugs. 'Some horses don't like being fussed over – like some people, I suppose. I'll just be taking the rugs off him so that you can be seeing him better.' He swept the heavy blankets off in one skilful swoop and flung them over the box door. 'There now, take a look at that,' he said proudly. 'He may be on the small side, but there's a lot of power in this fella too, I'm telling you.' He looked over at Toby, his eyes shining. 'We have a saying back home in Ireland: if we think a horse is something special, we say, "This one now, he'll change your address!" Well, Jacko here could be one of those. You wait and see!'

CHAPTER TWELVE

St James's Plaza Hotel
Lounging on Prince Hassim's great leather-upholstered bed, Lucy took a sip of the glass of champagne at her elbow and flopped back against the satin pillows. She had had time to smoke a small joint earlier, while she had been waiting for the chauffeur to pick her up at Elsinore Court, and was feeling more relaxed than she had done for some time. The past few weeks had been particularly hectic. She had never seemed to be in the same place for more than a few days and for once even she was tired of hotel living.

From an assignment for *Vanity Fair* in Palm Beach, she had flown directly to Rome for a picture session, then on to Scotland and the Isle of Mull. For several tedious days, while they waited for the weather to clear, she was trapped there, clambering in and out of fishing boats and being draped round bollards, for a feature for the *Tatler*. The money was derisory and she only did it as a favour to an old friend, an ex-model who was now the fashion editor of the magazine, and she got so fed up that she was stupid enough to sleep with the photographer. He was the latest magazine 'find': a young man of infinite ambition but, in Lucy's view, mediocre talent – and he had also turned out to be a very inadequate lover. Lucy suspected that he had only wanted to 'screw her', as he had described it, in order to swank to people about it afterwards. She also went to bed with a black actor she had worked with in Florida the week before one evening when they had both been snorting cocaine. He too turned out to be almost impotent, confessing that although he fancied her greatly he could really only 'get it together' with black women.

Both episodes were degrading and left her feeling self-disgusted and sexually frustrated, Lucy decided, as she took another sip of champagne. Through the closed door leading to Hassim's sitting-room she could hear the murmur of voices, talking in Arabic, interrupted from time to time by the shrilling of the phone. Ever since he had arrived from the airport earlier Hassim had been in conference with two of his most trusted financial advisers and when she turned up she had been shown straight to the bedroom. She hoped the meeting would not go on for much longer; after the joint and her experiences of the past weeks, she was beginning to feel randy. She knew, however, that Hassim had a typically Arab sense of time and, though he had insisted she be there by nine o'clock, he was quite capable of keeping her waiting for hours. She was about to slip her hand under her silk kimono and start to give herself a quick feel, as an hors d'oeuvre to the evening's fare, when she heard what sounded like moves towards departure in the next room.

Five minutes later Prince Hassim came quietly through the connecting door, looking grave and curiously dwarfed by his dark business suit. Lucy presumed he would change into one of the long white robes that he usually wore when they were alone together and which she thought made him look much more sexy. Arab dress enhanced his hawkish looks and gave him a definite presence; European clothes, on the other hand, made him appear much more ordinary, almost as though he was playing the part of someone far more lowly, a businessman or a run-of-the-mill commercial traveller.

'I must apologize for keeping you waiting,' he said softly, his eyes devouring her with relish. 'Particularly since it is some time since we met.' He sighed. 'My discussions this evening were, however, of great importance.' He turned away, starting to unloosen his tie, and headed towards the door of his walk-in wardrobe. Lucy suppressed a desire to giggle. His mixture of formal, almost self-conscious manners out of bed and rough intensity in bed always amused her. It was like dealing with two completely different people, but that did not bother her particularly. She wasn't interested in an emotional relationship with the man, after all, just a sexual one.

'I hope you are not too hungry?' he said when he eventually emerged. 'I have asked them to delay our dinner for a while,' he continued, pouring them both some more champagne. 'The video of Bahir's race this afternoon at Newmarket has just arrived and I wish to see that first.' He turned to her with an attentive look. 'No doubt you would like to see it too?'

'Not particularly,' Lucy replied, making a face. Having him standing there, so close to her, was making her feel randy again and she was also suddenly feeling very hungry. Hassim usually preferred to eat late, after their sexual congress. Lucy didn't mind what they did this evening, as long as they got on with satisfying one appetite or the other without further delay.

'Bahir is the horse I have in training with your father,' Hassim informed her, with a hint of irritation, 'the Sir Ivor colt. Have you forgotten? He had his first run today – and finished third, so I am particularly anxious to take a look at the tape. There was also a stewards' inquiry, I am informed.'

Lucy felt instantly contrite. 'Oh Christ! Daddy's horse! Oh, well, that's different.' She levered herself back against the pillows. 'Sorry!' she grinned. 'Sure. Of course I'd like to see it.' Third – on his first run! That sounded promising, she thought. It would be terrific if the colt turned out to have some real ability. Apart from keeping Hassim sweet it might also encourage other people to send their horses to Tod. At last it looked as though she may have done her father a favour.

It might not be quite that simple, though, she was forced to reflect minutes later, as Hassim replayed the tape for a second time.

'Look! That is where it happened. At the two-furlong marker,' he said, pressing the pause button on the remote control. He turned to Lucy, his eyes glittering. 'There, you can see quite clearly: my colt was bumped by that chestnut with the noseband. He lost his action completely. Look.' He pointed accusingly at the set.

Lucy put down her glass and peered at the picture. 'Well, there wasn't much room there on the inside, was there? – where Bahir was trying to get through, I mean. I'm sure the chestnut colt didn't bump him deliberately. They both seemed to veer off course at the same time.'

She had a horrible feeling that Jetlag, the colt Hassim was complaining about, was Alain's mount. They hadn't watched any of the preliminaries to the race on the video, so she wasn't sure, but it looked remarkably like him on the freeze frame. Her heart sank. Hassim was bound to make an issue out of this unfortunate coincidence. He was jealous enough of her relationship with the Frenchman as it was.

She did not have to wait long. 'Mmm ... it looks as though it was your friend du Roc who was the culprit,' Hassim said grimly, reaching over to pick up *The Sporting Life* and riffling through the pages.

'Yes, indeed.' He went on scanning the list of Newmarket runners and riders and flung the paper back on the floor. 'I cannot imagine why the stewards didn't take any action against him. He was clearly guilty of careless, even dangerous riding,' he complained angrily. 'I'll run the incident again.'

Lucy watched with some trepidation as he did so. As far as she could see it was just a question of both colts running a bit green, which was hardly surprising on their first outing. As Bahir, ridden by Jack Massam, moved up on the inside, he seemed to veer slightly away from the rails, startled perhaps by something in the crowd. At the same time, meeting the rising ground, du Roc raised his whip to encourage his colt, who then promptly ducked away from it, causing him to bump Bahir. Not surprisingly, both colts had temporarily become unbalanced but if anything, Lucy thought, it was Alain's colt who had come off worst, as he quickly faded whereas Bahir rallied again and ran on strongly to finish third, only a couple of lengths behind the winner.

'I don't know what you're making such a fuss about,' Lucy remarked languidly. 'It was no one's fault: both colts were just inexperienced, that's all. That's obviously what the stewards thought too. Anyway, Bahir finished like a train, didn't he?' she pointed out. 'You ought to be delighted.'

Why did the man have to be such a bad loser? Clearly his antagonism to Alain was affecting his judgement. She must try to bring his attention back to more pressing matters. She started to loosen the tie on her kimono.

'Of course I am pleased with Bahir; he ran an excellent race under the circumstances. That is not the point,' Hassim replied testily. 'Du Roc saw him going for the gap and tried to impede him.' He paused, glowering. 'Du Roc rode work on my colt the other day, you know. It was your father's idea: he wanted the man's opinion. Apparently it was very favourable.' He looked at Lucy accusingly. 'I imagine therefore that he saw the colt as a big threat to Jetlag today and was determined to spoil his chances. That's how I would read it.'

Lucy shook her hair, irritated. 'Oh, don't be ridiculous, Hassim,' she remarked, frowning. 'It was not Alain's fault. You're getting paranoid. Turn off the video and forget about it.' She swung her legs half off the bed and let the kimono fall open. 'Come here,' she ordered, holding out her arms. The sooner they could get on with the sex the better, she thought; it might improve both their tempers.

Hassim strode round the end of the bed, his eyes blazing. 'Why do you take that man's part against me?' he demanded angrily. 'It is disloyal and it offends me,' he added, his dark face taut with emotion.

'Oh, for heaven's sake! Don't be so pompous,' she protested. 'I'm not one of your possessions. Also, I can read a race as well as you can.'

She gazed at him seductively. 'You really are making a fuss about nothing.'

Hassim stared down at her, his whole body trembling with rage. 'Turn over,' he ordered.

'Why?' Lucy asked teasingly, opening her amber eyes wide.

'Because it is my wish,' Hassim replied. Bending over, he flung her over roughly face downwards on the bed and wrenched the kimono up over her slender waist.

Lucy, sensing her growing excitement, did not protest. At last she was going to get some proper sex to make up for the frustrations of the last few weeks, she thought with relief. She raised herself up on her elbows and wriggled her bottom lasciviously, waiting for Hassim to fling himself on top of her. He was bound to bugger her when he was in this mood. He always enjoyed it, and although the initial penetration was always painful, she did occasionally relish it herself. It was so much more brutal and intimate, somehow, than normal intercourse – exactly what she was in the mood for.

Instead she heard a slithering sound and, glancing sideways through a curtain of her hair, she saw that Hassim had removed the camel-hide belt he had been wearing round his waist and was running his fingers down its length.

'I do not like you defending du Roc, taking his part against me,' he hissed in her ear. 'I will not have it, do you understand?'

He slapped the end of the belt down hard on her buttocks, then started more lightly to hit her on either side, slowly, then faster, until the tingling sensation merged into pain.

'Ouch! That hurts,' Lucy yelped, trying to wriggle off the bed.

Hassim pressed a hand down on her back, pinning her to the satin sheet. 'Stay where you are,' he ordered. 'I haven't finished with you yet.'

Why the hell am I submitting to this? Lucy asked herself. It's really painful. Yet, at the same time, she realized that she was enjoying it. Sliding one hand down, she was amazed to realize how wet she was between her legs. As Hassim continued, panting with exertion, the rhythmical strokes began to transport her on to a new cloud of sensation, a blur of pleasure and pain, building up to an almost unbearable climax. At the same time, it also felt emotionally right, as though she was atoning for something – she did not know what.

'Say you are sorry,' Hassim hissed in a coarse whisper. 'Go on,' he repeated urgently, 'I must hear it.' He flicked the belt down harder. 'Go on. Do as I say.'

'All right! I'm sorry. I'm sorry,' Lucy heard herself cry out into the pillows.

The next moment she heard the belt drop to the floor and felt Hassim's naked body pressed against her.

'That is better. That is what I wanted to hear,' he said softly. Grabbing her bottom in both his muscular hands, he inserted his penis into her and rammed it in hard, then harder, ignoring her scream of pain. For a second Lucy imagined he was going to drive right through her, on and out the other side, doing her some terrible injury; then suddenly, with an overwhelming sensation of relief, she started to come in great protracted rolling waves of pleasure.

'Oh my God, my God! You bastard!' she wailed as she heard Hassim's own moan of triumph and felt his ejaculation pump into her. As though in a stupor, she flopped forward on to the satin sheets, her whole body dissolving beneath her.

The Old Rectory

It was as near perfect a May evening as she could ever remember, Kate thought, as she turned off the road that encircled Hazeley's green and crunched slowly up the Old Rectory drive. The change in the weather was unexpected – typical of the vagaries of the English climate; the previous few days had seen thunderstorms and squally showers over most of the country. It was also bell practice evening at St Peter's church on the far side of the green. Kate had heard the bells peeling out as she stopped at the T-junction outside the village; it was a sound that always made her feel nostalgic for childhood summer evenings, long ago.

The Old Rectory's drive was spotted with weeds, she noticed, as she parked her MG outside the stable block. She must remember to tell her mother to remind Davy to put down some of his lethal weedkiller. The trouble was that the old groom had not been too well this spring, and he and Lady Kitty had been concentrating all their efforts on keeping the herbaceous borders tidy and planting out the summer annuals that they had cherished from cuttings or seed in the greenhouse.

Getting out of the car, and leaning for a moment on the bonnet, Kate realized how glad she was to be home. She seemed to have been driving along motorways lashed with rain all week. She'd been to Warwickshire to photograph a successful showjumping family for the book, then down to Devon to take pictures of a couple who restored gypsy wagons for a feature in *Country Living*. She'd even called in at an Arab stud farm in Northamptonshire on her way up to Suffolk today. The most momentous piece of news, however, that she was longing to tell her mother, was that Achilles had done his first real piece of work this morning and it had gone very well.

She had also, with Lady Kitty's encouragement, made an offer for a small flat in Highgate. Driving past it one day and seeing an estate agent's notice, she had decided on a whim to take a look at it. When she discovered that it contained one large attic room, plus a small bedroom, bathroom and kitchen and quite spectacular views over the City and the rising ground of Kent on the horizon, she immediately decided she would like to buy it. It was expensive – £85,000 – for its size but she had managed to clear £46,000 from the sale of the Battersea house, and although £10,000 of that had gone straight into Achilles's training fund, she hoped that if she went on working as hard as she was at the moment there would be no problem in getting a mortgage on the remainder. Also, she wanted to get her share of the Battersea furniture out of store as soon as possible, since storing so much was proving expensive. The greatest advantage of the flat, though, was that it would be somewhere where she could be alone, unobserved, with Tod.

The purple lilac hedge flanking the end of the stable block was just past its best now, but she could still smell its sweetness, mingled with the scent of the stocks that Lady Kitty always planted beside the back door. It was only seven o'clock, so it was possible that her mother was still out in the garden. After dumping her things inside the back door, Kate headed out into the yard again and round the corner of the house towards the great copper beech tree, its young leaves glowing henna red in the evening light. The Old Rectory itself was looking particularly beautiful too, she reflected. The fading light flattered its proportions and concealed some of its increasingly obvious shabbiness. Apart from the continuing problems of the roof, the whole of the outside badly needed painting now with its traditional Suffolk pink wash. 'It will just have to wait until the autumn. Until we've sold poor Misty's little Grand Hotel filly,' Lady Kitty had told her the other day.

Glancing over towards the paddock, Kate experienced a severe pang of grief about the loss of the grey mare. Two days before she had been due to go back to the National Stud to be covered again by one of their stallions, she had gone down with a severe attack of colic and, despite all the efforts of the Three Swallows staff, had twisted a gut and had to be put down. Both the Levertons had been devastated.

Every time Kate drove up the drive now, although Misty had been away at the stud for over two years, she kept remembering how the mare had looked there under the trees, quietly cropping the grass. 'It's like losing one of the family,' she said miserably on the phone to her mother when she heard the news. 'Couldn't they have done anything to save her?'

'Apparently not,' Lady Kitty replied sadly. 'She was getting on a bit, you know. That didn't help.'

Pausing for a moment under the beech tree, Kate caught a glimpse of her mother over by one of the far borders. She was staking up some delphiniums, a tiny figure in faded dungarees almost obscured by the stalwart blue sprays around her.

Lute, followed more decorously by Liffey, saw her first and came hurtling across the lawn, leaping up, licking her face, sticking his nose up her skirt and generally giving her one of his more frenzied welcomes.

Her mother raised her head in the distance. 'Hello there,' she called out. 'I thought I heard a car and was hoping it was you. I'll be right over. We might have a drink on the lawn.'

'The weather's been playing havoc with the garden,' she complained as they sat, later, under the beech tree with their gin and tonics. 'It knocked some of the taller flowers for six and the weeds are growing like smoke.'

Her mother looked tired, Kate thought. Her face was more deeply lined than usual, and there was a preoccupied look in her faded blue eyes.

'I've got some great news,' she announced, cheerfully. 'It's about Achilles.'

Lady Kitty's abstracted look vanished and she turned to Kate excitedly, clasping her hands under her chin like a little girl.

'Oh! And what would that be, then?' she asked eagerly.

'Tod rang me this morning – caught me before I left. He said that Achilles had just done his first piece of real work – you know, a proper gallop, on the all-weather apparently because the last few days have been so wet. Jack Massam rode him and had great difficulty in holding him – the little devil really took off – but all in all Tod seemed delighted. He's going to work him with Bahir – that colt of Prince Hassim's who he's planning to run at Ascot next week – and see how they compare.' She leant forward excitedly. 'If all goes well, Tod thinks we might even see him on a racecourse some time in July! Isn't that amazing?' Propping her elbows on the table in front of her she gazed across the gold-streaked lawn to the paddock.

'I can't believe it, can you? It doesn't seem long since he and poor Misty were turned out together here, does it?' She looked sad for a moment. 'Anyway, Tod doesn't want to rush him,' she went on, more enthusiastically. 'He's got to be taught to settle a lot more before he sets foot on a racecourse, he thinks. But he wondered if you'd like to go and watch his next piece of work.' She made a face. 'I doubt if I'll be able to, I'm afraid – next week's going to be particularly hectic – but you can tell me all about it, can't you?'

Lady Kitty's eyes were shining. 'That's grand news, it really is,' she said delightedly. 'I knew the colt had ability – didn't I keep telling you? I wouldn't miss seeing him work for all the tea in China, but I wouldn't want him rushed either. Patience is essential at this stage. The little fella's got so much growing to do.'

She looked down for a moment at Lute, coiled on a cushion at her feet, her face clouding over.

'And will Tod be letting me know himself when the colt's going to be in action, or will he be leaving some sort of message with you?' she inquired casually.

'Oh, I expect he'll ring you direct,' Kate replied quickly, avoiding her mother's eyes. 'I'm sure that's more sensible than trying to arrange it through me.'

There was a silence, unusually awkward, between them. After a moment, Lady Kitty fished in the pocket of her jacket for a packet of cheroots and lit one slowly. 'Look, dearie, I don't want to interfere, but I'm not a complete *eejit*, you know: I do know what's going on. I know you and Tod are involved with each other and I can understand why: he's an attractive man.' She flicked a spent match on to the drinks tray. 'I can also see why you might be needing a man of his age at the moment,' she added reflectively. She leant back in her chair, exhaling the smoke very slowly. 'I'm sorry to coin such a cliché, Kate, but I just don't want you hurt again, that's all. It's not only that Tod's married – that's almost bound to lead to a problem, I'm afraid; but what really worries me is that I suspect he's a romantic, unwilling to consider any consequences his actions might have.' She sighed. 'I've met Myra only once and I can't say I took to her particularly, but she's a fighter all right. However badly she and Tod get on she wouldn't like the idea of a rival.' She poured out the remains of the tonic into both their glasses and turned to Kate with a weary smile. 'Right. There you are then: end of speech. I just thought it was time I said something. Might make it a little easier for both of us. I know you're not a natural deceiver.'

165

Kate picked up her drink and stared into the glass, her expression troubled. 'I never wanted it to happen, Kitty,' she said quietly. 'I don't approve of having affairs with married men any more than you do. You know that!' Her tone was indignant. 'But I just couldn't help myself: I just felt so incredibly drawn to him, right from the start. When I went over to Barons Lodge that first time and he showed me round the yard, I felt so close to him. Then, when he talked about Monique and how he felt when she was killed, and when I told him about Daddy and everything, we seemed so in tune with each other.' She frowned, her hands clenched on her lap. 'And then when he kissed me goodnight' – she shivered – 'well, that's when I knew I was lost.' She turned to her mother, her grey eyes shining. 'I think I am in love with him, Kitty. I'm sorry if that horrifies or upsets you but I just can't help it. I can't stop seeing him, even to please you. He's making me so happy.' She downed the remains of her drink defiantly.

Of course, she had really felt this way only for a week or so, ever since the last time they had made love, she realized. Up until then, her delight in being with Tod and knowing that he loved and valued her had begun to become tarnished by her frustration that they were not able to meet more often or openly. With the flat season now well under way, his visits to London had become rarer still and she could seldom risk ringing him up at Barons Lodge, but had to wait instead for his calls when Myra was out of the house.

Their last meeting, however, had been so memorable that all her reservations had been suddenly swept away. They had made love in Battersea, the day before she had finally moved all her things out, and for the very first time it had been breathtakingly successful. Their desire for each other became so strong during lunch that they abandoned the meal altogether and adjourned to the bedroom cluttered up with packing cases. Her mood was so loving and Tod stroked her and caressed her with such intense desire and tenderness that when he finally entered her and started to move, almost reverentially, inside her, to her joy and surprise, she began to experience a great rolling orgasm. This excited Tod so much that he climaxed almost simultaneously. As they shuddered and cried out together, Kate felt, for the first time in her life, as though she was actually part of another person, linked both body and soul. When Tod started to slip out of her again, she found herself clinging to him desperately, exhorting him to stay still. Taken aback by her own passion, she later tried to explain to him that she had felt she was losing part of her own body.

'I know, I know,' he replied, clutching her to him. 'You don't have to explain, darling. I feel that way too. I love you so much. You know that, don't you?'

He had not felt so intensely since he had lost Monique, he told her later as he lay back against the pillows, smoking one of his French cigarettes.

'I've never been in love with Myra, of course,' he said, with a hint of regret. 'She's always known that; we've never had any pretence. Right from the start we were a partnership – a partnership which we hoped would suit us both.' He sighed. 'It wasn't just that I was convinced I would never fall in love again. It was also that I didn't want to: I felt it would be disloyal.' He reached out to stroke Kate's hair. 'Can you understand that? I don't think Myra really knows what love is, poor old thing. She was devoted to her father, of course, and is very dutiful, but she somehow lacks the emotional equipment for anything more passionate.' He gave Kate a wry grin. 'Perhaps I shouldn't feel too sorry for her. Love, as we know, can cause infinite pain.'

'What about Marie Claire? Didn't you love her?' Kate asked with curiosity. Tod had told her about his long affair with Monique's best friend, describing her in such affectionate terms that Kate sometimes felt quite jealous.

Tod turned to her quickly, taking her hand. 'Oh, no! Not like this. She's been a marvellous friend to me, a real solace, but there was never any real passion between us.' He smiled at her boyishly, scarcely able to contain his delight. 'What I feel about you is totally different. I've fallen in love with you, for heaven's sake! I never thought it would happen again. Never.' He stared at her intently through the curl of blue smoke. 'I love you and want you and want to look after you. Just the thought of seeing you makes me feel ten years younger. Now that's love, surely?'

Recalling the scene gave Kate a shiver of delight. She glanced across at her mother who had been sitting in silence pensively stroking Liffey's snake-like head lying across her lap.

'Well?' Kate demanded, her eyebrows raised.

Lady Kitty turned to her with a resigned smile. 'Well, then. There's nothing more I can say,' she replied quietly. 'It would be churlish of me not to be glad for you. That sort of joy occurs so seldom – I know that.' She leant over, and took Kate's hand and squeezed it. There was no way the affair could continue without someone being hurt, of course, and she suspected that the most likely victim would be Kate. She got up abruptly, determined to shake off her sense of foreboding.

'Well, this won't do at all,' she said briskly. 'It's time for the dogs' dinner and ours, too, for that matter.'

Picking up her gardening gloves, she started to make her way across the lawn towards the house, both dogs trotting expectantly at her heels. As she stepped through the french windows into the drawing-room, the phone started to ring in the hall beyond.

'I'll get it,' she called over her shoulder to Kate. 'Bring the drinks tray in, will you, dearie?'

Gazing upwards at the canopy of purple leaves above her head, Kate closed her eyes and listened to the evening sounds all around her. The church bells had ceased but a blackbird was singing joyously somewhere near by and she could hear the purring of a wood pigeon in the branches overhead. In the distance, a couple of dogs were having a staccato barking match on the far side of the green.

It was all so peaceful, she reflected – in complete contrast with the swirl of emotions going on inside her head. What her mother had said was probably true – that Tod was a natural romantic – but that was one of the many things she loved about him.

It was true, though, that he could be irritatingly self-deprecating. It was understandable, in view of the setbacks and disappointments he had had over the past few years, but she did so hope that by loving him so much she would make his confidence return. She must encourage him to spend more time sketching, she thought. Those drawings of mares and foals he had in his Den were really very good: quite up to professional standards. Perhaps she should approach an old friend of hers who had a gallery in Notting Hill and see if she would consider including Tod's work in one of her exhibitions.

Letting her thoughts drift on she was startled by her mother's sudden reappearance. 'There's some worrying news, I'm afraid, dearie. That was Tod,' Lady Kitty's expression was concerned as she leant on the garden table.

'Heavens! What's happened?' Kate sat up, immediately troubled.

'There's a problem with Achilles's knee apparently. His off fore. He's developed some heat in it, Tod said. He sounded very fed up. He thinks it's just a banged knee but he's getting the vet to take a series of X-rays, just in case it's anything more complicated.'

'Oh dear, poor Achilles. Just when everything was going so well!' Kate frowned. 'How serious does Tod think it is?' she asked anxiously.

Lady Kitty shrugged her shoulders. 'I don't know. He just wanted to warn us that the colt may have to stay in his box for a week or so, which will set back his training programme, of course. Achilles won't like it one bit either, will he? We know how impatient he is.' She sighed. 'Anyway, Tod's getting him X-rayed tomorrow and will phone and let us know more then.' She pulled her cardigan around her more tightly. 'Come on. It's beginning to get chilly. How about a bath before supper? The water's piping hot.' She waited for Kate to pick up the drinks tray before taking her arm.

'I thought we might have our supper in front of the television tonight,' she said more cheerfully. 'There's that programme I so want to see on BBC2. You know, the one about Siberian tigers.'

'It's not good news, I'm afraid: the colt has chipped a bone in his knee,' Tod said grimly.

He had phoned the Levertons earlier and insisted on driving over to the Old Rectory after second lot rather than try to explain anything to them over the phone. 'I'm afraid it's more serious than we thought. I'll be over straight away.'

He spread the X-ray pictures out on the kitchen table so that both women could see them more clearly and pointed to a few flecks of white amongst the shades of black and grey. 'Look! There they are,' he indicated with his finger. 'Those are fragments of bone, just floating about in his knee.'

'But how did it happen?' Kate asked despairingly as she pored over the pictures. She looked so worried and upset, Tod thought with concern; he just wanted to fold her in his arms there and then and give her what comfort he could. Having been involved with racehorses for so many years, he was fairly immune to the sudden calamities that befell them, but he had to admit that he, too, felt considerable gloom. The little colt was so promising and the Levertons had both had such faith in him. He could hardly bear to tell them that there was now a possibility that Achilles would never get on to a racecourse at all.

'He's only a baby,' he replied bleakly. 'So there are bound to be structural weaknesses. He seemed spot on for his first piece of work but it obviously came too soon. He ran far too free, of course; that was the trouble. The bone must have shattered under the pressure, I suspect. Maybe I should have gone more slowly with him, given him more time to mature, but he seemed so keen to get on with it.' Tod shrugged his shoulders dejectedly.

'Now, stop it! Stop blaming yourself. There's no point,' Lady Kitty told him firmly. 'I've been around horses long enough to know that these things just happen.' She paused, looking at him anxiously. 'Can anything be *done* about it? That's what we ought to be discussing.'

Tod lit a cigarette and leant back against the dresser. 'I'm not sure, to be honest,' he said quietly. 'A year or so ago I would have said no, just bring him back here, turn him out and hope for the best – you might be able to keep him as a pet. He's not in any real discomfort, remember, but he'll certainly never race again. It happened to several horses I've had over the years and they were all finished. As racehorses, I mean,' he added quickly.

Kate and Lady Kitty were staring at him in dismay, their expressions frozen.

'But things have changed,' Tod went on. 'The past year or so has seen some remarkable advances in equine surgery.' He took a pull at his cigarette. 'There is a chance he could be operated on and put right. The same thing happened to a good filly of Gerry Carnegie's last year and he got her back on the racecourse. In fact, I rang him this morning before I left and asked him for his advice.'

'And? What did he say?' Kate asked impatiently, her face brightening.

'He suggested we try to get hold of this chap, Wayne Douglas, who operated on his animal. He's a genius, Gerry says, and the only vet he knows who can do this particular operation. It's called an arthroscopy apparently, and involves making a tiny hole in the knee joint and pumping the knee full of a saline solution; then they insert a tiny camera, take a look around, and pull out the bone splinters, one by one, with a pair of forceps.' He shook his head. 'I must say, Gerry made it all sound incredibly simple.'

'Well, we must contact this chap. What are we waiting for?'

'Well, there are a few problems,' Tod told her quietly. 'First of all, he may not agree to operate: he'd have to see the X-rays first, to make a decision on whether an operation is worth it or not.' He paused. 'Secondly, he's in Kentucky. Then, last but not least, there's the expense: none of the best vets are in it for charity, I'm afraid.'

'How much? How much did Gerry Carnegie have to pay him, do you know?' Kate pressed him, tight-lipped.

'All in all, Gerry says it cost his owners about three grand,' Tod replied. 'That included flying Douglas over here and back on Concorde – apparently he's a very busy man and insists on that. Then there were his fees and the cost of this special operating theatre he uses. It's somewhere in Surrey, Gerry says – not far from Heathrow, luckily. There's nowhere suitable at the moment in Newmarket.' He glanced from Kate to Lady Kitty, his brown eyes concerned behind his glasses.

'It's a lot of money, I'm afraid,' he added apologetically. He had no idea if they would be able to afford it. From what he had gathered from Kate, they had already made some considerable sacrifices in order to keep Achilles in training at all; and, attractive though it was, just by looking at the Old Rectory he could see that it was badly in need of a few coats of paint, not to mention structural repairs. Even if he had been in a position to lend them the money, which he was not, he very much doubted if Lady Kitty would have agreed – she was, he suspected, far too proud.

'Maybe, but never mind,' Kate said with determination. 'We'll just have to manage, that's all. I could take out a larger mortgage on my new flat, for a start,' she added thoughtfully.

Lady Kitty glanced at her sharply. 'We'll discuss that later,' she said. 'Is this operation guaranteed to succeed? That's what I want to know.'

Tod took off his glasses and began polishing them on his handkerchief. 'That I can't tell you. According to Gerry, yes, but I'd like confirmation on that. Gerry said his filly was fine afterwards – back on the gallops within weeks. Quite astonishing. She's been placed in a listed race this year, too. Remarkable.' He paused. 'But look, I really don't think we should raise our hopes too much until I've spoken to this bloke and he's seen the X-rays, do you?'

Lady Kitty began to lever herself up from the table. 'Absolutely right,' she said with determination. 'You get hold of him, then, as soon as you can and see what he says. If he thinks an operation would have a real chance of success we'll go ahead. Kate's right: we'll find the money somehow.' She stood up, looking around for her stick. 'We've got no option. That little colt was born to race, I'm sure of it. We can't let him down now.' She started limping towards the door. 'How about a stiff drink?' she suggested cheerily. 'I certainly need one. Then you must get back home, Tod, and get on to this chap in America straight away. The sooner we find out what our chances are the better.'

Barons Lodge

Carefully fastening the last of Southwold Jack's night bandages, Liam straightened up wearily and leant against the gelding's velvety neck. It usually gave him some feeling of satisfaction when he had 'set fair' all his charges for the evening and they were ready for their final inspection, but not today. He was feeling too apprehensive. Today was the day of Jacko's operation and he had felt sick with anxiety since first light this morning. Supposing the operation did not work, or that the colt responded badly to the anaesthetic? The staff at the Dorking clinic had reported that he had settled in reasonably well but were concerned about his temperament. 'We don't think much of his stable manners,' they had apparently reported to Tod on the telephone. It might have been different if he himself had been allowed to accompany him, Liam thought miserably. He had pleaded with Tod as hard as he could but he had been told, sympathetically but firmly, that this wasn't possible. Nobby, the travelling head lad, would take the colt down to Dorking in the box and pick him up again after the operation. Otherwise, the staff down there preferred to cope on their own; Liam was also needed at Barons Lodge, Tod had insisted. 'You know how short-staffed we are. Just before Ascot is no time for you to be taking a little summer holiday,' he'd joked.

He had not felt so anxious since he himself lay in the hospital waiting for the doctor's verdict on his foot, Liam thought as he straightened Southwold Jack's rug. Everything had been going so brilliantly, too, until Mr Beckhampton had been stupid enough to let Jack Massam ride Jacko in his first real piece of work. Liam was convinced that if he, or a more skilled jockey like Alain du Roc, had been riding the colt that morning, he would not have run so free and injured himself. He knew, at heart, though, that this was not fair and that his low opinion of Massam's horsemanship was partly prompted by jealousy. The jockey had been taking Angie out more than usual recently and they seemed to be getting on worryingly well. Massam would also have the ride on Angie's colt, Bahir, in the Coventry Stakes at Royal Ascot, which was giving the two of them further excuse to get closer. Only yesterday, when he was passing Bahir's box, Liam had glimpsed Jack's sandy head over the half-open door and heard Angie's peal of laughter as she led the colt out for first lot.

'You look as if you got out of bed on the wrong side this morning. Stop looking so sulky,' she chided him later in the morning as they jogged along with the string on their way back from Warren Hill.

'Look, Liam, I know what it's all about,' she added frankly. 'But you and I *did* go to the pictures the other day, didn't we?' She bit her lip. 'It's just that Jack's got a car and everything – it makes things a lot easier. Anyway, I enjoy his company,' she added defiantly, settling her filly back to a walk. 'I reckon you're just upset at the moment because of Jacko,' she went on, more warmly. 'I don't blame you, honestly. I'd be in a right state if anything like that happened to Bahir. But don't worry; I'm sure this operation will put things right. Anyway, just don't take it all out on me, OK? I'm your friend, remember?' She flashed him a quick smile before turning to talk to one of the other lads.

Of course he *was* particularly edgy at the moment, Liam admitted, as he bent down to pick up his grooming kit. He had tried to distract himself this afternoon by watching the racing from Sandown Park where Barons Lodge had had a couple of runners, but it hadn't helped. Behind the familiar images of summer racing – the runners streaming down to the start, silks fluttering, the close-ups of the triumphant winners, and the interviews with their connections – he kept seeing visions of Jacko, lying flopped out and vulnerable on his side, whilst a circle of strangers, masked and gowned, bent over him with their instruments. It was all so unfair, he thought angrily. There were so many moderate horses out there on the track, all of them hale and hearty, yet his colt, who he knew was something special, had to go and injure himself.

'It's incredible watching the horses come round after an anaesthetic. They try to get up, then just stagger around and fall down again, as though they're drunk. It's pretty alarming,' Charlie Kyle had told him yesterday, which had only worried him further. Charlie had been friends with a vet in Durban, apparently, and had watched quite a few operations, although nothing like the one Jacko was having. 'Don't worry! Equine surgery has come on in leaps and bounds since then,' he reassured him. 'Achilles will be fine, I'm sure.'

Liam leant against the side of the box and glanced at his watch. Where on earth had Mr Beckhampton and Sam Shaw got to? They should have begun their evening stable rounds a quarter of an hour ago and Southwold Jack's box was usually one of the first they visited. Suddenly, he heard footsteps striding urgently across the yard towards him.

'Liam, are you there?' Tod called out as he approached, clearly out of breath. 'I've just had a call from Dorking,' he reported, leaning heavily on the box door. 'I spoke to Douglas himself. The operation went splendidly. They got all the bone splinters out, just as they'd hoped. Isn't that amazing? Anyway, we can expect Achilles back in a few days' time when he's got over the anaesthetic.' He removed his glasses and wiped them with his handkerchief.

'Whew! I'm getting out of condition, I'm afraid,' he commented. 'But I thought you should hear the good news as soon as possible – I know what a state you've been in. To tell you the truth I've been more concerned about you than I have about the colt!' he joked, levering himself away from the door. 'Anyway, great news, isn't it? I must go and tell Sam before he starts on his rounds. We'll be back down here in a minute.'

Liam, still stunned with delight, turned towards Southwold Jack and impetuously flung his arms around the gelding's neck. Holy Mary be praised! His Jacko was going to be all right, after all. He couldn't believe it. As he buried his face in the horse's coarse mane, he wept tears of relief.

CHAPTER THIRTEEN

Ascot Racecourse

It was a humid grey morning, the first day of Royal Ascot, and already, by eleven thirty, the roads leading to the Berkshire course were clogging up with cars.

In an attempt to blot out her immediate surroundings, Kate was listening to a jazz programme on the car radio as she crawled along towards the Swinley Bottom roundabout. She turned up the volume for an old Sidney Bechet number, '*As Tu Le Cafard?*' It suited her mood exactly and reminded her of Georges and that first holiday they had spent together in the south of France, when he had initiated her into so many pleasures, including Sidney Bechet's playing, the Hot Club de France, Verlaine's poetry and making love after lunch. She could see him still, wedged in the window of their pension in Villefranche, in black T-shirt and jeans, blocking out the light from the bay and gesticulating to the tune, a cigarette drooping from his fingers. Kate wondered what had happened to him; she presumed he had married, become quite bourgeois even, as he entered middle age.

The prospect of going racing usually lifted her spirits, particularly if she was working, photographing horses and their connections as she would be this afternoon, but today she felt less cheer at the prospect. Accelerating across the Swinley Bottom roundabout, she caught a glimpse of the racecourse, its vast expectant stands and emerald lawns just visible through a gap in the trees, then swore as she was forced to brake fiercely to avoid colliding with a Daimler nosing out of a rhododendron-fringed drive on her right. It was packed with a jumble of fancy hats, grey toppers and intent faces perusing *The Sporting Life*; a cigar, clamped between two male fingers, poked out of one of the rear windows like the blunt nose of a gun. The occupants were not necessarily habitual racegoers though, Kate suspected: they were more likely to be devotees of this particular meeting, who, motivated by desire to be seen in the 'right places', would make their way to Ascot at least once this week in expensive new outfits, hired morning dress and the requisite Royal Enclosure badges.

Kate usually rather enjoyed Royal Ascot. Today, however, she was fighting off considerable feelings of gloom and despondency, entirely due to the latest problem with Achilles. She had almost begun to regret that she had ever agreed to her mother's scheme to get Misty in foal again or had the idea of keeping Achilles in training themselves. And she also, most certainly, wished she had never fallen in love with Tod. In fact, she was, she had to admit, feeling unusually and untypically sorry for herself.

Although it was only a week or so ago, she could barely recall the delight she had felt when Tod rang the Old Rectory to say that Achilles's operation had been successful. She and her mother had thrown their arms around each other, then opened one of the last bottles of vintage Krug that the Professor had sent them. They had discussed over supper when they would be able to get over to Barons Lodge to see the colt and what small gift they could take to Liam. The following day she had driven to London, feeling bouncy and cheerful and well able to tackle the extra amount of work she had taken on. She had also temporarily solved her accommodation problem, while she waited to see if the deal on the Highgate flat went through, by borrowing a small flat in Fulham from an old schoolfriend who had gone on holiday to Australia for a couple of months.

A few evenings later, when she had been out to the cinema until late, she was amazed to receive a phone call at about midnight from her mother.

'Sorry to ring you so late, dearie, but I couldn't go to bed without telling you,' Lady Kitty confessed shakily. 'Tod's been trying to get you all evening. We've got another problem with Achilles, I'm afraid. It looks like we're back to square one. The colt played up a bit when he was being boxed up to come to Barons Lodge and slipped on the ramp,' she explained. 'The Dorking people didn't think it was serious but when he arrived back at Barons Lodge, the knee was swollen worse than before.'

Kate felt as though she had been punched in the stomach. 'How on earth did they let that happen?' she wailed.

'God knows!' her mother replied bleakly. 'Anyway, he's haemorrhaged into his knee, it seems. It's full of blood and so swollen that he can't bend it properly. Tod sounded terribly upset.'

'He's not the only one,' Kate replied despairingly, flopping down on to a nearby chair. 'Well, what do we do? What sort of treatment does he need now, then?'

'Well, that's the trouble. There's not much we can do, apparently,' Lady Kitty replied. 'The only possible treatment is rest, continual hosing with cold water and the use of ice packs to try to get the swelling down. If that doesn't work, Tod says we've got to face the fact that he may never be really sound again, I'm afraid.' Her voice trailed off and there was a pause, both women obviously feeling too miserable to speak.

The previous evening, when Kate got back to the Old Rectory, Achilles was already back in his old box. She rushed to see him the moment she got out of the car and was appalled to see how wretched he looked. His head hung low over the bedding Davy had so lovingly forked around him, his eyes were dull and his lower lip was quivering. His coat was already beginning to lose some of its glossy summer bloom, she noticed, and his heavily bandaged off fore stuck out awkwardly in front of him. Even his attempt to nip her jacket as she went into the box to comfort him was depressingly half-hearted.

Later, over a subdued supper in the kitchen, Lady Kitty commented that Kate looked tired and she found herself snapping back that of course she was weary, she had taken on a lot of extra work after all, work that might not even be necessary now.

'It doesn't look as though we'll be paying any more training fees from now on, does it? Just vet bills, or worse!' She shivered with fatigue and despair.

Her mother came over and put an arm around Kate. 'I won't be listening to that sort of talk, Kate,' she said gently. 'It doesn't look too hopeful, I admit, but I've still got a feeling about the colt. I don't think he's quite done for yet. We'll get him better, even if I have to go down on my hands and knees and pray for it,' she added with a brave smile.

Kate's depression today was compounded by the fact that she had not heard from Tod for several days. He had promised to ring her after she arrived back at the Old Rectory but had then failed to do so. He was taking a runner to Windsor, he said, and would be going to stay with Basil and Pam Hunter in Fulham for the first three days of the Royal Ascot meeting after that. The others would all have gone out to a cocktail party by the time he arrived, so there would be plenty of time to call her.

When he still had not rung by eleven thirty, Kate felt so worried that she poured herself a large dollop of Scotch and was carrying the tumbler across the hall when she bumped into Lady Kitty.

'I've just let the dogs out. Why don't you take old Liffey up to bed with you as well as that nightcap you've got there? You look like you could do with something to cuddle!' her mother suggested.

Kate kissed her goodnight. 'I'm sorry I'm so edgy. It's just that Tod promised to phone and he hasn't. I'm just worried something's wrong, that's all,' she explained.

'I shouldn't think so for a moment. He probably just couldn't get to a phone where he wouldn't be overheard,' Lady Kitty replied in a matter-of-fact tone. 'That sort of thing happens in his situation, I'm afraid. Anyway, you'll be seeing him tomorrow at Ascot, surely?'

'Hmm . . . surrounded by "rabbit's friends and relations",' Kate replied unhappily. 'You know what the Royal Meeting is like: there'll be absolutely no chance to talk alone.' She shrugged her shoulders. 'Oh, well!' She looked down at Liffey and patted her head. 'Come on, girl, come and keep me company whilst I lock up and finish my drink.'

She paused for a moment in the open french windows, breathing in the warm scented air, and watched the whippet, standing alert at her feet, her nose twitching at the night smells, one ear cocked as an owl shrieked somewhere in the distance. It was amazing what comfort animals could give you, she reflected. Then she remembered Achilles out there in the darkness having to endure such pain and she wished with all her heart she could find a way to bring him some relief too.

There was absolutely no point in brooding about Achilles today, though, she told herself sternly. She had work to do. Crossing the busy Press Car Park now to the main entrance to the Royal Enclosure, Kate began to feel that she was rather underdressed for the occasion. She had bought a neat navy and white spotted silk dress, white linen jacket and navy Bally shoes on a flying visit to Options at Austin Reed the previous week. She had had so little time to shop recently, which was just as well, given the exorbitant prices of clothes she liked. She had made a quite definite decision, though, that whatever the weather she wouldn't be wearing a hat. She would be working, after all, darting around all afternoon, and couldn't risk the embarrassment of a hat blowing off and possibly frightening one of the horses. As it had turned out, that would be most unlikely to happen today. The weather was almost eerily airless and still.

All around her women were being decanted from the stream of cars and limos in an extraordinary variety of hats and elaborate, colourful outfits. A girl walking ahead of her, her arm tucked through that of a morning-suited male companion, was sporting an almost backless cerise and black striped taffeta dress with a hobble skirt that encased her bottom like clingfilm. She wore such high-heeled sandals that she was forced to lean forward as she walked, like some exotic stork.

As Kate waited in the queue to get her pass checked, she was nearly knocked sideways by a tall girl, swathed in blue organza, who looked more suitably dressed for a picnic with Marie Antoinette than for an afternoon at the racecourse.

'God, sorry! Can't quite measure my distance,' the girl apologized cheerfully, before bouncing off towards the Royal Enclosure.

Kate had not bothered to apply for the requisite badge. She would only be photographing people with their horses and horses did not get into the Royal Enclosure proper. She had never particularly liked the formality of the Royal Meeting anyway, finding the bulky officials who seemed to confront you at your every turn bureaucratic and forbidding.

She had just greeted a photographer acquaintance from the Express Group, working today for the William Hickey column, when his eyebrows shot up in delight under his ill-fitting topper and he hurriedly snapped someone behind her.

'Entry of the soap stars! Got 'em!' he remarked with satisfaction, as though he had just swatted several persistent flies. Turning round, Kate saw Bertie Diss, immaculate in a black satin topper and pearl-grey morning suit, walking towards her, followed by Sandy and another largish man who looked familiar.

'Who's that with Sandy?' she asked quickly.

'Larry Hagman, for Christ's sake!' The photographer was scornful of her ignorance. 'He and Sandy are old pals. She was offered a part in *Dallas* once, you know, but she turned it down – went on to do that other series.'

Sandy looked dazzling, rather like a lemon meringue pie, Kate decided, in a tight-fitting yellow silk suit, with shoulder pads and dramatically nipped in at the waist. On her head was an enormous white flying-saucer-like hat, sprinkled with white and yellow daisies, underneath which she wore her usual stuck-on smile. Catching sight of Kate as she sauntered past, she raised a hand in gracious, almost royal greeting.

'Hi!' she called out loudly. 'Good to see you! Work hard now. I'm relying on you! We're in Bertie's mother's box. Call in later, honey, if you have time.'

Kate found herself waving back. Despite her reservations, she had to admit that there was something rather impressive about Sandy. Her sheer chutzpah probably, as Geoffrey would say. They had finally had their lunch at Rockington one day in early May. The park looked enchantingly spring-like, dotted with blossom and lambs and the house, too, from the outside at least, was most impressive; it was so vast and old, like the house in Virginia Woolf's *Orlando*. Bertie, unfortunately, had been called away to London, Sandy informed them, but she was obviously primed to show them around herself. As they traipsed through the oak-panelled rooms, with their great fireplaces and mullioned windows, it was obvious that she was more interested in the commercial value of Bertie's family possessions than in any possible artistic merit they might possess.

'Yeah, sure that's a Gainsborough,' she replied at one point, in answer to a question from Geoffrey about a little portrait of a man with his spaniel. 'It's one of Bertie's favourites, as a matter of fact. Gawd knows why – the guy looks a real fairy to me! However, it's worth half a million bucks apparently. Crazy, isn't it? It's so *small*!'

Over the overdone roast beef at lunch, Sandy greeted all Kate's suggestions for the book with enthusiasm whilst at the same time insisting, implacably, that before she undertook any of these 'terrific ideas', Kate must photograph the list of subjects Sandy herself had drawn up. When Geoffrey commented that they all seemed to be friends of Bertie's or fellow members of the Jockey Club, she didn't disagree.

'Sure, that's the idea. That's what they like back home: the old English aristos – plenty of titles.' She flashed them a confident smile. 'Believe me, folks, I know.'

Kate decided there and then that there was very little point in arguing with her. She would take the pictures Sandy wanted, to the best of her ability, then she would follow up her own ideas without any further consultation. If Sandy didn't like them, she would just have to sell them elsewhere. There was no possibility, she realized, of any proper 'collaboration' on the book, and to continue to insist on it would only prove frustrating. She just hoped that Sandy knew the American market as well as she said she did, and that the US sales would be as good as their New York publishers were predicting. The enterprise would be worth it, she kept telling herself, if it made her some real money.

The Disses' racegoing seemed to consist of frequenting a series of boxes at all the smarter courses, interspersed with trips to the paddock if they had a runner or Bertie was stewarding. Kate would find the routine boring herself; she liked to have plenty of time on the track to browse around people, watching and observing the horses when they first came on to the course, or after the race was over. She had to admit, though, that she had been looking forward, more than she had realized, to seeing her family colours on show in the paddock. But it looked now as though that was never to be; the old Rathglin colours might as well have stayed packed away in the attic, she thought sadly, glancing across at the stands.

Out of the corner of her eye, she caught sight of Lucy Beckhampton, in an apricot-coloured suit, standing outside the weighing room with Alain du Roc. The girl kissed him briefly on both cheeks and turned to greet two other jockeys just coming on to the course before moving off gracefully. She looked remarkably elegant, Kate thought. Her slub silk suit was beautifully cut and her chestnut hair was piled on the top of her head under a particularly saucy black hat with a veil attached; as Lucy came closer, Kate saw that it was embroidered with tiny black butterflies.

'Hi there!' Lucy said, holding out her hand. 'I've been meaning to call you for months, but of course I never got around to it. I just wanted to tell you how much I liked those pictures you took of Alain. I thought they were great.'

'Thank you,' Kate said, gratified. 'I'm really glad you liked them.' Lucy was not only looking elegant, she thought, but so simply dressed as well; and unlike so many of the women here today she was totally at ease with her clothes. 'I like your suit,' she said warmly. 'It's such an unusual colour.'

Lucy smiled. 'It's from Valentino. It's Alain's favourite, too, so I'm wearing it today to bring him luck.' She smoothed her skirt over her thighs, pulling a face. 'He's just been telling me off about the butterflies on my stockings, thought – says they're *très vulgaire*. He's so bourgeois at times,' she complained, kicking up her leg so that Kate could see the clusters of black butterflies matching the ones on her hat, spiralling up the back of her stockings. 'I think they're rather sexy, don't you?' Lucy giggled, peering at her Cartier watch. 'Wow! I'd better get a move on. I'm lunching in the Turf Club tent, but it gets so hot in there. I thought I'd drop into the Sangsters's box first for a decent glass of champagne.' She frowned. 'By the way, you haven't seen Daddy, have you? When I got home late last night there was a message on my machine asking me to ring him urgently this morning at Basil and Pam's, but by the time I got up there was no reply – they must have already left for the course, I suppose.'

Kate's heart started thumping. 'No, sorry. I haven't seen anyone from Barons Lodge, I'm afraid,' she replied. 'They must be here somewhere, though. They've got a runner in the Coventry, haven't they?'

'Have they? Oh, God! Of course, *Bahir*! I nearly forgot,' Lucy grinned. 'I've been whizzing about so much this week, I've almost forgotten my own name! Thanks for reminding me.' She peered around her, short-sightedly. 'Right, must dash. Nice to see you – bye.' She turned and stalked over to a large, affable-looking man hovering near by, his pinkish face perspiring under a rakishly tilted topper.

Gazing after them, Kate wondered how Lucy would react if she knew she was Tod's mistress. She imagined that she would be surprised rather than shocked, possibly even delighted at any situation which could embarrass Myra. She knew from Tod how badly the two women got on. She was aware too that he loved his daughter deeply and would be happy if she and Kate could become friends. 'Lucy's so *flighty*,' he had complained once. 'She could do with a sensible friend like you.' Kate had been indignant about his remark at the time. She did not feel at all sensible, at least as far as Tod was concerned; neither did she think that she and Lucy had much in common. She liked the girl – she was not only beautiful but obviously warm-hearted too – but her whole lifestyle was far more hectic and louche than Kate would ever want hers to be.

She wondered again where on earth Tod had got to. Having heard what Lucy had said, she was now convinced that something was wrong. She just hoped fervently that it had nothing to do with her: that there had not been some sort of confrontation with Myra or anything like that. She seemed to remember that Tod was lunching with Stelios today, but she had no idea where that might be: there were, after all, so many restaurants and boxes on the course. But she wouldn't be lingering in any of them today, she thought ruefully as she headed for the Paddock Bar: she had work to do. It was just as well. Taking pictures was about the only thing that would divert her from her various worries.

Stella took another mouthful of dressed crab and looked around her. The restaurant was packed and though it was stiflingly hot, everyone seemed in a jocular mood, except for a small queue of latecomers who stood disconsolately by the door arguing with the manager and the harassed waitresses who were weaving their way through the crowded tables, plates balanced high. The lack of air was making people look more and more like the lobsters they were eating, pink and glassy-eyed, Stella thought unkindly.

She had always been in two minds about the Royal Meeting. The racing was brilliant, of course; it was the people she did not care for: the hordes of moneyed English who regarded the meeting as a purely social occasion and an excuse to dress up, and who were far more interested in fashion than they were in horses. She had decided to brave them today, however, as Kilmarron had a couple of runners, and since O'Donnell was not well enough to come over from Ireland, Nik was, as usual, in charge. They had high hopes that Rashkolnikov, their runner in the first race, the Queen Anne Stakes, might run well. The firmish ground, which would not suit some of the other runners, was definitely to his liking and he had been working with remarkable zest at home. The ground was definitely against their other runner, the three-year-old filly Isobar running in the Ribblesdale Stakes. She had not run at all as a two-year-old and was still rather leggy and backward, although she had won her maiden at the Curragh comfortably enough a few weeks previously. Nik had not wanted to bring her over today, believing that she was not yet ready for such a competitive race on ground that was too firm for her, but under pressure from her owner, a Californian dentist who wanted a runner at Royal Ascot, O'Donnell had insisted. There would be none of that when Nik took over the licence, Stella thought: owners would do as they were told and abide by Nik's decision as to when their horses should run.

Hot though it was, she was glad that at least her father had had the sense to arrange lunch in this restaurant – Number One Luncheon Room – rather than in some box or restaurant high up in the stands. Being at ground level and directly opposite the main entrance to the Royal Box, it was convenient for the weighing room and paddock. She glanced over at Stelios, sitting at the end of the table, squeezed into his morning suit, the contrast of its pale grey with his leathery tan making him look even more Levantine than usual. He was sporting an ostentatious pink pearl tiepin and his great head, with its oiled silvery hair, was inclined attentively towards Myra Beckhampton sitting beside him, impatiently scraping the meat off a crab's claw with her horsey teeth.

What on earth did the old fool think he was doing? Stella wondered again. Did he honestly think that he would get away with plans that might seriously jeopardize her own? Myra, she had already observed, did not seem to be particularly enjoying herself today. Although smartly dressed in a black and white silk coat dress and black tulle hat, she seemed ill at ease and restless, and had already left the table a couple of times to make a phone call. Stella had gathered that she was keyed up about the chances of the Barons Lodge colt Bahir in the Coventry Stakes, but she could not believe that this alone was causing her so much anxiety. There was obviously something else bothering Myra and Stella intended to find out what it was. It was high time, she realized, that she put her plan to befriend the woman into action.

She glanced across the table to where Tod Beckhampton was explaining something on the racecard to Mrs Palendiades, the wife of one of her father's shipping friends. Tod, too, seemed distracted today. He had eaten nothing, drunk a lot and looked up anxiously every time his wife had returned to the table after making her phone calls. He also seemed rather less attentive than usual to her father's heavy attempts at humour which he usually indulged. Maybe he had found out about Stelios's offer, Stella thought with some amusement. That would put the cat amongst the pigeons and perhaps save her the trouble of bothering to befriend Myra at all, but she did not think it was that. It was as though both husband and wife were united by some mutual anxiety.

Switching her thoughts away from the Beckhamptons and their problems, she looked across at Nik, his glossy black head bent attentively towards his neighbour as he poured her another glass of champagne. Neither she nor her brother had been given a particularly good draw at this lunch, she reflected. While she had to endure Basil Hunter, who had mercifully got up to go and talk to a trainer at another table, and that old bore, Mr Palendiades, Nik was sandwiched between Pam Hunter and Magda Borsche, a woman Stella knew he found particularly irritating. Magda was Hungarian, the widow of an American banker and art collector who had known Stelios for years. She was around sixty with a head of bubbly tinted curls and large animal-brown eyes that had acquired that startled look that so often results from a series of face-lifts. Although Stelios may have appreciated her coquettish, little-girl charm, Nik clearly did not. He did not particularly object to spoilt *pretty* women, provided they were under thirty-five and highly sexed, Stella knew, but mutton dressed as lamb, as he had once unoriginally described Magda, was not to his taste at all. The fact that the woman had absolutely no interest in horses did not help either and Stella was not surprised when a moment later he looked up and, tapping his watch, glanced meaningfully towards the door. He was anxious, Stella suspected, to get to the weighing room

184

before the arrival of the Royal party in their long fleet of open carriages made that much more difficult.

She was about to get up herself when Basil Hunter plumped back on to the seat next to her and put a hand on her arm. 'Stella! Please don't rush off,' he drawled. 'I wanted to ask you a couple of things about Devilry.' He leant back in his chair, gazing at her appreciatively.

Stella was irritated. Stupid man, she thought, why does he have to flirt with women in such a boring indiscriminate way? She really couldn't be bothered to answer his questions about Devilry now, she decided. There wasn't time. Also, although she very seldom sweated, she was beginning to feel uncomfortably hot and was longing for a breath of outside air.

'I'm afraid, Basil, I really can't go into all that now,' she replied. 'I have to be off. Why don't you have a word with Nik later? Please excuse me.' She smiled at him curtly before picking up her handbag and heading round the table in the direction of the door.

'Myra!' she said as she reached her chair, her expression visibly softening. 'We've had no time to talk, I'm afraid.' Her voice was silkily charming. 'I wondered if you'd like to lunch with me in London in the next week or so?' She put a slender hand on Myra's shoulder.

Myra jumped and turned round abruptly, her face flushed. 'Oh – er, hello Stella,' she said brightly. 'Lunch? Well, yes, that would be lovely.'

Stella's smile was feline. 'Good. Well, if I miss you later, I'll give you a ring.' She glanced towards the door where Nik was waiting impatiently. 'Right, I must be off. Best of luck with your colt in the Coventry.'

'The runners are going behind the stalls. They're starting the load-up now.' The commentator's announcement caused an immediate flicker of excitement all round and binoculars were raised and swung right, in the direction of the six-furlong start.

Kate was packed into the top of the stands in a section reserved for the press, with an exceptionally fine view of the whole course and surrounding countryside. Away to the left was the mile-and-a-half start and the long downhill sweep of the track to Swinley Bottom. In front lay the golf course and beyond a distant view of the Surrey hills. As Kate gazed to the right, towards the gates leading to Windsor Great Park, a jumbo from Heathrow came into view, cruising across the leaden sky like a great silver shark.

Minutes before, Kate had crammed hurriedly into the lift at ground level, packed with well-known owners, trainers and their wives. The favourite for the Coventry Stakes was Alcatraz, a grey colt owned by one of the Maktoums and trained by Michael Stoute; another fancied runner was Maurice Weinburger's chesnut, Rien Ne Va Plus, ridden by Alain du Roc. Apparently money had been pouring on to that all morning and Kate learnt with surprise that Bahir had drifted out to 8 to 1. 'Can't say I'm surprised. Did you see the way he was sweating up in the paddock? I reckon he lost the race there,' someone commented disparagingly. It was possibly true, Kate thought. Preoccupied though she had been earlier, even she had noticed that the colt was beginning to sweat up quite a bit in the pre-parade ring.

She had been photographing one of the real long shots in the race, a colt called Red Bird, owned by Lord and Lady Bradbury of Tern, relatives of Bertie Diss and two of the people on Sandy's list. Kate had taken several pictures of them standing outside the saddling boxes as their runner emerged, ears pricked, ready for the fray. While she was briefly chatting to them afterwards, she noticed Bahir being led around by his usual stable girl, a bouncy bright-faced blonde, who had been constantly talking to him in an obvious attempt to calm him down. The colt had appeared to be dancing around as though on springs, the sweat beginning to appear like foam between his quarters and his tail swishing irritably. Kate then suddenly glimpsed Tod walking slowly across the grass towards the paddock proper, preceded by a group which included Prince Hassim, a couple of bulky bearded companions, Myra and Charlie Kyle. Breaking off her conversation with the Bradburys, Kate sprinted impetuously across to the walkway leading down to the paddock and, leaning over the rail, managed to attract Tod's attention as he passed. His face beamed with joy as he caught sight of her.

'Kate!' he exclaimed, seizing her hand and gripping it tightly. 'I've been looking for you everywhere!' He lowered his voice. 'Look, I'm terribly sorry about last night. I just didn't get the chance to call you. We had a bit of a crisis.' He turned to acknowledge another trainer's good wishes for Bahir. 'Thanks, Guy. Yes, he is sweating up a bit, I know. But so am I for that matter!' He grinned briefly. 'I don't think it's serious,' He turned back to Kate.

'I'm sorry, I can't talk now – they'll be waiting for me in the paddock. Obviously I'll have to talk to Hassim after the race too, but whatever happens I'll get away after that. How about a quick drink before the Ribblesdale in that bar down by the paddock? There shouldn't be too many people we know down there. OK?'

He looked incredibly handsome in his morning suit, brocade waistcoat and black topper, Kate thought. He had exactly the right figure for such fancy dress, but her stomach was already churning again with worry. Had Myra found out something about them? she wondered. She wished that Tod had been able to give her a clue. He looked worried and rather flushed. Walking back towards the stands she realized that she was feeling uncomfortably hot now, her dress was sticking to her back and her feet felt swollen. She wished fervently that the weather would break and there would be a storm. The atmosphere and the tension combined were beginning to give her a nagging headache.

'The last of the runners are going into the stalls. That's it. They're all in now. They're off.' A hush fell over the stands at the announcement and once again all heads swung right. Kate could see very little as she stared into the middle distance just able to discern the posse of horses and multicoloured caps as they coasted downhill past the five-furlong marker, but as they came nearer she could pick out the grey, Alcatraz, running prominently on the stands but she could see no sight of du Roc's chestnut or the red and white cap of Bahir. As the volume of sound swelled around her she strained to hear the commentator's voice.

'It's Alcatraz now, Alcatraz still leading the field on the stands' side, followed by Darkness at Noon, Dancing Master, Red Bird and Rien Ne Va Plus right on the rails with nowhere to go. But here comes Bahir. It's Bahir now challenging on the far side.'

His words were drowned in cheering but as the horses surged towards the line way below Kate saw with amazement and delight that Bahir and Alcatraz were racing neck and neck, with Bahir seeming to inch ahead in the final strides.

'Photograph. Photograph,' the commentator boomed out.

Kate realized that she had been shouting out loud for Bahir, her headache quite forgotten. She couldn't believe it! It looked as though Tod had won one of the top two-year-old races of the season. Bumped and jostled on her way back to the lift, she hardly noticed the race-goers around her. She was so happy for Tod, so proud of him, and just wished that she had been able to watch the race with him, close by his side.

As the lift dropped downwards, there was an excited babble of conversation about the race.

'Can't remember when Barons Lodge last had a winner at this meeting, let alone a Group Two success, can you?' someone asked.

'Good old Tod! Obviously hasn't lost his touch after all,' another man remarked.

'I'm not sure Bahir got up, though. I think the favourite just hung on,' replied his female companion.

As Red Bird had not finished in the frame she need not bother to take any more pictures of him and his connections. She would take some of Bahir and Prince Hassim instead, Kate decided. They were hardly relevant to her book, but she might well be able to sell them profitably elsewhere and anyway it would enable her to photograph Tod as well. As the lift reached ground level, she was carried along with the tide of people towards the Winners' Enclosure. As Bahir was led in off the course his stable girl, who Kate seemed to remember was called Angie, was patting him ecstatically as they made their way towards the winner's slot. Judging by their applause, the crowds clearly regarded him as the victor, and Walter Swinburn, too, on the grey Alcatraz seemed in no doubt, walking quietly into the second slot. Jack Massam looked unusually animated, Kate noticed, his freckled face beaming as he slipped off Bahir's back. Dodging round a couple of other photographers, she took a few quick shots of Tod, standing there smiling broadly too, his hand on Bahir's neck as his travelling lad flung a cooler rug over his back. Behind him, Prince Hassim, his sombre face transformed, was accepting the general congratulations. As the result of the photograph was announced confirming Bahir as the winner, there was renewed cheering all around and Angie gave her colt another passionate kiss on the nose. At the same time, Kate observed Lucy Beckhampton, standing behind a gaggle of pressmen, turning to give Alain du Roc a sympathetic pat on the shoulder as he darted past her with his saddle. The next moment, swinging her camera leftwards, she got another glimpse of Prince Hassim's face contorted with anger as he witnessed this gesture. Lucy had better be careful, she thought with concern – the Arab was clearly a jealous man.

Presumably Tod would have to go off now to be interviewed by the BBC. Kate decided to try to push her way through the crowds towards the nearby Champagne and Seafood Bar where she knew there was at least one television. The whole area was desperately crowded but when she finally got there she could just hear Julian Wilson's familiar voice over the surrounding clamour.

'You've not had the best of seasons recently, Tod, what with the virus and so many of your owners going out of racing,' the commentator was observing. 'This win must give you particular pleasure. Does it herald a Barons Lodge comeback, do you think?'

Tod gave him his lop-sided grin. 'Well, I sincerely hope so. It's about time, isn't it? It's certainly what everyone in the yard's been hoping for and deserves. I've still got a first-class team at Barons Lodge, you know.' His next words were lost in a roll of thunder. Glancing towards the door, Kate realized that the sky outside had darkened dramatically and that people were already scurrying for cover. She would have to abandon the rest of Tod's interview, she thought, if she were to make it to the Paddock Bar before the deluge started. As she fought her way to the entrance, there was another loud clap of thunder and the rain started to hiss down in earnest.

She was still pondering on whether or not to make a dash for it when Tod himself came into view, loping along under a large umbrella. Darting out after him she grabbed his hand and let herself be pulled closer. 'Tod! Be careful!' she panted as he kissed her passionately on the mouth.

'Don't worry! No one can see us under this bloody great thing,' he reassured her, grinning. 'Come on though, we'd better find some proper cover. Whew! What a storm! It's almost tropical!' he commented, leaning back against the wall of the Tote building. 'Thank God the weather's broken at last. It's really been intolerably humid, especially in all this garb. I'm glad it waited until after the Coventry though. I very much doubt if Bahir would have performed as well in a thunderstorm.'

He tightened his arm around her as there was a dazzling zigzag of lightning and another clap of thunder. 'God, I'm glad to see you! I can't tell you how glad!' He looked down at her lovingly and squeezed her hand.

Kate smiled back at him. She felt immeasurably better now that she was just with him again. 'I was *so* proud of you winning just now,' she said happily. 'I was shouting my head off up there in the stands. People must have thought I'd backed Bahir to win thousands. Did you really expect him to run so well?'

Tod shook his head. 'Not really. I thought he'd give a reasonably good account of himself if he didn't boil over beforehand. I gave Angie Shaw full marks for preventing that. She handles the colt very well. Another crucial thing is that Jack rode him right this time. Brought him with a last-minute run on the wide outside. He's a bit of a claustrophobic character, you know. Hates being covered up.'

His face was still flushed with triumph and Kate was reluctant to bring him down to earth but she could wait no longer. 'Look, what's been happening, Tod? What's the problem?' she asked urgently.

Tod's face fell. 'What? Oh Christ! I'd almost forgotten in all the excitement. It's bloody Toby. He's disappeared. Gone AWOL,' he said despairingly.

Kate was ashamed to admit that she felt a slight relief. At least it had nothing to do with her and Tod – thank God for that.

'What do you mean, "disappeared"? What's happened?' she asked, puzzled.

'He was caught smoking out on the fire escape a couple of evenings ago, it seems – with his friend Giles. Matron caught them, apparently. Gordon, his housemaster, wasn't there at the time but when he sent for them both yesterday morning, they were nowhere to be found. They'd obviously done a bunk. Up to London, we presume. At least, that's the information Gordon managed to extract from the ticket man at Hadleigh Station.' He leant back against the wall as water cascaded suddenly from the guttering above their heads. 'Myra's going spare, as you can imagine.' He pulled a silk handkerchief out of his pocket and wiped his glasses. 'With all that going on I just couldn't call you last night, darling. I'm so sorry,' he said apologetically.

'Of course you couldn't, I quite understand. What a fearful worry,' Kate replied sympathetically. 'But I'm sure Toby's OK, Tod. He probably just panicked. I expect he'll get in touch soon.'

Tod made a face. 'I'm not so sure,' he said grimly. 'You see, when they searched his locker first thing yesterday morning, they found some dope, some marijuana. Well, that's absolutely *verboten* at Hadleigh. Gordon had no choice after that, I'm afraid. Toby's been expelled!'

CHAPTER FOURTEEN

Savoy Hotel

Crawling along the Strand in her BMW, hemmed in between buses and taxis belching fumes and an aggressive lorry driver who had just put up two fingers at her, Myra wished that she'd never accepted Stella's invitation to lunch. She'd always disliked London, even when she had worked there in the sixties and it was supposed to be 'swinging' – whatever that meant. Now it seemed an even more unfriendly, dirty and noisy place. The traffic jams were getting worse and there were foreigners everywhere, a lot of them black. As she was frequently telling Basil and Pam, she couldn't imagine why anyone chose to live there.

She was also, she feared, not looking her best. She felt as though she had been put through an emotional mangle by Toby and all the worry he'd caused by his disappearance and expulsion from school. Although he had rung them the evening of the Coventry, to say that he was all right and to stop them from calling in the police, he had not actually deigned to return to Barons Lodge for several days, saying he needed to 'think things over'. Myra's reaction to the whole business was a mixture of shame, anger and concern. Hadleigh had been her father's school, too; he was one of their more distinguished old boys, they were always saying. It was a slur on his memory that Toby should have got himself expelled. But she was also, of course, extremely worried about the boy. What was the matter with him that he had so little discipline and got himself into such bad company? she wondered. He had been very contrite when he finally came back to Barons Lodge, bursting into tears and apologizing for causing them so much worry, but he also insisted that he had been unfairly punished and had not actually been smoking anything other than ordinary cigarettes at school. Someone, he refused to say who, had 'planted' the marijuana in his locker, he said.

Since then, however, he had been sullen and withdrawn, refusing to discuss the matter with either Tod or herself. After much consultation with Gordon, they decided that the next step must be to get him into a crammers in Cambridge next term, to re-sit his O-levels. Much to her horror, Gordon even suggested they take him to a psychiatrist. 'Toby's exactly the sort of fragile personality who could be attracted by the drugs scene,' he warned. 'Even if he's living at home, you'll have to keep a very careful eye on him. I think both you and he are going to need some help.'

The other infuriating thing about all this fuss with Toby, of course, was that it meant that her plans with Stelios would have to go on 'hold'. An incident a few weeks ago, just before Royal Ascot, had further strengthened her resolve to take him up on his offer. Going along to the Den one evening to tell Tod that supper was ready, she had inadvertently overheard the end of the telephone conversation he had been having.

'*Ça me plaît beaucoup. A tout à l'heure,*' he said softly, before ringing off. She'd frozen, her heart pounding, outside the door. She couldn't believe it: he'd obviously taken up with that French woman, Marie Claire, again, which would explain why he'd been paying all those visits to London to his eye specialist recently. She had been aware of this affair for years, but after an initial storm of jealousy had decided that her best course of action was not to confront him but just accept what he was up to. After all, Marie Claire was heavily married, too, to an extremely rich and permissive husband; she was hardly likely to throw all that away for an insular life in Newmarket with Tod and horses, in which she had no interest. Also, as Myra had to admit to Pam, Tod was a great deal more interested in sex than she was herself and was bound to look for some outlet somewhere over the next few years. It was probably more sensible therefore to let him have his 'bit on the side', as Basil crudely put it, with someone safe who had no desire to disrupt the status quo.

She found herself surprisingly irritated, though, by this recent evidence that the affair was still continuing. But when she thought about it more calmly, she realized that it was rather convenient. She'd had considerable feelings of guilt about even thinking of leaving Tod for Stelios, but if he was still carrying on with Marie Claire, this was ridiculous – it would serve him right. The problem now was that, although she had decided to accept Stelios's offer, it must remain a secret for a while. Given his current instability, she could not possibly risk breaking the news to Toby until he had sorted himself out and taken his exams again. She was sure that Stelios would understand. Nevertheless, the last few weeks had been incredibly wearing, she brooded, as she swung right, across the traffic, into the forecourt of the Savoy. She couldn't imagine why Stella had asked her to lunch anyway. She had never even suggested it before. But perhaps it was fortunate timing. It would not only be a distraction but also provide an excellent chance to get to know the girl better. She knew that she did not get on well with her father but perhaps that was because they were too alike. Myra had always rather admired Stella – both the way she looked and her determination and professional skills. She had, after all, built up Mountclare into one of the most success-ful small studs in Ireland. If Myra was going to manage Ballinvale herself, Stella's advice and support would be invaluable.

Jerking on the handbrake, she stepped out of the BMW and handed her keys to the nearest doorman. 'Park this for me, would you? I'm running late,' she said imperiously, smoothing down the skirt of her Aquascutum suit and heading for the swing doors.

Stella, installed in the River Room at a table by a window, seemed genuinely glad to see her. She put down the copy of the American bloodstock magazine *Bloodhorse* that she'd been reading and held out her hand with a smile.

'Myra! Hello! Come and sit down. I'm so glad you could make it,' she said graciously. 'I've just been doing my homework on a young Blushing Groom stallion that I'm interested in,' she added, indicating the magazine. She was looking very striking, Myra thought, in a short-sleeved black linen shift and a pair of bold jet and gold earrings.

Immediately ordering them both a glass of champagne, Stella asked a few perfunctory questions about Myra's journey before proffering her the menu, and insisting she ordered anything she fancied.

'I'm just having melon, followed by the crab cake,' she announced. 'It's far too hot today for me to have much of an appetite. But please have something more interesting yourself.' When Myra had finally decided on dressed crab followed by grilled sole, Stella summoned the wine waiter and ordered a bottle of Pouilly Fumé without even bother-ing to look at the list.

'It's one of the better Loire wines they have here,' she commented, leaning back with a feline smile. 'Right, now we can relax.' She twisted her sleek head sideways. 'You're definitely looking better than the last time I saw you at Ascot,' she commented. 'I was concerned about you that day – you seemed a little on edge. Mind you, I do know about the strain of having a fancied runner. It's even worse when you've bred it yourself, I can assure you!' Disarmed by such unexpected concern, Myra found herself confessing that it had not been Bahir's presence in the Coventry line-up that had been worrying her, but Toby's disappearance and the trouble he'd got himself into.

'Of course, he came back eventually, but we were worried sick that day, I'm afraid,' she explained. 'Anyway, I do hope that Tod and I didn't cast too much of a blight over the proceedings,' she added more briskly.

'No, no of course not,' Stella replied. 'I'm sure no one else even noticed that both of you seemed – well – a little tense. I'm sure Father didn't. But then he's not the most sensitive of mortals, is he?' She picked up her spoon and carved a delicate sliver from the inside of her melon. 'I'm amazed, you know, at the capacity children seem to have for causing their parents worry and pain,' she continued in a conversational tone. 'I have absolutely no desire to be a mother myself – it seems so unrewarding. All those years of effort and devotion and then they invariably turn against you. Give me horses or dogs any day. Handle them with affection and firmness from the start and they never let you down, do they?' She raised her dark, unplucked eyebrows. 'But I'm sure your black sheep will be all right,' she continued. 'He's probably just hit a difficult patch – adolescence and all that. What are you planning to do with him now?' she inquired politely.

Again, her interest was seductive and Myra found herself explaining how they were going to try to get Toby into a crammers. 'It's important he gets good results. He wants to be a vet, you see. It was his idea, not ours. He thought it would be such a useful qualification to have if he was going to be a trainer,' she explained. She took a final sip of champagne. 'All I really want is for him to become a good enough trainer to take over Barons Lodge one day.' If only Stella knew how I intend to make sure that we still own Barons Lodge when that day dawns, she thought to herself with a certain amusement.

Stella, however, was still regarding her with disconcerting concern. 'Well, if there's anything I can do to help, just let me know,' she said briskly, pushing away her plate. 'Send him over to Mountclare some time when he's a bit older,' she suggested. 'We'll soon get him into shape. I was a great admirer of your father's, you know,' she went on before Myra could respond. 'I can quite see why you'd want your son to carry on the family tradition. I remember the first time I ever went to Newmarket. I must have been about ten. Sir Digby had two winners that day, I recall; one of them was a light-framed bay, by Connaught, in the Wood Ditton. Anyway, they were both beautifully turned out. That's what impressed me most, I remember. It's so important, don't you think?' She took a sip of her wine.

'I most certainly do,' Myra replied warmly. 'Tod's nothing like so fussy as my father was, I'm afraid. Left to himself, he'd have all our animals trailing round unplaited with their tails unpulled.' She made a face. 'Luckily, we've got a very good assistant at the moment. Chap called Charlie Kyle.'

'Mmm, don't think I've come across him,' Stella replied vaguely, as though she had suddenly lost interest in the conversation.

She'd been talking too much about herself and her preoccupations, Myra thought, and immediately asked about Devilry and his chances in the Eclipse at Sandown in a few days' time. Stella answered politely enough, with obvious enthusiasm for the colt, but Myra, with long experience of fending off inquiries about a fancied horse when there was a problem, sensed that she was not entirely happy about Devilry's well-being. She went on to ask about Mountclare and said how much she would like to visit the place one day.

'Ah, yes, of course,' replied Stella with alacrity. 'That's one of the reasons I wanted us to have this lunch – so that we could fix something up. I imagine you come over to Ireland quite often, don't you? I'm sure I've seen you at Goffs?'

'I doubt it,' Myra replied bitterly. 'I used to go over every year with Daddy, of course, and indeed with Tod some years ago, but he hasn't bothered recently.' Her mouth twitched down at the corners.

'Well, that will have to change,' Stella replied firmly. 'Anyway, if you are coming over, let me know and come on down to Tipperary for a few days.'

She went on to describe in some detail the various mares she had at Mountclare and possible mating plans she had for them in the future, but as Myra was finishing her sole she broke off suddenly and leant forward, as though something had just occurred to her.

'That's enough of all that,' she said abruptly. 'You'll be able to see it all for yourself when you come over.' She paused. 'I've been meaning to ask you – I nearly forgot – have you heard from Father recently?' she asked casually, her eyebrows raised.

Myra started. 'Er, no,' she replied warily. 'Not since Ascot. Why do you ask?'

Stella shrugged her shoulders. 'Oh, I just wondered. I know you and he keep in touch. He rang me yesterday from Athens. I wasn't here but he left a message to say that he was on his way to New York, to attend some charity do with that woman Magda Borsche. I was rather surprised, as I know he's planning to be at Sandown on Saturday. I just wondered if you knew what he was up to?' She fixed Myra with her intense blue eyes.

'No, why should I?' Myra replied defensively. 'Anyway, I don't understand. Magda Borsche? Who's she?'

Stella looked amused. 'She was at Father's lunch at Ascot. She sat next to Nik and chattered non-stop about nothing and made eyes at all the men. Surely you remember? She's Hungarian. Her last husband was a banker, a friend of Father's, but he died a few years ago. So she's on the loose!'

Myra remembered now, of course. She had been too preoccupied that day to notice much about anyone at the table, except for her immediate neighbours, but she did recall Stelios introducing her to a petite, overdressed woman who he said was a friend from New York. 'Oh *her*!' she replied, disparagingly. 'Yes, I remember her. Seemed rather a silly woman to me. Certainly didn't know anything about horses.'

'I think men are more her line. Or perhaps I should say husbands,' Stella replied evenly. 'She's had several, I believe, and it looks as though she's got Father in her sights, God help him! Still, he must be keener on her than I thought. It's unlike him to fly all the way to New York just to attend some charity function.'

Myra was experiencing a certain sense of shock. Was it possible that she had a rival in Stelios's affections? She couldn't believe it. The woman was an *idiot*. She'd never be able to run a stud farm. She must be careful, though, not to over-react to any of this information. After all, in Stella's eyes, why should she be particularly interested? 'You're not really saying that there's anything going on between your father and Magda, are you?' she asked, as innocently as she could manage.

'Who knows?' Stella said airily. 'Father's probably getting lonely, you know, and could well be thinking of marrying again. It's nearly ten years now since my stepmother, Elena, died, you know. I wouldn't put it past him, would you?'

Myra's heart was thumping uncomfortably. She had the perfect opportunity now to ask Stella how she would react if Stelios did remarry. She'd better make the best of it. 'Would you mind particularly if Stelios did decide to marry again? Not necessarily Magda, I mean, but someone else, perhaps?' she asked nervously, her long nails digging into the palm of her hand under the table.

'I couldn't care less what he does, as long as it doesn't interfere with any of my plans for Mountclare,' Stella replied tartly. 'Let's just hope that Magda isn't pursuing Father too seriously,' she went on more cordially. 'Anyway, if she is, I think I know how to put her off.' She smiled.

'Put her off? How?' Myra asked eagerly, unable to conceal her interest.

'By telling her about the Fairyhouse curse.'

'What on earth's that?' Myra's expression was genuinely puzzled.

Stella leant forward confidentially. 'If I tell you, you won't ever mention it to Father, will you? He would be very upset if he knew I'd told you. He doesn't even know I know, you see. Do you promise?'

'Of course I won't say anything to Stelios if you don't want me to. You have my word,' Myra reassured her.

'It all happened one day after the races at Fairyhouse,' Stella began, in a low meaningful voice. 'Father's car skidded in the mud as he and Mother were leaving and he hit some old tinker woman's lurcher – hurt its leg, apparently. The woman was hysterical.' She made a face. 'Father offered her money for the vet's bill, etc. At first she refused, then she agreed to accept if she could read his palm. He wouldn't have any of that, but Mother insisted – thought it might placate the woman, I suppose.' She took a slow sip of her coffee. 'She told Father that he'd be very successful, make a lot of money in foreign lands – all that sort of nonsense.' Her eyes narrowed. 'But then she gave him a warning. He brought bad luck to women, she said. He would marry three times, she prophesied, and all his wives would meet with accidents or painful deaths' – she paused – 'particularly the last one,' she added gravely.

'Well, at that point, apparently, Mother got into one of her rages and ordered Father to drive off. She told the gypsy she had no business inventing such rubbish: it was evil. But the woman was unrepentant. 'Your wives will be cursed, all three of them,' she called out after them as they drove off. Mother was furious, and she asked Father to put the whole incident right out of his mind. And as far as I know, he has. He's certainly never mentioned it to either Nik or myself. It was our grandfather who told us.' She looked thoughtful for a moment. 'I don't suppose he has forgotten it though, do you? I know those racecourse tinkers. I don't usually believe a word of their predictions but you have to admit that in Father's case the old crone got it right.' She paused, her face grave. 'I mean, poor Mother was drowned, as you know, and Elena, of course, died of particularly painful cancer.' She shook her head. 'God knows what fate awaits the third Mrs Alexandros – I dread to think!' She glanced at Myra. 'Anyway, it's all very odd, isn't it? It certainly could be enough to put Magda off, I'd have thought. She's bound to be superstitious – you know what Hungarians are like.' Before Myra could comment, she turned and signalled to the waiter to bring the bill.

Myra found herself shivering suddenly, despite the heat of the room. What on earth should she make of such an extraordinary story? She was not at all superstitious as a rule; she had no time whatsoever for gypsies' warnings and crystal-ball gazing or any of that sort of twaddle. She had to admit, though, that in this case Stella was right. The woman's prediction, about Stelios's first two wives at least, did seem to have come true. That really was rather spooky.

'I'd leave well alone, Stella, if I were you,' she replied sharply. 'What happened that day at Fairyhouse sounds unpleasant, I grant you; I'm not surprised that Stelios has managed to put it out of his mind. But I'm sure one shouldn't take it too seriously. It's just an extraordinary coincidence that she got it right – about your mother and Elena, I mean.' She pressed her napkin to her lips with shaky fingers. 'And I really can't believe that Stelios has got any real interest in that Borsche woman, either. I'm sure you've got that bit wrong.'

Stella extricated a gold fountain pen from her handbag and laid it carefully on the table. 'Really? Do you think so?' She raised her eyebrows. 'Well, let's hope you're right. I can't abide the woman myself! I probably won't say anything to her, though. It's really none of my business. If Father wants to go and make a fool of himself, let him.' She glanced at her watch. 'I'll have to dash now, I'm afraid.' She gave Myra a dazzling smile. 'I have enjoyed this. We must do it again some time.' As the waiter brought the bill, she sat back licking her lips, like a cat who has just tasted cream.

Thirsk Racecourse
As the horses surged past the winning post in the setting sun, Charlie Kyle's binoculars lingered on the Barons Lodge runner, Charcoal Burner, who was finishing way down the field.

'Oh well, that's that!' Charlie said with resignation, turning to Jack Crow at his side. 'The blinkers didn't seem to make any difference at all, did they? He just seemed to pack it in again, in the last furlong – did you notice? Absolutely hopeless! Well done, Mark!' He swung round to congratulate Mark Tennent, the young Newmarket trainer whose expensive Arab-owned colt had just won the six-furlong race.

'I'm not entirely convinced that your horse is ungenuine, you know,' Jack Crow remarked thoughtfully. 'I don't think he really gets five furlongs, let alone six – except perhaps on very fast ground.' He grinned. 'I think he's a four-furlong specialist. You get 'em sometimes, you know.'

Charlie snorted. 'That's a pretty charitable view. I'd say he was just chicken-hearted myself. Still, you could be right; he certainly showed blistering early speed again, didn't he?'

He looked around him at the attractive little racecourse, with its well-kept buildings and neat beds of flowers. Despite Charcoal Burner's dismal performance, he liked coming to Thirsk, particularly for the evening meetings in the spring and early summer. There was a friendliness and informality about the place, as there was at many of the small northern courses, which he often found missing down south. Also, thanks to Jack and Julie Crow, he'd made a few friends amongst some of the local trainers and farmers in and around the Vale of York.

Jack Crow paused and looked down at his racecard. Around the Winners' Enclosure people were already turning to applaud Mark Tennent's winner as he was led in by his smiling lad.

'Mmm, another million-dollar yearling, pot-hunting up north,' he remarked, frowning. 'God knows what Tennent is doing running him over six furlongs, though. Judging by his pedigree he should get at least a mile and a quarter and he was finishing like a train.'

'Tennent doesn't know his arse from his elbow about the right trip for his horses, if you ask me,' Charlie replied, grinning. He dug his friend in the ribs. 'Still, he did manage to win today, didn't he? Which is certainly more than we did.' He swung round, shielding his eyes from the dipping sun. 'Well, I'd better go and have a word with old Ted and see if the horse is all right. I'll see you later, up in the Members' Bar – OK?'

Jack's reference to the winner's high price tag was a common gripe amongst northern trainers these days, Charlie mused. With so many expensive Arab-owned horses coming up from the south to compete for even the most meagre of prizes, it was becoming harder and harder for small northern owners and trainers ever to win a race at all. One of the answers, of course, was to get the racecourses to put on more claiming and auction races for horses that had been bought cheaply at the sales. That at least would give the smaller-time players the chance of picking up a race or two.

Crossing the paddock, he came face to face with Charcoal Burner's rider, Ted Thorrowby, a veteran lightweight jockey now on the verge of retirement, whom Barons Lodge had had to book at the last minute, as Jack Massam was riding another, more fancied runner down south that afternoon. Thorrowby, scuttling wearily along with his saddle, was looking even more doleful than usual.

'Our lad didn't exactly cover himself with glory, did he?' Charlie remarked cheerfully.

'He's fucking useless,' Thorrowby replied with feeling. 'Practically pulled himself up after four furlongs. Got about as much guts as a toad. You won't get me riding the bugger again, I promise you that!'

'Can't say I blame you. Thanks anyway.' Charlie clapped him on the shoulder before striding on towards the saddling boxes. He could see in the distance that Liam had already started washing Charcoal Burner down. Charlie looked the horse over carefully before running his hands down his forelegs.

'By the way, where's Nobby got to?' he inquired, referring to Nobby Taylor, Barons Lodge's travelling head lad.

'He's gone to get a drink, Mr Kyle. Said he needed to drown his sorrows,' Liam replied quietly.

The boy looked so woebegone, Charlie noticed with concern. Charcoal Burner's performance wouldn't have improved anyone's mood, but it was not that that was making the lad look so miserable; it was the latest mishap with his little Greek Dancer colt, Charlie suspected. Everyone in the yard knew how devoted Liam was to his Jacko. Charlie also suspected that Liam was very attached to Angie Shaw and that things were not going very well for him there, either. Angie was going out more and more with Jack Massam these days and there was a rumour going round the tack room last week that the two of them might be planning to get engaged. Although strict with all the Barons Lodge staff and loth to have favourites, Charlie had considerable respect for Liam's capacity for hard work as well as his skill as a rider, and he felt genuinely sorry for the boy. 'You're still worrying about your little black colt, I can see, Liam. How is he, by the way?' he asked solicitously. 'I gather you go over to the Levertons every Sunday to see him.'

Liam put down his scraper and ducked under Charcoal Burner's neck. 'He's in a terrible state, sir. Not happy in himself at all,' he replied wanly. 'The knee's still awful swollen. The poor fella can hardly bend it.'

Charlie took hold of Charcoal Burner's bridle as Liam got to work on his quarters. 'It's always a mistake to get too attached to any animal, I'm afraid,' he said sadly. He patted the horse's neck. 'Even old Charky here has got his fans. His owner should have got rid of him last back-end if he'd had any sense, but he wouldn't. Anyway, go and get yourself a beer and something to eat when he's dried off. You've got a long journey home.' He reached in his pocket for some change. 'Here's a few quid. Go and treat yourself. And see you in the morning. I'm off after the next race myself.'

He didn't envy Liam his journey home, Charlie thought, as he made his way back to the stands. Charcoal Burner had shared a box up with Mark Tennent's two runners, the second of which didn't run until the last race. That meant that the boy wouldn't be leaving the racecourse until well after dark and wouldn't get back to Barons Lodge until the early hours of the morning. In his current depressed mood, it would also be particularly galling for him to have to travel with Tennent's lads, still jubilant about their winner.

Charlie hurried round to the front of the stands and bounded up the steps towards the entrance to the Members' Bar. As he went through the door, a couple of serious-looking punters on their way down to the bookmakers brushed past him, knocking him against a woman standing quietly looking out over the course. Apologizing, he quickly realized that it was someone he knew, Beth Arnott, Keith Warrender's old girlfriend, looking tanned and almost girlish in a round-necked, blue and white striped cotton frock, her dark hair tied back with a white ribbon.

'Well, well, it's Charlie Kyle,' she said with a wide smile. 'I thought I saw you in the paddock. Well, how are you, then? I've been wondering how you were getting on.' She moved her white jacket off an adjoining seat. 'Come and sit down. I was just keeping this seat for Bob. Goodness knows where he's got to – said he was just going to check if our dog was all right in the car. It's ever such a warm evening.'

Charlie sat down beside her. 'I've been meaning to get in touch with you since we met. But you know how it is in the middle of the season.' He pulled a face. 'Not that there's anything to report on the Keith Warrender front, I'm afraid. Look, can I get you a drink? What would you like?'

Beth held up her hand. 'No, thanks. I've not touched my lager and lime as it is – I'm not much of a drinker. No luck, then? With Keith in Australia, you mean?' she asked sympathetically.

Charlie nodded. 'That's right, absolutely none. I sent two letters to the address you gave me and both were returned, person unknown. Then I wrote to this bloke I know out there, Andy Johnstone. He was a mate of mine in South Africa and now works as a bloodstock auctioneer in Sydney; he knows all the trainers and breeders and their staff in the area. I asked him to ask around to find out if any of them had ever employed Keith, but he's had no luck so far.' He frowned. 'It's so frustrating. I don't know what to do next.'

Beth put a plump hand on his arm. 'Give it time,' she said soothingly. 'Something'll turn up. You know how closed the racing world is here. It can't be that different down under.'

'I wish I had your optimism, Beth. I just feel that the trail's gone cold. It's beginning to depress me,' Charlie confessed, heading towards the bar.

He watched the next race with her and her husband from the top of the stands. Bob seemed a good bloke, he thought: quiet but self-assured and devoted to his wife. He was intelligent too, judging by the comments he made on the race. Charlie wondered why they had not got any children; Beth was just the sort of kindly straightforward woman he would have liked to have had as a mother.

Apart from Charcoal Burner's performance, the visit to Thirsk had been a welcome distraction, he thought, as he said goodbye to Jack Crow and the Arnotts and headed for the car park. As well as his responsibilities in the yard, he seemed to have a number of things on his mind.

First of all, there was this worrying lack of progress in the search for Warrender. The last news Charlie had had of his father, from a doctor friend in Salisbury, had been worrying. 'Johnnie's not too good these days, I'm afraid. Seems very depressed and has rather taken to the bottle,' the man had written. Charlie knew the dangers of this. As well as depression, his father also suffered from angina and had been warned that heavy drinking could be dangerous.

Charlie was also uneasy about his relationship with Diana. They had been seeing a lot of each other recently, and the sex was still very good. Charlie could get an erection just by recalling the last afternoon they had made love, when she had seduced him as he lay dozing in the hammock in the garden at Keepers Cottage, ignoring his concern about possible passers-by. Her uncomplicated appetite for sex was still very appealing, but Charlie sensed that she was now wanting to take over his life further. 'It really is time you thought of moving on from Barons Lodge, you know,' she'd insisted the other day. 'You ought to do a stint with one of the really powerful stables – Stoute, Cecil or Luca Cumani, maybe. You could learn a lot from them, even in one year. Or if you want to learn the stud business, I know Daddy would take you on at Three Swallows. You could even move in during the busiest part of the stud season. That would be handy!' She'd said it jokingly, but Charlie sensed she was beginning to hustle him and he resented it. He simply did not want to get more involved with Diana, or anyone else for that matter at the moment. His search for Warrender had to be his first priority and somehow it seemed to take up a lot of emotional energy. He was not ready to leave Barons Lodge yet. Although Tod's philosophical approach to the yard's misfortunes often irritated him, he believed he was still a top-class trainer who had not lost his touch. His handling of Bahir proved that. The colt, in Charlie's opinion, had real ability, even classic potential, and he wanted to be around for his three-year-old career. Now that Bahir had come out of his Ascot race in good shape, Prince Hassim wanted him aimed at the Group One Prix Morny in Deauville in August.

As Charlie sped southwards down the A1, something else was nagging at his memory. Liam's description of Achilles and the sorry state he was in reminded him of something he'd been told, years ago, by Sixpence, one of his father's farm hands in Zimbabwe.

It must have been his first ever holiday out there when he was about fourteen. Eager as always to help, Charlie had volunteered to accompany Sixpence across to the far side of the farm to check on a dam that had been reported as leaking on to the main highway and to take a look at the nearby tobacco plantations to see how the crop was coming along. Petrol was, as usual, scarce and although they had an old Morris car and farm truck, Johnnie Kyle only allowed them to be used for trips into Salisbury or for ferrying essential supplies, so Charlie and Sixpence had made the journey on two of the farm's cob-like horses.

They had ridden home in a spectacular sunset, through gum-tree plantations, their pale leaves rustling in the breeze and with a strong scent of eucalyptus in the air. Although he had enjoyed every minute of it, it had been a long day in the saddle and, rounding a bend in the track, he had been delighted to see the familiar tobacco sheds ahead, clustered behind the long bungalow, its corrugated roof glowing fiery red in the evening light. This was his *real* home, where he really belonged, he realized suddenly, not Neville's cheerless house in

Kensington. Whatever his mother had to say about it, he intended to join his father out here as soon as his O-levels were over.

As they jogged homewards, Sixpence had been recounting a story about his uncle, a cattleman who believed in a series of strange animal cures and remedies. As a last resort, Sixpence had once taken him a mule who was so lame with a swollen knee that he was about to be sent to the knacker's yard. 'All swollen up like a coconut,' Sixpence had said. Nevertheless, his uncle had somehow managed to cure the animal. How he had done so Charlie could not remember, though he could recall thinking at the time that it sounded rather unpleasant.

As he drove on southwards through the darkness, an idea came to him: it was just possible that he had made a note of that ride in his diary. He must have a look. He still had all his old notebooks stashed away in a trunk at Keepers Cottage. Charlie determined to get home as quickly as possible.

Three hours later, Sumi curled up on his lap and an empty whisky glass at his elbow, he lolled in his armchair at Keepers Cottage, still wide awake. Looking through his old diaries had been a very nostalgic exercise; it had also increased his determination to try to clear his father's name. Despite Johnny Kyle's moderate success with the farm – they had had a series of excellent tobacco crops in the early seventies – Charlie realized once again, from some of his observations in the diary, how homesick his father must have been, missing his beloved Coombe Place and his old jumpers and the gentle, sinuous West Country landscape he feared he would never see again.

Realizing how late it was, Charlie eased himself up from the chair and, scooping up an indignant Sumi, strode over to the front door and threw the cat carefully out on to the lawn. There was an overwhelming scent of honeysuckle in the air and over towards Dullingham a barn owl shrieked as Sumi bounded off into the inky darkness. Charlie went back inside, his head still reeling with old memories. He *had* jotted down Sixpence's story about his uncle. 'He was a sort of medicine man who was a wizard healer of animals,' he had recorded. 'To cure swellings and blood clots and things like that, Sixpence said he used to use leeches! Ugh! He himself had been sent to collect some once, he said, from some swamp near Lake Kariba.' Leeches! So that was it, Charlie mused, as he turned off the lights in the hall and padded into his bedroom. All he really knew about them was that they lived on blood and looked rather disgusting, like slugs, but they did have some strange blood-cleansing properties too, he vaguely remembered from biology lessons at Marlborough. He had no idea whether they were still used medicinally or not – or, indeed, where one could find them – but he could make some inquiries. He might even mention the idea to Tod. He'd probably be told he was crazy, but never mind. Despite his advice to Liam, he himself had become oddly attached to Achilles. It was unlikely the colt would ever get to the racecourse now but anything was worth trying to at least get him sound again.

CHAPTER FIFTEEN

The Old Rectory
'Right, here we go then.' Crouching down on the swept floor of the box Charlie reached gingerly into the jar beside his foot and fished out the first of the leeches. Wearing a pair of rubber gloves and holding the slug-like creature between finger and thumb, he cupped his other hand underneath in case it slipped out of his grip.

Kate turned away, feeling sick. This was ridiculous, she told herself; she must pull herself together. The trouble was that she had always had an aversion to snakes and worms and suchlike, and she found the leeches, their shiny black bodies arching with excitement as they scented blood, quite repulsive.

Before Charlie had brought them into the box, he and Tod had prepared Achilles carefully, shaving the hair around his knee and covering the whole off foreleg in a stocking before making a hole over the swollen area. With a scalpel, they had then pricked the knee so that a tiny bead of blood appeared on the surface of the skin. Despite some initial irritation and laying-back of ears, none of this had seemed to exacerbate the discomfort the horse was already feeling. He stood quietly now, picking at his haynet in a depressed, desultory way, curiously unconcerned as Charlie fastened the first of the leeches on to his knee and watched it arch its neck and begin to pulse gently.

The strong sunlight streaming through the dusty window at the back of the box revealed the colt's lack of condition. His blue-black coat, usually sleek as a seal's, was patchy and staring and his ribs were beginning to show through the skin like those of a tucked-up greyhound.

On the far side of the box, Lady Kitty, unsqueamish as ever, peered at Achilles's leg with obvious fascination; as did Tod, bending down to assist Charlie fastening another leech in place. Only Liam, standing at the colt's head and murmuring to him softly, was also carefully averting his eyes.

Charlie's intent expression relaxed into a smile as he straightened up. 'Right, so far so good. Two more to go.' He rubbed his hands down his jeans as he bent forward again. 'Greedy little buggers, aren't they?'

'They don't seem to bother the horse at all, do they?' Tod observed, obviously relieved. 'Remarkable. How long do we leave them on for?'

'About thirty to forty minutes,' replied Charlie. 'Then they'll just sort of drop off, according to the Shrewsbury bloke. They won't need another meal for about six months apparently.' He glanced up at Liam. 'OK, Liam? You look a bit queasy.'

Liam swallowed nervously. 'I'm fine thanks, Mr Kyle. If my fella here can stand it all, then so can I,' he added in a small determined voice, still averting his eyes from Achilles's knee.

Charlie turned towards Lady Kitty, his mouth twisting into a brief smile. 'Extraordinary creatures, aren't they? Look at those blue and gold streaks on their backs. They're almost beautiful.'

Lady Kitty laughed. 'Well, I don't know about that, but they are certainly applying themselves to the job! Just look at them, the little sweethearts.' She reached for her stick, propped up against the manger. 'I'm not sure I want them making a meal out of me, though. Sometimes I'm glad I was born in the twentieth century, with the likes of antibiotics available, rather than leeches, I mean.' She looked around brightly. 'Well, now that they're all tucking in, can we offer anyone a drink? It's well past midday. Tod?'

Tod pushed back his glasses and leant against the wall of the box. 'What a splendid idea!' He turned to Charlie. 'Can I leave things in your capable hands for a while, then? You almost look like you're enjoying yourself!' he grinned.

Charlie waved his hand. 'Sure, I'm quite happy to keep watch.' He paused, glancing up at Liam. 'And keep Liam company, of course. He looks more in need of support than the colt does.' He bent over Achilles's knee again, his eyes alight with interest.

When, half an hour later, they were all gathered back in Achilles's box again, even Kate watched fascinated as Charlie gathered up the leeches and popped them, one by one, back in their bowl. Gorged now to almost double their previous size, they had obviously done their job.

'Well, that's that. Now I suppose all we can do is pray,' Charlie said cheerfully, peeling off his rubber gloves. 'I thought I'd take them back to Keepers Cottage to sleep it off for the next few months. Any objections? I don't imagine you'd want me to leave them in the pond here, Kate?' he added provocatively, sensing her repugnance. He looked across at her with a challenging smile.

'Feel free,' Tod said quickly before she could reply. He crouched down under Achilles's shoulder to take another look at his knee. 'I'm sure the Levertons have seen quite enough leeches for a while, and I certainly don't want them at Barons Lodge – they're not quite Myra's cup of tea either! There's not much change in the knee, I'm afraid. It's still unbelievably swollen.' He ran his hand gently down the horse's leg. As Achilles laid back his ears and snaked round, Tod caught his nose in the crook of his arm.

'Good lad, good lad, it's all over now,' he said soothingly. He turned towards Charlie, still peering into his jar of leeches. 'I'm not even going to attempt to bandage the knee. Best just to sponge it down and leave it till tomorrow, don't you think? I'll pop over and take another look at it then. Meanwhile, we'll leave him in Liam's capable hands. OK?' He glanced at the lad as he came back into the box carrying a bucket of fresh water.

Liam nodded. Some colour had come back into his face now and he looked a bit happier. Now that the leeches were off he was obviously just looking forward to fussing over his colt again, away from the bustle and distraction of Barons Lodge. Tod had been reluctant to spare him this week, with the season in full swing, but when Lady Kitty had told him that Davy had to go into hospital for a few days, to be stabilized on a new drug for arthritis, he had had no option. Liam, of course, had been delighted.

'Now then, Liam,' Lady Kitty was saying, 'we can make up a bed for you in the house, or there's a truckle bed in the old tack room, if you'd rather. Davy slept there when Misty was about to foal with Jacko and he said it was comfortable enough.' She smiled at him kindly. 'I know what I'd choose, but I also know what you lads are like with your horses!'

Liam managed a wan smile. 'A bed in the tack room would be grand. Thank you, ma'am.'

Lady Kitty clapped him on the shoulder. 'Right you are, then. And you'll have a bite of supper with Kate and myself this evening, I hope. We're having fish pie with peas from the garden and some of Kate's summer pudding and I know there's a drop of Guinness in the larder.'

Kate grinned to herself. There was nothing her mother liked so much as having someone around to spoil, she reflected. Especially, of course, if they were Irish.

Just before seven o'clock the following morning, stumbling down the back stairs still half asleep, Kate was startled to see Liam hovering inside the back door.

'Goodness! You gave me a fright,' she told him, pushing back her tousled hair. 'What's up? Is Achilles all right?'

The boy was quivering with excitement, just like one of the whippets. He nodded enthusiastically. 'I was so hoping you'd be up early, Miss Kate. I'd not be wanting to disturb you, but I have some good news!' He paused for breath. 'It's Jacko, you see. You'll never believe it: the knee's right down again, back to its proper size. I checked it as soon as it was light this morning. Come and take a look, Miss Kate, please?' His grey eyes were shining with delight.

Kate, suddenly wide awake, realized that her mouth had dropped open with astonishment. 'What? I can't believe it!' She seized Liam's hand impetuously. 'OK, come on, then. What are we waiting for?' Flinging open the back door, she hurried out into the yard, Liffey and Lute pattering in pursuit.

Ten minutes later she was back in the kitchen, hurriedly dialling the Barons Lodge number. 'Tod, Tod! Thank goodness I caught you before first lot,' she said breathlessly. 'I've got some terrific news. I've just been out to see Achilles. It's unbelievable – the swelling has gone right down, right back to normal. He seems to be able to bend his knee again too, perfectly. God, I can't believe it!' She flopped down on one of the kitchen chairs, her face beaming. 'What? No, Kitty doesn't know yet. I'm just about to take her up some tea. Yes, I know. Can you imagine her face? I can't wait,' she laughed, cradling the receiver to her ear. 'Can you come over at midday then? Great. See you then.'

'It's a miracle, I tell you. The miracle of the leeches,' Lady Kitty said ecstatically. 'Let's have some more champagne,' she ordered, looking fondly across at Kate and Tod, sitting side by side on the old garden seat, piled with cushions. Kate realized that she was already beginning to feel pleasantly inebriated. It was partly the midday heat, of course, and Tod's proximity, as well as the champagne. She felt so at ease with him always; and he seemed so at home here at the Old Rectory. If only they could be together all the time, she fantasized.

'Now, has anyone told Charlie the good news yet?' Lady Kitty was asking. 'After all, it's Charlie we should be raising our glasses to today. If it wasn't for him, none of us would ever have thought of the leeches, would we?'

It was perfectly true, Kate thought. He had spent a couple of afternoons reading up about leeches in some library in Cambridge. One of the things they did was to break down the viscosity of the blood; they also stimulated the circulation by injecting some sort of enzymes into the system. If they could get rid of the fibrous adhesions in Achilles's injured knee they might bring down the swelling, Charlie had said when he suggested the extraordinary experiment to Tod. From one of the scientific journals he had been reading he had then tracked down a man near Shrewsbury who was actually experimenting with leeches for medical research.

'No way!' Tod agreed. 'He deserves ten out of ten for effort. I thought the whole leeches idea was pretty barmy, to tell you the truth, but I couldn't put old Charlie off.'

'They give me the creeps!' Kate confessed, taking another sip of champagne. 'They're such horrible-looking creatures! Ugh! I could really hardly bear to watch just now. As Charlie obviously noticed,' she added with a certain acerbity.

Lady Kitty glanced at her sharply. 'Now, now. Just because you had that little contretemps with him at the sales that time, there's no need to take against him,' she rebuked her gently. 'You two just got off on the wrong foot, that's all.'

Kate made a face. 'Where's he gone today, anyway?' She turned to Tod. 'Can't you get hold of him somehow?'

Tod fished in his pocket for his battered pack of Gitanes. 'Sure. He's gone up to Catterick. Left at the crack of dawn, but I made him promise to ring the yard at midday, so Sam'll be able to give him the good news then.' He shook his head in wonderment. 'I must say I still can't quite believe it, can you? Incredible!'

'It's the best possible tonic all round,' Lady Kitty observed, beaming. 'I feel ten years younger than I did yesterday, and Davy will be over the moon when he hears.'

'If Jacko, as Liam calls him, is really sound again, what's the next step?' Kate asked tentatively. 'I mean, is there any chance at all that he could go back into training, or am I being too optimistic?'

Tod pulled slowly on his cigarette. 'Well, we'll just have to see what happens in the next day or so,' he replied thoughtfully. 'If the knee doesn't blow up again and he stays sound, I don't see why we shouldn't risk it. But we'd need to take him very slowly, of course.' He paused, obviously turning something over in his mind. 'I'm not sure that we should have him back at Barons Lodge yet, though. I think a better idea would be to send him on a little holiday – to the seaside.' He turned to Kate, smiling.

'What do you mean?' she asked, puzzled.

'Ginger Mann's place. Up at Holkham, on the north Norfolk coast,' Tod replied. 'Ginger's an astonishing character. Cockney born but with Romany blood, I suspect. He used to be a jump jockey.' He picked up his glass of champagne and drained it. 'He runs a little livery yard now. Specializes in cripples. He takes them wading in the sea every day and walking and trotting on the Holkham sands. The jumping boys swear by him. He's certainly had a lot of success in getting horses with dodgy legs back on to the racecourse again.'

Lady Kitty was leaning forward, her expression alert. 'Do you think he'd be able to take Achilles at short notice?' she asked eagerly.

Tod shrugged his shoulders. 'I don't see why not. I don't have a number for him, actually, but I know plenty of people who do. I'll ask around up on the July course this afternoon.' He got to his feet reluctantly. 'This sybaritic existence won't do at all, I'm afraid,' he announced. 'We've got a runner in the three o'clock and I must nip home to change first.' He stubbed out his cigarette and raised his hand. 'Please don't get up, Lady Kitty: just sit and relax and let the good news sink in. Miracles, after all, can be very exhausting! Kate will see me to the car, I'm sure.' He turned and smiled at her affectionately. 'If Ginger can take the colt, we might even go and visit him,' he suggested in a low voice as they turned away and strolled back towards the house. 'I don't know about you, but I'm getting desperate – desperate to see you alone, I mean. It's high time we had a whole day together, don't you think?' He squeezed her hand tenderly.

Fakenham, North Norfolk

'What did you say you were having for lunch?' Tod asked, turning to Kate eagerly.

'I didn't actually,' she replied, grinning. 'But since you ask – prawns in aspic, followed by a tortilla with a tomato and basil salad. Then just raspberries from the garden, of course,' she paused. 'Oh, and a bottle of Frascati, well chilled, I hope! Will that do?'

Tod licked his lips as he gazed at the road ahead. 'You bet,' he replied with enthusiasm.

He had picked Kate up at the Old Rectory just before eleven and they had made good time from Bury to Thetford, through the strange flat forests of Breckland and on to Swaffham and what Tod described as 'real Norfolk'. They were driving slowly now, along the main road to Fakenham, frustratingly stuck behind a cattle truck and a couple of lorries. On either side of the road, behind tall hedges, the rolling countryside basked in a haze of heat; bleached meadows dotted with sheep and clumps of poplar trees merging into sweeps of ripe umber corn, humped against the sky.

The traffic was so heavy that Tod suggested that they have their picnic on Fakenham racecourse, rather than try to drive on to the coast. 'I know it's a rather eccentric idea but I've got such happy memories of the place. There is a caravan park up there in the summer, I believe, but there'll be plenty of room beyond. What do you think?'

'Fine by me. Anything you say,' Kate replied happily, slinging a tanned arm round Tod's shoulders and gently nuzzling his ear. 'Tell me about these memories, then.'

Tod reached forward and lit another Gitane with the dashboard lighter. 'Well, believe it or not, I actually managed to win a rather "hot" hunter chase here once in my riding days,' he replied. 'It was entirely by luck, really. I was riding a horse of my father's which had a cast-iron mouth and I just couldn't hold him! I got completely carted for the first circuit. He was very fit, though, and we got so far ahead that no one managed to catch us!' He grinned at the recollection. 'Father was absolutely delighted, of course. I found out later that he had had a few at lunchtime and put twenty quid on me each way – a lot of money in those days, particularly since the horse had no form at all on the racecourse. We started at 33 to 1, I seem to remember.' He laughed. 'Father was in such a good mood he agreed to up my allowance. I was still up at Cambridge at the time. It was just before I met Monique.'

'Did you enjoy race riding?' Kate asked. 'It looks absolutely terrifying to me – crashing over fences at such speed. But I suppose it's pretty exhilarating too.'

Tod took a pull at his cigarette. 'On the right horse, it's pure magic,' he replied. 'The adrenalin soars and you want it to go on for ever. But I lacked the killer instinct, I'm afraid. I loved winning but I never wanted to push the horse too hard – was always just glad to get round in one piece. That attitude doesn't win races.'

A sudden growl from the back seat indicated that one of the terriers, restless in the heat, had disturbed the other. Tod glanced round quickly. 'Take it easy, girls. We're nearly there.'

As they turned off the main road and bumped slowly along the dusty track leading up to the racecourse, Kate felt a great surge of happiness. Resting her arm on the open window, she gazed out at the countryside bathed in heat and the hazy soft contours of the farmland all around, topped by huge clouds climbing lazily into the blue. It was so wonderful to be able to spend a whole day alone with Tod at last. She intended to relish every minute of it. Although the sun, beating down through the sun roof, made the car so uncomfortably hot that her dress was sticking to the back of the seat, she wouldn't have wanted to be anywhere else for the world. She was also getting very excited about seeing Achilles again later. Judging from the last phone conversation Tod had had with Ginger, the colt seemed to be progressing extremely well.

As Tod stopped the car in a small meadow beyond the caravan park he turned to gaze at her with such obvious love that she felt she might dissolve into tears.

'You look so innocent and French today, in that blue dress and straw hat,' he said tenderly. 'You remind me of a portrait by Berthe Morisot of a little girl in a cornfield.' He touched her hand. 'I wish I could convey how happy I am to be here with you, darling. I wish I could find some new words – the usual ones seem so inadequate, somehow.'

Kate flung her arms round him and kissed him passionately. 'I know, I know,' she murmured. 'I feel the same. Aren't we lucky!'

An hour later, lolling on her old tartan rug amongst the debris of the lunch, Kate was feeling splendidly replete as well as content. From the nearby copse came the soothing cooing sound of wood pigeons and, appearing from nowhere, a bee droned past her left ear. Leaning soporifically against Tod's side as he scanned the pages of *The Sporting Life* for the list of tomorrow's runners and riders, she felt that somehow the two of them had merged, both physically and emotionally, and were now inextricably linked, like Siamese twins.

As one of the dogs barked excitedly in the distance, Tod sat up abruptly. 'Bloody dogs,' he remarked affectionately. 'They're definitely up to no good. We can't have them going off hunting. I'd better go and round them up in a minute.' Languidly he indicated an item on a page of the newspaper strewn in front of him. 'The Saratoga sales seem to be up on last year, I gather. There's been a hell of a lot of competition between some of the English trainers. Buying for the Arabs, of course.'

'Wouldn't you like to be out there too?' Kate asked. 'You told me only the other day how much you like Saratoga and what a marvellous *Great Gatsby* atmosphere the place has.'

Tod shook his head emphatically. 'It has, but I'd much rather be here with you. No question about it.' He paused. 'Anyway it does now look as though I'll be getting to the sales at another of my favourite places this year – Deauville.' Hassim still wants to run Bahir in the Prix Morny and he's asked me to look at a few yearlings for him as well.'

Kate turned to him, surprised. 'You never told me, you wretch. That's terrific! We might even be able to spend some time together. You know *Tatler* have asked me to do a feature for them on the polo, don't you?'

'Er . . . yes . . . I think you did mention it,' Tod replied evasively.

Kate sat up with a start. 'Is Myra going to be there with you?' she asked.

Tod blinked behind his glasses. 'Well, yes. It does rather look like it,' he confessed. 'I didn't want to tell you till I was sure, but she fixed it all up last night, apparently. Toby's de Bernay cousins have asked him to stay for ten days with them at Lisieux. Myra's determined to pick him up there and then drive up to Deauville. It's not very far, you see.' He turned to Kate apologetically. 'So, it looks as if they'll both be with me, I'm afraid. Sorry about that, but there's really nothing I can do about it.'

Kate felt her good mood evaporate as suddenly as though a great shadow had fallen over the day. She'd been so looking forward to going to Deauville. She'd never been there before and she had, of course, been hoping that she might also be able to see Tod. Having him there for several days though, *en famille*, was something she hadn't bargained for.

Tod took her hand, noticing her expression. 'Please don't get upset, sweetheart,' he pleaded. 'Myra and Toby are bound to get involved in some social jaunts of their own. I'm sure you and I will be able to meet alone. There's a particularly good restaurant, right behind the *quai* at Honfleur, that I'd love to take you to. Maybe we could sneak off there one day for lunch, or even dinner. After all, you are one of my owners, aren't you?'

'I don't want to "sneak off" with you anywhere, that's the whole point,' Kate retorted angrily. 'I want to be with you openly, so that it doesn't matter who sees us. I want to be able to tell people how much I love you, how good you make me feel.' She thumped the ground with her fist. 'There's nothing wrong with that, is there? I would have thought it quite natural.' She turned to him, her face defiant. 'I hate all this deception and skulking around. I hate it. I hate you being married to someone else. Being a mistress is obviously just not in my nature,' she added despairingly.

Tod eased himself over to her, his forehead furrowed with concern. 'Please don't be upset, darling. Please don't sound so bitter – I can't bear it.' He put his arms around her shoulders. 'Look, I know it's difficult. I know I'm married to Myra. But it's you I love. You must know that by now, surely?' He paused, waiting for Kate's reluctant nod. 'Good. Well, then, it's possible that one day I could get unmarried, isn't it? People do, after all, all the time.' He frowned. 'It's obviously crossed my mind, but I didn't really want to bring it up right now. It is, after all, a very big step. We'd both have to be absolutely sure it was what we wanted.' He made a face. 'It would mean the most tremendous upheaval, of course. If I told Myra that I was in love and wanted a divorce, I'd imagine she'd kick me out of Barons Lodge straight away. After all, I couldn't expect her to leave: it's always been her home.' He stubbed out his cigarette on the grass with his shoe. 'And it's not just a question of what you and I want either, but what we could live with, too.' He went on gently stroking the back of Kate's neck. 'I'm not sure that either of us wants to grab happiness at the expense of others. I'm not sure either of us is ruthless enough. We'll have to see.' He disengaged his hand and got to his feet slowly. 'Anyway, whatever we decide to do, I don't think we should rush it. I really can't rock the boat at the moment, darling,' he pleaded, his expression troubled. 'You know what a fragile state Toby seems to be in.'

Kate turned back to him, her grey eyes suddenly contrite. 'I know, Tod, I'm sorry. The last thing I wanted was to spoil today in any way; it's been so wonderful.' She sighed heavily. 'I shouldn't have exploded like that, but I couldn't help it. I just needed to tell you how I felt, that's all.' She knelt upright and reached over to pick up her straw hat. 'And of course we can't disrupt anything just at the moment, I realize that, particularly now that Achilles is on the mend at last.' She glanced at her watch. 'By the way, talking of Achilles, hadn't we better get a move on?'

As she started packing up the picnic things, she felt a strange elation. She knew now that Tod not only loved her but that he had even thought of leaving Myra. Much though she was wary of causing pain and major disruption to other people just to accommodate her own desires, she found that very consoling. Perhaps, deep down, it was what she really wanted.

Holkham, Norfolk

'You'll be seeing quite a change in your colt, I reckon,' Ginger said as he led Kate and Tod across an unkempt lawn towards the stable block. They had found his run-down brick and flint farmhouse at the end of a long track, winding through water meadows dotted with cattle to a dip, sheltered by pine trees behind the sand dunes and the sea. 'Don't be put off by the general state of the place,' Tod had advised her. 'The horses themselves are very well cared for. It's just that Ginger lives on his own these days – his wife left him a few years ago – and he's a bit of a gypsy. Not too concerned about how the place looks or about material possessions. He used to gamble quite a bit in his riding days, I seem to recall.'

'I thought that was illegal,' Kate queried.

'Well, it is – against Jockey Club rules, anyway, for obvious reasons, but jockeys have ways and means of getting other people to do their betting for them.'

'What happens if they get caught?'

'They get banned from riding for a time. Like they do if they are found taking any sort of inducements not to try. The Jockey Club may be reactionary and snobbish but they do their damnedest to keep racing as straight as possible. Don't mention the Jockey Club to Ginger, though. They turned down his application to train, apparently, and he's pretty bitter about it.' He reversed the Saab carefully into a dilapidated-looking shed filled with a rusty harrow and bales of straw. 'This should be cool enough for the dogs. Come on, let's go.'

Whilst they had a quick cup of tea out of grimy mugs in Ginger's untidy kitchen, he and Tod swapped news of various mutual acquaintances. Ginger was a stocky man with grizzled cropped hair, alert blue eyes and a broken nose; he looked more like an ex-boxer than a jockey, Kate thought, as she followed him back out into the sunshine and down the cinder path. His shoulder and arm muscles bulged noticeably through his dark blue sweatshirt, but he also walked with a remarkably bow-legged swagger.

A couple of bay heads swung over half-open box doors as they approached the stables and one of the horses whinnied, but there was no sign of Achilles.

'He'll be enjoying his afternoon nap, I reckon,' Ginger explained. 'Not the most sociable of characters, is he?'

Approaching the end box, he kicked open the bottom bolt and gestured for them to wait. 'You wait there. I'll bring him out of his box so as you can see him better,' he ordered.

Tod grinned. 'Old Ginger doesn't change much. He always was a bossy character. Not with the horses, though – he's got all the time in the world for them.'

As Achilles clopped dozily out of his box, bits of straw clinging to his mane and tail, Kate could not believe how much better he looked. His ribs were no longer visible, he had filled out – even grown a bit, she thought – and his dark coat, dusty though it looked in the sunlight, was definitely beginning to bloom again.

As she approached him, fumbling in her pocket for the packet of Polos she had brought with her, the horse turned to her and whinnied, before lifting his lip to reveal strong yellow teeth.

'Look, Tod! He's really back to his old self, making those evil faces,' Kate exclaimed delightedly, as she offered him a mint on her outstretched palm.

Ginger, clicking his tongue and jerking on Achilles's headcollar, got him to alter his stance. 'There, that's more like it. Got to get him standing proper,' he observed with satisfaction. 'Sea air's doing him good, I reckon. I haven't bothered to clean him up special or anything for you, as you can see. I'm short-handed at the moment – only got a couple of girls helping me out and one of them's off sick. Anyway, he's well in himself and that's what matters.'

Tod walked round the colt, appraising him carefully before bending down to run his hands down both forelegs. 'Certainly no heat there now, is there? These legs are as cold as ice. Mmm . . .' He straightened up. 'He looks a different horse, Ginger. No swelling or stiffness at all since you've had him?'

Ginger held up two crossed fingers. 'Nope. But I've been taking him ever so slowly, mind you. Just wading in the sea, morning and afternoon, then a hack back over the sands. He's hardly broke into a trot since he's been here, but that'll have to change: he's getting impatient, I can tell – nearly had me off the other morning.' He chuckled and gave Achilles an affectionate pat. 'Didn't you, you devil? Bloody awful patient, aren't you?'

'How long till I can have him back?' Tod asked quietly.

Ginger scratched his head. ''Bout three weeks, maybe. We'll start trotting him on the sands in a day or two. If that goes OK, you'll have him back by the end of the month, I reckon.' He led the colt over to the nearest patch of rough grass and leant against his shoulder. 'Won't take much getting fit, I reckon. He's a tough little sod – all muscle and well put-together. You might even get a run into him by the end of the season – if he stays sound, that is, and you don't manage to bugger up all my good work.' He grinned, showing a couple of broken front teeth.

As Kate stood by Tod's side relishing seeing Achilles looking so well and relaxed again, the horse stopped cropping the grass suddenly and, lifting up his head, ears pricked, gazed out towards the sea. 'Look! He still stares into the distance in that strange way, like he used to as a foal!' she exclaimed. 'I'm sure he's going to be all right from now on. I can feel it in my bones. Kitty's right: his run of bad luck is over.'

Tod crossed his fingers hurriedly. 'Yes, well, let's just hope all this Leverton optimism is justified.' He grinned. 'I agree with Ginger, though. We'll have to take him very slowly. But if we can keep him sound, I see no reason why we shouldn't win a small race or two with him next year. He's an athlete and he's got the right competitive attitude – I'm certain about that.'

There had always been something out of the ordinary about the colt, Kate reflected, as she watched him cropping the grass, the afternoon light glowing around his silhouette like a halo. Despite his moodiness and size, he had a compelling presence; both Tod and Diana Saunders had remarked on it when they first saw him. He had also had quite an effect on all his connections already: not just Kitty and herself, but Liam, too, and even Charlie seemed to have fallen under his spell; he had also, of course, brought her and Tod together. Perhaps he had been sent by the gods as some sort of catalyst in all their lives, she mused. But that was ridiculously fanciful; he had just become very important to all of them and that was that. She had no idea right now how they were going to be able to afford to keep him in training next year, but she knew that somehow, they would find a way.

CHAPTER SIXTEEN

Deauville

'Do stop complaining, Father! You got Devilry for a snip,' Stella said impatiently. 'One and a half million for possibly the best middle-distance colt in Europe – you got a bargain. I'm amazed the owner agreed to sell; he must be really desperate.' She took another spoonful of her iced shrimp soup.

Stelios, a snow-white napkin tucked under his chin, was eating his way through a plate of *écrevisses* with great relish. The effort of dismembering them, added to the heat of the restaurant, was causing multiple beads of sweat to break out across his leathery forehead. 'Hmm . . .' he grunted. 'All that money for a horse that could well have lost his appetite for racing! That's hardly what I would call a bargain, my dear.' He wiped his mouth noisily. 'I just hope that Nik's faith in the horse is justified and that he'll be able to get him back to form.'

Stella looked at him with irritation. 'Oh, for heaven's sake! Of course it is,' she insisted. 'He just had a very debilitating virus, that's all. The vet thinks it may even be a new strain that we haven't encountered in Ireland before. One of Nik's other colts could have picked it up on a trip he made to Newmarket.' She took a sip of her wine. 'So we must just be patient. Nik's tempted to turn Devilry out for the rest of the summer – not run him again this season at all. I think he's right.' She indicated for Stelios to pass her the pepper. 'You wait until next year, though, when he goes for the King George and the Arc. You won't regret your investment then, I can assure you.' She leant forward, her eyes glittering. 'Look, I bred the horse, Father. We haven't seen him at his best yet, I'm sure of it. He's a late developer.' She ground the pepper carefully over her soup. 'No way has he lost his appetite for racing. Anyone who thinks that is a fool.' The discussion over, as far as she was concerned, she picked up her spoon again.

She and her father were lunching at a corner table on the upper tier at Ciro's, Deauville's smartest midday restaurant, on the day of the Prix Morny. Outside, under a grey and sultry sky, the beach was almost deserted except for a few scattered bathers and families picnicking beyond the forest of furled umbrellas, most holidaymakers having trudged back into the town for lunch. Far out, on the water, however, windsurfers were still criss-crossing the bay, skimming along in brief bursts as they caught the last of the morning breeze.

The restaurant was already packed with racegoers who had been filtering down since midday from the Normandy and the Royal hotels or rented villas high above the town, and the atmosphere was already thick with discussion of the afternoon's prospects and form.

Glancing round, Stella saw several familiar faces, including Mrs Arpad Plesch who had won the Derby twice with Psidium and Henbit, and two of the more gourmet-minded of the English trainers, Robert Armstrong and Jeremy Tree. Down on the lower tier, Tod Beckhampton was lunching very much *en famille* with Myra, Lucy and that troublesome boy Toby; and the far corner of the room was taken up by the Sangster party. At one of the tables by the door, she noticed Sandy Diss with Bertie, almost hidden behind his copy of *Paris Turf*, Diana Saunders and a good-looking man with striking iron-grey hair who she remembered having seen up at the sales the previous evening. He was Tom Dacre, Sandy Diss's elder brother, not in the bloodstock business himself but a 'hot-shot' New York banker, Nik had informed her. He was attractive, Stella mused, and seemed to be enjoying Diana's company. She herself had begun to have some respect for the girl and was even able to envisage her as a possible wife for Nik: they seemed to get on well together and Diana was certainly good-looking and tough enough for his taste; she was also rich which would, Stella suspected, turn out to be very useful. She was not taken in by Diana's easy-going Aussie exterior, either: behind that toothy smile, she guessed, there lurked a powerful ambition.

Wiping her mouth delicately on her napkin Stella glanced at her watch. Where on earth had Nik got to? she wondered. He had been playing golf with a Fort Lauderdale millionaire whom she knew he was trying to persuade to send some horses to Kilmarron; he had warned her that he might be late, but not this late, surely? It was unlike him. He had probably got caught on the telephone; she knew he wanted to put a call through to Kilmarron to find out how the fillies, and Isobar in particular, had worked that morning. Looking up, she was delighted to see him over by the door, immaculate in his racing clothes, dark-blue Ted Lapidus blazer and flannels, his hair glistening like jet as he bent over to greet Diana Saunders. As he threaded his way in Stella's direction, she realized that something extraordinary must have happened: her brother's blue eyes glittered and the expression on his face was one of suppressed excitement.

Stelios's face creased into a welcoming smile, but apart from briefly nodding in his direction, Nik ignored him, sitting down quickly and fixing Stella in his gaze. 'Well, we're off and running, my sweet,' he announced softly. 'The old man has finally obliged.'

Stella's whole body stiffened. So that was why he was so late: he must have been on the phone to McManus, O'Donnell's doctor in Ireland. 'When?' she asked tensely.

Nik unfolded his napkin and spread it slowly across his lap. 'About an hour ago. The call came just as I got in from my game of golf. It was a massive heart attack, apparently. They had the helicopter all ready to fly the old man to the clinic but there was no point. McManus said that ten minutes after the nurse called him, he was dead.' Nik leant forward, bracing his long fingers against the edge of the table. 'No one else here can possibly know about this yet,' he said in a conspiratorial tone. 'The news won't get out for at least an hour or so. I gave McManus orders not to talk to anyone till the yard office reopens again at two o'clock and the secretary comes back from lunch. The nurse won't be blabbing to anyone, either: she's very discreet, I've made sure of that.' He raised his dark eyebrows, a sanctimonious expression on his face. 'So, I shan't officially hear the news until I get back to the Royal. I shall then, of course, proceed to the racetrack, suitably shocked and saddened, ready to accept everyone's condolences.' He sat back. 'In the meantime, I intend to enjoy my lunch.' He looked around. 'Ah, here comes the wine waiter with the Veuve Clicquot I ordered. I thought a quiet little celebration was called for.' He smiled across at Stella, who was sitting very still, a distant look on her face.

Stelios, however, had been listening to him with a growing expression of disapproval. Refusing any champagne, he waited impatiently for the waiter to go away before inclining his head ponderously in Nik's direction. 'Sometimes I think I have sired two monsters,' he commented with displeasure. 'Your conduct is not seemly, Nik. Can you not show more respect? O'Donnell was a fine man. You owe him a lot: without his support you would never have had the responsibility you have so early, and gained such valuable experience in such a short time.' He paused, shaking his head. 'Yet before he is even cold, you wish to have a celebration. I find that distasteful.'

Stella, staring at him impassively, took a gulp of her champagne. 'Oh, come on, Father, don't be such a hypocrite,' she said, her lip curling. 'O'Donnell was good to Nik, sure, but he has more than repaid him. Who else would have given him so many Group winners in the past two years and let him take the credit? Since when did any of us have any real time for O'Donnell, anyway? While he was alive he was just in our way.' She smiled triumphantly. 'Now perhaps we can begin to get things moving – in a direction that would benefit you too, Father, if you could only see it.'

Nik, nodding in agreement, raised his glass. 'To the old man. May he rest in peace,' he said softly.

Half an hour later, as some of the lunchers, flushed and replete, were starting to leave for the racecourse, Stelios, his elbows propped on the table, was giving Nik his full attention.

'So, let's get this clear,' he said solemnly. 'You will take over the licence and O'Donnell's lease on Kilmarron. That much I expected. The lease expires at the end of next year, I seem to recall, but that is no problem: you have the right to renew it for another five years, or else it automatically reverts to his family.' He picked up a piece of bread and tore it in two. 'So why should you need any money from me at the moment? You'll have my horses – all this autumn's yearlings and any of the animals I've currently got at Barons Lodge. The ones you don't want can go to the sales.' He popped the piece of bread in his mouth and started chewing it laboriously. 'You can hardly expect me to finance any improvements to Kilmarron while you only have a lease on the place. Anyway, by this time next year, I predict that you will be wanting to move to England, to Newmarket, and you know I told you that I am prepared to assist you to do that.'

Stella, who had been sitting motionless throughout this monologue, now intervened brusquely. 'Nik has no intention of ever moving to Newmarket, Father,' she snapped. 'We've both told you that. I just wish you'd listen. We have a far better plan which we want to put to you. Nik, go ahead, tell him.'

Nik leant forward intently. 'I do indeed have the right to renew the lease on Kilmarron next year, Father, but there is now another more attractive option which you don't yet know about,' he said. 'I only got O'Donnell to agree to it himself last month – with the consent of his sister and the family solicitor, of course.' He paused, deftly extracting a sliver of white flesh from one of his lobster claws. 'At the end of next year, when the current lease lapses, I have the right to buy the whole property if I wish. The family were extremely reluctant to agree to this at first, of course – after all, Kilmarron has been theirs for generations; but there is no one to carry on the family training tradition now and they obviously have serious money worries.' He sat back with a self-satisfied smile. 'And so, I get first bite at the cherry if I can raise the money, that is. I am, after all, the devil they know, as you might say! They certainly know I will look after the place properly, not to mention build up its reputation. They care a lot about that.'

'How much?' Stelios asked abruptly, raising his heavy eyebrows.

Nik spread his hands, as the waiter began to clear the table. 'It's difficult to be precise. I'd get a special price, of course. We could probably get it for under two million. Irish pounds, that is.' He paused. 'And then of course I'd need at least another million to refurbish the yard and put in all the new facilities I need.' He rubbed his chin thoughtfully. 'Stella, as you already know, wants to expand and develop Mountclare,' he went on, staring at his father. 'She thinks – and I agree with her – that if it is to be really successful, it should become a public as well as a private stud, with facilities for at least two stallions. Obviously we hope that one of them will be Devilry.' He sat back as Stella waved away the menu and ordered them all some coffee. 'What we propose is a company incorporating both Kilmarron and Mountclare.'

Stella interjected, 'We would, of course, be prepared to offer you a one-third share in the whole enterprise, if you agree to back us – provided that you agreed to leave it to us, to be split equally between us. There must be no question of any outsiders being included.'

'Come on, Father' – Nik's tone was jocular – 'surely it makes more sense than you buying up a stud farm of your own and having to stock it from scratch? Stella's built up a first-rate band of mares at Mountclare, as you very well know.'

Stelios laid his tooled-leather cigar case on the table and extracted one of his Davidoff cigars with stubby fingers. Sticking it under his nose, he sniffed it like a well-trained dog. 'Hmm . . .' he said thoughtfully, reaching in his pocket for his cigar cutter. 'The proposition you have put to me is all very well. It has many merits, and in other circumstances I would be tempted, but there are certain drawbacks, I'm afraid. Unfortunately, it does not fit in with certain plans of my own – plans I have made entirely for my own future happiness. They may not interest either of you, I am aware of that, but I am committed, as a matter of honour.' He puffed away energetically at his cigar, his face impassive. 'As you know, I intend to remarry,' he said, lowering his voice. 'I have also been so bold as to make the lady concerned several promises. And one of those is that I will acquire a stud farm for her to manage.' He paused, waving away the cigar smoke before continuing. 'Horses have always been her life, and I can hardly expect her to abandon them completely at this stage, even for the privilege of being an ambassador's wife. Also, as you know, I am not convinced that Mountclare, if you do expand it into a public stud, would be the best place to stand Devilry.'

'But Myra Beckhampton has not finally agreed to your extra-ordinary offer yet, as far as I am aware,' Stella commented coldly, ignoring this last remark. 'I lunched with her in London the other day, you know. She's obviously got a lot of problems with her son at the moment. I would hardly have thought it was the ideal moment to go for a divorce. I didn't tell her that I knew what you two were planning, of course.' Her tone was scornful. 'By the way, her current husband is signalling to you right now,' she went on, glancing over to the door. 'Hadn't you better go over and say hello?' she added mockingly.

Stelios looked up, his cigar still clenched between his teeth, and peered towards the exit where Tod was indeed hovering, obviously trying to catch his eye. 'Yes, yes, indeed, I am forgetting my manners,' he murmured, his expression preoccupied as he got slowly to his feet and lumbered off between the tables.

Stella's expression hardened. 'Duplicitous old fool,' she commented. 'I'm still convinced that if we can just get Myra Beckhampton off the scene, we're home and hosed. It's perfectly obvious that it's only his stubbornness and ludicrous sense of honour that's stopping him from coming in with us straight away. I'll just have to renew my efforts to put the woman off, that's all.' She pushed back her chair with a sigh. 'Hadn't we better be getting back to the Royal? You're about to receive the tragic news about O'Donnell, remember?'

Nik drained his glass of champagne. 'You're absolutely right. Time ticks on.' He got up briskly, his eyes gleaming. 'What an eventful day this has turned out to be,' he said with satisfaction.

The crowd, a jumble of elegant clothes and tanned faces, was still packed around the Winners' Enclosure in front of the half-timbered weighing room as Lucy hurried across the lawns. She had dressed casually in a lime-green Ungaro suit and Ferragamo sandals, her tawny hair pinned back from her face with two Victorian tortoiseshell combs inlaid with diamonds that Alain du Roc had given her for her twenty-fifth birthday. Although Deauville was France's premier summer course, and numerous Parisians as well as most of Chantilly, both human and equine, decamped here for the whole month, there was always a frivolous, seaside air about the proceedings and hats, at least for women, were not *de rigueur*. Over towards the leafy paddock there were even young couples in shorts picnicking with their children on the grass and a benchload of gnarled old men in flat caps, fervently discussing the previous race through a haze of cheroot smoke.

Lucy had watched the race on the television set in Le Brantôme, the racecourse restaurant, where she had lunched with some Swiss banker friends. They had got very excited in the Prix Morny when it had looked for a moment as though du Roc and Bahir might get up to beat the favourite owned by the Aga Khan, but it had just been confirmed over the public-address system that he had failed to do so by a neck. Lucy was concerned, not only because she knew how disappointed both du Roc and her father would be, but also because she feared that Hassim would take the defeat badly. For some reason she had never been able to fathom, he was particularly envious of the racing success of the Aga Khan; and to have his best two-year-old beaten by one of the Aga's in such a prestigious race would, Lucy knew, put her lover in a bad mood.

By the time she reached the Winners' Enclosure, the horses were being led away, dark with sweat under their cooling rugs. Their connections, though, were still standing around, deep in animated post-race discussion. She caught sight of the Aga Khan, whom she had met several times in Sardinia, and gave him a cheery thumbs-up sign. He was looking understandably delighted, as he listened attentively to his veteran French trainer François Mathet. Her father, though, was looking unusually serious as he leant, hatless, against the rail, talking to Prince Hassim. The Arab was gesticulating fiercely as he turned round to address one of his habitual companions, or bodyguards. She had been right, Lucy thought gloomily: he seemed extremely put out by Bahir's defeat. She decided to hover on the edge of the crowd, hoping that he would not notice her, rather than to offer any immediate commiserations.

She had not actually seen him for several weeks; he had been on a trip to Jedda and she had been working on a couple of jobs in Spain and one in Monaco before flying into Deauville's tiny airport last night. There had been a note for her when she'd arrived at the

Normandy, asking her to have dinner with him this evening. It would be caviare and sex as usual, followed by baccarat or Black Jack at the Casino, she presumed, and wished she was looking forward to it more.

She was still turned on by the sex, but she had become increasingly alarmed by Hassim's jealousy and the pain he could inflict on her. A month ago, while they had been desultorily watching television she had glimpsed one of her previous lovers, an American actor, in a film. High on dope, she had foolishly remarked, giggling, that the man looked a little different from the last time she had seen him. She did not tell Hassim, of course, that on that occasion both she and Celeste had been in bed with him at his rented mansion in Bel Air, busy sucking *crème fraiche* off his penis when his agent had burst in. Her amusement, however, had been enough to get Hassim's jealousy aroused; and, after questioning her suspiciously, he had laid about her with a camel whip with such ferocity that when he finally stopped, the sheets were streaked with blood. The weals on her buttocks had caused her so much pain that she literally could not sit down for several days. When she had confided in Celeste, who was in London at the time, her friend had been appalled.

'For Christ's sake, you're all raw! The guy means business,' she exclaimed in horror. 'He could kill you, you know. I don't understand,' she added, bewildered. 'You can fuck anyone you like: everyone fancies you, sweetheart. Why bother with that kook? Dump him!'

Lucy was tempted to follow her advice. After all, out of bed, Hassim bored her completely. He had absolutely no sense of humour and even his 'remorse' presents were beginning to lose their appeal. Of course, she loved beautiful jewellery, but it was not much fun if she was forbidden to wear it and ordered to keep it in the bank. She and Celeste had decided to take two weeks' holiday and just 'flop' somewhere at the end of the month to give her the strength to break with him when she came back to London.

Lucy's heart sank as Hassim caught sight of her now and came stomping over, followed by his aides. His face was suffused with irritation.

'Hello. So you have arrived at last,' he said curtly as he shook her hand. 'We will meet later this evening, as arranged,' he added, lowering his voice, his black eyes boring into her. 'Your friend du Roc will not be riding for me again,' he went on angrily. 'I have just made that quite clear to him and your father. The jockey lost us the race. He was far too easy on Bahir; racehorses are not made of cotton wool, you know. They must learn to take the pressure.' His eyes raked around the enclosure as though defying anyone to disagree with him.

'I'm sorry you didn't win,' Lucy replied coldly. 'It's infuriating, of course, to come so close but if Alain was easy on your colt there's bound to be a good reason. He likes to win as much as you do, you know.'

Hassim snorted. 'There was no evidence of that today. No one makes a fool of me like that and gets another chance.' He turned abruptly on his heel and strode off.

Lucy shrugged her shoulders. Really, the man was intolerable, she thought: an incredibly bad loser! Quite unlike the other Arab owners she knew, the Maktoums or Prince Khalad Abdullah. To accuse Alain of deliberately not riding the colt out was insulting: everyone knew he was one of the straightest jockeys around.

She bounded over to Tod as he leant on the rail talking to a Chantilly trainer.

'Hello, Daddy. Bad luck,' she said, flinging an arm around his neck.

Tod turned around, his expression transformed with pleasure. 'Lucy! I wasn't sure if you'd make it or not. I tried to contact you this morning, to ask you to lunch, but the Normandy said there was no reply from your room. It's a real tonic to see you at last,' he said with affection. 'You saw our defeat just now, I suppose?' He pulled a face. 'I think Bahir ran an excellent race, considering the going was too firm for him. Alain says he was clearly feeling the ground when he asked him to quicken two furlongs out. You could see it, actually: he kept changing his legs.' He shrugged his shoulders. 'I'm afraid your friend Hassim does not see it that way, though. He blames Alain entirely – says he doesn't want him to ride for him any more.' He sighed. 'God knows whether he means it or not. I rather fear he does.' He turned away from the French trainer. 'He's wrong, of course,' he confided to Lucy. 'It made absolute sense for Alain to go easy on the colt in the circumstances. After all, none of us wants to break him down. Oh well, let's just hope it all blows over.' He tucked his racecard in his pocket. 'For God's sake let's go and have a drink. Myra's organized a table with the de Bernay cousins and I know they're longing to see you.'

Lucy leant across and kissed her cousin's wife, Alexis de Bernay, warmly on both cheeks. '*Au revoir, chérie*, I must go. I've got a rendezvous over at the polo.' She smiled her dazzling smile. 'It's been so lovely to see you and Bernard. Thanks so much for putting up with

Toby too, by the way. I'm glad you got him working on the stud, mucking out boxes and all that – it took his mind off himself for a change!' She waved at Alexis's husband, Bernard, sitting at the far end of the table, and blew him a kiss. 'Ciao, Bernard. *A bientôt, j'espère.*'

Stepping over to her father's chair, she touched the back of his neck. 'I'm off, Daddy – got to meet a girlfriend from New York over at the polo.'

Tod got up, downing the remains of his drink. 'I'll come with you. I could do with a little walk,' he informed her. 'There's someone over there I need to see, too. I'll just have a word with Myra. You go ahead.'

'I do think it was rotten of Tobes not to show up this afternoon,' Lucy complained as they were strolling round the main stands towards the racetrack. 'What's the matter with the little sod?'

Tod shrugged his shoulders. 'God knows. When he saw that this old James Dean movie was on in the town he just insisted on going to that instead.'

'I thought perhaps I'd take him out for a drink or something after racing,' Lucy volunteered. 'Try to have a talk with him, you know. I'm not dining till late.'

'Well, I'd be delighted if you could,' Tod replied enthusiastically. 'He might actually tell you what's going on in his head at the moment. I'd be the last to know!'

A fair number of people were drifting across from the stands now, making their way across the track to the polo grounds beyond, where two new teams were just emerging for their first chukka. It was less humid, too, and far out to sea, beyond the slate rooftops of the town, the clouds were breaking up, revealing clear strips of azure blue, and a faint but welcome breeze was blowing in from the bay.

Lucy clutched her father closer. 'I should have brought my *pull*. Never mind, you can warm me up instead!' She shook her hair. 'Don't worry about Tobes, Daddy. I'm sure he'll be all right. I think he should just re-take his wretched exams in November and then make a decision about whether he still wants to try for veterinary college or not, don't you? My bet is that he's gone off the whole idea but doesn't want to tell us. That's probably part of the trouble.' She looked pensive for a moment. 'In my opinion, what he really needs is a girlfriend. A good fuck, to be really crude about it!'

Tod stopped to light a cigarette. 'I can't think why you always think the cure for everything is sex,' he commented, amused. 'Women can be very distracting, you know.'

Lucy raised her eyebrows. 'Really!' She paused. 'Who did you say you had to meet over here?' she inquired casually.

'Well, I didn't actually,' Tod replied, embarrassed, 'just one of our owners: Kate Leverton. I think you've met her. She's a photographer. She's taking some pictures today for *Tatler* and a book she's working on with Sandy Diss.'

Lucy frowned. 'Kate Leverton?' Her face cleared. 'Oh yes, of course. That pretty girl with the snub nose. She's rather nice.' She nudged Tod in the ribs. 'Do you fancy her, then? Come to think of it, she's probably your type,' she commented.

'Of course I don't fancy her,' Tod replied sharply. 'I'm far too old to fancy anyone any more. Certainly anyone as young as Kate. She's only about the same age as you, you know.'

'So what?' Lucy retorted. 'Loads of men your age take up with women young enough to be their daughters. It gives them new vigour, so I'm told! Just what you need, Daddy. You could do with someone else, now Marie Claire's off the scene.'

Tod had told Lucy about his affair with her mother's friend when she was about seventeen, trusting her to keep it a secret, which she always had. He realized, of course, that she would be pleased rather than shocked. Anything that could in any way undermine Myra would always have Lucy's support.

'I told you,' Tod replied firmly, 'I'm past all that sort of thing!'

They had passed through the entrance to the polo ground now and were walking behind the stands fringing the edge of the field. There was quite a crowd gathered around the row of tea tables, the buzz of their conversation punctuated by the crack of mallet on ball.

'How many horses has Kate Leverton got with you, then?' Lucy asked innocently, shading her eyes against the sun as she looked around for her friend.

'Only the one. A little Greek Dancer colt – Achilles. She shares him with her mother, Lady Kitty. We've had endless problems with him, I'm afraid, but it does now look, touch wood, as though he might be properly sound again.' He took a pull on his cigarette. 'I can't wait to tell Kate that he's coming back into training next week. She'll be delighted – she's very involved with the colt.'

Mmm, that's probably not all she's involved with, by the sound of it, Lucy thought to herself with some amusement. 'Are you around for lunch tomorrow?' she inquired. 'It's my only chance to see you again – I'm heading back to Paris afterwards.'

'I'm not sure,' Tod replied cagily. 'Myra and Toby are lunching with the Carnegies but I managed to get out of that.' He paused. 'I might be free at lunchtime, but I'm not sure. I had vaguely planned to have lunch with Kate, actually,' he admitted, grinning. 'It's only a tentative date, though. She may well not be free. It's one of the things I thought I could find out now.' Screwing up his eyes against the sun, he peered towards the rows of polo ponies tethered in the distance.

'Well, perhaps we could all have lunch together then, somewhere in Honfleur perhaps or in the Courtyard at the Normandy, if you're sure I wouldn't be intruding,' Lucy replied sweetly.

She turned away in an attempt to conceal her amusement. She did not, for one moment, believe her father's denial. As he looked around for Kate anxiously, it was obvious that he was longing to see her.

Barons Lodge

Dropping the pair of reins he had been soaping, Liam hurried over to the tack-room window. Peering out through the drizzle he caught a glimpse of Barons Lodge's maroon-coloured horsebox bringing Bahir and Angie back from Stansted as it swung through the gates and turned into the lower yard. At last they were back safe and sound, Liam thought with relief. He was bursting to talk to Angie alone and had hoped that if he hung around the yard long enough now when all the other lads were off duty, he might get the chance. He wouldn't go down to Bahir's box yet, though; he'd give it at least ten minutes. Sam Shaw was already hurrying out of the office to greet his daughter and would want to get a full account of the race yesterday and to check Bahir over carefully without any interruption.

Angie had been more than usually busy recently. On top of her usual work in the yard, she had started a course of evening classes in bookkeeping and secretarial work in Cambridge so that she might be able to help her mother out in the office, and she hardly ever seemed to be free. By dint of much hard work, overtime and even a few careful bets Liam had managed to save £300 of the money he owed Rory. He was very reluctant to break into this to buy a car, but he did not have any alternative, he decided, if he wanted to compete with Jack Massam for Angie's affections. After asking around for weeks he had finally acquired a rusty Ford Escort for £100 in cash from one of the lads up at Warren Place. He planned to suggest to Angie today that they went out to her favourite pub for a drink together on Friday, a night he knew Massam would be away racing at Goodwood. He couldn't wait to see her face when she saw he'd actually got himself a car.

Angie was bending down, bandaging one of the colt's forelegs, when he leant over the half-door of Bahir's box.

'Hello there,' he called out softly. 'Did you enjoy your trip to France, then? I'm really sorry you didn't win, but the colt ran a grand race all the same, I'm told. How is he now? Is he all right?'

Angie looked up, surprised. Her face was flushed from bending over but she looked tired, Liam thought. There were circles underneath her brown eyes and they looked strained and devoid of their usual sparkle.

'Hello, Liam,' she said wearily. 'Deauville was great. I didn't have time to see much of the town, though, but it looked like there were some very posh shops and restaurants and things.' She made a face. 'We were delayed for hours at the airport on our way out – some stupid regulations – and then we had to leave very early this morning. Hostel was nice, though. Lovely chips in the café there, too.' She bent down again and ran her hand down Bahir's off fore. 'I'm worried about my baby here, Liam. He got ever so jarred up on that ground. Alain du Roc rode him as gently as he could, I know, but he's still quite sore all round.'

'Mr Kyle said the ground was really too firm for him, but Prince Hassim insisted on running him. Still, at least you had a good pilot,' Liam said sympathetically. 'You can trust du Roc to look after his horses.'

'Meaning there's some you can't, I suppose,' Angie snapped as she straightened up again.

'No, no, I didn't mean that at all,' Liam replied, defensively. 'I was just trying to cheer you up, that's all. It must be really disappointing to go all the way to France for a big race and just get touched off like your fella did. But at least he's come out of the race more or less OK. That's all I meant.'

'Hmm,' Angie replied, looking preoccupied as she checked the buckle at the front of Bahir's rug. She swung back to Liam, a purposeful look on her face. 'Look, there's something I ought to tell you,' she said quietly. 'Jack and I are getting engaged.' She pushed a lock of hair out of her eyes. 'We haven't announced it publicly yet. We want to wait till later in the week when Jack's riding up at Pontefract. He can tell his Mum and Dad in person then and they can have a little celebration. They only live about two miles from the course, you see.' She patted Bahir's neck, avoiding Liam's eye. 'I just thought you ought to know right now, that's all. Just so that we don't get any more sarky comments!' She bent down and picked up her grooming kit. 'Don't tell anyone else, though, will you? I'm sure I can trust you to keep it a secret. I've kept yours after all, haven't I?' She smiled at him quizzically. 'Well, did the cat get your tongue? Aren't you going to congratulate me or anything, then?'

Liam sagged against the box door feeling as though he had been winded. This was what he had been most dreading. There had been a rumour that Sam Shaw wanted Jack and Angie to get engaged but he had, quite deliberately, chosen to ignore it. Racing-yard gossip was usually exaggerated, he had told himself. Taking a deep breath, he pushed himself away from the box door.

'Yeah, sure, of course. I'll be off now, then. Got a lot of work to do,' he muttered. 'Don't you worry, though. I won't be telling anyone at all about you and Jack. Don't you worry about that.' He reeled round the corner of the stable block, his eyes half blinded by tears. He must get away from Angie and out of sight of the office too, he thought, unable to conceal his feelings. Stumbling across the grass into Achilles's empty box, he flung himself inside and crouched sobbing on the straw. All his hopes had crashed now, all his dreams of one day being able to tell Angie how much he loved her and wanted to look after her the way she deserved. As he sat hunched against the box wall, two things became gradually clear. One was that, whatever happened, he knew he would never be able to stop loving Angie: he was sure, in his bones, that she was the right girl for him. Somehow, he didn't know how, he would have to find a way of coping with seeing her every day. There was no way that he could leave Barons Lodge now that Jacko was coming back into training. Glancing around at the plain whitewashed walls of the box with its dusty oak-beamed ceiling, he also vowed that from now on, his energies would be concentrated on Achilles: all his skill and devotion must go towards getting the colt fit again and out on to the racecourse, where he belonged.

CHAPTER SEVENTEEN

Newmarket Gallops

'Aren't you taking a bit of a risk putting du Roc up this morning?' Basil Hunter asked. 'I mean, from what I gather Hassim has unofficially jocked him off and presumably that means he's barred him from riding work on his horses as well.' His face wore a petulant expression as he sat beside Tod, cursing his hangover as they drove swiftly up the hill out of the town and waited to turn right on to the approach to the Rowley Mile racecourse.

Tod shrugged his shoulders. 'I don't see why. The important thing is that Alain knows the colt better than anyone else and I am still not one hundred per cent sure he has not gone over the top.' He accelerated across the main road and towards the avenue of trees that led towards the racecourse, their russet leaves brilliant in the early morning light. 'After all, this is his final piece of work before Saturday. I've really got to make a decision today as to whether he runs or not; Alain's opinion will be invaluable.' He slowed down to observe a string of horses jogging along by the side of the road, ears pricked, coats still shining under their work rugs.

'Gerry's horses look bloody well, don't they? God knows what he's feeding them on. Caviare probably!' He wound down the window and peered out beyond the racecourse stables. 'Bugger it! There's no sign of my lot. Charlie must have met up with Alain and gone on ahead.' He had hoped to catch up with his string, led by Charlie Kyle on his hack, before they went out on the gallops, but he had been delayed just as he was leaving the yard by a phone call from a particularly tiresome and loquacious owner and he was obviously too late. 'Oh well, Charlie knows what he's doing. It's not the end of the world.' He wound his window back up again and swung left into the Members' Car Park. It was deserted at this hour of the morning except for a cluster of cars and Range Rovers belonging to other trainers and du Roc's red Porsche in the far corner.

'But suppose Hassim finds out? He'd be pretty pissed off, wouldn't he?' Basil persisted.

Tod grinned. 'Why should he find out? He's in New York right now, I gather. Anyway, in the unlikely event that he does get to hear about it, I'll probably just deny it – say we've got a du Roc look-alike amongst the lads.' He patted Basil's knee. 'Bit windy this morning, aren't we? Better go easier on the port tonight.'

Basil groaned. 'Never again, old chap. Doesn't seem to suit me any more. I must be getting old.'

Tod swung the car right towards the Members' Entrance and glanced at his brother-in-law, sitting wanly beside him. 'We all get a bit jaded at this stage in the season. Instead of trekking off to Keeneland you should have taken a week at that health farm, what's it called, Forest Mere, that Pam's always going on about.' He looked suddenly thoughtful as he eased the car to a halt. Talking of holidays, he must remember to ask Basil if he and Pam were intending to go to Barbados again this winter. If they were, it was imperative he encouraged them to take Myra with them again and Toby too, if possible. He desperately needed some time alone with Kate. He was worried about the way things were going with her at the moment. Her frustration and irritation at seeing him so seldom were obviously growing and he wanted to reassure her that at least in December or January they would be able to spend time together.

Despite the fact that Kate had always said she liked Lucy and wanted to get to know her better, the lunch in Honfleur had not been a total success. The two women had got on well enough but Kate was obviously upset that she and Tod were not lunching *à deux* and he had been the recipient of several definitely reproachful looks from her expressive grey eyes. Lucy, on the other hand, in an effort to be on her best behaviour, had curbed her usual flow of inconsequential gossip and had persisted in asking Kate a lot of questions, ostensibly out of genuine interest, but also, Tod realized, in an attempt to elicit more about their relationship.

His daughter had unnerved him further by darting amused looks at him under her lashes from time to time and he had not been a bit surprised when she had confronted him directly. 'Daddy! You naughty old thing!' she had said, giggling, when Kate went off at one point to the Ladies. 'It's quite obvious you two are mad about each other.' She snorted. 'Just one of our owners! Really! I feel seriously *de trop*, I can tell you.' Tod grinned, admitting defeat. 'Serves you right for inviting yourself,' he replied. 'I should have told you before, I know, but you

234

rather caught me off guard yesterday.' His face went serious. 'I am actually in love with her, Lucy, and believe it or not, she says she's in love with me. God knows what we're going to do about it.' He frowned. 'But it can't be that obvious, surely – can it? No one else seems to have noticed. We've had to be so careful. You know what a goldfish bowl Newmarket is.'

Lucy put her hand over his. 'Don't worry. It's only because I know you so well,' she reassured him. 'I'm delighted, of course. I would be, wouldn't I? My views on Myra haven't changed.' She drained her wine glass and looked at him thoughtfully. 'But play it carefully, won't you, Daddy? She's sweet and very pretty, but I think she's straight too, and probably not cut out to be a mistress. My guess is that if you are intending to leave Myra, you'll have to make a move soon or you'll lose her. I know it'll be difficult with Tobes in such a state and all that, but I'd do it if I were you. If it's what you and Kate both really want.' She glanced up smiling as Kate approached the table. 'Anyway, I'm on your side, remember?' she added softly.

Tod's brooding about Lucy's warning was interrupted by Basil tapping impatiently on the car window.

'Come on, Tod, for Christ's sake. Stop daydreaming. At this rate, all we'll see of Bahir is a distant view of his backside.'

Tod flung open the car door. 'Sorry, I was miles away,' he apologized, grabbing his binoculars from the back seat and loping off after his brother-in-law.

He trusted Charlie Kyle not to start Bahir and his companion off on their gallop before he was in position about half a furlong down the course from the winning post. The two horses would be working six furlongs across the flat on the broad strip of turf that ran parallel with the Rowley Mile racecourse itself, one of the best pieces of autumn galloping ground anywhere on the Heath. As he did not have another two-year-old in the yard good enough or mature enough to work with Bahir, Tod had decided to gallop him with one of his older horses, a four-year-old miler called Godless, a frequently unsound but speedy Red God colt who would be carrying one and a half stone more than du Roc. If Bahir went considerably better than Godless did, which he was certainly capable of doing, Tod would know that he hadn't yet gone over the top for the season. The colt seemed fine, very much on his toes recently, but that could also indicate that he'd had enough.

A pale gold mist still hung in patches over the Heath ahead and the clumps of horses moving purposefully at various speeds over the expanse of gallops were like parts of some unco-ordinated cavalry manoeuvre. Tod sniffed the air with pleasure as he strode across the track and headed down the far rail towards the furlong marker. He loved the sharp scent of autumn. It always made him feel nostalgic, reminding him of cubbing mornings years ago, hacking his pony to the meet with his father's old groom, heading westwards away from the arable land to the fringes of the Belvoir country, past hedges bright with berries and tufts of old man's beard.

His thoughts turned again to Kate. Lucy was right, of course. She would not be able to cope with the present situation for much longer. She was not a devious girl or a compromiser, and having to continue to share him with Myra would inevitably make her more and more unhappy, and he could not bear that. She would be busy this autumn – she had taken on a lot of magazine work and had to make the final selection of pictures for the book – but she would, he knew, be taking some time off over Christmas. By then, with Toby's exams – not to mention the sales and the flat-racing season – over, they would really have to sit down and work out what they were going to do. He was in love with her: there was no doubt about that. He had never thought it would happen again after losing Monique and he would be forever grateful; but he was also apprehensive that this love would be soured by all the unpleasantness and financial wrangling that a break with Myra would entail. He knew that he was more adaptable than most people who had been training horses for most of their lives and as long as he could have horses about him he would be quite glad to get off the daily treadmill; he could happily settle down to running a small stud, he supposed. But he would be left with little money and he was not at all sure that this was the right solution for Kate in the long run. He was, he knew, providing some sort of vital experience for her at the moment, fulfilling perhaps some emotional need caused by the early death of her father. But she would be thirty soon and would surely want a home with someone of her own age and children. Did he really want to start right at the beginning again himself? He was not at all sure. It was not the scandal or even the upheaval of leaving Myra that bothered him; it was just that he seemed to have been around for such a long time and had used up so much emotional energy already that he feared that there would not be enough left to sustain a new life with Kate. The whole business obviously needed a great deal more thought.

'By the way, I've been meaning to ask you, were you and Pam

thinking of jaunting off to Barbados again this winter?' he asked Basil as they leant on the running rail.

Basil looked a trifle taken aback. 'Barbados? Er, yes, well we were actually – Pam's particularly keen. Trouble is, if we do go we'd have to go over Christmas – that's the only time the house we want is available, apparently.' He bit his lip and gazed into the distance. 'Bit of a problem, really. I mean, we usually come to you for Christmas and we wouldn't want to upset anyone or anything.' His voice trailed off.

Tod raised his binoculars and raked the horizon in search of Charlie Kyle and his two colts. In the distance he caught a glimpse of the old Rubbing House and the sun glinting on the windows of the vehicles thundering along the main road beyond. 'Oh, I wouldn't worry about that,' he said airily. 'You'd be well out of it. After all, last Christmas was hardly a howling success, was it? Myra never stopped complaining about all of us, mainly me of course, and Lucy's sworn to be as far away as possible this year.' He grinned. 'So I'd book up, if I were you, and take Toby and Myra too, if you can face it. You can put it to her over dinner tonight.' He paused in concentration. 'Ah, they're lining up at last.' He swung his glasses leftwards as the two horses began to move towards them.

As the sound of their thudding hoofs grew closer, Bahir seemed to be going well enough; du Roc's face was intent as he crouched low over the colt's withers in his dark-blue Husky and blue bobble hat. As they drew level and the noise of their breathing and the creak of straining leather grew louder, Tod tightened his hold on his glasses. 'OK, now Alain, press the button,' he murmured gently. Right on cue, as they had agreed, the Frenchman bent lower into a drive position and, changing his hands on the reins, urged the bay colt to quicken. Without hesitating, Bahir lengthened his stride and, stretching his head out, began to cruise easily past his companion, his black tail streaming behind.

'Mmm . . . no way has that colt gone over the top! If he's not right on song, I'll eat my hat,' Basil commented, obviously impressed. 'At least you can tell Hassim now that you're all set for Saturday. That's one worry less.'

Tod did not reply. With his binoculars still trained on the quarters of the two horses as they drew level with the winning post, his grip suddenly froze.

As du Roc began to ease Bahir up, the colt seemed to stumble, causing the jockey to look anxiously downwards. Shouting something to the lad on Godless, he immediately began to pull his mount up.

'Sod it! Something's up!' Tod muttered. Dropping his binoculars, he began to sprint back up the track. By the time he reached the winning post, Bahir had slowed to a trot and was clearly hobbling. Reining him to a walk, du Roc slipped out of the saddle and, looping the reins over his arm, bent down anxiously. He turned to Tod as he hurried closer, his lined weatherbeaten face creased with concern.

'*C'est assez grave, je crois.* He was going so sweetly, and had quickened so well when he suddenly stumbled,' he said anxiously. 'I felt something go just as I was pulling him up.' He turned back to Bahir, who was standing on three legs, his off fore dangling; the colt's eyes were wide with alarm and a patch of sweat had broken out on his shoulder. Du Roc stroked his neck as he gazed downwards. '*Tiens! Mon pauvre petit, mon pauvre petit,*' he murmured softly.

Tod bent down to look at the leg. 'You're right,' he said tersely. 'Looks like a bad fracture to me.' He straightened up again. 'You stay with him. I'll go and phone the vet.' He glanced past Bahir to where the lad on Godless was circling around with a worried expression. 'Trot over and find Mr Kyle and the rest of them, will you, Steve, and tell him what's happened. Then give your fellow a pick of grass and walk him home slowly. Right, off you go. There's no point in you hanging around here.'

The colt could have just chipped a bone or fractured his pastern, he thought, as he hurried off towards the racecourse offices, but his experience told him that the fracture was more serious. He was used to sudden disasters; he'd been training for years, after all, and had learnt to be both stoical and philosophical about them. But this really was a blow. Bahir was the only horse in the yard with any real potential. Tod strode on with a heavy heart.

A quarter of an hour later, as he bent over Bahir's leg with the vet, he fought off a wave of sick despair.

'Nothing we can do, Tod, I'm afraid,' the vet announced. 'It's a spiral fracture of the cannon bone. No doubt about it.' He patted Bahir's neck, now awash with sweat, and looked apologetically from Tod to Alain du Roc, still holding the horse's head. 'Poor fella. And he's a good one, I gather, too. Always the way, isn't it? Sod's law. Oh well, better get on with it.' He crouched down on the grass and reached in his bag for the humane killer.

'You're pathetic. I thought you were finished with that creep Hassim – weren't ever going to see him again. That's what you said on holiday,' Celeste said accusingly, struggling to balance her box of multicoloured eyeshadow against the ledge of the taxi window. She peered at her reflection in the little mirror, smoothing some more silver on her eyelid as she did so. 'What made you change your mind, then? Sex, I suppose, or that necklace. For Christ's sake, how can you be such a tart?'

Lucy leant back against the seat, closing her eyes and fingering the eighteen-carat gold and ruby necklace with its serpent motif that curled snugly round her creamy throat. 'It's got nothing to do with the necklace,' she replied, unruffled. 'It would be a pity to give it back, though – it rather suits me, don't you think?'

'It's ravishing, honey,' Celeste replied, without looking up. 'As you well know. Keep it, don't be a fool. But finish with Hassim, for Christ's sake. The guy's a screwball.'

'He's a good fuck, though,' Lucy giggled. 'At least he can get it up, which is more than can be said for some.' She opened her eyes and gazed at the taxi ceiling. 'Grant is very sweet, I know, but he's useless in bed,' she said, referring to a successful criminal lawyer she'd had a brief fling with on holiday in Maine. 'I'm getting desperate. I suspect he's gay, poor man.'

Celeste peered out of the window at the sleek façades of Sixth Avenue and at the hooting, slow-moving vehicles all around them, shiny in the wet. The traffic had been terrible since they left Celeste's apartment in Bleeker Street twenty minutes ago. 'Christ, we're only coming up to Forty-second Street. I'm sure I'm going to be late.' She leant forward and banged on the grille. 'Driver, can you cross over to 8th and drop me at Columbus Circle. Thanks. I'll leg it to the Met from there,' she explained to Lucy. 'It's only four blocks. Otherwise I'll never make it.'

'I can't finish with Hassim this evening. It's just not the moment,' Lucy was musing. 'He's in a bad enough state as it is – been leaving messages for me all over town, which is very unlike him. You know how discreet he usually is.' She turned to Celeste, her amber eyes suddenly sad. 'It's Bahir. His best two-year-old, the one Daddy trains for him. He broke his leg on the gallops this morning, apparently, and had to be put down. Hassim's really upset.' She sighed. 'It's terrible. He was such a beautiful colt; I saw him win the Coventry at Royal Ascot. They're so fragile these thoroughbreds. I'm so sorry for Daddy, it's a real blow for him.' She peered out of the window, trying to make out where they had got to through the slanting rain. 'I can't walk out on Hassim tonight, Celeste. It would be cruel.' She shot her friend a lascivious look under her lashes. 'Anyway, as you so rightly suspected, I could do with a fuck. It might cheer him up too – usually does,' she said blithely.

Celeste glanced at her watch, its narrow diamond bracelet glinting in the street lights as they came up to the corner of Columbus Circle and Central Park South. 'Christ, I really am going to be late,' she said. 'This'll do. I'd better make a dash for it. Oh! There's something I forgot.' She leant forward, a mischievous smile on her face, and stuck one of her slender fingers between her legs for a moment. Withdrawing it, damp with moisture, she dabbed herself behind one ear and then the other. 'That'll take his mind off Janáček,' she grinned. She leant over and kissed Lucy lightly on the cheek, the scent of Joy mingling with the muskier one of her sex. 'Have a terrific evening!' she said sarcastically. 'And if you come home stripe-arsed and bleeding, don't blame me!' She flung open the door and, grabbing her umbrella from the floor, slid out into the wet.

Lucy grinned at the memory of Celeste and what she described as her 'old whore's trick' as she lay sprawling on the bed in Hassim's suite at the Plaza an hour later. Although the hotel had no links with his own establishment in London, he usually stayed there on his business trips to New York. Sipping champagne with a silver tray of caviare and toast at her elbow, Lucy was wearing nothing but her necklace and the minutest pair of black lace briefs.

Hassim, lolling against a mound of pillows in his white robe, gazed at her hungrily, stroking his beard. Dipping a finger of his other hand in his glass of champagne, he leant over and ran it lightly round one of her nipples until it sprung into a peak. Lucy shuddered, easing her long legs slightly apart.

'Ah, that is what I like to see. You have missed me then, after all, have you not?' Hassim asked softly. 'You think that maybe you don't like to see me too much any more. You think you prefer your all-American guy perhaps? He is more suitable, more available, you tell yourself. But it is me you want now, is it not? I am the choice of your body.' He bent over her urgently and with one powerful movement of his hands ripped the delicate fabric of her knickers in two.

Putting down her glass of champagne, Lucy sank gratefully backwards, her chestnut mane hanging over the edge of the bed, fringing the floor. How did he know about Grant? she wondered idly. Oh well, it was, after all, current Manhattan gossip and no doubt Hassim had his spies. Anyhow, what did it matter? She was obviously in for a good going over and that, for the moment, was all she cared about.

'If you have not been a good girl, I shall punish you later,' Hassim was murmuring. 'For the moment I just need to possess you. It will help me to forget.'

Lucy rolled over and started caressing him lightly under his robe with her slender fingers. 'I know,' she said sympathetically. 'I understand.'

Twenty minutes later when Hassim had exploded into her and they were still lying, slippery with the sweat of their exertions, immobile on the sheets, the telephone rang beside them. Lifting his head from her breasts Hassim swore lightly in Arabic as it continued ringing. Finally, with a louder expletive, he rolled over and picked up the receiver. 'I said no calls. I asked not to be disturbed,' he barked. 'Oh, I see, a call from England, from Newmarket.' He glanced at his watch. 'At this hour?' He looked puzzled. 'All right, OK, I'll take it.' He swung his legs off the bed and hurriedly pulled on his silk dressing-gown.

Lucy eased herself up on the pillows. It was two o'clock in the morning in England, she thought, puzzled. It was very unlikely to be her father at that hour. She wondered idly who it could possibly be.

Hassim sat motionless as he waited for the call, his eyes narrowing with impatience.

'Yes, hello, this is Prince Hassim. Yes. Yes. How are you?' His forehead creased into a frown. 'Yes, yes. A tragic accident. It is very sad. I will not be going to the racecourse on Saturday, so I shall not be lunching with you after all. Yes, yes, of course I shall be at the sales. I'm flying back on Concorde tomorrow. Yes, yes, if the Habitat filly is as good as you say she is, go ahead and bid for her. I'm prepared to go to half a million – more if any of the Maktoums are after her too. I'll call you tomorrow. All right?' Obviously keen to get off the phone, his voice was tinged with impatience. 'What? No, Beckhampton is not getting any more yearlings from me, I've told you.' He paused, his expression puzzled. 'No, no, du Roc does not ride any of my horses either, not any more. What are you saying? I don't understand.'

Lucy shot back against the pillows in alarm. The call was presumably from someone else who trained for Hassim. She couldn't imagine what had just been said but whatever it was, it was more bad news. Her unease mounted as she glanced up at Hassim. He clutched the phone tightly, his face darkening as he listened further.

'What! I cannot believe this! Are you sure?' he asked eventually. 'I see. Well, thank you for telling me. Yes, yes. Tomorrow. You will hear from me when I get to Heathrow. Goodbye.'

He banged the receiver back into its socket and turned to Lucy, his eyes glittering with anger. 'Do you know what I have just learnt? Your friend du Roc was riding Bahir when he had his accident this morning. I cannot believe it! Of course your father did not tell me that!' He spat the word out in his fury. 'Oh no! The man is a coward. He is also a fool to disobey my orders. I told him at Deauville that du Roc was never to ride any of my horses, under any circumstances, ever again.' Quivering with rage he picked up his champagne glass and flung it across the room, shattering it against the wall. 'How can he have been so stupid as to disobey me?' He thumped his fist down on the bed. 'It is his fault I have lost the colt. I shall not forgive him. I shall hold him responsible, do you hear me? Do you?' he thundered.

Lucy clutched the sheet more tightly around her, fervently wishing that he would calm down and stop being so horrid about her father. She also wished she felt less dozy. She had had several orgasms and, for the first time in weeks, felt sexually replete.

'Look,' she said, making a great effort to sound soothing. 'I'm terribly sorry about Bahir. It's such bad luck and so sad. But it's no one's fault – not Daddy's nor Alain's. Horses do sometimes shatter their legs on the gallops, you know. It's happened to Daddy several times, I know, but he didn't pick on the lad or the jockey or anyone. Why must you always find someone to blame? It's so childish.'

With a look of outrage, Hassim reached over and grabbed her shoulder, digging his fingers into her flesh. 'I only sent horses to your father to please you. It was you who persuaded me to give him a chance with Bahir and he has blown it. The man is a fool. How can you possibly defend him?' He glared at her with real hatred.

Lucy's patience suddenly snapped. Sliding off the bed she picked up the black silk kimono she'd left lying on the floor. 'Right,' she said quietly, struggling to keep her tone casual. 'I'm going to get dressed, then I'm going. I'm not prepared to listen to anyone running down Daddy like that. Bahir's accident wasn't his fault and you know it. He's a brilliant trainer, you told me so yourself before you lost your bottle at Deauville.' She headed towards the bathroom door.

Hassim grabbed her arm. 'You're not going anywhere! I haven't finished what I have to say to you yet. Get back on that bed,' he ordered, pushing her back down on the rumpled sheets. 'I blame you for a lot of this, you know. If you were not so friendly with du Roc, your father would not be so keen on him either. Is that not true?'

'Of course not,' Lucy replied indignantly, shaking her arm free of his grip. 'Daddy admires Alain because he's one of the best horsemen around – and I mean horseman, not just jockey. You're upset and you've lost all sense of proportion. Most people think they're bloody lucky if they can get Alain to ride for them. You're just jealous, that's all.' She got up purposefully, clutching her kimono around her. 'Right. I'm going to get dressed. You're being very boring.'

Hassim moved towards her with renewed fury. 'Don't speak to me like that. It is intolerable!' he exploded. Lifting his arm he hit her powerfully with his clenched fist, knocking her to the floor.

Lucy lay numb with shock, a burning sensation on the side of her face, her whole body trembling. She rolled over slowly and attempted to get shakily to her knees. 'You bastard! That really hurt,' she sobbed. Reaching for the clasp of her necklace, she ripped it off and flung it towards him. 'I hate you. I hate you and your presents,' she screamed. She staggered to her feet and stumbled across the room into the bathroom.

Slamming the door behind her she locked it quickly and slumped on to the floor. As well as the shock of what Hassim had done to her, she felt furious. How dare he hurt her like that! Punishment in bed was one thing but being seriously hit like that was definitely against the rules. No way would she put up with it any longer.

'Why don't you fuck off?' she shouted angrily through the door when she had got her breath back. 'You're just a jealous maniac, that's all. I wish I'd never got involved with you in the first place. I must have been mad.' Pressing her hand to her cheek, she sniffed loudly. 'Just fuck off and leave me alone. I don't want to see you again, ever,' she added tearfully.

After clutching herself for a minute, she got shakily to her feet and went over to the mirror. Much to her horror, she saw that Hassim's blow had left a great weal across the side of her face; and her left eye was already looking decidedly puffy, and beginning to throb alarmingly. Gingerly splashing cold water on her face, she blew her nose and looked around for the clothes she had shed so eagerly earlier. Luckily for once she had left them all in the bathroom, instead of all over the suite as usual. She put on her bra, suspender belt and stockings as quickly as she could and, dropping her black satin Dior dress over her head, smoothed it down over her body. Her face and hair looked frightful, she knew, but she couldn't do anything about it as her handbag and make-up were still in the bedroom. Anyway, she brooded, she wanted that bastard Hassim to see the damage he had inflicted.

Unlocking the bathroom door, she opened it warily. Hassim was sitting on the bed in his dressing-gown. He looked calmer, his rage obviously subsiding, but his expression remained grim.

'I am sorry,' he said gruffly, without looking up at her. 'I should not have hit you like that.' He scowled at the floor. 'But you do provoke me so. It is unbearable. Nevertheless, I should not have lost my temper. I hope you will accept my apologies.'

'No way,' Lucy retorted angrily. 'That's it. As I said, no one hurts me like that. We're through.'

Hassim stared at her in disbelief. 'I have apologized to you, have I not?' he asked indignantly. 'That is hard for a man like myself, you know. What more can I do? If I have hurt you, I shall make it up to you, of course. As I have said, I am sorry.'

'Too late,' Lucy retorted firmly. She picked up her black satin jacket and slung it around her shoulders. 'I'm off. That's it. Goodbye.'

Hassim stood up, still staring at her, his expression menacing. 'If you walk out on me now, just like this, I will not forgive you,' he warned, breathing heavily. 'I will call your father right now and tell him I am taking my other two horses away.'

'Go ahead,' Lucy replied with bravado, shaking her hair forward to conceal her injured face. 'Do what you bloody well like! Daddy wouldn't want your horses anyway if he knew you'd hurt me in any way.' Picking up her handbag, she turned on her heel. As she wrenched open the suite door with shaking hands, she heard Hassim pick up the phone behind her.

'Get me that number in Newmarket, England, I rang earlier, will you? Mr Tod Beckhampton,' he ordered loudly. 'Yes, I am aware of what time it is over there. Just get on with it, will you? I have some news I wish to convey to him as soon as possible.'

CHAPTER EIGHTEEN

Doncaster Racecourse

Charlie Kyle turned up the collar of his overcoat against the cold as he left the warmth of the emptying stands and headed across the tarmac towards the racecourse stables. He was at Doncaster on a raw foggy November afternoon, for the last meeting of the flat-racing season: two days of fairly mediocre racing attracting large fields as trainers struggled to get a final run into their charges before their long winter lay-off. Barons Lodge had one runner today: a four-year-old handicapper, Anzac Boy, whose owner would be sending him to the Horses in Training Sales at Newmarket in a few weeks' time, in the hope that someone would buy him to go jumping. The horse was a plodder, a one-paced but well-built gelding by Oats who, much to everyone's surprise, had managed to run into third place today, thanks to a determined ride from Jack Massam. It was a run his connections hoped would enhance his chances of finding another owner.

This modest success had not had much effect on Charlie's mood, though, as he strode towards the gaggle of rails bookmakers packing up hurriedly in the dusk, a carpet of torn-up betting tickets softening his tread. He felt tired and dispirited for a number of reasons. It was the end of a long and arduous season; one which in the early summer had seemed to be full of promise. There had been Bahir's Royal Ascot win and the prospect of him making up into a classic three-year-old, and a series of encouraging runs from some of the older horses. But since Bahir's accident, little seemed to have gone right for the yard. Prince Hassim's decision to take his two remaining two-year-olds away and cancel his plan to send Tod any more yearlings in the future had shaken everyone at Barons Lodge and, worse still, seemed to have discouraged any more new owners. Now that Nik Alexandros had taken over the licence at Kilmarron, Stelios Alexandros would be taking his horses away too. Even stalwarts like Jack Weston and his northern friends were cutting down the number of animals they were keeping in training next year. It really did look as though Tod's early-summer change of luck had been only temporary and the yard would be reduced to less than thirty inmates next season.

Charlie's private life was not going particularly well, either. He had come to an unavoidable crossroads with Diana, who had just flown off to Australia for her annual visit to the Melbourne Cup. He had cooked her a special dinner at Keepers Cottage the night before she left. It had been a pleasant enough evening, punctuated by some energetic lovemaking in front of the fire, but over the pheasant casserole, she had delivered him an ultimatum.

'Look, Charlie, we get on great, in bed and out, but if we're to stay together next year, I've got to have more commitment,' she announced with her usual honesty. 'I mean, I understand that you can't spare the time to come to Australia with me and meet some of the family, but you don't seem to want to come and stay in Daddy's house in Barbados in February, either.' She poured herself some more wine and smiled at him, shaking her head. 'I don't understand you, kid. You don't seem to want to have any fun any more. When you're not worrying about Tod and Barons Lodge, you're brooding about that bloke Warrender.'

She leant back in her chair, the firelight flickering on her strong, features. 'I understand that you want to clear your father's name and all that, but it may just not be possible. Has that occurred to you? You've done your best to find Warrender but he's obviously disappeared or certainly left the horse business.' She glanced across at him, a determined look on her face. 'I think you've really got to make the decision to move on, Charlie – concentrate on your own career for a change. It's no good hanging on with Tod just out of loyalty. You should quit now, before the end of the year, to give him plenty of time to get someone else for next season. I'm sure that one of the really big boys would be happy to take you on. You've got a good reputation for being professional and smart. Or, as I've said before, you're welcome to come and help me at Three Swallows; that offer's still open – for the time being.'

She picked up her knife and fork and attacked the remains of her pheasant with enthusiasm. 'Either way, there's no point in drifting on like this. We're getting nowhere. I'd like a decision by the time I get back from Oz at Christmas.' She smiled at him ruefully. 'If you feel you can't make the sort of commitment I want, that we get engaged next year some time, then that's it. We'll stay friends, I hope, but nothing else. I've got ambitions, Charlie, things I want to do with my life, even if you haven't.'

Charlie had not known whether to feel annoyed or amused. Diana's directness had always appealed to him and he still appreciated it but he also realized that she did not really understand him at all. He, too, was ambitious but for the moment that ambition took the form of learning his trade and trying to prove his father's innocence. He would, of course, have liked to have continued with Diana just the way they were. The sex suited him and the hitherto casual nature of their emotional involvement even more so. But he knew too that to expect that to be enough for Diana indefinitely was unrealistic. He did not love her; he was sure about that, so there was no question of their getting married. If he ever got married at all, which he doubted, he had no intention of marrying a woman who had so much more money than he had himself – he would find that demeaning. He had considered accompanying Diana to Australia – it would have given him a chance to make some inquiries about Warrender, after all – but he had decided that if his old mate Andy had not had any success he was unlikely to fare better himself. Instead he had drafted a small advertisement, asking anyone to contact him if they knew of Warrender's whereabouts, for Diana to put in a couple of racing journals out there. For the moment, frustrating though it was, that was all he felt he could do.

'You know my views on marriage. Even you can't change them. It's nothing personal – if that doesn't sound insulting. I'm just not ready to give that sort of commitment, I'm afraid,' he told Diana. He got up to clear the table, feeling a pang of sadness. 'So, if that's what you really want, you must go ahead and find it from someone else.' He bent down to kiss the back of her neck. 'There's no shortage of candidates, is there?' He slipped his hands under her breasts. 'I'll miss you, though. Very much, actually. But that's my bad luck – and some other bloke's good fortune!' He felt his erection stirring. 'I may not be husband material, but I challenge you to find anyone who appreciates you more sexually.' He tweaked one of her nipples affectionately. 'In fact, I wouldn't mind convincing you of that before the pudding. Come on, come over to the sofa!'

Laughing, Diana had of course complied and, as usual, they had fused remarkably well together.

Now, as he headed across the road in the darkening light towards the racecourse stables, Charlie was feeling strangely bereft. He had meant what he'd said. They had been friends as well as lovers and

247

although he was extraordinarily self-sufficient, he was missing her already. This winter, he suspected, would be long and lonely. He was planning to take two weeks off at Christmas and fly to Zimbabwe to see his father. Johnnie Kyle had sounded so low in his last letter that Charlie was now worried more about his mental than his physical health. As well as trying to cheer him up he also felt the need to see a few of his old friends in Salisbury again and get a blast of proper sunshine. Already, as usual at the dreary onset of the English winter, he was feeling homesick for the African heat and the scents and strong colours of the landscape.

But the trip was at least six weeks away and he put it out of his mind as he headed towards the racecourse stables. He had two horses to check over this evening. Anzac Boy would normally have started on his long journey home to Newmarket, but Tod had decided he should stay put so that he could travel back with Achilles who was having his first-ever run tomorrow afternoon.

The colt had recovered remarkably well from all his leg problems, Charlie reflected with pleasure. He had come back into training in September and had been working so well recently that Tod was determined to try to get a run into him before the end of the season. In both their views, the colt had potential and could come on a lot over the winter, so it was essential to try to get some racecourse experience into him as soon as possible. He was still moody in his box, though, and had shown a slight tendency to claustrophobia, both in the starting stalls and in the horsebox. Tod therefore felt that he might travel better with a calmer, older horse in the box with him, so he had accompanied Anzac Boy up this morning and would be going back home with him tomorrow after his race. As a result both horses were, most unusually, spending the night in the racecourse stables.

Charlie had a growing affection for Achilles, or Jacko, as everyone in the yard now called him. Having been responsible for finding the leeches to treat his knee he felt particularly involved with his progress. However, he was less certain than Tod, and certainly than Liam, about the horse's ability to run well tomorrow. Judging by his behaviour on the gallops, he would prove extremely hard to settle and Jack Massam, in Charlie's view, did not possess that rare combination of strength and tenderness necessary to get the best out of him. Few jockeys did. The colt was certainly fit enough but Charlie's fear was that by fighting for his head, he would burn himself out in the early stages of the seven-furlong contest – if he went through the stalls all right, that was. Such misgivings, added to his own feelings of depression, were beginning to convince him it had been a mistake to bring the colt up to Doncaster at all. As he looked around the drab racecourse stables he wished he did not have to hang around the place for another day; he would have much preferred to have checked over Anzac Boy earlier, sent him on his way and have been halfway home by now.

Most of the boxes in the yard were empty. The majority of to-morrow's runners would not arrive at the course until the morning, but a few scattered lights and open box doors indicated where the handful of lads were settling in their charges for the night.

Tod had another reason for wanting to run Achilles tomorrow, of course, Charlie mused, as he looked around for Liam: he wanted to keep the Levertons sweet. They had had so much worry and frustration with their little colt that it was understandable that he wanted to give them the pleasure of seeing their colours in public at last. Although he had not said anything to anyone, not even Diana, he was also certain that the trainer had become involved with Kate Leverton in some way. He'd eagerly grabbed the office phone on a number of occasions when she'd rung up, and had also let slip that she had accompanied him on that visit to Ginger Mann in Norfolk. Having disliked the girl at first, Charlie now admitted that she was undoubtedly pretty and intelligent and a far better photographer than he had imagined; her pictures of Alain du Roc had been remarkably good. It was hardly surprising that Tod needed a romantic fling, given his relationship with Myra, but Charlie hoped, for some reason, that Lady Kitty did not know about the liaison: he had a great deal of respect and liking for her. He was hoping, too, that she would not be too disappointed if Achilles did not run all that well tomorrow and feel that her journey to Doncaster had been wasted.

'Everything all right then, Liam?' he asked, spotting the boy filling up his water buckets in a little alley between the boxes.

Liam turned around, startled. 'Yes, thanks, Mr Kyle. Anzac seems to have come out of his race OK. He's eating up fine.' His anxious face softened. 'And my little fella's settling in grand. Travelled well, too – putting him in with a sensible animal like Anzac sure seems to have done the trick.'

Charlie nodded. 'Good. Now for God's sake get yourself a decent meal later, won't you? You're looking even more starved than usual.'

Liam managed a grin. 'I don't think I'll be eating too much tonight, Mr Kyle. I'm too nervous about tomorrow.'

Charlie shook his head. 'I don't know. You and Jacko here – you make a fine pair!' he commented, putting his hand on the boy's thin

249

shoulder. 'Now don't go hoping for too much tomorrow, will you? I know you think the colt's something special but it is his first-ever run, remember, and you know better than anyone how difficult it is to get him to relax.'

Charlie knew that Liam had once had ambitions to become a jockey, before he had had that accident to his foot, and would have given anything to be riding the horse himself the following day. He also knew that there was no love lost between him and Jack Massam, though Liam seemed to be keeping his opinions of Jack's riding more to himself since Angie Shaw had announced her engagement.

Liam turned off the water tap. 'He'll be all right – if Jack gets him through the starting stalls OK and doesn't let him run too free,' he observed gloomily.

Charlie clapped him on the shoulder. 'Jack'll manage all right. Don't you worry!' He shivered and stuck his hands in his coat pocket. 'Right, I'm off then. It's freezing. Oh, by the way, don't forget to tell whoever's keeping an eye on the horses tonight that Anzac has a tendency to get cast in his box, will you?'

Liam picked up the full bucket of water. 'Sure, sir, of course. The nightwatchman comes on about eight thirty, I think. Some bloke called Warrender, they told me down the office.'

Charlie froze on the spot, his heart thumping. 'What? What did you say his name was?' he asked urgently.

Liam looked at him in surprise, startled by the tension in his voice. 'Warrender, I think it was, Mr Kyle.' He put down his bucket. 'Or could have been Warren. Sorry, I can't remember. I wasn't really paying all that much attention.'

Charlie stared at him for a moment, unseeingly, before turning on his heel and sprinting off in the direction of the office.

Pushing open the door without ceremony, he leant over the stable manager's desk.

'Do you employ a man called Keith Warrender here, as a nightwatchman?' he asked abruptly.

The burly Yorkshireman who had been sitting with his feet up, contemplating a mug of tea, looked taken aback.

'Well, we do, as a matter of fact, lad, when our regular security bloke's away on holiday. Except his Christian name's not Keith, it's Ray. But what's it to you, anyway?' He sniffed disapprovingly. 'And there's no need to come barging in here like that, you know. What's happened to your manners?'

Charlie took a deep breath and gripped the edge of the desk. 'Sorry,' he said quietly. 'The thing is, I've been looking for a man called Warrender for some time,' he explained as calmly as he could. 'He used to work as head lad for my father, the trainer Johnnie Kyle, down in Somerset years ago, and there's something I need to talk to him about.'

The manager shrugged his shoulders. 'Doubt if it's the same bloke, then. This one's been in Australia for years, he says. Certainly showed me a reference from out there somewhere. Got ill, though, and had to come home.' He took a long noisy gulp of his tea. 'Doesn't look like he'll last too long, if you ask me. Terrible colour he is sometimes. Bad-tempered bugger too. I doubt if you'll get much out of him, lad. If it's the same bloke, that is.'

It must be the same man, Charlie thought excitedly. Even if the Christian name was different. There couldn't be two men called War-render in the horse business who had been living out in Australia, surely?

'What time does he come on duty?' he asked.

'Oh, not for a while yet. 'Bout eight thirty.' The stable manager glanced at the clock on the wall opposite. 'He usually has a few pints over at the Pig and Whistle round about now,' he volunteered. 'It's only a few minutes from here. T'other side of the main road, past the roundabout, turn left, then right at the bus stop. If you really want to see him, lad, you'll likely catch him there.'

The Pig and Whistle was one of those pubs that from the outside looks so unappealing that you feel someone should actually pay you to go in, Charlie reflected. It was at the end of a long street of decaying red-brick terrace houses, a squat two-storey building with a grimy sludge-green stucco front and peeling dark-brown paintwork. The sign itself just said 'Pig and Whistle' in faded gold on green lettering; there had been no attempt to illustrate the combination. As Charlie opened the door of the saloon bar, this impression of dinginess increased and there was a powerful smell of stale tobacco and alcohol. Taking a deep breath, he stepped forward into a narrow room, made even more cramped by a long curving bar and dark, shabby furniture, including an outsize Victorian hat and umbrella stand right by the door. Faded prints of racehorses mingled with a handful of brasses hung on the dark flock wallpaper, presumably as some sort of reminder of the racecourse just up the road. Looking about him, Charlie saw a cluster of men sitting over their pints at the table nearest the bar and a couple of solitary customers beyond them in the far corner. Behind the bar a large woman with streaked blonde hair, her figure bulging through a tight blue wool dress, was languidly polishing some glasses. She was the epitome of a typical barmaid, Charlie thought: blowsy, over-made-up and, he hoped, approachable. He hung up his overcoat and stepped up to the bar.

'Half of John Smiths, please,' he said with a diplomatic smile.

'Right you are, love.' She flashed him a quick, appraising look before reaching for a glass.

Charlie leant forward over the bar. 'I'm looking for a bloke called Warrender. Ray Warrender. They told me up at the racecourse stables that this was his local. Is he here, by any chance?'

The woman looked up from pulling the beer and raised her plucked eyebrows. 'Ray?' she said, seemingly surprised. 'What would you be wanting with him, I wonder?' She indicated the far corner of the room with a tilt of her lacquered head. 'Yes, he's here, over there. The one in the corner hidden behind his flipping paper.' She handed Charlie his mug of beer. 'Hey, Ray. You've got a visitor. From up at t'racecourse,' she called out cheerily.

Charlie felt his adrenalin rising as he neared Warrender's table. It must be him, he thought, his heart pounding. Now that he was so near his quarry, he felt elated but also nervous. The Barons Lodge horses very rarely spent the night up at Doncaster racecourse; he had found Warrender only by some extraordinary fluke of fate. He must be very careful in the way he handled the encounter. He mustn't be too aggressive or the man might feel threatened and clam up altogether, he told himself.

Warrender put down his paper and looked up, frowning. 'Yeah? Who are you, then?' he asked suspiciously. 'I ain't seen you before. Got a message from Jack up at the stables, have you? Ain't I needed then this evening after all?' His voice was a straight blend of cockney and Australian twang with no hint of any other inflections.

Charlie would hardly have recognized him, but it was definitely his father's old head lad. He was thinner and more weaselly than he remembered, and had the sort of yellowish complexion that often clings to Anglo-Saxon people who've spent some time in the sun. The dark hair greased back over his scalp was thinning and going grey now, but the eyes hadn't changed: they were very dark, black as pebbles, and still had the same insolent look.

'Well, what's up? Cat got your tongue?' Warrender inquired.

Charlie's usual instinct was to hold out his hand when introducing himself, but he had no desire to touch Warrender if he could help it and he kept his hands firmly clenched at his side.

'My name's Kyle. Charlie Kyle. Johnnie Kyle's son. You probably don't remember me,' he said, quietly indicating the spare chair. 'May I sit down?' He put his beer on the table. 'This is quite an occasion for me, I can tell you. I've been looking for you all over, though your name used to be Keith, not Ray, didn't it?'

Warrender was gazing at him in amazement, his mouth dropping open to reveal a row of uneven stained teeth. 'Strewth!' he said, 'Johnnie Kyle's kid. Well, I never! You've changed a bit since I last saw you.' He shook his head. 'I'd never have recognized you.' He leant forward and peered at Charlie more closely. 'Dunno, though. You've got your mother's eyes all right.' He sat back again, rubbing the side of his nose. 'Quite like your father, too, I suppose – same build. Quite a chip off the old block, I reckon.' He regarded him warily. 'Well, what do you want with me, then, after all these years? And how come you found me here, anyhow? This is not exactly the most popular pub in town. Come to think of it, Doncaster's hardly the centre of the universe either. You in the racing business, too, then, are you?'

Charlie nodded. 'I'm assistant trainer to Tod Beckhampton in Newmarket,' he explained. 'We've got a couple of horses staying overnight at the racecourse stables and the chap there just happened to mention your name.' He shook his head in disbelief. 'I still can't believe it! It's such an extraordinary coincidence. I've been looking for you for over a year. I thought you were in Australia. At least, that's what one or two people down in Yelperton told me,' he added quickly. He had decided that he would not mention Beth Arnott's name to Warrender or tell him that he knew her. It might have been simpler to do so, but he had promised that if he did ever find Warrender, he would not disclose her whereabouts; he liked her too much to want to jeopardize her current happiness in any way.

Warrender started to roll a cigarette, frowning as he did so. 'Yeah, well, I was in Australia. Been in Brisbane for the last five years, working in the garage business. Changed my name to Ray there. My partner's name was Keith, too, so it all got too bloody confusing. Still, means I got away from the bloody horses for a while, thank goodness, though they seem to have caught up with me again now.' He made a face. 'Doing quite well for myself out there, I was – until I got sick, that is. Got cancer, I have – nasty business. Had to have half of one of my lungs out an' all.' He tapped the tobacco tin with a bleak grin.

253

'Shouldn't be smoking, of course, but what the hell? Got to die of something, haven't you?'

Charlie was surprised at the man's openness about his situation. He had had the impression from Beth and others that he was an unforthcoming character. He had observed, however, from a limited experience, that people who knew they were dying of something like cancer either never talked about it at all or tended to refer to it frequently, even to strangers. 'So when did you get back from Australia?' he asked Warrender politely, trying to conceal his impatience.

''Bout six months ago. Came home for my operation, didn't I? Good old National Health Service. I couldn't afford to get proper treatment out there – wasn't insured or anything.' He gave another crooked grin. 'Who'd have thought it, having to leave all that lovely sunshine just in order to come back to the bloody north of England to have my bloody lung removed? Joke, isn't it?' He rolled the end of his cigarette into shape and reached in his pocket for his matches.

'Why did you come back to Doncaster?' Charlie persisted. 'By the sound of it, you're a Londoner and a cockney.'

Warrender snorted. 'I ain't got no family left down south and if I had I doubt if they'd be pleased to see me.' He darted Charlie a scornful look. 'I never liked it down in the West Country, either, in your part of the world. Dozy bloody place I always thought it was, and full of nosy parkers.' He lit a match. 'A mate of mine in Brisbane had a sister living up here. A widow she was, he told me, took in the occasional lodger. She was lonely, he said – needed a bloke to look after.' He inhaled his first puff of the cigarette and immediately started coughing. 'So, he fixed me up with her,' he went on when he had recovered. 'Nice enough woman. Lives just around the corner. She's been good to me, too. More than most bloody women have – cows, most of them, in my experience.' He lifted his head and stared at Charlie suspiciously through the cigarette smoke. 'You still haven't said why you are here, why you want to see me.'

Charlie took a deep breath, his heart thumping. 'I want to know about the fire at Coombe Place, the fire that destroyed the yard and my father's reputation. I want to know what really happened that night,' he said purposefully.

Warrender's face froze. 'What do you want to go digging all that up for, after all these years?' he asked sharply, flicking a piece of cigarette paper off his lower lip. 'It was a bad thing to happen, we all know that, but there's no point in going over it all again now, is there?' he complained. 'Anyhow, you know what happened, surely? I know you were too young to come to court and that, but your Ma must have told you what happened, and explained it all to you at the time, didn't she? Bad business it was, very unfortunate,' he added.

Charlie leant across the table, his hands clenched tightly. 'I've never believed that my father started that fire, either deliberately or accidentally,' he said in a low vehement voice. 'I never thought he was guilty at the time and now I know he wasn't. I followed him out to Zimbabwe, you know, and talked it all over with him many times. He could never have done anything so dishonest or anything that could possibly harm the horses.' He paused, struggling to control his anger. 'But it was mainly your evidence that got him convicted, wasn't it, Warrender? That and the comments of other "well-wishers" in the area,' he added sarcastically. 'After all, you were the only other person who was down at the stables that night – apart from my father and my mother, that is.' He was about to add 'and she's dead', when the barmaid came clattering past the table on her high heels, heading for the Ladies just beyond. 'Everything all right, then, lads?' she asked cheerily. 'Old friends, then, are you? You seem to have a lot to chat about.' She hurried on without waiting for a response.

'Now look 'ere,' Warrender said angrily, ignoring her, 'what is this? Are you suggesting my story ain't true or something?' He gave Charlie a black glare. 'That's bloody cheek, that is. Everyone believed it at the time, I can tell you. Not bloody surprising. Your father was guilty all right, whether you like it or not. All the evidence was there to prove it.'

'I know there was a lot of evidence to support your story; I'm not disputing that,' Charlie insisted. 'I just believe that you know more about what really happened that night than you told the court at the time. I don't believe you told them the whole truth, that's all!'

Warrender banged his beer mug down on the table, his face twisted with anger. 'Oh, don't you? Well, you're in for a fucking disappointment then, mate, because that's all there is to tell.' His dark eyes narrowed. 'Look, laddie, your father was desperate. He was so far into debt that he didn't know where to turn. I heard him on the phone only the week before the fire telling this farmer chum of his that his only solution was to burn the bloody yard down himself and claim the insurance.' He held up his hand. 'Yeah, OK, OK, I know what you're going to say. I thought it was meant as a joke at the time too, but then when I saw him carrying a petrol can down to the yard a few days later I was not so sure. Going to mow the grass, he said at his trial, but that was bollocks. We never used the motor mower for that piece of grass – seeing it was so small, we always did it by hand.' He lit another cigarette and broke off, bent low over the table, in a fit of coughing.

When it had ceased he looked up at Charlie, his eyes bloodshot. 'Your Dad was desperate enough before that night, I can promise you that. I knew how much money he owed, how many bills he couldn't pay. I was his head lad, remember? Then comes the final straw. That very evening your mother tells him she's having a ding-dong with this bloke up in London and wants to marry him. Wants out – from Coombe Place, the marriage, the lot.' He stopped in mid flow, flashing Charlie a mocking glance. 'You knew that bit, did you, or was it a case of not in front of the children, eh? You never know with you lot.' He raised his eyebrows. 'I mean, you knew the two of them had a real humdinger of a row that night, did you?'

'Yes, I know all about the row. My father told me,' Charlie replied icily.

'Well, then, it was obvious what happened, wasn't it?' Warrender continued. 'They had this flaming row – excuse the pun – down by the stables. Bloody woke me up, it did. They were arguing at the top of their voices, just under my window. Your Ma tended to park her car there when she couldn't be bothered to put it away in one of the garages.' He succumbed to another fit of coughing. 'Bloody fags. I'll give 'em up tomorrow,' he muttered. 'Well, then she buggered off into the night, roared off down the drive as though the hounds of hell were after her and I went back to sleep. When I woke up about twenty minutes later the bloody yard was on fire!' He stubbed his cigarette out and sat back gasping for breath.

'So that was that,' he finally continued, wiping his brow with a grimy handkerchief. 'Your Dad must have flipped and decided to do the deed right there and then.' He drained his beer mug and looked around. 'I could do with another pint when that bloody woman comes out of the toilet.' He turned back to Charlie. 'Mind you, I don't blame your Dad for going a bit loco. Your Ma's a bloody good looker. Or was in those days, at any rate. Not surprising she had so many blokes after her. If it hadn't been that one up in London it would have been someone else. He was a loser, your Dad, and she doesn't like them.' He pulled a sympathetic face. 'I reckon it must have broke his heart to lose her as well as everything else.'

Charlie felt his rage rising. It was more than he could stand to hear this despicable man talk about his father like that. 'My mother's dead,

256

didn't you know?' he informed Warrender grimly. Warrender's jaw dropped for the second time that evening. He looked genuinely upset. 'Dead? Old Suzie? Well, I never. I didn't know that.' He shook his head. 'Well, I never,' he repeated. 'She kept in touch with me for quite a while, you know. Always got a Christmas card from her and that rich bloke she married – till I went to Australia, that is!' He shook his head again. 'Oh dear, what a shame! What a shame!'

Charlie was unable to contain his rage any longer. Leaning across the table he seized Warrender by the shoulders, digging his fingers into the cheap cloth of his jacket. 'Yes, it is a shame, isn't it? You would be upset, wouldn't you? You two were hand in glove, weren't you? Both of you knew more about what really happened that night than either of you let on in the trial.' He had pulled Warrender to his feet by now and was shaking him violently, his anger out of control. 'My father is totally innocent. I know it. If you don't tell me what really happened that night, I'll bloody well kill you,' he heard himself shouting. He was suddenly aware of the barmaid's not insubstantial presence as she prised his hands away from Warrender's neck.

'What the bloody hell do you think you're doing?' she thundered. 'Assaulting one of my customers and a poorly one at that. You ought to be ashamed of yourself.' Pushing him aside, she turned to Warrender who had slumped, shaking, against the wall.

'You all right then, Ray? Here, take it easy, love. Come and sit down and take a deep breath. That's it.' She guided him back to his chair. 'And you lot can mind your own business and all,' she shouted over to the group of men at the other end of the bar who had got to their feet and were peering down the room with considerable interest. Charlie stood there, still quivering with rage, but already horrified at what he had done. By losing his temper he knew he had blown his chances. Warrender would never tell him what really happened now. If only he had been able to stay calm; but hearing the man run his father down like that had been more than he could bear.

Warrender stared up at him, his face twisted. 'I ain't never going to talk to you again, and that's a promise,' he said vehemently. 'Who the hell do you think you are, going for me like that just because you don't like what you hear? Don't like the truth about your bleed-ing Daddy.' He almost spat the word out. 'Bloody public-school bully!'

'I'll get you another pint, love,' the barmaid said solicitously. 'On the house. How about that? I reckon you've earned it.'

She turned to Charlie, her expression fierce. 'And as for you, I want

257

you out. Now. Got it? And don't try showing your face in here again.'
She moved off, her mouth pinched with disapproval.

Charlie gripped the table tightly. 'I'm sorry I lost my temper,' he
muttered, staring at the floor. 'But I don't take back what I said. I'm
convinced that something else happened that night which only you
and my mother knew about. I don't know why you kept quiet about it
at the trial but you did and that was unforgivable.' He bent lower
across the table, looking Warrender straight in the eye. 'I love my
father very much,' he said with passion. 'I know better than anyone
how much he's suffered, both in prison and afterwards with all the
disgrace. I'm never going to give up trying to clear his name. Never! I
want you to remember that.' He levered himself away from the table
and strode, stony-faced, towards the door.

Doncaster Racecourse

'*Will the jockeys please mount?*' The request came suddenly over the
public-address system, preceded by the clanging of a bell. The runners
for the second race, the Steel Plate Autumn Stakes, clopping round in
the murk, were jerked to a halt by their handlers and turned into the
centre of the parade ring. Kate tightened her hold on her mother's arm
as they followed Tod, Toby and the dwarf-like figure of Jack Massam,
weaving their way through the throng of trainers, owners and their
hangers-on.

There, at the far end of the paddock, was Achilles, flanked by Liam
and Nobby, looking about him with interest, ears pricked as he took
in the unfamiliar scene. His black tail and mane were unplaited as Tod
had decided that, with his temperament, it would be unwise to put
him through any fussy or unnecessary preliminaries. Evidence of his
winter coat was visible under his rug and he looked distinctly woolly,
but otherwise Liam had done his best to make him look smart. His
hooves were oiled, his long white stocking dazzled and his tack was
gleaming. He waltzed sideways as they approached, his quarters swinging away in a semi-circle like a dinghy swirling on a painter.

'Whoa, fella! Whoa,' Charlie Kyle said soothingly, suddenly materializing at the colt's side, clad in a dark-blue overcoat and trilby. He
patted Achilles's neck before sweeping off his rug.

'Right! Here we go, then!' Tod said cheerfully, turning to Jack
Massam standing quietly at his side. 'Remember what I told you, Jack:
do your damnedest to settle him the moment he comes out of the gate,
but if you're not successful in the first furlong, don't fight him, let him
stride on. What we want to avoid at this stage is souring him in any

way. We want him to enjoy himself. Good luck, then. Up you go.' He legged the jockey up into the saddle.

Stepping backwards, he gave horse and jockey an appraising look before turning to Lady Kitty. 'There you are! Your splendid Rathglin colours back in the plate at last. I expect you thought it would never happen.'

Lady Kitty laughed. 'I never doubted it for a moment. I was the least faint-hearted of the lot of you. I knew the poor lamb would come right if only we all had the patience. Look at him! Doesn't he look like an old hand already?' She watched with delight as Liam led the horse quietly back into the line of mounted colts still circling round the paddock.

Jack Massam, his freckled face pale beneath the old gold cap, knotted his reins as they jogged around, before bending down to catch some comment from Liam. The boy's face was even more tense than usual as he eased Achilles to a halt to avoid bumping into the quarters of the colt playing up ahead of him. It was the favourite, the flashy chestnut Applejack, who was very much on his toes; a mature-looking two-year-old standing well over sixteen hands, he made Achilles look very puny.

'I hope Liam's not leading Jack astray and countermanding any of my orders,' Tod joked. 'I get the distinct impression that he'd like to be training the horse as well as riding him himself.' Grinning, he glanced round at the others. 'Oh, well! There's nothing we can do now. It's all in the lap of the gods. We'd better hop it to the stands before they fill up.' He offered his arm to Lady Kitty. 'Come on, Kitty, no more loitering.' He turned to Kate who was standing behind him with Toby. 'I think we'll watch the race from the top of the steps in the stands. Easier than trying to cram into the escalators, and we'll see just as well from there in this visibility.' Hitching his binoculars over his shoulders, he swung back to Lady Kitty.

'I'm awfully nervous, aren't you?' Toby confessed shyly to Kate as they threaded their way through the crowd. 'For Liam really, as well as for Jacko. He thinks so much of the colt!' He pushed a lock of hair out of his eyes.

'We all do,' Kate replied, smiling. 'Come on, then. I don't want to miss a moment of the action, particularly since I thought I'd never get here at all.'

Tod had driven her mother and Toby up from Newmarket much earlier that morning, before the fog had got really dense but, because she had been working in London the previous day, Kate travelled up to Doncaster alone on the train. It had been grey and dismal when they left King's Cross but between Peterborough and Grantham the visibility had worsened down to a few hundred yards. As the train crawled along through the ghostly grey flatness of south Lincolnshire she started to panic. It would take hours to get to Doncaster at this rate, she feared. No way would she be there in time for Achilles's race, or maybe the whole meeting would be fogged off. It looked as though their hopes of seeing the colt on the racecourse at last were going to be dashed yet again. But suddenly as the train picked up speed, the fog began to thin, revealing clusters of farm buildings and trees, the mist still clinging to them like strands of dirty cotton wool.

When they finally arrived at Doncaster Station, there had been a long queue for taxis and she had only arrived on the course as the runners for the first race were filtering into the saddling boxes. She found the others, ensconced as promised, in the Owners and Trainers Bar on the ground floor of the vast stand, a pile of smoked salmon sandwiches and a bottle of champagne on the table between them.

Tod leapt up, his face a mixture of relief and pleasure as she came into the bar. 'Kate! At last! We were all getting so worried. We thought you'd never make it.' He kissed her affectionately but formally on both cheeks.

'Come and sit down. Grab a sandwich. Was the journey absolutely ghastly?'

Kate kissed her mother quickly and shook Toby's hand before flopping down in the chair next to him. 'Not really, just slow.' She made a face. 'The train stopped completely just before Grantham. I thought we'd be there all day.' She took off her scarf. 'Anyway, I'm here now – that's all that matters.' She glanced across at her mother, who was wearing her favourite heather-coloured tweed suit and the Victorian amethyst and silver brooch that she always wore for luck. She was also sporting a dark purply-coloured beret with a jaunty feather which Kate hadn't seen before. 'You're looking very smart and perky,' she remarked, smiling. 'How was your journey, then? Were you very held up by the fog too? I was worried about you driving all that way.'

Lady Kitty reached for her glass of champagne. 'Oh no, we were fine,' she replied gaily. 'Tod was very clever. He insisted that we leave extra specially early, so we got here before the fog descended in fact.' She turned to Tod with an appreciative smile.

'Isn't it a bit premature to be drinking champagne?' Kate had inquired. 'I'm not complaining or anything – I can't imagine anything more welcome after the journey I've had – but it won't bring Achilles bad luck or anything, will it?'

'Of course not,' Tod replied firmly. 'Look, the colt may well run disappointingly today. I have warned you all of that.' His face was suddenly serious. 'Jack's not the ideal pilot for him, to be honest. He hasn't quite got the hang of settling him yet but I didn't want to upset him by jocking him off in favour of one of the really top boys.' He turned to Lady Kitty. 'Also, as I was saying to you the other day, I would have preferred to run Achilles first time out over a turning course to help Jack slow him down, but that just wasn't possible, either.' He grinned. 'So, let's just celebrate the miracle of getting him to the course at all, shall we? After all, it hasn't exactly been a doddle!' He raised his glass. 'Here's to Achilles. And to all of us. Cheers!'

Lady Kitty's small face was pink with excitement as she too lifted her glass. 'I just wish my brother Tom was here today,' she said ecstatically, glancing down at her racecard. '"No. 11 Achilles, black colt by Greek Dancer out of Mystical",' she read out. 'I can't honestly remember when I was so excited.'

She looked like a little girl on her birthday, Kate thought. Her china-blue eyes were huge and she looked ten years younger. Even if Achilles disappointed them later, to see her enjoying herself like this was heartwarming and well worth the most tedious of journeys.

'There was a terrible scare just before you arrived,' Lady Kitty informed her. 'The visibility was so bad that the stewards considered calling the whole meeting off, would you believe? But then the fog cleared slightly and we were on again, thank the Lord.' She rolled her eyes.

After a couple of glasses of champagne, Kate finally began to relax. But now, as the race was about to begin and she climbed the steps of the stand, her mouth felt dry with apprehension. As Tod had said, they were not expecting Achilles to win, of course, but it would be dreadfully disappointing if he ran really badly. She looked up to where her mother was standing between Tod and Charlie, a tiny figure, between two tall human pillars, the tip of her jaunty feather only coming up to their shoulders, and climbed up the steps on Tod's other side.

'Can't see a bloody thing,' he complained, gazing down the course through his binoculars. 'At least we are spared the usual view of the slag heaps beyond the straight mile start, but unfortunately we can't see the horses either!' He dropped his binoculars and started polishing his glasses.

'Achilles went down a bit too freely, I'm afraid,' he told Kate. 'Jack managed to canter him down quietly for the first two furlongs, but then one of the other runners took off past him and Jack had a real battle with him – and lost, from what I could see.' He sighed. 'Oh, well, I hope to God he goes into the stalls OK. I've requested they put him in one of the last, so that he's got less time to panic.' He turned to Kate, his face relaxing slightly, and squeezed her hand surreptitiously. 'Are you all right, darling? I'm so sorry I wasn't able to call you yesterday. I've been missing you so,' he said softly. 'You're looking amazingly pretty today in that grey outfit, by the way; it matches your eyes.' He bent closer towards her. 'Look, there's a chance I could get away for a night in London next weekend. Next Saturday. You couldn't possibly be free, could you?' he pleaded urgently.

Kate nodded, her spirits soaring. 'Of course,' she replied, returning the pressure on his hand. She hadn't seen him alone for several weeks now, which had been making her edgy and depressed. She had been very busy, organizing the little Highgate flat, putting together the final pictures for the book and working on several magazine features, but she'd experienced a certain sense of futility about it all. What was the point of working so hard and getting a new London base together if she was so seldom able to share any of it with Tod? She'd wondered quite seriously last week if it wouldn't be better to break off the whole thing with him as soon as possible. But now that she was back in close proximity to him, that seemed unthinkable. Also, as Tod himself kept reminding her, they did have Christmas to look forward to. Now that Myra and Toby were definitely going off to Barbados with Basil and Pam Hunter, there would be plenty of time to be alone together then.

Raising her binoculars, Kate took a look down the course. Tod was right. The seven-furlong start was hidden behind an impenetrable bank of fog, as indeed was the far side of the course. As she peered down to the five-furlong marker, past the stately old-fashioned stand she was startled by the public-address system booming out the announcement that the runners were finally going behind the stalls. She took a deep breath, her heart pounding. Achilles, carrying their colours, was down there somewhere in the murk and would shortly burst into the view of all these people. Her horse! She could hardly believe it. She leant round Tod to clasp her mother's hand. 'Well, this is it. Achilles's big moment. I'd no idea it would be so nerve-wracking!'

Lady Kitty agreed, her face glowing. 'Don't worry, though. He won't disgrace himself,' she added firmly.

She indicated Charlie standing on her right, his binoculars trained

on the start. 'Charlie tells me he's gone out to "double carpet" – 33 to
1,' she said with relish.

'Oh goodness, I've forgotten to have a bet,' Kate wailed. 'In all the
excitement I completely forgot. How stupid can you get?'

Tod nudged her side. 'It's all right,' he said quietly, still gazing
down towards the start. 'I put on £50 each way with my usual rails
bookmaker. Half of it is for you. If we run into a place I'll take you
out to dinner at the Connaught. How's that?'

'*They're off,*' the racecourse commentator announced dramatically.
At once the clatter of conversation all around ceased and heads swung
leftwards. '*And as they settle down to race, it's Gingerbread Man on
the far side, who breaks quickly, followed by the favourite Applejack
and Teeming Bar. They're going at a pretty good pace, a pretty good
clip in the first furlong, Gingerbread Man taking them along.
Gingerbread Man in the lead.*'

Kate gazed blankly into the distance, her whole body trembling. If
this was racehorse ownership, she didn't know if her nerves were
strong enough to stand it! She felt almost sick with excitement. Keeping
her binoculars trained down the course into the gloom, she strained to
catch the commentator's words.

'*It's still Gingerbread Man, Gingerbread Man with his white face on
the far side, followed by Teeming Bar ... it's difficult to see the
colours in this visibility ... followed by Harmony Bridge and
Applejack.*' The commentator paused for a moment, his tone surprised.
'*But here comes Achilles, here comes Achilles, bursting into the lead
up the centre of the course as they come up to the five-furlong
marker.*'

Tod groaned aloud. 'Oh no! Bloody hell! Jack's obviously not been
able to hang on to him. Good God, I can begin to see them now. Look
at the little sod! He's coming away from them as though he's got
a rocket up his arse.' He nudged Kate urgently. 'Can you see? It's
amazing!'

Kate's hands were trembling so much that she could barely focus
her binoculars, but picking up the line of horses thundering towards
her in the fog she could just make out one horse, out in front, power-
ing up the middle of the course, his head held slightly to one side.
As they grew closer, she could see quite unmistakably that it was
Achilles.

'Go on, Jack! That's it! Now he's gone, keep him up to it. And for
God's sake keep him balanced,' Tod was muttering excitedly.

Kate gave up trying to focus her glasses and, dropping them

abruptly, just stood on tiptoe, gazing eagerly down the course. As the runners approached the furlong marker Achilles was still out in front, Jack Massam crouched low over his dark mane. As Kate watched, holding her breath, Achilles seemed to falter and veer away from the stands slightly as the roar from the crowd grew louder.

'The noise just hit him,' Tod observed tensely. 'He's never heard anything like that before! He's also coming to the end of his tether. Look, see, he's changing his legs. Go on, Jack! The favourite's closing on you, lad. Keep him up to it, for Christ's sake!'

'Go on Jack! Go on then! Hang on in there!' Kate heard herself shouting as the crescendo in the roar around her rose.

Waving his stick furiously, to encourage Achilles and to keep him straight, Massam seemed to crouch even lower as he drove the colt towards the line, the chestnut behind him edging closer with every stride. Stretching out his neck, Achilles changed his legs again but kept on galloping and, ears flat back, flashed past the post, a clear length's winner.

Kate lolled weakly against Tod's side, her legs turned to jelly. Achilles, their Achilles, had won! She simply couldn't believe it!

'He did it! He did it!' Tod was saying in astonishment. He hugged her impetuously. 'How about that, darling? Wasn't that brilliant?'

'What did I tell you? What a performance! The little angel ran a blinder,' Lady Kitty crowed.

Minutes later, her emotions still in a whirl, Kate was hurrying through the crowds towards the Winners' Enclosure when Charlie Kyle bounded alongside her and put a hand on her arm.

'Wasn't that amazing!' he exclaimed, abandoning his usual reserve. 'Jacko ran far too freely, of course, but he still managed to hang on. Incredible!' His eyes glittered with excitement. 'Well, come on, then,' he exhorted. 'If you hurry, you can be the first to greet him as he comes in!'

Kate, grinning back, quickened her step. She was in a state of advanced euphoria, she knew, but she was surprised that Charlie of all people seemed so delighted. Earlier in the afternoon, as they were all walking from the saddling boxes to the paddock, he had seemed even more taciturn and preoccupied than usual, so much so that she had actually mentioned it to Tod.

'Mmm, well, he had rather a bad time yesterday, I'm afraid,' Tod replied, frowning. 'The most extraordinary coincidence: the man he's been looking for all this time – Warrender – turned out to be working up here in Doncaster, at the racecourse stables! Charlie finally ran him

264

to earth last night but the meeting went very badly, apparently. I'll explain later.'

Whatever had happened, Achilles's victory had certainly succeeded in putting it temporarily out of Charlie's mind, Kate reflected, as she followed him towards the weighing room. She had never seen him look so genuinely happy.

A smattering of applause broke out amongst the groups of professionals and press waiting expectantly below the weighing-room steps as Liam led Achilles towards them. The colt's dark coat was flecked with mud and sweat but he still looked around him with his usual curiosity and he was clearly in no way distressed by his exertions. Liam, at his head, looked the epitome of happiness; he seemed to have almost lost his limp in the excitement and with his shoulders thrust back in the new dark-brown suit he had bought specially for the occasion he looked several feet taller. He led Achilles proudly into the winner's stall and stood there smiling, his usually peaky features transformed.

As the colt threw up his head, jangling his bit, Jack Massam – mud-spattered but beaming – threw Liam his reins and kicked his feet out of the stirrups. 'Good lad, good lad,' he said, patting Achilles's damp neck before slipping off his back. 'I thought he was going to tie up, Mr Kyle, but he kept on galloping. He can motor all right.' He shook his head in happy disbelief. He turned to Tod who, followed by Lady Kitty, was hurrying towards him. 'I'm sorry, guv'nor,' he said breathlessly, 'I just couldn't hang on to him when we left the gate. He took hold of his bit and was off like a flippin' rocket. Like you said, I didn't want to fight him, so I let him stride on.' He shook his head again. 'Must say I never thought we'd still be in front when it mattered!' Still looking bemused, he undid Achilles's girths and surcingle and posed happily for the photographers before heading off to weigh in.

Tod, grinning broadly, was questioning the clerk of the course. 'Don't know what the winning time was, by any chance, do you?' He raised his eyebrows in surprise. 'Good heavens, was it really? One minute 28.02 seconds.' He glanced at his racecard. 'Well, that's not bad, is it? Not bad at all. Only .02 of a second under the previous best! In fact, it's bloody good considering the ground's definitely on the soft side.' He went up to Achilles and patted his neck enthusiastically. 'Good boy. Good lad. You're a star.' He pulled the horse's rug straight and grinned across at Liam. 'OK. OK, Liam. You were right. I admit it. Nijinsky couldn't have done it better,' he joked.

Liam nodded solemnly. 'That's right, sir. But we'd have won by a distance if only he'd settled,' he added quietly but firmly, reaching up to pull Achilles's browband back over his ears. 'Still, we won all right, didn't we, fella? We showed them!' He gazed at the colt lovingly.

Tod, already surrounded by a group of pressmen, notebooks at the ready, was being subjected to a barrage of questions. He dealt with them rapidly but amiably, explaining how well Achilles had been working at home but how headstrong he was and hard to settle. 'We owe a lot to his lad, Liam Byrne here,' he stressed. 'We've had a hell of a time keeping him sound, too. Had to have him operated on for a bone chip in his knee, you know, earlier in the year.' He gave brief details of this and of the leech treatment while they all scribbled it down.

'Blimey, leeches!' said someone from one of the populars. 'That's a rum idea! Never heard of that before.'

'It was Charlie Kyle's idea. I'm sure he'd be delighted to give you all the gory details if you want,' Tod informed them, winking across at his assistant.

'Will Achilles stay beyond a mile, do you think? What plans do you have for next season?' a man from *The Sporting Life* asked.

Bill Sink stepped forward. 'How much ability do you actually think he's got, Tod?' he inquired brusquely. 'Not in the same class as Bahir, the colt you lost, surely?'

Tod shrugged his shoulders. 'It's difficult to say. I doubt if he's as good as Bahir, Bill, no. But he's got plenty of speed, as we saw today. I don't want to announce any firm plans right now. Let's just see how he comes through the winter, shall we?'

Lady Kitty, detaching herself from a group of well-wishers, ducked into the throng, her feather dancing. 'Nonsense,' she said firmly, smiling round at the pressmen. 'You trainers are always so cautious. So reluctant to stick your necks out!' She indicated Kate who was standing just behind her. 'My daughter and I bred the colt ourselves so we've always known he was something special.' She paused for a moment, her head on one side. 'I don't think we'll bother with the Guineas,' she pondered. 'We'll need to take him slowly next year and it would be bound to come too soon for him. Also, judging by his pedigree, he should get further than a mile. We'll be entering him for the Derby, though,' she insisted. 'That's right,' she nodded emphatically, 'next stop Epsom.'

PART THREE

CHAPTER NINETEEN

Rockington Manor, Leicestershire

'Here come hounds, the little beauties!' exclaimed a ruddy-faced man in a coat to match and black topper, draining his stirrup cup at one gulp. He reined his cob backwards, narrowly missing Stella and a collision with the Disses' butler hovering behind him with a silver tray laden with glasses of port and ginger wine. Stella gave him a withering glance as her horse threw up his head and passaged nervously across the raked gravel. Patting his neck with her gloved hand, she wheeled him round, positioning him more safely behind a large, clipped yew tree.

It was the first Saturday morning in January: the traditional day that hounds met at Rockington, an occasion made much of by Sandy Diss. Against the backdrop of the massive rose brick and timbered house, with its twisting Tudor chimneys and gleaming mullioned windows, an army of specially recruited retainers circulated briskly through the throng of people and horses with drinks and trays of mince pies, canapés and sausages on sticks. Stella, refusing any such sustenance, looked on with disapproval – it was not a cocktail party, after all, she thought, and her adrenalin was running high enough as it was – but she had to admire Sandy's organizational skills. The meet had fallen off in popularity in the seventies, Bertie Diss had told her last night at dinner, but Sandy had been determined to change that. Contrary to the usual practice of keeping quiet about the locations of meets for fear of attracting the attention of the anti-blood sports brigade, she had actually sent out invitations for today and quite apart from the usual hunt 'cap' had charged all car followers £2 a head just to drive through the main gate. She had also installed what had, so far at least, turned out to be an efficient team of security guards operating between the gatehouse and the house itself, in order to keep all possible 'antis' out.

There was no sign whatsoever of any of those idiotic people here today, Stella thought with relief, as she turned to watch the huntsman and his whippers-in trot purposefully up the drive, the bitch pack of hounds flowing gaily around their horses' feet. All along the avenue of limes, their slender branches etched black against the wintry sky, immaculately clipped and turned-out horses had been unloaded, eager and snorting, from their boxes. Mounted now by their smartly dressed riders, they mingled with people in caps and waterproof clothing stomping about, greeting each other cheerily or leaning out of the windows of mud-streaked Range Rovers.

There must have been well over a hundred people present, Stella reflected as she bent down to tighten her girths. It was a far more elegant and sophisticated meet than those she was used to in Ireland where anyone who could clamber on a horse was encouraged to do so and foot followers were few. She loved hunting locally in Tipperary and Limerick but always enjoyed a day with one of the top English shire packs as well, provided, of course, that she had a decent horse to ride.

Today she was hoping she had exactly that. She was riding Zante, a young sixteen-hand thoroughbred by the National Hunt stallion Menelek whom Bertie Diss had bought in Ireland several years ago as a 'store' for possible hunter chasing, and whom he had only introduced to cubbing and hunting the year before, none too successfully.

'He's got scope all right, but he's just too hot for my needs, I'm afraid,' Bertie had confessed to Stella at the Newmarket December Sales. 'There's so much to do on the estate that I can't spend the time on him that I'd like, and I'm not as fit as I was, either. He actually threw me the other week and galloped halfway across Leicestershire. Frightfully embarrassing! Someone told me you were looking for a young hunter,' he added hopefully. 'If that's so, I've got one for sale. Just thought I'd mention it.'

Stella had been immediately interested. Her favourite hunter was fourteen years old now, frequently unsound and beginning to lose his zest; he would be pensioned off at the end of the season and she was definitely looking for a replacement.

'Good show,' Bertie said later over a drink as the last of the mares and foals trooped through the ring. 'Tell you what, there's no point in your coming all the way to Rockington just to sit on him for ten minutes, is there? Why don't you come and stay for the weekend in January when hounds meet at the house? Then you could try him out properly.'

Stella liked the idea. It would fit in well with her plans after Christmas. She was due to join Nik and a small party, which included Diana Saunders, skiing in Davos in January and before that she would be staying in London at the Savoy for a few days while she had her annual medical and dental check-ups and a meeting with her account-ants. The idea of a day's hunting with one of the best packs in England on a tricky young horse made the trip infinitely more inviting.

She liked the look of Zante the moment she saw him. He was a lean, athletic-looking animal, slightly over at the knee, a fault that never particularly worried her, but with a good length of rein and a bold eye. A rich, almost liver chestnut, with nothing flashy about him, he was nevertheless as hot-blooded as Bertie Diss had led her to expect; and in an effort to keep him from boiling over at the meet, she was deliberately keeping him to the edge of the mêlée. Already on his toes, he reared up suddenly, rolling his eyes in mock terror as a couple of hounds, exploring the crowd, feathered eagerly around his feet.

Stella did not budge in the saddle as he came back down on to his quivering forelegs again. 'Steady, now, steady,' she soothed, the reins slack on his withers, her hand on his neck.

'I'd say you've got your hands full with that one,' drawled a soft American voice behind her. Tom Dacre, Sandy Diss's elder brother, was watching her with interest from the back of a tall raw-boned bay.

Stella shrugged her shoulders. 'He'll be all right once we get moving,' she retorted.

Dacre had been paying her a lot of attention since she had arrived at Rockington yesterday evening and, according to Sandy, had insisted on sitting next to her at dinner. The main reason she remembered him from Deauville was that he was good-looking in such an unusual way. Lean and tanned, he had the same large blue-violet eyes as Sandy but it was his short, almost cropped iron-grey hair that was so striking in someone who was still so young. He was a banker, and like Sandy had been brought up in Kentucky and was reputed to be an excellent rider who had been shortlisted for a place in the US show-jumping team when he was still at Harvard. He had married a du Pont girl a few years ago but only last spring, Stella gathered, his wife had been killed when her Cessna crashed in the Nevada desert; and in order to try to distract him from this tragedy, Sandy had insisted that he spend some time with her and Bertie this winter in England. If he was still grieving, he did not show it, Stella had reflected last night at dinner. He had been an attentive companion, relating entertaining anecdotes from his showjumping days. She had also found him less brash than his sister.

'Sandy's hell-bent on keeping this old place going, you know,' he informed Stella over the soup. 'She's even talking of returning to acting: taking some part in a film being made over here in the summer, to pay for some of the work needed on the roof and those crazy chimneys.' His voice was soft with only a hint of a Southern accent. 'What do you think of Rockington, anyhow?' he asked with interest. 'Do you like it?'

Stella shook her head. 'No, I don't,' she replied with candour. 'I've never liked Tudor architecture. I wouldn't like to live here at all.' She shivered. 'But it's no doubt a remarkable house in its way and should be properly cared for. That takes a lot of effort and money, I know. I wish Sandy luck.'

'Oh, Sandy has always liked challenges,' Tom replied, smiling. 'You should understand that, I guess.'

'What do you mean?' Stella raised her eyebrows.

'Well, Bertie tells me you're trying out a real difficult horse of his tomorrow – a pretty explosive type.'

'Yes, I'm looking forward to it,' Stella replied coolly. 'No horse is that difficult, anyway, unless it's been mishandled, of course, and Zante doesn't come into that category.'

When, a few moments later, Dacre leant across her to answer some query from Bertie about the Dow Jones Index, he quite deliberately brushed her arm with the sleeve of his dinner jacket, glancing up quizzically into her eyes as he did so. He would be hunting, too, tomorrow, he told her over the pheasant, borrowing a couple of horses belonging to a nearby landowner who was on holiday in New Zealand.

'They are keen but sensible, I've been told,' he informed her. 'Just as well. I'm pretty out of practice, I can tell you. Ring rusty, you could say,' he added with a smile.

Nevertheless he looked very much at ease in the saddle, Stella now noted with approval. Not being a habitual member of the hunt, he was not entitled to wear scarlet, but his plain black hunting coat and breeches were well cut and his boots polished to perfection. She approved of that: if you were intending to hunt with a good pack, it was essential that you and your horse were as smartly turned out as possible, in her opinion.

She herself had already received several compliments on her appearance, which was perhaps not surprising. The finest hairnet kept her bobbed black hair in place under a velvet cap; her dark-blue jacket with its Tipperary hunt buttons fitted her like a glove; her breeches had been cut by her Dublin tailor who'd learnt his trade at Peal and Tautz; and her long legs were encased in the lightest of Lobbs leather boots. Just as another admirer, a pompous local solicitor whom she had met at dinner last night, was threading his way towards her through the crowd, his face aglow with anticipation, the huntsman, much to her relief, blew his horn to gather the hounds around him. She eased Zante gently behind the line of horses preparing to move off in his wake. Today the horse was going to be seriously tested: that was the priority and Stella had no time for small talk with strangers. She nodded politely to the riders on either side of her as she shortened her reins, then, looking straight ahead between his flicking chestnut ears, let him walk on.

It was a perfect hunting morning, still and misty grey with a sprinkling of overnight rain to freshen the scent. Ahead of her lay some of the best hunting country in England: hundreds of acres of pasture and only occasional plough, separated by inviting, well-trimmed hedges, rolling away from copses riddled with foxes, their earths far more efficiently stopped than they ever were in Ireland. A bevy of rooks wheeled raucously down from the nearby elms as she settled herself towards the back of the long line of horses jogging along ahead, curb chains jangling, their breath rising pearl white in the damp air.

As they passed the entrance to the stable yard, she caught a glimpse of John Brown, the Disses' groom, and Rory Byrne, loading up the two spare hunters into the Rockington horsebox. Despite his misgivings, she had insisted on bringing Rory with her on this jaunt. He'd got his parole just before Christmas, several months earlier than expected, and had come back to Mountclare on New Year's Day. Stella had been delighted to see him: the stud season would be starting again soon and his help would be invaluable. She had immediately upped his wages and assured him that he would be replacing Desmond as head stud groom in July. She'd also told him she was taking him to Rockington. 'Do you good to have a break in England – catch a glimpse of life in the shires! It will confirm all your worst prejudices,' she joked. 'Anyway, I need your opinion of Zante. You can look after him while we're there.'

Not surprisingly, Rory looked leaner and harder than he had before his spell in prison, but he had certainly not lost any of his enthusiasm for the cause, Stella soon learnt. 'I met this man in Mountjoy who's got a lot of useful contacts for us in the States,' he told her as they sat talking in front of the fire in her study the first night he was back.

'There's even a chance we may be able to buy some hardware through him over there later this year – sophisticated stuff, SAM missiles, warheads, detonators and the like,' he said with relish. 'If we can get the funds together, that is,' he brooded, gazing into the flames.

They had already made love, coupling briefly but hungrily on the floor, like animals, but once that was over, and their lust satisfied, no further physical contact was required by either of them. Rory just sat quietly in the chair, answering her questions, as he might have done with some trusted male ally. 'I've to lie low for a while, of course,' he said solemnly. 'I'll have to be careful. But the general plan now is to switch our activities to the British mainland in the next twelve months – try to up our profile over there.' He reached in his pocket and handed her a carefully folded piece of paper. 'Here are some of the bastards we'll be after: politicians, generals, judges and the like. I hope none of them are friends of yours!' His mouth twisted in a sardonic smile.

Glancing idly at the unevenly typed list, one name alone sprang out at Stella, causing her to catch her breath. 'Ashley Spence!' she exclaimed. 'What on earth's he doing on your list? I thought he was just a second-rate old MP!'

Rory shrugged his shoulders. 'I've never heard of him myself. I'm not as well acquainted with what's been going on at Westminster as I'm going to have to be, I'm afraid. But this bloke Spence has been getting right up some of the lads' noses. He's been making a lot of ignorant speeches pressing for the reintroduction of internment. He's hand in glove with the Ulstermen on the matter.'

Stella sat cradling her whisky, her whole body tingling with excitement. If, incredibly, Ashley Spence was now on an IRA hitlist, this could be extremely fortunate. She had not for one day forgotten her intention of somehow paying Spence back for his treatment of her mother. Encouraging Rory and his friends could be the perfect opportunity. She would assist them in any way she could, without telling him why, of course. Rory knew she was in general sympathy with the IRA's aims, if not all of their methods; it would be wiser, though, to keep her real motive to herself.

She was thinking about Spence again now as she trotted along towards the first covert. Bertie Diss had actually mentioned his name last night at dinner, in connection with some recent speech he'd made that had been widely reported in the papers. Apparently, according to Bertie, Spence was now a prominent member of the 1922 Committee, whatever that might mean. Stella was not in the slightest bit interested in the minutiae of British politics; what was relevant, though, was that the man had clearly become a pro-Ulster bigot. Well, he might well regret that, she thought with satisfaction.

Rory had done an excellent job on Zante today, she decided, forcing herself to concentrate on the present. Except for his legs, he had been completely clipped out and his mane meticulously plaited. His tan coat, though, was already stained with sweat as he bounced along, impatient to get going. As the long line of riders streamed through a gateway ahead, she noticed that Tom Dacre had dismounted and was courteously holding the gate open for the rest of the field. As she came level with him, she swung her reins over and urged Zante on to the verge.

Dacre looked up, grinning. 'Hi! How are you doing?' he asked cheerily. 'Fine. I'll ride with you to the first draw, though, if you don't mind. I want to keep at the back of the field for the moment and some of the idiotic chit-chat I've been listening to is driving me mad. You'd think some of the women out today were at the hairdressers, the way they prattle on.' Stella indicated a couple of heavily made-up blondes, giggling at some private joke as they splashed noisily through the gateway.

'Sure, you can ride with me, it'd be a pleasure,' Tom replied, eyeing her appreciatively. 'You look great on a horse, as you probably know. As though you'd both been sculpted out of the same mould, somehow.' The man clearly fancied her, Stella decided, as they trotted expectantly up the track together, towards the dark strip of woodland ahead. He was extremely rich: not just in his own right, she had gathered, since on his wife's death he had inherited all her du Pont money as well. Maybe it would be a good idea to ensnare him further, she brooded, even make a serious play for his affections. After all, if her father planned to get married, why should she not do the same? Also, if he proceeded with his ludicrous plan to buy Ballinvale both she and Nik would have to look elsewhere for the financing they so urgently needed. Dacre could be her best alternative. There would be no question of any emotional involvement on her part, of course: she felt no more for him than she did for any other man, though she had to admit that he was good-looking and probably tough enough to earn her respect. Also, if it did come to marriage, she could always divorce him after a few years. Rather taken with this plan, she changed her hands on the reins and allowed Zante to break into a slow canter.

All thoughts of Dacre, however, were forgotten when the hunt seriously got under way. Stella had had to use all her skills to control

Zante at the first two blank coverts, where he'd got into a lather of frustration with all the hanging around, but once the hounds really got going, she managed to settle him in the middle of the field with little difficulty. Jumping fluently and with great enthusiasm across the well-tended patchwork of fields, the music of the hounds in her ears, she decided that Zante would suit her very well. He was not too clever at one of the fences, a particularly trappy post and rails on the edge of some plough, but that was due to inexperience. He was green all right, but as brave as a lion and that was what mattered. As she shortened her reins for the wide ditch and blackthorn hedge ahead, he flew over it brilliantly. She might even take him hunter chasing in a year or two, she mused. It was what he had been bred for, after all, and he certainly had the scope and ability to jump at speed. He had, she realized, glancing round, managed to take her right to the front of the field, just behind the Master and up with the real 'thrusters', as Bertie Diss called them. She galloped on, perfectly in tune with the horse and revelling in the pleasure of being on his back.

Minutes later, after sailing over a five-barred gate into a small meadow, she felt Zante stumble and lose his stride. Swearing to herself, she immediately eased him to a trot, then to a walk, and gazed down anxiously at his off fore. Blood trickling from a cut just above his hoof indicated that, as she feared, he'd struck into himself on landing. As she slipped off his back to examine the damage closer, there was a crashing sound and a horse and rider landed beside her in a flurry of mud and straining tack: it was Tom Dacre on his bay, both breathing heavily now and flecked with mud and sweat. Pulling up, they circled back towards her.

'What's up? Is it serious?' Dacre called out, anxiously.

Stella, bending over Zante's fetlock, looked up, her pale face unusually glowing from her exertions. 'No, I don't think so, just a slight over-reach,' she said, in a matter-of-fact tone. She patted the horse's heaving flank. 'But that's him finished for the day. Pity, as he was enjoying himself, but there we are.' She shrugged her shoulders.

As Dacre jumped down from his horse and bent to take a look for himself, his knee brushed against her thigh and she felt the heat of his body through his thin breeches. Much to her surprise, this gave her a sudden frisson of sexual desire and she stepped back quickly. So . . . she did find the man quite attractive, after all! She must be careful. It would be unwise to give him too much obvious sexual encouragement at this stage.

'I'd better start looking for the Disses' box. I don't suppose you've any idea where we are, have you?' she asked briskly.

'Not a clue,' Tom replied easily, leaning back against his horse's shoulder as it snatched a quick mouthful of grass. He indicated behind him with his whip. 'You could be in luck, though. I noticed a by-road back there with a couple of boxes parked along it and I'd swear one of them was Bertie's.' He glanced at her admiringly. 'You're a damn difficult lady to catch up with, you know – a regular Lucy Glitters.'

Stella raised her eyebrows. 'A Surtees reader – well, I never!' she replied, with a hint of a smile. 'As the purpose of coming out today was to see what Zante was capable of, there wasn't much point in hanging about, was there?' she said coolly. 'Hadn't you better get a move on, too?' she suggested, running up her leathers. 'Won't do your horse any good standing around here in the cold, will it? He's had a breather.' She raised her hand in a greeting of farewell as Dacre prepared to get back in the saddle.

He was right. It was Bertie's horsebox in the distance, she noticed with relief as she rounded the far corner of the field, Zante clopping behind, and started trudging slowly down the long lane towards it. Rory jumped down from the driver's cab as she approached and hurried towards her.

'I was having a read of my paper. Didn't realize it was you until you were almost upon us,' he apologized. 'What happened then?' he asked, concerned. 'The last time I caught sight of the two of you, you were going as sweetly as Arkle round Cheltenham.'

Stella made a face. 'He got a bit tired and struck into himself, that's all,' she replied. 'It's not serious – won't require any stitching. You can deal with it in a minute.' She patted the horse's neck. 'Good boy! Is my other horse ready?'

Rory nodded as he took the reins. 'Sure. Looks a bit of a plodder, though – not in the same class as this one. You'd best get going straight away if you want to catch up with the rest of them.'

'Mmm ...' Stella halted in the middle of the lane, regarding him thoughtfully. 'Why are you on your own? What's happened to Brown, the Disses' old groom?' she inquired.

Rory indicated a cluster of brick cottages backed by a line of poplars about half a mile down the road. 'He's down there, beyond those cottages. The road bends sharply there and some stupid sod put his Mercedes into the ditch when the hounds were running across that plough just now. Some pal of His Lordship's, apparently. Brown's gone to get him out with one of the farm tractors. Wanted me to go and help but I refused. Not our job, I told him. I'm staying here with the lorry.' He led Zante up the ramp of the horsebox and into one of the empty stalls. Stella, looking preoccupied, followed Rory up the ramp and stood watching him as he took off Zante's tack, put a head-collar on him and flung a rug over his back. When he turned back towards her, she stepped forward and put her gloved hand on his crotch.

'That can all wait for five minutes.' She fixed him with her lazer-blue eyes.

Rory's mouth twisted in surprise as he divested himself of the saddle and bridle. 'You'd not be wanting it here and now, just like that, would you?' he asked softly.

'Why not?' Stella started to unbutton her breeches.

He shrugged his shoulders before wrenching at his belt. 'Well, then, you'll not be disappointed.' Staring back at her impassively as he unzipped his flies, he pressed her roughly back against a bale of hay and forced open her legs.

Dunwich Heath, Suffolk

'God, it's cold here, but so beautiful,' Tod exclaimed, pulling his cap down more tightly over his ears. 'Look! Look over there; at those cormorants skimming the waves.' He swung back towards Kate. 'And look at that extraordinary squadron overhead.' As he spoke, a flock of Canadian geese, honking majestically, flew overhead in tight forma-tion, their silvery necks arrowed towards the marshes.

He reached for Kate's arm and pulled her closer. 'What a clever girl you are to bring us here today, our last day together!' he said en-thusiastically. His scarf, caught in a gust of wind, whipped over his shoulder, a sliver of canary yellow against the gun-metal sea.

Kate shivered. 'You make it sound like you were going back to the condemned cell,' she replied miserably, scuffing the shingle with the heel of her boot.

They were walking with the dogs along the beach at Dunwich Heath, near Sizewell, on a ferociously cold January morning, the stinging north-easterly wind driving the waves on to the shore in an explosion of foam.

Tod looked around. 'Hey, Gert, Daisy! Out of there!' Leaning against the wind he put two fingers in his mouth and blew a piercing whistle at the two terriers scampering along the bank separating the beach from the Minsmere bird reserve.

It was a favourite beach of hers and Lady Kitty's, Kate had told him, frequently deserted in winter except for the occasional birdwatcher or dog walker. It was a bit of a drive from the Old Rectory, about an hour and a half perhaps, but it was worth it.

'We might even see a seal,' she'd announced, her eyes shining. 'They like the warm water around the new power station. We saw an enormous one last year, right by the Minsmere sluice, with a great pitted face and amazing whiskers. The dogs couldn't believe it.'

Tod couldn't see any sign of her whippets now. God knows where they had got to. Jamming his glasses back on his nose he searched the low dunes with their scanty covering of winter grass, the sinister grey hump of the power station behind. Suddenly, he saw them, two dark shapes hurtling flat out towards him on the sands, teeth bared, eyes enormous, ears flat back against their snaky heads.

They slithered to a halt in a flurry of sand, circled, and came bounding back to where he and Kate were standing; both dogs were panting furiously, their tongues lolling out, eager for praise.

'Good boy! We ought to send you racing – make you earn your keep, eh?' Tod said, as he bent down to fondle Lute. He glanced sharply up at Kate, still standing with her back to him, gazing out to sea. 'Cheer up, darling,' he said. 'Please don't be sad. It's such a beautiful day.' He stepped over to her and put a hand on her shoulder. 'We'll have more good times together, you wait and see.'

Kate shook off his touch and, stuffing her hands in the pockets of her Barbour, turned slowly towards him, hunching her back against the wind. She felt on the brink of tears. The decision she feared she must make had become more and more apparent in the past twenty-four hours, and now she knew she could avoid it no longer.

'I can't cheer up, I'm sorry,' she said miserably. 'I know it's spoiling our last day, but I can't help it.' She made a half-hearted attempt to tuck her hair, streaming across her face, under her collar. 'That's just the trouble,' she complained. 'It is our last day together and we haven't decided anything because you said we should just enjoy being together. Then ever since Christmas, although we keep saying how much we love each other, we just keep restating all the problems. Toby. Money. The difference in our ages. We never seem to discuss what we could do about any of them, do we?' She stared at Tod accusingly.

He stepped over to her and wrapped his arms around her, burying his face in her hair. 'I know we don't,' he said gently. 'For a very good reason: we still don't know what's the right thing to do.' He kissed the tip of her nose. 'I love you so much. You know that. You've transformed my life in the last year, given me so much happiness. But I am just not certain that I am the right man for you to spend the rest of your life with, that's all. It's fine now, but you'll want children, and what happens when I'm sixty and an old man and you're still under forty? I said it all to you the other night. Also, it's a major decision for me to leave Barons Lodge and Toby, quite apart from Myra. You know that.' He stood back, holding her tenderly at arms' length, oblivious to the cold. 'We have to be absolutely sure it's what we both really want.'

Kate swung away, her face flushed with emotion. 'I know what I want,' she insisted. 'I want you. I want to marry you despite all the difficulties.' She turned back towards him, clutching her arms around her for comfort. 'It's you that isn't sure. You don't love me enough to leave Myra, that's the trouble. If you did, you wouldn't hesitate.' She strode off towards the sea, Liffey trotting at her side and gazing up at her plaintively, her long blue nose butting Kate's jeans.

When Tod caught up with her, she was crouching on a strip of sand, her arm round the whippet's neck, the wild sea dissolving into a carpet of foam behind her.

'I just can't stand it any more,' she said tearfully. 'Having to share you, I mean. It's unbearable.' She paused, wiping her eyes on her sleeve. 'I want you to do something for me,' she gulped. 'I want you to promise not to contact me at all for a while, to leave me completely alone.' As she bent over the dog, clutching it's worried face to her chest, an outsize wave slammed on to the shingle, covering her with spray. Shaking her drenched head like a spaniel, she got slowly to her feet. 'It's the only way, I'm afraid,' she said wanly. 'If we don't see each other at all, perhaps you will find out what you really feel: whether you love me enough to leave Myra or not. We have to know.' Fumbling in her pocket for a handkerchief, she blew her nose, hunching her back against the wind. 'I'm afraid I've reached the point where I want all of you or nothing at all. It's as simple as that.'

'Well, if it's really what you want, of course I'll stick to it,' Tod said dejectedly, half an hour later when they were sitting by a crackling fire in a nearby pub.

'It's not what I want. I want to be with you all the time,' Kate replied, exasperated. 'It's just that I think it's the only way to find out how much we really love each other.' She sighed and took a gulp of her whisky mac. 'I wish I were different. Didn't need things so cut and dried. Weren't so sensible, if you like. But I can't help it, I really can't.' She smiled forlornly. 'I'm a Taurean, remember?' She reached for Tod's hand. 'I'm sorry.'

After collecting all the dogs together and trudging back to the car park, they had driven to the pub in silence, Kate gazing out of the window at the heathland bright with gorse and purple heather, her face stained with tears.

She had disappeared into the Ladies the moment they had arrived at the pub and had emerged looking pale but surprisingly calm. There was a new, more determined set to her mouth, Tod noticed, indicating that she intended to stick to this plan not to meet for several months. How on earth he was going to manage without seeing her for that long, he had no idea. Ever since he'd first met her, she had brought him joy. Even when he was not able to see her very often, he'd always been cheered by the thought of their next encounter. To have no contact with her whatsoever would be like withdrawing from a powerful drug. To ease the pain he could already see himself reaching for the bottle.

He glanced down at his glass, empty on the table in front of him. 'I need another,' he announced. 'How about you?' Wearily he got to his feet.

Kate shook her head. 'No, thanks. I don't want to drink too much. I'll only get over-emotional again.'

'How long are you going to give me to make up my mind, then?' Tod asked bleakly as he sat down again. 'Three months? Six months? A year?'

Kate glanced at him in dismay. 'Oh, no! Nothing like that,' she replied sharply. 'It won't take you a year to decide what you really want to do, surely?' She leant forward, biting her lip. 'Look, I'm probably going to the States with Sandy to publicize the book in May. Maybe we could meet again and talk the whole thing over when I come back?' She frowned. 'That'll be long enough – four months, surely? It seems an eternity right now!'

'Well, there will be one or two things I need to discuss with you and your mother during that time, you know,' Tod said evenly, lighting up another Gitane. 'About Achilles, I mean,' he continued, throwing the spent match into the fire. 'In the unlikely event that I do think he's good enough for a Derby preparation, there'll be lots of things we have to decide between now and the middle of May. Where he should have his prep races, for a start. Also, you really should make up your minds whether or not you want to sell a third share in him to help with the training fees, as your mother mentioned the other day. We ought to be looking round for possible takers if you do.'

His tone was casual, but Kate could sense the hurt behind it. She looked across at him, her eyes pleading. 'Look, Tod, I'm not suggesting this separation for fun, you know,' she insisted. 'I shall hate it just as much as you will.' She sighed. 'I just can't see any alternative, that's all. I can't go on like this. I have to force you to choose: it's the only way.' She sat back, screwing up her eyes as though in pain. 'As far as Achilles is concerned, you'll just have to talk to Kitty,' she went on, more briskly. 'She can pass it all on to me. I can't see that that's a problem.' She reached for her drink.

She was sounding so sharp and businesslike, she thought, that she hardly recognized herself. It was as though she and Tod had suddenly become strangers. Looking up she realized that he was gazing at her, his expression tender.

'I'm sorry,' he said contritely, 'but all this has come as a bit of a bombshell to me, you know. I'm not really sure how to deal with it, to tell you the truth.' He leant forward and took her hand. 'You did enjoy our Christmas together, though, didn't you, darling?' he asked anxiously. 'I was so determined that you should.'

Kate looked away, her eyes once again filling with tears. 'Of course,' she said miserably. 'That's just the trouble. It was one of the happiest times I can ever remember.' That really was true, she thought, mainly because she had forced herself to put her concerns about the future out of her mind for a few days and just concentrate on the present. Tod had not actually stayed at the Old Rectory, partly to save Lady Kitty any embarrassment and also because since Charlie Kyle was away in Zimbabwe and Sam Shaw had time off too, Tod needed to stay at Barons Lodge to keep an eye on the horses. He'd come over every day for four days, though, for both lunch and dinner, and had got on splendidly with the Professor, whom Kitty had invited over again for the holiday period. As usual, Tod had seemed remarkably at home at the Old Rectory, Kate had noticed, and there had been so much laughter and mutual affection, particularly on Christmas Day itself, that she had felt at one point as though someone had waved a magic wand and spirited Myra away for ever, rather than merely arranging for her to be away temporarily in Barbados. 'I shouldn't be so happy ... it's not real somehow, is it?' Kate had said, perplexed, to her mother, as they were stuffing the goose. Lady Kitty gave her a searching look. 'Now come along, dearie, it's Christmas. This is no time to go agonizing about things. We're all going to have a lovely day together. Don't spoil it for yourself.'

Kate's favourite present had been from Tod, a beautiful silver brooch in the shape of a whippet from Tiffany's, but the biggest surprise of the day had undoubtedly been the Professor's to her mother.

'I'm afraid it looks dreadfully unexciting,' he apologized, handing her a long envelope spattered with gold and silver stars.

'Nonsense! Nothing you've ever given me has been unexciting,' Lady Kitty retorted, turning the envelope over and opening it carefully. She fell back in her chair, a stunned expression on her face, when she glimpsed what was inside. 'Now come along, Desmond. You've really gone too far this time,' she exclaimed as she pulled out a cheque. 'How could I possibly accept this? It's out of the question!' She looked across at him, her astonishment mingled with concern. 'And how did you get your hands on such an amount, I'd like to know? You've not been robbing a bank or anything, have you?'

The Professor sat there beaming. 'Now calm down, will you? It's only £2,000 for heaven's sake. It's the amount you'll be needing to enter your little colt for the Derby. At all the stages, of course. I checked it out with Wetherby's.' He drained his glass of champagne. 'Of course you'll accept it. I'll never speak to you again if you don't. It's fairy gold, you see, Kitty. I won it in the Lottery last month, would you believe it! But then I've always been lucky.' Chuckling, he mopped his brow with a large spotted handkerchief. 'I thought at first I'd take you on a little holiday, a cruise or something.' He looked across at her fondly. 'But then when you told me what an eejit you'd made of yourself at Doncaster, telling everyone that your colt would be running at Epsom, and when I realized that you were serious, I began to think that there was an even better use for it!' His eyes sparkled with satisfaction.

Lady Kitty was still staring at the cheque, shaking her head in disbelief. 'What a man you are for surprises, Desmond,' she said quietly. 'For once, I tell you, I'm speechless. I don't know what to say, except thank you, of course!' Levering herself out of her chair she limped over and with great affection planted a kiss on the top of his bald head. 'I'll tell you what,' she went on firmly. 'I'll accept your ridiculous generosity on two conditions.'

'Oh, and what would they be?' the Professor asked, winking at Kate sitting opposite him on the sofa.

'That you'll let me refund it all to you if we never get to Epsom, and that if we do, you'll be our guest, all expenses paid, and I mean all – the flight over from Dublin and everything. How about that?'

'For heaven's sake, there'll be no question of you not getting to Epsom, woman,' the Professor replied emphatically. 'I know what you're like when you've set your heart on something. I've never known you not to get what you want.' He held out his glass for a refill. 'And of course I'll come to the Derby with you all – I wouldn't be anywhere else for the world.'

Tod, grinning, topped up his glass with champagne. 'Splendid! Well, all I've got to do now is to improve Achilles by about two stone I'd say,' he said with irony. 'Oh, and keep the little sod sound, of course!' He raised his own glass. 'Well, here's to Achilles – and the rest of you, too, crazy optimists! Happy Christmas!'

They had indeed come back from Doncaster in a state of euphoria, Kate recalled, as she gazed into the fire, but the person who had been least surprised by Achilles's win, of course, had been Liam. Not only had it confirmed his conviction that his colt had talent but, according to Tod, he had won nearly £400 on him as well.

'He was over the moon about that, as you can imagine,' Tod had reported. 'I asked him if he was going to replace that old banger he bought last summer, but he said no, he owed one of his family some money and he had to settle that debt first – sounded a bit mysterious to me.'

The flames in the fire were glowing an extraordinarily pure blue, Kate noticed suddenly. They must be burning driftwood off the beach; she'd meant to collect some herself earlier but in the midst of all the emotion, such a mundane task had been forgotten. Why did people who loved each other make each other so miserable? she wondered yet again. Perhaps it was because they often seemed to meet at the wrong time, when any attempt to grab happiness for themselves meant destroying bonds of habit or affection somewhere else.

'A penny for them,' Tod was asking her gently.

'I was just thinking that it's probably best to avoid all passionate entanglements,' Kate replied sadly. 'Perhaps arranged marriages are the answer.'

'I hardly think so,' Tod snorted. 'That's more or less what I had with Myra and you know only too well how successful that's been!'

'Mmm. It hasn't been all that unsuccessful either, I suspect,' Kate said. 'As a working partnership it's actually, until recently at least, been quite good.'

'Maybe, but I don't love her,' Tod replied plaintively.

'I'm not sure that's all that important,' Kate replied. 'After all, you do love me – or so you say, and I believe you.' Her forehead creased into a frown. 'And yet you're still not sure that it's me you want to live with.' She held up her hand impatiently. 'Yes, all right, I know. You've got very good reasons to be doubtful – you think you're too old for me, I deserve something better, you're all washed up, etc., etc. But I really don't find that convincing. If you really wanted to live with me, none of that would matter.' She flopped back in her chair, feeling suddenly weary. 'Oh God, it all seems so complicated!'

'Would you like a sandwich or something?' Tod asked quietly. He glanced at his watch. 'We ought to be leaving soon.'

Kate shook her head. 'No, no thanks,' she replied in a listless tone. 'I couldn't eat a thing. By the way, what time is Myra supposed to be phoning?'

Tod shrugged his shoulders. 'Oh, whenever the plane gets in – she didn't say exactly. That's not the reason I want to get home. They're certainly not expecting me to meet them at the airport or anything.' He sighed. 'No, the thing is, I've got the vet coming before evening stables. Two of the older horses are coughing, which is rather alarming.' His voice was unusually gloomy. The thought of facing up to another problem-ridden flat season, this time without the comfort of Kate, was suddenly more than he could bear.

Barons Lodge

Pouring himself another slug of whisky, Tod settled back to his perusal of the Racing Calendar. He was searching, without much enthusiasm, for a suitable three-mile hurdle race for Southwold Jack. Amazingly, he had kept the gelding sound all season and had even managed to win a small novice hurdle race with him at Market Rasen in December, which had convinced his owner that he was good enough to be entered for the Stayers Hurdle at the Cheltenham Festival meeting in March. Tod was hoping to find a competitive race in February that would prove Jack Weston wrong: in his opinion the horse simply didn't have the toughness to handle the hurly-burly of Cheltenham.

As he peered through his glasses at the yellow pages spread out in front of him, he was aware of footsteps striding down the passage outside. There was a knock at the door before Charlie Kyle opened it cautiously.

'Tod! Hello! Sorry to disturb you in the Den but I wanted a word before I headed off home. Can I come in?' he hovered expectantly in the doorway in his stockinged feet.

'Sure, come and sit down,' Tod said warmly. 'I'm only pondering on where we should run Southwold Jack. I think I'll leave the decision to you, actually. You're much smarter at placing animals like him than I am. Have a drink.' He indicated the whisky bottle on top of the fridge.

Charlie shook his head. 'No, thanks. I've got a heavy evening ahead, I suspect. The Carnegies have invited me to dinner and you know what their hospitality is like!' He flopped down on the sofa, next to the two terriers, and stretched his long legs out towards the fire. He was looking tanned and a lot more rested after his trip to Zimbabwe, but from what Tod'd gathered in the past few days, the visit had not allayed any of his worries about his father. They had had a pleasant Christmas together, apparently, with lots of socializing with old friends, but a talk with his doctor pal had confirmed that Johnnie Kyle had got worrying arterial problems, exacerbated, of course, by his drinking, his refusal to give up smoking and brooding about the past. This conversation had made Charlie feel wretched, he had confessed to Tod earlier in the week as they were sitting in the kitchen at Barons Lodge having their usual lunchtime snack of soup and sandwiches.

'If only I hadn't blown it with Warrender,' he'd said angrily, banging the table with his fist. 'If only I'd been able to get something out of him, Dad might have been able to come home.'

'I doubt if he would have told you anything, even if you had kept your temper,' Tod replied consolingly. 'Even if he does know more about the fire than he's ever let on, why should he suddenly decide to change his story now? It's not logical. You mustn't let the man become an obsession,' he added, clapping Charlie on the shoulder. 'You've really done everything you can.

'Well, then! What can I do for you right now?' he inquired, lighting up another cigarette.

Charlie leant forward, his hands on his knees. 'It's about Achilles,' he said. 'You mentioned the other day that the Levertons want to sell a third share in him before the start of the flat.' He looked across at Tod, puzzled. 'It that really so? It seems so out of character, somehow.'

Tod made a face. 'Well, no, you're right, they don't particularly want to sell a share in the colt, but I don't think they've got much option. They've got real money problems at the moment, I gather. Lady Kitty's been very frank with me.' He took a pull on his cigarette. 'They can't actually afford to keep a horse in training at all this year, I suspect. Kate's working extremely hard, but she's got a mortgage to keep up and they've just had to fork out yet more money for repairs to the Old Rectory roof.' He sighed. 'I'm rather worried about them, as a matter of fact, but what can I advise? They've been through so much with the colt and now they've got this crazy idea of aiming him at the Derby!' He shook his head. 'Selling a third share in him does seem some sort of solution. It'll give them a little help with the training fees, after all. They're only asking for £10,000 plus a third of the running expenses, you know. It's not really enough, but Lady Kitty insists that they've no interest in making a profit out of the transaction.' He took another gulp of his whisky. 'Even so, we're going to have some difficulty in finding a suitable taker, I suspect. I suggested a friend of Jack Weston's who wants to get into the game, but Kate's turned him down flat, apparently, according to Lady Kitty. Says it's got to be someone they know and like. I'm going to make an approach to Diana Saunders next week. She's away skiing somewhere at the moment, as you know.'

The mere mention of Kate's name made him feel miserable. Only a week had passed since that last day they had spent together but already he was missing her dreadfully.

'Mm . . .' Charlie replied thoughtfully, staring at his feet. 'Do you think they'd accept me?' he asked after a moment, his eyebrows raised.

Tod looked at him in astonishment. 'You? Good God, I never thought of that,' he exclaimed in surprise. 'Well, yes, I'm sure they would. Lady Kitty likes you a lot, I know. She was most impressed with your determination over the leeches.' He paused, frowning. 'Look, I don't want to sound insulting, but I didn't realize you had any spare cash floating around at the moment. I thought everything you'd got was tied up in your stepfather's house or something. Isn't that right?'

Charlie nodded. 'Sure. Mother only left her half of the house to me on the strict proviso that I don't get the money until Neville wants to sell.' He shrugged his shoulders. 'Which won't be until he dies, I suspect! He's devoted to the wretched place. It doesn't really matter, of course, until I want to set up training myself. Then that sort of money will be absolutely vital. But I very much doubt if Neville will oblige me by popping off before then. Shits always seem to live for ever, don't they?' He gazed broodingly into the fire.

'Well, where are you going to raise the money from then?' Tod asked, interested.

'I shall borrow it!' Charlie replied firmly. 'Using my share of the house as collateral. There's nothing in the will to prevent me from doing that! The place must be worth at least £400,000 by now. Even my bank – not known for their imaginative powers – aren't going to refuse to loan me £13,500 on my half share of that!' He paused, stroking Daisy's back absently, his eyes gleaming. 'I'll need nearly £14,000 of course, to cover the running costs for this year as well.' He looked at Tod expectantly. 'Well, what do you think?'

Tod stubbed out his cigarette. 'Well, quite honestly, I'm a bit taken aback,' he admitted. 'I mean, it's a bit of a gamble, Charlie. After all, there's no guarantee that we can keep the colt sound this season, after all he's been through. Also we've no real proof that the form of his Doncaster race was up to much, have we? He may have just beaten a field of extremely moderate horses.' He made a face. 'And the little sod hasn't got the easiest temperament in the world. For all we know he may not even have trained on.'

'I'll bet he has,' Charlie replied enthusiastically. 'I was impressed by that Doncaster run, you know. I've watched it again and again on the video. He was at the end of his tether half a furlong out but he really battled on gamely. He's certainly no quitter, and held up properly I see no reason why he shouldn't get a mile and a quarter at least this year. He's filling out too and becoming a bit less moody. Liam's idea of putting Watson in the next-door stall was inspired.' He paused, his expression reflective. 'You've got to hand it to the boy, Tod. He really seems to have got inside the horse's head.'

'Yours too, by the sound of it,' Tod replied, amused. 'You don't want to listen to him too much, you know. He's wildly optimistic. According to him, Jacko could *win* the bloody Derby!'

Charlie grinned. 'I know, I know. He thinks Jacko is another Nijinsky. I don't go that far, of course, but I do think the colt's got potential. That's why I'd like to take this share in him. Put my money where my mouth is, so to speak. Quite apart from helping the Levertons out, I honestly think he's a good investment.'

Tod shrugged his shoulders. 'Well, it's up to you. I can't stop you, though I think you're taking a big risk. After all, you'll need every penny you can lay your hands on when you take out your own licence, remember.' He raised his glass. 'Still, good luck to you. Lady Kitty's not at home tonight, I know – she's gone to London. But why don't you give her a ring tomorrow and see what she has to say about it? My guess is that she'll jump at the idea.'

Kate might not be so enthusiastic though, he mused later, after Charlie had gone. She had reservations about the assistant trainer, he knew, finding him cold and judgemental; but in this case, Tod suspected, she would be overruled. He'd meant what he said. Lady Kitty did genuinely like Charlie and could sense the passion and strengths that lurked beneath his reserved exterior. She had appreciated his determination too. She might well regard selling him a share in Achilles as an apt reward for his efforts with the leeches.

Tod had just poured himself another whisky when he heard a door bang in the distance, followed by the sound of Myra's high heels clattering purposefully across the hall in his direction. She had returned from holiday in an energetic, irritatingly bossy mood which, in his present gloomy state, he was finding hard to tolerate. As usual, she burst into the Den without knocking and stood in the doorway, looking around critically. 'We really must get Tracy to do this room more often, Tod. It's an absolute tip!' she announced, stepping over to the sofa and plonking herself down next to Gert, who growled softly in her sleep. 'I want to discuss this with you,' Myra went on, waving a letter. 'It arrived this morning, from Stella Alexandros. She wants me to go over to Mountclare for a few days at Easter, to see round the stud and everything.' She nodded. 'I'll go, of course. Stella and I get on well, and anyhow, I shall find it interesting.'

She settled back against the cushions. 'She's invited Toby too. For the whole holidays. I think it's an excellent idea, don't you? It will take him out of himself and give him valuable experience. Stella will really make him work, too; she's adamant about that. It's just what the boy needs right now, in my opinion.'

'Well, yes, I rather agree,' Tod replied thoughtfully. 'If he does still wish to pursue this idea of becoming a vet, a stint at Mountclare could be very useful.' He reached in his pocket for his Gitanes. 'And of course we should have his exam results by then, so at least we'll know whether or not veterinary college is still even on the agenda.' He lit a cigarette slowly.

Toby had, recently at least, been rather more co-operative at home, offering to help out in the yard at weekends. Also, ever since the lad had had the brainwave of putting Watson in a stall opening on to Achilles's box to give him some company, Toby had struck up quite a friendship with Liam, Tod noticed. He was still, however, reluctant to ride out, insisting that he had too much work to do and that his shoulder was still playing him up. Tod was not convinced by this but, anxious not to push him too hard at the moment in the hope that he would regain his nerve, he was only putting him up on horses who were, for various reasons, on the 'easy list' and confined to roadwork and trotting. This could not go on indefinitely, of course. If Toby was to continue living at home for the next two years, Myra was right, he would have to pull his weight about the place more than he was at the moment. But Mountclare could just be the break he needed to rekindle his old interest. Perhaps he could put off any kind of a showdown with him until he got back from there, Tod decided with relief.

'By the way, how was your Christmas Day with the Levertons? You haven't really said,' Myra inquired.

'Fine. Very pleasant,' Tod replied casually, pulling on his cigarette.

'Who was there, then?' Myra persisted.

'Oh, just the four of us: Lady Kitty and Kate and an old Dublin friend of theirs who was staying – Desmond something or other. I forget his surname; the Levertons always call him the Professor. He's quite a distinguished historian, I gather. A very jolly old boy too.' He grinned at the recollection.

'Hasn't that girl Kate got a boyfriend or anything?' Myra asked sharply. 'I mean, she's quite attractive but she must be coming up to thirty. You'd think she would have acquired some sort of permanent or semi-permanent man by now, wouldn't you?' She flashed Tod a keen look from under her mascaraed lashes.

'She's been married actually. To a chap called Hugo, who's a wine writer,' Tod replied evenly. 'It didn't work out, though, I'm afraid. He's remarried now and living in California, I gather.'

Myra stared down at her hands, obviously pondering something. 'Basil and Pam think you've got a thing about the girl,' she burst out suddenly. 'They kept on about it in Barbados. Basil says he noticed you giving her particularly doggy looks in Deauville.' She paused, frowning. 'You're not having an affair with her or anything, are you?' she asked, her eyebrows raised.

Tod took another pull on his cigarette. 'Of course not,' he replied indignantly. 'Basil's imagination has taken off with him again, I'm afraid. I wouldn't be at all surprised if he didn't fancy Kate himself,' he added quickly.

Myra did not reply. Pursing her lips, she continued to stare at him suspiciously.

'Of course I'm not having an affair with Kate,' Tod repeated, with as much reassurance as he could muster. 'She's a very attractive girl, of course, I admit that. But she's half my age, for heaven's sake.' He gulped down some more of his whisky.

'Mmm . . . since when did that have anything to do with the price of fish?' Myra retorted sharply.

'I like both the Levertons a lot, as a matter of fact, and regard them as friends,' Tod continued. 'I would have thought you would have appreciated them, too,' he added. 'They are, after all, two of the few "civilized" owners we've got left, wouldn't you say?'

'Hmm – and whose fault is that?' Myra got abruptly to her feet. 'I must go and see about supper,' she announced. 'Dorcas made one of her better fish pies, by the look of it. It should be ready in about ten minutes. We're eating in the kitchen.'

She strode through the door, banging it behind her. She was feeling oddly upset, she realized. She wasn't really sure what had prompted her to confront Tod about that Leverton girl – probably the fact that both Basil and Pam had gone on about it so much on holiday – but she wished now that she hadn't. Tod's insistence that there was nothing going on between them had not been altogether convincing, yet surely it didn't matter to her what he got up to now? After all, if she was just biding her time until she left him anyway, why should she care who he got involved with? Yet, for some reason, the idea that he might be infatuated with such a pretty and much younger girl made her feel rattled, very rattled indeed. It was all very confusing.

CHAPTER TWENTY

Mountclare

Sitting on the worn stone steps under the great fanlight above the front door, Stella let the softness of the April afternoon fall over her like a cloak. The air was filled with the chirp of birdsong and the distant bleating of the lambs; and in the paddock beyond the lawn, through half closed eyes, she watched two of her wispy-tailed yearlings sparring. Teeth bared, eyes rolling, they boxed for a moment until one of them wheeled round sharply and cantered off towards the far railings.

Stella was tired, as usual at this stage of the stud season. She had been up for two of the last four nights foaling a couple of her mares, one of which had been a bit tricky. The results had been satisfactory, though – two healthy but dissimilar foals: a brown filly by the Irish National Stud stallion Lord Gayle and a more robust chesnut by Coolmore's Be My Guest. Basking now like a cat in the tepid sunshine Stella forced her thoughts away from animals and on to certain recent developments on the human front.

Suitably, for this time of year, romance or certainly lust was in the air, she mused cynically. As she had guessed at Rockington, Tom Dacre was definitely smitten and had made several attempts to get her to have dinner with him in London before he had gone back to the States. Then, the other night, she had another call from him informing her that he was back in London, staying at the Dorchester, but would be returning home via Dublin as he wanted to purchase some Waterford glass. With her father still proving stubbornly unco-operative, she agreed to meet Dacre for dinner. It was time, she decided, to ensnare him further.

There was also, she noticed, a growing closeness between Nik and Diana Saunders. It had begun on their skiing holiday, when they spent most of the time together and, both being expert skiers, they frequently ventured off piste in what other members of the party regarded as recklessly dangerous conditions. Since then they had met several times in London and, despite Diana's reluctance to leave Three Swallows during such a busy time in the stud season, Nik had even persuaded her to fly over to Kilmarron for the weekend. Dining with them there, Stella had observed how proprietorial Diana had become, looking keenly around the house and its contents and making suggestions as to possible improvements. Although ideally Stella did not want any stranger muscling in on her and Nik's plans, Diana was as suitable a sister-in-law as she was ever likely to get and the way things were going, her money would come in extremely useful.

Myra Beckhampton's visit had been less satisfactory. The woman had gone out of her way to be pleasant and was obviously very impressed by what she saw at Mountclare, but she had asked a great many questions, presumably anxious to glean as much as she could in case she did ever manage Ballinvale. It looked as though her attempt to put Myra off marrying Stelios by telling her about the Fairyhouse curse was not proving successful, Stella had reluctantly concluded.

She had also heard a disturbing rumour recently that Ballinvale might indeed be coming on to the market. Her father was in the Far East at the moment, but it would not be long before the news reached him too. It was therefore imperative to find some other way of trying to stop the marriage. One possibility had already occurred to her. Toby, she suspected, was Myra's Achilles heel. Listening to her talking about how concerned she was about his recent behaviour, and how much she wanted him to take over Barons Lodge one day, Stella was convinced that anxiety about how it might affect her son was the main reason why Myra had not actually left Tod already.

'Toby's so easily led, I'm afraid. Seems to just drift into bad company,' she confessed one day as they were driving over to Kilmarron. 'I'm quite convinced that the other boy, that wretched Giles, planted those drugs in his locker. Toby's housemaster even hinted that they might be having one of those unhealthy liaisons! Would you believe it?' she added indignantly.

The most effective way to get at Myra would be through Toby: enlist him as an ally, Stella realized. She herself would not be surprised if the boy had had some sort of homosexual experience at school. When she had inquired whether he still saw his friend Giles, he'd shaken his head guiltily, his cheeks immediately flooding with colour. She did not think, though, that he was irredeemably gay. She had observed him carefully since his arrival at Mountclare and, from his reactions and eagerness to please, sensed that he was already in her thrall. Her next move was obvious, she decided, getting slowly to her feet. She must seduce the boy at the earliest opportunity.

Toby awoke slowly, prodded into consciousness by a heavy blast of rain slamming against his bedroom window. For a moment, he lay quietly under the bedclothes, his mind still comatose, until he began to recall the events of the night before. As the relief and excitement flooded through him, he turned and hugged the pillow tightly. It had all been real, not a dream; it had also been without doubt the most remarkable thing that had ever happened to him. He had actually made love to a woman – well, to Stella of course – for the first time ever, and it had been absolutely wonderful. This must surely mean that he didn't have to worry any more: he was not, as he had feared, basically gay or some sort of freak. He felt like jumping out of bed and yelling out his delight. It was as though he had emerged suddenly from a thick fog of guilt and confusion into bright sunlight.

He had grown to admire Stella more and more since he had arrived at Mountclare. She was so involved with her mares and young stock, so competent in the way she handled animals, whom she almost seemed to prefer to people. She was also, he had decided, very beautiful, with her peculiar Siamese cat's eyes and alabaster skin. But he was afraid of her too, as were most of her staff. He soon observed that they were all expected to conform to the high standards she set herself and if they didn't, as he gathered from one of the girl grooms, they were dismissed, usually without a reference. Only Rory Byrne, who by an extraordinary coincidence turned out to be Liam's eldest brother, though he didn't seem very like him, did not appear to be in awe of her.

Yesterday, therefore, when Stella had suddenly turned her full attention on him, he found it gratifying, but alarming too, as though he had stumbled suddenly into a powerful beam of light.

'You've done well with him. He looks almost respectable. Don't forget to do his feet, though, will you?' she said, coming into the box where he had been strenuously cleaning the mud off one of the yearlings. 'I'm not expecting any of the mares to foal tonight. I've got a free evening, as a matter of fact,' she added casually. 'I thought I'd watch the Marlon Brando film, *Last Tango in Paris*, on the television in my study. Why don't you join me?'

It had been more of an order than a request, Toby sensed, but he willingly agreed. The film, he knew, was what Giles would have described as 'steamy' and certainly not the sort of thing his mother would have encouraged him to watch.

Stella offered him an Irish whiskey the moment he went into the study and sat down on the sofa next to her. As the film got under way he felt a strange intimacy developing between them, fostered presumably by the nature of the film and the alcohol. He kept thinking how uncomfortable he would have been watching the sexual scenes with his parents, but somehow with Stella, lounging so still and contained next to him, he felt barely self-conscious at all. At one point, early on, when Brando was almost raping Maria Schneider, she turned to him and gave him the strangest smile, a blend of complicity and reassurance, and brushed his knee with hers.

By the end of the film, despite its disturbing finale, he was therefore in an uncomfortable state of tumescence. Stella poured him another whiskey and, curling up gracefully again on the sofa, began to stroke Tara's head, which was resting against his knee.

'Tara doesn't like many people, particularly men. You're quite favoured, you know,' she commented, her fingers brushing his thigh as she leant over to straighten one of the dog's ears. Feeling an instant and delicious shiver of sexual excitement run through his groin, Toby closed his eyes for a moment. When he opened them again, Stella was staring at him with her disconcerting blue gaze.

'That's right, relax,' she ordered in a soft, compelling tone. Much to his surprise, he did so, as though hypnotized, letting his hand flop back against the silk cushions. As Stella's long fingers began to explore his thighs and then, very gradually, massage his crotch, he felt his erection stir and he wriggled with embarrassment.

'It's all right, it's all right, let it happen. You're quite safe with me,' Stella said in the soothing tone he'd heard her use so effectively with her fractious mares.

When she finally started to unzip his flies and began to caress his penis, the pleasure became almost unbearable. Sensing this, she pulled him gently down on the floor and, easing off her own jeans, knelt over him, flicking her tongue deftly round one of his nipples. 'Relax. Go with it. You're going to fuck me in a minute,' she insisted, before rolling over on to her back and pulling him on top of her. 'There now, that's better,' she whispered. 'Go on. Don't disappoint me, Toby. It's what you want, anyway. Go on. That's it. Just slide in.' As she opened her legs, guiding him with her hand, Toby thrust downwards, finding himself suddenly inside her, caught in a delicious warm trap.

'Oh! Wow! That's wonderful,' he cried out, unable to control himself.

He could feel Stella's small, firm breasts through his shirt and realized that this was exciting him further. As though reading his mind, she pushed up her blouse and pressed herself more closely to him.

'There. You like the feel of them, don't you? There's nothing wrong with you, Toby. Nothing at all. Mmm, that's it. Go on. That's it. Go on. Harder!'

As his rhythm built up and he felt his ejaculation coming, Stella suddenly contracted her vagina, taking him completely by surprise, and sending him gushing into her, like a dam breaking, moaning uncontrollably as he did so.

That evening would be imprinted on his memory for ever, Toby told himself as he lolled in the old oak bed. He loved Stella now, of course, bonded to her by what she had proved to him more than anything else, but, oddly enough, he did not expect the emotion to be reciprocated. She was out of his reach, he knew, a grown-up woman who could have no real need for a boy like himself. He accepted this completely. Quite unlike his experience with Giles, their sexual encounter had calmed him and given him confidence. From now on, he told himself, he would be content to love her from a distance, just treasuring the memory of what had occurred and grateful that someone he so admired had shown such an intense interest in him, if only for one evening.

Jumping out of bed, he stood gazing out at the rain-lashed landscape. The chestnut trees along the avenue, usually so stately, were being buffeted hither and thither in an undignified fashion and beyond them he glimpsed a handful of yearlings, huddled together in an open shed, their woolly backs hunched miserably against the wind. Stella would probably want them brought in in this weather, he thought in a sudden panic as he searched around for his clothes. It was particularly important after what had happened last night that she did not think he was slacking. Not that there was any real danger of that. His visit to Mountclare had been momentous in more ways than one. By giving him responsibility for some of the yearlings and letting him assist at the foalings, Stella had rekindled all his original interest in horse care. It wasn't a lack of that that had been putting him off the vet idea, he now realized: it was his loss of nerve about riding out, on top of a general inability to concentrate on his studies in the midst of so much emotional turmoil. He would have to face up to this problem now, he thought, perhaps even discuss it with his parents. They would be baffled and disappointed in him, of course, particularly Myra who would be horrified that any member of her family had any fear of horses, but at least he was not going to have to confess to them that he was gay, which had been his greatest dread. Getting into veterinary college would be a real struggle, though. Although his O-level results had been better than he had expected, he had still only got eight, which meant that he'd have to get good grades in all his three As.

As he pulled on his sweater, he felt a new determination to try, at least, to achieve this objective. Sprinting over towards the door, he noticed that a white card had been pushed under it, a note in what looked liked Stella's small, incredibly neat handwriting: 'You slept well, I hope! Come and see me in the study at nine o'clock, will you? There's something we need to talk about.'

An hour later, walking along the long stone-flagged passage leading to Stella's study, he experienced the same feelings of nervousness that he used to have at Hadleigh whenever the headmaster sent for him. What on earth did Stella want to talk about? he wondered. He did hope she did not regret what had happened last night; that would be awful.

'Come in,' she called out briskly in response to his knock. He stood awkwardly in the doorway, hardly able to believe that the tall room, filled now with clinical morning light, was the same place that had cocooned their erotic activities of the night before.

Stella swung round in her chair, flashing him a cool smile. 'Hello. Sit down.' She indicated a chair. 'You look well,' she added drily.

As Toby sat down, biting his lip, Tara lifted her head and gazed mournfully at him across the room, her yellow eyes unblinking.

'Don't look so nervous,' Stella insisted with a faint look of amusement. 'I'm not going to bite you, I promise.' She propped an elbow on the desk and regarded him thoughtfully. 'There are a couple of things I want to say to you,' she said softly. 'First of all, I want you to know that I don't regret what happened last night; I enjoyed it, as a matter of fact – and presumably you did, too, so that's fine.' She paused. 'But it won't happen again, Toby, and I don't want you to worry about that either. You'll understand later on, even if you don't right now, that that would not be wise.' She leant forward and fixed him with a compelling look. 'And of course what happened is a secret. Our secret. No one else must know. I'm sure that's understood.'

Toby nodded, flooded with relief. She didn't have any remorse over what had happened, then. That was wonderful. Staring across at her, looking so pale and fine in the pearly light, he felt suddenly overjoyed.

'Good. We are agreed on that, then,' Stella said, glancing up at the long windows as another squall of rain hammered on the glass.

'Something else has happened, rather important, that I want to share with you, too,' she went on, turning back to Toby. 'You're leaving soon, so it's important that I tell you now.' She paused, examining her hands with interest, her long pale fingers pressed together as though in prayer. 'It's about your mother and my father – Stelios,' she said deliberately. 'They are friends of long standing, as we all know. But what you do not know is that their friendship has become rather more serious than that.' She paused again, her eyes narrowing. 'As a matter of fact, Toby, my father has gone so far as to ask your mother to marry him – after she has obtained a divorce, of course! He is retiring from Alexandros Maritime this year and has been offered the post of Greek Ambassador to Dublin.' Her mouth twisted into a cynical smile. 'He therefore wants to remarry and thinks that your mother would be the ideal candidate. She is on the verge of accepting this offer, I fear, ludicrous though that may seem!' She glanced calmly across at Toby, who was staring at her in complete disbelief, his mouth hanging open.

'What!' he said eventually. 'I don't believe you! Mother going to leave Dad and me to go off with Stelios?' He shook his head dismissively. 'That can't be true. I don't believe you!'

Stella's blue eyes blazed briefly. 'I don't invent things, Toby,' she replied coldly. 'Preposterous as it may sound, I can assure you that it's true.'

'But Mother wouldn't even consider it, surely? Leaving us and Barons Lodge for an old man like Stelios,' Toby burst out. He bit his lip. 'Sorry, I know he's your father and all that but I think it's a horrific idea!'

'Well, maybe, but she has more or less accepted the proposal, I gather,' Stella replied calmly. 'You must remember that my father is a very rich man, Toby. He could provide her with financial security for the rest of her life. You can see why your mother might find that attractive.'

'No, I can't!' Toby exploded, his face flooding with colour. 'I simply can't believe that she'd leave Dad just for money! She doesn't love Stelios – she couldn't do,' he added incredulously. 'Anyway, if she's even thinking about the idea, why hasn't she talked to you about it? After all, you're supposed to be her friend.' He stared at Stella accusingly.

'I am her friend, Toby,' Stella replied soothingly. 'The reason she hasn't confided in me is, I think, because she has not yet entirely made up her mind whether to leave your father or not.' She paused. 'And the main reason for that, of course, is you.'

'Me!' Toby looked astonished. 'You mean Mother might have actually left already if it wasn't for me?' He leant forward, his hands clenching and unclenching in his lap.

Stella nodded. 'Of course. She loves you a lot, you know. She's been very worried about you recently and concerned about all that turmoil you've been in – as well as the trouble you've caused.' She lifted an eyebrow. 'She's obviously apprehensive about upsetting you further. At least, that's what she told my father. That's why she's asked him to wait till later in the year before they make an announcement, I gather.' She leant back and folded her arms. 'So, you see, all is not quite lost and you are the key factor in all this, Toby. You are obviously the only person who could persuade her to come to her senses.

'It would be a great mistake for her to marry my father, in my opinion,' she continued gravely. 'I have nothing against her, of course – I admire her greatly – but I don't believe that the marriage would work. She doesn't love my father, I agree with you about that, and she would be bound to have regrets about leaving you and your father.' She leant forward and threw another log on the fire. 'Also Nik and I have urgent business plans, which we want to include Father in – for his own good, of course. But, at the moment, he is stubbornly refusing to co-operate – says our ideas are in direct conflict with some scheme he's involved in with your mother. So, you see, I have practical reasons for opposing the whole thing as well.' She stared at Toby reflectively. 'I'm sorry if all this has been a terrible shock but I felt it was my duty to tell you,' she said softly. 'After all, I'd say you were grown up now, wouldn't you?' Her mouth flickered into a smile. 'So I thought you'd want to know. Presumably you love both your parents, too, despite any difficulties you may have had with them recently, and you want them to stay together, don't you?'

'You bet!' Toby replied with vehemence.

Stella's smile was sugar-sweet. 'Right. Well, we must put a stop to my father's plans then, mustn't we? Or rather you must. You're the only one who can, you know – I'm sure of that.'

CHAPTER TWENTY-ONE

Barons Lodge

'Whisky?' Tod asked, sloshing some more into his own glass.

Toby nodded, his face tense. 'Yeah, please. Just a small amount, Dad, with lots of soda.' He lifted Gert gently out of the way and perched apprehensively on the sofa.

Tod handed him his drink, glancing at him with concern. 'Whatever's up, Tobes? You're looking awfully grim.' He sank back into his chair with a sympathetic grin. 'There weren't any problems in Ireland, were there? I thought the whole thing had gone rather well.'

Toby took a gulp of his drink and made a face. He wasn't sure if he really liked the taste of whisky but he needed a drink to steady his nerves, and whisky was all Tod seemed to have on offer in the Den these days. His father was certainly drinking more again, he had noticed.

'No, no, Mountclare was fine. I really enjoyed it.' In fact, it made me see lots of things differently. About my future plans, I mean. I'm pretty sure what I want to do now – or at least try to do,' he added earnestly, gazing into his tumbler. 'I want to have a talk with you about all of that, Dad, but not right now. I needed to see you alone today because there's something else much more urgent.' He looked up, his expression strained.

'Well, go on, out with it, whatever it is,' Tod encouraged him.

Toby took a deep breath. 'I've found out something really awful about Mother,' he said shakily, taking another gulp of his drink.

Tod leant forward, his curiosity aroused. 'Good God! That does sound serious. Well go on, then, let's have it.'

Toby glanced at him, summoning up his courage to go on. 'It's unbelievable, Dad, but Mother is planning to leave you,' he burst out, his heart thumping. 'She's planning to leave you and me and Barons Lodge and everything and go off with Stelios Alexandros. Apparently, he proposed to her some time ago, saying she could take her time to think about it. Unbelievable, isn't it? But I promise you it's true!'

To his amazement, Tod seemed to be amused. 'What? Myra run off with old Stelios! Don't be ridiculous, Toby! I simply don't believe it! Where on earth did you hear such twaddle?' He reached for his drink, shaking his head wryly.

Toby leant forward on the edge of his seat, his body rigid with emotion. 'I know it's unbelievable, Dad, but it's true, I promise you,' he insisted. 'But I can't tell you how I know, Dad, I promised I wouldn't. You've just got to trust me,' he pleaded.

Tod held up his hand in protest before reaching for his Gitanes. 'OK, OK, calm down. Of course I trust you,' he said soothingly. He lit a cigarette and blew the smoke out slowly. 'Right,' he said eventually. 'Let's start again, shall we?' He looked across at Toby, his expression quizzical. 'You tell me that your mother is about to leave me and run off with Stelios. Hmm. You learnt this in Ireland, presumably. The information didn't come from the little people, I trust, did it?'

Toby bit his lip. 'Don't send me up, Dad. I'm deadly serious. Please, you must believe me,' he begged. 'I can't tell you who told me: I promised I wouldn't.'

Tod raised his eyebrows. 'Well, then I see absolutely no reason why I should be prepared to believe you,' he replied lightly. 'Oh, don't worry, I believe that *you* believe this extraordinary piece of information – you wouldn't be so stirred up otherwise. But until I know your source I shall absolutely refuse to take it seriously.' He sank back in his chair and took another gulp of his drink.

Toby dropped his head in his hands. 'Oh, Lord,' he said despairingly. 'OK, all right, then,' he said, looking up after a moment, 'you win, Dad. I will tell you if you promise not to tell Mother. That's absolutely essential. Promise?' He regarded Tod anxiously.

'Of course I promise,' Tod reassured him. 'I give you my word. So . . . how did you come by this bizarre information, then?'

Taking a deep breath, Toby began to explain how Stella knew and what she had told him.

Tod did not comment for a moment. Leaning back in his chair, a preoccupied expression on his face, he let his half-smoked cigarette dangle from his fingers. 'Well, well, well,' he said eventually. 'Who'd have thought it? Old Stelios actually proposing to Myra! What a sly old fox he's turned out to be!' He sat up suddenly, snorting with laughter. 'It's rather touching, in a way, that he should want to rescue her from me and Barons Lodge and all the problems and give her a worry-free old age and make her ambassador's wife to boot, for God's sake!' He shook his head, bemused. 'I always suspected he rather fancied her, of course, but running off with her at his age – well, well, that does surprise me, I must admit. It's almost romantic, wouldn't you say?' He glanced at Toby inquiringly.

Toby stared back in amazement. What was the matter with his father? he wondered angrily. He seemed to think it was all a bit of a joke. Didn't he care that Myra was about to run off with Stelios. Didn't he see the humiliation?

Unable to control himself, he leapt up and stood over Tod, his face contorted with emotion.

'For Christ's sake, Dad! What's the matter with you?' he shouted. 'Don't you care that Mum's about to leave us, and go off with someone who's supposed to be your friend? Just because he's stinking rich?' He banged his fist on the arm of Tod's chair. 'We can't let that happen, we really can't. You've got to stop her.' Tears welled up suddenly in his eyes. 'You've got to tell Mum she's got to stay here, that we need her. Otherwise we won't be a family any more.' He started to sob.

Throwing his cigarette into the fireplace, Tod unfolded himself urgently from his chair and put his arms around Toby's quivering shoulders. 'There, there, Tobes. I'm sorry. Don't be so upset, please. I'm sorry.' He stood rock still, letting Toby cling to him until his distress had subsided. 'This must have been an awful shock to you, I understand that. There, there now. Of course I'll do something about it. I'll talk to your mother as soon as I can.' Patting Toby on the back, he disengaged himself gently, before picking up the whisky bottle and pouring them both another drink.

'I'm sorry, I shouldn't have sounded so flippant,' he said apologetically. 'It's just that this is all a little unexpected, you might say.' His mouth flickered in a grin. 'And shock takes people different ways, you know.' He looked down at Toby thoughtfully. 'Nevertheless, you must realize that things may not be quite as simple as you'd like them to be, you know.'

Toby blew his nose forcefully. 'What do you mean?' he asked.

'Well, things are pretty ropy here at Barons Lodge, you know,' Tod explained gravely. 'With so many empty boxes, we're nowhere near breaking even. We've got debts all round as well as owners leaving. Myra's done the best she can over the past few years.' He sighed. 'We'd probably be in a far worse mess if it wasn't for her, and it's been a hell of a struggle for her, I realize that.' He fumbled in his pocket for his packet of cigarettes. 'And the future looks anything but rosy. So,

302

you see, she may well feel she's had enough – wants to get out before the situation gets even more desperate.' He shrugged his shoulders. 'I can't say I'd blame her, in a way! There's no doubt about it, she might well be better off with Stelios. Not just financially, of course – that's indisputable – but emotionally, too. He could certainly afford to look after her properly . . . I very much doubt if she loves him, or anything as dramatic as that, but she might well find his offer very appealing.' He lit a cigarette, his expression preoccupied.

Toby stared at him, astonished. Why was he taking it all so philosophically? he wondered. He really didn't understand his father at all. 'But what about us, Dad?' he asked anxiously.

Tod put a hand on his arm. 'Your mother wouldn't want to do anything to hurt you, Toby: I'm absolutely sure of that. She wouldn't want anything she decided to do to alter her relationship with you.' He blinked behind his glasses. 'We both love you, you know. Very much indeed. I know we don't always show it and things haven't been very easy between all of us recently, but that doesn't mean we don't love you enormously. You must always remember that.'

Toby's face was creased with anxiety. 'I know, Dad, I know. I've been a bit of a pain in the past year or so, I'm afraid, and I'm sorry, but I have had a few worries of my own, you know.' He frowned. 'But it's not just me I'm thinking about, Dad: it's you, too. What will happen to you if Mother goes? I mean, I'll be leaving home in a few years anyway, I suppose. So then you'd be alone, and that would be awful.' His eyes were wide with concern.

Tod, touched, felt an immediate wave of guilt. Perhaps he should come clean with Toby right now about Kate: confess how he had fallen in love with her and admit that far from being horrified at the idea of Myra going off with Stelios, it would give him something he had been longing for, a chance to try living with Kate. He had missed her acutely in the past few months but he was still not certain that he was the right man for her. His self-confidence had been slipping badly again and he frequently felt too old and wearily secondhand to be of much use to anyone. He had almost resigned himself to thinking that he should let Kate go so that she was free to find someone more suitable and younger. But now, suddenly, everything had gone topsy-turvy. It was Myra, it seemed, who was so desperate and unhappy that she was on the brink of breaking up their marriage. It was essential that the two of them talk everything through, no holds barred, before he confided in Toby, Tod decided. To do that now would not only be disloyal to Myra, but might upset the boy further.

'I think you're jumping the gun a bit, Tobes, you know,' he said soothingly. 'After all, your mother hasn't even told us she's thinking of going yet, has she? Let alone actually left.' He drained his glass and replaced it purposefully on the table. 'It's sod's law, of course, that she's in London today and the Craven meeting starts tomorrow. I probably won't get a chance to talk to her till the weekend. The house'll be full of people all week.' He turned to Toby, his face grave. 'But I'll confront her with all this then. You have my word, I promise.'

Barons Lodge: Achilles's Box

'I just didn't want Rory to know where I am – where to find me,' Liam said despairingly as he started brushing Achilles's mane with brisk, methodical strokes.

'But why?' Toby asked, bewildered. Liam really was in the most peculiar mood, he thought. You would have imagined he'd be pleased to have news of his elder brother, but the reverse seemed to be true. The moment Liam had heard about his having met Rory at Mountclare, he had become tense and preoccupied.

Toby secured Watson's hay-net more firmly above the manger and leant on the partition dividing his pony from Achilles's more spacious box. He regarded his friend with a baffled expression. 'But why not?' he persisted. 'He certainly seemed to be pleased to have news of you. I told him all about Jacko here, of course, and what a world-beater you thought he was. Rory seemed very interested. He wanted to know when and where Dad was likely to run him.'

Liam looked even more disconsolate at this information. 'To be sure he did. Just so as he can track me down and start upsetting things again,' he replied tersely.

'Oh, for heaven's sake! Why should he want to do that?' Toby asked, exasperated.

Liam stopped his grooming for a moment and turned towards him, his narrow face solemn. 'Because I took some money from him to get myself over to England, and I imagine he'd be wanting it back,' he said grimly. 'It's OK, I can pay it back, thanks to Jacko,' he added quickly, patting the horse's neck. 'But Rory's not to know that.' He sighed. 'I was planning to send the money over to our Ma to give to Rory when he came out of Mountjoy this summer – if she promised not to let on where I am, that is.' He looked down at the straw, pulling some of Achilles's coarse black hairs out of his brush as he did so. 'But now, seeing as he's got his parole or whatever it's called earlier than we expected, he's bound to find out what I did and then he'll come looking for me all right. There's no doubt about that!'

Toby stared at him in astonishment. He did not, he realized, know Liam at all. He had always seemed so straightforward and honest, the last person he would have suspected of stealing anything, let alone money from his own brother.

Also Stella had never mentioned anything about Rory having been in prison. Perhaps she didn't know, but that seemed unlikely. She knew everything about the people who worked at Mountclare.

'I never realized Rory had been in prison,' he exclaimed. 'Whatever for?'

Liam picked up his grooming bag and clucked at Achilles to move over. 'He and his friends were involved with some arms smuggling down Wexford way, or so the Garda thought,' he replied.

'Arms smuggling! Whatever would he get involved with that for? What are you talking about?' Toby asked, bewildered.

'Rory keeps bad company, that's what I'm talking about,' Liam snapped.

'OK, OK, keep your hair on,' Toby retorted, still confused. He had had quite enough of this conversation. 'Look, Liam, I'm really sorry if I've landed you in any sort of trouble with Rory, but I really don't think it's my fault,' he said defensively. 'How on earth could I have known that things were so complicated? You should have warned me.' He raised his hand. 'Anyway, I'll see you in the morning.'

He couldn't understand, either, why Liam was not more excited about the prospect of du Roc working Achilles on the gallops for the first time tomorrow. He himself certainly intended to be out on the heath to watch the partnership in action. It would be a welcome distraction from his other preoccupations. Although he was greatly relieved that Tod now knew what was going on, there had been something disturbingly casual about his father's reaction, almost as though he didn't care that much whether Myra left him or not. Perhaps he had been drunker than he'd appeared. Anyway, at least the whole thing was out in the open now, or would be after the weekend. Toby intended to avoid being alone with his mother until then. He was too enraged by her behaviour to be able to pretend he didn't know about it, but Tod had promised that as soon as possible they would have a proper 'family' conference and he could have his say then.

Myra slammed the front door shut thankfully as Jack Weston's Jaguar crunched off down the drive. Thank God the last few social days were over, she thought, and she could now relax. There had been twelve for lunch today, including the Westons and a couple from Huddersfield who were now part-owners of Southwold Jack. The Yorkshire brigade had also insisted on dropping in for a drink after racing as well, definitely the worse for wear. They had all backed the long-shot winner of the big race, since it was trained up north and they knew the owners, and their raucous celebration had left Myra with a throbbing headache. She had been irritated, too, by the fact that all her other guests, including Basil and Pam, had left for London straight after the racing, leaving her to entertain the Weston party on her own. Tod, as usual, had had the excuse of evening stables and Toby, who seemed to have been avoiding her deliberately ever since his return from Ireland, hadn't even gone racing at all. He had announced at lunch that he was going to a film in Cambridge with a friend and wouldn't be back until late. According to Stella, his stint at Mountclare had gone very well: he had worked hard and seemed eager to learn, she had reported. Nevertheless he seemed to be in a peculiar mood and had given her some very baleful looks over lunch.

As she headed back to the drawing-room, she realized that she was feeling unusually tired. The dirty glasses and ashtrays could wait; what she needed was a stiff drink. Pouring herself a large gin, she sank down on the sofa and kicked off her shoes.

Tod, too, had been behaving rather oddly in the last few days, come to think of it. She had caught him staring at her across the dinner table with a look of genuine interest the other night, something she could not recall him doing for years.

They had been in the middle of a discussion about Achilles, that colt of the Levertons that Alain du Roc had ridden for the first time that morning and with whom he had clearly been impressed.

'He's got ability, Tod. He's headstrong, of course. I'm not at all sure that you shouldn't try running him with a dropped noseband or one of those Australian bridles, but I liked the feel of him. Vroom . . .' he made an expressive gesture with his hands. 'He's got some acceleration, that one! I'd be delighted to ride him for you on the racecourse, if I'm not committed elsewhere. Where will you go, do you think? York for the Dante? Or Lingfield, perhaps? You might even think about Chester, you know. A tight track would suit him very well, in my opinion. His action is *très economique*.'

'Surely you don't go along with this crackpot idea of running him in the Derby, do you?' Basil asked, pouring himself some more wine.

The Frenchman shrugged his shoulders. 'If he runs a decent trial, I don't see why not. He's very inexperienced, *bien sûr*; it's a pity you couldn't get a run into him earlier. But he's a quick learner, I'd guess.'

Tod nodded in agreement. 'He's certainly that. I'm prepared to risk it, personally.' He grinned. 'It's more than my life's worth to disappoint his owners. Lady Kitty has set her heart on seeing her colours on Derby Day!'

'I think you're all barmy,' Myra interjected. 'After all, the colt didn't beat much at Doncaster and we don't even know he stays a mile, let alone further. He's fast, of course, any fool can see that, but he could flop completely in one of the serious trials. He could make us all look ridiculous!'

'Oh well, it wouldn't be for the first time, would it?' Tod retorted good-humouredly enough, but the comment was accompanied by a quizzical glance in her direction.

He had been drinking again recently, too, she'd observed, and had resumed that lackadaisical approach to Barons Lodge's problems which irritated her so. The only horse in the yard that seemed to really engage his interest was Achilles, God knows why. The animal had too much temperament to be a top-class racehorse, in her opinion. But what did it really matter? She'd be away from it all by the end of the season. She was due to lunch with Stelios in the next week or so, as soon as he returned from the Far East. They would decide then when they were going to inform their immediate families about their plans. They would also need to discuss her initial financial settlement and possible legal manoeuvres, should Tod be unwilling to agree to a quick divorce. She herself was reluctant to confront Tod until after Royal Ascot: memories of last year still lingered and she wanted to give Toby at least half a term to settle in at the Perse, his new school.

She was delighted he had done so well at Mountclare. Stella seemed to have had a more positive effect on him than even she had hoped and the fact that he had enjoyed stud work could only bode well for the future, particularly if she and Stelios were to be living at Ballinvale. She had come around to the view, albeit reluctantly, that after she left, Toby would have to remain with his father at Barons Lodge during term time but spend all his holidays with her in Ireland. That seemed the most reasonable arrangement all round.

She was so involved with her thoughts that she did not hear Tod come into the house until he was actually crossing he hall. He flung open the drawing-room door, shooing the two terriers towards the

Den. 'God! Evening stables were a chore tonight,' he complained, leaning against the doorway. 'Every bloody animal seemed to have a problem and this spring flu's certainly mowing down the staff. Poor old Liam had to do five horses tonight! Oh well!' He looked around. 'Our northern friends have departed, I see. Bit Brahms and Liszt, weren't they? Jack Weston at least. Talking of which . . .' He headed purposefully towards the drinks cupboard.

Myra snorted. 'Why on earth they wanted to come back here after racing I cannot imagine. They'd had quite enough to drink already.'

'You're not dashing off to the kitchen in a minute or anything, are you?' Tod asked as he turned back to her again, a large whisky in his hand.

Myra looked puzzled. 'No, why do you ask?'

'Because I want to talk to you, that's why,' Tod replied firmly, sinking down into the armchair opposite her. 'About us.'

Myra's heart thumped with panic. God, he hadn't got wind of what she was up to, had he? she wondered guiltily. How on earth could he have found out? And what was she going to say about it all? She took a quick gulp of her gin. Tell the truth, she supposed. Just confess that she had come to the end of her tether with him and the situation at Barons Lodge and had decided to do something drastic about it. It might be quite a relief in a way.

Tod was regarding her quizzically as he lit his cigarette. 'It's all right, Myra. Don't look so panic-stricken. I'm not going to create a scene or anything,' he observed calmly. 'But the game is up, I'm afraid. You've been rumbled. I know what you're planning to do: leave me and do a bunk with old Stelios, I mean. I found out the other day.' He eyed her keenly through a haze of blue smoke.

Myra felt peculiarly calm. Now that her secret was out in the open it all sounded unreal somehow, almost as though it was someone else's life they were discussing – nothing to do with her at all.

'Yes, well. That's rather a vulgar way of putting it, don't you think?' she retorted. 'Stelios has asked me to marry him, if that's what you mean, and I have agreed.' She smoothed a strand of hair back into her French pleat. 'I'm sorry you had to hear about it from someone else, though. I was about to tell you myself, as a matter of fact.'

Tod seemed amused by this reply. 'Really! You surprise me! I imagined that I'd be the last to know. I gather that Stelios made this extraordinary approach to you some time ago,' he went on casually. 'I wish you'd discussed it with me at the time; it might have saved a lot of time and trouble.'

'Discussed it with you!' Myra said with astonishment. 'How on earth could I have done that? It never occurred to me.'

'Well, I don't see why not,' Tod replied, stretching out his legs. 'I am your husband, after all, aren't I? For the time being, at least!'

Myra looked at him in disbelief. 'But Stelios was asking me to leave you, to abandon you completely.' Her voice had become more agitated. 'I tell you, the whole proposition came as a terrible shock to me. It took me weeks to absorb it. I hardly felt I could discuss it with you!' She was genuinely bewildered. 'How did you find out, anyway?' she demanded, keen to return to surer ground.

Tod shook his head. 'Sorry. Can't tell you that. I'm under oath not to. Let's just say, though, that the information came from someone who wishes you well, not ill, so you've no need to get paranoid about it. Anyway, it doesn't really matter, does it, if you were about to tell me anyway?'

Myra scowled at him. 'I suppose that cow Pam told you – she never could keep a secret. She was just the same at school – leaky as an old boot.'

Tod shook his head again. 'No, Myra, Pam didn't tell me,' he said quietly. 'Though it doesn't surprise me at all that she knew. It explains all those odd half-pitying looks she's been giving me recently.' He banged his drink down on the table beside him, suddenly exasperated. 'For God's sake, Myra, you might have talked the whole thing over with me before telling half Newmarket,' he complained.

'I haven't told anyone but Basil and Pam,' Myra replied indignantly. 'Basil is my brother, after all, and I had to tell someone!'

Tod sighed, pulling at his cigarette. 'Look, Myra, I know things have been difficult in the last few years. I know how disappointing and frustrating it's been for you, particularly in contrast with the past. I also appreciate how much you've done to try to keep the yard together. Perhaps we should have talked more about it all, instead of just brooding in our separate corners.' He shrugged his shoulders. 'Trouble was, I always found going over it all again and again only depressed me further! You must have been flattered, though, by Stelios's proposal?' he inquired more cheerfully. 'You are still very handsome, of course, but not many women of your age get proposals from millionaires, do they? Particularly if they are already married! You must have been tempted to bunk off right there and then.'

Draining her glass Myra got up abruptly. 'For heaven's sake, you make it all sound like a bloody picnic!' she exploded. 'It's been bloody hard for me, you know, trying to work out what's the best thing to do. I've been at my wits' end.' She stomped over to the drinks cupboard and poured herself another gin. 'Barons Lodge has been my home all my life. You know how much it means to me.' She swung back to Tod, her face tense with emotion. 'Daddy left it in our care, and just look what's happened, look how we've let him down. I'm so ashamed.' She banged down the gin bottle angrily onto the table. 'The whole place is falling apart,' she went on indignantly. 'We owe the bank nearly £100,000 now, you know!' She walked slowly back to the sofa, biting her lip. 'I have struggled and struggled to keep the place going, as well as boost everyone's morale, particularly yours . . . We'll definitely have to remortgage the place this summer, the way we're going, and within a season or so we could well have to sell up altogether.' She flopped back on to the sofa, her face puckered with despair. 'You know I couldn't bear that – having to sell the yard to a stranger. I'd never forgive myself for letting Daddy down like that. So when Stelios made me this offer, it was not just the promise of an end to my personal worries and financial insecurity that was tempting: it was his offer to save the yard as well that really appealed. Surely you can understand that?' she asked, exasperated.

Tod, who had been sitting quietly, a resigned, almost sympathetic look on his face, seemed stung by this last piece of information. 'Save the yard? How do you mean? By buying it, I presume,' he queried, frowning.

Myra nodded. 'Yes. For Nik to train here initially and then for Toby maybe to take over in the future.' She spread her hands emphatically. 'Christ, Tod! It's a very generous offer. Stelios would certainly give us a good price and it would mean that the future of the yard was secure, at least in our lifetime. That's quite something, don't you think?'

Tod stared at her, his face clouding over. 'God Almighty, Myra! What a benefactor Stelios is turning out to be,' he said bitterly. 'He seems to have thought of everything. Except making me an offer, in an open and friendly way, of course!' He shook his head in disbelief. He couldn't bring himself to do that, it seems. He had to sneak along and offer to marry you behind my back. That's not a very friendly gesture, is it?' He got up and strode over to the drinks cupboard. 'A decent offer for Barons Lodge would suit me very well right now, as a matter of fact,' he said vehemently. 'I care what happens to this place, of course, but I, too, oddly enough have had about enough of struggling to make ends meet. I'd be delighted to get off the treadmill at the end of this year – pack it all in and do something else.' He swung back to face Myra, cradling his glass in both hands. 'Your father wasn't an easy act to follow, you know,' he informed her. 'Yet despite that I did become a champion trainer. I proved that I was as good as he was, didn't I?' He sighed. 'But I certainly haven't got the will or the energy to do that again. Sorry!' Pushing up his glasses, he wearily rubbed his eyes. 'Left to myself I'd probably have packed up training altogether in the past two years, you know. I've forced myself to keep going, largely for your sake – and Toby's perhaps. Ironic, isn't it, given what you have been planning!'

'Well, I've never even considered giving up on Barons Lodge,' Myra retorted defiantly, stung by Tod's martyrish tone. She was the only one who seemed to be prepared to take drastic action to save the yard, however much unpleasantness and disruption it might cause, she thought. She was damned if she was going to be made to feel guilty about it. Also, other than showing a certain resentment about Stelios's going behind his back, Tod did seem to be taking the whole situation remarkably calmly. She had been so busy justifying herself that she hadn't had time to question him about what he had been up to.

'And how about you, anyway?' she asked accusingly. 'You've been busily grilling me about my plans, but don't tell me you haven't got some of your own. What about you and the Leverton girl, then?'

'What about her?' Tod replied calmly.

'Well, there's something going on between the two of you, isn't there? I know you denied it before, but you weren't very convincing, let me tell you! I'm not the only one who's been leading a secret life, now, am I? Go on, own up!' She leant forward, glaring at him balefully.

Tod stared at her thoughtfully for a moment. 'If you'll calm down a minute, I'll tell you about it,' he replied eventually, stubbing out his cigarette. 'Pam was actually right for once, yes,' he went on, his face solemn. 'Kate and I were having an affair, as she would put it. We love each other, believe it or not, very much. But I haven't seen her for nearly five months,' he added quietly.

Myra's mouth had gone dry with shock. Tod loved the girl, he said. She hadn't bargained for that. She'd presumed he'd just been having a little sexual fling. 'Why not?' she asked, her voice shaking.

'Because Kate insisted we have a trial separation. She said she couldn't cope with the deception and secrecy of our relationship any more and having to share me with you.' He shrugged his shoulders. 'So, if we didn't see each other for some time, she hoped I'd be able to work out how much she meant to me.' He glanced at Myra, his eyebrows raised. 'Whether I'd be prepared to leave you for her, I suppose it really came down to.'

Myra's heart thumped in her chest. 'And are you?' she asked tensely, reaching for her drink.

'Well, to tell you the truth, I wasn't absolutely sure,' Tod replied candidly. 'I do love her, very much – I've already admitted that; but I wasn't sure if that alone justified destroying everything here. There was Toby to consider, and you, of course, and all the humiliation and upset I thought it would cause you.' He gave her a lop-sided grin. 'Seems rather ironic now, doesn't it? Also, to be perfectly honest, I wasn't sure if I was really right for her,' he went on quietly. 'After all, she's so much younger and will certainly want a family and all that.' He sighed. 'I wasn't sure, at my age, if I really wanted to embark on all that again!' He paused. 'But now, since you seem to have torn up the form book, I think I'll risk it. If she still wants me, that is,' he added ruefully. 'She may well have found someone else by now.'

Myra sat rigidly in her chair, transfixed with indignation. How could Tod take it all so lightly? It was their marriage he was talking about, a partnership of many years' standing. How could he discard it so easily and consider taking on this Kate girl just like that? But she was planning to leave *him*, she had to remind herself sternly; she had already accepted Stelios's offer, after all. The news that Tod was also involved with someone else should therefore have been extremely welcome; it presumably meant that there wouldn't be any sort of trouble over the divorce, and she wouldn't have to feel guilty any more about what she had been plotting. What was the matter with her? Why on earth was she feeling so displaced and shaken? Tod leant forward, his expression concerned. 'I'm really sorry that things haven't worked out better between us, Myra,' he said earnestly. 'I owe you a great deal, I know. You put me together again after Monique's death, and gave me a real chance to prove myself. And we've not had such a bad life together, have we? After all, we did have some real triumphs with the horses in those early days and we've got Toby, haven't we?' He frowned. 'We'll both have to try very hard to explain to him why it's best for us to split up, though. He won't like it one bit, I'm afraid.' He took another pull at his cigarette. 'We must explain that we both love him, whatever happens, and hope he'll get used to the idea in time.' Catching sight of Myra's grim expression, he got up and gently gave her a peck on the cheek before gently prising her glass out of her hand. 'Cheer up, old thing,' he said affectionately. 'I reckon all this calls for another drink. We must toast the future, both our futures. That would seem appropriate, don't you think?'

Myra, her hands clenched, stared silently down at her lap, unable to articulate her feelings. Tod repeated, 'Cheer up! We've both had a hell of a shock over all this, I know. I can't really take it all in myself yet.' He shook his head. 'But somehow all sorts of extraordinary, unexpected things seem to be falling into place. It'll all work out in the end, I'm sure of it.'

Myra suddenly experienced an overwhelming feeling of panic. 'Will it?' she asked in a muffled voice. 'I doubt it.' Leaping up, she clapped her hand over her mouth and fled from the room.

The Old Rectory

'I'm just sorry that Kate can't be here today,' Lady Kitty remarked wistfully. 'Still, she seems to be having the time of her life in America. And I'll be ringing her in New York tonight, of course, to give her a blow-by-blow account of Achilles's race.'

She was sitting with Charlie in the kitchen at the Old Rectory, having some coffee before they started off on their journey down to Lingfield Park for the Derby trial. Lady Kitty had wanted to make her own way to the Surrey course, by train, but Charlie had insisted on coming to pick her up and driving her there and back himself. 'No problem,' he had said. 'I'd be delighted to be your chauffeur for the day.'

'Kate will be pretty fed up about missing the race, I should imagine,' he said thoughtfully, stirring some more sugar into his coffee. 'Still, the book now has to come first, I suppose, and if the launch is going well, that should make up for it.' He glanced across at Lady Kitty. 'I admire her work a lot, you know. Those pictures she did of Alain du Roc last year were brilliant, I thought.'

Lady Kitty nodded. 'Indeed they were. But she lacks self-confidence. That's why the success of this book is so important.' Her eyes twinkled. 'Mind you, tagging along with Sandy Diss will help. That one's got enough confidence for ten! She's a generous soul too, you know. The moment she heard I was thinking of flying over to New York for Kate's birthday next week, she insisted we borrow her Park Avenue apartment. Kate says it's quite splendiferous.' She clapped her hands together in childish delight. 'Neither of us know New York well – Kate's been far too busy to do any exploring – and I'm so looking forward to us seeing the sights together!'

The moment the American trip had been mooted by the New York publishers Kate had cheered up, her mother recalled. She was obviously finding the separation from Tod hard to endure and although she had been working flat out since Christmas, that alone had not proved much consolation. This jaunt with Sandy, which seemed to entail a frantic round of TV and radio interviews and signings in both New York and Kentucky, was exactly the sort of distraction she'd needed.

'I never knew it was Kate's birthday next week. I wish you'd told me,' Charlie complained. 'I'd have asked you to take a card over or something. Still, you'll give her my best wishes, won't you? I'm sure you'll have a great time, the two of you.' He drained his cup of coffee. 'You get on so well together, don't you? More like sisters than mother and daughter. I envy that in a way. I love my father very much, as you know, but I'm always very conscious of the difference in our ages, in our attitudes.' His face clouded over. 'I feel so responsible for him now, too, of course. If only I hadn't blown that meeting with Warrender! I just couldn't bear him being so disparaging about Dad and so sympathetic about Mother. Still, I shouldn't have lost my temper. That was really dumb.' He shook his head vehemently.

'You shouldn't be so hard on yourself,' Lady Kitty remarked gently. 'You were upset, so you let it show. That's not a criminal offence, you know! You don't seem to have had much time for your mother, though. Was she really that wicked?'

'Wicked? Is that what I make her sound?' Charlie queried, surprised. 'Well, perhaps that's not fair. I can be too harsh on people, I know.' He frowned. 'I just didn't like her, I'm afraid. I know that's unnatural, but there you are. She was beautiful, of course, but spoilt and very shallow. I could never trust her, either – certainly not after the fire.' He gazed broodingly out of the window at the rain lashing down outside.

Lady Kitty regarded him thoughtfully. She had begun to like the boy a lot, she realized, despite his reserved exterior. There was an openness and determination about him that appealed to her. His face in profile was striking, with its alertness and strong bone structure, but there was a definite vulnerability about his mouth and those grey-green eyes, with their ridiculously long lashes. His unfortunate relationship with his mother could well have left him with a deep need for feminine love which he would find difficult to acknowledge, let alone assuage, she suspected. He had been involved with Diana Saunders recently, she gathered, but much though she liked the girl, Lady Kitty did not imagine that Diana had been able to cater for Charlie's emotional needs. She was too tough and masculine herself. But such maternal maunderings really wouldn't do, she told herself sternly as she caught sight of the clock. It was time they got going.

'Oh dear! Poor old Achilles won't like this weather at all. He's such a fastidious creature,' she observed, glancing out of the window as Charlie helped her on with her raincoat.

'Well, he'll just have to put up with it, won't he? It'll be just as unpleasant for all the others, after all,' he replied briskly. 'I just wish we'd been able to get another race into him, that's all. But his blood count wasn't quite right all last month, you know. We just couldn't risk it.'

Holding open the front door, he followed Lady Kitty out under the porch. 'You're looking a bit worried, all of a sudden,' he commented, glancing at her sharply. 'What's up? I'm not that bad a driver, you know!'

Lady Kitty slipped her hand under his arm. 'It's not that, silly!' she replied pensively. 'It's just that I suddenly had rather a sobering thought, that's all: Achilles is not the only one on trial today, is he? My judgement's really on the line, too. After all, it was my crazy idea to aim him at the Derby in the first place, wasn't it? I could look a proper old fool in a few hours' time.' She tugged at his sleeve, her expression relaxing. 'Oh well, it serves me right. Come on – if we don't get a move on, we'll miss the whole caboodle!'

Lingfield Park Racecourse

Packed uncomfortably into the top of the little Members' Stand, Lady Kitty again felt her confidence slipping. Achilles had looked so small in the paddock compared to the other runners and, as they had anticipated, he was clearly not enjoying the rain. Heavily protected in a waterproof hood as well as a paddock sheet, he had slouched around the ring, his lop ears flicking back and forth irritably.

'He looks like a horse in one of those nineteenth-century sporting prints,' Tod had remarked. 'A bit like the one I've got, of horses being struck by lightning on Middleham Moor – though the weather today's not quite that bad, thank goodness!'

Alain du Roc was finding the wet equally distasteful, Lady Kitty observed with some amusement. Although as relaxed as ever about the actual race, he was clearly anxious to get on with the job. '*Alors, mon vieux. Allons-y.* Let's get this over and done with as soon as possible,' he said briskly, as Tod legged him into the plate.

Leaving the paddock, Lady Kitty was surprised when Tod turned back towards her, a look of urgency on his face. 'Just in case we don't get the chance to talk privately later, I wonder if you could do me a favour,' he requested, guiding her gently under his umbrella. 'I've written a letter to Kate, care of you at the Old Rectory,' he explained, lowering his voice and glancing up to check that Myra and Charlie were out of earshot. 'I wondered if you'd mind giving it to her in New York next week. It's not just that it's her birthday: there's also been a rather dramatic development on the domestic front that I thought she ought to know about.'

Heading up into the stands Lady Kitty had somehow managed to get separated from the others and felt suddenly claustrophobic, hemmed in by so many tall people and the overpowering smell of wet raincoats. She wished she had taken Charlie's advice and watched the race on the television in the comfort of the Seafood Bar. She wouldn't be able to see much up here, she realized with a pang of disappointment.

'We lost you. Are you all right?' Charlie asked her anxiously, suddenly materializing beside her.

'I'm grand, thanks. I can't see much though, I'm afraid. Thank heavens you are videoing the race at home.'

'There you are! I told you we should have stayed downstairs,' Charlie reproached her. 'Never mind. I'll just have to be your eyes for a while.' He trained his binoculars across the course to where the runners were being loaded into the stalls. 'Achilles went down OK,' he reported. 'And he seems to be going in all right. But I am rather worried about the early pace.' He tensed suddenly. 'Hang on. This is it, Lady Kitty. They're off!'

Clutching her racecard tightly, Lady Kitty cocked her head to one side as she strained to catch the racecourse commentary.

'Sod it! Just as I feared,' Charlie muttered at her side. 'They're going no pace at all. Alain's having a hell of a time restraining our lad. He's chucking his head about all over the place – look, can you see?' He took Lady Kitty's arm. 'Oh no! I don't believe it!' he wailed suddenly. 'Alain's letting him go on. He's taking up the running. What does he think he's doing? He's supposed to be holding him up.'

Standing on tiptoe and peering between the shoulders of the people in front, Lady Kitty caught a brief glimpse of the field streaming along on the far side of the course. It was clear indeed that du Roc had taken up the running. Crouched low in the saddle in his rain-drenched silks he had already rocketed at least four lengths clear of the rest of the field. Lady Kitty felt her confidence ebb away further. This was just what they had hoped to avoid, of course. After all, there was no guarantee that the colt would stay the trip today. Both Myra and Sam Shaw, she knew, had real doubts about his ability to do so. Maybe this was it, she thought unhappily: the end to all her silly romantic dreams of having a Derby runner. Tod would never let Achilles take his place in the Epsom line-up if he flopped this afternoon. But he hadn't flopped yet, she told herself sternly. And after all, it wasn't Jack Massam riding him today but Alain du Roc, one of the best jockeys around. If he'd let the colt go on and make the running, it must have been because he felt it was the only thing to do in the circumstances. Pricking up her ears, she heard the commentator confirm that Achilles was now six lengths clear of the others as he came out of the dip on the far side of the course and headed up the hill.

'Alain's totally slipped his field. Some cheek!' Charlie gasped admiringly. 'Steady, though, steady. The ground's a bit slippery on that turn,' he added.

Lady Kitty tugged at his sleeve. 'It all hinges on how he comes down the hill. How he handles that,' she said urgently. She could hear from the commentary that Achilles was still ahead, with the favourite Antrim's Pride back in third, but the next half furlong, she knew, would be crucial.

Frozen like a pointer, Charlie stood rock still, his eyes glued to his binoculars as he watched the field make the descent down into the straight. 'Brilliant! Quite brilliant,' he murmured excitedly. 'Smooth as silk. No problem. The only thing that matters now is that he doesn't tie up on the run in.'

'*And as they come into the straight and pass the three-furlong marker, it's still Achilles, the outsider Achilles, who's being given a very enterprising ride by Alain du Roc, still out in front. But the favourite Antrim's Pride is pulling out now. Beginning to make his challenge. He's been switched to the outside now and it looks like he's beginning to close on the leader.*'

As the noise of the crowd started to swell, Lady Kitty turned anxiously to Charlie, her heart pounding, her eyes huge with apprehension. Oh no, she prayed. Achilles mustn't let them catch him now, not when he'd led them so resolutely from start to finish.

Charlie clutched her arm with his free hand. 'Don't worry, don't worry,' he reassured her exultantly. 'He's absolutely walking it. None of the others will catch him now. Brilliant, Alain! Bravo! Well ridden!' He turned to Lady Kitty in delight. 'You were absolutely right. We've got to have a crack at the Derby with him now.'

As du Roc and Achilles powered up to the line, he threw his sodden trilby up into the air and whooped with triumph.

CHAPTER TWENTY-TWO

Epsom Downs

Drumming his tanned fingers on the wheel of the Bentley Continental, Tom Dacre turned to Stella with relief. 'Well, it looks like we finally made it!' he said. 'The traffic is quite something, though. No wonder you prefer the helicopter ride!'

Stella lifted an eyebrow. 'We're not there yet. This last bit is the real crawl,' she cautioned, leaning forward to adjust her sun visor. She wanted to obscure the view of the open-topped double-decker bus which they had been following for the last half hour: its upper deck, hung with placards and streamers, was packed with noisy, casually dressed punters, already drinking champagne and intent on energetically waving the ice-blue Bentley goodbye as they bumped off in the direction of the Derby Arms pub.

Stella smoothed her black Ungaro skirt over her knee with a sigh. 'Thank God for that! I'd certainly seen enough of them for one day,' she remarked languidly, gazing out of the window as the car slid forward again. On her right, the famous gaunt Epsom grandstand, flags fluttering, stood stark on the ridge of the downs. Its weatherbeaten roof rust-pink in the sunshine capped tier upon tier of terraces, antiquated boxes and bars already filling up with people. Beyond the winning post, decked out in the black, red and gold colours of the Derby's sponsor, Ever Ready, rows of open-topped buses faced the stands like an army drawn up for battle, and way beyond, high above Tattenham Corner and the serried rows of cars in between, the great fairground wheel turned slowly in the haze.

Stella did not really appreciate the jostle and razzamatazz of Derby Day. The crowds, the traffic jams, the powerful aroma of frying hamburgers and fish and chips, the brass band music, all of it almost made her want to turn tail again and head back to the tranquillity of her suite at the Savoy to watch the race on television. It was ironic, she mused, that as a serious breeder, so much of her efforts were devoted to producing a middle-distance champion, a Derby winner, yet she found the occasion itself an ordeal.

Years ago, as a child, she had found it exciting, though. She recalled her first-ever visit, when she and Nik had fled from Stelios's elaborate picnic in the Owners' and Trainers' Car Park and scampered across the course to mix with the informal Derby crowd milling round the tents and gypsy caravans in their shirtsleeves. There had still been the occasional old Romany wagon on show down there then, with lurchers and goats tied up underneath it in the shade; nowadays, the gypsies' patch was more like a glittering space-age caravan park with its lines of metallic mobile homes, festooned with television aerials and frosted glass and neat vases of plastic flowers.

Craning her neck, she could see them now, spread like a great silver carpet on the slope of the downs. Above them, at the top of the Derby course, where the track swerved leftwards towards Tattenham Hill, the sky was dark with helicopters, buzzing down in droves to decant their well-dressed cargoes before spiralling noisily back towards the centre of London again. Normally, she and Nik would have been amongst the passengers but today, at Diana Saunders' insistence, they had been persuaded to return to tradition and picnic in the car park behind the stands. Tom Dacre had willingly co-operated, providing both the perfect car to picnic from and the meal itself, which he had organized through some contact at Searcys. Diana, though, had insisted on driving Nik independently to the course in her new toy, a brand new Toyota.

The girl had really been getting her hooks into her brother recently, Stella had observed. She had spent the last two weekends at Kilmarron and had already got a lot of refurbishments in the house in hand, much to the dismay of O'Donnell's old housekeeper. When Stella had asked Nik the other day if he was planning to get engaged, he had shrugged his shoulders and said, 'Why not? Diana suits me as well as anyone. Besides, we could do with the money.'

It was perfectly true. Stella had to accept that, despite all her efforts, her father's plans to marry Myra Beckhampton seemed to be going ahead. She was therefore accelerating her efforts to get Tom Dacre to fall in love with her and had even begun fantasizing about a possible double wedding some time later in the year.

Glancing at Tom now, as he sat casually behind the wheel, *The Sporting Life* spread out across the dashboard in front of him, she congratulated herself on having made such a suitable catch. She would never have any real feeling for him, of course – she had no real feeling for anyone except Nik – but she had to admit that the American was very pleasing on the eye. With his unusual hair, which looked as though it had been specially dyed to match his morning suit, he looked tailormade to sit behind the wheel of a Bentley Continental. She was also rather enjoying playing her new malleable, flirtatious role and observing the success it was having. Tom had already suggested a trip to Kentucky to meet his parents, and had begun questioning her urgently about her past affairs – always an encouraging sign.

'They've none of them been important,' she had reassured him over dinner at the Waterside Inn at Bray the previous evening. 'I've always known exactly what I want, of course – just never found it.' She reached across the table to touch his sleeve. 'Perhaps my luck has changed,' she added, flashing him a suggestive look.

He was smiling at her indulgently now, easing up the handbrake as a traffic policeman halted the stream of cars ahead. 'Do you think the others will be here yet? What do you bet?' He grinned.

'You know I never bet,' Stella rebuked him with mock severity. 'They're probably at the stables. Devilry flew over last night, you know. Nik will certainly want to check he's settled in OK before we start lunch.'

Tom slid the big car forward again. 'I know you don't like being put on the spot, honey, but what are Devilry's chances tomorrow? Do you expect him to win?'

Stella looked thoughtful. 'I don't know. He's still a bit ring rusty after that long lay-off, but he's certainly fit enough to do himself justice. The Coronation Cup is just a prep race for the ones that really matter – the King George and the Arc, of course. But we'd obviously like to get it in the bag too, if we can.'

Tom nodded with interest. 'Diana seems quite sweet on the colt, Achilles, who runs in the Derby today,' he remarked. 'She had him as a yearling at Three Swallows, she was telling me. She seems to think he's got a chance, if he gets through the preliminaries. He's a touch temperamental, I guess. What do you make of his chances?' he inquired as they bumped off the road on to the grass of the Owners' and Trainers' Car Park.

Stella made a face. 'Well, I suspect Diana's being over-optimistic,' she replied. 'Achilles did win the Lingfield Derby trial but the race was run at such a muddling pace. It's hard to know what to make of the form. I suspect she's just rooting for him out of sentiment. He's by her stallion Greek Dancer you know. If Achilles does win today Greek Dancer will become flavour of the month. He could do with a boost: Achilles has been the only winner out of his first crop so far.'

'I see. But I wouldn't have thought Diana was a particularly sentimental type though,' Tom queried.

'All breeders are when it comes to animals they bred themselves,' Stella said firmly. 'It's a weakness that has to be conquered. Anyway, we'll know soon enough. I've asked one of my stud grooms, someone I can trust, to go up to the stables and take a look at the colt, and judge whether Diana's confidence is justified. His younger brother happens to "do" the animal, I gather, by some extraordinary coincidence.'

She raised her hand in greeting as the Bentley drew level with some familiar faces, the Newmarket trainer Jeremy Hindley and a group including the ex-jockeys Jimmy Lindley and Joe Mercer. One of their party, a frothily clad blonde, swinging her legs on the bonnet of an MG, waved back cheerily as they passed.

'Who's that?' Dacre asked with amazement.

'Daytripper, by the look of it.' Stella's tone was disparaging. She had just caught a glimpse of Tod Beckhampton stalking along in the distance like a heron, in his grey morning suit. He had not assisted her plan at all, she thought with irritation. From the emotional letter she had received from Toby after his return to Barons Lodge, she had gathered that the boy had had yet another shock: his father too was involved with someone else, Kate Leverton, one of the owners of Achilles. Far from being devastated at the prospect of Myra leaving him for Stelios, Tod actually seemed to give it his blessing. 'I can't believe it. My parents are pathetic,' Toby wrote. 'I think they've both gone mad.'

Stella wished she had known about Tod and the Leverton girl earlier. She wouldn't have wasted her time trying to put Myra off or bothered to seduce Toby if she had suspected that Tod was actually looking for a way out of his marriage.

Still, all that was water under the bridge now; she must just throw all her energies into her new scheme instead.

'Well driven, Tom,' she said enthusiastically, slinging a slender arm around Dacre's neck. 'I never thought I'd drive to the Derby again but with you it's really been remarkably painless.'

Her companion grinned. 'Swell. Maybe I can persuade you to enjoy a few more things in the future?' he suggested meaningfully.

Stella returned his gaze unblinking. 'I don't see why not,' she replied sweetly. 'Who knows what surprises lie ahead?'

*

Less than half a mile away, in the centre of the course, Toby Beckhampton was sitting munching a hamburger. The atmosphere around him was very different from that in the Owners' and Trainers' Car Park. It reminded Toby more of a Bank Holiday crowd he had mingled with once on the beach at Skegness on a jaunt from Hadleigh than any crowd he had ever encountered at a race meeting before. The nearest group of picnickers were a raucous lot, a collection of middle-aged couples with strong cockney accents, who had spread themselves out on the grass in varying states of sunbathing undress and were clearly enjoying themselves hugely. Already reddened by the sun, they were swigging back drinks from a series of bottles of spirits and beer and enthusiastically digging into two large buckets full of jellied eels. Their loud good humour was adding to the general cacophony of noise all around: the pop music blaring from a nearby stall selling gigantic teddy bears, cheap straw hats and sunglasses, unintelligible announcements booming out intermittently over the public address system, and the constant whirring of helicopters overhead.

Although it was barely midday, the temperature, Toby reckoned, must be in the mid seventies and with his fair skin he was already feeling uncomfortable. Following the example of most of those around him, he had shed his jacket and tie and was using his copy of *The Sporting Life* as a sun hat. God knows what his mother would have said if she could see him, he thought with some satisfaction. But there was not much risk of that: she never ventured out of the Members' Enclosure on Derby Day, except to go to the paddock. She was lunching with Stelios in one of the boxes today, he had gathered. Where Tod was right now, he had no idea, nor did he particularly care: probably with Kate Leverton and her mother. He was absolutely fed up and disillusioned with both his parents at the moment. He intended to stay as far away from both of them as possible today, except in the paddock, of course. It would be incredibly difficult and embarrassing to have to greet the Levertons and possibly Stelios as though nothing was going on, although his whole upbringing in a racing yard had taught him that on the big occasion personal problems were put aside: the race itself was all that mattered.

He had better start making his way back to the paddock area now, he thought, getting slowly to his feet. He had promised to try and meet Liam there for a quick cup of coffee before the lad returned to the stables to put the final touches to Achilles.

The colt had been remarkably well behaved out on the course

early this morning. He had looked about him eagerly in the sunlight, taking in the change of scenery with interest. He had given a couple of fly jumps when Tod legged Liam into the saddle but had then proceeded to canter up the course, past the vast empty stands, in a calm workmanlike fashion.

'It'll be a different ball game this afternoon, I fear. We've done what we can, but God only knows how he'll handle the parade,' Tod commented to Charlie. 'We'll put cotton wool in his ears, of course, and I'll lead him past the stands with Nobby in attendance, but I want you and Liam to take over when he's back in the paddock area. He's bound to be thoroughly wound up by then!' Dropping behind the others as Liam led Achilles back to the stables, Toby had to admit that whatever his irritation with his father at the moment, his admiration for his skill as a trainer was undiminished. Not only was Achilles at peak fitness and looking very well in himself but everything possible had been done to prepare him for the rigours of the occasion. Liam, accompanied by Sam Shaw or Charlie, had spent hours leading the colt round the small back paddock, to the accompaniment of loud band music and crowd noises from a tape recorder and amplifier they'd rigged up under a tree.

'It's from an old record we got from the police years ago,' Tod explained. 'They used it to train their horses for coping with demonstrations and riots and things. It worked a treat for old Mafioso, but God knows if it'll help Jacko here; he's a very different sort of character.' He gazed at the colt reflectively. 'Oh well, there's no point in our sweating up about it. It's a miracle he has got back on the racecourse at all after his leg problems, let alone into the Derby line-up. We shouldn't forget that, whatever happens.'

'Hello there, brother mine,' Rory called out softly over the box door. 'Well, well, fancy finding you here, then!'

Liam, busy putting a final shine on Achilles's quarters, was so startled that he dropped his brush on to the straw. He had been expecting Rory, of course, but not here, not on Derby Day. 'Heavens above, Rory!' he exclaimed, straightening up. 'It's a heart attack you'll be wanting to give me.' He took a deep breath. 'But then you always were one for surprises.' He could not imagine how Rory had got into the stable area without a special pass. Security today was extra tight, but here he was all right, looking just the same and leaning on the box door, his head and shoulders casting a shadow over the straw.

324

'You're right there,' Rory agreed softly. 'Fancy you doing such a smart colt as this, then! There's quite a bit of each-way money going on him, I hear.' He unbolted the door and pushed it open. 'Well, let's get a good look at him, then! Stand him up properly, will you?' he ordered, stepping lightly into the box.

After a moment's hesitation, Liam did as he asked. His natural pride in his colt and desire to show him off to his brother overcame all other, conflicting, emotions. Talking to him the while, he nudged Achilles into a better stance.

Rory stared at the horse intently, his skilled eye raking him over from top to toe. 'Hmm, not much of him, is there? He's well made though. I'll grant you that.'

'He's something special, I'm telling you,' Liam replied fiercely. 'He'll see the lot of them off today. You wait and see.'

Rory's lip curled. 'OK. Take it easy. I'm impressed with your loyalty. I didn't know you had it in you,' he commented sardonically. 'You'd better get on and finish him right now. Then I thought you and I might have a little talk. There's plenty of time.' Without waiting for Liam's response, he stepped out of the box and leant back against the door, arms folded.

How dare he come here today and try to upset things, Liam thought angrily. It was Jacko's big day, his 'High Noon' as Mr Kyle had put it, and nothing must distract anyone from that. If Rory gets angry about the money, I'll just insist that I always intended to pay it back. After all, he can check with Ma if he doesn't believe me, Liam told himself.

'There's no problem about the money, I've told you,' he insisted again wearily as he and Rory were sitting in the crowded paddock cafeteria about fifteen minutes later. 'I have it. I can send it to you wherever you want. First thing tomorrow morning, if you like – just tell me where.' He ripped open a sachet of sugar with his teeth and shook it aggressively into his cup of tea.

Rory glanced at him, his face impassive. 'You can send a cheque for the full amount to this bank account, then. At the Bank of Ireland in Cashel. Made out to Mr Kevin O'Leary.' Picking up Liam's racecard he produced a pen and scribbled some details down on one of the inner pages.

'Hey, there's no need to go scribbling all over my card like that,' Liam protested, grabbing it back. 'I'll be wanting to hang on to this one, you know. Today being such a special occasion.'

Rory looked up at him, his eyes narrowing. 'For the life of me, I can't see how you thought you'd get away with it – stealing the money instead of doing as I asked. It was very foolish. It's a long memory I have, you know.' He tapped his forehead significantly.

'Look, I've told you. I needed to get away from Ireland and make a new start,' Liam replied wearily. 'I didn't want to have anything to do with what you and your friends were up to. He wiped his brow with the back of his hand. 'I know it was a stupid thing to do, but I've said I'm sorry. Anyway, you'll be getting it back in a day or two – or Kevin O'Leary will, whoever he may be. What more do you want, for Jesus's sake?' he asked defiantly.

Rory stared at him for a moment. 'I'm not sure, but I'll think of something, all right. That bloke in Wexford – the one you didn't bother to go and see – didn't take too kindly to being let down like that, you know. He's got just a little bit of a grudge against us as a result, I'm told. Very unfortunate.' He paused, examining his hands with care. 'So you owe us one, I'm thinking – some favour that we'll get around to asking one of these days,' he added lightly.

Liam reached for his packet of cigarettes, his hands shaking. It was just as he'd feared: Rory hadn't changed. He was still the old manipulator, still issuing threats. He'd have to put Rory out of his mind for today, though, Liam told himself; he needed all his concentration and cool for the business in hand.

Glancing up, he noticed that Rory was staring over towards the door. 'Ah, here comes your pal, Toby Beckhampton,' his brother remarked. 'He'll be delighted to see us here together, having such a cosy little chat! He was quite a hit at Mountclare, you know, was Toby. You must get him to tell you about it some time.'

Liam was both surprised and relieved at Toby's appearance. Although they had made a plan to meet he had not expected his friend to show up. There was such an enormous crowd here today and Toby would be bound to bump into all sorts of people he knew and get delayed. But now here he was, bang on time, threading his way eagerly through the tables towards them.

'Hello! Hello, Rory,' he said with surprise. 'I didn't expect to see you here, I must say.' He looked at Liam with sudden apprehension. 'Look, I'm not interrupting anything important, am I? I'm sure you two have a lot to talk about.'

'I'm just off, as a matter of fact,' Rory replied, pushing back his chair. He paused for a moment. 'I'll be seeing the boss, Miss Alexandros, in a bit, I reckon. I'll give her your regards then, shall I?' he inquired mockingly, his eyebrows raised.

'Er, yes, of course,' Toby replied, blushing. In an effort to change the subject, he fished in his pocket for his racecard and flourished it enthusiastically. 'I've had a really hot tip for a horse in the first race, by the way,' he announced, flicking through the pages. 'From someone I talked to up on the downs. It hasn't got much form, he admitted, but he insisted that it had been especially laid out for today. Look, it's that one there.' He pointed to the list of runners. 'No. 7 Delta View. It's trained here at Epsom, I see, and owned by some bloke called Ashley Spence.' He looked up, puzzled. 'Isn't he an MP or something?'

Rory, who had got to his feet, snatched the card from him abruptly. 'Hmm, well, well. Fancy me missing that,' he mused under his breath as he scanned the page.

'What's up with you? Don't tell me you've become a betting man, have you?' Liam asked him incredulously. 'You never left off warning me against it in the old days.'

'It's not the horse I'm interested in, it's his owner,' Rory said tersely. 'I might be doing some business with him one of these days.' He handed the card back to Toby. 'Thanks a lot. I'll be off then. Good luck with your colt. Maybe I'll be seeing both of you later in the Winners' Enclosure.' His tone was sarcastic. 'And don't forget, Liam, I'll be in touch.'

'Look! Look! Here he comes.' Lady Kitty clutched Kate's arm more tightly. She was standing on tiptoe, the brim of her new hyacinth-blue hat brushing Kate's shoulder. 'Doesn't he look smart, the little angel!' she added.

Kate, following her gaze to the far end of the paddock, watched eagerly as Achilles, led by Liam, came into view. The black colt, looking about him as usual, was dancing along, his lop ears flicking back and forth, his tail streaming behind. A few puffy clouds now clustered around the sun but it was still very warm and, in common with most of the other runners, he sported a light paddock sheet with his name and number clearly marked on it. He looked seal-sleek as he jig-jigged around, his coat shining like polished ebony, not a hair out of place in his well-pulled mane and tail and his hoofs oiled and glistening. As he came nearer, Kate was relieved to see that although he was definitely on his toes, he was not, as yet, showing any serious signs of sweating up.

'Doesn't he look magnificent?' she agreed with rapture. 'Liam has really excelled himself today.' She squeezed her mother's arm more tightly. 'Oh, Kitty! I still can't believe it: our own colt right here in the Derby paddock! It's a miracle! Tell me I'm not dreaming.'

'Of course you're not. You're wide awake, you silly girl. Anyway, didn't I tell you he was something out of the ordinary?' Lady Kitty replied happily. 'And he knows it,' she added with amusement as Achilles, being regarded with some interest by the Royal party, chose to give a sudden buck of *joie de vivre*.

'He's such a show-off,' Kate agreed affectionately. Liam was looking very solemn, she thought, as he led the colt round, talking to him the while. He looked extremely smart, though, in well-pressed grey flannel trousers and the black anorak, trimmed with red and emblazoned with the gold Ever Ready emblem, that the Derby sponsors had given all the lads.

He was keeping his eyes firmly fixed on the horse ahead or on Jacko himself, though clearly avoiding looking into the crowd, she noticed. She didn't blame him. It was a daunting sight. The racegoers, six deep, were packing the white rails and the little paddock stands beyond, and subjecting all fifteen colts on parade to the most careful scrutiny. There were also, of course, millions of people across the world watching the scene on their television sets. Standing in the Derby paddock was pretty unnerving for everyone – for the owners as well as their horses, she reflected, rather like being rare and unusual animals in the zoo. She just hoped she looked smart enough to do Achilles justice. She was pleased with the fuschia-coloured Calvin Klein suit she had bought in New York especially for the occasion, though she had been horrified at what she had had to pay for it. 'Oh, don't be so stingy!' her mother had rebuked her at the time. 'How many times in your life are you going to own a horse that's good enough to run in the Derby? Anyhow, the cut's perfect. So is the colour – makes you look remarkably pretty.'

Ever since she had stepped on to the course today Kate had been aware that she had somehow undergone a substantial change in status. She had always found the racing fraternity pleasant enough, particularly when she had been working amongst them as a photographer, but she had also always felt herself to be an outsider. Today, as the owner of a Derby runner, that had all changed. In the paddock itself and walking down from the stands, just behind the Royal party, she had been astonished at the number of nods and smiles she and her mother had received from other owners and trainers, people she only knew by sight, like the Sangsters and the Cecils, Lord Howard de Walden, even some of the Maktoums' entourage. Down by the saddling boxes, Lady Kitty had been accosted with great enthusiasm by a former senior steward of the Jockey Club. He had known her father, apparently, and wanted to tell her how delighted he was to see the Earl's Rathglin colours back on the racecourse again, particularly on such a distinguished occasion. It was ironic, she reflected: she and her mother had barely been able to afford to keep Achilles in training at all, let alone see him through all his vicissitudes; it had been a real strain on their determination and financial resources. But none of that mattered any more. By earning a place in the Derby line-up the colt had ensured that they were now competing on equal terms with some of the richest owners in the world.

But Achilles was not the only catalyst in her life at the moment. So much seemed to have changed recently, it was alarming – as though events had suddenly gone into fast forward, out of her control. Only a few weeks ago, when she had left for New York, she had been convinced that it was all over with Tod and that she would somehow have to adapt to just regarding him as a friend. She did not know if that would be possible, and she would have preferred to continue not seeing him at all, but with Achilles in his care that was clearly not feasible. Then, much to her surprise, she had had such a hectic time in America and had so enjoyed herself with Sandy that, as she waited for her mother at the airport, she had realized that she had hardly had time in the past two weeks to miss Tod much at all; it gave her a pang of guilt, but it had boded well for the future.

But then had come the bombshell of his letter, which Lady Kitty had handed to her the moment she'd arrived in Sandy's apartment. Suddenly it seemed that the kaleidoscope of her life had been vigorously shaken by someone else's hand and all the patterns looked different again. Myra's extraordinary plan to marry Stelios meant that she and Tod would shortly be free to continue their affair in the open, possibly even try living together if that was what they both still wanted. 'What a sneaky old thing Myra has turned out to be,' Tod had written. 'All the time I was worrying about not hurting or humiliating her, she was planning to do a bunk herself. Ironic, isn't it?'

Now, also, as the book was already selling well in the States and would be launched in England in a week or so's time, the publishers were keen to sign her up for another book – on the Irish and their horses this time. The magazine *Town and Country* had approached her about a feature on breeders of the Blue Grass, about the top studs in Kentucky, followed by another one on the August scene in Saratoga. Being so much in demand had given her a new confidence in herself, she realized, as she stood looking about her in the paddock. She also had a strange certainty that whatever happened today her life had somehow, irrevocably, changed.

'Charlie's just told me that Jacko's gone out two points in the betting, would you believe?' Lady Kitty was saying. 'He's out to 9 to 1, the fools! Haven't they got eyes?' She glanced lovingly at Achilles as he strode past her, walking more decorously now, but impatiently jangling his bit. 'Oh well, it doesn't affect me. I got him at 50 to 1 before Lingfield.' She was looking years younger again today, Kate observed, the bright blue of her suit and hat matching her eyes and making them look even larger and more childlike than ever. The Professor, too, was looking remarkably youthful and spruce in his rented morning suit. She had never seen him in a hat before, except his battered old fishing cap, and he had looked so respectable when he had come to pick them up at the Stafford Hotel that morning that she had hardly recognized him.

'Will you not rattle on so about our wagers, then, Kitty,' he pleaded. 'It'll only be bringing the colt bad luck.' He took off his topper and mopped his brow with a large white handkerchief.

'Do you like Jacko's new browband, then, all woven in our gold and green colours?' Lady Kitty asked Kate. 'Smart, isn't it?'

'I noticed it earlier over at the saddling boxes,' Kate said enthusiastically. 'I meant to ask Tod if it was his idea but I didn't get the chance. He seemed a bit preoccupied!'

Lady Kitty pursed her lips. 'Hmm, I have to tell you, dearie, that it was Myra's suggestion, apparently. I've already thanked her, as a matter of fact – thought it might be easier if I did it,' she added briskly. 'She told me that it was an old tradition of her father's to fit browbands in the owner's colours whenever Barons Lodge had a classic runner.'

'I see. Well, it's a nice touch.' Kate glanced thoughtfully across at Myra standing on the fringes of a small group which included Tod, Charlie and fellow Newmarket trainer Clive Brittain. In a tight-fitting cream suit and a pink cloche hat, Myra reminded her of an elegant flamingo as she stood there, one leg crossed over the other, looking tensely about her at the horses. Stepping back suddenly as the colt nearest her shied at something in the crowd, one of her high heels caught in the turf and she clutched Tod's arm for support. Kate felt a stab of jealousy. The sooner Myra and Stelios made their liaison public and took off together the better, she thought. Myra had come to the course with the Greek today and they had even lunched together in one of the boxes, but she was still insisting that other than their immediate families, no one should know of their plans until after Royal Ascot. In the meantime, Kate thought that the situation was extremely embarrassing for all of them. She had no idea what she herself was supposed to say to Myra about it all. The two of them had shaken hands earlier when Myra turned up unexpectedly in the Owners' and Trainers' Bar, and although the woman had made some effort to be pleasant, she had also given her several very frosty looks. What was the matter with her? Kate wondered. After all, she was about to get what she wanted: an end to all her financial worries, quite apart from the cachet of becoming an ambassador's wife. As far as Kate could work out she had been contemplating abandoning Tod well before that wonderful New Year's Eve she herself had spent with him so she couldn't possibly be jealous. She also thought that Myra's behaviour today was unnecessarily proprietorial, both when she came to rout Tod out of the bar during lunch and later when she insisted on walking ahead with her arm tucked into his on their way down to the saddling boxes; and she looked oddly tense. Perhaps it was just the anxiety of having a Derby runner, but behind the heavy make-up her eyes looked anxious and strained.

Kate's musings were interrupted by Charlie Kyle who came to stand next to her, and much to her surprise, complimented her on how smart she was looking.

'Well, thank you very much.' She smiled. 'You look pretty dandy yourself!' It was perfectly true. Although Charlie did not wear his morning dress uniform with the same ease and nonchalance as Tod, the formality of it suited him. He would be an attractive-looking man, she thought, if only he could loosen up a bit and take himself a little less seriously. Still, there was every reason why he might not be feeling very relaxed today, she had to admit: she herself was getting increasingly apprehensive.

'I'm feeling awfully nervous, I'm afraid,' she confessed. 'Doncaster was bad enough, but this is far worse. One feels so self-conscious out here too, with all eyes on the paddock.'

Charlie grinned sympathetically. 'I know. It's beginning to get to me, too, I'm afraid. Jacko's obviously got a real gift for getting under our skins. Some horses, the real characters, can always do that.' He glanced over at the colt keenly. 'Still, he seems to be reasonably calm so far.' He crossed his fingers with an exaggerated grimace. 'That's all that matters. It's the parade that really worries me, though. That and the long journey down to the start.' He stood on tiptoe, his expression alert. 'Ah, here come the jockeys at last,' he observed with relief. 'Thank God we've got Alain today. Other than Piggott and possibly Swinburn, he's the most nerveless big race jockey in the business. I must go and have a quick word.' He turned to Kate with a boyish shrug of the shoulders. 'Oh well! This is it, best of luck!'

'Heavens above! Can they not get going? I've not been this nervous since I landed my first salmon, and that was further back than I like to remember!' The Professor, tilting his topper backwards, mopped his forehead anxiously. 'Is the little fella loading up all right?'

'It's no use asking me, Desmond, I can't see a thing. I've not got the height for it,' Lady Kitty replied impatiently. Propping her elbows more firmly on the rail in front, she trained her binoculars again in the direction of the start. All she could see, however, beyond the brilliant green of the turf and the scarlet splash of the Guardsmen around the winning post, was a vast multicoloured blur of people and vehicles, tents and awnings, stretching across the downs to the trees on the far side of the course. 'What's happening? Can you see?' she asked Kate urgently.

Kate, pressed tightly against her in the crush, was fighting hard to stop her hands from shaking as she too tried to focus her binoculars. 'I think they're just beginning to load up now,' she replied, standing on tiptoe. 'There doesn't seem to be any delay.'

Tod had detailed Basil Hunter to look after them the moment they left the paddock. With the aid of some rather undignified pushing and shoving, he had managed to find all three of them a place at the front of the flower-fringed balcony jutting out above the Winners' Enclosure before departing for his usual vantage point in the press room higher up in the stand. A few minutes later, when the parade had started, it had become impossible to move in any direction: all the stairways and steps as well as the stands themselves were packed solid.

Glancing down at the crowded lawns below, Kate saw that Tod had managed to make his way to the wall just below Brough Scott's commentary box and was standing there, hatless, as he had been since he'd left the paddock, talking to Diana Saunders, Nik Alexandros and the burly silver-haired Irish trainer Mick O'Toole. She could also see Lucy Beckhampton in a lilac-coloured suit, her chestnut mane hanging down her back, leaning on the rail of the Winners'. Circle talking to the French breeder Alec Head. Glancing up suddenly, Tod caught sight of her and grinning, gave her the thumbs-up sign before shrugging his shoulders as though to say, 'Well, this is it, then! It's all in the lap of the gods now!' Charlie Kyle, she presumed, was still making his way back from the downs. She hoped desperately that Achilles wasn't playing up down at the start and would go into the stalls all night.

As the band of the Welsh Guards across the course concluded their selection from *My Fair Lady*, the public-address system crackled suddenly overhead. A shiver ran down Kate's spine as the racecourse commentator announced excitedly that the runners were now beginning to load up.

The parade, of course, had been a pretty nerve-racking experience. Preceded by a mounted policeman and flanked by Tod and Nobby, Achilles had led it, the runners parading as on the racecard, in alphabetical order. When the commentator had announced that 'the first horse out on the course was No. 3, Achilles, winner of the Lingfield Derby Trial, owned and bred by Lady Kitty and Miss Kate Leverton, trained by Tod Beckhampton in Newmarket and ridden by French champion jockey Alain du Roc', she thought she would explode with pride. There could not be anything in the world more thrilling than this: seeing your own, homebred colt parading out there in front of the enormous crowd.

Glancing at her mother she could see that she was similarly moved. 'Look at them! Aren't they the grandest sight you've ever seen?' she breathed. 'I just hope your grandfather's looking down from wherever he is,' she added, her eyes moist. 'He'd have given ten years of his life to have been here today.'

The Rathglin colours looked particularly good on du Roc, Kate had to admit. The bright gold cap shone brilliantly in the sunshine, enhancing his tan, and the dark-green jacket fitted him like a glove. But he had already had to prove his skill as a horseman. Achilles had been remarkably well behaved during the parade, very much on his toes but only sweating up slightly, his nerves clearly under control; but when Liam, with a final pat, released him and he turned to canter back past the stands towards the paddock, he grabbed his bit and bounded forward in such a dramatic fly jump that it caused a great gasp from the crowd. Du Roc, however, weathered this with the ease of an old rodeo hand and, to scattered applause, kept the colt under control. 'Whew!' Lady Kitty observed with relief. 'Alain would enjoy the hunting back home, don't you think, Desmond?' she commented admiringly. 'If only I were a year or two younger I'd take him out with one of the Tipperaries myself!'

Kate had been concentrating so hard on Achilles that she had barely taken in the other runners. Tamarind, a flashy chestnut colt by The

Minstrel who had won the Mecca Dante at York, was the favourite and she liked the look of another fancied horse, the grey French colt Sirkhan. The second favourite, a neat bay called Nightjar who'd run the Dee Stakes at Chester, was owned, she recalled, by that awful man Prince Hassim. She noticed, too, that a handsome chestnut colt of Luca Cumani's, who Achilles had easily beaten at Lingfield, was also in the field, looking particularly well.

But now, suddenly, as the band ceased playing, a great quiet fell like a cloak over the vast crowd. A tangible tension gripped the vast packed stand and way above the downs two glittering air balloons hovered expectantly in the blue.

'They're all in now. They're under starter's orders. They're off.' The announcement, slicing the quiet as brusquely as the fall of an axe, was followed by an eerie silence. Everyone all around strained forward, desperate to get a glimpse of the field now surging ahead in the distance.

Even standing on tiptoe, Kate could see nothing but a jumble of bright caps bobbing along above the far rails. Tilting her head sideways, she tried to listen to the commentator, willing him to mention Achilles's name. But all she heard was much mention of Tamarind, a habitual front runner, and Sirkhan, followed by a mumble of unfamiliar names as the caps swept on towards the top of the hill. Then, suddenly, she heard it.

'And Achilles is improving his position now. As they come up to the mile marker, it's Tamarind, followed by Sirkhan going easily in just behind, these two at least two lengths clear of the rest of the field, followed by Nightjar and Achilles making up some ground now on the outside . . .'

Kate felt Lady Kitty clutching her arm, her small fingers gripping her painfully tight. 'That's right, that's it. Alain's quickening at the right time, the angel. He knows he's got to have a good position at the top of the hill,' her mother muttered.

As the volume of noise all around grew louder, heads swung left as the field began the descent down Tattenham Hill. Kate could hear little of the commentary and certainly no mention of Achilles. Maybe he couldn't lie up with the pace: maybe it was too hot for him? Closing her eyes for a moment she imagined the horses streaming down the hill, as she had seen them do so many times on television. 'Go on, oh, go on Jacko. You show them. You can do it. Go on, I'm willing you!' she wailed silently.

Raising her binoculars again with trembling hands she focused them on Tattenham Corner. As the horses came surging round towards the four-furlong pole she saw that Tamarind was still in the lead, his white blaze clearly visible. Behind him a small group of horses had burst out of the pack and seemed to be closing. One of them was the grey colt Sirkhan, another Nightjar and a third, on the wide outside, was unmistakably Achilles, du Roc's gold cap glinting bright against his dark neck. With the crescendo of the crowd's roar sweeping up the course, she realized that Achilles, like a smooth black torpedo, was making relentless progress in the middle of the course. As Tamarind, tiring now, changed his legs passing the two-furlong marker and began to roll towards the far rail, Achilles was overtaking Sirkhan, attacking the ground with neat powerful strides, and drawing level with Nightjar's quarters. As the two dark colts passed the faltering favourite, they seemed shackled together, heads outstretched, ears flat back, legs pounding like pistons, both of them striving their hearts out as they headed for the line.

Kate, yelling uncontrollably now like everyone around her, watched, thunderstruck as, unbelievably but perceptibly, Achilles's black head began to edge in front and du Roc, putting down his stick, urged him past the post just hands and heels the clear half-a-length winner.

The next few minutes passed in a complete daze. She had a vision of her mother's face, transfixed and radiant, before they hugged each other, crying with delight, unable to speak. She could have sworn that there were tears, too, on the Professor's face as, pulling off his topper, he seized Lady Kitty in a breathless embrace.

'Kitty, what a wonderful woman you are! I don't believe it, you only went and won!' he panted before hurling his hat in the air. There was laughter and clapping all around as someone in the crowd below caught it and tried to hand it back. As the cheering subsided, people were already turning towards her with smiling faces but Kate hardly noticed them. She had only one aim in mind. Somehow, she must get her mother and the Professor down from the stand in time to lead Achilles in. Miraculously, as she shepherded them urgently along, the crowd seemed to part to allow them through, their progress actually assisted by a battery of congratulatory pats on the back. In no time at all they seemed to have floated down the stairway to ground level and Kate found herself face to face with Tod. He seized her in a bear hug, swinging her off the ground.

'Kate, darling, wasn't that absolutely heart-stopping!' he exclaimed delightedly. 'We've won. We actually did it. I can't believe it!'

335

Kate nodded, speechless. As he put her down, she was immediately accosted by Diana Saunders who also threw her arms around her, jigging up and down with excitement.

'Strewth, Kate! Who'd have thought it? Our little Achilles winning the Derby! Our little runt that no one wanted!' She held Kate at arms' length, grinning from ear to ear. 'Well, he sure put them all in their place today. He showed them!'

Nik Alexandros stepped forward and held out his hand. 'Congratulations,' he said with a polite smile. 'Your colt won well. I hope you'll consider running him in the King George after today. Then we can take you on with Devilry.'

His sister, standing beside him, stared at Kate with her weird blue eyes. 'Why not?' she nodded. 'It would be quite a contest. Well done!'

Kate caught a glimpse of a dark-bearded figure, his expression grim beneath his topper, pushing his way through the crowd in front of her, aided by two burly companions. It was Prince Hassim, she realized, obviously heading out on to the course to greet his runner-up. The colt had run a gallant race but the Prince looked angry and Kate recalled Tod telling her that, unlike any of the other major Arab owners, the man was an extraordinarily bad loser.

She halted in her tracks, suddenly concerned about how her mother, being so small, was coping with the throng behind. Turning round she saw that she need not have worried. Lady Kitty, supported on the one hand by the hatless Professor and on the other by a smiling Tim Neligan, boss of United Racecourses, was talking animatedly to the bevy of pressmen, who were bending forward to catch her comments.

Catching sight of Kate, she waved cheerfully. 'Go on! You go ahead and lead him in,' she ordered. 'I've got my hands full with this lot for the moment.' She turned enthusiastically back to her wall of admirers.

Kate, jostled on all sides, was just beginning to panic when she felt a familiar arm around her once again and, folded against Tod's shoulder, breathed in the usual faint comforting blend of French tobacco and Eau Sauvage.

'Sorry, darling. We got separated. I never knew I had so many fans!' he joked. 'Wasn't Jacko absolutely brilliant? Alain gave him a lot to do by bringing him as wide as he did, but that didn't stop him. And it certainly avoided all that scrimmaging at the top of the hill.' He pushed his glasses back, his eyes shining. 'God! What acceleration! Wasn't it breathtaking?' He pulled a triumphant face. 'And we beat that sod Hassim, too, which gives me particular satisfaction!' He grabbed her hand. 'Come on, then. Let's go and lead him in.'

The next few minutes seemed to pass so quickly that Kate barely had time to take them in. One moment she was battling through the throng in the middle of the course, dodging under the necks of the police horses, to greet an ecstatic Liam and grab Achilles's bridle; the next, they all seemed to have been propelled out of the mêlée into the comparative tranquillity of the Winners' Circle.

Alain du Roc leant over impulsively and took her hand as Achilles flung up his head and came to a trembling halt. *'Il était magnifique, votre petit Jacko. Formidable!'* he exclaimed with relish, his lined face relaxing into a delighted smile.

'You were sensational, too. You rode a terrific race. Absolutely brilliant!' Kate retorted.

Du Roc shrugged his shoulders. 'It was a piece of cake, as you say,' he grinned. 'All I had to do was to sit tight and steer. He was always going well: settled far better than we'd expected.' He leant forward and patted Achilles's neck. *'Bravo, mon petit, bravo,'* he murmured affectionately before kicking his feet out of the stirrups.

I will never forget this moment, never, Kate thought to herself, breathing in the pungent warm horse smell of Achilles as he stood there, still trembling and flecked with sweat, his nostrils distended. Then there was the joy and delight on the faces of all his connections, some of the individuals she loved or liked most in all the world. Glancing up at the great tiered wall of the stands, packed with people still gazing down at her and buzzing with excitement, she felt an incredible surge of happiness.

Turning to Tod beside her, she flung her arms around him again oblivious to all those watching. 'Oh, Tod, I'm so happy,' she announced, her eyes filling with tears. 'It's all been so wonderful. Being here with you today and Jacko winning. Aren't we lucky?'

As she disengaged herself, still feeling as though she was dreaming, she caught a sudden glimpse of Myra over Tod's shoulder.

Pressed back against the rail, her hand clapped to her mouth, she appeared to be silently screaming. But that was nonsense, Kate told herself sternly. The woman was obviously just overcome with emotion – as she was herself. Nevertheless, the image had been disturbing. She turned with relief to her mother at her side.

'Go on, Kitty, you're on,' she urged, indicating the podium. 'You're keeping Sir Gordon White waiting. Hurry up. Go and get us our trophy then.'

PART FOUR

CHAPTER TWENTY-THREE

The Old Rectory
Lady Kitty inclined her head to one side. 'What is Achilles worth now, after the race?' She took another pull at her cheroot. 'Well, several million pounds more than he was beforehand, would you believe? Astonishing, isn't it? We really can't take it in. But we're not complaining!' she added with a mischievous smile.

She and Kate were conducting one of the many press interviews they had done in the past two days, this time with a feature writer from the *Sunday Times*, a foxy-looking redhead who was faithfully scribbling down what they were saying on a large notepad balanced on her knee. Des, her Australian photographer, was roaming restlessly around the drawing-room, taking innumerable shots from different angles.

'That's a helluva lot of dough!' he commented. 'What did you say you paid for him again?'

'We didn't. We bred him ourselves,' Lady Kitty explained patiently. 'We did it for a bit of fun, and to give my mare Misty some company out there in the paddock. We also hoped to make a pound or two out of selling him as a yearling, of course,' she added.

It was a dismal June day, with rain lashing the long french windows, but inside the room was bright with the many gifts of flowers and cards the Levertons had received since their Derby win.

'We had a few repairs that needed doing here at the time,' Lady Kitty continued, looking around at the faded wallpaper and cracks in the drawing-room ceiling. 'There still are, to tell you the truth. Achilles proved to be a little more of an extravagance than we had imagined! The poor lamb was constantly in the wars as a two-year-old. But he's certainly come right now, the angel!' She reached over Liffey's slumbering form for the glass of Fino on the table beside her.

Des, who had been squinting at her through his lens in a dissatisfied fashion, instantly bounded over. 'That's it, Lady Kitty,' he said enthusiastically. 'Just hold it there, can you? And you, too, Kate. Just raise your glasses to each other, will you? Come on, Kate, relax for Christ's sake. You're supposed to be celebrating.'

'Sorry, I'm just not used to being on this side of the camera,' Kate apologized, grinning. 'Makes me feel very selfconscious. Now I know what my victims are always complaining about!' She turned to her mother, raising her glass. 'Well, cheers, Kitty! Here's to Jacko!'

'The ridiculous thing was that no one wanted him when we sent him to the sales. He didn't even reach his reserve. It must have been fate.' Lady Kitty chattered happily as Des snapped away. 'So we decided to take a gamble and keep him in training ourselves. It's what I'd dreamt of doing from the start, of course, though I didn't care to admit it to Kate. She's the practical one around here!'

Kate pulled a face at her. 'Oh, come on, Kitty! That's not fair. You make me sound such a killjoy. I was as much in favour of the whole adventure as you were, right from the start,' she said indignantly. As she spoke, the phone rang again, for what seemed like the fiftieth time that morning, and she leapt quickly to her feet. 'I'll take it in the hall,' she said. 'It's probably someone else from the press. If they want a quote from you, Kitty, you'll just have to relay it through me. Liffy'll never forgive you if you disturb her again.'

'It could just possibly be Desmond. I asked him to let me know when he'd got home safely,' Lady Kitty called over her shoulder. 'The way he sounded on the phone last night, he could well have ended up in Dubrovnik rather than Dublin. He'd had a punishing evening at the Irish Club, I gathered.'

Prowling around over to the fireplace, Des picked up the little gold Derby trophy from its pride of place on the mantelpiece and gazed at it with interest. 'Is this it?' he asked disparagingly. 'Not very big, is it? But I suppose it's worth a few quid. How about a shot of you holding it, Lady K? That would look true blue!'

'I don't suppose we should have it on show here at all,' Lady Kitty said, taking the trophy from him good-humouredly. 'I'm sure the insurance people wouldn't approve. But we just couldn't resist it. Anyway, we'll need it for our party in July. We've decided to have a little celebration party here on my birthday, 14 July,' she went on, stubbing out her cheroot. 'Of course, there might be cause for a double celebration by then. If Achilles has really come out of Wednesday's race all right, I would dearly love to have a crack at the Irish Derby,' she rolled her eyes. 'To win at the Curragh would be heaven on earth!' She picked up the Epsom trophy again and gave it a quick kiss. 'But Achilles doesn't have to prove anything to anyone any more. The party's on, whether we win in Ireland or not. You can both come along if you like,' she suggested. 'Kate's being a bit of a gloom about the weather, I'm afraid,' she added. 'She's worried it's going to be wet like today but I've reminded her that it never rains on my birthday!'

'Well, I'd love to come, thanks,' the red-haired reporter replied, taking an appreciative gulp of her sherry. 'But tell me, didn't you all have some sort of celebration on Derby night itself? That's customary, isn't it?'

'We did indeed,' Lady Kitty told her. 'We had a delicious meal at the Connaught. Just Kate and myself and Desmond, an old friend from Dublin, and Charlie Kyle, of course. He's got a share in the colt, too, as I told you, as well as being Tod's assistant trainer. We were invited to Annabel's, as a matter of fact,' she continued. 'Alain du Roc and the Beckhamptons had booked a table there and wanted us to join them, but we decided to do the Cinderella act and be back at our hotel by midnight. I thought a nightclub might just finish poor old Desmond off. He was already in a high state of excitement as a result of his flirtation with the Princess of Wales!' She smiled to herself in recollection of the Professor's enjoyment of the company in the Royal Box and of his reluctance to leave. He had always been such a Republican too, which had made it even more amusing.

It had been Kate, though, who had actually vetoed the idea of going on to Annabel's, although she didn't tell the *Sunday Times* duo that. She herself had been going to take up Tod's invitation. The whole day – the miraculous win followed by all the post-race euphoria, the conference with the press and being interviewed by Brough Scott on the television, going up to the Royal Box for tea and then the exciting lift back to Battersea in one of the sponsor's helicopters – it had all been so wonderful that to end the day with dancing would have somehow seemed fitting, but Kate had had understandable misgivings.

'Look, Kitty, I hate to be a wet blanket,' she'd said on the journey home, 'today of all days – it's all been so fantastic. You and the others go to Annabel's if you like but I absolutely cannot face any more time with Myra. She's been giving me the most peculiar looks on the racecourse. And I really don't know what to say to the woman. The whole situation's impossible. Sorry!'

Lady Kitty had patted her hand consolingly. 'It's all right. I understand,' she said. 'And so will Desmond. I think we'll let Charlie go, though, don't you? There's no reason for him to feel uncomfortable about such complications.'

Glancing up now she realized that Kate was standing in the doorway, beckoning, a distinctly troubled look on her face.

'Can I have a word, Kitty?' she called over brightly. 'Sorry to break things up.'

'What's up, dearie? You look worried,' Lady Kitty said immediately after she had limped over to the door and closed it behind her. 'Who is it on the phone, and what do they want?' she asked, concerned. 'One of the newspapers?'

Kate nodded, her expression distracted. 'Yes, yes. *The East Anglian*. They want to come over to do a brief feature on us. I told them to come round about four. Is that OK? I thought it would give you time for a rest after lunch if you want one. But that's not the problem,' she continued urgently, lowering her voice. 'It's Tod. That was him on the phone earlier. Something's wrong. He wants me to go over to Barons Lodge straight away. I called you out here because I didn't want to say anything in front of the *Sunday Times* people.'

Lady Kitty's eyes were wide with alarm. 'Oh, heavens! What's up, do you think? There's nothing the matter with Achilles, is there?'

Kate shook her head. 'No, no. It's nothing to do with Jacko. He's in great shape apparently.' She paused, frowning. 'It's Myra. She's been taken ill or something. It's obviously serious, though Tod wouldn't say any more on the phone. But he sounded pretty strained.' She shrugged her shoulders. 'Whatever it is, I had better go and find out. Sorry to abandon you like this, but I am sure you can cope with our visitors. The sooner I know what's happened the better.'

Barons Lodge

Parking the MG in the front drive at Barons Lodge, Kate turned up the collar of her raincoat and hurried down the little flagged path that led between the laurel hedge and the house, and through the red-brick archway into the yard. As usual in the early afternoon the whole place seemed remarkably tranquil and deserted. None of the lads would be back until the start of evening stables and most of the horses were dozing in their boxes, with the exception of one or two who swung their heads in her direction as her footsteps crunched across the gravel. She would go and see Achilles later, she thought, when she'd talked to Tod and found out what had happened.

Skirting the tubs of drenched geraniums and petunias she knocked cautiously on the back door. 'Just let yourself in. There'll be no one around,' Tod had said on the phone, but she still felt uneasy creeping into someone else's house like this. What on earth could have happened? she wondered yet again. Perhaps Myra had had a car crash or something awful, though, from the little Tod had said, it all sounded more complicated than that.

The walnut-framed clock on the kitchen wall informed her that it was only half past one; she had made good time from the Old Rectory despite all those irritating roadworks on the A45. She was feeling surprisingly nervous, though, at the thought of what Tod was about to divulge. She had a presentiment that it might be disturbing. But there was no point in delaying the moment. Taking a deep breath, she headed across the hall and down the long passage to the Den.

Tod was sitting at his desk, an empty glass at his elbow. He was on the telephone with his back to the door; the two terriers were curled up in their basket by the side of the fireplace; and the air was thick with French cigarette smoke, indicating that he had been there for some time. He turned and beckoned for her to sit down, his face anxious and preoccupied. 'Yes. Yes. I understand. I didn't expect to see him anyway this morning,' he was saying. 'I had to get back to Newmarket. I'm phoning from there now. Yes, yes, of course I'll be back to see my wife again this evening. Perhaps I could have a word with the doctor then. OK. Well, I'll leave that to you. Thanks. Goodbye.' He put down the phone and heaved himself wearily out of his chair.

'Kate, darling. Thank you for coming over so promptly. I had to see you,' he said, coming over to the sofa and folding his arms around her. He buried his face in her damp hair. 'Ah, you smell so sweet,' he murmured, 'I do love you so.'

Kate disengaged herself gently. 'Tod, what's happened? What's happened to Myra?' she asked anxiously.

Tod sat back, fumbling in his pocket for his packet of cigarettes before replying. 'She's only nearly gone and done herself in!' he replied eventually, with a weary grin.

'What!' Kate exclaimed in horror. 'I don't believe it! Why on earth would she want to do that?' She gazed at him, her grey eyes incredulous.

Tod lit a cigarette carefully before flicking the match into the fireplace. 'Well, she insists it was a mistake, of course.' He flopped back against the cushion. 'Says she had no intention of taking an overdose, or anything melodramatic like that. She just hadn't realized how many various pills she'd actually taken or how much alcohol she'd drunk. Who knows?' He sighed and closed his eyes for a moment.

345

'She's going to be OK, Kate, but it looked pretty dicey at one stage, I gather.'

'But what on earth did she take?' Kate asked urgently.

'Some very powerful headache pills that she'd got in Barbados, apparently. And some sleeping tablets. On top of a hell of a lot of booze in the course of the previous day and evening. She was drinking far more than usual, I noticed. Anyway, it was all a pretty lethal cocktail.' He took a pull on his cigarette.

Kate felt torn by a variety of emotions: relief that Myra wasn't seriously hurt coupled with irritation that the woman had cast such a shadow over what should have been a perfect week. She also felt considerable anxiety about how this new development might affect her and Tod. She felt she had so many questions to ask, she didn't quite know where to begin.

'Where actually is she then?' she wanted to know.

'In the London Clinic. They took her straight there from the Savoy when they found they couldn't wake her up.' Tod sighed. 'She was conscious by the time I got back to London. They'd pumped her stomach out and all that sort of thing. She looked absolutely ghastly.'

'But I don't understand,' Kate shook her head. 'When did all this happen? Obviously after we spoke on the phone yesterday morning. You didn't know anything was wrong then, surely?'

Tod rubbed his chin. 'No, of course not. It was absolute chaos here at the time with the press ringing up non-stop about Achilles and photographers prowling about all over the yard getting in everyone's way. I decided to go out with the second lot just to get away from them all! But when I got back there was this urgent message to ring the Clinic. I'd no idea what it could be about. I left the Savoy at the crack of dawn, as you know. I was back here by eight. Myra was sleeping extremely heavily. That I did notice. So I certainly made no attempt to wake her. Also I knew she'd had a bad night. What we'd had of it, that is!'

He paused, frowning. 'I suppose in retrospect I should have suspected that something was wrong. She looked such an odd colour and was breathing so heavily, but she tends to do that when she's tired.' He took off his glasses and polished them on his handkerchief. 'We left Annabel's reasonably early, actually, long before the others. Myra had been complaining of a headache all day and said she was exhausted. She didn't go straight to sleep, though. I heard her banging about in the bathroom for ages. That's why I didn't want to disturb her when I got up.' He shoved his glasses wearily back on to his nose.

346

'Christ! So you had to drive straight back to London, then? The moment you'd heard what happened?'

Tod nodded. 'I tried phoning you at the Old Rectory last night but you were constantly engaged. I only got back here two hours ago. I called you straight away then. I haven't told anyone else.'

'Toby knows, surely? And Basil and Pam presumably?' Kate inquired.

'Oh yes, sure. I told them all straight away. They've been in a hell of a state, particularly Toby. It seems to have hit him very hard. He's with Myra right now.' He shook his head in disbelief. 'God, Kate! All this drama, the day after winning the Derby. It's too much! I seem to have been through the most extraordinary gamut of emotions, including those I didn't even know I possessed, in the last forty-eight hours!' He flopped forward, his face in his hands. 'Christ, I'm tired.'

Kate gently took his arm. 'The last few days have been unbelievable for all of us, Tod. Even without this latest drama,' she said softly. 'Of course you're upset about Myra. I wouldn't love you if you weren't. But she's not dead or anything really awful, is she, and you have just won the Derby, remember? It was an incredible triumph, darling, it really was.'

Tod sat up slowly, his expression preoccupied. 'Mmm . . . maybe. But I'm afraid everything else seems to be in a fair bloody mess!' He forced a wry smile. 'I need another drink. How about you?' He got up and, picking his glass up from the desk, poured himself a large slug of whisky.

Kate shook her head. 'No, thanks. Kitty and I were just toasting Achilles, knocking back some of her Fino, when you rang. God! That seems like hours ago already,' she added quietly. 'But Tod, what I really don't understand is why Myra's in such a state,' she continued, puzzled. 'She may well not have wanted to kill herself, but she must have been pretty desperate about something to start swallowing all those pills, mustn't she?' She made a face. 'And why did she have such a terrible headache on Derby Day? It can't just have been pre-race tension. I thought her behaviour all day was pretty odd. She certainly gave me some very peculiar looks. What on earth's the matter with her? She's got what she wanted, hasn't she? Stelios and financial security for herself – and the yard – for the rest of her life. I don't understand, it doesn't make sense.' She spread her hands in bewilderment.

Tod stared into his whisky, his face grim. 'It's not quite as simple as that, my darling,' he replied quietly. 'You're not going to like this at all, I'm afraid.' He paused, frowning. 'But about the only thing she's made clear in the last twenty-four hours is that she's changed her mind: she doesn't intend to marry Stelios at all! She simply can't face it, she says.' He stubbed out his cigarette, his expression bleak. 'She's going to call the whole thing off. At the eleventh hour! Stelios will go berserk! I don't blame him.'

Kate stared at him in disbelief, clenching her hands together in an attempt to keep calm. 'What! You can't be serious! You mean after all that dithering, she's changed her mind again? I can't believe it. She can't do this to all of us. She really can't,' she wailed.

Tod shrugged his shoulders. 'I know, it's unbelievable, I agree. But what can I do about it? Shaky though she is, she's quite adamant about that. She just can't leave Barons Lodge. It's where she belongs, she says. She feels terribly guilty about Stelios and knows that he'll be furious but says there's nothing she can do about it. She'll just have to face up to telling him as soon as she feels strong enough.' He sighed. 'She keeps bursting into tears and asking me to try to understand. It's all very unnerving, I can tell you – completely out of character too!' He took another gulp of his drink.

Kate, devastated, was unable to speak. She felt as though the emotional structure of her life had collapsed like a broken hammock, depositing her ignominiously on to some stony ground. 'But if she can't leave Barons Lodge, where does that leave you? Or more to the point, us?' she asked eventually, her voice tense.

Tod got up abruptly and stood with his back to the fireplace, leaning against it while he lit another cigarette. 'Good question! I honestly don't know, my darling,' he admitted ruefully. 'I haven't really found my bearings in all this chaos yet. I'm not sure.'

'Well, I am,' Kate exploded. 'If she can't leave Barons Lodge, that means she can't leave you either, doesn't it?' she asked angrily. 'Which means we can't go ahead with any of our plans, doesn't it? To see each other openly. Even try living together. Doesn't it?' she repeated accusingly.

Tod came over and sat next to her again, reaching for her hand. 'Please don't be angry, darling,' he replied with concern. 'That'll only be temporary, won't it? Nothing that's happened with Myra changes the way I feel about you, does it?' He gazed anxiously into her eyes. 'I still love you. I'll always love you. You know that. We'll work something out, you'll see.' He took a long pull at his cigarette, gazing into the fireplace. 'Look! It's not my fault that Myra's changed her mind,' he added defensively. 'The whole thing's come as as much of a shock to me as it has to you. I thought everything was going to be fine at last. But I can't just abandon her now, can I? Not when she's in such a state,' he pleaded. 'Anyway, I feel sort of responsible. She is, after all – for the moment, anyway – still my wife.'

Kate pulled her hand away. 'Hmm ... have you any real idea why she has changed her mind then, causing maximum disruption all round? Did you manage to ascertain that, amidst all the tears?' she wanted to know.

'Well, no, not really. She says that she finally came to her senses on Derby Day – realized that she belonged at Barons Lodge and just couldn't leave. She'd never been one hundred per cent sure about marrying Stelios anyway, despite all that money and security, she says.' He walked over to the desk to pour himself some more whisky. 'She actually wanted me to stop her, she says now,' he snorted. 'God! Some people are so perverse! And then, apparently, when not only did I make no attempt to do so, but actually rather encouraged the whole idea – when I told her about you – she says she felt furiously hurt and jealous.' He turned back to Kate with a shrug. 'When Achilles actually went and won on Wednesday, that was the last straw. She felt so proud and kept thinking how delighted her father would have been. The real panic about leaving it all to marry Stelios set in then, apparently. The woman's having a breakdown, if you ask me!' he added, shaking his head.

Kate leant forward, her eyes blazing. 'And what about you? What role do you play in this touching little scenario, I wonder? It isn't just her attachment to Barons Lodge that made Myra change her mind, is it? It's her feelings for you, too. It is just possible that the woman loves you, you know. In her own odd way. Don't tell me that that hasn't become glaringly obvious in the last twenty-four hours.' Her tone was sarcastic.

'Well, not really,' Tod countered, taken aback. 'She needs me more than she realized, maybe. Certainly at the moment. But I wouldn't go further than that.' He looked at Kate anxiously. 'Look, darling, please don't get so cross and upset. It's you I love, not Myra, that's what matters, surely?'

'What's she said? I want to know exactly what she's told you. About her feelings for you, I mean,' Kate asked with intensity.

Tod looked thoughtful. 'Well, she hasn't said all that much really. What has come out seems rather sad, actually. She told me she thought she was probably emotionally dyslexic or something, and that the feelings of affection – and exasperation – she has had for me were probably the nearest to love she would ever get! She said they were certainly stronger than anything she had ever felt for Stelios.' He reached for his glass of whisky with a wry smile. 'It was rather touching, really – unnerving too. She's always had so many barriers up. Even with me. She seems so vulnerable, somehow, when they're all down.'

Such concern for Myra was too much. Overwhelmed by a surge of fury, Kate leapt up and, seizing his glass, hurled it into the fireplace. 'I don't give a damn how vulnerable she is!' she shouted, forgetting all her usual inhibitions about losing control. 'What about me? What about my feelings?' She grabbed his arm and shook it, her face scarlet with rage. 'How can you stand there drivelling on about Myra and her problems after what you've put me through? How dare you, you bastard!' she went on, her whole body trembling. 'I'd just about steeled myself to the idea of doing without you when I went to the States – and bloody painful that process was, too. Then I got your letter, and everything had changed. It was all going to be wonderful.' Her tone was sarcastic. 'And why was that? Because Myra had made a decision. *She* had decided that *she* was going to leave you. Not the other way round. So suddenly everything was different.' She paused, panting as Tod took another step backwards, a look of deep, almost comical surprise on his face. 'And now what's happened? Dear old Myra has changed her mind again. Just when we thought we were home and hosed. Instead of which we seem to be right back where we started.' She stamped her foot, the tears welling up in her eyes. 'I just can't stand it, Tod! I really can't! I can't go on being subjected to your bloody wife's emotional whims.' Sobbing, she sank down on her knees beside the fireplace, burying her head in her hands.

The two terriers, thoroughly alarmed by this outburst, whined anxiously and sat up on their haunches, gazing at Tod for reassurance. 'It's all right, girls, it's all right,' he said soothingly, dropping to the floor. 'She's not shouting at you. It's me she's angry with, I'm afraid.' He moved towards Kate and attempted to put an arm around her. 'Darling, I can't bear this. I can't bear to see you so upset.'

Kate swung away from him angrily and, hooking her arm around Gert, buried her face in the terrier's rough coat. 'Sorry, dogs!' she said in a muffled voice. 'It's all right, you haven't done anything wrong. It's all right now. It's over.' She took a handkerchief out of her pocket and blew her nose loudly. 'I'm sorry,' she went on eventually, turning to Tod, still crouching at her side. 'About losing my temper and breaking the glass and everything. I didn't mean to do anything like that – it just happened.' She got shakily to her feet, brushing down her jeans. 'It's just that I can suddenly see it all so clearly, as though for the first time, and I just can't bear it,' she sniffed. 'It's not just that you can't leave Myra now, Tod. You'll never be able to leave her. She will always call the shots. She's stronger than you are. And she's certainly not going to let you go now, is she? Not when you're back on top.' She held up her hand. 'Don't say anything, please,' she pleaded as Tod, too, got to his feet, his face stricken. 'Don't deny it, and certainly don't come any closer. Don't touch me, Tod, please. I couldn't bear it.' She bit her lip, her eyes once more filling with tears.

'You do love me, Tod, I know that. I also know that you don't love Myra in the same way. But your links to her are stronger: you're tied to her by years of habit and feelings of responsibility as well as gratitude and affection.' She fumbled in her pocket for her handkerchief again. 'You'll never be able to leave her now, I'm sure of that. Not for me or anyone else. Not when it's obvious how much she needs you. You're not ruthless enough, I'm afraid. It's probably one of the many reasons I love you.'

Stepping quickly over to the sofa, she picked up her handbag and slung it over her shoulder. 'I'm going now. There's nothing more to say. I love you so much but it's all over between us. It absolutely has to be if I'm to survive. I've got to go and get on with my own life now. Please leave me alone to do it. Don't get in touch, I beg you.' Her hand on the door, she turned back to Tod, who was still standing rock still, his face contorted with emotion. 'Believe it or not, everything else is going rather well at the moment,' she said shakily. 'I'll just have to build on that, won't I? Goodbye then. Be lucky!' As Tod finally lunged towards her, his expression anguished, she fled through the door, banging it behind her, and ran along the passage to the hall, her eyes streaming with tears.

Newmarket Heath
'Steady, girl, steady,' exhorted Liam as the grey Absalom filly cavorted sideways, alarmed by the sound of a motorbike backfiring on the road ahead. Patting her neck, he eased her to a walk and waited for the rest of the string to catch him up.

'She's a right liability in traffic, that one,' Pat, one of the lads, commented as he passed. 'Best tuck her in here, on our inside. This filly's as quiet as an old sheep.'

Swinging his reins leftwards, Liam did as Pat suggested. He had had trouble with the Ulsterman ever since he had arrived at Barons Lodge. Not only did Pat seem to despise all Catholics, but he also appeared to resent Liam's skill as a work rider and the way he was given the most promising horses to ride.

But now, thanks to Achilles, that had changed. Barons Lodge was once again basking in the spotlight of success – something the younger lads like Pat had never experienced, and the few older hands who had been around in Tod's heyday thought would never return. Now, not only would the lads benefit from the Derby win through the general prize money pool, but Lady Kitty had insisted they should each be given an extra £50 out of her own share of the winnings. The Levertons had also invited the entire staff to their celebration party at the Old Rectory in July. Overnight, Liam's popularity had rocketed and even hitherto hostile lads like Pat were going out of their way to be pleasant.

It was over ten days now since the Derby – the Royal Ascot meeting actually began today – but the reality of Achilles's victory and what it meant to Liam personally was only just beginning to sink in. There was the money, of course. Not only had he risked £100 on Achilles at 10 to 1, but thanks to the yard's share-out system he was also due to receive an additional £10,000, a sum that seemed like a million pounds to him. He was already looking around for a really good car, a Ford Capri maybe, and had given the hostel notice that he would be moving out at the end of the month. He planned to find more pleasant accommodation to rent: or even buy a flat or cottage on the outskirts of town.

But more important than any of this was the glorious proof that all the confidence he had had in Achilles had been justified. The colt was now a household name, one of the most-talked-about horses in racing. Every time Liam heard him being discussed or saw his name in the racing press, his heart swelled with pride. It was his Jacko they were all on about! Hadn't he always had total faith in him and known that he was something special? The colt's victory had given him a confidence he had not known he possessed. He'd found himself whistling as he went about his work yesterday and he was even able to think about Angie again without bitterness. The kiss she had given him after the Derby when she had come rushing impetuously into the Winners' Circle had been so affectionate that he had actually summoned up the courage to ask her out for a celebratory drink in one of her favourite pubs. He planned to tell her that he had now paid Rory back in full and recount what had happened on Derby Day. He wouldn't say anything about Rory's threats, though; he had decided to put them out of his mind for the moment, and certainly didn't want any such anxieties about the future to dim his pleasure at being alone with Angie again. Neither did he intend to mention Jack. There were rumours going around the yard that the couple weren't getting on too well and whilst Angie was taken up most evenings with her business course in Cambridge, Jack had been seeing his ex-wife again. Two of the lads reported seeing them having a drink together in a very friendly way in a pub over Risley way.

Now, as second lot jogged towards the gallops, Liam had a clear view of Angie riding ahead on a powerful chestnut colt by Final Straw that she'd looked after since he'd arrived in the yard as a yearling. He was a good-looking animal, but headstrong, and had already run away with a couple of the girls. Up until now, despite her pleadings, Angie had never been allowed to ride him. Today, however, the yard was particularly short-staffed, so Tod had reluctantly agreed to let her have a go. 'Make sure she goes carefully. Just a slow canter alongside one of the older horses,' Liam heard Tod instructing Sam before he left for Ascot. From the concerned way he was eyeing his daughter earlier, the head lad was none too happy about all this, Liam suspected. The colt looked magnificent, his coat gleaming like copper in the sunshine, but he had already been playing up, rearing up and bouncing back on his hocks like a dressage horse. He looked altogether too full of himself for Liam's liking.

But a quarter of an hour later even his anxiety about Angie was forgotten as, balanced motionless over the grey filly's withers, he sped over the perfect turf. It was the balmiest of June mornings, the larks were singing their lungs out, the air smelt of mown grass and the well-tended gallops stretched invitingly ahead. He could not remember when he had felt so content, probably not since that time on the Curragh when he had ridden his first winners and his future as a jockey looked so assured.

Liam was so taken up with his thoughts and with this tremendous, unfamiliar feeling of well-being that it was only when he was reluctantly pulling his filly up that he noticed something of a commotion in the distance. As the group of Barons Lodge colts came cantering up the gallops, two abreast under the watchful eye of Sam Shaw sitting motionless on Tod's hack, one of the lead horses stumbled, almost going down on his knees. The animal following him jinxed sideways to avoid a collision, then seemed to cock its jaw and take off at a tangent across the grass. To Liam's horror, he realized that it was the Final Straw colt and, judging by the way she was battling with his head, that Angie was not in control. She was also heading for one of the roads that intersect the Newmarket gallops in such a hazardous way. Most local drivers had the sense to slow down if they saw a lad in trouble, but there was always the passing maniac who without looking to left or right found the straight expanse of road leading to the town only too inviting.

Snatching the grey filly up, Liam decided to try to get to the road before Angie did and head her colt off. Out of the corner of his eye he saw that Sam Shaw had had the same idea and had rousted his old hack into a canter. Liam's filly, however, was nearer and faster and without further hesitation he kicked her into top gear. She responded well and he was already easing her back to a canter when he saw what he had been dreading: the dazzling beam of a motorbike's headlights scorching along the road towards them. Hoping that his filly's nerve would hold, he stood up in his stirrups and gesticulated frantically for it to slow down. The driver, impervious behind his goggles, merely crouched lower and blazed on. The Final Straw colt, suddenly noticing him out of the corner of his eye, swerved abruptly to the left, throwing Angie over his shoulder, before slithering to a halt just as the bike flashed past only yards away. Jerking the reins out of Angie's hand, he then proceeded to trot back sedately in the direction of his stable.

Liam slipped off his filly's back and, looping his reins over his arm, ran towards Angie, who was lying in a crumpled heap, her white shirt bright against the turf. He knelt down and gently put his arm around her, his face pinched with concern.

She gave a yelp of pain as she felt his touch. 'Oh Liam,' she whimpered. 'I think something's broken. There was an awful crack when I hit the ground.' Her face, pallid beneath its summer tan, twisted in pain. 'I was so frightened just now, Liam. I thought we were going to be killed! I just couldn't hold him, the naughty monkey!' She tried to smile.

Liam, still crouching beside her, put both his arms around her and tenderly eased her back on to the ground, ignoring his filly who was jerking impatiently at her reins. 'You'll not be moving now until we get the ambulance,' he said. He laid his cheek against hers. 'Now don't ever do that to me again. Don't ever give me such a fright,' he said forcibly. 'I love you, you see, I really do. I'd die if any harm came to you.'

Angie looked up at him, her eyes huge. 'Oh Liam, dear Liam. And I love you too,' she murmured before lolling against his shoulder in a dead faint.

CHAPTER TWENTY-FOUR

The Old Rectory

As the Dog Collar Five – the little group that Charlie had found, made up of Cambridge theology students – struck up ''S'Wonderful', Lady Kitty looked around happily. It was one of her favourite Gershwin numbers and seemed to sum up perfectly what she felt about today. She was thrilled to have so many of her favourite people gathered together here at the Old Rectory on such a special occasion and, as she had predicted, the weather was perfect. There was only the faintest of breezes, and whilst the garden shimmered in the heat, under the canvas arch of the open-sided marquee, it was cool and inviting. She had been determined that the Rathglin colours should be much in evidence and all the flower arrangements, the hanging baskets of trailing nasturtiums, marguerites, clematis and lady's mantle and the table centrepieces of roses and camellia leaves were a fusion of gold, yellow, white and green. Even the marquee itself had gold and green striped poles and pennants, giving it the air of a medieval jousting pavilion.

Most of her guests had already sat down to lunch, but glancing back to the house she could see a few latecomers drifting in from the drive; and several people still hovered by the long trestle tables laden with food laid out under the beech tree.

In the harsh mid-summer light even the Old Rectory itself was not looking as shabby as she had feared. Thanks to the enormous amount of potash and tomato fertilizer she and Davy had piled on them last spring, her pink and white climbing roses were rampant this year and mingled with the late-flowering clematis, covering up the cracks and faded paintwork very well. Kate was right, though, they would have to get the whole of the outside of the house painted this winter after the roof repairs had been carried out. At least, of course, they could afford to get it done properly. She and Kate between them had netted over £100,000 from Achilles's Derby win.

Screwing up her eyes against the sun, she could just make out the shape of Watson contentedly cropping the grass in the paddock beyond, a buttermilk blur against the grass.

'Will you stop your daydreaming, for heaven's sake, Kitty?' the Professor was saying. 'It's time you said a word or two. Everyone's waiting to get started on the eating and drinking.' He bent his head to sniff the yellow rose in his buttonhole. 'Well, off you go then, woman. Get on with it!'

Lady Kitty, startled, obediently rose to her feet. He was right, she realized. The noise and clatter of conversation in the marquee was dying down and a hundred or so faces were gazing at her in expectation. What a terrible hostess she was turning out to be! Gripping the edge of the table tightly she leant forward with a welcoming smile.

'Hello there, everyone,' she began. 'I hope you've all got enough to eat and drink – for the moment that is, anyway.' She held up her hand. 'Now, it's all right, don't worry. I'll not be subjecting you all to a long sort of a speech or anything like that. I'd just like to welcome you all here, on behalf of Kate and myself, and Charlie Kyle, of course, Achilles's co-owner.' She indicated the adjacent table, where Charlie was sitting. 'As soon as we all got over the shock of winning the Derby, the very first thing we started thinking about was the celebration,' she went on cheerily. 'There was the odd argument, I must admit, but there were two things we all agreed on straight away. One was that we should have our party here, at the Old Rectory, where Kate and I hatched our harebrained scheme of breeding Achilles in the first place. We were also determined that as many people as possible who had helped him along the way should be invited.' She gazed about her with affection. 'So, we are particularly pleased to see all those from both Barons Lodge and Three Swallows who could make it here today.'

She paused, frowning. 'In fact, our only disappointment is that Tod can't be here, too. We owe him more than we can ever repay. He believed in Achilles right from the start and handled him so brilliantly and patiently through all his vicissitudes and triumphs! Success, though, has its penalties, and Tod had to be away at the yearling sales in Kentucky this week, spending a fortune of somebody else's money!' She grinned mischievously. 'We all know that however much he spends he won't find anything as good as Achilles over there! But we wish him luck, anyway, and Myra, too, who is with him.' She peered round the nearby tables. 'Anyway, Tod is very ably represented here today

357

by his son Toby and by Lucy Beckhampton, too, of course.' She flashed a smile at Lucy, who she had managed to locate sitting at a table in the corner with Alain du Roc and a couple of Newmarket-based jockeys. 'We are even delighted to welcome some of the ladies and gentlemen of the press,' Lady Kitty continued, scanning the far end of the marquee. 'Earlier in the year, some of them, Mr Sink in particular, made it quite clear that they thought we were mad to even contemplate running Achilles in the Derby – but come to think of it, they were not alone in that view! Some of my nearest and dearest were of the same opinion.' She swung round to make a face at Kate. She spread her hands in a gesture of blessing. 'However, I'm prepared to forgive you all!

'But there were other staunch believers who always had faith in the colt,' she continued, when the laughter had died down. 'Alain du Roc was one, and we would particularly like to thank him for all his brilliant piloting, particularly on the big day itself.' She paused for another ripple of applause. 'We would also like to pay particular tribute to those closest to our colt at Barons Lodge: his lad, Liam Byrne, whose dedication has been total. He's been with the colt day in day out since he first set foot in Barons Lodge, and his hard work and rapport with him have been crucial. The little monkey could pull the back teeth out of your head when he first went out on the gallops, I was reliably informed. We'd certainly not have won a race at all with Achilles, let alone the Derby, without Liam's help. And then, of course, there's Sam Shaw, Barons Lodge head lad; Nobby, Tod's travelling head lad; Jack – Jack Massam who rode Achilles on his first ever outing; and Ginger Mann up at Holkham, who built up his health and strength so well and gave him such a splendid seaside holiday.' She looked around her, her eyes shining.

'We'd like to thank you all. From the bottom of our hearts. Without your help we certainly wouldn't be having the party here today.' She clasped her hands together, waiting for the applause to die down. 'It's all right now. I shan't be much longer, I promise. We all want to enjoy our lunch, after all,' she went on quickly. 'I would just like to remind everyone, though, that we'll be showing the race again after lunch on a gigantic screen in the drawing-room, so don't you all be rushing off without taking a look at that, will you? Last but not least, I want to say something about Achilles himself.' She paused, her expression serious. 'When we planned this little occasion, we had absolutely no idea that he would be able to join us! As you know, the plan was to run him in the Irish Derby, but a pulled muscle put paid to that.' She made a face. 'So we decided to take him out of training altogether, let him down completely for a few weeks and send him back for a crack at the big races in the autumn.' She spread her hands with a beaming smile. 'So we brought him home. I'm sure you'll all agree that it's a real bonus that he's here today for all of you to see.' She leant forward and picked up her glass of champagne.

'So . . . before you all tuck in, I'd like to give you a toast.' She raised her glass. 'To Achilles, who has brought Kate and me more excitement and glory than we'd ever imagined. Certainly more than we deserved, God bless him!'

As the little band struck up 'See the Conquering Hero Comes', Achilles, led by Davy and wearing his Derby winner's rug, emerged with perfect timing from the far side of the beech tree and passaged across the grass towards the marquee with the sedate gait of an old dressage hand. As the applause broke out, however, and people got to their feet clapping and cheering, he stopped suddenly, laid back his ears and reared up, nearly dragging Davy over.

Lady Kitty turned to Liam, hovering anxiously nearby. 'Off you go, then. Give poor old Davy a hand. What are you waiting for?' she ordered cheerily.

Kate, furiously clicking away with her new Leica, paused for a moment to get her breath. She had built up an impressive portfolio of pictures of Achilles by now and some good shots of him today were essential. She had also been glad of the diversion that his appearance had provided. When her mother had referred to Tod earlier, she had once again felt a stab of pain. Memories of that last afternoon in the Den, when she had realized that she had to break with him, had come flooding back and her stomach lurched with misery. Luckily, what with the English launch of her book, a magazine feature she was working on for Geoffrey on Literary Lions and organizing the party, she had had very little time to brood about Tod recently; but her distress at losing him was still acute.

She did not, however, regret her decision. Even when she had been driving back to the Old Rectory that afternoon, her vision blurred by tears and the rain lashing the windscreen as though in sympathy, she knew it was the right one. It wasn't that Tod had been deliberately deceitful – he did, she knew, love her – but his ties with Myra were too strong. He certainly was not ruthless enough to abandon her now and even if she had put pressure on him to do so, his resulting guilt would have ruined everything. There had been absolutely no point,

359

therefore, in hanging on in the hope that some time it would all change, she told herself. As she neared Hazeley she had stopped the MG for a moment and winding the window down, let the soft rain drift on to her face. Gazing out at the field of rape in front of her, glowing brilliant yellow against the gun-metal sky, she had been amazed to find that instead of the wave of self-pity she had anticipated, she actually experienced a definite sense of relief. It was as though she had sloughed off a burden which she had been carrying for some time and which had become uncomfortably heavy.

This did not mean, though, that she felt strong enough yet to face Tod in public and she was grateful that he had had to go to Kentucky and decided to take Myra with him. Thanks to Achilles, he now had orders for half a dozen well-bred American yearlings for next season, which would more than make up for the loss of Prince Hassim. Kate was delighted. Although she felt that Tod had let her down, she was not a vindictive person and did not in the long run wish him ill.

Achilles's latest setback had been another problem that had preoccupied them all in the past few weeks, of course. When he had worked deplorably just before the Irish Derby and they had realized that he had pulled a muscle in his back, they had decided to abandon all plans to run him in the King George as well, let him down completely for the summer and bring him back for an autumn campaign, culminating in a crack at the Champion Stakes or the Prix de l'Arc de Triomphe. It had been very disappointing, particularly for Lady Kitty, who had set her heart on running him at the Curragh, but as usual she had accepted the situation with equanimity.

'We said at the start that we would never run him, even at an evening meeting at Wolverhampton, unless he was one hundred per cent,' she reminded Tod. 'No way will we ever go back on that.'

Liam and Charlie brought the colt over a few afternoons later, accompanied, as usual, by Watson. Achilles seemed to recognize his old home, immediately setting off at a canter round the perimeters of the paddock, as though to mark out his territory, before stopping to stare, motionless, out over the parkland beyond, just as he used to do as a foal.

Charlie watched him affectionately for a moment before vaulting over the gate and looking around him. 'Now Liam, I want you to walk round with me and check all the fencing again,' he ordered. 'I know that Lady Kitty regards Jacko as a family pet, but we mustn't forget that he's a pretty valuable property now, too, you know!' He grinned. 'We certainly can't risk him jumping out or getting in any mischief,' he insisted. 'There are quite a few mares around the village. I saw a couple on the other side of the parkland as we drove in just now. I presume they belong to Winterton over at Hazeley Hall?'

Lady Kitty nodded, leaning forward on her stick. 'That's right. He's a funny old buffer. Nearly blind now, but he likes to have his mares around him in the summer. He may have to sell most of them soon, though. Money's pretty tight, I hear.'

She straightened up, an amused look on her face. 'But look here, Charlie, a sentimental old fool I may be but I'm not completely witless. I promised Tod that Davy would check all our fencing. We've actually replaced quite a few of the posts and railings on the far side. Didn't Tod tell you?'

Charlie shook his head. 'No, he didn't mention it. But then he's had a hell of a lot on his plate since the Derby, hasn't he? Problems with Myra and all these new owners to butter up,' he said casually.

Kate wondered again how much Charlie actually knew about her and Tod, and what he thought about it. Tod swore that he'd never discussed their relationship with his assistant, but Charlie was very observant and must have put two and two together, particularly since Myra's collapse. Kate had to admit he had seemed to be making a great effort to be friendly recently, particularly over the plans for the party, and had even complimented her a few days ago on some of the photographs in her book. She only hoped he wasn't feeling sorry for her in any way. That she couldn't bear.

'He probably thinks you were very sensible to break things off,' Lady Kitty had commented bluntly. 'He's fond of Tod, I'm sure, but he knows his shortcomings. I suspect he's come to the same conclusion about the two of them that you have – that although it's certainly no love match, they rub along all right in an odd sort of a way and it would be quite out of character for Tod to leave the poor woman now.'

By the time Kate got back to her seat, Geoffrey Barlow was in full self-congratulatory flow, regaling the table with news of how her book was doing.

'It had terrific reviews in the racing press and in some of the qualities, particularly the *Telegraph*,' he was boasting, helping himself lavishly to some more mayonnaise. 'Of course Achilles's Derby win was an absolute godsend. It helped enormously. Kate and Sandy Diss were frantically busy signing copies at Ascot. Didn't you see them on TV? Sandy's hat attracted a lot of attention – it looked like a multicoloured eagles' nest!' He took another mouthful of lobster. 'I don't know anything about horses but I didn't think Achilles looked too happy just now,' he commented, glancing up at Kate.

She laughed. 'No, you're right, he wasn't! He was definitely living up to his name and sulking, I'm afraid. Davy took so much trouble getting him ready that he must have thought he was going to the races, rather than just doing a few laps of honour around the garden!'

As she tucked into her plate of smoked salmon, her other neighbour, Basil Hunter, who had been paying great attention to the pretty vet's wife on his left, swung back towards her again with an unctuous smile.

She had been none too pleased when Basil had come and sat down next to her; she found him pompous and embarrassingly flirtatious. He had undoubtedly known about Myra's plan to go off with Stelios and her own relationship with Tod, too. She had no idea what his views on all that would be. Presumably he would be delighted that his sister had decided to stay put. She did hope that he was not going to gloat over this in any way. She decided to take the initiative and inquire after Myra's health before Basil could make any reference to it himself.

'Oh, she's all right,' he replied airily. 'Bit of a mid-life crisis, that's all. But she'll be back to her old self again soon, I'm sure. Now that she knows where she is.' He gave Kate a meaningful glance. 'After all, Barons Lodge is definitely on the up and up again, wouldn't you say? Tod's taking her off to Martha's Vineyard for a week after the sales – did he tell you?' he continued casually. 'That should do her good. Pam and I are flying out to join them, actually. We're able to take a little break ourselves. Thanks to your colt, of course.'

'Oh, you backed him, then? Good for you,' Kate remarked politely.

Basil's smile was complacent. 'I should say,' he drawled. 'I got on for the Derby before Lingfield. Against Tod's advice, of course. If I listened to him I'd never have made a penny on the racecourse. But then he's not much of a risk-taker, is he?'

She'd had enough of this, Kate decided. She had to get rid of the man before she lost her cool. 'Why don't you have some more lobster, Basil?' she suggested. 'There's plenty for seconds, you know.'

'Hmm,' he ran his tongue round his full lips. 'Do you know, I think I will. What a good idea. It's all quite delicious.' He pushed back his chair.

As Kate sat back with a sigh of relief, Diana Saunders, catching her eye, waved to her cheerfully from a nearby table. She seemed to be getting on very well with Charlie now, despite their break-up. Kate did not suppose that she and Tod would ever be able to be that friendly again, she thought sadly.

Being engaged seemed to suit Diana, too. She was looking even more healthy and glowing than usual in a simple but well-cut green linen dress from her favourite Australian designer, and with her streaked blonde hair tied back in a ponytail she looked ridiculously young. She was also sporting a large emerald and yellow diamond engagement ring which she had made a point of showing Kate earlier.

'Terrific, isn't it? I had to work very hard on Nik to get this, I can tell you!' she said, grinning. 'You can try it on if you like. Emeralds should suit you. Why don't you get one? After all, you're a rich woman now. You ought to splash out a bit.'

Kate had laughed good-humouredly but the remark had again made her think of Tod. He didn't like emeralds, she knew. He thought they were unlucky. He had given Monique an emerald and diamond engagement ring, apparently. She found herself wondering what sort of ring they would have chosen together had things worked out differently. Certainly something more discreet and less flashy than Diana's: a sapphire perhaps, or a ruby, probably her favourite stone.

'Hello! What a terrific party!' Lucy Beckhampton, looking particularly French in a white jump suit and Jules et Jim yachting cap, was standing beside her with a dazzling smile.

'Come and sit down. Here, have Basil's seat,' Kate insisted. 'He's gone to get some more to eat. Thank goodness!'

'I know, isn't he a bore?' Lucy replied sympathetically, flopping down next to her. 'God! It's hot! Perfect day for a party though.' She turned to Kate, her amber eyes concerned. 'Look, I know this isn't really the time or the place or anything, but I really had to tell you how sorry I am about you and Daddy,' she said tentatively. 'I gather you just felt that it couldn't work out – after what's happened with Myra, I mean.' She sighed. 'Daddy's dreadfully upset, you know.'

Kate stiffened at this implied criticism. 'Well, I am, too. But I'm just learning to live with it!' She bit her lip. 'I'm sorry, I didn't mean to snap. But I've been pretty miserable, too, you know,' she confessed. 'It was absolutely the last decision I wanted to make. I love Tod very much, as I think you know, but I don't think I had any option.' She turned to Lucy, her grey eyes imploring. 'It just couldn't have worked, I'm sure of that. I know you were rooting for us but I'm afraid you were on to a loser. We all were.' She frowned. 'Tod can't possibly leave Myra now. Not when it's clear how much she needs him. Surely you can see that?' she pleaded. 'You know him better than anyone.'

Lucy made a face. 'That bloody woman!' she replied petulantly. 'Why does she always have to spoil everything? I was over the moon about the idea of her clearing off with Stelios and you and Daddy living together. I was really thrilled. I thought maybe he'd be happy at last.' She leant forward, clasping her slender arms round her knees. 'I'm not convinced you're right about him, though,' she said earnestly. 'I know he's got a ridiculous conscience and all that but it's you he loves, not Myra! I'm absolutely sure of that!'

Underneath her make-up the girl was looking strained, Kate noticed. Her amber eyes, so disconcertingly like Tod's, were underlined with dark circles of fatigue. 'Are you OK? You're looking a bit pale,' she inquired, concerned.

'I'm knackered, actually,' Lucy admitted. 'Alain was lecturing me about it on the way here today. He thinks I should stop gallivanting around, if you know what I mean. He didn't put it quite so politely.' She giggled. 'He even had the cheek to suggest that I ought to settle down with someone – you know, get married!' She rolled her eyes comically. 'I told him that he's the only man I know who could cope with me more or less full time and he's not on the market. He's never going to leave boring old Françoise!' She twisted a strand of chestnut hair around her finger, her expression pensive. 'I absolutely dread the idea of being married, you know,' she confessed. 'I mean, even when I fancy someone like mad, I hate the idea of having to have breakfast with them every day or sleep with them when I've got a cold or the curse very badly.' She peered across the room. 'Oh Lord! Here comes Basil again, I'm off,' she announced, promptly getting to her feet. 'Come over and join us, do. Alain wants to thank you again for those amazingly beautiful gold cufflinks you and Lady Kitty gave him.' She smiled.

'I'm glad he likes them. We wanted him to have something special. They belonged to my grandfather, the Earl of Rathglin,' Kate said.

Lucy grinned. 'Gosh! How grand! No wonder Alain's so delighted. He's such a snob – like all the French! Anyway, ciao. See you later.'

Diana held up her hand, her engagement ring glinting as the Dog Collar Five swung into another, familiar, number. 'Hey, listen. This one's definitely for us. "Yesterday."' She grinned at Charlie. 'Still, we had some great times, didn't we?' She took a swig of her champagne. 'I've been thinking, kid. Isn't it time you found a replacement?' she inquired. 'A proper girlfriend, I mean. Not just the odd one-night stand. It would take your mind off that Warrender business, too. There's nothing more you can do about that now, you know.' She tapped him affectionately on the knee.

'Don't rub it in,' Charlie replied bitterly. 'And just because you've decided to become respectable doesn't mean I have to follow suit. Anyway, you know perfectly well that I don't want to get too involved at the moment. It was the main reason we split up, for Christ's sake.'

Diana sat back. 'OK, OK, keep your hair on,' she protested amiably. 'I didn't mean you should get engaged or anything drastic like that. Just that you should find a regular girlfriend, that's all. I know you like being a loner and all that crap, but I think you need a woman more than you realize.' She leant forward, a mischievous look in her eyes. 'For companionship, not just sex, I mean. Though it seems a great pity you're not exercising your talents in that direction, too. Think what some poor girl is missing!'

'Flatterer,' Charlie grinned. 'Well, you could be right, but I really haven't got time for anyone right now. It's been incredibly busy, you know, with Tod away for such a long time. Days on end seem to be spent driving back and forth to the racecourse. I'd be happy never to see a motorway again. I hardly ever seem to get to bed before one in the morning. Even you wouldn't put up with that!'

'Oh, I dunno! I'd find a way of getting your juices flowing somehow,' Diana replied cheerfully. 'Anyway, this hectic stint at Barons Lodge won't last for ever, will it? When things ease up a bit, you should start looking around a bit more. Accept a few more invitations. Newmarket's full of talent, you know.' She glanced across the table. 'What about Kate? You two seem to get on pretty well now. She's a very sensitive type, too.' She frowned. 'Trouble is, I suspect she's having some sort of number with Tod. They looked pretty lovey-dovey on Derby Day. She must be really pissed off that he's not here today. She's on to a loser there, though, I fear. Tod'll never have the balls to ditch Myra.' She picked up a strawberry from her plate and bit into it with relish.

Charlie pushed back his chair abruptly. He knew perfectly well that Kate and Tod had been involved but he didn't like gossip and was not inclined to discuss it even with Diana. He also guessed, from the way Tod's communications with the Old Rectory these days were always conducted through Lady Kitty, that the affair was finally over. Presumably Myra's collapse had seen to that. For some reason, he had not stopped to analyse why, he was glad. The two of them would not have been happy, in his view. Quite apart from the age difference, Tod was too world-weary for Kate. There was a toughness and ambition about her that he himself was beginning to respect. It would take an altogether stronger, more determined character than Tod to cope with that, he suspected. 'Mmm . . . maybe. I wouldn't know about that,' he replied non-committally, glancing around the marquee. 'Anyway, I must be off. It's time I circulated a bit. I am supposed to be one of the hosts, after all.' He got to his feet.

'Go ahead. I'm not stopping you,' Diana waved airily. 'We'll return to the subject of your sex life some other time. Anyway, I've got some serious wheeling and dealing to do myself in a minute – in connection with the stud. Greek Dancer's the flavour of the month now, you know. I've had to turn one or two mares down for next season already!'

She hadn't wasted much time, Charlie reflected later, when he'd finally got away from a breeder acquaintance who was complaining bitterly about his mare's rejection. Criticizing small breeders' mares was like attacking their children, he thought to himself, as he strolled over to the beech tree and helped himself to some iced coffee. They invariably took it personally. He was delighted that Achilles's win had given Greek Dancer such a boost, though. There would be a great deal of interest now in his third crop, the yearlings coming up for sale this autumn.

Glancing up, he caught sight of Kate crossing the lawn towards him and raised his hand in greeting. There was no doubt about it, his views on the girl had changed remarkably in the past six months, he realized, recalling Diana's cheeky suggestion. It had never entered his head, though, that they could be more than friends. She'd been Tod's property, and even if the affair was now over, she would be hurt and bruised for some time, he suspected, and in no mood to contemplate anything new. She was looking very attractive today in her old-fashioned, Alice in Wonderland sort of frock but there had been real anguish on her face when she'd been talking to Lucy Beckhampton earlier, he'd noticed. She looked flushed but happier now as she hurried towards him.

'Hello,' she said. 'I've been looking for you all over. Do you think the party's been a success?' she asked eagerly. 'It's so hard to tell when you're giving it yourself. I think everyone's had a good time, though, don't you?'

Charlie glanced towards the drive where an ancient van packed with some of the Barons Lodge lads and their girlfriends was revving off, tooting its horn, a cluster of gold and green balloons streaming like a parachute behind. 'I don't think there's much doubt about that!' he reassured her. 'Several people have told me that it's the best party they've been to for ages, and they can't all be lying!' He grinned. 'I think actually seeing Achilles in the flesh was quite a thrill for some people too,' he commented. 'He's none the worse for his parade, by the way – I checked myself just now. Davy will turn him out in the paddock again when the mob have finally departed.'

Kate sank down thankfully on to one of the large garden cushions. 'Gosh, my feet are sore. Must be the heat,' she complained, kicking off one of her sandals and rubbing her toe. 'Several people have asked me what we're doing about syndicating Achilles and all that,' she said. 'I said I'd really got no idea at this stage.' She turned to Charlie, her grey eyes pleading. 'Look, you wouldn't like to handle those negotiations for us later, would you? Kitty and I'd be very grateful. We're complete innocents in that field, I'm afraid.'

'Of course, I'd be delighted.' Charlie plumped down on the cushion next to her. 'There's a surprising amount of interest in the colt's future now,' he remarked thoughtfully. 'Diana was talking about it – she said they obviously couldn't stand him at Three Swallows but Stella Alexandros was very keen to get him for Mountclare. I told her they'd all just have to wait. I'd no idea what you and Lady Kitty want to do when the time comes. After all, anything could happen this autumn. We haven't even got him back on the track yet, for heaven's sake!'

Yawning, he stretched his hands above his head and gazed upwards at the great canopy of purple leaves arching above them. 'I love your beech tree. It's got such grandeur.' His stare intensified. 'Oh, look! I can see something up there: a sort of platform. Is there a tree house up there, or something exciting?'

Kate nodded. 'Yes. Daddy built it years ago – one school holidays. Kitty and I keep meaning to get someone to take a look at it. It's probably completely rotten by now and rather dangerous. We're worried that bits of it could fall on someone's head!'

'I'll check it for you. I'd love to,' Charlie said eagerly. 'Not right now, of course – that wouldn't be very sociable! Also, I'd need to organize proper ladders and everything. But I'll certainly have a go some time soon. I'm a bit of a tree-house specialist, actually. I built myself one at Coombe Place, I remember.' His face clouded over. 'It's very unlikely that I'll ever get the chance to see that again, so I'd really like to have a crack at repairing yours.' He flopped back against the cushion again. 'You ought to look after it for future generations, quite apart from anything else! Lady Kitty may be inundated with grandchildren here one day, so the least we can do is to make sure it's safe before then.' He gave Kate a mischievous grin.

'That doesn't look very likely, at the moment,' she retorted, taken aback. She'd never known Charlie make such a personal comment. It must be the effect of the champagne.

'You never know,' he replied, lolling back, his eyes closed. 'I'd like a great gang of kids myself. Probably because I'm an only child and I know how lonely that is.' He sighed. 'The real problem is finding the right person to marry. Someone who could put up with me, I mean. Even Dad says I'm difficult to live with!'

'How is your father, by the way? Have you had any news of him recently?' Kate inquired, seizing the opportunity to deflect the conversation. She was distinctly thrown by Charlie's sudden confidences; it was so unlike his customary reserve.

He sat up, his face darkening. 'I had a letter this week from his doctor pal. The news is not good: Dad's very depressed and getting more angina pains. If only I'd been able to get something out of Warrender.' He pushed back a lock of hair. 'You heard about that fiasco, I suppose?'

Kate nodded. 'Yes, Tod told me at the time.' She looked at him thoughtfully. 'Look, couldn't you have another go at trying to talk to Warrender or getting that nice woman who used to be his girlfriend to do it? You know, the one you went to see in Yorkshire. What was her name?'

'Beth. Beth Arnott,' Charlie replied. 'No. I don't think so. Warrender's too wary to talk to anyone now, even Beth. I don't want to involve her any more, anyway. She's happily married now; the last thing she wants is to get mixed up with Warrender again.'

He got up abruptly, his expression still grim. 'Oh, well, there's no point in brooding about it, I suppose. I've just blown it, that's all.' He looked over towards the marquee. 'Come on, we're neglecting our duties as hosts. There are quite a few people waiting to say goodbye.'

As he strode off, Kate felt a great wave of concern. It seemed so tragic that despite all his efforts to track down Warrender, when he had finally found him, he'd not been able to find out anything new about the fire, anything that might have helped him clear his father's name. She and her mother owed Charlie a lot, she mused. If it hadn't been for his efforts with the leeches, Achilles might never have been sound again, let alone triumphed in the Derby.

It may have been the euphoric effect of the champagne but as she too got to her feet she resolved to think of a way to help him.

Keepers Cottage

Charlie lay stretched out on his sofa, Sumi at his feet, listening to the final movement of the Chopin E Minor Piano Concerto. It was one of his favourite pieces of music, particularly this old recording by Artur Rubinstein that his father had given him years ago. As the last notes died away he continued to lie still, absorbing the evening sounds all around him: Sumi's rhythmic purring, a dog barking somewhere across the fields and the thrush just outside the open window, trilling its last song of the day. In the dusk, the little room was fragrant with the scent of the tobacco plants he had grown himself from seed and with the heavy perfume of the Old Rectory roses that filled the bowl at his side.

His thoughts flicked back to the extraordinary events over at Hazeley that Liam had described to him on the phone earlier. As it was a Sunday, Charlie had had plenty of time to digest them and he was now clear in his mind as to what he should persuade Lady Kitty to do.

The sultry July weather had broken with a vengeance the night before and there had been electrical storms all over East Anglia. The gale force winds had abated by this morning but because he knew that both the Levertons were away in London, Liam had been concerned about Achilles and had driven over to the Old Rectory at about eight o'clock to see if everything was all right. 'I knew Davy would have brought himself and Watson in for the night, surely, but I just thought I'd check they were OK,' Liam had explained. 'And I thought that Angie might like a ride in the new car, the Capri, too, maybe,' he had added shyly. 'She likes to get out now her collar bone's mending so well.'

After the dramatic incident on the heath the other day, when by all accounts Liam had saved Angie from serious injury, the two of them seemed to have become very close. Much to Sam Shaw's chagrin, Angie had broken off her engagement to Jack Massam who had decided to move back up north and try to make a go of it with his ex-wife again. Charlie was not unhappy about this development. He liked Jack but he had never been convinced that the self-effacing Yorkshire-man was a good enough jockey to be retained by Barons Lodge and if his departure left the way free for Angie to take up with Liam again, Charlie was delighted. Angie was a pleasant girl and her affectionate good-humoured support could be just what Liam needed.

369

When the two of them had arrived at the Old Rectory this morning, they had apparently bumped into Davy heading back to his cottage in a state of excitement.

'You'll never be guessing what he'd just seen – only our Jacko having a go at covering a mare, would you believe?' Liam reported incredulously.

The old groom had let both Achilles and Watson out in the empty paddock as usual, it seemed, then returned home for his breakfast. On his way back he heard some agitated whinnying and was amazed when he rounded a corner of the drive to see Achilles attempting to mount a dark bay mare. After quietly obliging him for a moment, she lashed out as he slipped off her back and cantered off, bucking and squealing. 'She was in a right old lather by the sound of it and had a nasty cut on her off fore. Davy hadn't a clue how she'd got into the paddock or whether our fella had covered her properly or not. But she's in season all right – he's sure about that,' Liam recounted.

The old groom had led the mare back to the stables straight away and bandaged her up the best he could and was now on his way to telephone the vet in case she needed any stitching, Liam told Charlie.

'I've already checked Jacko's OK, Mr Kyle. He doesn't seem to have a mark on him, the little devil, though he's in a right evil mood. He's back in his box now, too, and won't be coming out, to be sure, till we have the fencing mended. We reckon the mare must have come across the parkland looking for trouble. There's a lot of trees been damaged out there and a great big branch has come off one of the oaks and crashed through our paddock railings. The mare must have skipped over them there and found herself in with Jacko. Her lucky day, you could say!' He chuckled down the phone.

'Do you know who she belongs to?' Charlie queried sharply.

'She's one of Major Winterton's, Davy says. He recognizes the head-collar. It's got her name, Seafret, on it. She's a nice enough mare, he says. Got quite a presence to her!'

'It won't matter if she's Sceptre herself if she turns out to be in foal! That would really put the cat amongst the pigeons,' Charlie muttered. 'Anyway, thanks for letting me know straight away, Liam. You did the right thing. I'll get on to Winterton's groom straight away.' He paused. 'I shan't say anything about a possible covering, though, and I don't want any of you to do so either. Certainly tell Davy not to mention it to the vet. Is that clear?'

'Sure. As a bell, Mr Kyle,' Liam reassured him cheerily before ringing off.

Charlie managed to locate the groom about an hour later. Winterton himself was apparently away but his staff had been out looking for the mare already and the groom sounded greatly relieved to hear where she was and that the vet had been summoned.

'I told the Major to expect trouble if we didn't replace that fencing,' he said forcibly in a strong Yorkshire accent. 'He agreed. Mind you! Just never came up with the money!' he snorted. 'Ah well! All's well that ends well. As long as she's safe and more or less sound!'

The mare was by Blakeney out of a Forlorn River mare, he told Charlie. Winterton had bred her himself and had had high hopes of her potential, but she'd been something of a disappointment all round.

'He put her into training but she got sore shins at two and never stayed sound enough to get to the racecourse. So, he retired her to stud but she's not been much use there, either. She's a shy breeder, you could say. We've only managed to get her in foal twice. She did produce a grand little colt by Mummy's Pet, though, last year – it was sold to Japan – but try as we might we couldn't get her in foal again after, either last year or this. The Major'll be sending her to the sales this autumn, I reckon. Mind you, the way things are going round here, I could be out of a job myself by then,' he'd added gloomily.

Charlie got up and poured himself a large whisky. Lady Kitty had been out all day, he knew. She'd taken some friends down to the gardens at Wisley in Surrey and then out to an early supper in London afterwards, but surely she would be back by now. He reached for the phone.

'Hello! Is that the Stafford Hotel? Could I speak to Lady Kitty Leverton, please?' he requested. As he waited, Sumi uncurled himself suddenly from the far end of the sofa and leapt effortlessly in two inky movements on to the window sill and into the near darkness beyond. 'Lady Kitty? Hello, it's Charlie. I hope I'm not disturbing you? Good.' He paused. 'Look, you know you are always saying that you'd like to find a replacement for Misty? A nice mare to look at in the paddock when Jacko's gone back into training? Yes?' He raised his eyebrows, grinning. 'Well, I think we've found just the one. I haven't seen her myself yet but she's a pretty little thing, I gather. By Blakeney. She's called Seafret. What? All right, OK, I'll explain.' Cradling the receiver against his ear, Charlie settled back and began to recount what had happened and what he was convinced they should do about it.

CHAPTER TWENTY-FIVE

Mountclare

Stella stood by the open window watching one of her more forward yearlings, a colt by Ahonoora, plunge across his paddock, chasing his shadow in the evening light. These were his last few weeks of freedom: he'd been sold privately to an American and Rory would be taking him up to trainer Jim Bolger's yard in Coolcullen next month. Where the hell was Rory right now? she wondered. He'd agreed to come up to the house at seven and it was unlike him to be late. She needed him urgently. It had been a week of accumulated frustrations which she needed to work off in the most effective way.

She now had the architect's plans and the money to begin work on the stallion extensions to the stud – her bank manager had been almost obsequiously eager to lend her what she wanted the moment he'd heard about her wedding plans. But, infuriatingly, her father was still refusing to promise her Devilry. She was even more determined to stand him at Mountclare after his impressive win in the King George, of course, but Stelios was still dithering. He hadn't decided what to do about Ballinvale yet, he insisted. He'd make a final decision next month, after Devilry had run in the Arc.

It was Myra Beckhampton's fault, of course. Her last-minute rejection had infuriated Stelios, who was still sulking about it. If only the stupid woman had changed her mind earlier, Stella was sure she could have won her father round. But she was too deep into her game with Dacre to abandon it now. She had just returned from a taxing trip to Kentucky to meet his parents and discuss wedding plans. With considerable guile, she had managed to persuade everyone to keep them simple. After all, as she had piously pointed out, it really wasn't very long since Tom had tragically lost his first wife. A lavish occasion would therefore be unseemly and would also take the spotlight away from Diana and Nik. Their wedding, by all accounts, was likely to be one of the most ostentatious of the year.

Stella had also been thwarted this week in her approach to the Levertons about Achilles. They had no idea what their syndication plans would be or where they would like to stand their colt, she had been informed by Charlie Kyle. Well, to hell with them, she thought. If they ran Achilles in the Arc she was certain that Devilry would beat him anyway. She was nevertheless anxious to have some future stake in the colt. His Derby win had impressed her.

Tara, squatting beside her on her haunches, stared up at her with her mournful yellow eyes. Animals were so loyal and predictable, Stella thought, so much easier to form relationships with than people. The best way to treat people was just to manipulate them like pieces on a board. The trouble was that just when you'd got them where you wanted, they tended to move again without permission, behind your back. It was infuriating!

Tara stiffened suddenly, ears cocked – a sure sign that someone was approaching.

Knocking briskly, Rory came in and sat down in his usual chair.

'Sorry I'm late. I went to check out the mare again. She's as right as rain again after that bout of colic, would you believe? She's a tough one, that, all right.' He shook his head in admiration.

'It's the family – they're survivors,' Stella said. She fixed Rory in her hypnotic gaze. 'You can have a drink later. Right now there's something more urgent you need to attend to,' she said softly, starting to unbutton her shirt.

Rory stared back at her calmly. 'Is that so? Well, could it wait just a couple of minutes. There's something I think you ought to know first.'

Stella raised her eyebrows. 'Really! What?' she asked impatiently.

'You remember that Spence man we talked about?' Rory said. 'The one who couldn't keep his mouth shut? Well, he's gone and blabbed his way to the top of our little list now, hasn't he? I thought you'd like to know.'

Stella froze in her seat. 'When? What's the plan?' Her voice was tense.

The groom shook his head. 'Now I'd not be telling you that, would I? The less you know, the better. Let's just say that the man has undertaken a public engagement, just after Christmas, that I think he'll be regretting!' His mouth twisted in a smile.

'I see.' Stella frowned. 'Well, what do you want from me, then?'

'Your help with a little negotiation,' Rory replied softly. 'We need to know whether or not we can count on you before we go ahead with certain plans.' He leant forward, gazing into the fireplace. 'You'll be going to Florida for the Breeders' Cup in November, will you not? As part of your honeymoon trip. Am I right?' He raised an eyebrow.

Stella nodded. 'Yes. So?'

'We've got ourselves a valuable contact over there. Someone who works as an electronics systems engineer for one of the airlines. He's a big sympathizer, you might say. A member of Noraid. Anyway, we might be asking you to make contact with him in Miami. Negotiate a few little purchases for us, triggering devices, maybe even a warhead or two – that sort of thing.'

Stella stared at him intently. 'What sort of money are you talking about?'

Rory shrugged his shoulders. 'I'm not absolutely sure at this minute. Ten thousand. Fifteen thousand, maybe. Dollars, that is. Certainly no more.'

'All right. Just let me have all the details as soon as you can, will you? After all, I've got other things to do on my honeymoon, you know.' Her smile was sardonic. 'And now let Tara out and come and attend to me, will you?' she ordered, her hand on the dog's collar. 'For some reason the information you've just given me has made me want it more than ever.'

Hatchards Bookshop, Piccadilly

Signing her name with a flourish, Kate handed the copy of *The British and Their Horses* back to the smartly dressed woman standing in front of her.

'Thanks awfully,' she gushed. 'My daughter will be absolutely thrilled. She's obsessed with wretched quadrupeds at the moment – can't seem to concentrate on anything else.' She turned to her companion, a military-looking man with a moustache. 'Well, it's preferable to sex, I suppose. That'll be next, you realize.' Grimacing comically, she moved away.

Kate turned her attention back to the next person in the queue, a studious-looking boy of about Toby Beckhampton's age, dressed in black with horn-rimmed glasses, who did not look in the least horsey.

'It's a favour for my sister,' he explained, apologetically. 'I'm interested in books on chess myself but she bribed me to come along today and buy your book for her birthday. She's at Pony Club camp this week, somewhere in the back of beyond. Ugh!' He pulled a face. 'Anyway, it would be great if you and Sandy could sign it for her.'

Kate, amused, took the book from him, sneaking a look at Sandy alongside her as she did so. Her collaborator seemed to be hustling away with her usual energy though she had had an extremely late night at Annabel's the night before. Either she had the constitution of an ox or she was a better actress than she was usually given credit for, Kate reflected. She herself was beginning to feel rather weary.

It was gratifying how many people had actually turned up today, though. Those radio and TV interviews they'd done last week had been worth it. Geoffrey, of course, was over the moon; the last time she'd glimpsed him he had actually been rubbing his hands with delight. Sandy was looking particularly eyecatching today in a turquoise cat suit from Charivari and a pair of matching ostrich boots, and her striking presence seemed to be drawing even casual visitors to the bookshop in her direction like a magnet. She was talking animatedly to two of them now, a bewildered-looking middle-aged couple in plastic raincoats who looked like American tourists.

'Yeah. Sure I was Nurse Julie. Great series, eh?' she flashed them a radiant smile. 'I'll sign the book "Nurse Julie" as well, if you like. Sure you're going to buy a copy. It'll cost you twice as much back home!' She fixed them with a steely look. 'Anyhow, you'll offend my feelings if you don't. And Kate's too. She's very sensitive and a brilliant photographer, as you'll see.' She thrust a copy of the book firmly into the man's hands.

Apart from such amusing diversions Kate would be glad when the session was over. She never knew what to say on such occasions and her smile was getting more and more fixed. No one had made any very interesting comments about her work, either, except for a nice woman from Norfolk who'd liked the picture of the ploughing match that Kate had managed to sneak into the book despite opposition from Sandy.

'Well, how's it going, then? I hadn't realized that you were such a celebrity!'

Looking up, Kate was amazed to see Charlie Kyle hovering on the other side of the table, looking remarkably spruce in a well-cut grey suit.

'Actually Lady Kitty told me that you'd be here this morning. I was just passing so I thought I'd drop in and say hello. Even buy a copy of the book maybe. Why not?' He smiled. 'Anyway, I hope I'm not interrupting.'

'Absolutely not. We're just finishing. Run out of punters – almost,' Kate reassured him. She was really glad to see him, she realized. She had meant to get in touch with him this week but had been so busy that she'd just not got around to it. There was so much to do before she left for New York in a few days' time.

'Good. Well, then, perhaps I could take you for a drink?' Charlie suggested. 'I can't offer you lunch, I'm afraid, as I've got to be back at Barons Lodge for evening stables. Tod's gone racing today and won't be back until late.' He paused. 'Still, perhaps we could have a glass of champagne and a snack somewhere. How about the Ritz?'

'Gosh! Well, that would be lovely. What a treat!' Kate replied enthusiastically. 'But isn't the Ritz rather extravagant?' she queried. 'We could just go to a pub or something.'

Charlie shook his head. 'Nonsense,' he replied firmly. 'They'll be incredibly crowded round here and besides, I want to show off my suit!' He grinned, fingering the sleeve of his jacket. 'I've just collected it from Dad's old tailor, just around the corner from here. He used to be cheap, in the sixties, I'm told, but that's certainly not how I would describe him now!' He grimaced. 'Anyway, now that I've got over the shock of paying for it, I might as well show it off somewhere civilized, don't you think?'

Kate laughed. 'Absolutely. The Ritz it is, then. The suit looks very smart, by the way.' She glanced at Sandy and the dwindling queue in front of her. 'I'll be with you in a minute. Five at the most. It looks like we're nearly through.'

Charlie seemed to be in a very relaxed mood, she thought, as she bent over the table again. She did hope that that wouldn't change when he heard what had happened in Yorkshire. Just in case there were any repercussions, it would be best, she had decided, to tell him before she left for the States.

The Ritz Bar

'I've got a confession to make to you,' Kate announced casually as the waiter brought their drinks. They had been chatting inconsequentially ever since they'd arrived in the hotel's ground-floor bar with its elaborate gilt decoration and ornate mirrors but it was time now, she decided, to broach a more important matter.

'Really!' Charlie raised an eyebrow. 'Well, let's hear it, then. I hope it's not too serious!'

'I told you I was going to Middleham last week, to take some pictures of Neville Crump for this series on Racing Characters I'm doing, didn't I?' she inquired.

Charlie nodded. 'Sure. Neville's perfect for your series. He's a really genuine character and still one of the best trainers of staying chasers in the business. I told you to look up my friends the Crows, too, didn't I? How did it all go up there?' He raised his glass expectantly.

'Fine. Crump and I got on splendidly. But that's not the point.' She bit her lip. 'I didn't look up the Crows, actually. I just didn't have the time, but I did have a talk with Beth Arnott . . .'

Charlie's fingers froze on the stem of his glass. 'You did what? Why, for heaven's sake?' he asked, his face immediately wary.

'Because I wanted to try to help,' Kate explained firmly. 'And going to talk to Beth was the most positive thing I could think of to do. I was practically in Leyburn, after all,' she pleaded. 'I couldn't resist ringing her up and popping over to see her.' She leant forward, her grey eyes earnest. 'Look, you've been so helpful with Achilles, Charlie. Without all your efforts with the leeches he might never have been sound again. Both Kitty and I owe you a lot.' She smiled. 'We realize what it would mean to you to get the truth out of Warrender. We thought it worth one more try. I told Kitty what I was going to do.'

Charlie stared at her coldly. 'But I didn't want to involve Beth any more. I told you that. I wish you'd listened.'

'But she didn't mind my getting in touch at all,' Kate assured him. 'In fact, she seemed rather relieved to be able to discuss it all with me.' She took a gulp of her champagne. 'The whole business had been preying on her mind quite a bit, she said. She'd been concerned about you and also about Warrender himself, she confessed. She hates to think of him being so ill down in Doncaster, more or less on his own. She'd actually been thinking about sneaking down to see him, without telling her husband, of course. I got the impression that she really wants to go and see him to say goodbye. She's a soft-hearted person, isn't she? Doesn't seem to bear Warrender any sort of grudge about the old days. I really liked her a lot.'

She helped herself to an olive. 'If she does go down to Doncaster she'll try to bring up the whole business of the fire, she says – see if she can find out if he really is hiding something. But she couldn't promise, she said. It would depend on what sort of mood he was in.'

She turned back to Charlie. 'Anyway, we got on splendidly, so no harm's been done. There's even an outside chance that she might find out something new. We both agreed it was worth a try,' she repeated cheerily.

Charlie stared at her, stony-faced. 'Well, I think you are both being ridiculously optimistic,' he snapped. 'Beth will just upset herself for nothing. Warrender won't talk to anyone now – not even her. I wish you hadn't encouraged her to go and see him, Kate. It's really none of your business.' He picked up his drink, his nostrils flaring.

Kate sat back, struggling to control her irritation. Charlie really was being quite rude, she thought indignantly. And extraordinarily pessimistic, too. If his failure with Warrender was still preying on his mind so much, why was he so averse to making one last approach to the man, particularly if Beth was willing? It didn't make sense. She had expected him to be surprised by what she had done but certainly not angry. She didn't understand him at all. The whole business must be really eating into him.

She felt suddenly concerned about their holiday. Lady Kitty had insisted that Charlie join them on the last-minute trip to Italy with the Professor that they had arranged. The villa they were renting near Siena – La Cenerentola it was called – looked so lovely, too. It had a splendid pool, judging by the pictures, and there would be a cook as well as a maid and a gardener, so there would be absolutely no chores for any of them to do. They should really be able to relax. She did hope that inviting Charlie had not been a mistake and that he was not going to be moody and bad-tempered like this out there, as well, and spoil everything.

She glanced at him as he reached for the bowl of nuts, his expression still tense.

'Look, Charlie, I'm sorry if I've upset you. That was certainly not my intention. I was actually trying to help,' she said. 'Anyway, whether you like it or not, I gave Beth our address and telephone number in Italy. We presumed that if she does go and see Warrender and find out anything new at all, you'd like to know about it. Maybe we were wrong but I could have hardly predicted you'd react like this!'

Reaching for her glass of champagne, she drained it defiantly.

La Cenerentola, Tuscany

'But surely if we don't take on Devilry and the others in the Arc it will look like we're chickening out!' Kate protested. 'We had to pull Achilles out of the King George and now you're suggesting that we give the Arc a miss as well. People will accuse us of bad sportsmanship!' She sat up abruptly, adjusting the strap of her bikini. 'They'll think we're deliberately avoiding meeting Devilry at all,' she said, glancing at her mother for support.

They had been quietly sunbathing down by the pool, watching Charlie complete length after length of leisurely crawl until, as he was drying off, he had mooted this extraordinary suggestion that they take

378

Achilles out of the Prix de l'Arc de Triomphe and go straight for the Champion Stakes at Newmarket, followed by the Breeders' Cup Turf in Florida instead.

'Let them!' Charlie countered, towelling his hair vigorously. 'We'd like to take on Devilry, sure, but not when all the cards are stacked in his favour, as they will be at Longchamp.' He sat forward and studied his feet. 'Everything in France will suit Devilry better,' he insisted. 'The ground will be soft, which he loves, and the track is ideal for such a long-striding animal. Also, given the importance of the draw, it can be a pretty rough race and he's much more mature and experienced than we are.' He frowned. 'Even with Alain on board I'm convinced that we're asking too much of Achilles to beat him in the hurly-burly at Longchamp, this year at any rate. The Arc would be a completely different prospect next year, of course, when he's bound to be stronger.'

Lady Kitty, sitting decorously under an umbrella in a green linen sundress and straw boater, took a thoughtful puff at her cheroot. 'Hmm ... what about the American "hurly-burly", Charlie?' she queried. 'Big races can be pretty rough out there, too, I imagine. There's so much money at stake, for a start. Also they have a completely different type of running from the European one, don't they?'

Kate nodded vigorously. 'That's right. I was amazed in Saratoga at the speed at which all the races, even those over a mile, were run. They seem to go absolutely flat out from the gate to the "wire" as they call it.' She turned to Charlie. 'And what about the travelling? Surely that would be a problem? Flying the Atlantic takes for ever. Achilles will hate that, surely?'

Charlie grinned, draping his towel back over his shoulders. Although he'd only been in the sun for a few days, he was already tanning nicely, Kate noticed. She had been apprehensive about seeing him again after that episode at the Ritz. Although he had eventually apologized for his rudeness he had remained preoccupied throughout their lunch and she had been relieved when, after ordering a salad which he'd hardly touched, he'd paid the bill quickly and left. He seemed to be much more relaxed here in Italy, though, and appeared, thank goodness, to have put Warrender out of his mind.

'OK, OK. Calm down. I know it all sounds very problematic, but I really don't think that it is,' he reassured her. 'I think it's our best option.' He took a swig of his beer. 'I know that Jacko used to be claustrophobic,' he continued, 'but he seems to have got over that now, certainly when Watson's with him, doesn't he? We'd have to send Watson out there, of course. Expensive maybe, but essential. Liam would fly with them, too, as well as the specialized flying grooms.'

He put down his beer and stared into the middle distance. 'I honestly think that the conditions at Gulfstream Park would suit him very well. He likes being up with the pace, after all, and with his speed and economical action a tight-turning track would be ideal. It's left-handed, too, which he prefers.' He turned to Lady Kitty. 'Even the weather would suit him, wouldn't it? We all know how he hates the wet!' he added, grinning.

'Hmm,' she replied with a frown. 'I'd still be worried about the American style of running, though. You've all worked so hard to get the colt to settle. The poor lamb won't be able to readjust just like that, surely?' She glanced across the glinting blue water of the pool towards the steps, fringed by geraniums and rosemary bushes, that led up to the house and watched the Professor descend them slowly, dressed in a cream shirt and slacks and a panama hat.

'Ah! Here comes Desmond at last. Bursting with questions about what's for lunch, no doubt,' she commented with affection. 'We'll see what he has to say about your crazy idea, Charlie. He has a high opinion of your judgement as a rule. I can't imagine why!'

Kate flopped back in her chair with a sigh. It really was too hot and idyllic here to have such an important discussion about Achilles, she reflected. At last, she was beginning to unwind after the rigours of her American trip. She'd loved Saratoga, as Tod had predicted she would: the place was magical, caught in some moneyed elegant time warp, quite unlike anywhere else she had ever been to in America. Up most mornings at five to photograph the horses and their handlers out on the track, she had then entered into an exhausting schedule of lunches, dinners, cocktail parties, concerts and balls, not to mention afternoons on the racecourse and evenings at the sales; the opulence of some of the houses of the Saratoga regulars on North Broadway had been incredible, a glimpse into a vanishing era. She was on the whole pleased with the pictures she had taken, as were *Town and Country*. Only when she was leaving her last session with them in New York had she realized how her adrenalin had been working overtime and how tired she actually was.

She had come to the right place to recuperate though, she reflected. Although the temperature was in the eighties, there was a refreshing breeze down by the pool today and the air was fragrant with the scent of fresh hay, thyme and lavender. Built a few hundred yards below the farmhouse in what was still an orchard, the pool was wedged into the side of the hill with the ground dropping so steeply away on one side that swimming along one had the impression of being suspended in space. Through half-closed eyes she gazed out at the view beyond, shimmering in the midday heat, a pastel patchwork of interlocking rounded hills, pastures, olive groves and vines, with clusters of dark cypresses marking the presence of other farmhouses and pink-roofed villas. Over towards the foothills of the Massa Maritima, she could even see the faint outline of a medieval castle silhouetted against the sky. What she really loved about the landscape with all its sweeps and contours was that it looked so old, so unchanged since the fourteenth century when it had been painted by Duccio and Lorenzetti. She'd been struck most forcibly by this the first time she had seen the frescoes in the Palazzo Pubblico in Siena.

Still pondering Charlie's suggestion, a sudden suspicion crossed her mind. 'You're not insisting that we send Achilles over to America just for the money, are you?' she asked him sharply. 'I mean you're not just attracted by the Breeders' Cup "purse", as they call it over there?'

Charlie's nostrils flared. 'No, I am not,' he replied indignantly. 'I'm concerned with what's best for the colt primarily, but I don't think you ought to be too sniffy and English about the prize money, Kate. After all, it could come in very useful. Someone's got to think about you and your mother's future, you know.' He flopped huffily back on to his chair.

'Hear, hear, well said,' the Professor intervened, his eyes twinkling. Carefully placing his glasses and hat down on the table, he wiped his brow with a spotted handkerchief. 'You're both as daft as donkeys when it comes to finances,' he told Kate cheerfully.

'I've thought of a way of educating Achilles for America, too,' Charlie continued quietly, leaning back in his chair. 'We could send him to Kilmarron.'

'Kilmarron! Whatever for?' Kate, clutching a bottle of sun-tan lotion, stared at him in astonishment.

Charlie sat up slowly, flicking back a lock of hair. 'It's the obvious solution,' he explained. 'Nik Alexandros has actually got everything we need over there. He's laid out a tight, banked, oval grass gallop and he's just got some American-type starting stalls as well. He wants to train a few horses specifically for the States, apparently. And of course going over there would give Achilles valuable flying experience, too,' he added, taking a swig of his beer.

Lady Kitty regarded him with amused affection. 'Goodness! You have given it all a lot of thought, Charlie,' she said. 'Such diligence alone deserves respect! But what makes you think that Nik Alexandros will co-operate with such a plan? After all, he's not the most altruistic of mortals, is he?'

Charlie snorted. 'Hardly. But that's exactly the point. He'll help us out because it'll suit him to do so. After all, as we know, the Alexandros camp is already interested in Achilles. Stella will be even more keen to stand him at Mountclare if he distinguishes himself at Gulfstream Park, won't she? Also Nik himself is touting around for more American owners at the moment, so Diana tells me. A good show by Achilles in Florida would be an invaluable advertisement for Kilmarron. So, all in all, you see, he'll be only too delighted to give us a hand. Cheers!'

Looking around triumphantly he downed the remains of his beer and dived neatly back into the pool.

'I must say, Charlie's getting very forceful these days, isn't he?' Kate remarked. 'Not only has he got us halfway across the Atlantic with Achilles already, but we seem to have acquired a dodgy brood mare as well. I'm longing to see her.' Reaching for another peach she bit into it with relish. She was feeling delightfully relaxed and sleepy after so much Frascati. She might even consider a short siesta before her next swim, she decided.

'Seafret is the prettiest thing you ever saw,' Lady Kitty said. 'If you judge her by her conformation alone, she'd be worth every penny of £15,000, I'd say, though Charlie insists that we got her for a snip. Well, I suppose we did, if she turns out to be in foal to a Derby winner!' she added, her blue eyes twinkling.

They were sitting on the main terrace, overhung with fig trees and vines, after a delicious lunch of artichoke and spinach soufflé and stuffed veal scallopini, followed by a salad of sweet, plum-shaped tomatoes and slabs of Parmesan and Pecorino cheese.

'You don't honestly think that's possible, do you?' Kate asked, wiping her hands on her linen napkin.

'No, I do not!' her mother replied firmly. 'Winterton's groom was very graphic about her shortcomings as a brood mare. He's never known a mare that's so difficult to get in foal, he told Charlie. That's why he was so surprised when we offered to buy her. Charlie's getting the vet to check her over again, though, when he gets back.' She looked up, puzzled. 'He's been the devil of a long time getting that coffee, hasn't he?' she said. 'It'll be teatime before it arrives at this rate and I know some people are dying to take a siesta.' She glanced affectionately at the Professor dozing off in the sun at the end of the table, his glasses slipped down to the end of his nose.

Kate got to her feet. 'It's OK. I'll go and hurry him up,' she said.

As she padded down the terrace, past the vast shuttered sitting-room, a couple of lizards bolted hysterically for cover under the terracotta pots of verbena and scented geraniums. How Tod would have loved it here, she thought again. She still missed him acutely at times, particularly the way he used to look at her so lovingly and the gentle sound of his voice. She wondered how he was getting on with Myra these days. The two of them had been over in Deauville again earlier in the month, Charlie had told her yesterday as they were driving back from Siena.

There had been a pause in the conversation, Charlie glancing at her quizzically. 'I'm sorry things didn't work out between you and Tod, Kate,' he sympathized. 'I'm fond of him, too, you know. But I don't think he ever had as much room for manoeuvre as he thought, if you follow me.'

'Quite,' she replied briskly, turning to gaze out of the window. She had been tempted, for an instant, to discuss Tod further, but remembering how Charlie had turned on her at the Ritz, decided against it. Also, he had to work closely with both Tod and Myra, after all, and he might have found it embarrassing.

What on earth was taking him so long with the coffee? she wondered. He was a domesticated creature as a rule, but perhaps he had got into difficulties with the espresso machine, which was certainly very explosive.

She peered into the cavernous kitchen with its uneven stone-flagged floor and massive beams, festooned with bundles of herbs and garlic. To her surprise Charlie was sitting motionless at the long oak table, staring intently at the pages of a letter spread out in front of him.

'Hello. I just came in to give you a hand. Is everything OK?' she asked, concerned.

Charlie looked up at her, his expression dazed. 'I'll say so. I'll say it is!' he replied emphatically, shaking his head as though in disbelief.

Focusing on her properly, he levered himself up from the table and, seizing the letter, waved it at her excitedly. 'This has just arrived by Special Delivery. It's from Beth, Beth Arnott,' he explained breathlessly. 'I simply can't believe it. She's pulled it off. She actually did it – got

Warrender to tell her everything! Beth, you're a genius!' Lifting the pages to his lips, he kissed them passionately.

Kate's heart thumped with excitement. So going to see Beth and encouraging her to help had been the right thing to do, after all; her instinct had been spot on. So much for Charlie's disapproval, she thought triumphantly. 'Oh Charlie! How wonderful. How on earth did she manage it?' she asked with genuine delight.

Charlie perched on the edge of the table, running his hand abstractedly through his hair. 'I can't tell you what this means to me,' he went on, ignoring her question. 'At last I can clear Dad's name. I thought it would never happen. I still can't really take it in!'

'But what happened? How did she manage it?' Kate asked him again, this time more impatiently.

Charlie shrugged his shoulders. 'Actually, she said it wasn't all that difficult in the end. Warrender seemed so pathetic and glad to see her. Not at all how she remembered him, she said. He didn't care about anything anyway, he told her – didn't give a sod. Why should he? After all, he was dying, wasn't he? So she seized her opportunity – said he must tell her the truth; he wouldn't die with a clear conscience unless he did. She got the impression that he was quite relieved in a way – to get it off his chest, I mean.' He looked up at Kate, his green eyes pleading. 'I owe you a huge apology. It was your idea to go to see Beth and encourage her to tackle Warrender, after all. I was dead against it. As I made quite clear, I'm afraid. I just thought you were interfering. I'm sorry, Kate. I hope you can forgive me.'

'Of course I can. I'm just delighted that my visit paid off, that's all,' Kate replied firmly. 'But what exactly did Beth find out? What did Warrender confess? At least tell me the gist of it.'

Charlie's face clouded over again. 'He told her what I've always suspected: that my mother was the villain of the piece,' he replied, his voice bitter. Picking up the letter again, he scanned it with care. 'Ah, here we are, this is the bit,' he said eventually, holding a page up to the light. '"Keith said it wasn't your father who started the fire at all. You were right about that,"' he read out slowly. '"It was your mother. She did it accidentally."' He paused, struggling to control his emotion. '"After that furious row your Mum and Dad had down in the stables, Keith actually saw your mother throw a lighted cigarette out of the car window before driving off to London. He says he was half asleep and couldn't be bothered to do anything about it, so went back to bed. When he woke up a short while later, the whole place was ablaze. He remembered then that there had been a pile of rope lying outside

384

one of the empty boxes. He supposed that that must have caught fire first, then smouldered like a sort of fuse!"' Charlie stared at the floor.

'But why on earth didn't he speak out at the time?' Kate asked indignantly. 'Why did he pretend that he thought your father had started the fire when he knew, for a fact, that he hadn't? That's criminal, surely? In every sense!'

'He didn't speak out because my mother bribed him not to,' Charlie replied, his face grim. 'When Warrender first told her what she had done, she was appalled. But then, being the monster that she was, she saw how she could turn the whole situation to her advantage. If she could persuade Warrender to say that he believed my father had started the fire deliberately – and there was, after all, plenty of evidence to back that up – it would give her the chance she'd been waiting for, to ditch him and go off with Neville; it would also get her a lot of sympathy, too, of course. So she paid Warrender £10,000 to keep him quiet. That was a lot of money in those days, you know.'

Suddenly without warning he smashed both his fists down on the table. 'The bitch! How could she do that to him?' he cried out. 'How could she cause him all that pain and suffering? I was right to hate her. I was bloody right. I never trusted her! I'm glad she died a painful death. She bloody deserved it!' He turned away, his whole body trembling.

Kate sat there, horrified. What an awful thing to find out, she thought: that your own mother had behaved in such a selfish and callous way. No wonder Charlie was distressed. His outburst, though shocking, was quite understandable. It was so far removed from anything in her own experience, however, that she did not know what to say to comfort him.

'How could she do it to him? He never did anything to hurt her, never!' Charlie raged on. 'He's had to suffer so much. It's so incredibly unfair!' He turned slowly back towards Kate, his expression determined. 'Well, he's not going to suffer any more. At least I can make sure of that,' he announced with resolution. 'Beth seems to think that she can persuade Warrender to make a proper statement about the whole thing and sign it. If she succeeds, we'll get it to the police as soon as possible and then on to the Home Office.' He stalked over to the window and stared out unseeing at the drowsy Tuscan landscape. 'I'll make sure everyone knows about it, too. Just so that all those bastards in the Jockey Club and everywhere who were so happy to believe that Dad was guilty know what a mistake they made!' He clenched his hands together so that the knuckles glowed white. 'I'm going to do everything I can to make sure Dad lives out the rest of his life with some peace of mind and the respect he deserves. Back in England too, where he belongs.' He stared at Kate, his face intent. 'And then I'm going to do what I've dreamt of doing for so long – go for a Free Pardon!'

CHAPTER TWENTY-SIX

Longchamp, Paris

Instructing his chauffeur to hand him his box of Davidoff cigars, Stelios settled heavily back on to the rear seat of the Mercedes. He felt most agreeably suffused with euphoria and mildly drunk. What a day this had turned out to be! What a triumph!

Even before the race and Devilry's great victory, he had sensed a change in people's attitudes to him. He had noticed it particularly at lunch, amongst those members of the English racing establishment who had also been guests of the Prix de l'Arc de Triomphe's sponsors. A couple of members of the Jockey Club had come over to his table to wish him luck with Devilry; and one of his neighbours, an elderly peer who had actually bred a Derby winner, had deferred to his opinion several times when discussing the possible outcome of the race. It was all very satisfactory, Stelios thought as he selected a cigar and stuck it between his lips, and due no doubt to his new status as an ambassador elect, as it were. At last, after all those years of being an outsider in the most exclusive European racing circles, despite his wealth and business success, he was to be shown respect. Devilry's win had been the *coup de grâce* and he had to confess that he had been near to tears as he watched his own green and white colours surge into the lead in the last half-furlong and later almost choked with pride as he stood in the smoky autumn light listening to the Guarde Republicaine playing the Greek National Anthem in his honour.

He had been congratulated by people that mattered, too: the Aga Khan, the Queen's racing manager, the French Prime Minister and a first cousin of the Comte de Paris. It had been overwhelming. Never again would they look down on him, he thought with relish. He had won one of the world's most prestigious races, with a colt bred and trained by his children. That was some achievement!

Relations with the twins were far from satisfactory at the moment, though; but that was partly his own fault. Maybe the time had come to patch things up a bit, certainly with Nik.

It was too late to prevent him and Stella from going ahead with a commercial merger of their operations at Kilmarron and Mountclare, but he might still be able to curb some of their other schemes. He was delighted by Nik's engagement to Diana. It seemed an ideal match in every way and he was greatly looking forward to the wedding in December which promised to be the most lavish that Newmarket had seen for a long time. He sensed, too, that he had an ally in Diana: who although happy to provide the money for the purchase of Kilmarron, was not keen on the idea of being based in Ireland long-term, and, like him, believed that Nik would be better off in Newmarket. He must have a private talk with her soon, Stelios decided, and persuade her that they should present a united front on this. The fact that Barons Lodge might not now be available was of no consequence; there would be other equally attractive yards coming on the market in the next few years.

His rift with Stella was, he knew, more serious. They had had an acrimonious meeting recently when he had informed her that although he had abandoned his interest in Ballinvale he was still not persuaded to stand Devilry at Mountclare. He had, in fact, a more ambitious plan in mind. He was still determined to keep the colt in Ireland, despite the growing interest in him from America. Not only were the financial advantages considerable – the income from stallions standing in the Republic was tax-free – but it could give him an opportunity to advance his status in Dublin even further. If he were to accept the Irish National Stud's offer to stand Devilry there, he would perhaps donate a few shares to the President of Ireland through the Irish Government, a gesture that would be very well received in diplomatic as well as bloodstock circles. He did not intend to tell Stella about this, though, until a deal had been struck. In the meantime, he had told her, it was time she concentrated less on impractical schemes for the expansion of Mountclare and more on her own personal future.

'Nik is getting married, and it's time you thought about it, too,' he insisted. 'How about this guy, Dacre? He seems very attentive and his financial circumstances are excellent, I am told. I would gladly give my support to such an engagement.'

Stella's eyes blazed. 'If you stand Devilry anywhere else in Ireland other than Mountclare I will never forgive you,' she replied. 'And as far as Tom Dacre is concerned, it's absolutely none of your business.'

It was not natural for his only daughter to talk to him like that. Why could she not have more respect? Presumably she was still, most unfairly, blaming him in some way for her mother's death. He loved his daughter and was very proud of her, but she was deeply flawed, he realized. It was not normal to be so vengeful and ruthless, irrespective of other people's feelings. He had always cherished the hope, sentimentally no doubt, that if she ever found love, her heart would soften. But he saw no sign of this with Tom Dacre. She clearly found the man an agreeable companion, but if she was considering marrying him it was for the power she would get from his money rather than because of any emotional attachment, Stelios feared. The man was a fool to allow himself to be manipulated so. But who was he to pass judgement? His own relationships with women seemed to be completely doomed. He was still furious with Myra. How dare the woman string him along for so long, then reject him at the last moment? It was unforgivable! So humiliating. Thank God he had not made even more of a fool of himself by making any public announcement of his intentions! Myra would regret her decision, of course. Tod's current renaissance as a trainer was due only to the exploits of one colt, after all, and he had *au fond*, Stelios was sure, lost his enthusiasm for the game. You only had to contrast his attitude to Nik's to see that.

As a result of Myra's rebuff Stelios had unfortunately allowed himself to become involved with Magda Borsche. She was all right as a companion in the rarefied atmosphere of Manhattan, where her late husband's collection of modern art gave her some status and where her preoccupations with money, appearances and the latest developments in plastic surgery seemed perfectly normal, but she would be completely out of place in Dublin. Her little-girl looks, limited intelligence and total lack of interest in Irish culture or history would leave her fluttering like some exotic hot-house bird in an alien temperate wood.

Although she was in Paris today, the woman had not even bothered to come to the course, he thought with irritation. She had one of her migraines, she had said, though that would not prevent her from nipping out to Chanel to collect a dress for this evening, he suspected. Win or lose with Devilry, he had arranged a supper party for a dozen people at the Tour d'Argent and Magda would have no intention of missing that. She was looking forward to showing off the sapphire and diamond brooch she had persuaded him to buy for her recently from Cartier in New York. He would lay evens, therefore, on her headache miraculously having disappeared by the time he got back to the Crillon.

Vexed by all this, he leant forward and vented his irritation on his chauffeur, castigating him in fluent, guttural French, for picking the slowest-moving line of traffic.

Ahead of them, a slender figure wrapped in a russet-coloured cloak stepped swiftly out of a Porsche and slammed the door angrily behind her. As she stalked down the line of cars towards him Stelios realized with surprise that it was Lucy Beckhampton. What on earth was the silly girl doing? It was raining heavily now; she would get soaked. Lowering the car window, he leant ponderously out and called her name.

Lucy, looking pale and preoccupied, glanced up crossly. 'Oh hello, Stelios! How are you?' she said in a totally disinterested manner.

'What on earth are you doing wandering around in the rain, Lucy? Your clothes will get ruined. Here, you'd better get in quickly.' He leant forward to open the car door.

Lucy tossed back her hair. Her tiny felt hat with its long dainty feather was already bedraggled, he noticed.

'No thanks,' she said petulantly. 'I feel like a walk. I'll go back to the stands and call a taxi.'

'Don't be ridiculous. You have no chance whatsoever of getting a taxi for hours. Get in,' Stelios ordered. He turned his great head around and glared at the car behind which was impatiently sounding its horn.

Startled by his peremptory tone, Lucy meekly did as she was told, slipping gracefully into the back of the car as it once again jerked forward.

Stelios, taking another pull at his cigar, regarded her with benign affection. 'That's better,' he said, patting her knee. 'I hope my cigar does not upset you. I would have refrained from lighting it up had I known I was to have the pleasure of your company.' His heavy features creased into a smile. 'We are heading back to town eventually,' he said, peering impatiently out of the window, 'to the Crillon, to be precise, but we can drop you wherever you like.'

'Thanks. I'm staying in the Place des Vosges,' Lucy replied tersely.

Stelios watched her under his heavy lids. She had had a row with Alain du Roc, presumably. He was not surprised. In France at least, du Roc tended to put his wife first and Lucy was no doubt becoming bored with that. He had known Lucy, of course, most of her life – ever since she was a small child, then a skinny headstrong teenager causing

390

so much friction between Tod and her stepmother at Barons Lodge. Myra was always complaining how difficult she was to handle, he remembered. He had often been tempted to defend the girl – partly because she was so spirited and fragile-looking, like some elegant russet-coloured doe; merely observing her flit about the house in Newmarket had given him the same frisson he got from watching thoroughbreds in action. Now, as she suddenly turned towards him, the sheer force of her beauty, despite her mood and pallor, quite took his breath away.

'God! I'm so sorry!' she exclaimed with a disarming smile. 'I haven't even congratulated you on Devilry's win! How rude can you get?' She laid a hand on his arm. 'He was magnificent, wasn't he? You must have been so proud.'

Stelios beamed. 'Yes, indeed,' he replied, through a cloud of cigar smoke. 'It is, of course, a race I have always wanted to win.' He spread his hands expansively, his gold rings glittering. 'And with a colt bred and trained by my family. That made it doubly satisfactory, of course.'

Lucy shivered, pulling her cloak more tightly around her. 'Of course,' she agreed politely.

Stelios leant forward with concern. 'You are cold, my dear. We must adjust the heating,' he suggested.

'No, no. I'm fine, thanks. It's perfectly warm enough.' She gave him a wan smile. 'It's just me, I guess. I'm tired as well as pissed off!' She rolled her eyes. 'I've had a row with Alain, as you've probably realized. He's so ratty with me these days. I can't stand it!'

'It is probably because he, too, is weary,' Stelios said soothingly. 'It has been some effort to win the French championship again this year, has it not?' He pulled at his cigar. 'I think perhaps he should be thinking of retirement. Quit whilst he is still the best. That is the time to do it, in my opinion.'

Lucy nodded. 'Absolutely. I agree. He's always lecturing me about packing up modelling and settling down and all that. But it never occurs to him to take the same advice himself!' She gazed mournfully out of the window as the car finally swung out of the car park and on to the main road. 'Oh well' – she shrugged her shoulders – 'I probably won't see him again for a while – not until the Breeders' Cup in November. If he does go over to ride Achilles, that is. Probably just as well,' she added, her tone *triste*.

Stelios looked at her thoughtfully. 'Mmm ... well, now. If, as I understand it, you are at a loose end this evening, my dear, why don't you join our little celebration at the Tour d'Argent?' He placed his massive hand on her knee. 'It will just be a few old friends, from New York and Athens, and Nik and Diana, of course.' He paused, a cloud flitting momentarily across his brow. 'Stella is unable to be with us, I am sorry to say.' He glanced at Lucy, his eyebrows raised. 'Join us, please? It would give me much pleasure,' he insisted. It would also annoy Magda, he thought with satisfaction.

Lucy hesitated for a moment, propping her chin on her fingers as she gazed out of the window. 'OK, why not?' she said, turning back to him with a dazzling smile. 'I like dining with winners!'

Stelios beamed. 'Good. That is settled then. I will send a car to pick you up at nine.'

Le Tour d'Argent

Nibbling at a petit four, Lucy glanced around the gradually emptying restaurant. She had not been to the Tour d'Argent for years and had always regarded it as something of a joke: a place for well-heeled tourists, or where provincial bankers took their mistresses to impress them. Also, the celebrated view of Notre-Dame and the Île St.-Louis was almost obscured tonight by the continual heavy rain. Yet inside the opulent room there was an air of luxurious urgency that she found rather comforting. No matter what went on in the world or with the weather outside the elaborate ritual of the *canard à la presse* would continue.

She had also, surprisingly, quite enjoyed the company. Stelios had insisted on seating her between himself and Marcus Lemkos, an old friend from Athens, the head of an international salvage company, who looked remarkably like Spencer Tracey. Basking in the cross-glow of their combined admiration Lucy had not felt obliged to make any effort, which suited her mood very well. Heads had turned, as usual, as she came into the restaurant. She was, she knew, looking particularly good this evening, despite her fatigue, in a black almost backless Balenciaga dress and simple pearl choker. She was aware, too, that her presence was irritating Magda Borsche sitting on the other side of the table next to another old friend of Stelios's from New York. That, too, had quite amused her as, although she had only encountered the Hungarian woman a few times, at Royal Ascot and at a charity ball in Manhattan, she found her pretentious and her little-girl act embarrassing. How on earth Stelios could spend time with her she had no idea, but then he clearly had no taste as far as women were concerned; his pursuit of Myra had proved that.

What a pity it was that that had not worked out, Lucy mused, as the waiter bent solicitously over her shoulder. She liked Kate Leverton, who she could see suited her father in so many ways. She feared, though, that Kate's insistence that he would never be able to leave Myra was probably true. When she had taxed him with it he had turned to her, his face bleak. 'Well, I don't know about that but I certainly can't abandon her now, can I? Not when she's made such a fool of herself with Stelios. I'd feel a complete shit. She's so vulnerable, somehow.'

Her stepmother was about as vulnerable as a Chieftain tank, in Lucy's opinion, but if her father was determined to play the martyr there was little she could do about it. The only positive thing about the whole situation as far as she could see was the effect it had had on Toby. He was so much happier now and seemed to have settled down well at the Perse and be concentrating seriously on his A-levels at last.

Perhaps it was time that she, too, got her act together; or at least that's what Alain kept insisting. What had really annoyed her earlier was not so much that he had announced at the last minute that he couldn't take her to the Weinburgers' party as planned this evening – Françoise was perversely insisting on accompanying him – but his reaction to her mild complaints.

'Ca suffit, Lucy. We are copains, bien sûr. Best friends. But you know the rules. It is time you found your own man, as I keep telling you. But you had better kick on, chérie. You won't be able to pull any man you want for ever!'

He had no need to be so brutal, Lucy brooded. Anyway, who on earth could she possibly marry? None of the men who had proposed to her in the past few years had any appeal as husbands: they were either too boring and besotted or so self-centred and ambitious that they only really saw her as a decorative appendage. She was sick of young men anyway; they were narcissistic and selfish. Successful older men were far more relaxing and with their failing sexual prowess they were always so appreciative, and grateful, too.

She realized that Stelios, beaming with pleasure, was waiting impatiently to introduce her to a thin gnomish-looking man of about sixty with cropped grey hair and gold-rimmed glasses, who had stopped by the table to congratulate him on Devilry's victory.

'The Prince is a Hohenzollern, you know,' he said in a loud impressed whisper. Lucy held out her hand, grinning. Stelios was a fearful snob, she thought with amusement, and curiously un-sophisticated for a man of his wealth. Yet he was clearly enjoying himself tonight, basking in everyone's admiration. She found that rather touching. She also suspected that he was not immune to her physical appeal. As she was thrown lightly against his side in the car going round the Place de la Concorde earlier, he had jumped as though stung; and the kiss he gave her as she got out of the car in the Place des Vosges had been clumsy, but certainly not avuncular.

Chatting inconsequentially to Lemkos over her *rougets à l'anis* a wicked plan began to formulate itself in her mind. She was feeling extremely randy, probably because she had not had any sex for over a week. It might be amusing to try to seduce Stelios. She seemed to remember Tod telling her that, according to Myra, Stelios was impotent, but she found that difficult to believe. It was obviously an excuse to avoid all sexual congress with Myra, understandable in Lucy's opinion; or even if that were sometimes true, it would only constitute an even more interesting challenge. She had already decided that, rather than go on with the rest of the party to a nightclub, she would plead a headache and ask Stelios to give her a lift back to her apartment in the Place des Vosges. She would then invite him in for a final drink, an invitation which she was sure she could get him to accept. She also remembered that he had a sweet tooth, despite his diabetes, and might well be tempted by one of the little crumbly pieces of fudge that she would offer him with his drink. What he would not know, of course, was that they were 'hash cookies', bought from a jazz musician friend in the Rue de l'Odéon. Since she was fairly attuned to their contents they did not have much effect on her, except as a mild relaxant; but Stelios's reaction might be much more dramatic. At least they would rid him of his inhibitions, she thought with private amusement.

Intercepting another hostile look from Magda, she pressed her long fingers lightly on his sleeve and launched into a completely spurious account of why she had changed her mind about going on to Castel and wanted to go home early.

As though in a trance, Stelios removed his tuxedo and, draping it carefully over the back of the sofa, went on gazing at Lucy. Sitting curled up on the chaise-longue opposite him, she had kicked off her shoes and shaken her hair loose so that it rippled over one bare shoulder like a great chestnut mane. She was regarding him lazily, managing to look both abandoned and content, like a big cat basking in the sun.

He leant forward to pop another fudge cookie into his mouth. Lucy had insisted that he try some with his Armagnac and although sweet, which pleased him, they had an almondy aftertaste which was oddly bitter. He was beginning to feel rather strange, as if he was floating above the ground, and all his limbs felt heavy and disconnected like those of a puppet held together by string. Maybe it was too much alcohol playing havoc with his blood sugar, he wondered uneasily, or perhaps it was just the heat of the room. But whatever it was, the very sight of Lucy, lolling there in front of him, her breasts faintly visible through the dark material of her dress, seemed to be making him increasingly intoxicated. He also felt that she was exerting some strange control over him. He had so enjoyed his friends' company and all the admiration he had received over dinner that he had even agreed to accompany them to Castel, something he rarely did these days; but when Lucy asked him to take her home instead he immediately complied with her wishes. Even more surprisingly, he then agreed to join her for a final digestif. It was as though ever since their meeting earlier at Longchamp, she had looped an invisible thread around his will and was leading him wherever she wished. The odd thing was that he wasn't resisting, he was doing exactly as she asked. He realized, of course, that despite his sexual infirmities, he desired her fiercely. He probably always had, but had just had to repress his feelings.

He had also always been averse to taking up with a much younger woman from his own social circle. Such a public liaison was, he had always believed, just not seemly. But here was Lucy making a blatant play for him and he was revelling in it, although all too soon, he thought sadly, he would have to confess the extent of his sexual inadequacies. But what game was she playing? She was one of the most desired women he knew, with many young lovers on both sides of the Atlantic. Why was she bothering with an old man like him? It didn't make sense.

His head was beginning to ache and he closed his eyes for a minute. When he opened them again, Lucy's image seemed to loom closer, then retreat again in his vision as though he was focusing on her with a zoom lens. Suddenly, without a word, she got up and, unzipping her dress, shrugged it off in one slow sinuous movement until she stood there in front of him, completely naked. As he watch her, spellbound and stunned by the beauty of her body, she sank gracefully back on to the cushions with a bewitching smile. He shook his head, unable to believe what he was seeing. Lying there so confident and tawny, her breasts so perfect, her hand resting lightly on the chestnut tuft between her legs, she reminded him of one of his favourite pictures. It was quite astonishing, he thought, beginning to tremble.

'You look so beautiful. Just like a Goya's *Maja Desnuda*. It's unbelievable. I never thought I'd see anything so beautiful, in the flesh, ever again,' he heard himself murmur.

A sudden unexpected sadness engulfed him. What Lucy was radiating was not so much sex as innocence, and it reminded him of all he had lost. There was Tessa whom he had loved so much but who had died so tragically before he was able to prove it to her. Then there were her two children, so uncannily alike, who had been so pure and beautiful and whom he also seemed to have lost. He would never forget them walking hand in hand that dreadful day of the funeral, ashen with grief and gazing about them blankly with those strange blue eyes. They had needed him then, to comfort them, but now he suspected that they had both grown up to despise him. And now here was Lucy, so glorious and desirable, yet he was unable to make love to her, to worship her body as he would wish. It was all incredibly sad. Much to his horror and embarrassment he experienced a great heaving of emotions and, dropping his head in his hands, he began to cry uncontrollably.

The next thing he knew, Lucy, a silk shawl flung round her shoulders, was kneeling beside him on the floor, her hand on his knee, her eyes huge with concern.

'I am so sorry, so sorry. This is shameful,' he muttered, shaking his great head. 'I don't know what came over me. To see you there so beautiful and beyond my reach somehow reminded me of all I have lost and can never regain.' He gave a long shuddering sigh. 'I would like so much to please you, you see. But I am not what I was. It is not possible.' He straightened up slowly, his face contorted with pain, and fumbled in the pocket of his trousers for his handkerchief. 'Lucy, forgive me, please. I feel so strange. I don't seem to know what I'm saying or doing.'

Lucy levered herself up on to the sofa beside him and took his hand in hers. 'It's all right. It's not your fault,' she murmured softly, leaning her cheek against his shoulder. 'It's I who should apologize, I'm afraid. I'm really sorry. I'd no idea you would react like this.' She started to unbutton his dress shirt and, slipping her hand inside it, began to caress his chest.

Stelios slumped back against the sofa. He suddenly felt unbelievably weary but was aware too of an unfamiliar tremor of desire. 'There, there. It'll be all right, you'll see. You don't have to make love to me.

It doesn't matter, it really doesn't,' Lucy was murmuring. 'What can I do to cheer you up, to make it better? Tell me, tell me,' she said softly.

Opening his eyes, Stelios glanced down as she deftly unzipped his flies. After a moment's hesitation, he took her hand and, gently prising it away from his crotch, placed it between her legs. 'There. That's what I want you to concentrate on. I want to make you happy. I want to watch you come,' he whispered. 'Do as I ask. Caress yourself and I will tell you a story,' he went on, pressing her hand in encouragement.

Lucy looked up at him, her eyebrows raised in surprise. 'You naughty old thing,' she replied with a giggle, settling back against his shoulder.

As her fingers started to move, Stelios bent over, cupping his hand around her breast. Taking the nipple in his mouth he began to flick it delicately with his tongue. Feeling an immediate sizzle of desire, Lucy snuggled closer and started to speed up the rhythm of her fingers. Stelios watched her dreamily, his heavy features suffused with pleasure.

'Don't hurry. Don't hurry, my beautiful one,' he murmured. 'I want to tell you about the first girl I ever made love to, as in some ways you remind me of her,' he continued. 'Strangely enough, I feel right now very much as I did then, all those years ago.' He caressed her nipple lightly.

'It was when I was just fifteen and on holiday on Athosini, my father's island near Ithaca. Still for me it is the most beautiful place in all the world. Maria was just a village girl, the daughter of one of the fishermen, but I had always noticed her. She was so lovely, you see. Long black hair, clear skin and eyes like a seal. I was sitting alone on the beach one evening. There had been a family row up at the villa, and I had been encouraged to go out for a walk. It was one of those magical late summer evenings that we get in Athosini. The sea looked like wine, dark wine, Richebourg, with a great spill of gold spreading across it in the setting sun. Maria was swimming all alone in the little bay just beyond our jetty. She slid out of the sea like a mermaid and lay down on the beach next to me, pulling down her costume so that I could see her breasts; they were tiny but she was so proud of them.' He smiled at the recollection, glancing down at Lucy's rapidly moving fingers. 'That's it. That's it. Don't stop,' he ordered softly, continuing to caress her.

'She let me stroke her, as I am stroking you. I don't think I'd ever felt so excited. I thought I would explode. Then she said we should race to the nearest rock and if I beat her, she would show me something really interesting: the place where she had hair down below, she said. Well, I got to the rock first, of course, but then she went all shy. She would only let me look and touch with my fingers and eventually with my lips. I lay there naked, bursting for her, in a great pathway of gold. It was out of this world.' He paused, a faraway look of delight on his face. 'I crouched over her like an animal, like a cat, licking her all over. In between her legs she tasted of oysters, I remember; it's one of the reasons I've always enjoyed them so much.' He sighed. 'But she would not let me inside her. She would not let me fuck her, as I so longed to do.' His fingers quickened again on Lucy's nipple in conjunction with the speeding rhythm of her own.

'But soon I could not control myself any longer. I came all over her. A great explosion of juices and joy. It was wonderful! I will never forget it. It was the first time ever, you see – with a girl.' He glanced down again. 'Go on. Go on, my darling. That's what I want. Come too. Come. Come,' he whispered insistently, as Lucy's body began to tremble and, crying out, she brought herself finally to a shuddering climax.

When she eventually flopped back, exhausted, against him, her hand limp between her legs, to his amazement he felt his penis stir. Gently, he pushed Lucy's head towards it, his heart pounding.

'Take him in your mouth, my darling, please,' he pleaded. As she did so skilfully, he felt himself stiffen further. There was a chance one day, he now knew, that he might be able to make love to her properly. He also knew, without any doubt, where the best place would be to try.

'We will go to Athosini, my sweetheart,' he murmured joyfully into her hair. 'It will make everything right for us. Not just sex – everything. You will see.'

CHAPTER TWENTY-SEVEN

Newmarket Heath

Tod dropped his binoculars with a grunt of satisfaction. 'Well, that was a bit of all right, wasn't it?' he observed. 'He left the others looking very flat-footed and that Sharpo colt is no slouch. If Jacko can quicken like that on Saturday, he'll slaughter them.' He and the Levertons had driven out to the gallops on a blustery blue morning to watch Achilles, ridden by Liam, do his final piece of work before the Champion Stakes later that week. Kicked in the knee at evening stables the night before and still feeling sore, Tod had handed over the actual supervision of first lot this morning to Charlie.

Screwing up his eyes against the sun, he watched his assistant trot purposefully back towards him now on Silverlight, the old grey hack. 'Well, what did you make of that?' he asked him expectantly.

'Mmm . . . well, Jacko's fitter than I thought. He hardly blew at all,' Charlie reported. 'Should be spot on for Saturday, all being well,' he added cautiously.

'Of course all will be well. He looks cherry ripe to me,' Lady Kitty said impatiently. 'Keen as mustard, too, wasn't he? He's certainly lost none of his enthusiasm, the angel.' She shivered, pulling her old sheepskin coat more closely around her.

Tod took her arm. 'Right, come on, then. Let's get you back to the car,' he ordered. 'It's real brass-monkey weather out here this morning!'

Lady Kitty hesitated for a moment. Standing on tiptoe she waved to Kate, still packing her cameras away over by the running rail. 'I'm taking a lift back to Barons Lodge with Tod, dearie,' she called over. 'Don't hang about too long in this wind, will you? Remember you've only just got over a cold.'

Zipping up her camera bag, Kate came stomping across the grass, her cheeks whipped healthily pink by the cold. 'Don't fuss, Kitty. I won't be long, I promise,' she reassured her. 'I just want to get a few shots of Jacko walking back with the string. I'll see you back at Barons Lodge.' In actual fact she had no intention of hurrying back for breakfast. There was always the possibility she might be left alone with Tod, or even Myra. Something she was still anxious to avoid.

As she watched her mother and Tod limp rather touchingly away together, arm in arm, she fished in her pocket for a packet of Polos and offered one to Silverlight. The old chaser took it eagerly, crushing it between his long yellow teeth.

'I got some good shots, I think, of Liam too,' Kate said to Charlie. 'He seems even more bullish than usual about Jacko's chances on Saturday.'

Achilles had returned to Barons Lodge from his holiday at the Old Rectory at the end of August and had then been prepared for the September Stakes at Kempton Park where he had easily defeated his three rivals. 'He hacked up, didn't he? Not bad, considering he's only half fit,' Tod had commented afterwards. 'Mind you, we frightened off all the decent opposition today. It won't be like that at Newmarket. I hear that François Boutin's sending over that colt that won the Prix d'Ispahan. He'll be a tough nut to crack.'

'Do you think we'll beat the French colt on Saturday?' Kate asked Charlie now, looking up at him intently.

'Hmm . . .' He pursed his lips. 'I wouldn't bet on it, I really wouldn't. The Boutin colt's a top-class animal, you know. He's got a brilliant turn of foot. We'll be hard pushed to catch him if he's still running on coming out of the dip.'

'You're so cautious always,' Kate complained, laughing. 'Still, I suppose that's a good balance to the ludicrous Leverton optimism. We make a good team in a way!'

Charlie pushed a lock of hair back under his safety helmet. 'Well, yes. Perhaps we do!' He glanced down at her grinning. 'Not everyone thinks so, though. Tod's very critical of our decision to go ahead and register Achilles properly as a stallion and make the covering official and everything, you know.' He made a face. 'So is Myra. She was storming on at me again about it last night. Says it'll make nonsense of the stallion statistics, put breeders off, make us all look ridiculous – all the usual arguments.' He picked up the reins as Silverlight shifted impatiently from one leg to another. 'I said I'd had my reservations about the decision, too, but I'd simply been overruled, and that was that: you and Lady Kitty were just determined that the foal would be eligible to race,' he added casually.

Kate stepped back indignantly. 'You liar,' she protested. 'You were as much in favour of bringing the whole thing out in the open as we were! Though I know you don't share our sentimental belief that the mating was fate!' She turned up the collar of her Barbour. 'Anyway, if there is any argument about the whole thing at breakfast, I shall expect you to pitch in on our behalf,' she said firmly.

Wheeling Silverlight round, Charlie raised his whip in a gesture of farewell. 'But of course,' he replied teasingly. 'I won't let you down. I promise!'

'I don't suppose you've seen the *Daily Express* this morning, have you?' Tod enquired, slowing the Saab down as they approached the Clock Tower roundabout.

Lady Kitty shook her head. 'No. Should I have? It's not my preferred reading as a rule, I have to confess. Have I missed something fascinating, then?'

'Well, I'm not sure that's exactly the right description. Mind-boggling might be more apt,' Tod replied. 'Still, I must say it has its amusing aspect.' He rubbed his ear thoughtfully as he waited to cross the roundabout. 'There's an item in the Hickey column, under the heading "Tycoon's Last Fling?",' he explained. 'It says that there's something going on between Stelios and Lucy. They were seen together last week on his island of Athosini, apparently.' He snorted in wry amusement.

'Can you believe it? In the circumstances it all seems like a particularly improbable game of consequences, doesn't it? Anyway, I'm just hoping to God that Myra doesn't see it. She's been in such a good mood recently. This news will certainly put an end to that!' He accelerated boldly across the roundabout and swung left along the Cheveley road.

'But are you sure it's true?' Lady Kitty asked incredulously. 'You know what these gossip columnists are like! They're hardly the most accurate of reporters!'

'Mmm ... I know, but I've an awful feeling they may be on to something here,' Tod replied. 'I got a call last week from Lucy from Athens. That in itself is not unusual – she rings me from all over the place, usually late at night. But she did sound rather giggly and mysterious. To tell you the truth, I thought she must have been smoking – you know, marijuana. She does from time to time, I'm afraid. Anyway, she was taking a little holiday she said, having a terrific time; she'd tell me all about it when she got back to London.' He shook his head.

'Lucy and Stelios! It's too ludicrous. What's the matter with the man? He seems to find my family irresistible! Can't leave them alone! Myra will be absolutely furious. She keeps insisting how happy she is that she decided to turn him down and stay at Barons Lodge, but she certainly wouldn't want Lucy to take off with him!' He sighed. 'The two of them have never got on, you know. They used to fight like cat and dog.'

'How are things going with Myra, then, if I may be so bold as to ask?' Lady Kitty inquired.

Tod shrugged his shoulders. 'All right, I suppose. She's certainly far more amenable and friendly than she's been for years. It's rather disconcerting, to tell you the truth.' He pulled the car into the side of the road abruptly and switched off the ignition. 'Look, I would just like to say how sorry I am that it didn't work out between me and Kate,' he said, turning to Lady Kitty. 'I really am. I haven't had the chance to talk to you about it alone up until now, but I do want you to know that I love her very much,' he insisted, his brown eyes pleading. 'It's just that I couldn't leave Myra after she had got herself in such a mess. It wouldn't have been right. I hope you understand.' His tone was dispirited.

Lady Kitty regarded him with a kindly expression. 'I do, as a matter of fact,' she reassured him. 'I also think that things have actually turned out for the best,' she continued briskly. 'I honestly don't think that it would have worked out between you and Kate in the long run. I never did, as a matter of fact. Nothing personal: I just don't think that you'd have made each other happy, that's all.'

Tod looked surprised. 'Really? Well, you seem very sure about it. Oh well, you're probably right. I'm far too old for her, apart from anything else.' He glanced at her sharply. 'You haven't got anyone else in mind for her, by any chance? Someone more suitable in your opinion?' he asked, his eyebrows raised.

'I certainly have not,' Lady Kitty replied firmly, her blue eyes innocently wide. 'Kate's her own woman and anyway she's not over you yet.' She tapped him on the knee. 'Now let's get a move on, for heaven's sake. You seem to have forgotten about the breakfast you promised me. And if, as we hope, Myra hasn't seen that item in the *Express* yet, we don't want to risk putting her in a bad mood ourselves by being late, do we?'

Rowley Mile Racecourse, Newmarket
'But what about his head? He didn't do himself any serious damage,

402

did he?' Kate asked anxiously. Clutching her trilby to prevent it from blowing off in the wind, she craned forward to catch Alain du Roc's reply.

The jockey reached up to remove Achilles's saddle, his face grave. 'I don't think so,' he replied cautiously. 'He gave himself a hell of a crack though.' He turned to Tod standing disconsolate at his side. 'You'll get the vet to take a look at him straight away, won't you?' He glanced at Kate with a mournful shrug of the shoulders. '*Je suis désolé,*' he said with feeling. Hitching the saddle more firmly into the crook of his arm, he headed back towards the weighing room, zigzagging against the gale.

Although a large crowd had formed around the Winners' Enclosure where the presentations to the French colt's connections had already begun, Achilles, standing on the losers' lawn near by, was still the centre of considerable attention. He looked thoroughly out of sorts, flinging his head up and down irritably, his ears laid back as Nobby made another attempt to fling a rug over his quarters in the gusting wind.

'Get him back to the box as soon as you can, for God's sake!' Tod ordered. 'We don't want any more mishaps. I'll be over to check on him myself in a minute.' He turned back towards the others. 'In the meantime what we all need is a drink!'

As Liam, his thin face pinched with anxiety, finally managed to secure Achilles's rug and led him away, Kate gazed after them with concern. She still really hadn't taken in what had happened. Although none of Achilles's connections had been completely confident about beating the Boutin colt today, particularly with such a powerful cross wind sweeping the course, it had never occurred to any of them that he might refuse to take part in the race at all. He had been no more edgy than some of the others in the paddock, and although he had done his usual fly jump when he got out on the course and had fought for his head all the way down to the start, there had been no hint of any serious trouble until he was being loaded up. Just as he was being led into the stalls, they'd been struck by a particularly fierce gust of wind, causing the colt next to him, already installed, to lash out noisily in panic. Achilles, startled, had then reared up himself, banging his head against the top of the stalls before dropping down again and backing out sharply. Despite all du Roc's coaxing and the efforts of the skilled handlers he had then mulishly stuck in his toes and refused to go in again. The starter, aware that the other runners were becoming increasingly restive, had had no alternative but to let them go without him.

Kate was just thankful that Lady Kitty had not been on the course today. As well as the shock and disappointment, there had been the behaviour of some disgruntled punters to contend with. Achilles had been the short-priced favourite for the race and although he had not actually come under Starters Orders, which meant that most bets on him would be refunded, there had been a wave of boos and slow hand claps when du Roc finally brought him gently back past the stands.

It had been Charlie who had finally persuaded her mother to stay at home. 'Look, you've got bronchitis. The doctor thinks you ought to be in bed. Listen to him for once!' he'd insisted. 'If you don't, you could get really ill and then you'd have to miss America. Think about that!'

Watching at home, on television, Lady Kitty would actually have had a far better view of the incident at the start than any of the rest of them had had from the stands. She would be dreadfully worried, Kate knew; she'd ring the Old Rectory in a minute and tell her what Alain du Roc had reported.

Glancing over towards the weighing room she saw that Tod, with Myra at his elbow, her raincoat billowing about her like a spinnaker, had been waylaid by a group of pressmen including Bill Sink, Basil Hunter and Derek Thomson from Channel 4 Racing. Catching her eye, he beckoned her and Charlie over.

'They want a quick word with me on TV,' he informed them. 'Not surprising, I suppose, but God knows what I'm going to say about the Breeders' Cup after this débâcle today.' He frowned. 'We may even have to scrub the whole plan. Even if the colt is physically OK, you can bet your boots that he'll have been psychologically affected. Oh well, I'll just have to busk it!' He turned away. 'OK, Derek, I'm all yours.'

Myra came stomping towards them, her mouth turned down grumpily. 'God, what a day! Sympathy from the likes of Bill Sink is more than I can stand! Tod won't say it on television, of course, but he's got serious reservations about going to Florida now,' she went on, lowering her voice. 'So have I, I can tell you. There's no point whatsoever in us all trekking over there, with all that effort and expense, if there's a risk that Achilles won't even deign to go into the stalls, is there?' she asked indignantly. 'Bolshie animal! It's always been his temperament that's worried me,' she added tetchily.

Kate felt a surge of anger. 'Oh, come on, Myra! That's not fair,' she burst out. 'He could have hurt himself quite badly today, for all we know. Any horse would have been put off by banging its head like that. It's not his fault, surely?'

'It was no one's fault. Certainly not the colt's, I agree,' Charlie intervened quickly. 'It's very worrying, though,' he added, frowning. 'We might well have to take America off the agenda. We'll just have to see how he is in the next few days. If he seems OK, I'd still want to take him to Kilmarron. I don't think we should make any sort of final decision until then.'

Myra raised her eyebrows. 'Well, I think you're being wildly optimistic,' she retorted, flashing a chilly glance at Kate. 'If I were the colt's owner, I'd scrap the whole plan here and now and retire him for the winter,' she continued. 'Horses take ages to get over an incident like that, I know. It happened once to a filly of Daddy's and we couldn't get her anywhere near the stalls again for weeks.' She stepped backwards to avoid being jabbed in the face by a couple striding along under a large umbrella. 'God! Some people have certainly left their manners at home.' She glared after them. 'Anyway, I'm off to get a drink. See you in the bar.'

'How dare she blame Jacko like that,' Kate muttered indignantly as she watched her stalk off. 'I shouldn't have snapped at her so rudely, I know, but I couldn't help it. I don't think she's got any real empathy with animals at all!'

Charlie took her arm. 'Well, she's more imaginative with them usually than she is with people,' he remarked. 'I don't think she'd have made a very good diplomat's wife, do you?' He grinned. 'That's better. I've made you smile. Come on. It's freezing out here. Let's go and get ourselves a whisky mac.'

CHAPTER TWENTY-EIGHT

Miami, Florida

'I still can't actually believe we're here, can you? It all seems like some amazing technicolour dream,' Kate said, flopping back, bleary-eyed, on to her seat.

It was not yet seven in the morning but she and Lady Kitty were already nearing the Gulfstream Park track, speeding along the freeway from the hotel in Fort Lauderdale, cocooned in the white Cadillac stretch limo that had picked them up from the airport the night before. It had been dark then, certainly too dark to see much of their surroundings, apart from the ruby dazzle of the taillights ahead and the brightly lit condominiums.

They had been more fascinated, anyway, by the interior of the limo itself. With its mock-leather upholstery, shag-pile carpet, stereo, TV, telephone, scented air conditioning and bar, it was more like a dwarf version of a tycoon's office than any car they had ever travelled in before. At one point, reaching for the control panel, Kate had managed to turn on both the TV and the telex machine at the same time, which had reduced them to helpless laughter.

This morning, however, they had awoken to clear sunshine and now, clutching her beaker of orange juice, clinking with ice, Kate gazed out through the tinted windows at the buildings that lined their route. Tall apartment blocks fringed with palm trees were interspersed with an extraordinary variety of motels and fast-food restaurants, advertising such delights as 'garlic crabs' and 'sausage and pancake breakfasts' as well as the usual burgers and fried chicken. An occasional massive art deco hotel reared up in their midst, like an ornate rococo wedding cake, iced in faded pink. As the limo halted at a busy intersection, Kate noticed a long ranch-type building to her left with what looked like a swimming pool on its roof and flashing neon signs announcing 'The Nude Pussy Kat Nite Club'.

She pointed it out to her mother. 'Perhaps that's where we should go to celebrate or drown our sorrows after the race,' she suggested, laughing.

As Achilles had suffered no obvious ill effects from his Champion Stakes experience, after much deliberation his connections had decided to risk going ahead with the plan to send him to Kilmarron and then on to Florida. From what they had gathered from Charlie, the colt had finally gone through the stalls all right in Ireland but they were still deeply apprehensive about how he would behave on the big day itself. Had he developed a real stalls phobia or had the Newmarket débâcle been just a one-off? Even if the flight over went all right, would he recover in time to do himself justice on the day? Such worries had been running through everyone's heads for days. Only Lady Kitty seemed determined not to let them get her down.

'Look, we plumped for Gulfstream Park rather than Longchamp because we thought that the track and conditions would suit Jacko better,' she'd pointed out yesterday on the flight over. 'Well, they haven't changed. And as far as his head's concerned, I'm certain that his spell in Tipperary will have put that straight. He passed the stalls test, didn't he? Anyway, I intend to enjoy myself out there in Florida, even if the rest of you don't!' she added firmly.

'We must nearly be there,' she commented now, handing her beaker of orange juice to Kate. 'Pop one of those splits of champagne into this, will you, dearie? I know it's early, but I've got a feeling that a Bucks Fizz would perk me up nicely!'

The Backstretch, Gulfstream Park Racecourse

'Steady now, fella. Steady there,' Liam said soothingly as Achilles flung up his head, startled by the sudden blaring of a transistor radio from the stall next door. Although it was early still, the temperature on the backstretch had climbed into the seventies and several of the American horses were already out cantering on the track. The European runners, housed in a special 'isolation' barn, separated from the other stabling by a high wire-netting fence, would be pulling out later. Already though, a cluster of people, mainly photographers and press, were milling around outside the compound, peering in through the wire like visitors to the zoo.

Liam was glad that they had not been able to see Achilles earlier. The colt had been lying down half the night and when he had deigned to get to his feet to be mucked out, pieces of straw still clung to his coat, making him look more like a tinker's pony than a Derby winner.

Although the quarantine regulations in Florida had meant that neither Achilles nor Watson had yet been allowed out on the track, the colt was already attracting considerable media attention. It had been a very sensible idea of Charlie's to insist that his final preparations be conducted in the relaxed atmosphere of Kilmarron, rather than in the full beam of publicity here. Things hadn't gone all that easily in Ireland, though. Achilles had broken out in a muck sweat at his first sight of the American starting stalls and refused to go anywhere near them. Only after several days, dismounted and following Charlie and Watson, had he allowed Liam to lead him through. When they eventually managed to load him up, mounted, he shot out again like a bullet from a gun.

'Well, if we can get him in at Gulfstream, he'll certainly break fast, no problem about that!' Charlie had joked. 'We'll have to get permission for Watson to lead him down, though, and an undertaking from the Clerk of the Course or whatever they're called over there that they won't let the stalls handlers touch him. They swarm all over the gate like monkeys, grabbing hold of the horses' ears, I gather. We haven't a hope in hell if they subject Jacko to that.'

Achilles had no problem whatsoever, though, in handling the tight oval gallop at Kilmarron, even at full speed, and on non work days they hacked around the estate's tracks and downland to give him a change of scenery and help him relax.

The flight over had also gone better than any of them had expected. All the horses, even Achilles, slept a lot, surprisingly unperturbed by the noise and movement of the plane. Liam wished he could have said the same for himself. Forced to make themselves as comfortable as they could on the floor, he, Charlie and the other lads and specialized flying grooms travelled in pitch darkness, as the sides of the horses' stalls covered up the plane's windows. They also had to endure a cabin temperature that fluctuated between icy cold and unpleasantly stuffy heat. As a result Liam spent most of the journey wrapped in an old horse blanket, alternately shivering or sweating on the floor, and it was a real relief to emerge after over twelve hours into the balmy heat of a Florida evening and get a first whiff of the ocean. A room was reserved for him at a hotel near the track but so far he had only used it for showering and changing his clothes, preferring to actually sleep outside Achilles's stall. Security at the track was tight – no one could even enter the backstretch area, let alone the isolation barns, without several badges and passes, and armed security men with dogs patrolled day and night – but Achilles was a fancied European runner and Liam was leaving nothing to chance.

He had spent some time studying American form and talking to the local work riders, and was now convinced that if they could get him into the stalls all right, Achilles only had two serious rivals. One was the American turf star, Slew's Best, and the other the four-year-old French filly Mamoushka who had won the Prix Vermeille and finished close behind Devilry in the Arc. Those two, Liam concluded, provided Jacko's only real threat.

But right now he must finish getting the colt ready for his first canter on the track. Charlie and Angie would be here any minute and the Levertons, too, he gathered, were expected on the backstretch this morning.

Tired and apprehensive though he was about Saturday, Liam felt much happier now that Angie had arrived. He had not been able to conceal his delight when he'd learnt that she was coming over in place of Nobby, the travelling head lad. 'I can't spare Nobby this year. Not with so many good yearlings coming in,' Tod told him. 'I reckon Angie can cope, don't you? With a little help from you!' he added, grinning. She had arrived at Miami airport yesterday afternoon and came straight out to the track.

Liam then took her for a meal at Pumpernick's Famous Diner opposite the racecourse gates, where she was too excited about being in America for the first time, as well as amazed at the size of the milk shakes and portions of 'French fries' that were on offer, to give him much of her news. But she seemed overjoyed to see him again, which was all that mattered. They had become so close recently that he had been dreading coping with such an important event as the Breeders' Cup without her. He told her all about Kilmarron and how much he had enjoyed being back in Ireland, hearing the familiar accent all around him again and breathing in the soft damp air, so different from the harsher climate of Newmarket. He'd appreciated the Kilmarron cooking, too. 'The head lad's wife made us colcannon one night – my favourite,' he reported. The only unpleasantness, he confessed, had been his encounter that last evening with Rory.

'What do you mean he threatened you? How dare he? What did he say?' Angie asked, chewing her T-bone steak.

'He told me to expect an approach from a contact of his over here. Someone who would ask me to do them "a favour",' Liam said. 'I would agree, of course. I owed him one, he insisted.'

'What sort of favour?' Angie asked, wide-eyed.

Liam shrugged his shoulders. 'I've no idea, and I don't care either. I told him to get lost – him and his murdering bunch of friends,' he replied angrily.

Angie grabbed his hand across the table. 'OK, OK, keep your hair on,' she said, concerned. 'Look, I don't know anything about Irish politics but I'm sure that if Rory's friends are as wicked as you say they are, you shouldn't have anything to do with them.' She gripped his hand more tightly. 'But you must stop worrying about it, love. We've got a race to win, remember?'

Angie was right, Liam reflected as he ducked under Achilles's neck and began grooming his shoulder. He must put that conversation with Rory right out of his mind and concentrate on the present.

It was only when the colt suddenly threw up his head, snorting with alarm, that Liam was aware of a tall, slim figure, dressed in a black T-shirt and jeans, standing at the entrance to the stall behind him. At first he thought it was one of his neighbours, a pleasant girl who worked for the English trainer Guy Harwood, who had a runner in the Breeders' Cup Mile, but as he turned around, facing into the sunlight, he realized with surprise that it was Stella Alexandros. He'd glimpsed her in the distance down by the barns yesterday and someone at Kilmarron had told him that she'd recently got married to some American bloke and was now on her honeymoon; but it had never entered his head she would want to talk to him. What on earth could she possibly want? he wondered nervously.

'Hello there. Morning, miss,' he mumbled, giving her an apprehensive nod.

Stella stood there, expressionless, staring at him with her extraordinary blue eyes.

'You're Liam Byrne, aren't you, Rory's brother?' she inquired eventually. 'Hmm . . . you look quite alike, I suppose.' She paused, her head on one side. 'I'm Stella Alexandros. As you probably know,' she added eventually. 'How did you get on at Kilmarron? They looked after you all right there, I hope?'

Liam nodded enthusiastically. 'Yes indeed, thank you, miss. We were made to feel very much at home. Particularly Jacko here.' He gave the colt a pat.

'Good,' Stella replied briskly. 'How is his stalls problem, then? Over it now, I trust?' she asked, regarding the colt keenly. 'It'll be a waste of time running him here if he isn't! He's still very small, too, isn't he? No wonder you didn't want to take Devilry on at Longchamp!'

'It wasn't his fault, what happened at Newmarket. He hit his head a terrible crack,' Liam replied defensively, stung by her note of criticism.

Her presence was making him feel distinctly uneasy. He was aware of her reputation for toughness; even Rory had respect for her, he knew. But it was not just that that alarmed him. Every time she looked at him with those hypnotic eyes, he felt as though she was trying to draw him somehow into her power.

'I thought we ought to get acquainted. We will be flying back together, after all. As far as Shannon anyway,' Stella went on easily. 'I've just bought a little Secretariat filly. Out of a full sister to one of my best mares. She runs here tomorrow, but after that she'll go into training at Kilmarron. She's very highly strung, so I've decided to fly back with her myself.' She frowned. 'I don't want one of those flying grooms jabbing sedatives into her unless it's absolutely necessary.' She paused, flashing Liam a seductive smile. 'I thought perhaps you could help me keep an eye on her on the flight.' She paused. 'And do me another small favour, too: help me load something else on to the plane. Just a few things of my own – a couple of crates, that's all.'

A shiver ran down Liam's spine. As he bent down to retrieve his body brush, he tried to figure out rapidly what he should do. It was such an innocent request – to help Stella load a crate or two on to the plane – but 'favour' was the word Rory had used and this must have been what he was referring to. Heaven knows what Stella Alexandros was doing mixed up with Rory and his friends but he had no time to bother about that now. What he did have to hang on to was his resolve, expressed again last night to Angie, to turn his back on Rory's activities once and for all.

'Well?' Stella inquired pleasantly, her eyebrows raised.

Straightening up, Liam shook his head sullenly. 'I'll give you a hand with the filly, sure – no problem. But I'll not be helping you out with anything else.'

Stella looked annoyed. 'Why not? Rory was quite certain you would co-operate.'

'Well, he got it wrong, didn't he?' Liam replied, suddenly angry. 'I told him I'd not be doing another thing to help him and his pals. I made that clear when we spoke at Kilmarron. He can't have been bloody listening.'

'Don't swear in front of me – I don't care for it,' Stella rebuked him, her eyes blazing.

Picking up the tension of this exchange, Achilles laid back his ears and cannoned sideways, nearly crushing Stella against the side of the stall.

'Do keep your colt under control,' she said tetchily. 'If he shows this sort of temperament on the flight back, we'll all be in trouble. My request has got nothing to do with Rory and his pals, whoever they may be,' she continued impatiently. 'I am simply asking you to do me a small favour, that's all. Don't you think it's churlish to refuse just because you've had some stupid quarrel with Rory?'

He mustn't believe her. His instinct told him she was lying, Liam told himself doggedly. 'I'm sorry, miss, I can't be obliging you,' he replied, avoiding her eye.

Stella stared at him for a moment, obviously weighing up whether or not it was worth trying to persuade him further.

'Move over now, there's a good fella,' Liam murmured to Achilles, his hand trembling on his flank.

Stella levered herself away from the side of the stall, her face taut with anger. 'You'll regret this, you know,' she said. 'I don't like being crossed – particularly for no good reason. I would have thought your brother would have told you that!' She paused at the entrance to the stall, her long figure casting a shadow over the straw. 'There's something else I should make clear, too,' she said menacingly. 'This conversation never took place. If I ever find out that you've mentioned it to anyone, anyone at all, I will make sure that you lose your job at Barons Lodge and never work for a decent yard again. I hope that is understood.' She turned on her heel and strode out into the sunlight.

The Enclosures, Gulfstream Park Racecourse

'Off you go then, cock! It's all yours. Good luck!' With an attempt at a cheery grin, Tod legged Alain du Roc into the saddle and stepped back into the centre of the paddock.

The colt, flanked by Liam and Angie in their smart purple Breeders' Cup jackets, had been jig-jogging around the paddock for only five minutes but his ebony coat was already dark with sweat.

'Nothing to worry about. It must be over eighty out here,' Tod tried to reassure them; but it was obvious that the colt was even more on his toes than usual. Liam was in a terrible state, too, Charlie confided to Kate as they were going into the saddling boxes.

'He's awash with sweat himself, poor lad. Angie's doing her best but the tension's really got to him, I'm afraid. There's been a hell of a lot of pressure out there on the backstretch in the past few days, what with all the media attention and hype. Let's just hope Jacko calms down when Alain gets on board!'

There was no doubt about it: the tension of the occasion was affecting them all now, Kate realized. It was not surprising. Not only was there a distinct possibility that Achilles might refuse to go into the stalls, but even if he broke all right, he was up against some of the best middle-distance horses in the world, competing for a staggering 'purse' of nearly a million dollars.

Even Lady Kitty was having difficulty in maintaining her usual sang-froid. 'I'll not be worrying about him,' she said unconvincingly, as the colt bounced by, flicking his long black ears. 'He's just keen to get on with it, that's all, and there's nothing more we can do for him anyway. He's in the best possible hands. Alain's as cool as ice.' She took Kate's arm. 'I've really taken to this place, you know,' she commented, looking around with enthusiasm. 'It's got such a grand carnival atmosphere, don't you think? I just wish that Desmond could be here too, instead of insisting on attending that conference of old fossils in Stockholm. He must be out of his mind.'

'Now Kitty, don't start on that again,' Kate replied, laughing. 'You know perfectly well that he couldn't get out of it. He was giving the main paper, for heaven's sake.'

What her mother had said about Gulfstream Park was perfectly true. From the moment the limo had decanted them outside the entrance to the course that morning, there had been a continual buzz of excitement. The thousands of racegoers that were pouring through the gates in the scorching heat, dressed in an extraordinary variety of clothes, from expensive silk or linen suits to suntops, miniskirts, alligator thigh boots and cowboy boots, all seemed to be hell bent on enjoying themselves.

There was an appetizing smell of grilling food in the air and tents all around the paddock were advertising French fries, hamburgers, beers and pizzas. Although everyone, except the lads and horses circling round the paddock, had patriotically jumped to attention before the first race when the band had struck up 'The Star-spangled Banner', there was a general, and most refreshing, lack of formality about the proceedings, very different from most major European race meetings. Kate noticed, too, that even in the most expensive bars and restaurants Arab owners, millionaire Kentucky breeders, Hollywood film stars and the smart, East Coast moneyed brigade, mingled quite unselfconsciously with other, more ordinary racegoers. Racing in America, it seemed, was truly democratic.

The course was particularly attractive; rows of tall palm trees and Florida pines fringed the paddock, with its elaborate centrepiece of purple and white flowers, the Breeders' Cup colours. Neither could any racegoer be ignorant for long of any of the action. Above the saddling boxes and out on the course, huge electronic boards relayed information about everything from the ever-changing state of the pool betting to the temperature on the course and the exact number of minutes to the off, or 'post time' as the Americans called it. There were also giant television screens depicting the horses in the paddock and re-runs of the live action from the moment the runners jumped out of the gate. As Charlie remarked earlier, everything about American racing, from the shape of the tracks to the facility of betting, was geared to the convenience of the spectator; it was all so different from many of the English courses which often gave the impression of being organized solely for the benefit of the professionals or even of the horses themselves.

'It's odd, isn't it? I'd always imagined that racing over here would be rather colourless without the bookies,' Tod had observed over lunch. 'Far from it, though. Look, they're showing some sort of water-skiing contest out there right now.' He'd gestured towards the giant TV screen, easily visible through the window.

They had all had lunch in the large air-conditioned restaurant overlooking the course. It had an enticing variety of local seafood on offer, including red snapper, mussels, swordfish, soft shell crabs and lobster, but apart from Basil and Pam Hunter, whose appetites seemed to be unaffected, Achilles's connections had all been too nervous to consume much except large quantities of iced water and Californian white wine.

The Alexandros party, consisting of Nik and Diana, Stella and Tom Dacre – there had been no sign of Stelios – had come over to their table at one point to wish them luck. Stella had been agreeable enough but despite their good looks, there was something chilling, reptilian almost, about the twins, Kate decided: they had a superior withdrawn air about them, a strange lack of spontaneity, as though they were weighing everyone else up and finding them wanting. Myra had seemed particularly pleased to see Stella and Kate recalled Tod commenting ages ago on their new-found friendship. 'Most odd! Stella keeps inviting Myra out to lunch. She must want something. I don't trust those twins an inch!' he'd remarked.

Kate'd actually seen quite a lot of Myra in the past few days which had not been as awkward as she had feared, perhaps because they were all, including Myra, bound together by a mutual bond of excitement and apprehension in the last few days before the race.

Kate had caught Tod gazing at her wistfully on several occasions since they'd been in Florida, but he had not actually talked to her alone until earlier today when he had grabbed her hand as they were leaving the restaurant, slightly behind the others.

'You look so pretty, Kate, and you're such a celebrity, too. I enjoyed your interview on television this morning,' he said admiringly. 'I still love you, you know. Very much indeed. I always will.' He gave her an apologetic grin. 'I hope that one day you'll be able to forgive me – for not being free to marry you, I mean. Though Kitty thinks that it would have been a disaster, I'm afraid.'

'Well, we'll never know, will we?' Kate replied, blushing. 'I was incredibly miserable for a while, Tod, I have to admit, but I'm over it now,' she replied firmly. It was the first time he had touched her since that afternoon in the Den and she found it disturbing. 'I still love you too, in a way,' she added, on impulse.

Observing him now in the paddock, she thought how extraordinarily English and traditional he looked in his blazer and flannels and panama hat. Kitty was right, though: he was too old for her and there was something else that could have been a problem too, his reluctance to have any more children. That strange conversation she had had with Charlie under the beech tree the day of the Derby party had set her thinking: she actually wanted children herself, far more than she had realized. In fact, now that her career was going so well, it had become a definite ambition. But this was no time to be brooding about the past or the future, she rebuked herself. The horses were filing out on to the walkway leading to the course and she wanted to give them her full attention.

Passing her now was the French mare Mamoushka, a tall rather angular bay with a plain head but as tough as teak and as professional-looking as anything else in the field. Behind her came the Oaks winner, Adieu, a neater, more compact bay filly who looked to have slightly gone in her coat. She was followed by Tallahassie Bridge, a dark grey colt by Valdez who had run brilliantly earlier in the season, winning the Turf Cup at Hialeah in April, but who had rather lost his form this autumn, Kate gathered. Then came another American runner, the Florida-trained Fappiano colt Fabled, followed by the favourite, Slew's Best. Trained in California and owned by the film producer Cy Steinholz, the four-year-old chestnut had already won the Arlington Million in Chicago and the Belmont Turf Classic. A powerful sinewy chestnut, with no flashy markings, he had a magnificent presence. He was ridden by José Santos, one of the top American jockeys who had just won one of the previous races, the Breeders' Cup Juvenile, and who was exuding confidence as he rode past, knotting his reins.

Had they done the right thing in not putting up an American jockey? Kate wondered in a sudden flash of panic. Alain was brilliant, of course, and got on with Achilles so well, which would certainly be an asset at the start; but after watching the earlier races she was beginning to wonder if any European jockey could equal the skill of the best American riders in actually negotiating their own peculiarly tight left-handed tracks.

But it was too late to worry about that now, and as she turned to watch du Roc swing by, Kate felt instantly guilty at having entertained such doubts. Achilles looked as though he were about to explode with energy and although the patches of sweat had spread under his girth and along his shoulder, he did not seem particularly agitated in any way. Du Roc's lined face was impassive as he knotted his reins but as he turned out of the paddock he bent down, smiling, to pull one of Achilles's ears and mutter some endearment to him in French.

Liam, at the colt's head, still looked desperately tense. She must have a word with Angie the moment the race was over and see what they could all do to help him unwind, Kate decided.

The next moment, as du Roc raised his whip, as though in salute to someone in the crowd, Lucy Beckhampton, wearing a pink, tube-like dress, ducked under the rail of the walkway and ran back towards the paddock.

'Daddy! Hi!' she called out excitedly, her hair streaming behind. 'God, we're so late. I thought we'd never make it. The traffic on the freeway coming from the airport was diabolical. I just had to wish you good luck.' She flung her arms around Tod's neck.

Behind her, Kate could see the bulky figure of Stelios Alexandros, his ponderous features creased into an indulgent smile. Wearing a silvery grey suit, he had an exotic-looking black girl on his arm. She, too, was smiling and looking up at him as though sharing some private joke.

It must be true, then – all the gossip in the press about Lucy and Stelios – Kate thought with amazement. As Lucy detached herself from Tod, she caught her eye and waved her over.

'Hi, Kate, how are you?' Lucy asked breathlessly, kissing her on both cheeks. 'Isn't this incredible? Achilles actually running in the Breeders' Cup Turf. I do hope he's going to be a good boy and go into the stalls today.' She pulled a face, crossing her fingers in an exaggerated manner. She looked tanned and radiant, far better than the last time Kate had seen her in Newmarket.

'I know, we're all on such tenterhooks,' Kate confessed. 'He was fine at Kilmarron but it's a very different ball game today. He's pretty wound up too, as you can see.'

'Yes, indeed. Me, too,' Lucy replied gaily, flinging back her hair and glancing affectionately over her shoulder. 'Look at Stelios with my old friend Celeste. Aren't they sweet? We're having such a laugh. It's a real *ménage à trois*,' she giggled. 'It's doing him the power of good, you know, and he's so grateful, too.' She lowered her voice. 'He's actually asked me to marry him!' She rolled her eyes. 'I'm quite tempted, as a matter of fact. I rather fancy being an ambassador's wife. Think of all those attachés or whatever they're called that I could have at my beck and call. And it would certainly put Myra's nose out of joint, wouldn't it?' she added gleefully. 'Anyway, I must dash. Best of luck. See you later.'

As Kate digested this latest, extraordinary piece of information, she caught a sudden glimpse of Myra, standing ahead at the entrance to the track tunnel, her expression frozen in a comical mixture of disapproval and disbelief. Lucy was absolutely right, she thought. If Stelios's intentions towards her were that serious, Myra would not like it one bit. She felt a hand on her arm.

'Come on, slow coach, chop chop,' Charlie was saying urgently. 'It's time we got back to our seats.'

'*There is two minutes to post time. Two minutes,*' the public-address system boomed out over the stands. Kate peered anxiously across the course to the row of white starting stalls in the distance, searching for a glimpse of Achilles.

'Where is he? I can't see him. Is he all right?'

'For heaven's sake girl, relax,' Lady Kitty ordered, seemingly unaware that as she raised her glasses again, her own hands were trembling. 'He went down like a lamb. He's in a tip-top mood, I can tell.'

'Maybe, but they could still mess him about at the start. I don't trust those handlers,' Kate replied unhappily.

'He's still circling round. So far, so good,' Charlie informed her tersely, his glasses glued to the start.

'There you are. I told you. Stop panicking, for heaven's sake. Just take a deep breath and count up to ten,' Lady Kitty advised.

Taking her eyes off the start, Kate turned her attention to the crowds, packed expectantly into the enormous stand all around her. There were no front lawns at Gulfstream, unlike at most English courses, so the area of tiered seats in which they were sitting along with most of the other owners and trainers ran right down to the track. They were surrounded by 'serious' racing money, hemmed in by some of the world's leading owners – the Maktoum brothers, Prince Khalad Abdullah, the Sangsters, the Aga Khan, the Wildensteins from France, the American, Eugene Klein – all with their retinues of trainers, racing managers and bloodstock advisers. Just below her, down by the gangway, Kate noticed that the Steinholz party from California included at least two film stars.

So much of this Florida trip had seemed like something out of a movie: the limo, the red carpet treatment they had received throughout, their suite at the hotel in Fort Lauderdale with its vast canopied beds and gold-plated hot tub, the pre-race party where she had drunk too many mint juleps, danced with a millionaire Senator on a jetty right over the water and watched a live alligator do a cabaret turn with its wet-suited trainer. Even the course at Gulfstream, with its palm trees and glittering ornamental lake, seemed like a film set; but when she had actually heard her own name over the public-address system earlier, when Achilles had come out on the course, she had realized with a shock that it was all for real. It nevertheless seemed light years away from that chilly autumn afternoon at the Old Rectory when she and Lady Kitty had first decided to embark on this adventure. That seemed now like another life.

She felt her arm gripped violently by Charlie.

'Oh my God, he won't go in! Alain's had to take him right back again. Hell and damnation!' His voice was trembling.

Kate turned to him, panic-stricken. 'Oh no! I can't bear it. Please, Jacko. Please. Go on, get in there, please,' she pleaded. Glancing at her mother she observed that Lady Kitty, her eyes shut, her face screwed up like a baby's, seemed to be muttering something remarkably like a prayer.

'It's OK. I think it's OK. He's half in now. Good baby. Good boy,' Charlie muttered, his voice barely audible in the general buzz of excitement. He dropped his binoculars slowly, his hands shaking. 'Alain's done it. Thank God!' He shook his head in dazed relief.

'And they're off!' the commentator's voice boomed out over a suddenly hushed track. 'And Fabled breaks alertly. Achilles, too. Achilles, the English colt, hits the gate running. Slew's Best on the outside breaks well. Slow out of the gate is the Oaks filly Adieu. But it's Fabled now. Fabled the Florida horse, the local fancy, taking them along now. Fabled followed by Tallahassie Bridge, Slew's Best and Achilles.'

'We did it! We did it! He flew out of the stalls like a rocket. Whoopee!' Charlie danced up and down. 'Now all we must do is hold our position to the turn.'

Taking a deep breath, Kate leant forward again, straining her eyes on the far side of the track. She could see du Roc's gold cap now, in fourth position, Achilles apparently going sweetly on the rails. Already the rest of the field were strung out, with the filly Adieu struggling to keep up with the pace, plumb last.

'*And it's Fabled going on now, increasing his lead by half a length. Fabled zips the opening quarter in twenty-four and five.*'

As the horses hurtled round the bend, led by the Florida star, Kate could see that Achilles was handling the turn well, hugging the rails, his short powerful stride grabbing the ground.

'They're going so fast already,' she exclaimed. 'They'll never be able to keep up this pace, surely?'

'You want to bet?' Charlie replied, grinning. 'This is America, remember? Anything's possible here.'

'*It's Fabled. Fabled still out there, blazing the trail. Slew's Best improving his position now, on the outside. The French filly Mamoushka goes with him. But it's still Fabled winging it with Tallahassie Bridge chasing him now. Achilles, the English colt, still holding his position on the rails.*'

Charlie jogged Kate's arm as the horses flashed past, a blur of colour and pounding limbs. 'Go on, Jacko. Go on. Keep at 'em,' he urged under his breath.

The commentator's voice slid up an octave as his excitement mounted. '*And now as they head towards the back stretch again, it is still Fabled. Fabled from Florida, the long-time leader, heading them still but Slew's Best is chasing him now. Slew's Best really beginning to roll. Mamoushka, the French filly, staying close up, too. The two of them now, showing they mean business. Tallahassie Bridge races neck and neck with Achilles on the rails.*'

As the leader finally started to come back to his field, Kate could see that the grey, Tallahassie Bridge, had indeed drawn level with Achilles on the outside and was matching him stride for stride, hemming him in against the rails.

'Hell's teeth, we've got no bloody room,' Charlie wailed. 'Alain's got a double handful but that effing jockey on the grey is keeping him boxed in.'

'*And as the leaders head for the final bend, Achilles is in trouble now. Achilles on the rails needs racing room. Slew's Best moves boldly*' *past Fabled. Mamoushka right behind. The pace really hotting up now.'*

'The bastard. He won't let us out. We can't possibly win now!' Charlie exploded in despair, slapping his fist on his thigh with frustration.

As the horses swept into the final bend, the crowds in the stands rose to their feet in one great rippling wave, roaring their applause. As the long-time leader Fabled began to drop back tamely, Slew's Best and Mamoushka were locked in battle out in front. Achilles, as far as Kate could see, was still hemmed in, in an impossible situation on the rails, but as she, too, shot to her feet, she realized with amazement that Alain was somehow managing to force him through a seemingly non-existent gap, driving him forward like a man possessed.

'It's Slew's Best now, heading for the wire. The favourite Slew's Best and Santos, really getting into overdrive now. Cauthen and Mamoushka going with them still. But here comes Achilles. Achilles, the Derby winner, a late bloomer on the rails. Achilles and du Roc in a brazen display of speed, really starting to fly!'

As Kate yelled them on, she could now believe what she was seeing. Aided by every ounce of du Roc's skill and strength, Achilles was simply devouring the ground and, ears flat against his snaky head, was managing to close the gap between himself and the leaders.

'It's Slew's Best, Mamoushka, Achilles, the three of them in line now. But Achilles heads them now. Achilles will not be denied. Achilles takes the race.'

Engulfed by the crescendo of noise all around, Charlie turned to Kate, his face scarlet. 'My God, Kate, we've won,' he choked, seizing her in a triumphant hug.

As they clung together, Kate could feel his heart still pounding in his chest with excitement. As he slowly released her, Tod leapt up from the row below and grabbing both her hands, pumped them ecstatically. 'We did it! We did it! Wasn't it unbelievable!' he exulted, his glasses misting up with emotion. At Kate's side, seemingly oblivious to anything else, Lady Kitty had stepped forward and was gazing, transfixed with delight, at the giant TV screen across the track showing a close-up of Achilles pulling up behind the caption 'Unofficial Winner'.

'The little angel. The little treasure. He showed them,' she muttered, the tears streaming down her face.

Swept up in the congratulations and the chaos of pressmen and photographers swarming up into the stand, flash bulbs and microphones at the ready, Kate felt herself being almost physically lifted down on to the track.

The next few minutes, passing like a dream sequence, were marked by certain indelible images which she knew would be for ever etched on her memory. As Achilles stumbled to a halt in front of the winning post, the floodlights were suddenly and dramatically switched on and the massive purple and yellow Breeders' Cup garland placed around his neck as the band struck up 'God Save the Queen'.

When the last bars had died away, Alain du Roc raised his fist in one final gesture of triumph before slipping, exhausted, off the colt's back.

'Il est formidable.' He turned to Tod, his eyes shining. 'This is a colt in a million, tu sais? It was a miracle how he got through a gap like that. No other horse could have done it!'

Liam, too, looked radiant, as though he had just seen a vision, as he limped round, Achilles's reins looped over his arm, his usually peaky features transformed by a beatific smile.

Only Lady Kitty, it seemed, had regained some control over her emotions. 'Yes, indeed. We all had complete faith in the colt,' Kate heard her informing the bevy of pressmen at her elbow, somewhat breathlessly. 'There were a few problems with the stalls, yes, but we put all that right in Ireland. Horses can be cured of most things over there, you know! Of course this has been the most exciting occasion of my life and it's not over yet, I'm telling you. We'll be having a little party tomorrow. Can't tell you where or when, but you're all invited!'

Laurie's Lobster Restaurant, Fort Lauderdale

'Come on, Charlie! You should be dancing, too. Don't be such a wallflower,' Kate called gaily over her shoulder. She was gyrating energetically, partnered by Tom Dacre on the edge of the small dance floor to Elton John's 'I'm Still Standing'. The banker was looking even more handsome than usual in an ice-blue tuxedo and matching bow tie, Charlie observed with a twinge of jealousy.

Kate herself was looking enchanting this evening, he thought. Her green silk dress enhanced the creaminess of her skin and with her shining grey eyes and dark hair tied back with a velvet ribbon, she looked touchingly innocent, too, like a young girl at her first grown-up dance. He was definitely falling for her, Charlie realized with a certain apprehension. It wasn't just her prettiness and her character he admired, it was the growing certainty that he could trust her, something he'd never been able to do with a woman before. He didn't enjoy the jig-jog of modern dancing much. Strangely enough, for someone of his generation, he was a good ballroom dancer and would have preferred to sweep her up in an old-fashioned foxtrot or quickstep, but he would nevertheless request a dance with her soon, he decided. Dacre was by no means her only other admirer this evening: she had hardly sat down or had time to enjoy her supper since the party had started.

They were at Laurie's Lobster, a fashionable seafood restaurant, right on the main waterway at Fort Lauderdale, which they had only been able to book at such short notice because Laurie, the proprietor, had turned out to be a passionate racegoer. Within minutes of Lady Kitty's impulsive announcement after the race yesterday, he had introduced himself, telling them that against all the advice of his track buddies he had actually backed Achilles to win and would be honoured if the colt's connections would hold their party at what he called 'my joint'. As well as his usual fare, he had insisted on serving jambalaya, a sort of Cajun risotto with shrimps and spices which he believed would provide perfect blotting paper for the champagne. He had also managed to create a pleasantly festive atmosphere with music, piped from the restaurant down below, candles on all the little check-clothed tables and a chain of multicoloured Chinese lanterns strung along the verandah overlooking the water.

Charlie was lounging under one of them now, watching a rakish-looking motor launch power out to sea, its bow cutting a silver furrow through the inky water. There were more such craft moored on the bank opposite, some of them so massive and top-heavy with all the modern paraphernalia of deep-sea fishing that they practically obscured the view of their millionaire owners' homes behind, set in designer lawns, their swimming pools glinting like sapphires in the darkness. It would be fun to come to Florida for a proper holiday some time, he thought. Maybe he'd suggest it to Kate and Lady Kitty. They had had no time at all on this trip to explore the Everglades or even take a proper look at a flamingo, let alone visit the Florida Keys or go shark fishing or anything exciting like that.

As he turned away from the water, Diana came sashaying along the balcony towards him. 'I've been dancing with José Santos – you know, Cy Steinholz's jockey,' she said. 'He's terrifically sexy. If I could shrink by a foot or two I'd break off my engagement right now,' she grinned. She had persuaded Nik that they should stay on for the party tonight, particularly as some of Achilles's closer connections had had to return home. Tod was worried about one of his most expensive yearlings, who was apparently running a high temperature, and Alain du Roc, still pursuing the French title, was riding at Maison Lafitte the following morning.

'Stella can't make it either, apparently,' Diana reported. 'She's got some business to attend to in Miami itself on Sunday evening, Tom says. Sounds very mysterious to me, but it's probably only some sort of horse deal. Stella's very secretive, you know. Anyway, loads of other people have decided to stay on, so we're hardly going to be short of punters.'

It was odd that Liam and Angie had not shown up yet, though, Charlie mused as he headed back into the restaurant. Maybe they had decided to check Achilles and Watson again before leaving or had run into traffic problems on the freeway.

Glancing over towards the corner of the room, he noticed that Cy Steinholz, who had proved to be a very sporting loser, seemed to be getting on famously with Lady Kitty. She'd receive an invitation to his Beverley Hills mansion before the evening was out, Charlie guessed with some amusement, narrowly avoiding a collision with Laurie who was weaving his way towards him with a tray of drinks, his swarthy face beaming.

'Great party, eh, Charlie? Some folks is really letting their hair down!' He indicated Lucy Beckhampton, dancing erotically just behind him with her friend Celeste, whilst Stelios, his bulk spreading on to two chairs, looked on benignly. 'Oh, by the way, there's a phone call for you. Some chick who says it's urgent. I'd take it in the booth at the top of the stairs if I was you.' Laurie indicated with his head before hurrying on.

Who on earth could be calling him here? Charlie wondered. As he hesitated, puzzled, the music changed and 'Let's Twist Again' merged into a track he liked much better, Phil Collins's 'You Can't Hurry Love'. Damn it. This would have been the right number to dance with Kate, he thought to himself ruefully. How infuriating that he had to take a phone call instead.

'Yep! Charlie Kyle here,' he barked into the receiver.

'Oh, Mr Kyle. Thank goodness it's you. I've been hanging on such a long time. I thought they couldn't find you or something.' Angie sounded breathless and upset, most unlike her normal self.

'Angie, what's the matter? What's happened?' Charlie asked, immediately concerned.

'It's Liam. He's been hurt, in a fight. We're waiting for a cab to take us up to the hospital right now,' Angie told him shakily.

'A fight! How did that happen, for Christ's sake? Where are you anyway?' Charlie asked, alarmed.

'I don't know exactly. Some bar near the track. We only popped in for a couple of drinks after we'd seen to Jacko. Liam said he needed to steady his nerves before the party – you know what a shy one he is. Well, anyway, this bloke turned up the moment we'd got in there. Pretty sozzled he was, too. When he realized that Liam was Irish, he wouldn't leave him alone and kept telling him he was Irish, too, and supported the IRA. Freedom fighters he called them.' Angie paused, gulping. 'Liam only went and lost his temper with him, didn't he? Called him a bloody fool who didn't know what he was talking about! The next thing I knew they'd got themselves into a fight. The barman managed to separate them but not before the bloke had knocked Liam through a couple of tables. He's in real pain, Mr Kyle. I think he's broken something.'

Charlie thought quickly. 'OK. Don't panic,' he said soothingly. 'Find out from the barman the exact name and address of the hospital you're going to, will you? Yes, right now. I'll hold on.' Cradling the receiver against his ear, he fished in his breast pocket for his diary and a pen. 'Yes, yes, I've got that. It's near Hialeah, I think. OK.' He scribbled the details down hurriedly. 'Well, get him there as soon as you can and make sure he moves his arm as little as possible. I'll tell Kate and Lady Kitty what's happened and borrow their limo if I can. If not, I'll get a cab. But don't worry, Angie, I'll be with you within the hour, I promise.'

Excelsior Beach Hotel, Fort Lauderdale

'Thank heavens for Stella Alexandros! That's all I can say,' Lady Kitty remarked cheerfully, lighting up a cheroot. 'I don't like the woman, as you know, but she's certainly done us a favour.'

'Absolutely,' Kate agreed. 'But how did you know she was flying back with the horses this morning?' she asked Charlie, puzzled. 'We'd assumed she'd be travelling back with Tom and the others via New York.'

'Liam told me up at the hospital,' Charlie explained. 'When he was told that he'd broken his arm and couldn't possibly fly any horse home, he got fearfully upset and kept on about Stella being on the plane, too, which only seemed to worry him more, for some inexplicable reason. I thought it was great news, of course. If she's so keen on Achilles, she could keep an eye on him and Watson as well as her own filly on the journey, I reckoned.' He frowned. 'I could have insisted that Angie went with her, too, but when I spoke to Tod about it all on the phone, he agreed that those flying grooms are pretty skilled people and that she'd probably be more use here, looking after Liam. He's still pretty shaken, poor boy.'

Stretched out on the balcony of the Levertons' penthouse suite, the three of them had been pondering the momentous events of the last few days as they basked in the last of the afternoon sunshine.

Despite the colour he had picked up earlier down by the pool, Charlie was looking tired, Lady Kitty noticed. It was hardly surprising. Although the party had continued merrily without him, it had been over by the time he got back to Fort Lauderdale and he had barely had time to change and shower, let alone make phone calls to both Stella and Tod, before heading back again to Gulfstream to assist Angie in loading up Achilles and Watson and accompanying them to the airport. They had had some trouble in getting Achilles into his stall on the plane, apparently, but they had finally managed it.

'It's such a shame you can't stay on till mid week and relax a bit,' Lady Kitty said. 'Can't we tempt you? We thought we might drive down and take a look at places like Corkscrew Swamp and Royal Palm Hammock one day. They have such quaint names in Florida!'

Charlie made a face. 'There's nothing I would like better than to stay and be your chauffeur,' he said. 'But I really can't, I'm afraid. Tod's been more than generous with time off recently as it is and I've got so much to do before I leave to bring Dad back from Zimbabwe. I'm hoping to fly off there directly the December sales are over.'

'I bet your father's getting excited. Any chance of getting the Free Pardon by the time you get back, do you think?' Kate asked with concern.

'I don't know. The papers are with the Home Secretary right now but it all seems to take so long.' Charlie's eyes gleamed. 'But I'm really hoping it'll be through by Christmas. That would be the best present Dad will ever receive!' He stretched his arms back behind his head. 'What I'd really like to do, of course, is to buy back Coombe Place some time in the near future – as a home for Dad and me, and also to turn it into a working yard again. But that's cloud cuckoo land, I know.' He sighed. 'The present owners show absolutely no signs of selling and even if they did, I couldn't afford it. I'll need my share of Neville's house before I can do anything like that.' He stared out to sea, his expression preoccupied.

'You never know. I have the feeling that if you want something badly enough, you'll get it,' Lady Kitty told him sneaking a glance at Kate, lying supine on her lounger at his side.

As she spoke, the telephone rang somewhere in the recesses of the sitting-room. Glancing at his watch, Charlie hauled himself wearily to his feet.

'I'll get it,' he said. 'It's probably Cy Steinholz. He said he'd call round about now. He's very keen to get involved in our syndication deal. By the way, you know Achilles is insured for ten million pounds now, do you? I spoke to the brokers in London at lunchtime. Crazy, isn't it?' He pushed back a lock of hair. 'Cy's bound to want a word with you, by the way, Lady Kitty. You made quite a hit there, you know! He'll be going to give you a part in one of his films if you're not careful.'

Lady Kitty waved him inside impatiently. 'Get on with you,' she ordered. 'And when you're through with Cy, order us up three of those delicious frosty concoctions with gin and fresh limes they do in the downstairs bar, will you? I've got a terrible thirst all of a sudden.'

She turned and leant over the balcony rail, screwing up her eyes against the setting sun. The scene below looked like a thirties travel poster, she thought: the palm-fringed beach, the sailing boats tacking across the bay, the sleek white liner slipping out of Port Everglades into the rose-gold path of the sun. It all looked too painted and idyllic to be real, as Kate had remarked earlier. Her daughter was very quiet today, she reflected. No doubt, like all of them, she was trying to recuperate from all the excitement and emotion of the last few days, but she suspected it was more than that. When Kate went this silent it meant she was brooding about something important, usually her feelings. In this case, Lady Kitty suspected, these related to Charlie. It had been obvious to her for weeks that the boy was smitten but Kate herself had probably only just noticed it.

'I'm really going to miss Charlie when he goes,' Lady Kitty observed lightly as she stubbed out her cheroot. 'I've got so used to him taking charge of everything for us. I'll feel quite lost without him. Won't you?'

Kate sat up abruptly, reaching for her towelling robe. 'We'll manage,' she replied. 'But you're right, Kitty. He's become very much a part of our lives recently, more so than I'd realized.' She paused, looking thoughtful. 'Oh well, I think I'll go and change. I'm getting quite chilly.'

She'd just got to her feet and was searching for her espadrilles when

Charlie reappeared in the doorway, swaying slightly, his face extraordinarily pale.

'I think you'd both better sit down again,' he said in a strangled voice. He stared down at the floor in front of him, his eyes glazed, as though unwilling to meet their gaze.

'Charlie! You look awful. What on earth's the matter?' Lady Kitty inquired, overwhelmed by a sudden feeling of dread.

Charlie slumped down on the seat opposite her without replying and buried his face in his hands.

'Charlie, what on earth is it? What's wrong? What on earth did Cy say to so upset you?' Kate asked, bewildered.

Charlie raised his head, his expression anguished. 'There's terrible news. Absolutely awful. I can't bear to tell you.' He took a deep breath in an obvious attempt to pull himself together. 'That wasn't Steinholz, it was Tod,' he went on shakily. 'He's just had a call from the airport at Shannon. From the Garda there. There's been a dreadful accident, I'm afraid. He wanted us to know before the press get on to it and start calling us up.' He dropped his face in his hands again.

'What sort of accident? What's happened? Tell us, for God's sake,' Kate demanded, her voice shrill with apprehension.

Charlie stared at her, his face ashen. 'The plane has crashed, apparently,' he said quietly. 'The plane with Achilles and the other horses on it. Somewhere off the west coast of Ireland.' He let out a juddering sigh. 'No one knows what really happened yet. The pilot radioed to say that one of the horses was giving trouble and then they lost contact . . .' his voice tailed off. 'They're certain that there won't be any survivors, though. Some wreckage has been spotted already but they were some way from land and conditions were very stormy.' He shook his head, dazed. 'I can't believe it, I really can't. It's too horrible.'

Kate was staring at him, aghast, her face drained of all colour. 'Oh, no! No!' she wailed. 'It can't be true. It can't be.' She leant forward clutching her stomach as though she were about to vomit. 'Oh no! Please! I can't bear it. Poor, poor Jacko!' Screwing up her face unrecognizably she began to whimper like an animal.

As though in a trance Charlie got to his feet and, stumbling across the floor, slumped down next to her, pulling her to him.

Lady Kitty stood there, still clutching the back of her chair for support, struggling to absorb the dreadful news. Achilles couldn't have been killed, just like that – just when he had had such a glorious triumph. It was too cruel to comprehend. Yet, even in her state of shock, she realized that the news could have been even worse. If Liam had not hurt himself in that stupid fight both he and Angie would have been on board as well. As it was, the only person they had known who had perished was Stella Alexandros, poor woman. Perhaps it was all some awful nightmare, Lady Kitty thought, closing her eyes in the vain hope that she would wake up in a minute and find that all was well. But, forcing them open again, she realized that it was all horribly true. There, in front of her, Kate and Charlie were still clinging together, Kate sobbing uncontrollably now, her head buried against Charlie's shoulder.

It was too painful to observe, Lady Kitty thought, turning back to the sea. What was so devastating was that everything looked precisely as it had done a few minutes ago: the setting sun, the flotilla of sailing boats, the liner steaming into the sunset – they were all still there. And yet, Lady Kitty knew, things would never be the same again. A vital presence that had warmed and enriched all their lives had been suddenly and violently snuffed out. Kate and Charlie were young – they had many adventures to look forward to; but for her, the glory days were over. Thanks to Achilles, this year had been quite extraordinary. Life would never be as exciting or rewarding without him again.

When she felt composed enough to turn back to the others, Kate and Charlie were still sitting hand in hand, unable to speak, their faces still totally stricken.

She limped over and put an arm round them. 'We must comfort each other all we can,' she said tenderly. 'We'll have to break the news to Liam and Angie later, God help us.' She shuddered. 'In the meantime, Charlie, when you feel able, get on to Tod, will you, and British Airways. There's no question of any of us staying on here now. We must all get back home as soon as we can.'

EPILOGUE

The Old Rectory

'Easy, girl, now, easy,' Davy said gently as Seafret, still breathless from her exertions, lay heaving on the straw. He indicated for Liam to help him lift her foal to the corner of the box so that she could see it better. It lay there shivering, a soaking wet bundle, its ears flat back against its head, its long black legs twitching.

'It's so tiny! Except for its legs!' Kate exclaimed. 'It looks like it's going to be black, too, just like Jacko, doesn't it?'

Charlie bent over the foal intently. 'Hmm ... I don't know,' he mused.

'His coat may well lighten up when he dries out. And look – he's got more markings on him than Jacko, too. Two white socks at the back and a star on his forehead, just like his Mum.'

As he spoke, the big bay mare lifted up her head and whinnied anxiously before starting to lick the foal dry.

Davy stroked her neck in encouragement. 'There, there, girl. That's it. That's the way. You get the little fella's circulation going, then,' he murmured.

Lady Kitty clutched her dressing-gown around her. 'Now they are going to be all right, the two of them, aren't they, Davy?' she asked with concern.

'Will you stop fretting, m'lady,' the old groom replied. 'They're both grand. The mare might have a little pain now that she's lost the afterbirth, but if she's distressed at all, I'll be giving her some of the foaling draught I have at the ready. It's that same old opium mixture we used to use at Rathglin.' He hooked his arm around the foal's body and shifted it nearer its mother. 'The little fella is tip-top, as you can see. Maybe he's on the small side, but then so was his Da.'

Lady Kitty stepped back, reassured. In the harsh naked light of the foaling box, her small face without make-up showed her age, lined and vulnerable, but her blue eyes were shining.

'Right, then. We can start thinking of names for him. I'd not even let myself consider any till now in case it brought bad luck.' She gazed rapturously at the foal, her hands clasped together. 'Should we choose something classical again – to keep the tradition going, do you think?' she asked, her head on one side. 'I'll have a hunt through Homer later, to refresh the memory a bit.'

'Mmm ... I'm not sure. Maybe we should forget ancient Greece this time,' Kate replied thoughtfully. 'We ought to wait a bit anyway, to see what this little one's temperament's going to be like. Achilles was such an apt name for Jacko because he was moody as well as being so brilliant.' She turned to Angie at her side. 'Dear Jacko. I miss him every day, don't you?' she added wistfully.

Angie nodded. 'I know. Liam and I talk about him all the time. We'll never forget him. Never.'

A sudden sadness fell over the foaling box, everyone preoccupied with their private most vivid memories of the colt.

Kate could hardly bear to recall that last night in Florida when, in between fending off calls from the press, they had tried desperately to get more information about exactly what had happened. By four in the morning, they were little wiser. Shannon reported that the pilot had radioed in to say that one of the horses was in difficulties, but that was the last anyone had heard. The black box flight recorder had never been found, though a fishing boat in the area had reported that it had heard an explosion. The only clue that the crash might have been caused by a horse lashing out and kicking through one of the boarded-up windows came from a piece of fuselage which was recovered and which had severe dents in it, clearly made by a horse's hoof.

As a result of this lack of information as to the exact cause of the accident, the insurance company had been reluctant to pay up the full compensation. Only a few days ago, under considerable pressure, had they finally agreed.

The racing world had been absolutely stunned by the tragedy, of course. Not only Barons Lodge but the whole of Newmarket had gone into mourning and for several days afterwards, in tune with the particularly dismal November weather, a dark pall of gloom had hung over the town. Liam had been inconsolable. It was only when Angie had announced they were getting engaged on Christmas Eve that his spirits had seemed to visibly recover.

Nik Alexandros had been so devastated by Stella's death that he had immediately cancelled his wedding and barricaded himself away at Kilmarron, refusing to see anyone. When he had emerged at the start of the flat season, he'd looked ten years older, people thought, and a lock of his hair had turned completely white. But the shock had not affected his skill as a trainer: whilst his own personal future and his plans for Kilmarron and Mountclare lay in the balance, he had still managed a brilliant win in the Irish One Thousand Guineas for one of his new American owners.

Stella's death would have had a shattering effect on Stelios, too, if it had not been for his romance with Lucy. Much to everyone's amazement, they had announced their plans to marry some time this summer. 'Well, why not?' Lucy had said when Kate had met her for lunch at Harry's Bar recently. 'It's time I settled down. Alain was right. And I've always found Dublin very *sympathique*. Stelios really loves me, too, and wants to look after me, you know.' She rolled her eyes. 'Anyway, I'm pregnant, I think, and I can't face another abortion!'

She had ceased to be surprised by anything her friends did any more, Kate had decided. Since the tragedy of losing Achilles her own emotions had become engaged in a way she had not anticipated, either. Apart from her increasingly successful career, her relationship with Charlie was becoming the focal point of her life, she mused now as she watched the little foal thrashing about in an attempt to get to his feet. Sticking his legs out in front, he had just succeeded when he toppled over again comically, his eyes wide with alarm.

'Oh, isn't he sweet!' Angie exclaimed, beaming.

'I don't know about that, Angie,' Liam commented from his crouching position at Seafret's head. 'I'd say he's a pretty determined little fella. Just like his Dad!' He reached forward to pull one of the mare's ears. 'Right then, girl, I think it's time we gave you your bran mash,' he announced, getting stiffly to his feet.

Kate followed him out of the box, anxious for some air. Dawn was already breaking now. The first few primrose streaks of light glimmered on the horizon and high up in the beech tree a thrush and a blackbird had started a duet. Despite her fatigue she felt remarkably content, delighted that Achilles's foal had at last arrived safely and seemed healthy and sturdy. Thank goodness they had had the good sense to register the mating officially. It would have been another tragedy now if Seafret's little colt had never had the chance to race.

'You look cold. Would you like my jacket?' Charlie had stepped out of the box and was standing beside her.

She shook her head. 'No, thanks. I'm just a bit tired, that's all. I'll go back in and organize some tea.'

Charlie took her arm. 'I'll come with you. I've something amazing to tell you. I've been bursting with the news all night but somehow it didn't seem appropriate to say anything till we knew the foal was all right.' He propelled her towards the house. 'You remember that estate agent I contacted in Yeovil? Well, he rang last night to say that Coombe Place is definitely coming on the market! Any minute now, apparently. He wanted me to know as soon as possible! Isn't that incredible?' He waited eagerly for Kate's reaction.

She stopped in her tracks. 'Oh, Charlie! That's wonderful news. I'm delighted.' She gazed up at him, her eyes shining. 'And you'll be able to afford it now presumably, now that the insurance money has come through?'

Charlie nodded. 'I think so. Anyway, I've arranged to go and talk to my bank manager tomorrow and thrash out all the details then.' He paused, looking down at her tenderly. 'You will come down and see Coombe Place with me as soon as possible, won't you? You can't imagine how often I've dreamt of showing it to you, whilst thinking, of course, that it would never happen.' He paused. 'I'd like you to see it as your home, too, if you can. You've made me feel so welcome here, I'd like to do the same for you.'

Kate reached up and hugged him impulsively. 'I'm not sure exactly what you're suggesting, Charlie.' She grinned. 'But whatever it is, the answer is yes.'